To Phillip

Feta

A Mother's Imprint
THE SAGA OF SHELLY WATERS

Maria Greka Delaney

MGD PUBLISHING, LLC

NAPLES ◇ FLORIDA

ISBN: 0-9771546-1-0

Library of Congress Catalog Card Number: Pending

Edited by Dyrel P. Delaney
MGD Publishing, LLC ◈ *Naples, FL*
Design & Illustration by Laura M. Connaughton
Laura Connaughton Fine Art & Design ◈ *Naples, FL*
Manufactured in the United States of America
by Rose Printing Company, Inc. ◈ *Tallahassee, FL*

FIRST EDITION: October 2005

Dedicated to Delaney Vineyards. Roots in the soil and toil in the sun for the production of wine birthed of romance, of life with love and affection never ending. Because I know of the work, the sweat, the dedication, the self-sacrifice...and the emotions that must be endured to keep the nector of romance alive.

Maria Delaney

Introduction

by Dyrel Delaney, the author's husband

A Mother's Imprint

All characters are fictional

Author: Maria Mary Greka Delaney (deceased)
Death came on an operating table from a face-lift procedure.

This introduction is by the author's husband about her death and why this book.

The why? It was the author's dream to write a novel of literary significance. In her lifetime she went from immigrant peasant girl to Congressional Aid in the halls of the United States Congress. She was the holder of a Master's degree in Medieval French, a foreign language teacher at the secondary level in five States, a translator, and master of five languages. For all of her accomplishments, however, it was this book that she wanted as her legacy; her personal stance against the spiraling decline of literary standards.

The four years of writing herein were not unduly difficult; but finding a publisher was impossible. To the many publishing doors to which she went, all turned her away; with the advice that she was not sellable. Chief among the reasons for rejection was that she did not possess a youthful face. In today's world of tinsel, she was advised; it is essential that the cover of any new book be glorified with the face of a youthful author.

"It might work in her favor", she was guided, "that she give consideration to having a face-lift".

A supposition on her part that she found revolting. Regrettably, it was I, her husband, who encouraged and convinced her to have the surgery.

Now it is I, her husband who carries a guilt that does not weaken with time. Her's was a senseless untimely death stemming directly from senseless unnecessary pursuit toward vanity. While she would not want it so, I shoulder the blame. How insanely stupid were my unsolicited actions. In some twisted decisions that made up our daily lives, her death is directly tied to this novel.

Her native land was Greece and in comparative analysis the consequence of it all parallels the sadness of real life Greek Tragedy.

I am now alone and she is gone; and the pain does not diminish with time. I owe her so much of which I can never pay. The one thing I hope I can do is let history judge whether her writing is of literary value. In my debt to her I vehemently hold a vile hideous curse to the collective publishing houses and have turned instead too private publishing. I believe her work is complete enough to be judged. The one notable deviation from the norm is the page numbers, which are not numerically continuous but still in individual chapters. I have elected to publish it just as she left it. It has not been critiqued or otherwise modified. If her work is deemed a literary contribution I want the recognition to be hers and hers alone. I do not want my fingerprints or anyone else's fingerprints on her work.

I am asking you, the prospective reader to please buy a copy. It will be redemption to me and a compliment to the life she lived if you find it a good book. In our lives together she and I have stood together on the principles of level, plum, solid and square and I do not now wish to alter that posture.

Thank you for your graciousness and may God Bless.

Dyrel Delaney

A Mother's Imprint
THE SAGA OF SHELLY WATERS

An emotional novel...

———————————————————————

That our emotions answer a call to be free...
In hide from a world that lives in twine
A tear in precious can be thine
In private now journey free
Away stay stress, harsh and disagree
Forbid yea entry now this place...
For emotions set free...are gifts of grace

by

Maria Greka Delaney

(Deceased)

Prologue

Pittsburgh, Pennsylvania in the Strip District, there once lived two men; a storyteller and a listener. Each not-liking himself, each being envious of the other and each being of the notion that it would be preferable to meet an enemy on a field of battle than to be alone in a darken room with his own soul. Thus each was secure in the knowledge that the other would never leave. Each accordingly felt no limitations on expressing their views of one to the other.

"Friend of mine," the listener said one day, "talking to you is like Noah saying 'It looks like it might rain'. You are totally out of touch with reality. Why must you argue? Admit it. The Strip District is the most miserable place on the face of the earth. Twenty below zero, blowing snow and I'm, we, are locked in this miserable hole."

"Hark!" responded the storyteller, "that the creative vernacular of William Shakespeare should have ever been subjected to such thrashing of the spoken word. Without rhyme in pattern or pause in phrase, you sit with five days growth of beard. You are oblivious to beer cans and empty bottles of distilled spirits askew on the floor, and an ashtray overflowing with repugnant cigarette butts. Your fly is unzipped, you have a stench that would cause a swine to seek relief, and yet... you complain. Such a disposition; but one that nonetheless can be gleamed and molded into the prognosis of your shortcomings.

"Namely," the storyteller continued, "your misguided perception, otherwise known as outlook on life, which is perpetually on the negative side, my card shark, bail jumping, hot car wiring, vagrant, looking-for-something-suitable in a line of work friend."

"Uh huh," rebuked the listener. "Look who's talking, you reject from a mental health ward. If dynamite were brain you wouldn't have enough to blow your own nose. If you, even in a drunken stupor, can find something nice to say about this place you are a candidate for the funny farm.

"I can tell you for an absolute fact", the listener continued, "that Satan, the one and only devil himself claims the Strip District as His own private Hell on earth. This...for Christ's sake is where Satan winters.

"Yes sir," the listener would not be interrupted, "regular as the clock ticks. When winter comes to Pittsburgh Satan comes to the Strip District. You might turn out for his arrival sometime. He always comes in on a big ass barge floating down the Allegheny River. Like Cleopatra coming down the Nile, he pulls up to the bank at the end of Liberty Avenue, gets off with all of his entourage, lets a big ass fart, belches, scratches his belly, raises his three prong fork above his head, makes a few sweeping waves and says 'This is it. Let Hell freeze over.' And bingo you and I are caught in this rat hole for another winter."

"That supposition," the storyteller quickly responded, "is totally preposterous. The conception that life in the Strip is a creation of Hell is not only absurd it is a diabolical contradiction to its real intent.

"Not withstanding," his rebuttal continued, "that you are mentally handicapped I will nonetheless endeavor to explain the reality. In fact of the matter the Strip is a heavenly engineered proposition which was personally created by God as an avenue of bestowing humble blessings."

"Humble blessings? What are you, sick or drunk? Which one?"

"Both." *burp.* "What's your response?"

"Evidently," the listener turned to a window, "you haven't taken a good look outside. In case your pickled brain can't grasp the situation we are snowed in, frozen in, locked in, by a howling blizzard that's been blowing for three days...and you, you inebriated poet, your smell would gag a maggot."

"Ah Ha! Inebriated. Not drunk, plastered or soused, but inebriated. Finally, a word of refinement has drifted into your erstwhile inept, annoying, slurred slaughtered vernacular. There may yet be some slim hope that the beauty of the English language may somehow find its way into that two inch thick skull which houses your half size brain.

"With your unsolicited concurrence I will reiterate. There is more good than bad in this conglomerate of warehouses, fish markets, truck terminals and whorehouses."

"Oh, two inch thick skull. Ha, you pseudo intellect. Let me put it this way. If I owned the Strip and I owned Hell, I'd rent out the Strip and live in Hell."

"Commendable, I like it. How about I fix another round?"

"Whisky, no ice, no water."

"This is the last of this bottle."

"Last is as good as the first."

"Correct me if I am wrong," the storyteller continued as he rose, "but I believe the credit for that little sagacious comment is properly attributable to General Sheridan around the end of the Civil War. For some military purpose he took his gluteus maximus out to Ft. Bliss in West Texas. Arriving, as he did, in a blinding sand storm he would later say words to the effect that if 'he owned Texas and he owned Hell he would rent out Texas and live in Hell'."

"Sand storm, snow storm, same thing."

"Ah, but that's where you err in comparative analysis my friend of marginal intellect. The Strip has West Texas bested by a substantially greater number of easily accessible watering holes."

"And of course right now accessibility is certainly the big item."

"If," the storyteller emphasized for effect, "I may finish without being interrupted. Those oases in the desert of life where a man can go and find comfort of thirst and flesh. In the darken night of loneliness there are angels of love."

"You must be insane," the listener sighed. "Have you ever really taken a sober look at the bar flies that hang out in these Strip District gin mills. Every oddball female reject in the City of Pittsburgh eventually drifts off down here. I don't suppose you would have any recall of this but a few nights back you ended up with a ghoulish beast that a radar wouldn't pick up."

"And," he stressed, "how about that torrid kinky sex encounter which you had last summer with that two hundred pound female wrestler?"

"That."

"What?"

"That. You imbecilic incompetent butcher of the English language. You continue to misuse the pronouns that and which. How many times must you need correcting? You said an oddball beast which."

"So what's the big ass difference?"

"Not that there is the slightest hope that you will grasp the error, but for clarification 'that' is properly reserved to introduce a restrictive nature; meaning restricted to the word or words to which it applies. Since you made reference to a singular oddball the intent is restricted and the proper introduction to the element is therefore 'that' and not which."

"Un huh. Could I ask you a question?"

"Rhetorical, doesn't call for an answer."

"Why do you always insist in putting me down?"

"I should think by now it would be obvious. Do we have any more beer?"

"Half a six pack," the listener responded to the change of subject. "Look on top of my dresser, back room. No wait; look on the floor beside my bed. Christ, listen to that blowing wind whistle in around the windows. Since you're up getting the beer let's exchange places. You take this damn spring sticking arm chair and let me stretch my fine little bo-hine out on the sofa."

"Stretched out. One of your favorite job searching positions."

"So what's your answer?" the listener came back to his question. "What's with this proper language bullshit you always throw in my face?"

"It's my arsenal of equalizing our relationship."

"Ah shit. Not back to that again. I thought we were just pretty good drinking buddies. I never thought of us as needing to be equalized or anything else for that matter."

"Exactly my point."

"Don't tell me I'm finally right about something?"

"I'm referring to your point. Most assuredly you would assume that you are the rightful heir to the dominant position in our relationship. Why would you think otherwise? You being 6'1", 190 lbs. and me being 5'5", 135 lbs."

"Ah, that's bullshit and you know it. The fact is you're frigged up in the head and I'd like to know why. I mean why in the hell are you down here. Me, I can understand. I'm a thug. But you, you're educated, a famous actor, performances on Broadway. Why, may I ask, do you wallow in this hole?"

"Foul! You have again lunged your fencing blade at my point of weakness. As in times past I have swirled your dull rusty saber aside with the supposition that every one has to be somewhere."

"But you, here, a great..."

"Actor?"

"Exactly. If I were in your shoes with all you have going for you I sure as to hell wouldn't be..."

"Down here? Can I take that to mean that the only place where a drama can be played out is on some musty smelling, by-gone era stage to be performed before a stuffy audience of pompous stuff- shirts and pseudo critics?

"Friend," the storyteller spoke in a tone of sincerity, "trust me when I share with you two profound thoughts. First, and perhaps the strongest, can you envision a man of my size or stature playing the lead role in Othello or Hamlet? Even beyond that, let me point out that the great performances of the world are those that are played out on the stage of life. Why I recall..."

"Crap!" the listener cut in. "Pure unadulterated crap! You are an actor and you belong on stage. The rest of us are just the world. So answer my question why do you insist on living down here when you could be living a life..."

"Of luxury?" the storyteller softened his point. "Whatever that means. I suppose from your perspective you are entitled to an explanation. The only answer I can give you my one best friend is a mother's imprint.

"Arguably," he felt compelled to clarify his answer, "an adjective phrase but for present purposes I'll call it a term which encompasses the big why in life; my why, your why, everyone's why. Why did Eve have such a compulsion to taste the apple? Why did the great and powerful Mark Antony shun the thousands of beautiful Roman women and allow his self to be enslaved by the sexual dominance of Cleopatra? What so possessed Vincent van Gogh to cut off his ear as a futile lunge at loneliness? I am down here, as you say my dear friend, because the Strip provides me with the forbidden fruit of sex and affection of the lowest order. A destiny that I know is rooted in self-destruction.

"Or..." the storyteller paused in search of words he had never spoken before, "for want of a better explanation, a tragedy which I am compelled to act out without benefit of a stage or an audience."

A silence came over the room. While outside, the wind howling around the building seemed to magnify the distance between these two wayward souls. Then finally the listener spoke his point of view.

"Crap. I may not be very smart but I do know that if you are acting out something it has to be on a stage. Otherwise it's just copping out."

There again followed a pause as the storyteller searched for a direction that would bring some solace to his self imagined plight.

"Very well," he began in an obliging tone, "for the sake of debate I will redefine the perimeters."

"What does that mean?"

"It means," he snidely reverted, "you annoying, wasted life, dimwitted, insensitive accumulation of drunken questions, because of my mother."

"Your Mother?"

"I was reared by my mother. My father died when I was three years old. And... my mother was so unduly possessed of confusion, drive, strength, of challenge and complexity so as to defy description.

"A giver of love but a pusher to achieve. As the twig is bent so shall the tree grow. A believer in Greek philosophy that pleasure seeking is a myth; it does not exist. Why should it? The greatest rewards in life come from being all that you can be. That the one single thing which has ruined more lives than all other things combined is to be concerned about what other people think."

"Uh..."the listener attempted to interject but was cut off.

"If!" the storyteller stressed, "I may continue uninterrupted. There were other thoughts as well. Such as the spoken word being mightier than a swinging sword; the depth and eminence of a man's mind and not the scope of his body will be the determining factor of his net worth; believe the words of Shakespeare when he said 'all the world is a stage'.

"And," his rhetoric now flowing as lines to a play, "to a stronger degree still, he who giveth the world a powerful Greek Tragedy will be held in higher esteem than the rulers of the masses; because stories told are the only possible escape from the brutalities of life.

"And to this day, I do not know her. She wanted me to be someone great; someone great. I hesitatingly repeat a term that stands without definition. Alas, destiny is a cruel taskmaster. Faith just never saw fit that her dreams would materialize."

His words stopped as quickly as they had started and a silence again fell upon the room. The storyteller finished his lines the listener had no cue as to his part and the howling wind held the suspense.

Finally the listener fell compelled to speak. "And that's the reason you ended up down here; because you could not make your mother's dreams come true?"

"Because I loved her more than life itself."

"Uh... excuse me for interrupting, but I couldn't help but notice. You are confusing me with present and past tense. You do not know her; present tense, but you loved her; past tense. I thought you once told me she was alive. Which is it? Is she dead or alive?"

"Sometime she is, sometimes she isn't. Mothers have a very profound influence on our lives; wouldn't you agree? I, there, uh... could you excuse me dear friend? I seem to be in need of a moment of silence. Embarrassing, very embarrassing. A deep breath is helpful but temporary. Oddly enough I have concocted an escape mechanism.

When these spells overcome me my thoughts seem to always turn to another person, a young woman, who suffered a similar destiny and who finally found peace."

"Is," the listener quickly interjected, "that the one about the weirdo doll that owns all them X-rated theaters? What's her name; Shelly Wateringhole? Every time you get slobbering drunk you start telling that story again."

"Waters, her maiden name was Shelly Waters, not Wateringhole you leech on society. Now, would you please grant me the gift of your silence?

"My recalling of the story is for my benefit, not yours. I realize that your limited mentality is incapable of comprehending my motive. Nevertheless, in dissecting her manifesto my hope is that I will somehow find a solution of my own. So when I am talking, you third grade drop out, I am talking to myself not you."

"Yeah, uh huh, then why do you always go into all sorts of convulsions? You can't be content with just talking. No sir, not our very own Einstein genius. You have to rake over every last detail, mimic all sorts of different people, whores, lawyers, sob sisters; the whole nine yards.

"Just answer me one question," in the listener's mind his question was important, "just what good does all that motion and moving and jumping up and down do?"

"That..."the storyteller held the word for commanding emphasis, "which you so ineptly refer too as jumping up and down, you accidental conception from the pre-human era, is properly defined as melodramatics; a dramatic presentation characterized by the use of suspense, sensationalism, conflict, romantic identification and finally a happy ending. I find it all of absolute necessity because I am an actor.

"If I am nothing else I am first, last and foremost an actor. To tell her story with any less zeal is to forsake and mortally wound my own soul."

"O.K. Whatever. Go ahead, I'm getting drowsy anyway and hearing that story for the umpteenth time ought to be good for a couple of hours of sleep. So do it."

"Thank you. As I recall it all started..."

"Just don't forget to put in a pause for-a-pee clause somewhere along the line."

"Funny. As I was saying, it all started unfolding back in 1960, the story actually goes back much further than 1960 but for now we'll pick up with her one night in mid-October; clear night, full moon, balmy autumn weather.

"She had just gotten her baby pink little gluteus maximus arrested and charged with about eight different counts; including assault and battery on two deputies sheriffs."

"That I can picture; bar fly, smeared makeup, bleached hair type. Who else would own a string of skin flick theaters?"

"That all comes later, you nitwit."

"Let's just say that it is the only part of the story which whets my interest."

"I assume as much; her porn, but not the circumstances of her young life. Nor..., in turn..., her own untenable influences of her own mother. Is there no end to the persecution I must endure that my performance be staged before a singular audience who has less depth than a puddle of rainwater; but I will continue.

"Shelly's decision, as the saying goes, to punch out their lights most certainly had unanticipated repercussions. It's not at all difficult to picture her being escorted off to jail by two deputy sheriffs and how the sound of their footsteps echoed ahead of them as the three walked without talking down the long corridor to the women's holding cell..."

Chapter 1

"The year", the storyteller started, "was 1960. The season..."

"Is", the listener cut in, "this the part of the story where she's in jail and some cripple guy comes down to visit her?"

"Arrested, you interrupting unenlightened sub-bourgeois reject. She had just been arrested and..."

"I just thought I'd make mention that I've heard that part many times before."

"Well hear it again you uncaring lifeless form of insensitive mass. You might well hear it again after this; ever how long it takes. Somewhere in this backward look there is something I have consistently overlooked. Something of such significance so as to explain who she is and why I am who I am.

"Now, as I was saying, this particular time frame was mid- autumn; trees all turned, good time of the year to get out and take a country drive. All of the crops have been laid by. Long rows of shocked corn were still standing in fallow fields, and bright orange pumpkins still attached to frost killed vines. In general it was an atmosphere of balmy days and cool nights; a bright full moon was on the eastern horizon each evening. Out east of town the annual Allegheny County Fair was in full swing and by 8:00 P.M. each night the mid-way was already packed, all fairly typical. Just about what one would expect.

"Hoards of people aimlessly milling around in a setting of amusement rides, food stands, bright lights, waving streamers, and barkers in front of side show tents.

"Shelly was there but Morgan Smithfield wasn't. He came later in the night. In case you've forgotten the name, he's the cripple guy you referred to as coming down to visit her in jail. The reason he wasn't out at the fairgrounds earlier in the evening was because he was in town, on 5th Ave. During that era he was the owner of the stately landmark downtown Stran Theater. On that particular night he was in his office, impatiently waiting for the last feature to end.

"Sitting slouched in his desk chair he was unconsciously pinching his thick black eyebrows between his callused thumb and index finger. In the way of physical description Morgan's head was either too large or his neck was too short; either way it was almost a mismatch for the rest of his stocky, slightly overweight body. He also had a prominent mustache which most of the time needed a trim. His shaggy coarse black Greek hair forever lapped at his shirt collar and flakes of dandruff tended to blend in with sweat lines. He had a twisted leg and walked with the aid of a cane; a silver handle cane to be exact which had become his trademark

"At the particular moment he was thinking about his stepdaughter, Shelly Waters. It was Saturday night, she was nineteen, out, most probably by herself and trouble would always find her.

"The wall clock had just sounded the chimes at 11:00 P.M. On most nights he normally took his shoes off and spent the waiting time with his stocking feet up on his desk. On this night his twisted leg was hurting more than usual. As he was sitting there his judgment told him to get up and move around but his motivation told him it would do no good. Judgment won out. Using his cane for support he grimaced an awkward get-up and flinched at the first few steps. Pausing for a moment he rested against the corner of his desk and his eyes came to focus on a wall calendar; compliments of Hill's Funeral Home. The top half was a glossy picture for October showing a full harvest moon shinning down on a field of corn shocks, pumpkins and squash.

'Damn, another month almost gone', he thinks as he continues his way across the office. *'Where in the hell does time go? Sixty years old, it doesn't seem possible that I am damn near sixty years old'*.

"'Father Time' "he murmurs aloud as he opens the office door, "'if there be you, why do you taketh away from me in my sensible years that which you so generously gave me in my impetuous youth?'"

"The air is cooler as he steps out into the massive empty lobby;

silent at the moment. However, that will rapidly change when the last showing ends at 11:36 P.M. His motor muscles are slow to respond and he has a natural tendency to look down.

For no cognizant reason his attention is attracted to the carpet and his thoughts flash back to when it was a new, rich smelling, luxurious, deep pile maroon. Back to the time when it had provided the finishing touches to the lobby's grandiose rotunda dome ceiling, ostentatious shinny brass ornamentation, twin circular balcony stairways with brass handrails and massive chandelier. To this setting of elegance, the carpet had been the magic bridge over which patrons passed to the majestic world of the silver screen.

Passage that was first secured by the purchase of a ticket at the outside ticket cage, torn in half by an usher at the swinging doors and enter the world of fantasy. A magical world which beckoned patrons to stop at the oasis of refreshments before continuing through the second set of doors and down the long raked aisle to the wide expanse of velvet sink-back seats.

However, all of that was a long time ago. The crowds are thinner now. Moreover, the magic of the carpet has been reduced to no more than floor covering. Tufted and thread bare, it now serves as a legacy to the throws of patrons who have come, entered the land of dreams for awhile and then passed on.

The ringing of his office telephone suddenly startles Morgan's gaze at the carpet. He instinctively wonders who would be calling his private number at this hour. He turns and attempts to hurry but assumes the ringing will stop before he can make it. In his jake leg shuffle he gets through the office door and to the front edge of his desk. In a rush fumble he makes a grab reach and in a shortness of breath answers.

"Hello."

"Hello," the other end responds, "Mr. Smithfield, please."

"Speaking."

"Mr. Smithfield, this is Desk Sergeant O'Reilly at the Allegheny County Sheriff's Office. Do you have a minute? I need to talk to you."

"Why, uh yes, of course. What? Could I ask what's...?"

"Mr. Smithfield this is an official call. I am making it on behalf of someone who claims to know you."

"Who, uh...?" He was cut off.

"Mr. Smithfield do you know or would you be acquainted with a Miss Shelly Waters?"

"Why yes, of course but why? What has happened? Has she been in an accident? Is she hurt?"

"Mr. Smithfield what is your relationship to Miss Waters?"

"She's my stepdaughter. Now tell me what...?"

"By regulations I must ascertain that we are talking about the same Miss Waters. I am going to read the information from her booking sheet and ask that you verify that we are talking about the one and same person. Are you there?"

"Yes, yes please."

"Very good. I am reading now. The person we have in custody is a white female, unmarried, 19 years old, height 5'4", weight 123 lbs., hair color honey blond, medium length, eyes blue, no visible scars or tattoos. Mr. Smithfield, from that description can you reasonably assume that the person we have in custody is your stepdaughter?"

"Yes, absolutely, now please, if you don't mind can you tell me with what she is being charged?"

"Mr. Smithfield we are holding Miss Waters on two counts of assault and battery, one count of resisting arrest, one count of destruction of private property, one count of using obscene language and one count of seeking to incite a riot."

"Good God," Morgan sighed as he let out exhausted breath.

"Hello, Mr. Smithfield, are you still with me? Good. Mr. Smithfield, Miss Waters asked that you come down to the county jail. Are you an attorney or do you have an attorney?"

"Yes, of course, I'll be down, I have to close up here. Uh do you take messages? Tell her I'll call an attorney. For now though, I would like to ask, is she OK? Hurt? Injured?"

"No, Mr. Smithfield she is not hurt. If she were injured we would have seen to her medical needs. Right now she is being held in a holding cell with other female prisoners. If you come down you will be allowed brief visitation privileges. That is all I can assist you with at the moment. And I do have other calls, now if you will excuse me." Click.

In Pittsburgh Pennsylvania, to enter the world of criminal justice is to enter the domain of sovereign power. The realization that man in many is governed by the power in few. Intimidation and subservience to that authority are established at the Allegheny County Courthouse and Jail. Built in 1885-88 of Romanesque architecture characterized by deep entrance arches and massive bluish tent quarry stone construction. Those who enter through the arched, massive doors and go to the jail sector find as their stopping point, a cold insensitive repugnant smelling smoke filled Operations Room that is already characterized by peeling walls and barren concrete floor. The officer in charge is stationed at an oversized oak veneer desk on an elevated platform sectioned off by banister rails. An authoritative nameplate with the words Front Desk establishes without explanation that this is the first point of business.

It is after midnight when Morgan arrives and gets in line with the nightly collection of foul smelling, slouch standing, hack coughing, cigarette smoking human dregs. It is after 1:00 A.M. before it becomes his turn. After relating his business to the desk sergeant he is ushered by a female deputy sheriff through a maze of security doors and led to the women's compound. An iron-cage affair, roughly forty feet by sixty feet with floor to ceiling iron bars on two outside walls and flat barren brick on the back two sides.

The cell appears to Morgan to be filled to capacity or even overfilled. The female deputy turns to leave but first gives him curt instructions to remain behind a yellow floor line. She then leaves without making any announcement of his presence to the inmates. He suddenly feels embarrassed; like a schoolboy standing conspicuously out in a long corridor.

Why couldn't Shelly have been right up front, he mentally mumbles.

As his eyes gradually adjust to the dimmer light he starts searching for her inside the cage; weaving and nudging along the yellow line that he is restricted from crossing. The inmates are not helping matters. Especially those crowded against the front bars with their arms hanging out. Drunk and rebellious, they are venting their frustrations and combativeness by banging on the bars and hurling insults.

He attempts to look deeper into the compound. Searching among the inmates who are seated either on the floor or one of the end-to-end wood benches along one side. At first he has little success.

Shelly is down out of sight. She is sitting on the floor propped against one of the back brick walls. With her head resting on her folded arms across her pulled up knees she has been impervious to her surroundings. Gradually noticing the commotion of a man being in the women sector causes her to abruptly spring to her feet and shove her way to the front. As she squeezes in between the inmates she sees him and blood rushes to her face in embarrassment.

Seeing him standing there, alone in the middle of the corridor, she is shocked at his apparent strain. His necktie is loose and askew, his clothes wrinkled and the crown in his black fedora hat is crumpled. His weight is shifted to his good leg and he is using his cane for support.

For the first time in her life she realizes that he is showing age. The stoop in his shoulders seems to make him bigger at the top than bottom. His head of coarse black hair with its strands of gray falls unruly from under his hat and shags around his neck.

Her eyes water as she thinks to herself, '*there he is Mommy. He's still watching over us.*' Wiping her eyes on the back of her hand she puts her face to the bars and calls out; even as her voice has a choked composure.

"Hey! You! Stranger. How is it they let you into no man's land? You got permission to be in here?"

"Shelly," he responded, "what on God's green earth?" Making eye contact he intuitively started to move closer to the cell but from nowhere the watchful eye of the female deputy yelled him back behind the yellow line.

He then asked the deputy if there were provisions where he and Shelly could be alone. The deputy inquired whether he was an attorney. "Yes, I am," he responded, "and I would like to be alone with my client." Satisfied with the answer, Morgan and Shelly were ushered into a small conference room with the door closed and locked.

"Always remember that," he commented to the clanging sound of the locking door. "When you are dealing with bureaucrats, tell them what they want to hear. Their job is to carry out a set of rules and that is the extent of their concern. In this case the rules allow an attorney to be with a client. She can truthfully say that she asked if I was an attorney and when I answered yes, she is cleared."

Shelly paid no heed to his comment; it was just initial small talk. Their meeting had not yet been sanctioned by a hug. Lovingly, she stepped to him, put her arms around his mid-chest and hugged herself to his body. She could feel his free arm return the response by hugging her in close. She gave him a second firm squeeze and looked up as he looked down and emotions came to both their eyes. In a soft, constrained voice she said, "Thanks for coming."

"Honey, you're my baby," he spoke as he again squeezed her close and her head came under his chin. "You know I'll always be here for you." That said, they both knew the rules. To avoid the brutalities of emotions, their lifelong decorum of toughness immediately surfaced.

As she stepped slightly back he cupped her chin in his hand. With her face slightly upturned he slowly moved her head from side to side in a mock inspection. After meticulously scrutinizing the cuts and bruises he commented in a reserved, slow voice.

"That looks like a pretty nice busted lip you have there Baby-Doll. I would say you took a pretty good right cross. I don't suppose anyone ever told you anything about ducking?"

She did not respond but continued to remain silent as he then pulled her chin slightly down and observed the dirt and straw matted in her hair.

"My goodness," he implied surprised. "All of this dirt and grass on the back of your head," he picked with his fingers, "You didn't end up on bottom? That would be a little unusual for you wouldn't it?" At this point it was all a facade and she knew it; the prelude to the substance of what they had to face.

"Baby," he finally said with a sigh, "when will you ever learn to control your hair-trigger impulses?"

"Uh..."she was about to respond when he cut back in.

"I see we have benefit of two straight back metal chairs. How about we get off of our feet? My leg is acting up a tad." Without waiting for her answer he pulled his dragging foot over to one of the chairs, seated himself, stretched out his leg and welcomed the relief. She complying pulled her chair up along side of his and with her arm partially around his back she laid her head on his shoulder. As she gave him another hug she hoped he wouldn't detect her fight to keep the wetness out of her eyes.

"Baby, Baby," he said as he reached around, with his free arm and patted her head. "This isn't your first ruckus. Is a little busted lip that painful?"

"You know me better than that," she sniffled as she raised her head and slightly wiped her eyes on her blouse collar. "It's not the pain and you know it. It's just... it's just everything. Why do I always end up in trouble? I can't seem to keep my mouth shut. Things come along which are none of my business and before I know it, bam I'm in it.

"Sometimes I think I hate the whole world. The only time I seem to be happy is when I go looking for trouble. Knowing full well that every time I do, I'll hurt you. And each time and every time, I swear that I will never do it again, but then I go right out and it's all over again.

"Morgan," she asked as she fought to hold back an outpouring of emotions, "what's wrong with me?"

"Baby. Sweetheart. Right now let's not concern ourselves about what may or may not be wrong with you. Right now just tell me what happened."

"Same ol' thing. I got into a fight."

"Uh... from the list of charges," he countered, "assault and battery, resisting arrest, destruction of private property, inciting a riot... I would say that this is not quite the same ol' thing. Now suppose you tell me exactly what happened."

Making a facial gesture to indicate it was a lengthy involvement she inhaled deeply through her nose and as her chest expanded she responded, "It's a long story."

"Well," he obliged, "we don't seem to be going anywhere. Now from the beginning and every word."

She scooted her chair around to where it was easier to talk face to face and again made a slight wipe of her wet eyes on the back of her hand. Then with collected composure she began; strained hesitating words at first but then with more control.

"Where-o-where?" she questioned herself. "First. Well first of all, it all happened out at the County Fair Grounds; actually on the mid-way area of the carnival. And to tell you the truth Daddy Morgan, I don't even know what I was doing out there. I really don't have any interest in that kind of kid stuff," she slightly shrugged for emphasis.

"You know the theme. Ferris wheel, thrill rides, kiddy airplanes, merry-go-round, lots of hype, bright lights, waving flags and streamers, music blearing from loud speakers. Crowds of people all milling around. Barkers standing out in front of the side shows..." She abruptly halted with the thought that additional explanation was needed.

"Actually, "she reverted back, "it all started much earlier in the day. By happenstance I was glancing at the morning newspaper and saw where the carnival was in town. Instantly for some unexplainable reason something just kind of stung me. A weird resentment tingled through me and I felt an immediate offense at it even being here.

"For no reason I just felt anger. Anyway, nothing happened right then. The rest of the day I just went on about my business. Nevertheless, the thought of that carnival continued to linger on my mind. So, by the time night came I just decided to go.

"I got out there around 8:00 or so and the first place I went was out on the mid-way. It was just about what I expected; crowded with the usual Saturday night go-seeers. I was by myself. I didn't have any interest in being with any one; just my own company. At first I mostly just ambled along and watched people. For something to do I did try my hand at throwing a few darts and tossing a few pennies.

"But that wasn't my real interest. I know I was looking for something I just didn't know what. But I sure don't believe it was trouble and it sure wasn't romance. You can see what I had on," she pointed to herself. "Just jeans, blouse and loafers; real plain Jane. I was wearing my hair the way I have it now; swept back with side combs but no lipstick. It wasn't like I was dressed up trying to be somebody; though I did get a couple of whistles from some roving guys.

"But honestly Daddy Morgan, I had no mind set on anything. I was just wandering and people watching. But then I happen to pass by a couple of the side shows; and that's when something inside of me clicked."

"Clicked?" he interjected in a tone of surprise. "What the hell kind of side shows?"

"Well," she flinched at his question, "the first one I came to had a giant canvas mural of a fat Arabian sheik dressed in fancy silk clothes and wearing a white turban with a bright red ruby in front. Lord and master there he was. Bigger than life he was sitting on satin pillows with his arms crossed and a harem of scantly clad, sex starved young slave girls with great big bulging boobs sitting at his feet. Hungry expressions on their faces looking up drooling; just waiting to serve him. The implication being I guess was that he had tons of money and he can simply buy as many hard nipple women as he wanted.

"I kind of burned a little, but the mural wasn't *that* big of a deal. The worst part was the tent barker and his bullhorn, out in front bellowing for people, mostly men, to come inside and see the sex chambers of some mysterious Arab sheik."

Morgan was not expecting anything of this nature as to her reason for getting into trouble and frowned his eyebrow to express his surprise. "That's it?" he cast an unbelievable look. "You see a faded mural on the front of a side show carnival tent and you get into a beef?"

"No. Of course not," her tone implying that she understood how he could be surprised. "I resented the implication, but that was not where the fight started. I think that must have just been the first spark."

"Well," his tone clearly showing his impatience, "please do continue. I surely do want to know what was so damn cynical about a carnival side show that we both ended up here in the County Jail at two o'clock in the morning on a Sunday morning."

Shelly looked at him with an apologetic expression and responded, "I said I'm sorry. I know it's inexcusable. I..."

"No, no it's OK Baby," he cut back in. "I just want to know what happened."

"Well," she started again, "it just happened. First though I will tell you something. Aside from hurting you it was one of the sweetest moments of my life." The manner in which those words came out caught her by her own surprise and she quickly explained.

"Uh, no wait. That didn't come out exactly right. I mean the moment I got busted in the mouth. I'm not going to try and explain why. I'm just going to tell you that the split second when I felt that iron fist smash my mouth, the feel of my lip splitting and I felt my own blood gush out, that moment. It was an indescribable sensation. I have never felt anything so sweet in my life.

"It was like every pent-up frustration, hate and resentment of my entire life had just been set free, and I had been handed a no-holds-barred, blank check to take on anybody in sight."

"Shelly..."he was about to comment when she cut back in.

"OK, sorry, I got a little carried away there. Back to where and how the fight actually started."

"If," he sniped a slight curt, "it's not too much of an inconvenience. What was so damn earth shattering this time?"

"This time," she responded to his gruff, "it was a freak show. I had moved on from the fat Arab tent and generally got mingled back in with the crowd. Then a couple of hundred feet on down the midway there's another one; this time a giant size mural blearing out in bold letter FREAK SHOW. Talk about a blood boiler! I hadn't fully cooled down from the first rub when I get a second dose.

"How about that?" she reinforced her viewpoint. "A freak show.

Note if you will. The wording did not say live people with birth defects. Oh, no, nothing as cordial or sensitive as that. Just tell it like it is in nice big glowing red letters, FREAK SHOW. But, if I'm truthful I really didn't give the mural all that much notice right off. Everyone's attention, including mine was being overpowered by the bellowing bullhorn of the tent barker. 'Yes Sir, ladiesss and gentlemennn step right up. Don't be bashful, come one, come all. See the world's largest collection of living breathing human freaks'."

As she finished her mimic of the barker she glanced directly at Morgan to see if he seem to understand. When he just looked back and said nothing she drew her own conclusion and continued. "OK, I know. Why should it bother me? But then, listen to this. Not only is it degrading to the poor unfortunate people on the inside, the barker was adding insult to injury by insinuating that there may be some sort of forbidden sex orgies going on in there.

"And... it was along about here that I glanced back over for a little closer look at the mural which showed a faded, mismatch collection of people; and talk about an implied suggestion? I instantly detected a common denominator. For the most part they were women; and further for the most part, women with big round bulging sexy breast.

"Ha! What a degrade! Right there on the mural front was a picture of Siamese twin girls with big sexy boobs, sexy faces, bedroom eyes and connected at the abdomen; suggesting that somehow they were as happy as they could be and for the man who was a bargain hunter they could offer twice the fun for the price of one.

"Then there was the picture of the fat woman with massive huge breast hanging down on an overflowing belly; sitting there with bedroom eyes and a box of chocolate cookies; appealing I suppose to the man who likes a little snack of milk and cookies before bedtime.

"And of course we have to have a bigger than life Amazon spear throwing wild woman, dressed in a loincloth and halter top. Her oversized boobs showing a deep, foot long cleavage and her muscular legs standing spread eagle suggesting that down in the good old Amazon there are spear throwing wild women roaming the jungle looking for men they can turn into mammary gland sex slaves.

"Oh… and mustn't forget the female Space Alien. Another bigger than life sexy woman with big oversized tits, tiny waist, muscular legs and the head of an outer space creature. Standing right there with her Buck Rogers' ray gun blasting away at whatever.

"Yes sir, all with big round firm bulging breast; if you've got it, then by God flaunt it. To be fair, the mural also had a smaller scale background painting of a midget, a skinny thin man and a young man born without arms. Nevertheless, can you imagine…"she emphasized her point with a shrug and ended?

Feeling that she had adequately explained the starting circumstances she briefly glanced at Morgan. To her surprise, Morgan said nothing; transmitting a strong signal.

"I know" she instantly retorted, "I know what you must be thinking. I should have simply walked on by, but I didn't. I just kept listening to the hype of that barker. Bellowing through that bullhorn about having the world's largest collection of freaks, assembled from the four corners of the world for our viewing pleasure I just…"

It was at this point that Shelly was abruptly interrupted by the clattering sound of keys unlocking the iron door. As the door half opened a female deputy sheriff stuck her head inside and asked, "Is everything OK in here?"

"Uh, Yes… fine," replied Morgan.

"How much longer you going to be?"

"A while yet. We'll let you know."

"Just knock on the door when you're through," she responded closing and re-locking the door.

"Daddy Morgan," Shelly asked in uncertainty, "this is getting too drawn out. Do you…?"

"Yes, yes I do," he finished her sentence, "but just get to what happened. Who hit who and how did it start?" As she looked at him this time their eyes made contact. In a split second she had a flash that the actual fight was not that big of a concern. He was looking for something much more important. He too wanted to know of what it was she was searching. *He's right*, she thought. *What is it that makes me do these things? For ever how much he wants to know, I want to know a thousand times more* Thence she pushed her hair back on both sides, reset her hair combs and proceeded; not only to Morgan but also to herself.

"OK, at this point I was standing kind of further back in the crowd. Well, what happened was I sort of pushed my way through and got up pretty close to the front and got a closer look at the barker.

"A real Mr. Cool Cat, he was. Standing up there on a platform; young 24 to 26, tall 6 foot, 165 lbs. broad shoulders, trim waist, full head of jet black oil shiny hair, baby face, unblemished smooth skin and a soft neat little mustache. If he wasn't a cocky looking dude; all dressed up like a riverboat gambler. Stiff brim straw hat cocked to one side, white shirt with a stiff high collar, black bow string tie, a black garter on each sleeve, red satin vest with a gold pocket watch chain dangling across the front. A real lady-killer; black, peg leg trousers.

"Well, before I knew it I found myself making mental comparisons between him and the people being exhibited. By what divine providence, I'm starting to wonder was he on the outside and they were on the inside. More still, the despicable manner in which it all was being flaunted. Then I started listening to his insinuations. 'Just inside, ladiesss and gentlemennn, there is a room full of human rejects. Nature's jokes really. Brought to you at great expense from the four corners of the globe. Now it's a natural inclination to be curious about such freaks. Sooo, without any self imposed guilt, step right up, buy a ticket...'

"Looking back," Shelly continued without pause, "I was probably ripe for a mad-on because I started comparing his hype to that of Adolph Hitler and his crap about a super race," Her tone and idiom showing indignation. "It's awfully easy," she continued, "to mock the unfortunate when one is on the more perfect end of the human scale. Well, the more I listened the hotter I got and before I knew it something inside me just snapped. I pushed my way on through the crowd and stepped right up in front of our perfect specimen Mr. Barker.

"From there, I just started it. 'Hey, fellow!' I remember shouting,

'How do you like your job? I'd like to ask you a question. Do you like what you do for a living?'

"As I heard my own words come out I instantly felt blood surged to my face and I could not believe it was me. But in the next instant or two the embarrassment went away and I immediately started feeling self-righteous. Who was he, one human being, to stand up there and ridicule the misfortunes of others?

"So I just laced into him. 'You think this makes you a big man?' I shouted. 'Standing up there and yelling about the birth defects of others?'

"He didn't react at first; probably considered it just routine haggling, cause he went right on. 'Step right up ladiesss and gentlemennn,' he continued. 'I tell you what I'm a gonna do...'

"But along about here I cut him off again 'Hey, excuse me, excuse me, I'm sorry but I didn't hear your answer. Why don't you answer me?' I yelled. 'Look, Lady I...' he tried to respond but I out shouted him. 'Don't lady me', I continued. 'I'm very particular who calls me a lady, and degrades like you do not qualify'."

Shelly then paused as she felt a warm sensation in her face. Saying the words here in front of Morgan was not the same as when she had shouted them at the barker. This time it all seemed too much. What good was it doing? Lost in her own thoughts, she simply stopped. At some point in the pause her own awareness returned and she glanced at Morgan. He was sitting silently and watching. With his twisted leg outstretched and both of his hands resting on his upright cane, he was patiently waiting; like an understanding father letting a confused child work out its own answers. He didn't have to say it. She knew; his leg was in pain.

"Do you really want me to continue?" In a tone that was neither commanding nor impatient he simply replied, "Yes."

Then, in a voice that was not quite as exuberant she took a deep breath and started into the details of the fight. "OK. So, now I have got it going and I can't back down, even if I wanted to; which I didn't. I will admit that in the initial moment or two I had a fleeting wish that it had not got started; but by then it was to late to back out.

"Mr. Barker was already firing back. 'Are you crazy?' he shouted or words to that effect. 'If you don't like the show then move on. What in the Hell is wrong with you?' he ended with a stare. So now one thing was building on another. And I think it was probably along about here that I started cupping my hands up to my mouth so I could holler louder.

"'That's right BUCK-O', I probably shouted words to that effect, 'I am crazy, and I don't like the idea of this *freak* show as you call it, and kiss my back side if I will move on. You may not know this but it makes my blood boil for one person to make fun of the misfortunes of others. In fact,' I continued shouting, 'when I see one person putting another person on display and then charging admission I have an uncontrollable urge to punch that someone's lights out'."

Her exuberance in explaining that part caused her to feel slightly embarrassed and she toned down as she continued. "Well, by now the crowd was starting to get involved on my side and was goading me on. I think the barker started to sense some danger because he stepped backward; which was another one of those things that built one on another... because what happened was he lost his balance and fell off of the platform.

"As he was scrambling to get on his feet he must have felt a compulsion to defend himself because he was now at my level. Staring directly at me he started shouting, 'Hey You,' he finished getting up and stepped in my direction. 'Yeah you. Loud Mouth. What are you? One of them lizzies that Pittsburgh's so damn famous for. Maybe we could use you in our freak show. How about it? Would you like to join up?'

"Uh, Oh. Wrong choice of words. Now he was insulting yours truly. I saw rage and I suspect he realized his mistake because he instantly tried to tone it down.

"'Look, lady, no one is forcing these people to be in there. They can leave of their own free will anytime they like. We are actually doing them a favor by providing them with a means of making a living.'

"My only thought at that remark was dear God. First you display them as freaks and then brainwash them into believing you are doing them a favor.

"At that point I just exploded. I lunged forward and, I guess you could say that's where it actually started. At first it was just me and him locked in a man to man, uh woman, clinch and rolling on the ground dirt fighting; half hitting, kicking, nothing sensational."

"Just you and him?" Morgan spoke in a surprised tone. "If that's the case where did all of these charges come from; inciting a riot, assault and battery?"

"Daddy Morgan," she paused, inhaled a deep breath and searched for words, "I... it just exploded. Like I said. In the beginning I was on top and mostly trying to stay there and getting in a few short hits; he was mostly trying to get out from under me and getting in a few side hand hits but neither of us was doing any real damage to the other.

"I remember glimpsing around while we were wallowing in the dirt and all I could see were people's feet; and of course lots of yelling and goading on. On that account I may have been a little distracted cause along about then is when it happened. I don't know how because I sure didn't see it coming. But he came up with a hard bare knuckle fist and landed a straight blow to my mouth."

At that point Shelly put her hand to her mouth and wiggled one of her loosened front teeth as if to illustrate to Morgan. Then, realizing that he was not going to comment, she continued. "I think he may have loosened a couple of teeth but at the time I didn't notice. Blood just squirted out and all it did was make me madder. It may have also been the punch that caused things to really start getting out of hand.

"Cause a couple of young men from the crowd jumped to my defense, which I didn't need, but over my objections they pulled me aside and now they're involved; and what else? A couple of carnie workers then jumped in.

"From there on it just kept getting worse. The crowd got more boisterous with yelling and goading. The commotion could be heard to the far end of the mid-way and of course that meant that every carnie worker on the circuit came a running, which causes other Pittsburgh steel workers to jump in."

"And," Morgan summed up, "the bottom line is you are the one who gets charged with inciting a riot? I don't suppose you would care to enlighten me on exactly how you managed to end up in the slammer while everyone else walked?"

A conspicuous silence came over the room at the sound of Morgan's question. She had hoped to avoid that part of the story but now there it was.

"I guess..."she finally responded in a meek tone when she could no longer delay the answer. "I guess the main reason is because I mistakenly punched out a couple of deputy sheriffs."

"You what?" he resounded in disbelief. "You guess... you mistakenly punched out a couple of deputy sheriffs? Is that what you're telling me? You saw a freak show that you didn't like so you just decided to punch out a couple of deputies? Is that your way of releasing your pent-up frustrations? Get in a good brawl with Pittsburgh's finest. Is that it?"

"No," came her meekish reply.

"Well, then what did happen?"

"Daddy Morgan," she commenced in a low docile tone, "I didn't know they were deputies. The best explanation I can give is mob brawl. Like I have already told you I was right in the middle; crowd shoving and fist flying. From who or why I don't know but I got a couple of hard blows to the back of my head that made me see stars.

"Then from nowhere I felt a big powerful set of a man's arms grab me in a bear hug and whirl-threw me out to the edge of the crowd. I can still feel myself just flying some ten or twelve feet through the air and as I landed I felt a chest-crashing thud that knocked the wind out of me. I landed face down first and just skidded across the hard dirt. My face, especially my nose was skinned to where loose skin was hanging down.

"I had dirt in my eyes and I could taste dirt and blood in my mouth. The crowd was blocking out the light so I couldn't see who did it but I didn't care. Ever who it was, he was going to pay. It took me a split second to get my breath, spit out some of the blood and dirt but then I was ready.

"I was just getting up on one knee when I saw out of the corner of my eye the crowd was moving back and that a male body was coming at me.

"And for once in my life I got lucky; at least I thought it was lucky at the time. Just as he got within hitting distance I clenched my fist, sprang full up on my feet, came all the way around with a whirling right hand and caught him exactly square in that big ol' beautiful left eye.

"Pain instantly shot through my fist and wrist but at the same split instant I saw his knees slightly buckle and oh man did it give me a feeling of being invincible.

"But somehow in the next split second I got shoved back into the crowd; or else the crowd just shoved in around me. At any rate I'm jammed tight in a smothering mob. By now every carnie worker in the carnival was running over with a club in hand. Which means that every eighteen and twenty year old steel worker in Pittsburgh had jerked off his Saturday night shirt, handed it to his date and jumped in for a good ol' free for all; what a mess. There must have been over a hundred people all-trying to kill each other.

"At that point I was just trying to keep from getting knocked down and kicked to death. The force of the crowd sort of pushed me into the front opening of that now famous freak show tent; and guess what? Low and behold, bigger than life, there's our perfect Mr. Barker. Only right then he wasn't quite so perfect. He was standing upright but not too steady on his feet. And those fancy duds he had on? They didn't look quite so fancy painted with a little blood and dirt. I don't know if it was from me or from some one else but in a glimpse of light I saw him wiping blood from his mouth. Moreover, in the same glance that I saw him, he saw me.

"From there it seemed like there was an instant metaphysical flash of lightning that we go after each other again. Some inherent code of honor that the two of us finish what we had started; and I knew I had to do it.

"Daddy Morgan, can you imagine? In all of that crowd, the yelling the shoving, the swinging of fists, the two of us we were drawn to each other like magnets."

At the end of that statement she paused to find new words. Words that she had never before relate to anyone. The thought of someone else knowing what she was about to say caused her to become clammy. She turned and shifted herself up right in her chair; as if good posture would give her more strength.

In feelings she had never experienced before she wanted Morgan to finally know. Yet, simply knowing was not enough. The knowing had to be of such magnitude and understanding so as to pardon the blame for all of this; and all of that which had gone on before. Finally she continued.

"Daddy Morgan, I'd be lying if I said I wasn't God awful scared. He was a man and I'm a woman. And I had no illusions that if he took me down, one minute under his weight down on the ground in the middle of those mob stomping feet is all it would take.

"But...be that as it may, I wasn't backing down. So... I just said to myself...this is where I die. But I wasn't going to die until I settled one final score. The score for my mother was going to be squared right then and there.

"'Mother,' I remember saying as if she was standing right there on the sideline looking on, 'This is for you, I love you. If I die... please find me in Heaven'."

There, she had said it. The words had come out. She had stripped herself naked and now stood totally exposed; but nothing happened. Only silence. Morgan said nothing nor made any motion. No consoling, no overtures of understanding. No chide words about self-pity.

For her total exposure she had received no reward, no benefit, no authoritative acceptance. She felt only an instant panic of mistake to which she tried to recover by choking back her emotions and fleeing back to their life long decorum of toughness.

"Looking back," she attempted to pick up where she had left off. "I think," she continued in an explanatory tone, "that the thought of meeting mother in Heaven must have given me a super charge of adrenaline because I lunged at him in a blind rage. In some warped sense of justice if I died I wanted to take him in particular out with me. I..."

"So," Morgan abruptly cut in with delayed words of understanding. "That's the reason. All these years. It's been your mother all the time. Baby, you'll never know; after all these years. I finally know for sure what I have always felt. This is how it finally erupted. The thought that your own mother could have very well been one of the people sitting inside that tent."

Morgan's response did not get an answer. It got a silence pause. A pause and a look from an insecure set of blue eyes that were at odds with the world and a set of emotions which were strained to the breaking point and fighting to hold back a flood of tears. To that inner turmoil came a renewed defense mechanism as she continued to hold on by sheer threads.

"But guess what?" she answered rhetorically. "In Pittsburgh, the steel workers take care of their own and taken care of I was. From out of nowhere I see a big heavy set, barrel chest, red-faced Swede stepping in. He didn't do anything at first just stood between my self and Mr. Barker. Like I say the barker was as determined to get at me as I was at him. The Swede, however, didn't know all of this and so when the barker gave a hard shoving push and tried to get past it was Kattie bar the door. To nobody's surprise a powerhouse fist the size of an anvil came out of that Swede's hip pocket and in a roundhouse swinging blow, connected square on the barker's jaw and I heard the bone crack. I know it's terrible of me but I couldn't help but feel good.

"I shouldn't have been so quick though cause mine was coming. Just at that minute there was a roaring yelling to make room and a fast clearing back of the crowd.

"And Uh Oh! That powerhouse punch I told you I threw. The one that landed square in the quy's eye? Uh, in hindsight it may not have been quite as lucky as I had thought. As it turned out the eye that I so squarely hit belonged to a deputy sheriff and now he has me squarely in his sights.

"He was slobbering at the mouth, charging like a bull and clutching a nightstick. Right at that instant it didn't take a rocket scientist to figure out that I was rear-end deep in a whole different kind of trouble.

"The fight in me instantly turned limp. I impulsively threw up my hands to show no resistance but it didn't help much. From out of nowhere a second deputy hit me on my blind side and down I went. Followed by both of them. In the next instant I was being crushed beneath about four hundred pounds of law meat, my face shoved into the dirt and the next thing I knew I'm hand cuffed with my arms behind my back."

Finally finished, she felt a sense of relief; like a child in a stage play who had successfully delivered her lines. However, this was not a stage play and there would be no applause. There was only reality. She looked at the starkness of the jail, of herself tired and dirty and the sadness in Morgan's eyes. The momentary silences made her feel even more self-conscious and she felt obliged to speak.

She was about to say something when Morgan reached over and took her skinned-knuckle hands in his. As he held them, he gently rubbed his large thumb over the oozed dried blood and then gave a gentle squeeze. In the silence he inhaled a deep breath, looked into her eyes and consoled, "Baby you must miss your mother more than I can ever hope to imagine."

The manner in which his words came out, his tone of inter-soul understanding, a revealing of emotions she had never before seen, it was the plank which broke her last frail resistance and the dam holding back her emotions broke and crumble. Returning his gaze her eyes instantly watered. Streams of tears swelled out of control and flowed down her cheeks as she answered in sobs.

"Every day, every moment of every day I think of her." In hysteria she buried her face into Morgan's chest and sobbed. "She is always there; lingering in the back of my mind. And every day I miss her a little more."

Hugging her closer into his arms Morgan stroked her hair as he attempted to find words of comfort. "Bless your tender little heart," he murmured in a tone that watered his own eyes.

"Baby that which God decreed on your mother He did so for reasons of His own. It was something between her and God. While we all can feel sorry for the apparent inequity, it is not for us to seek revenge.

"My precious Darling," he spoke soothingly, "God in Haven knows you've been pulled from pillar to post. Never a real home or a real mother and father." He held a consoling hand on her shoulder as he looked down.

"Your mother was a wonderful person Shelly and I understand why you were so enraged. I feel the same way, maybe even more so. And for ever how much you miss her, I miss her even more." Impulsively they hugged again and as they released each other she found her own strength.

"Did you know," she spoke as she wiped tears from her eyes with the back of her hand, "that I have four pages of her pictures?" She intuitively knew that the statement was a surprise.

"That's another thing," she tried to interject a touch of humor, "that the long arm of the law may get me for someday; destruction of public property. How do they say it? One each; in this case one each Encyclopedia of Rare and Unusual Genetic Birth Defects." She didn't wait for Morgan to ask, she simply continued.

"I've known for years. When I was younger, I used to go out to the Carnegie Library almost every day. I'd take down the medical encyclopedia, go to a quiet section and have myself a good cry looking at her pictures.

"Then a couple of years ago I just tore out the pages and I have kept them ever since. I sleep with them every night. Do you know that those are the only existing pictures of her?"

What followed then was a terrible, awkward silence. Shelly wanted to say that Morgan had been the most wonderful person in her life, but she said nothing. Morgan wanted to say that he missed her mother as much as she does but he could not find the words. Feeling a need to control their emotions he interjected a different frame of mind.

"What's past is past, Sweetheart. None of us can un-ring a bell. What we have to do now is to think of the future." He paused to allow a moment of time and then carefully asked, "Honey do you know what you want to do with the rest of you life?"

Shelly sensed what he was doing and was thankful for the change. She also slightly paused to genuinely reflect the nature and depth of their conversation.

"I think I know, Daddy Morgan. At least it is the only thing that always seems to be in the back of my mind." This was a welcome for Morgan because he had never before heard her even make mention.

"What Baby?" he encouragingly asked. "College, law school, medical school, what? You name it and its yours."

Shelly was surprised by his choice of suggestions. Because it was generally assumed, or at least she thought it was generally assumed that there was something in her life that she had to come to terms with before there could ever be talk of tomorrow.

"Heavens no Daddy Morgan," she responded in a clarifying tone. "A college campus is not where I belong. I realize that all of you have encouraged me in that direction. It doesn't seem to me though like that is the route that I am supposed to be taking. For now," she slightly emphasized, "I think what I want to do is to follow you in the theater business."

"'But Honey," he pushed for something more, "what about your young life? Baby, here your are, in the prime of young womanhood and you seem to be letting it slip away. Why aren't you out in the world with young friends; going to socials, partying, dancing the night away?" At this point Morgan was being forceful because he believed it was needed.

"Sweetheart, let's get serious for a moment. Between, Jenny, Frank, Aspen and me there have been a stream of young men knocking on your door. Now, I would like to know why we end up with nothing?" For reasons she could not explain, Shelly welcomed the subject. The moment seemed right for her to tell her thoughts.

"Morgan, in the boy friend department, no girl could have had a wider choice. Name it and you all have seen that I tried it. From banker, to lawyer, to lonely GI, to movie projector operator; and for that I love you all.

"I know that you all keep looking for some semblance of love, marriage, kids and a white picket fence. And... I need to tell you that I have tried. I wanted to do it for no other reason than to please all of you. Once I even set out to fall in love. His name was Jeffrey Ellis; how do they say it, a promising young banker.

"But there was just nothing there. We even had sex, not once but several times. And each time, all I could think of was mother.

"I felt a little something only one time, when I pretended she was watching and approved, but then nothing.

"Morgan, having the four of you by my side has meant four times the pleasure of growing up. More than that I have had benefit of four different outlooks on life.

"Somehow it is all inside of me and I seem to know so much. It's just that I haven't figured how to put it all in order." As she finished she had expected him to express some sort of understanding.

It was not understanding however that interested Morgan. He was determined not to let the moment slip away. "But baby, don't you have something special you want in life? You surly can't be serious about the theater business. That's no kind of life's expectation. Don't you have any secret dreams? Surely there is something?"

At this moment it was Shelly who made and held the two in eye contact and then said, "Look at me Daddy Morgan. What do you see; really?"

Morgan had no need to break their eye contact. With a returned tone of equal sincerity he said, "I see a little girl. A little girl who I have helped raise since she was a beautiful baby. And now she is a beautiful woman." A swell of emotions again rose up in Shelly. It was sufficient to make her blink but she retained their eye contact as she said.

"And I am a woman, Daddy Morgan; in every way a woman. Complete with all the emotions, desires, dreams and feelings.

"And I firmly believe in the natural order in life of woman coming to man; that the man is intended to be the dominant figure. About that there is no question. But there is also something else."

She paused for a moment to think of the words she needed. Then, as if there were no words, she simply turned back to Morgan and said, "Don't ask me what it is because I don't know. All I know is... there is something that I have to find. Maybe," she hesitated in a manner intended to show that she did not want to discuss the matter any further.

"Maybe," she shifted to a lighter hearted tone and signaled the ending. "My dream is to fly away with a handsome prince on a *magic carpet* to some far away mysterious land."

Panic within Morgan was instantaneous and without bounds. There came a stabbing pain; a contracting shooting hurt directly through his heart. *Please God,* he prayed. *Don't let it show; don't let her see.*

And there is a merciful Deity, because at that very instant there was a loud, offensive intrusion as the attending deputy sheriff unlocked the door and announced that time was up.

In a rush they hugged and said good-by. Morgan reassured Shelly not to worry, that Frank Buckwilder would be her lawyer and he would be there as soon as possible. Shelly was then led back to the holding compound and Morgan was escorted back to the front. The lobby that had been so crowded when he arrived was now empty. The desk sergeant looked up from a book he was reading but said nothing.

As Morgan opened the door and went out into the street the first traces of morning light were just becoming visible across the sky. He glanced up at the zigzag collection of thin red lines and gazed into the promise of a new day. Streetlights reflecting on the early morning dew simmered across the empty avenue and cast an eerie glow. He inhaled a deep breath of the damp air and adjusted his fedora hat. When the circulation in his leg had improved he stepped out on the cobblestones. A lone figure in a silent street; walking cautiously, placing his cane and then prodding his jake leg forward as he moved into the night. His body was headed home but his thoughts remained at the jail.

"How, how, how?" he asked himself aloud. "How could she possibly remember? How is it possible at age three or so to remember something so long ago?"

Chapter 2

The storyteller briefly paused and silence again fell over the room; pierced only by the sounds of a howling wind whistling in around the double-hung windows. Finally the listener spoke.

"I'll say this much, my storytelling friend, you always manage to keep that part of the story interesting. And I especially like it when you put in a little extra tid bit of change."

"Tid bit? What extra tid bit?"

"That extra tid bit at the end."

"I didn't put in any extra tid bit, as you call it, you thick headed pile of elephant dung. I am aware of my own words. I know what I said. I should know. I have repeated them often enough. So if it's not too much of an imposition would you please reframe from casting dispersion on my verse? As in times past, I will again define the rules. You are at complete liberty to lunge your scraggly rusty blade at the women of my life. But dare you not puncture my composition."

"Then quit changing it."

"Listen... my listener friend, of few things am I more sensitive. I have just this instant come to the realization as to why you reside in the State of Pennsylvania.

"By some means unbeknownst to me, you have ascertained that murder is illegal in this State. Following that bit of jailhouse legality, your inept logic has led you to a false sense of security that I will refrain from doing the world a favor by making you a candidate for the County morgue.

"Lest you become too secure in your erroneous logic however, be aware that there is also such a thing in this State as justifiable homicide. Before I perpetrate that pleasurable act on you I herewith give you the fairness of liberating yourself if you will immediately disavow your accusations.

"For the sake of argument I will grant you liberties far beyond your actual capabilities. Let's assume that by stretching your intellect, you actually do know the complete alphabet of the English language.

"Nay, I will go even further. I hereby disregard the bounds of impossibility and concede for the moment that somehow or another you are capable of putting together a complete sentence.

"Would you now tell me, the judge, jury and executioner, on what evidence you make the claim that I have, as you say, added a tid bit."

"Because you put in that last bit."

"Don't push me you death-wish addict. I always put in that last bit."

"This time it was different."

"Impossible. Unless you are deliberately trying to accelerate your demise I suggest you stop joking. I fail to see the humor."

"Who's joking? You changed the ending."

"Death may be just a bare hands choking breath away. Therefore, I beseech thee to choose thy words carefully. How did I change the ending?"

"You put in that part about her wanting to fly away on a magic carpet."

"Do not attempt to further infuriate me my listener friend. Tell me I have spoken of that before."

"Nope."

"Never?"

"Nope, never."

"Never ever ever?"

"Nope. First time I ever heard it."

"Please. Let us be extremely precise. We are both speaking of the same her flying away on a magic carpet with a handsome prince?"

"Same one. I think you also mentioned something about a mysterious land. But it's the first time I've ever heard it."

"Oh, for heaven's sake," heavily sighed the storyteller as he hopelessly shook his head.

"Better that I be struck by lighting. Is it possible after all these years? Could I have been so blind? That the clue I have so arduously been searching for has always been right at the end of my nose?"

"Are you talking to me or to yourself?"

"Silence you annoyance. Can't you see the significance of this? I vaguely remember something about the silent movie era, something about one of the ol' Arabian Nights series.

"But...but, that was in the 1920s; maybe even further back. Was it the era of the big money or the depression? OK calm...down. Start far enough back to include everything; go as far back as her grandparents. Surly, that's far enough. Grandparents...

Both of Shelly's grandparents were Irish immigrants; how be it they came over at different times. The grandfather was a scheming unsavory no account by the name of Michael 'Mike' O'Riley who came to this country one step ahead of the law. Shelly's grandmother's maiden name was Colleen Sayer; a simpleton woman with good looks but few brains. Mike came to Pittsburgh with expectations of nothing more than being a coal miner and a life being spent deep down in the bowels of the earth.

Before too long however, he became influenced by the vogue of his fellow coal miners; aptly named Coal Mine Financiers; meaning *talk-making it* while breathing coal dust. In substance the era when Pittsburgh had the reputation of being the wealth capital of the world; where great fortunes were routinely made by seemingly non-descript men.

In those days talk of money was everyone's mania. Business owners, blue collar workers, bankers, taxi cab drivers, housewives and politicians; everyone was obsessed with who had it, who was currently making it, who had the most of it and how they made it; and in the bowels of the even earth more so.

Dark dreary shifts down in the bowels of the earth were passed by tales being spun of money; easy money, everywhere money, so plentiful it was just lying in the streets. Miners making a dollar a day talked in terms of millions. Every man down in that dungeon boasted of personally knowing someone who had made it; and...'I tell you Mike O'Riley my boy, if you had just of (so and so), why today you'd be worth millions'.

Andrew Carnegie, worth over five hundred million, came from Scotland in 1848 when he was only thirteen. He first worked in a cotton factory as a bobbin boy for $1.20 per week.

He eventually owned railroads, steel mills, coalmines, office buildings, and banks.

William G. Johnston, purported to be worth twenty million, made his fortune as a printer and bookseller, and became the president of Duquesne National Bank, Pittsburgh Steel Casting Company and the Hainsworth Steel Company.

Henry J. Heinz, the son of a brick maker, began by cultivating horseradish in the family back yard garden. Seward B. Hays started out in life by building a flatboat to haul coal on the Allegheny and Monongahela Rivers. During the civil war he sold coal to both sides and became known as King Coal. George Westinghouse, inventor of the air brake, began operations in a small factory that occupied only two city lots at the corner of Liberty Avenue and Twenty-Fifth Street. He went on to perfect the alternating electrical current system and made hundreds of millions. Donald O'Neill, publisher of the Daily Dispatch in 1865 made a fortune in publishing the first penny newspaper.

Glasswork, petroleum, coke, natural gas, railroads, machine companies; success was the rule rather than the exception. And before long Mike O'Riley could no longer endure the sweat, black dust and misery of mining coal.

In 1914 when he was 40, he went to a marriage broker where he was introduced to and subsequently married Colleen Sayer; then age 19 and whose level of intelligence, if not retarded, bordered thereon. For the sum of twenty-five dollars Mike was able to negotiate a bargain because, as the Agency noted, she was a little touched in the head but she would work hard and do as she was told.

Quite coincidentally, a wife who would do as she was told was exactly what Mike was looking for. He took her home, bought her one new dress, a bottle of cheap perfume, a tube of bright red lipstick and set out to enter the world of investments; via the avenue of Colleen's sexual favors.

He first started by hanging out at brokerage houses and would thrust himself upon anyone who would be of potential help. For those lecherous entrepreneurs who were willing to divulge inside stock tips or other financial gossip, sexual encounters were readily available.

The strategy was clumsy at first but little by little it began to show results but then came a mishap; Colleen got pregnant. Nine months later she gave birth to a baby girl whom they named Patricia and shortly thereafter they were back in business.

From this meager beginning their niche in society gradually took hold and grew. As it did Mike devoted ever more attention to refining Colleen's image. As they increasingly attended more formal affairs her dresses changed accordingly. Eventually he graduated her to low cut, full length, satin gowns patterned after European aristocracy.

Her trade mark, whether appropriate for the occasion or not, was a diamond choker necklace and diamond dangling earrings, be they gotten by less than scrupulous means, and she attempted to mirrored the antics of royalty, court, intrigue and infidelity.

The long cleavage of a bulging, firm bosom in the body of a twenty plus year old is indeed a thing of beauty. Her unblemished complexion suggested youthful virtue; not a virgin but close enough, and as the circle of gossip went, certainly above Mike's class. When she was introduced to men, she had a talent for flirtatiously extending her hand, flashing a wide smile of pearly white teeth that accented her dimples, slightly dropping her eyes and executing a suggestive little curtsey. Then holding the introduction just a tad too long, she would end with a squeezing hand and alluring eye contact. While her antics were laughable by other wives, in Colleen's mind it reflected stately protocol.

Having displayed the merchandise, Mike would slightly pull her back and assume the conversation. In cases where an interest was shown he would convey the terms; stock tips first, sexual favors later. Things went well enough, or one could say even better than expected through the early and mid 1920s. Everyone was making money and Mike even managed to get a token membership into the elite Webster club.

Token meaning he was there simply for the amusement of the other members. Initially he had been invited into the power circle because someone, in a moment of humor, decided it would be amusing to have a-touch-of-slumery in the Club. A mascot of sorts to which everyone could toss a few investment crumbs. Eventually he simply became community property and the focal point of condescending remarks.

His status was indicated by his reference as a coal miner in a business suit. But all of that had been just fine with Mike. He played his role and accepted the subservient status as the price he had to pay to get where he wanted to be. In reward for his bootlicking, the money boys would toss him advanced stock tips and little by little he was making the climb; by his standards. Nevertheless, in the eyes of money his gradual progress was nothing more than a reason to turn up his sweat threshold. They had a mania for dropping names such as J.P. Morgan, Rockefeller, or Ford that they knew would cause him to have an intimidating attack.

Stories of rags to riches always flamed his discontent and to make him drool it was common to dribble out stories about the ease with which great fortunes had been made. A favorite was the night of the Millionaires Banquet back in 1901.

'I tell you Mike, my boy if you had of been there that night', he was frequently told, 'why you would be a very wealthy man today'. That particular story was about the first days of the United States Steel Corp. Nearly 100 millionaires had gathered at the Schenley Hotel for a big money, big name banquet to celebrate the formation of America's first billion dollar corporation.

'Let's see now,' the money would mimic, 'as I recall the Mellons were there; so were the Guggenheims, the Rockefellers, ol' J.P. Morgan himself, and of course H.J. Heinz, Charles Schwab and Lawrence C. Phipps. Funny thing though, ol' Andy Carnegie didn't show.

'At's a shame too, because I wanted to talk to him about that three or four hundred million he had', and so it went. The club members baited and Mike drooled. In overall generalities, history tells a fairly accurate account of the way the financial world was in those days.

As the years past Mike was able to start dressing in style, buy a spanking new four door Packard automobile and acquire a nice home out in Avalon; how-be-it, life in that new house was not keeping pace. In fact it could be said that his home life was going in the opposite direction.

As Mike's status and wealth flourished his attention to family, if they're ever was any, completely diminished and along the way Colleen dropped completely out of the business picture. Her beauty took a rapid decline, her mentality deteriorated and she regressed to taking care of Patricia.

Factored into the circumstances, Mike had hired a full time maid to run the house and there was very little for either Colleen or Patricia to do.

On a personality scale both wife and daughter were somewhere below meek and mild; and family discussions, in the normal sense of the word, simply did not exist. When either wife or daughter did talk with Mike it was usually on the level of 'Yes Dear, No Dear' and 'Yes Daddy and No Daddy'. Whenever their presence became a nuisance to him he would simply let out a roaring bellow that would result in the two fading from sight. Lacking an interest from anyone else, mother and daughter turned to their own company.

From early on Colleen had a strong bonding instinct and possessively showered Patricia with attention. It wasn't so much that she acted in the role of mother teaching the child, as it was a regressing down to the child's level. What started out as reading nursery rhymes progressed to fantasies of her own.

By the time Patricia reached her ninth birthday or somewhere therein both mother and daughter started playing with lipstick and make up.

When Patricia was age 14 or so she quit going to school; mostly because her chest was becoming odd shaped and other kids made fun of the way she looked. With no objection from Colleen she simply started staying home and their days were spent dressing up and pretending. Mike never noticed that Patricia no longer went to school. Nor did he notice that Colleen was creeping toward imbecility. He was busy making money.

But, all good things must come to an end. The year 1929 arrived on the scene and the world of Michael 'Coal Miner in a Business Suit' O'Riley was about to come tumbling down on two fronts; home and work. The home front part pertained to daughter. The work part stemmed from the stock market crash. Destined for collision, it was a happenstance of happenstances that the two separate factions would collide on the same day.

For some time Colleen had noticed that Patricia's breast were not developing as normal; rather they were becoming elongated. At first it appeared that just the nipples would be long. But the pattern continued and soon her young breast started to dangle.

As the months passed her 15th birthday arrived and the elongation continued. Finally on a Tuesday morning like any other Tuesday, Colleen took Patricia to one of Pittsburgh's few women doctors. After a thorough examination and consulting the medical books and journals, the diagnosis was mammopendulopathy. The prognosis was that she would develop into womanhood with breast in the shape of long cucumbers. On that same Tuesday, Mike was at his brokerage firm. Sadly it wasn't long cucumbers but long strings of ticker tapes cluttering the floor that was on his mind. And by closing time the first half of his world was known. The date was October 29th and would become chiseled in the annals of financial history as Black Tuesday.

Mike had borrowed heavily against everything he owned included his house and now it was all worthless. That was during the day. The evening would bring the news that his family life just about equaled the value of his stock.

His energy drained he left the brokerage firm of Gene, Wiley & Witt and despondently drove the seven miles out to a home that was no longer his. In a daze he pulled his big shinny black Packard into the circular driveway and got out without locking the doors.

As he stepped up the steps and onto the porch the front door opened and he was surprised to be greeted by both Colleen and Patricia. Never before had either of them troubled to acknowledge his presence. In a fleeting instant he welcomed what he thought would be words of sympathy and comfort; a surge of warmth that he had someone to share. But it was a short-lived feeling. A rare conversation started taking place. Confusing at first, but nonetheless it was a conversation as the Irish accent of Colleen greeted her husband.

"Hus'band, me dear man', thank heaven yea be finally home. An awful day tis been." The tone of her voice clearly implying an emergency. Mike paused on the porch, not for a wifely kiss but to agree.

"Aye. Terrible, blooming' bloody terrible. I can't yet be'lieve it. Faith that we should come this far and then 'ave it 'appened," he then push past both Colleen and Patricia and entered the house.

"Tis God. He's punish'ing us fer' the bad deeds we've done, don't yea see,"Colleen continued as she and Patricia followed.

"I've al'ways known He'ed punish us, I did. In me own mind I knew it, and that's a fact. I even told Father Meehan down at St Ann's, don't yea know. When I was a'making me confession, I did. And yea know wha't he said? He said God would punish us. That's what he said."

"Fait'h wife,"Mike admonished, "God had damn lit'tle to do with the mat'ter. Greed, that's what caused it now. Greed. That's what's at the root of this whole blooming busi'ness. Too many people a try'ing to get rich, when they got no right."

His tone reflecting resentment as he crossed the room to a liquor cabinet. Bringing down a bottle of Irish whiskey, his hand shook as he poured a double jigger. He then dropped into an easy chair, took a stiff swallow, and was continuing his rage when he noticed Patricia.

"What' be the matter with yea lass?"he yelled. "Yea worr'ied that ye'll 'ave to be out and earn'ing yea own keep now? How old yea be, 15, 16?

"When I was you'r age I was work'ing 16 hours a da', I was. Moreover, hard work let me say. Maybe that's what yea be need'ing now. A little hard work will do yea good. Make yea a'ppreciate all the things I've given yea."

"Now Dar'lin hus'band don't yea be blaming yea daugh'ter,"Colleen quickly intervened. "Tis not her fault what 'appened. Tis God's de'cision it tis. She's a 'aving to pay for the sins of 'er parents, she is. And a sad day tis, to 'ave this 'appen to your only daughter."

"Faith woman,"Mike roared, "would yea be doing me a favor and tell me, where is the son? A son I could start over with. A daughter I 'ave. Tell me now if yea will, the wor'th of a daughter?

"The men,"he rose to his feet in wrath, "with whom I do business; the fellows down at the Board Room; the right sort of fellows, all of 'em.

"They tell me to make it in this world; everything has to be measured in terms of money. Money is capital. What's more, there be only three ways of getting capital.

"Ye can either steal it, borrow it, or s'weat it out of yer employ'ees. So now I'll be asking yea wife, 'ow will I be re'gaining me wealth from the sweat of a daughter?"

"I know my dear man. I know, that I do. Tis me own fault and I ad'mit it. A son she's not, but she's still yea flesh and bones, that she be. I'll be ask'ing yea as your duty to be fix'ing that what's wrong with 'er. It would be no prob'lem for the likes of a man such as yeself. Yea could do it in no time a'tal and it would mean so much to 'er happi'ness don't yea see."

Mike took another swig from his glass and again grimaced at the sharp bite. Hundreds of thousands of dollars he had just lost. What was he doing holding this conversation. In response he blurted out.

"Woman, don't yea know what 'appen to'day?"

"I know, and I know it ta be a fact, that I swear."

"Then sup'pose yea ex'plain ta me what 'appen today,"he shouted; expecting her to say she had heard about the stock crash.

"What 'appened ta day was we found out that yea daughter, yea own flesh and blood is suf'fering from a deform'ity. I've been a'trying to tell yea but yea won't listen. Your own daughter, she tis."

"Deform'ity?" He questioned as he abruptly turned to Patricia. "Faith in me Christ woman, what be yea talking a'bout? What kind of a deform'ity?

"Come 'ere child. Speak up. What 'ave you gone and done to yeself that yea 'ave some sort of a deform'ity?"

"She's done nary a bit to 'erself. Born with it she was. Now she's a coming into a woman yea have to be fix'ing it yea do. It's a father's re'spons'ibility, it tis.

"Now if it pleases yea I want yea to look at yea-own daughter's breast. They're not right, they're not,"Colleen continued as she started unbuttoning Patricia's blouse.

"No, Mommy,"Patricia quickly protested. "Mommy, please don't. Please,"she begged as she held her hands to her breast.

"Come now child, tis only yer fath'er. We who brought yea into this world we did. Now I'll be asking yea 'ow is he going to be a fix'ing what's ailing yea if he can't see,"she continued to open up the blouse and then turned to Mike.

"What on 'arth do we have 'ere woman?" Mike bellowed in reaction. "What is the mean'ing of this?"he moved to Patricia and with an open hand reached out and lifted up one of her breast.

"Faith woman, what 'ave yea done to yea self. Look at this,"he rolled first one of her breasts then the other between his thumb and forefinger. "What are yea 'alf cow? Wife, is this yer idea of a joke?"he turned in rave at Colleen. "Tits like a cow; on me own daughter.

"Is this what yea give me for tak'ing you in when there was nary a'nother man what would 'ave yea. Wo'man, a sorry wench yea be. What would yea 'ave me do with this, this cow?"he flipped away Patricia's breast.

"Tis like I've been trying to tell yea,"Colleen attempted to explain. "We'll 'ave to spend some mo'ney to get 'em fixed. It shouldn't a'tall be that costly don't yea see. Not seeing as 'ow she's still young and fine and 'tall. We can sure'ly find a doctor to do some operations. It's what we've got to do fer 'er 'appiness, don't yea see."

"Woman I don't have any money,"he roared. "Faith, what will it be tak'ing to make yea understand! The money is gone. Maybe you would like it if I could just sue somebody and get it all back. Would that be making you happy now? Just march right out and sue somebody; *sue somebody, sue somebody'.*

The rest of the night he sat in his armchair and thought. And by morning he looked upon Patricia's mis-genetics as a Godsend; a Heaven sent windfall to offset some of his stock losses. Somebody had done something to deform his daughter's breast. Ever who that somebody was, doctor, hospital, anesthesiologist, they were going to get sued. But first he had to find out exactly what mammopendulopathy was. And the only place he could think of to find that out was at the Carnegie Public Library.

In all probability he didn't get much sleep that night because he was out of the house before dawn. By all accounts, heavy predawn fog still shrouded the streets as he got in his car and first drove down to a newsstand at 12th and Avalon.

There he bought an early edition of the *Gazette* and then proceeded across town to the library. Knowing that he would be early he had planned on scanning the paper while waiting. But time waiting while in a state of anxiety does not make for reading and the paper was kept rolled up instead. Pacing and clock watching he would occasionally whack his leg.

When the library doors did open at 8:30 he simply tossed it in an outside trash container. In an impatient huff he stepped inside, and met his first experience of a different world.

The colossal magnitude of so many books came as a shock. He was instantly taken back by the library's sheer magnitude; walls and tiers of books, 2nd and 3rd floors of books. As for as the eye could see books; it was his first time ever in a library.

For a split second it all seemed too overpowering; but that misgiving was quickly squelched. After the hell he had just gone through there was no way that he was going to be intimidated Neither was he going to embarrass himself by seeking out some snooty librarian, having to explain his predicament and meekly ask for assistance; not while he still had a single ounce of self respect.

Without stopping at either the reference desk or the checkout counter he plunged headlong into the endless maze of shelved books; searching through one long row and then another. The deeper into the maze he got the more aggravated he became. He was not, on that day, or any other day for that matter, the least bit interested in fiction, romance, history, mysteries, or home improvement. On that day his only interest was the elusive part of the library that housed the books on human anatomy.

Saving face, he cornered an innocent looking young shelving clerk and asked for directions. Proceeding to the second floor he experienced a small bit of relief as he came to the rows of medical books.

Tilting his head back to read the top shelves and squatting down to read the bottom he nudged along in his search. Finally he came to something that seemed promising. A single volume, three inches thick book with the title Encyclopedia of Rare and Unusual Genetic Birth Defects; the thickness and weight of which, required the use of both hands to handle. Taking it from the shelf he carried it to a reading table and as he sat down he intentionally opened it up in the middle; which was unfortunate

If he had not been in such a rush, if the circumstances had been different, if he had not been so overwrought...he may have opened the book at the front; at the prologue. In which case he would have read, in part, that the book was published in the interest of science. Explaining as it did that the natural evolution of life does not always produce perfect specimens and the reader is advised that some of the material may appear extremely graphic.

Within the book contents, the prologue would have further related, are depiction's of a female born with two fully functional heads, various cases of Siamese twins, several examples of persons being born with a claw shaped hand, cases of females with accessory mamma (mammary glands in excess of the normal number of two), mature females with two inch nodules nipple, as well as many others.

But Mike was not interested in the prologue. His concern was the oddity of his own daughter's breast. For that reason he opened the encyclopedia at the letter M. Hurriedly he flipped the pages until he came to the word mammary; and with his index finger he began scanning the lines:

mammary (mam'er-e) [L.] mammarius. Pertaining to the breast...

mammiform (mam'i-form) [mamma+L. forma]. Shaped like the mamma, or breast...

mammogen (mam'o-jen). A hormone of the anterior pituitary: m. (1) stimulates growth of the ducts; (2) stimulates growth of the lobules of the mammary gland...

mammopalasia (mam'mo-pla'ze-ah) [mammo-+Gr. plasis formation+-ia] The development of breast tissue. *Adolescent m.* the development of ...

mammopendulopathy (mam'mo-pendu-lopathy) [L.] *mammary gland* a milk producing organ in female mammals: *pendulous* hanging loosely, suspended so as to swing or sway: *pathy* [Gr.] denoting morbid condition or disease. **MAMMOPENDULOPATHY:** A rare genetic defect wherein the mature female breast develops in an elongated configuration. Length may vary from five to eight inches. Circumference may vary from three to four inches. Cause of defect unknown. Suspected latent gene of prehistoric era. Possibly pre-*Homo sapiens* when the evolutionary mammal was thought to have walked on four extremities and female breast hung down in the shape of similar four feet mammals. Not considered life threatening. Not known to adversely affect nursing capability. No known corrective or reconstructive surgery. (Circa 1925)

Mike scribbled down notes of the definition on a piece of torn tablet paper, re-shelved the book, and headed for the nearest telephone. Calling his lawyer from the lobby he was curtly advised that the case in point was genetics and that one could not sue on the grounds of genetics. As an ending comment he was then given an even sharper curt to the effect unless one felt that the wrong color of one's eyes or the pigment of one's skin was sufficient grounds to seek damages.

With the revelation of that news, the world of Mike O'Riley again plummeted into total despair. Hanging up the telephone he slowly made his way back to the front doors. Leaving the quietness of the library he stepped out into a city in chaos; stock market panic, congested streets, honking horns and crowded trolleys. In a very short time it was a world in which he would again get caught up in; but for the moment his mind was still at the library.

As he meshed into the crowded sidewalk he unconsciously started talking to himself. "Mamm mopen, Faith an' St. Patty," his Irish brogue came out. "I can't even pro'nounce it an' me own daugh'ter has it. Mam-o-penn-lo," he tried again. "Leave it ta the glor'ious medical pro'fession. If there be a diffi'cult way to sa' something, they'll find it. Why in the begorey 'ell don't they just call 'em hang'ing tits an' be done with it. I have a daugh'ter who will grow into grown woman with eight-inch long dang'ling tits. Hang'ing down like tits on a cow, they will. A real jewel. Getting her married off? Ha! How in 'ell am I ever going to gat her married off?"

He was so preoccupied that when he reached the street corner he absent mindedly stepped off of the sidewalk and almost into the path of an on coming taxi. To the sound of screeching breaks and a blowing horn a fist weaving driver bellowed out, HEY, YOU, IDIOT FACE. WHAT'S THE MATTER? YOU CRAZY? STAY OUT OF THE MIDDLE OF THE DAMN STREET. WHAT'S WITH YOU, YOU CRAZY? YOU TIRED OF LIVING OR WHAT?

Shaken and embarrassed, Mike O'Riley finished crossing and as he reached the other side he turned south and proceeded toward the Webster Hotel.

"She must not be my kid," he unconsciously continued his own conversation. "I've al'ways said that she wasn't my kid. She can't be. Nobody on my side of the fam'ily ever had any'thing like that."

As he came to the next intersection he waited in the cluster of other pedestrians and when the light changed he mindfully moved with the crowd. Once across his mind again turned to his self-pity; only now he walked in silence.

Life's a real jewel, he thought. *For fifty years I've kissed ass, crawled, groveled, and licked boots. And all for what? I end up busted flat on my ass without a penny to my name; not one damn red cent. Overnight, in just one fucking overnight my stocks are worthless. As if that's wasn't enough,* he continued thinking, *I have an idiot for a wife and now I find out I have a daughter who will have foot long tits and can never get married off. Great. Just fucking great.*

I had always thought that whenever I made it big I would get rid of 'em both; wife and daughter. Get me a sweet young thing with rock hard tits and finally start to live a little. But, thanks one Hell off a lot to you, Lady Faith you ol' battle ax now it doesn't look like it's ever going to happen. Of all the rotten lousy luck.

He moved with his head down and tightness in his body, frequently taking in deep breathes to expand his lungs as he continued walking toward the Webster. *Money is everything and everything is money. Life is money,* he persisted in thinking. Then without knowing why, he happened to think of one of the richest men in the world, Henry Clay Frick; and the 100 rooms Frick mansion called the Clayton that Frick lived in.

His thoughts about Frick then caused him to start recalling other wealthy estates around Pittsburgh; the forty-room mansion of George Westinghouse, called Solitude, the spectacular view, and grounds of the Lawrence C. Phipps' mansion called Grandview, the William Thaw mansion called Lyndhurst, the A.A. Frauenheim mansion...

His mind now raging with resentment his thoughts then jumped to entire neighborhoods; of all the money out in Squirrel Hill, Shadyside, Wilkinsburg, Mt. Lebanon and of course Sewickley.

Walking with his clenched hands shoved in his pants pockets and his head still bowed he was impervious to anyone else on the street. Fuming at his destiny he started recalling all of the great buildings that had been constructed since he came to Pittsburgh; and he didn't have a penny in any of them.

To argue his own point that somehow he had been wronged he started curling a finger to count as he started recalling building names.

First finger, the Frick 19 story annex in 1906. Second finger, the six million dollar Carnegie Institute in 1907. Third finger, Union National Bank also in 07, forth finger, the Mellon National Bank in 05 no wait 02 1902, the Baer-Kaufmann Store in 1913, the Mellon Bank in 1923, the 34 story Koppers Building, the H.J. Heinz Company...

It suddenly dawned on him what he was doing and he relaxed his hands as he entered the elite Webster Hall Men's Club where he would be attending a meeting being held by a group of very wealthy men in a very expensive place. The Webster cost four million dollars to build when it opened in 1926 and was herald as an unsurpassed millionaires club.

And back in 1926, millionaires were plentiful. At the height of the market, Westinghouse stock had gone up from $30.00 per share to $280.00. U.S. Steel moved from $36.00 per share to $250.00 per share. It was a one-way market. Everything went up and nothing came down; until the day before.

He took the elevator to the top floor and proceeded toward the conference rooms. In a preparatory mode he first stopped at the rest room, found it was full, lit a cigarette and waited his turn. When a urinal became empty he stepped up and unzipped his fly. Squinting one eye to avoid smoke irritation he glanced towards the ceiling; an etiquette of respect to the wealthy gentleman next over.

The pressure which he had been holding was released with a forceful stream and as the strain relaxed he slightly shifted up closer and allowed nature to continue. With his head dropped slightly, he took another drag from his half smoked cigarette and in a repeated show of respect he again tilted back and blew the exhaled smoke upward.

Having communicated his subservient position, he relaxed nonchalant and looked indifferently at the graffiti scrolled on the urinal wall. As his leak finished he noted, in passing, the scribbling of an outhouse philosophy, *...we are all responsible for our own orgasm....* *Christ,* he thought, *the whole damn world is falling apart and someone is worried about my orgasm.*

As he came out of the rest room he glanced down the hall to the Board Room. A crowd of stately dressed men were milling around waiting for preparations to be completed. Inside the unoccupied room, male waiters dressed in white serving jackets and black trousers were busy setting drinking glasses, pitchers of ice water and writing pads on a long conference table. One of Pittsburgh's most famous meetings of Bankers and Financiers was about to come to order; or disorder.

These were men who were not as wealthy on this day as they were the day before. Nor would this meeting be one of lavish lunch, Chardonnay wine, Havana cigars and back slapping comraderie. This meeting would be a battle of accusations; a shouting of double-crosses and charges of lying and cheating. Rich people who have lost their money are not very nice people at all.

The level of wealth represented at the meeting was reflected by the nameplates on the seating order; Henry Clay Frick, Andrew Carnegie, Author Vining Davis, Howard Heinz, A. M. Byers, etc. By these standards Mike O'Riley was a pauper. His net worth before the crash had never made it to the first million.

As straggling members continued to filed into the Boardroom Mike mingled in and took a seat; not at the long mahogany conference table but against the back wall. When the meeting was called to order, he listened and said nothing. Today, the Money was not in a tolerant mood.

For anyone to give even a hint of credence to Michael 'Coal-Miner-In-A-Business Suit' O'Riley would have been unthinkable. The best he could hope for was to listen and hope to learn what action, if any, was available to recoup his losses.

The meeting opened with the money tycoons shouting in allegations.

All of them had lost a lot of money but none of them, except Mike, had lost it all. Accusations and counter accusations herald in a capital brawl. After lengthy shouting and accusing there surfaced only one course of action. A course of action, which they, the Money, could take but he could not.

The Money strategy was to go out and buy additional stock while the prices were on bottom. In a process called dollar averaging a market comeback would eventually bring them back up.

When the meeting adjourned Mike remained behind as the others left and the echo in the quiet empty room made him realized how alone he was. He had no place to go. The world outside was in panic and he knew that it would only be a matter of days before the bank started foreclosing on his house. From the ninth floor window of the Webster he looked down at the crowds of people clamoring outside the banks; fanatically trying to make withdraws.

Most of the institutions had already run out of funds and simply closed their doors. It was too late to even get survival money. For no conscious reason he opened one of the large boardroom windows. As the windy breeze rushed in he reached inside his coat pocket and took out a silver whiskey flask; a once-upon-a-time status symbol. As he stood before the open window he unscrewed the cap and took a long swig. In no hurry to swallow, he held the whiskey in his cheek for a long instant then gradually let it ooze down his throat. He looked out at the breezy Pittsburgh skyline and made note of the Koopers Building, the Gazette Square, and the Union Trust Building. He looked at the steel mills out in Homestead and along Carson Street. He looked at all the city bridges and mentally counted ten silhouettes of arching steel across the Allegheny and the Monongahela River. Still he gazed.

After a while his attention drifted back to the presence of a pigeon sitting on the window ledge. Remaining very still he looked directly at the red ring eye that was peering back. The two held eye contact for a moment and then Mike began to speak.

"Hello there Mr. Pigeon, top of the day to yea." He held his flask in toast took another stiff swig and let it again ooze down.

"Are yea a mem'ber of this club?" he mocked. "It's a ver'ry ex'clusive club yea know. No Jews, no blacks, no women, no Prot'es'tants; no one has ever said any'thing about pigeons.

"I suppose yea would be a good re'publ'ican now wouldn't yea. Sure now, I can tell by the way yer feathers are smoothed back that yer a re'pub'lican. Still if yea not be a member the moneymen would frown on the likes of yea coming in. Even if yea is the fine up'standing chap yea be. What, with such a nice red ring about yea eye and ta'll.

"Tell yea what Mr. Pigeon, 'ow about I just come out on the ledge and we can 'ave our selves a nice lit'tle chat. I never could talk through a win'dow, I swear it." Out on the ledge Mike paid no heed to the bustling traffic nine stories below. He leaned against the window opening, held the flask to his lips, and swallowed the remaining swig of whiskey. Wobbling slightly on the ledge he turned and tossed the flask inside the Boardroom. Regaining his balance he looked down at the pigeon and continued.

"Tell me Mr. Pigeon, 'ow er yea hand'ling the stock market crash. No prob'lem yea say? Yea al'ways put every'thing yea 'ave on Pittsburgh real estate.

"Yea be sug'gesting er yea, that I should start get'ting the feel of real estate. Rock solid yea say. In'ter'resting, very in'ter'resting. Say I wan'ted to get in touch with some good down'town pro'perty, 'ow would I do that?

"Yea recommends something which is access'ible by air do yea. Most in'ter'resting. When yea say by air, am I cor'rect in as'suming that yea mean by wings? I see, of course yea do. Sort of a spec'u'lative venture. Something a few of the others are 'aving a go at. Well, yea certain'ly seem to be a very smart pigeon so may'be I'll be follow'ing yer invest'ment ad'vice.

"After all 'ow 'ard can flying be. Just lean over and let the soft cool air cur'rents take control. So if yea be ready my new found friend, let's fly away..."

As the storyteller pause the listener intervened. "Uh... I'm curious, my storytelling friend. The babe with the long tits, the one you called Patricia. Who did you say she was?"

"What?" The storyteller responded in surprise. "Of all the...I didn't say... idiot face; not specifically anyway, but her name was Patricia, Patricia O'Riley and Patricia was Shelly's mother. I assume that is sufficient clarification even for you."

"Shelly-the-porn-queen's mother. That makes long tits your grandmother doesn't it?"

"IT..., you gob of spit, makes her Shelly's mother."

The manner of the question asked and the manner it was answered sparked a fleeting touch of awkwardness. The listener, feeling the onus to say something, but still not being too apologetic, made the comment.

"You say 'good-ol'-boy O'Riley' had a fleeting impulse of sensitivity about any and all human deformities when he first opened up that book?"

"If he did I think we can assume it was probably a very fleeting impulse."

"And...?"

"And the sensitivity must have been very short lived because in a split second his impulses focused right back to his own interest."

"Let me ask,"the listener interjected, "That book, that Encyclopedia of Rare and Unusual Genetic Birth Defects, why is there such a book anyway? I mean for what?" In response the storyteller inhaled a deep breath in a subconscious preparation for what he knew would be a lengthy answer.

"I suppose", his words being intentionally hesitant,"the earlier versions were buildings block of sorts in the evolution of medical books. I believe that the intent was honorable, meaning that the primary interest was to make the world aware of the thousands of things that can go wrong in the cycle of life.

"Back then wrongs were generally referred to as deformities. In that regard there has at least been some progress in that they are now medically referred to as birth defects." Here the storyteller should have concluded, but his impulse pushed him on.

"In my own pursuit of mind I have looked at the earlier versions of that encyclopedia. All of the earlier hardcopy of course have long since been out of print. However, Carnegie Public Library has them on Micro-Fish.

"And", he slightly paused knowing in a moment of weakness he was about to disclose something he didn't really care to be known. "I have actually seen pictures of Shelly's mother."

"What?" The listener responded in his insensitive character. "You mean to sit there with your bare face hanging out and tell me that you've seen picture of your grandmother's tangling tits. How'd they look?"

"Yes, you repulsive gob of whale puke, I have seen pictures of Shelly's mother. They're there for me to see, you to see, or anybody else to see. In case you happen to have a warped sense of curiosity..., which you do, go out to the Carnegie Library and see for yourself.

"It might even be possible that you will conclude that the pictures are in fact a thing of no importance.

" What is important is the impact which they had on Shelly."

"Ha," the listener resounded, "why'ent you go ahead and say it. Mommy, Your mommy?"

"Since," the storyteller disregarded the remark, "I started it, I will say it. But you, you mental case, let me ask, have you ever pictured your mother...assuming you did have a mother, did you ever actually see her having sex?"

"Hey..." the listener quickly responded, "hold on here. Mother? My mommy having sex. What? You crazy?"

"Uh huh, kind of out of bounds isn't it. So if you will be so kind as to hold thy tongue I will attempt to get this out. Meaning my statement that the pictures of Shelly's mother and her birth defects are probably the cause and effect that has put me here today."

"I get the feeling this is going to be long?"

"Feel whatever you like, I'm not doing it for you anyway. What I'm saying is for me. Shelly nursed, or to put it in a vernacular which your deranged mind can comprehend, Shelly sucked on these elongated mammary glands until she was past age three, resulting, if you will permit my use of the word, in a lifelong association with warmth and love."

As his own words came forth, the storyteller experienced a never before self-question. Can, the question took on silent form, effects of bygone eras, in actual fact, drift down to later generations? An involuntary pause then followed as he took in a deep breath that expanded his lungs to capacity. Thence, there materialized his conclusions. He had only two choices. One choice was to search. The other choice is to live a life of always wondering. Since he knew he could not live a life of the latter, there was really only one legacy before him.

Chapter 3

After a while the listener again spoke. "About the ol' man. You mean the ol' boy just took the quick and easy?"

"What?" The storyteller was jolted out of his silent thoughts, then responded. "Uh, I suppose that's as definitive as any."

"Then what happened?"

"What happened was Colleen raised Patricia. Patricia got married; actually an arranged marriage that lasted one night, and one night only. Nine months later she gave birth to Shelly. Shelly, among other things, if I may borrow your words, grew up and became a porn queen; the evidence of which we can look out the window at the marquee on the old movie house across the street and see."

"You leave one hell of a lot to be explained you know that?"

"Such as?"

"Unless I'm mistaken somewhere along the line you have been trying to convince me that if you, or me, or anybody else who has some unconventional sexual pursuits it's probably because of something which happened when they were a child."

"I think what I have said in times past, has been words to the effect that the imprints on one's own mind are apt to be strongly influenced by one's mother and whatever happened in the mother's life will flows to the child. And the life which Colleen and Patricia had after the ol' man took his own life, was ten years of hell."

"You mean the great depression?"

"I mean ten years of absolute living hell which society and history has seen fit to sugar coat by calling it a depression."

"Ah, come on now. Sure it was bad. Everyone knows that. But that's not what we've been talking about anyway."

"It's exactly what we've been talking about, but do me a favor. Don't attempt to become understanding you misguided disarrayed moron. In fact of the matter you are really all I have to insult and if you become understanding then I'll have nothing. In my self-imposed fear of that great loss, I will back off a bit.

"I can see how your dimwitted mind might be confused. Perhaps it will help if I put things on a little more personal note.

"Do this. Cast your eyes around this fleabag flat that we are living in. Would it interest you to know that these very same paper peeling walls, splintered floors, rusty plumbing, dirty double hung windows and sagging doors bore witness to those ten years of depression hell?"

"So?"

"So...? So, don't you think that maybe living through something like that might have some small minuscule influence on one's outlook on life? There was a time", the storyteller continued, "when the people who once lived in this rat-trap went hungry. Maybe even two or three whole families."

"So? How's that different from me. I'm out of work. And I don't happen to see me going into any suicidal panic."

"Uh huh. Such a tower of strength! What, with your unemployment check coming in every week and moonlighting on the side, I don't see how you are able to survive. Allow me to contrast that with a few statistics.

"The first thing that happened to Colleen and Patricia was they had to move out of that nice home out in Avalon and go on public relief. For that matter, so did thousand upon thousands of others. That within its self however really doesn't tell you much. The entire city as well as the whole county went into panic. The first reaction was the clamoring at the bank doors; and from there it got worse. Gloom over Pittsburgh grew as dark as the black smoke that once belted from the smokestacks of thriving steel mills. Manufacturing instantly cut production and almost overnight thousands upon thousands of workers were dismissed.

"Within the next two years more than 175,000 people in the Pittsburgh area would be looking for work. Emergency funds were quickly depleted and on January 16, 1931, the County relief agency issued a public statement that as many as 50,000 Pittsburgh metropolitan residence would be on the verge of starvation. Still it got worse. On June 30, 1931 over 5,000 hungry workers paraded the streets. On January 5, 1932 Father James Cox led 15,000 jobless workers from St. Patrick's Church at Seventeenth Street and Liberty Avenue in a demand-for-help march to Washington, D.C. Thirty-three banking institutions closed their doors. In April 1932 matters had deteriorated to where free milk had to be distributed to some 20,000 children in public schools. And time moved at a snail's pace. For the first five years after the crash, each day seemed to bring news that was worst than the day before.

"In an endless sea of idle time, lonely days and feelings of despair, people lived in hope that maybe tomorrow things would start to get better; but things did not get better. In February 1935, as thousands of sad eyed spectators looked on, the largest industrial dismantling project ever attempted got under way with the disassembling of the National Tube Company. A message to all those present not to even hope. Day by day public morale dropped a little lower. As it did, time honored deeds of chivalry and compassion fell by the way.

"Hungry men, both young and old, standing in long food lines had little inclination to assist those even more destitute; and Colleen and Patricia were among those many. On the City streets, idle men passed the time by gazing at others passing. They quickly learned to judge those who were worse off and turned away to avoid eye contact. Younger men drifted to their own circles and generally congregated in the doorways of closed bank buildings. Spontaneous humor would sometimes ignite as a relief valve and passers-by became the focal point of bleak jokes. A man hobbling past on a crutch became Hop-A-Long, a patch over another man's eye earned the title of One-Eye-Jack, and a frayed bowler hat worn by a small man with a mustache gave Pittsburgh their own Charlie Chaplin. And while they never knew it, Colleen and Patricia were given the Mohawk Indian name of Cow-ah-Tavd; which by some strange coincidence was an acronym for crazy old woman and her tag along virgin daughter.

"It wasn't that Patricia didn't attract attention. She possessed her mother's features of a creamy complexion, sparkling eyes, and long flowing hair. While not overly striking, neither was she homely. As she matured into womanhood her imperfect breast were kept hidden by high collar blouses and loose fitting garments. When it did happen that she would venture out alone she usually received her share of calls and whistles.

"Nevertheless, the character of romance in times of depression is not nearly as sparkling as romance in times of prosperity. Extravagant evenings of the Nineteen-Twenties became austere moonlight strolls in the Nineteen-Thirties. City parks were free admission. Similarly, the feature entertainment was nighttime spooning on the backside of Elm trees where the lawn grass was shaded from streetlights. Tree Shadow Marriage became another way of saying shotgun wedding and by either name the results meant more worries; a gripping fear which held a check on unmarried sex.

"With the demise of husband Mike, Colleen instinctively knew that the security of her own future would depend upon how wisely Patricia married. Wisely, she was not about to permit either of their futures to be jeopardized by a moonlight blanket on the grass in the shadow of an Elm tree.

"Resultantly, the prospects of Patricia getting married were not very promising. Prospective suitors who had a job could do better than a penniless uneducated girl living in a ghetto. On the other side of the coin, would-be callers from the same ghetto were stonewalled at the door by Colleen's fury. Resultantly...Patricia never dated. Of necessity, mother and daughter simply existed and the problem of her elongated breast was not their most dominant concern. As the months drifted into years, their expectations rose no higher than the economic level of the times.

"For the city of Pittsburgh, it was toward the end of 1935 before the first flicker of hope would appear. The American Iron Works of Jones and Laughlin announced a $40,000,000 dollar expansion program and two thousand men would be put back to work. If it's true that God works in strange and mysterious ways, not necessarily always good, then that advent bore out the proverb.

"Because during the same time frame Pittsburgh was again slammed head on with another disaster. This time in the form of floodwaters; not from one but two rains swollen rivers; the Allegheny and the Monongahela. On St. Patrick's Day, March 17, 1936 floodwaters from two hundred miles up stream came roaring down to empty into the headwaters of the Ohio. Cresting at 46 feet the entire downtown area of Pittsburgh was submerged under 20 feet of water. Over 100,000 men, women, and children were left homeless.

"From the bottom of the bottom however, Pittsburgh did start to rebound and on January 1, 1937 reported business was up almost 30 percent. United States Steel initiated expansion plans of $60,000,000 and Carnegie-Illinois Steel broke ground on a $63,000,000 plant in West Mifflin.

"By 1938, the prewar effects of World War Two were beginning to ripple through the local economy. In January 1939 a $5,000,000 Monongahela River front improvement project was started. In April 1939, construction started on the widening of Bigelow Boulevard at a cost of $1,900,000. In May a public-housing project was authorized for the expenditure of $19,000,000 in Federal Funds. On June 2, 1939 Westinghouse made full restoration of pay cuts that had been necessary in earlier years. Finally...the notion of things becoming normal began to emerge.

"On November 3, 1939 Pittsburgh had a *world premiere* movie showing of Allegheny Uprising at Loew's Penn Theater (a 4,000 seats, domed ceiling structure, built in 1926 at a cost of $2,500,000). Prosperity was gradually returning and at the end of 1939, as the demand increased for wartime ships, both Colleen and Patricia got full time jobs at the shipyards at Neville Island. Thankfully at Christmas that year they had hot eggnog and the cold of winter did not seem so harsh.

"Other silver linings were also starting to bring brighter days. It was in early January when the postman delivered a 'Please Forward' letter.

To: Mrs. Colleen O'Riley,

From: Merchants State Bank, Real Estate Loans Dept.

Dear Mrs. O'Riley,

We at Merchants State Bank have been attempting to reach you for some time. It is imperative that we contact you in the matter of the incomplete foreclosure proceeding on your residential property in Avalon, Pennsylvania.
There is a sum of money awaiting you upon the final release of title.

Sincerely,
J. Hocksworth Smith
Chief, Loan Officer

The foreclosure on the O'Riley house, as with any foreclosure property, left a cloud on the title which lawyers have a duty to clear. In exchange for her signing a Quit Claim Deed on the Avalon house, the Bank paid to Colleen the sum of two thousand dollars. The month was February. The year was 1940. Patricia was 25, not married; not dating and her natural mating instincts were yearning for fulfillment.

It may have resulted from the feeling of security that the two thousand dollars windfall brought. The feeling of well being of steady employment may have brought it on. Just as likely, it may have simply been the inherent order of life and the natural flowing of youthful hormones. For whatever reasons the lives of Colleen and Patricia experienced a transition that spring.

"Mommy," Patricia asked one morning in April. "Do you think I will ever get married?" The question was asked in an implying tone that finding a husband was a responsibility to which Mother Colleen should start giving attention.

"O' course yea will Dar'ling,"Colleen responded in a tone which clearly agreed that the matter was in fact her duty. "Tis just a mat'ter of time, it tis. I've been a looking with me own eyes fer some time now don't yea know.

"All the young men what work at the ship yar'ds, they look at yea they do. And that's a fact."

"Oh, Mommy,"Patricia responded. "None of them would ever want me. All they're interested in is joining the Army and running off to war."

"Tis not a fact daugh'ter. Fer some time now I've had me eyes on a fine young Irish lad over in welding. A fine upstanding lad he be. I've had me thoughts that he'd make a fine and proper husband for yea. And you know what baby daugh'ter? I'll be asking 'im about the prospects any day now. That I will."

Patricia felt satisfied with the answer. She understood that her mother had not been neglecting the matter; it had just been the times. However, with all of that now coming to an end it was proper that she should be taking her place as a wife. She felt a warm glow from the thought and went to bed that night pretending her pillow to be a new husband. Once the notion did set in however it became foremost in her thoughts and it was difficult for her to contain her restlessness. Three days later she again asked Colleen.

"Mommy, did you talk to the man in welding like you said you were going to?"

"Aye that I did me Dar'ling. And I'm sorry to say I was mistaken about me thoughts. Not 'alf the man I thought he was, he's not. But that's no matter. There's a plenty more there are."

"Mommy,"Patricia asked in panic, "what caused him to say no? Does he know about my breast? Is that the problem? That's it isn't it. You told him. Shouldn't we have waited? Mommy it seems to me that..."

"Now, now Dar'ling, course I didn't mention such a minor thing. Tis of no importance it tisn't. The man is just not manly enough to live up to his respons'ibil'ities. He's not, and tis a lucky thing we found out a fore hand. Now there's no need to be getting excited. There's more prospects there are. I've been watch'ing all the while, I 'ave."

"At lunch time, that's the best time,"Colleen answered as if finding a husband was in the same category as shopping for groceries. "The young ones col'lect together out on the docks at noon they do. Now daugh'ter, you know wha'? I got me a plan, I 'ave. Star'ting to'morrow I'll be 'aving me sack lunch and talk'ing around a bit. Tis me feeling we'll be 'aving you fixed up in no time atoll. You're a vir'gin right enough. And that's the important thing now don't yea see."

The fantasy of a mother; fruitful to dream, not so fruitful to fulfill. The husband search of the docks produced no prospects. After a week or so, Patricia again brought up the subject.

"Mommy, I know something must be wrong. I've been watching you go out on the docks every day at noon. And I've seen how all the men laugh. Its not that I have been spying but I did want to see. I found a good peeking place over by a window inside the building so no one knows. I just wanted to watch. Have you found anyone you like? What do you say that makes them shake their heads? You must joke or something cause I see them laughing when you leave. Why do they do that? Do you mention that I am a virgin?"

"Aye, Dar'ling. I do tell 'em that you're a vir'gin right enough. A' ourse 'tis the natural thing that they want a vir'gin; but so many of 'em tell me how tis. Most of 'em have old folks at home and they're having to help out with money matters don't yea see. The truth is that they're not in a position right now to be taking on a wife. But times are a get'ting better you'll see.

"They're good-natured lads though, the lot of 'em. Tis good that I share a laugh at the hard times they be hav'ing and not being able to start a family of their own."

Still later.

"Mommy, it's almost the end of April. Will I be getting a husband this spring?"

"You'll be get'ting your husband right e'nough Dar'ling. I've made up me mind to get down to business. I put an advertis'ment in the *Post*

Gazette and I have put aside a $1,000.00 for your dowry, I 'ave."

Still later.

"Mommy, it's almost the end of May. Why can't we find me a husband?"

"Tis not yea fault Dar'ling. A sorry lot the bunch of them. Nary a one worth his salt. A wan'ting the dowry in ad'vance, before the wedding, they do. A man is no good what would want his wife's dowry a fore he has taken her for his wife, he's not."

"Mommy, I'm never going to get married. I know it. Look at all the men we have already asked. Even with the $1,000.00 dowry. It's cause I'm the way I am. Nobody wants me."

"Don't be go'ing and saying silly things like 'hat Dar'ling. Ye dear ol' mother won't be letting you down. The month of June tis the wedding month, it tis. And married yea'll be. I 'ave been busy I have. Talking at work where I know'ed that yea wouldn't be listening."

"Talking? Talking about what? What is it that I don't know?"

"I've 'ound a marriage bro'ker, I have; a Gypsy lady. She calls herself Madam Rose, she does. Claims she has loads of a'vailable men wan'ting to get married. Fact of the matter she swears she 'as one in par'tic'ular. A real wealthy prize catch he be if we have enough money for her services."

"How much are her services?"

"A pretty penny to be sure. She want'ed $1,000.00, she did; a $1,000.00 up front. But I wasn't going to be taken in by that. I told her $500.00; that's all I had. I told her $500.00, not a penny more and then I just sat and looked her in the eye, I did."

"Mommy!"exclaimed Patricia. "What happened? Did she refuse? If she has a good man it's worth it, isn't it?

"Mommy please say yes. We know that all the men my age are going off to war, please? Did she describe what he looked like?"

"Dar'ling if what she says is true, he's a real genu'ine re'fined gentle'man, he is. Comes from good stock. Has a beautiful home over in Philly. Part of the old-line folks over there. That's what she says. Over 6 foot tall and she swears he's a real gen'teel man, he is. But very de'ter'mined in what he wants. Madam Rose made that clear to me, she did.

"He wants a wife what ain't been spoiled. He's ab'so'lutely firm that she has to be a vir'gin. According to Madam Rose he wants to start a family, he does. And the wife has to be young enough to produce good quality children. A family man sort. Gentle and considerate and after the honeymoon he won't have any ob'ject'ions to me living with yea. A big house he has, lots of room. Now how does that sound Dar'ling? Is your sweet ol' mother looking out fer yea, or not?"

"Oh Mother, he sounds perfect,"Patricia ran and gave Colleen a big hug. "Just perfect,"she continued with exuberant hugs. Then just as quickly she became frightful.

"Mommy... what if I'm not what he is looking for? Mommy, if he refuses I'll just die. I know I will. Does he know about me?"she sought reassurance. "I mean about my breast and all?"

"There, there Dar'ling, I have already thought of everything. What I told the Gypsy 'ady was that you are vir'gin and she has al'ready told him about yea; especially that you're a vir'gin. And...he says that's the most important thing. Nevertheless, he is asking for one other thing. According to Madam Rose tis of little im'portance to him but he also says there has to be a dowry. It's not the money that he's in need of, mind you. It's the custom thing."

"Did you tell her we had a dowry, did you tell her we did?"

"Aye, Baby, that I did right enough. She said that we should make it as much as poss'ible in order to make a good im'pression, so as not to scare him off so to speak. Well, I did a tad of lying I did, I told her a $1,000.00 was all we had."

Patricia's face became flush, her eyes were sparkling, and tiny tears ran softly down her cheeks. Colleen felt warm as she continued. "So accor'ding to Madam Rose, she convinced him that the money was not the important thing. The important thing is that ye're from good stock and ready to start 'aving babies. So to make a long story short, if the dowry is no less than a $1,000.00 then he's given his word he'll marry yea."

"When! When!"shrieked Patricia as she excitedly cupped her hands to her mouth. "Oh, Mommy will it be in June, pleeease?"

"All in good time Sweet'heart. I still had a fight on me hands over the fee for her services, I did. That Gypsy woman likes to shout and yell a bit about 'ow she is being chea'ted; but she wasn't going to get the best of me, don't ye see. She finally agreed to the $500 but swears she must have the money before the wedding. So what we did was, we came to an a'gree'ment, we did. She will bring him over from Phil'adel'phia and we will all meet at St. Ann's Church. I will swear before the 'ouse of God that you are a vir'gin, that I'll do. Then if we like 'im and he says he'll marry you, then she gets her $500. And after the Priest has pro'nounced ye man and wife then I'll give him your dowry, that I'll do."

Colleen's emotions swelled up as she shared in Patricia's joy. Then as an added bit she continued. "Now, me Dar'ling can ye keep a secret?"she paused with a coy smile. "I'm not sup'posed to tell yea, but the lady Madam Rose, yea know what she said? She said yea new husband, to show you that he doesn't care about the dowry money, he's going to use part of it to take you on a honeymoon, that' he's going to do. You'll be starting out yea-new married life in a fancy room right here in the William Penn Hotel. Now what do yea 'ave to say about that?"

"Oh Mommy,"Patricia again cupped her hands to her face and squealed. "Mommy I'm so happy. My very own husband. I'm so excited. Thank you, thank you, thank you."

"And now my baby daugh'ter we 'ave to get busy. A wedding gown and arrange'ments we'll be needing to make."

When Madam Rose met Edger Waters at the train depot there was immediate anger on both of their accounts. Madam Rose was expecting a gentlemanly sort of man in his early thirties dressed in attire befitting a prospective bridegroom. What she got was a man in his early thirties, unshaven, dirty, and destitute.

Edger Waters had anticipated that a welcoming committee would meet his arrival. As a minimum there would certainly be a representative sent by the bride's family to take care of his immediate hotel and dining needs. From what Madam Rose had led him to believe, he could also expect that there would be a formal dinner, a meeting of the prospective bride, a show of the full and complete dowry, an inspection of living quarters and finally a job offer.

As the train unloaded, Madam Rose was searching the arriving passengers with anticipation; and Edger Waters was searching the waiting crowd with anticipation. If their searching eyes crossed each other it went unnoticed.

When all the passengers finally cleared and the train pulled away there were only two people remaining on the boarding platform. One was a dumpy, painted up, middle-aged woman dressed in a bright red flowers on white patterned dress, a large black floppy straw weave hat, matched by an oversized black purse and carrying a black umbrella. The other was a tall, lanky man dressed in grubby clothes, needing a shave, unruly reddish blond hair and carrying one small frayed suitcase. In skepticism they finally addressed each other.

"Are you by any chance Mr. Waters?" Madam Rose asked across the platform; feeling sure her man had not arrived.

"Aye, that would be my name right enough. May I ask who might you be?"

"Mr. Edger Waters!" Madam Rose's voice rose sharply as she moved in his direction.

"The... Mr. Edger Waters who is supposed to get married today?"she questioned.

"Madam,"Waters responded in his own suspicion as they moved closer. "Pleeease tell me that you are not the prospective bride."

"MR. WATERS,"Madam Rose's voice rose in anger, "You sir are a disgrace!"

"MADAM,"retorted Waters in an equally combative tone. "You did not answer my question. Are you the prospective bride because if you are..."

"Don't... be silly you despicable excuse for a man!" she said tyrannically as she moved directly into his face. "Of course I am not the prospective bride, you idiot. Your bride-to-be and her mother are waiting for you at St. Ann's Church this very moment; assuming of course they are stupid enough to accept you."

"Madam."

"Quiet! You miserable reject! I'll do the talking. I've spent too much time and effort putting this thing together to let your miserable incompetence screw it up."

"Madam, I must protest. I have not yet agreed to the terms. I..."

"Let me assure you Mr. Waters, you are agreed to the terms. You are getting married today! You will marry a beautiful young woman by the name of Patricia O'Riley. She is 25, still a virgin and comes from a wealthy family out in Avalon. You will get an initial dowry of $1,000.00 cash paid to you at the church. You will pay me $500.00 out of that dowry as my fee. The remainder of your very overly generous dowry will be presented to you by the bride's father at an elaborate formal dinner which is still being arranged."

"Madam," Waters attempted to speak, "has anyone ever told you that you..."

"Silence, you scum. I took the precaution of checking your background. You do know what a background check means don't you? You bag of scum? In your case it means you make your living by fleecing lonely women and widows. Your arrest record reaches from here to where you supposedly just came from, Philadelphia.

"'I suspect that the reason you are dressed like a bum is to avoid the law. From what I hear the law is on the lookout for a sophisticated gentleman who would be traveling in style. NOW, Mr. Waters, if you will turn slightly and look off to your right you will see one of Pittsburgh's finest. Better known as Patrolman Schultz, pride of the force. Do we understand each other?"

"As I was about to say Madam... you do have a way with words."

"Good. Now that we understand each other, what is the meaning of this?" Rose demanded an explanation as she poked his grubby clothes with her umbrella.

"A matter of necessity," mellowed Waters. "An urgent need for a new identity so to speak. A trading of clothes with a sporting sort of chap whom I chance to meet under a railroad bridge. A fair exchange

I would say. The fashion jacket I was wearing at the time badly needed cleaning."

"Amusing,"slurred Rose. "I don't suppose you have any of your old identity in that rag you call a suitcase?"

"I, uh I wish I could be of more help," gestured Waters as he shrugged his shoulders and cast a helpless look.

"And money?"she forcefully demanded.

"A might short in that department; strictly a temporary situation," he attempted a slight smile.

To this Rose was not buying. Her sharp tongue quickly intimidated him into her control. She first rushed him to a public bath with instructions to shower, shave, and apply plenty of the free after-shave lotion. In the meantime she went at a whirlwind pace to a pawnshop, tuxedo rental store and a florist. In a short time she returned with a second hand wedding band, a freshly pressed tux, black shoes and a bouquet of roses.

Within an hour after his arrival, Edger Waters and Madam Rose arrived by taxi at St. Ann's Catholic Church where Colleen O'Riley, daughter Patricia and parish priest Father Shannahan were patiently waiting. With instructions to the driver to wait, Edger and Madam Rose stepped from the cab; then with the aggressiveness of a predator she moved in on her prey.

"Mrs. O'Riley," she initiated the introductions. "How lovely to see we all made it. Mrs. O'Riley, may I present Monsieur Edger Waters. Monsieur Waters this is Mrs. Colleen O'Riley and your lovely bride-to-be Patricia." Her words purred at the formalities of nodding and hand shaking.

"What a wonderful occasion, just wonderful," she vibrantly continued. "Now, lovely people I think it's best if we proceed right to that slightly unpleasant but very necessary part of our arrangement. Mrs. O'Riley do you hereby swear before Father Shannahan that your daughter Patricia is a virgin, and that she will accept Monsieur Edger Waters in marriage?"

"I so swear it, that I do 'ere in front of God and Father Shannahan.

And if yea don't mind me say'ing so Mr. Waters, tis a fine woman ye be getting. I gave her a motherly talk a fore the wedding I did. You're to be treated grand while on your 'oneymoon. To be made to feel like a real gentle'man, ye are..."

"Yes! Yes!" Madam Rose abruptly cut in. "Mrs. O'Riley I am sure that Monsieur Waters will not be disappointed. But we have not yet finished with the arrangements. Now, do you, Edger Waters agree to take Patricia O'Riley as your wife in accordance with our marriage agreement?"

"I so agree," nodded Waters.

"Good, now I believe that my part of the arrangement is complete. My further presence here will only be an intrusion into this beautiful and blessed event. Therefore I will take my graces and leave. If I may say this without sounding too crude, Mrs. O'Riley I believe you have something for both me and Monsieur Waters."

"Aye, that I do, and mighty proud to be giving it to yea, I am. In an envelope 'ere I have it. For you Madam Rose, I have fi..."

"'Mrs. O'Riley!" Rose sharply cut in. "Really, Mrs. O'Riley, I don't think it's necessary to mention any amounts. After all we are in sight of a house of God. Now if you will just present Mr. Waters with his envelope and me with mine."

Feeling embarrassed at her apparent social blunder, Colleen lost her determination to hold the dowry until after the wedding. She meekly handed Madam Rose her envelope and at the same time handed the $1,000.00 dowry envelope to Edger Waters.

"Wonderful," exclaimed Madam Rose as she moved to finish. "Now if you will excuse me I have one more bit of private business with Mr. Waters," Rose gestured in confidence as she turned her back to Colleen in a manner of shielding herself and Waters.

"Congratulations Mr. Waters, I am sure you will be handsomely rewarded in your new married life. For your first night, the expenses are on me.

"Here is a key to an already paid for room at the William Penn Hotel. Now, if you will be so kind, my agreed gratuity and I will take my graces."

With $500.00 from Waters and $500.00 from Colleen, Madam Rose stepped back into the waiting taxi and left. An awkward moment of silence fell as the remaining four watched the cab disappeared. An impatient usher in a frayed tux had been standing just inside the church door and now stepped out. Pointing to his wristwatch he whispered to Edger of being late and nodded instructions for him and Colleen to walk together with Father Shannahan down the isle to the church alter.

From the choir loft an organ started to play as the usher and Patricia stood in the foyer. Upon Father Shannahan upward look the tune changed to the bridal march and the young usher extended his escort arm. In a veil of white and cradling a bouquet of roses, she accepted his lead and they marched down the isle. In a brief ceremony, witness only by Colleen and the young usher, Father Shannahan united Edger Waters and Patricia O'Riley as husband and wife in the bands of holy matrimony.

The ceremony over, the bride and groom lightly kissed and made their way out of the church. On the outside steps Colleen dabbed her tears with a white linen handkerchief. She and Patricia hugged and as they were holding each other close Colleen whispered, "Congratulation Dar'ling, we did it. Now don't yea be for' getting. Tonight yea get in bed first. Be sure and have on yea baby-doll top so as to hide yea know what. When he comes out of the bathroom, yea want him to see the virgin part first. Trust your dear ol' mother, he'll nary notice anything else."

Inside a taxi, Edger and Patricia sat in silence as the cab moved through the Pittsburgh traffic and were inside the hotel lobby before their first words were spoken. As a stiffly starched uniformed bellhop wearing a matching round head cap escorted them from the registration desk to the elevator, Edger looked at Patricia and said, "Welcome to your first night away from home." They looked at each other and exchanged slight smiles but nothing more was said.

Inside Room #1027, Edger took Patricia in his arms and as he pulled her close he commented, "Tonight my new wife we stay here but tomorrow morning they will be waiting for us at your folks' place out in Avalon. That is the plan isn't it? If I am correct that's what Madam Rose mentioned; that you have a fashionable home out in Avalon," he murmured as he turned her face up and planted a forceful dominant kiss.

Reactively he also reached to her bosom and slipped his hand inside. When he felt her elongate breast his slobbering hard kiss froze, his eyes jerked open and he squeezed again in disbelief. Blood pulsated to his face as he stepped slightly back in a burst of fury; an instant sensation that he had been duped. In a frenzy he then jerk and ripped away the front of her wedding dress. Then with a second vengeful grab he yanked at her brassiere and as the clasp gave way he watched as her dangling eight-inch long mammary glands uncoiled and hung down.

"What on Earth!" he exclaimed. "I, uh Cow! Good God! You're a Cow! A Blooming Bloody Cow!" he bellowed.

"No wonder your father is paying a king's ransom to get you married off. Sweet Jesus in Heaven! Would it be worth all the gold on earth that a man should have a cow for his wife."

But for whatever rage Edger Waters felt at first, moments latter he would feel even more as he learned that Patricia had no father, there was no fashionable home out in Avalon, no generous dowry and that Madam Rose had got the best of him by $500.00.

On that last thought his rage manifested into an insane laugh. As Patricia stood frightfully still, he hysterically flung himself backward on the bed then recoiled to his feet. As his demented laugh became more intense he waved his arms, slapped his leg and wildly stormed about the room; that he, a professional at scamming, could possibly be scammed by a woman. The thought was inconceivable. The irony was too much. What he needed was a drink; a good strong drink of straight Irish whiskey. Still laughing in hysteria, he slammed the door as he left the room and headed for the hotel bar.

Left all alone in the room, Patricia sat in silence and waited. When it finally started getting dark she followed her mother's instructions and prepared herself for her wedding night. Lying in bed she continued to wait. At some time after midnight she could no longer stay awake and drifted off to sleep. It was bar closing time before Edger Waters returned to his honeymoon suite. And in that time line. The time from the wedding at 2:00 P.M. to the bar closing at 2:00 A.M. there passed in the night, that which might have been, and that which was.

That which might have been was the dreams inherent in their wedding vows:

When Edger Waters married Patricia O'Riley, he vowed he would take her for his lawful wedded wife, to have and to hold, in sickness and in health, to provide and protect, for better or worst, till death do thee part.

To these words and to this marriage Patricia had brought a young woman's trust and innocence. She had also brought to their wedding bed a virgin body. A testament of inner grace. Between her long beautiful white flawless legs had been an untouched hymen. Nestled in a bed of velvety soft fluffy hair and carried with the frailty of a soft white cloud. Her maturity from young girl to womanhood had precipitated fantasies of the day when a prince would arrive and claim it for his own. She had carried it with the feeling of entrustment. That it was hers only to guard and protect until that day when the crown of all jewels would be delivered to its royal prince. It being intended that the acceptance of this sacred gift be sanctioned upon satin sheets by a gentle tearing of the flesh, in nature that the blood may flow without pain and act as a blending ointment. The time-honored rituals of merging two bodies into one; wherein the sum of the union is greater than separate souls.

For this sacred moment on her wedding night Patricia had dreamed out her part a thousand times. She laid her nude body out upon the bed and beneath her buns she placed a pillow of satin white so the transfer of ownership could be in the highest reverence.

That which was, was abhorrence; the loathing product of deceit and subterfuge under which she had become a bride.

Edger Waters returned to Room #1027 in a drunken stupor. Reeking of alcohol, cigar-smoke and body odor he loudly barged into the unlit room holding an opened bottle of whiskey and flung himself fully clothed onto the bed.

Letting the bottle drop and spill on the floor he feverishly grabbed his bride and pushed his slobbering mouth down on her soft unresponsive lips. As she squirmed to escape, he exerted more strength. In a captive, helpless posture he held her with one hand and unbuckled his trousers with the other. As he unzipped his fly she could feel his bulging, blood engorged muscle. With an unwashed searching hand he guided his stiffen rod into the unprepared dry vagina. His shoes still on, he anchored his feet into the footboard and with explosive force rammed his copulating organ to the depths of her womanhood. She screamed at the excruciating pain as her hymen seared and the delicate dry walls of her vagina tore. As the intruding cock pulled out in preparation for another thrust, virgin blood gushed forth. Her attempts to resist were met by brutal slaps across the face and head. In hunching strokes that lasted no more than a minute he drained his bank of semen. When the last of his sperm had emptied into her bloody vagina he boorishly rolled over and fell into a drunken sleep. As his breathing became heavy she maneuvered from beneath his sprawled body and the satin white pillow slid with her. She rose up to a seating position on the edge of the bed and was attempting to stand when she felt the pillow still stuck. As she carefully pulled it loose she felt faint at the touch of hemorrhaged blood and sticky semen. She turned her head at the thought of the desecration and with an uttered shrill cry pushed it away. Released from her trembling hands, the pillow fell to the floor and came to rest; not with the sanctity of heavenly honor and the softness of purity but in the sewer of humiliation, shame, and disgrace.

She sat silently on the bedside until she was overcome by exhaustion. When she could no longer endure she slowly pulled back her side of the sheets. Trembling with fright she very quietly lay back down beside her husband; for she was married to Edger Waters.

The sounds of the City start early in Pittsburgh. The clanging of garbage trucks rises easily to the tenth floor window of a downtown hotel. The piercing noise startled Patricia from an uneasy sleep and she instantly remembered. Frightfully she looked to the other side of the bed. The side where her husband had gone to sleep was empty. She then looked about the room. It too was empty; he was gone. In a cataclysmic time warp she was overcome by a strange detachment from her own body.

She rose from the bed and moved about without any emotions. In a pain induced trance she packed her few items in a canvas bag and also left.

Patricia had never heard of the Gypsy proverb that, *it is destiny not God that works in strange and mysterious ways*. When Edger Waters left he had sneaked out the West exit, the lowly direction of a sinking Sun. The significance was not yet hers to see but the door from which she parted on the same morning faced the East, to a rising Sun. Still, Gypsy proverbs are easier to say then life is to live.

Chapter 4

The storyteller said no more. The listener made no comment but rose to his feet and went to the kitchen. From the living room the storyteller followed his sounds. He heard as the refrigerator door opened and then closed. He heard the noise of metal cans placed on the kitchen cabinet. He heard the snap hissing sound of a tab being pulled. Then heard the sound a second time. He mentally tracked the footsteps moving back into the living room and looked up as he was handed a beer. He watched as the listener returned to the sofa, took a swallow, and then wipe his mouth with the back of his hand before speaking.

"How do you know all of this?"

"I just do."

"You seem to know a lot about these people."

"There's more; a whole lot more."

"Like what?"

"Like Patricia's marriage. It didn't work. Like Colleen going insane. And like Patricia giving birth to a baby girl whom she named Shelly."

"Shelly? Don't tell me? The Shelly? Our very own one and only porno queen Shelly?"

"The one and only."

"How do you happen to know all of this?"

"How... you ask? How do I happen to know all of this? I guess I know all of this because Shelly is my mother."

Again there was silence. When the silence could endure no more the listener was the first to speak.

"I'm sorry I didn't know."

"It's all right."

"You want to talk about it?"

"No."

"Could I ask why?"

"Because."

"Because? What kind of answer is that? You think maybe you could tell me how you just happen to go from having a porno mother to getting down here?"

"How come there was beer in the frig?"

"What...?"

"I thought the last came from your bed room."

"Of all... there was a couple of cans left. Now are you going to answer my question or not?"

"I could but I'm not going too. I don't mind making conversation about them... but I'm not in the mood right now to discuss my own life."

"Then finish telling me 'about the them' part."

"From where I left off?"

"Yes, from where you left off."

"Other people start getting involved."

"Like who?"

"Like Morgan and Jenny for starters."

"Who were they?"

"Morgan, Morgan Smithfield. At the time he was the owner of the Stran Theater over on 5th Ave. And Jenny, Jenny Craig was a whore; a young, at least at the time, good looking hooker."

"How did they play into Shelly's... uh your mother's life?"

"How did they play into Shelly's life? To understand that you first need to know how the two of them met and how their own lives became intertwined.

"I suppose," the storyteller spoke to himself, "the best place to start that piece of the puzzle would be along in 1939; middle of winter. Probably in weather about like we are having right now.

"Pittsburgh was paralyzed by the overlapping grips of two record breaking cold fronts. It started with a snowstorm moving in from the Ohio Valley and dumping almost twenty-four inches of dry white powder. Thence a chilling Siberian Express came hollowing down out of Canada causing the temperature to drop below zero and the knife-cutting winds to whip the unconsolidated snow into blinding whiteouts. Schools were closed, public employees were sent home, and traffic came to a stand still. Travel advisories were broadcast over the radio and authorities issued warning for people to stay indoors. As faith would have it Morgan Smithfield was caught inside the Stran Theater.

"Figuring that prudence was the better part of valor he complied with the advisories. For two nights he slept on the leather sofa in his office. And sometimes in such cases, when a man spends three days and two nights of prudence it can have results that are different than normal times.

"The combination of cozy warmth on the inside and the midnight sounds of howling wind on the outside are circumstances under which a man might be prone to find comfort in good sipping whisky. Whisky, which everyone knows has a gentle glow that floats up from a half empty bottle and is apt to bring dreams of grandeur.

"In Morgan's case it may have come from being the owner of the Stran. Or it may have just been that the time was ripe but on those two particular nights Morgan allowed him the pleasure of uninhibited no-limits fantasizing about being a famous movie director/producer.

"His physical stature not being of the tall, dark and handsome mode of the day, he surmised he would be a director of the stocky build, short neck, full head of thick shaggy black hair, deep seated sparkling blue eyes, mischievous smile accentuated by a jet black mustache and spontaneous personality sort.

"In his mind he already had a couple of things going for him. One, he wore a fedora hat and two, he had a brand new 1939 black four door Buick Roadmaster with twin spare tires fully encased side mounted in the front fenders. It seems that during that era both the hat and the car were standard trademarks of West Coast movie moguls in motion picture business.

"If it should ever happen that Hollywood desperately needed him

Morgan would be ready. The fact that he had not already been called was a no-never-mind. He understood their reluctance to bother him with anything that was not of monumental proportions. In guessing their minds he judged that a remake of the Napoleonic wars would be something worthy of his time and imagination.

"He vividly pictured how he would direct the opening scene. It would start with a distant shot gradually coming in for a close-up of the wind-whipped stern face of Napoleon in full military uniform mounted on a gray stallion. The camera would then zoom back out to some degree to show him with flowing cape at the head of an army on the march.

"The setting of this monumental epic being Napoleon's crossing of the vast plains of Russia and his line of moving troops would extend back against a diminishing horizon. Again zooming the camera in directly behind Napoleon there would be close up scenes of horse soldiers with sabers and lances, gradually zooming back the view would bring in the artillery caissons, thence the marching foot soldiers; all wearing uniforms trimmed in gold braid. As Morgan envisioned, that would be the opening scene from Napoleon's side.

"Then, under his stern dictatorial authority, Morgan would direct the camera to break to the other side of a rolling hills to bring in massive numbers of advancing Russian troops. In sequence, the two armies would come together at the crest of a ridge and a battle royal would begin.

"Cameras in numbers would concentrate on panoramic views of exploding shells, cannon smoke, lofty ranks of charging lancers, falling horsemen and dying men....

"When Hollywood called, Morgan had no doubt he would be ready. Smooth drinking whiskey can do a lot to mask the pain of a twisted leg... and the loneliness of an empty heart. In his return to reality he wonder again, as he had wondered in the past, why his fantasies were of such nature; rather than dreams of finding a woman to love.

"But three days were enough. He was getting restless from being closed in by the walls of his office. On the third day some of the main roads had been opened and a few patrons had even manage to get in and attend an evening showing. Not many but he figured if they could get in he could get out. He looked at his gold pocket watch; it was almost midnight. From habit he wound the stem and returned it to his vest pocket.

"The last feature had ended a few minutes earlier and the ushers and projection operator had all said good night. It was time to lock up and leave. With topcoat buttoned and his fedora hat pulled down close to his face he left his private office, crossed the lobby to the front doors and peered out one of the small eye-level oval window. The outside whiteness made it almost as bright as day. The wave-like pattern of swirling snowdrifts glistened under the streetlights and gave off an effulgent hue. As expected, Fifth Avenue was deserted; though in a glimpse it seemed to him that he saw a shadow move in the doorway across the street.

"'*Jesus*', he thought. '*Some poor bastard down on his luck and caught out on a night like this*'. Impulsively he strained his eyes for a better look but the whirling snow again caused a whiteout and his thoughts reverted back to himself. He visualized his ordeal of walking to his car parked in the all night Metro Parking Garage. It was only three blocks, but it would be a long three blocks. '*What a picture that's going to make*', his mind returned to fantasyland. '*A crippled man with a walking cane and a dragging foot, on a deserted street, out in a blinding snowstorm in the middle of the night*'.

"The effects of the alcohol now causing him to slightly weave. '*It would be a good opening scene for a murder mystery. We could have the camera open by panning the neon lights of the bars along skid row. The camera would then zoom in on a second story hotel to a cheap flophouse room. Old and junky it would be furnished with a double bed, sagging mattress, rusty coil springs, rusty lattice design iron headboard, battered dresser with a cracked mirror, cast iron steam radiator sizzling out heat, and a single exposed incandescent light bulb hanging from the center room ceiling. The inside walls would be covered with peeling wallpaper and a single dirty, cracked, double hung window would overlook the street and a flashing neon hotel sign. The lone occupant in the room would be a woman; make her an old hooker. For effect, one who is long past her prime and now works the skid row bars. Tonight she could find no takers and gave up early. The rouge on her face is smeared and her dyed blond hair with black roots is matted and falls haphazardly around her sagging cheeks and down-turned mouth. She has taken off her good dress and is wearing a wrinkled red satin slip. She has a cigarette in one hand, a half glass of straight whiskey with no ice in the other, standing in a posture of spread legs and gazing out at the street.*

In her youth men had clamored to lie between her thighs but now it is a place where mostly drunks come to dwell. She shivers at the snow swirling under the streetlights. It is a terrible night to be alone. She is wondering how it all could have happened; that she ended up here at the end of the road.

"'She's deep in melancholy thought when she suddenly notices a movement in the street. It is blurred at first; half hidden by swirling snow. As she is watching, the swirling suddenly lulls and a brief clear view is visible. She sees a lone figure moving alone the sidewalk. A man, a crippled man trudging along with the aid of a cane. He is wearing a long dark topcoat and a black fedora hat. His head is bowed into the bitter cold and he is dragging his leg as he struggles against the blowing wind.

"'With a silver-handled cane in one hand and his coat collar pulled up over his face with the other he makes his way through powdery snowdrifts. She watches his silhouette under the eerie lights. Swirls of blowing snow are quickly filling in the trail of footprints as if to cover up the evidence.

"'Evidence! What! Oh God. That's RAZOR CALWELL. They've finally found me...'

"Morgan abruptly stopped. *'I must be going crazy,'* he thought as he quickly brought himself back to reality for a second time with the thoughts, *'I sure must hate the thought of leaving this warm lobby'.* In quick movement he then braced himself, swung the door open, stepped out under the marquee and was instantly hit with a blast of freezing air; even colder than he had anticipated. Without removing his glove he locked the double doors, turned, and started into the wind. Head down and one hand holding his coat collar around his face he stepped out on the sidewalk. His mangled leg seemed void of feeling as his cane sank into the powdery snow. He had only gone a few feet from the marquee when it seemed liked he heard something in back; a voice...or some sound behind him. Paying no heed he continued a few more slow shuffling steps through the swirls of snow. Then, there it was again.

"Date Mister?"

Date? What in the world? He stopped and slightly turned just as he felt a young woman's hand reaching to touch him. Surprised, he further shifted around to where the wind was to his back. Letting his coat collar drop from his face he look at a silhouetted obscure body in a mid-calf top coat, pulled up collar and wrapping herself in her own shivering arms.

"What? What did you say?" he asked.

"I asked you if you would like a date, you know... you, me together like a date," answered the shivering young voice.

"You... You want to date me?" he asked in astonishment. Without waiting for her answer he cautiously looked up and down the street. He could not see anyone else so it appeared that she was alone.

"Young lady," he responded in a demanding inquiring voice. "What could possibly have you out on the street on a night like this?"

"Didn't you hear?" she repeated. "Would you like a date? I asked if you would like a date? You do know what a date means don't you?" her collar still turned up as she hugged herself. Morgan remained silent for an instant as he adjusted his body weight to his good leg.

"Sure," he answered. "I know what a date is. And yes, I might be interested; if you're legal. How old are you?"

"I'm twenty four," she replied. "Is that old enough for you?" By then Morgan had nudged up a little closer, to where he could block the blowing snow with his body as he answered.

"Twenty four. Certainly, twenty-four is fine, just fine, but before we go any farther how about we move in under the theater alcove. It won't make you mad if we get in there for a little windbreak will it?" As the two jointly shuffled in behind the ticket cage the area was darker and the young woman sensed a slight danger. She welcomed the break from the howling wind but she was also out of protection of the open street.

"Now", Morgan continued, "let me look at you". He steadied himself on his cane and slowly removed one glove. Unprotected the hand tingled at the cold exposure. He gently reached out and raised her chin. By the subdued light of the street they looked at each other and for an instant came into direct eye contact.

"What's your name?" he asked as he lightly cupped her jaw and slightly moved her head from side to side.

"Jenny."

"Jenny... very nice. Very nice indeed."

"Glad you like it," she moved her face away from his hand. "Now what's your answer? Date, or no date? Make up your mind. In case you haven't noticed, it's ass freezing cold out here."

Morgan was slipping his glove back on and shifted both hands to the top of his cane as he answered. "Well Jenny, how much money are we talking for this date... as you call it."

"Oh brother," she reacted. "Everybody knows the going price. Ten bucks. Take it or leave it."

"Ten bucks," he mimicked surprised. "That's a lot of money Jenny. I would have to get a lot of date for that kind of money. "You do know, don't you that the going rate for day labor is five dollars a day?"

"Yeah... Well, maybe that's why I'm out here. Instead of chasing ten cent tips as a waitress in some all night dinner. Anyway I am not standing here in bone chilling weather to discuss my finances. Yes or No," she ended on a demanding note.

"Maybe," he responded. "But I'm just curious. The light is not the best back in this alcove, but how far off am I when I put you at about eighteen?"

She recoiled slightly and pulled her coat collar back up around her neck. "It would put you off about six years. Now how about an answer? Do we have a deal or not?"

"If six years is about right then I would say that there's a pretty good chance that we can come to some sort of an arrangement."

In a surprised voice she asked, "Really? You mean it?"

"Of course I mean it. That is if we can continue the negotiations someplace where it's a little warmer."

"I thought you would never ask," she agreed. "Do you know a place that's handy?"

"I would say about as handy as it gets," he commented as he was taking the door keys out of his pocket. "How about just inside here?"

"In here?" her tone reflected surprise. "Who do you know that you happen to have keys to the Stran?"

"I know the owner."

"And who is that?" she continued.

"Me."

"You... you own the Stran? I..., I don't believe it."

"Believe it. Are you impressed?"

"Well, yeah, sure. It's only the swankiest spot in town."

As he opened the door the warm air rushed out to greet them and the two quickly moved inside.

Morgan then re-locked the door and turned to Jenny. The night light in the lobby was dim but when their eyes adjusted he took his first close look. *Dear God*, he thought. *If there was ever a poor soul down on her luck...*

"How about the money?" she asked. "I'm supposed to be getting some money along about here."

"Ah yes, the money," he mimicked. "We do need to get to the money don't we.

"First, though," he asked, "how would it be if we move into my office? I am getting tired standing on my bad leg and it would be helpful if I could sit down. Do you think that would be acceptable?" His voice slightly patronizing. Forgetting that she should be cautious, Jenny replied, "Oh... of course, I'm sorry, I didn't realize your leg hurt so much. How did it happen?" she inquired as they moved across the lobby.

"It's a long story. I'll tell you about it sometime."

As they entered his office Morgan switched on a low watt floor lamp. And to Jenny's surprise, the room was a model picture of what an executive office should be. Impeccably decorated, it was complete with a dark mahogany desk, deep dark red leather sofa, matching leather chairs, thick oriental rugs on a highly polished dark stained wood floor, a medieval suit of armor holding a lance standing in one corner, an upper torso portrait of a Spanish Conquistador in a large gold frame on the wall behind his desk. And to reinforce that it was a man's domain, one side wall was adorned with a full length portrait of a beautiful nude woman standing with a wide, red velvet ribbon draped across her shoulders in a pose showing her full round breast, pronounced body curves and one leg slightly bent across the other to show just the suggestion of pubic hair.

The decor was warm and the room temperature was warm. The change from outside was intoxicating; the atmosphere of a man's room romantic. Without her realizing it, Jenny's position of dominance as hooker on the outside had been melted away.

She watched as Morgan took off his hat and topcoat and methodically placed them on a clothes tree. When he finished he turned and was surprised to see she was still standing.

"My goodness," he said. "I'm forgetting my manners. Here, let me help with your coat."

She shifted slightly as she slipped out of her coat and as she turned back their eyes made a darting contact. "This is rather new for me," he remarked. "I think I may even feel a little awkward or embarrassed."

"You, embarrassed? A sophisticated man like you," she spoofed. "Embarrassed at negotiating a trick with a street hooker like me. Who you kidding?" she spoke as she stepped over and seated herself on the sofa. From habit he moved around to his desk, sank down in his office chair, leaned back and placed his good leg up.

"Is that what you think? That I'm sophisticated," he responded. "Ha! If you only knew. Maybe someday I'll tell you the story of my life; but right now we should be getting acquainted. Are you hungry? Have you eaten...?" he watched for an expression.

"Yes, I mean no, I'm not hungry. I really don't care for anything to eat." she ended on an implied note.

"Something else?" he asked the question.

"Uh... since you asked, I could use a shot of good stiff whiskey to break this bone chill; if you happen to have one handy?"

Morgan reached in the bottom drawer of his desk and took out a bottle and one glass. "Am I going to be drinking alone?" she asked as she watched him pour.

"I just caught the wagon about an hour ago," he replied as he reached across the desk and handed her the drink.

"Thank yea very much," her voice had a little caught to it as she held up a slight toast then put the glass to her mouth and savored the first biting sip.

"Jenny..." he spoke as he leaned back and squeezed his thumb and forefinger across his brow, "this could all prove much more interesting than I had anticipated.

"For reasons I don't know why," he lowered his hand back down and looked at her, "I would like to know more about you. How is it that things are so bad that you have to be out in a blinding snowstorm? That sort of thing. Or maybe I should say that one sort of thing." He paused for a moment to gauge her response. When none came he continued. "Let me ask, is it imperative that we get right down to the business of this date, or is it permissible to first make small talk?"

"Well," she hesitated, "this is certainly different. I'm generally more accustomed to standing on a street corner and talking through an open car window.

"I mean I do like being in here where it's nice and cozy; a handsome man, cold winter night, wind howling outside. Too bad you don't have a roaring fireplace and a soft bear skin rug. We might even be able to make it a freebie," she paused in a conciliatory tone. "But the thing is, I need the money. Moreover, I don't know yet if I am going to make anything out of all of this. Now, you tell me and I will tell you," she finished.

"O.K. The first thing I'm going to tell is a question. It's important to me to know this urgent need you have for money that you are out on a night like this?"

"Ask a good question, get a good answer," she responded. "And that good answer goes something like this. Aside from such little incidentals as rent, utilities, food and clothing, life has decided that it is in my best interest to have one little additional problem."

"And."

"And, it seems that some uninvited, wayward sperm from some unknown man has found a nesting place in one of my very fertile eggs."

Dear God... pregnant, his thoughts flashed. Pausing to give her an understanding look, he shifted his posture and without even being cognizant of his actions he assumed guidance of the conversation.

"Jenny... let's do this... How about I give you the ten bucks, no wait. Make that twenty. Twenty bucks. Here," he took the money from his wallet. "I'll give you the twenty, but I would like to reserve for myself the right as to whether we do or do not have sex."

"Uh Oh! Now I am curious," her tone cautious. "Before I reach out and take that twenty spot I want to know more about what you have in mind. My ol' Poppy always used to say to watch out where you stick your hand, someone may whack it off." Morgan smiled at her reaction. The mood was becoming more relaxed and they both were starting to feel more comfortable.

"Look, Jenny, just since I've met you, thoughts are coming to my mind which were not there earlier. Call it impulsive, but suddenly I want to know about you; you understand what I am saying?"

"I have the same feeling," she responded. "I could ask you a million questions. But one of us has to keep things in perspective. You ask me what you want to know and I will ask you what I want to know. Fair enough?"

"Deal," he responded. "You first."

"First," she asked, "what's your name? You know my name but I don't know yours."

"Morgan, Morgan Smithfield."

"Smithfield... Wow... you mean Smithfield, like in one of Pittsburgh's famous landmarks. Smithfield Bridge?"

"Just coincidental. Don't believe everything you hear."

"Then how come all of this," she asked as she looked around the room indicating her awe. "Does everyone whose name is Smithfield have money?"

"Jenny..." he spoke in a slow methodical tone. "To you all of this may seems like a lot; but it's not. From your standpoint it probably looks like I've really made it to the top of the mountain. And, in a way I suppose I have.

"But it's a funny thing about the top. When I finally made that climb I found out there were only two things, no wait make that three. To me the top only showed me three things of any importance. You think you would be interested in hearing what they are?"

"Sure... Why not... assuming that twenty spot is still on the table."

Morgan didn't catch the wit nor did he respond in a manner that indicated he needed her approval. He had passed into his own need as he continued. His eyes were looking her way but the look was more in simple direction than to her.

"The first thing I learned is that all there is at the top is a view. That's it; a good view. And that taught me the second thing. When you're up there looking around it makes you realize just how small and insignificant all of us actually are. None of us mean anything to that ol' mountain Jenny. We all climb up and we all slide back down but that don't concern that ol' mountain one way or the other. Not in the slightest. That ol' Mr. Mountain, he just keeps right on taking care of mountain business and this ol' world keeps right on turning, he..." his pause and tone indicating a loss in thought.

"And the third?" she asked in a manner of continuing on.

"What?"

"The third. You said there were three things you had learned. You've only given me two."

The question, the way it was asked, struck Morgan that the

circumstances and the discussion were not in perfect harmony. Yet he did not know what to do but respond. He gave her a direct look and she was looking directly back. There was softness in the exchange. Not a deep eye contact but an open looking.

He then inhaled a deep breath and with slow emphasized words he said, "The third thing that I learned Jenny is what's important and what's not. Even Moses came back down from the mountain. And the reason he came back down was because there wasn't any work that needed to be done on the top. The purpose of all work Jenny is to make things better. God's real interest is the poor souls at the bottom of the mountain... not at the top."

"I'm sorry," she spoke as he paused. "But... you've lost me. I mean I must be missing something. Is this all leading somewhere?"

"No, not leading. It's a rambling impulse that I'm having. And most likely, most very likely this little ol' mind flash which I'm having right now will end up costing me one hell of a lot of money and cause me one hell of a lot of grief. But..." he paused slightly for emphasis, "seeing you like that... Out in that ass freezing cold trying to make it. Dear God... if I can use that word in the present context. There has to be a better way of selling sex than being out in blinding blizzard freezing your firm little ass off."

"Uh... don't you think maybe that that's my choice. I..."

"For the life of me," he ignored her comment. "I don't understand how something as beautiful and wonderful as a sexual experience can be displayed from a street corner, price bargained under the most unromantic conditions and more times than not consummated on a flea infested mattress."

"Uh, Morgan... I guess I can call you by your first name. Is this all part of that twenty bucks? I mean is there something...?"

"What a degradation," he again ignored her comment and continued speaking, "that something which is so magnificent that it should be reserved for an alter... is in fact dispensed in squalor. There has to be a better way," his tone indicating he had reached the end of his thought.

"I get the feeling," she started her response as she slightly shifted on the leather sofa, unconsciously crossed her legs and tugged her skirt down, "that you are trying to tell me something but I have no idea what it is."

"What I am trying to say," he looked at her as if she of all people should know what he was trying to say, "is grace; grace, dignity, decorum. The sale of something as beautiful as sex should have dignity, elegance, grace, and decorum. Instead it is just the opposite."

"Uh... look, Morgan," she started getting to her feet as she spoke, "this doesn't seem to be working out. I think it would be best if we..."

"It has dropped to the lowest possible level," he repeated. "To me it's a travesty. That the highest should drop to the lowest. I just think that it deserves better. The entire realm of mon-for-fun, pay-for-play is ludicrous. The laws that forbid it, the manner in which it is dispensed, the image it bears... Everything is basackwards. There needs to be a total overhaul." He paused to finalize his point. "One of the great misguided issues in the evolution of man is the illegality of buying and selling sex. To me, it is a perpetuating iniquity. In effect what we have is a clash between natural instincts and law wherein man has seen fit to voluntarily shackle himself. My question is why? Why should something so natural be so illegal?"

"Yeah... Uh huh. Well I sure can't argue with you there. Listen, this twenty. It be O.K. if I just slip it in my pocket? It's getting awful late and I..."

"As far as I know," he continued his thoughts, "there are no laws forbidding the satisfying of hunger. One can eat as much or little as the circumstances permit. Nor are there any laws prohibiting the satisfying of shelter. So why sex?" He ended in a rhetorical tone.

She offered no response and the silence made him realize by the sound of his own words that it was all out of character for the present circumstances. "I know that it will always be illegal," he attempted to bring things back the present with an explanation. "But does it seem to you that there would be anything wrong if it were given a little more respectability? Maybe dress it up a bit, take it out of the back alley and move it into the high rent district?"

"No argument from me. We'll have to get together again sometime. Now, I hate to talk and run but I think I can still catch a cab so..."

"What I'm saying," he continued, "is that sexual needs are as much a part of life as living and dying.

"And for those whose private life does not provide for sexual fulfillment, there should be respectable outside sources."

"Excuse me," she pushed her point. "But I believe when we came in I saw you lock the front door. Uh, you think maybe, you know... a little matter of you unlocking, me leaving... you stay... I go."

"And to me respectable means a lack of fear of being caught doing something illegal. Now, we've already said that we can't do much about the legality. But with the right person it might be possible to initiate a plan of improvement. I would be willing to provide the financial backing but there would have to be that one certain right person to undertake the actual doing. Now... having said all of that let me ask you, in a yes or no answer, would you be interested and if so, why?"

A momentary silence followed. She looked at him as he was looking at her and waiting for an answer. "Well... I'll... be damn," came her surprised words. "A crusader; a real honest to goodness crusader. I didn't think they existed anymore."

"Funny," he responded. "Yes or No!"

"You mean that's what this has been all about. You want to start your own whorehouse. Man you sure like to take the long way home. We could have established all of this in ten words or less out in the alcove. In a yes or no answer the answer is Yes! You must be out of touch with reality. There's not a hooker on the street that doesn't dream about having her own house. Does that answer your question?"

"What about the why?" he reminded.

"As to why... the why is... it seems like I have been looking for you most of my life. Not you in particular of course but that certain someone who would materialize and become a type of mentor. I feel certain that I have a destiny in life but until this moment I never thought I would ever actually realize my dream. If you are sincere in what you say, with your help," she reinforced, "I can do in life what I know I am supposed to do."

"And?"

"And., what I am suppose to do, what it is intended for me to do in life is to provide the highest quality of sexual services and bring the best possible comfort and feeling of well-being to men in need."

With those brief words Jenny experienced a feeling of satisfaction that she had finally been able to make that statement to someone of apparent significance.

Inhaling a full breath she added. "When I achieve that goal, then I will have achieved my calling in life.

"Believe it Mr. Smithfield," she now emphasized respect, "being able to ease the sexual needs of haunting men is a gratifying experience. It gives a woman, at least this woman, a feeling of worth; a natural sensation that she is fulfilling her intended role. It is the answering of a natural order that all of the laws on earth will never be able to change. So... all of the things in which you believe are also the things that I believe, only more so."

Here Jenny paused. Like Morgan, she also knew that the subject was too deep to continue. Feeling that she had answered his question she finished by asking, "But could I ask? What sparked this impulse in you? I mean here and now; in a snow storm, on a night like this?"

"Who knows Jenny? Maybe it *was* destiny that brought us together. The sale of sex in this town, as in every other town, basically takes place in the gutter. I see it every day, down along Liberty Avenue and out in the Strip District. I have never liked it but up until just now I never thought of doing anything to improve it. This country is already gearing up for the next big war. Call it my contribution to the war effort if you like but if I can I want to do something to improve the system; at least within the limits of my... our power."

What Morgan was thinking about were all the hookers around Pittsburgh who hung out on the street corner and flagged down passing cars. He was thinking of all the young GIs home on leave from boot camp, who want to dive headlong into manhood by losing their virginity before shipping out to war. He was thinking of every young man's desperate need to hold and embrace an American woman before he faces the prospects of dying on foreign soil. One would assume that society would understand and even condone such a benevolent deed.

But in fact of the matter, the degree of society's understanding seldom extends past a final home cooked meal. So, without society's blessing, young hero's everywhere seek fulfillment of their needs under a cloak of darkness.

After their respectable home-from-boot-camp family gathering around a home cooked meal of white wine, carved turkey with cranberry sauce and hot apple pie, all served on special-occasion chinaware, America's young recruits finish up by touching a white linen napkin to their face and exercise good manners by asking to be excused as they get up from the table. And across the land young men in their Class A Dress Uniforms and their shaved head haircuts put on their uniform jackets and relate to their family that they are going out for the evening and may be late getting in.

On their last night home-on-leave they venture out from their middle class homes and middle class neighborhoods. They congregated in pubs of Irish, Italian, Polish or some other ethnic bar or a high school hangout. They meet with other young GIs; and in comraderie head down to the lower west side with the intent of making a final deposit of their American sperm in the love canal of American womanhood.

But more often than not, that which they seek is not what they receive. The love canal they seek ends up not between a pair of soft silky thighs but the putrid, black waters of the Allegheny River after getting knocked in the head and robbed by thugs and pimps. In Morgan's mind this was not a befitting tribute to gallant young men going off to war. In a noble impulse, he wanted to improve the situation. At the moment though that's all it was; an impulse. He did not have a solution; so he didn't answer Jenny's question. Instead he simply answered a question with a question.

"Suppose we talk about you?"

"About me?" she asked rhetorically. "I suspect you mean about me and sex; not about me and what kind of an all-American family did I come from." She looked at Morgan to see if he agreed with her little bit of levity. When he made no motion she continued.

"The thing about me and sex is, I like it. I like it a lot and a lot means as much as eight or ten times a day," she confided before she thought... and then felt a touch of embarrassment.

"Uh Oh, that didn't come out just right did it. It's true though, lots of times I have it ten times in one day; I just didn't want to mention it right up front," she justified.

"But since we have this started, let's finish. It seems to me that the sole driving force in my life is sex. It's all I think about, care about, or talk about. Since I was 12 years old it has been the only thing on my mind. I have never had any dreams of going to college, or to be a doctor, lawyer, nurse or even a housewife. I don't want to be a mother or to be a teacher. The only thing I know about, think about or care about is right between my legs." Feeling that she was now on better footing she talked more openly.

"Sex, in some form or another, seems to be the only thing I think about. Wherever I am, whomever I am around, my reason for being there in some way is because of what's between my legs. I have an overpowering sensation that I am supposed to be using it to help others in life. I don't look upon it as being different; I look upon it as being a special gift. I want to help others and others to help me. For me, the urge for an orgasm can come at any time and without any warning. And when I do get an urge, there is no control. It takes precedent over whatever else I am doing. I have no desire to suppress it; just the opposite, the more active the better.

"The thing is, I don't necessarily need any foreplay or anything like that. I just want a fast explosive orgasm. When an urge does surface, I want instant gratification. I don't like using the phrase of 'doing it and getting it over with' but for now it conveys the picture." She paused for a moment to collect her thoughts; not to justify so much as saying it in plain words.

"I have tried working a few regular jobs," she continued. "And surprisingly I get along pretty good in the business world; good typing skills, good at taking dictation, good at working with people.

"But what happens is," she felt a need to be explanatory, " I can be right in the middle of an assignment, say typing a letter, and from out of no where I get an urge and that means problems. At least it's a problem if I'm working in an office.

"Because to solve that problem I need to have a quick orgasm. Unfortunately, not very many business offices happen to have a handy, dandy, desk top, rapid fire orgasm satisfier."

Jenny felt instinctively what Morgan must have been thinking. *'So what's the big problem. Any gal in any office can always get a quick fix from any one of the helpful young testosterone loaded executives'.*

'The problem is,' she wanted to mentally offset, *'office help means involvement; and involvement misses the whole point'.*

"Don't misunderstand," she went on, "it's not a personality thing; like I am lonely, or insecure or need the feel of a man.

"It's simply my nature to get instant unexplainable sensations in my crouch and when I do I need a quick, intense fix before I can continue with whatever it is I happen to be doing. How it is achieved is not all that important. If society had some sort of futuristic sex machines, that would do just fine. Then I could work in an office. When an urge hit, I could run back to the back room, get a few fast strokes, have an orgasm, and get back to work. I know how crass that must sound but it's true.

"There, now you have that part of it," she continued her view of herself. "And from there it has lead me to other thoughts. Surely I'm not the only person in the world who's wired that way. If frequent sex urges have such an effect on me isn't it reasonable to assume that there must be men who are affected the same way?

"Women and men?" Her tone implying a self-evident answer. "Say men. Good men, family men, church going men, who truly love their wives and family and believe in God; who do not want to hurt anyone but none-the-less have sex drives similar to mine?"

"And?" prompted Morgan.

"And," she continued, "I put myself in their shoes. If, when I am hot,

I had a quick fix available I would be very appreciative. So, that's what I do. I do for others what no one would do for me. I am there for whoever needs uncomplicated pleasant relief of a very wonderful natural human function."

Then, as a signal that she had complied with her side of the implied agreement she spoke to Morgan in a tone that it was now his turn to confide.

"Now, how about we talk about you. What do you have in mind to do with all of this information?"

Morgan did not respond directly to her comment but continued in his mind set theme. "What would you say is your biggest problem right now?" he asked and she responded.

"Right now I would say that I have two problems. One, I need money for an abortion.

"And two, I need to find someone who will do it. I mean a doctor. I am not about to let some midwife run a rusty coat hanger up inside me."

"How do you feel about the life of the fetus?" he asked. "Do you have any guilt feelings, remorse, or religious doubts; anything in that respect you would care to discuss?"

Jenny felt embarrassing blood rush to her face and answered somewhat forcefully.

"Could I ask just how my religion, or remorsefulness, or lack of remorsefulness, or anything else figures into the picture? For your information, no I am not remorseful. I do wish that some man had not planted a sperm inside my belly but he did and that is that. What we might do is rush out and initiate a citywide search to find that wayward individual, whoever he is, and ask him if he is remorseful about indiscriminately shooting out precious life sperm. I... I don't know who he was and I don't care. My problem now is to get it out as quickly as possible.

"I do not," she continued without stopping, " repeat do not, think that human life starts in that great blinding flash of light when a sperm wiggles his wiggly swim up the love canal and makes that sensational penetration into a nice fertile egg.

"Now, if that happens to be your belief," this she spoke directly to Morgan, "then fine; I respect your beliefs. But I don't and I request that you respect my beliefs.

"If this is something you can't deal with then let's terminate this conversation, I'll still take the twenty bucks, and we can consider the deal closed."

During the course of their talk Morgan had spent most of the time leaning back in his chair with his good leg on the desk. He had a mannerism of resting his elbows on the chair's arms, holding his hands in prayer fashion and flexing his palms in and out; in what as a child he called a spider doing pushups on a mirror. Jenny had scooted an adjusting scoot back on the leather sofa but her now frequent twisting indicated she was either tired or restless. He glanced at the wall clock. It was later than he realized. He had been fascinated by the night's events and would like to have continued. But he felt a stiffness in his back and his leg was again aching. They had discussed enough for now.

"Jenny," he spoke as he was getting up from his chair. "I am please to tell you that I have no problems with anything I have heard or seen. In fact the more I learn about you the more I like. With respect to abortion I have no feelings one-way or the other. And I will be most happy to respect your feeling. However, I also respect the beliefs of those who oppose abortion. In substance, it is an issue in which I have not allowed myself to get involved one way or the other." Then with strong emphasis to establish a firm understanding he replied. "On that matter the issue is closed.

"You mention that you are in need of a medical doctor to perform the abortion. With your permission there is a doctor I would like for you to go see. His name is Doctor Daniel Owise, MD. Here is his number. Use my name and tell him I sent you. Have him send me the bill. He knows my address. I can't say that he is a friend or that I even like him; but I do know that he is a competent practicing physician.

"And whatever you decide, I think he will provide it without concern for the law. Now, it's past 3:00 A.M. and I suggest we give thought to calling it a night. Where do you live and I will drive you home."

They did not spend that first night together, this solitary man with lines on his face and who walked with the aid of a cane and the radiant younger woman of the night. Nevertheless, their paths had crossed. At his home later that night when he was alone in bed he sought relief from pain as he took a pill and waited for sleep to come. She, in her double bed kept feeling the magnetism of the man surging through her thoughts. The words he had used...grace, dignity, poise, decorum... must surely be a reflection of inner grace. For the first time in her life she was mesmerized by something other than physical features. *With a man like that by my side,* she fantasized. *I could rule the universe.* As she dropped off to sleep she hugged the extra pillow to her bosom and whispered, "Goodnight Morgan."

The listener did not hear the final portion. Somewhere in the night he dropped off in a deep sleep. Of this the storyteller was aware and was not offended. The story, in part or in some manner, had been told before.

The purpose thereof always was being the storyteller's own. *Mother,* for she was on his mind, *may that my quest be laid to rest. In countless numbers I have searched your saga and still I do not know. There is a torment to which I am hopelessly shackled; words once said from you to me '... the person that we are, each of us, is the sum total of all the people who have ever come into our lives'. It follows that to know who I am I must first know you. But in your life there were so many; Morgan, Jenny, the lawyer Frank Buckwilder, the banker Aspen McGee, Dr. Owise, the ballet instructor Sidney Griffin, the carnival scout who solicited Patricia; and friends of these friends. How did all these people influence you to do the things you did. If therein an answer lies then let me go one by one.*

Morgan and Jenny now on my mind let me continue; God that I can recall. I remember it being said that he was always lonely; and that...

Chapter 5

The life of Morgan Smithfield started each day before the rising of the sun. In a seldom changing routine from bedroom to grooming to streets that were not yet busy, he would step into the outside world; from side door to black Buick to downtown newspaper stand to Metro Parking to the front door of the Stran.

With the unlocking and opening the front door part two of his routine continued. As he entered the quiet cool lobby, an inescapable feeling would start to materialize. In the time he cane-walked across the lobby, entered his private office, heard the door click behind him, hung his hat on the clothes tree and sat down at his desk the feeling was complete; he was lonely. And his late night encounter with Jenny Craig the week before now lingered constantly on his mind.

God how thrilling she would be to hold, he fantasized; *sparkling eyes, beautiful complexion, youthful body radiating the promise of spring. A woman like that would appeal to any man.*

The point word of any man being the exact point that he held against himself.

When she can have any man she chooses, why would she want a man like me; a cripple. Besides, even if it did happen, and then it didn't last, I think it would finally be more than I could bear.

Don't even think it, he admonished himself. *If a man my age knows anything he knows to be realistic. I don't know who's the woman for me, maybe never. Whoever she is though she will need me as much as I need her.*

The thing I have to look for is need. If she needs me as much I need her then we'll have something. Then we have a bond that will hold two people together through thick and thin. Things like having something wrong with the body or differences in age simply won't matter. At least that's what I hope.

On that particular morning he had followed his normal office ritual of slightly pushing his chair back from his desk, putting his feet up, leaning back, starting to read the daily news and then quietly dosing off as the paper slid from his hands. A ringing telephone in the middle of a nap is apt to trigger a slight irritation. Occasionally it might be good news but more likely than not it will be a problem that can be better handled later in the day.

"Hello," he answered in a monotone.

"Hello...? Is this Morgan? Hi Morgan. This is Jenny, Jenny Craig."

"Well, for... little Jenny," his tone perked up. "Jenny Craig how you been? You been around?"

"A little, you know, here and there. Staying alive. Are you surprised to hear from me?"

"Surprised? It's as good a word as any. I have been hearing good things about you though. I hear you weren't in a family way after all; just a little off balance."

"What? How'd you find out? Is nothing sacred in this town?"

"My ol' buddy Owise. He called me after you left his office. He said something to the effect that you were lucky this time but that you should learn to be a little more careful, whatever in the hell that means."

"I can't believe that he would broadcast things like that around town. I thought doctor-patient relations were supposed to be confidential."

"Don't worry too much about it Jenny. First of all, Dr. Owise doesn't know the meaning of the word ethical. His telephone call to me actually had very little to do with you. It goes much deeper. You just happened to be the instrument that gave him an excuse to jerk my chain. But that's enough about him. Back to us..."

"Now that's a subject I could learn to like," she cut in with a purring voice.

"And just what subject is that?"

"Us spelled U S, as in US states, or to put it another way, a state of us, you and me."

"You sound pretty chipper this morning," he detected her little flirtation and ran up his own little caution flag. "What's on your mind?"

She in turn detected his tone and she slightly drew back. "Well, you did mention something about us getting together to do a little business. Is that still a possibility?"

"As possible as ever. At least the thoughts are still going around in my head. Several things in particular I want to discuss, but not right at this particular moment.

"How about you drop around to my office a little later in the day and we'll spend some time chewing the fat."

"Deal," she replied. "See yea."

As Morgan reached to hang up the phone a sharp pain shot through his leg and triggered the remembrance as to how he and Dr. Owise had come to cross trails.

Actually, he quickly recalled the larger picture. *There were three parties to that junction; himself, Owise and Frank Buckwilder, Attorney at Law. Three persons, none of who previously knew the other, drawn together in a bitter lawsuit.* And without even thinking Morgan heard himself blurt out loud, "Owise you no good son-of-a-bitch! Frank, now you on the other hand, what can I say, you're just one hell-of-a-man"; and he was again reminded.

It all started in the early 1930s when there were ten men for every job. Morgan was working in the steel mills, got injured, was treated unfairly, and wanted to sue. His association with Frank came about because he was looking for a good courtroom lawyer. As he had put it, the lawyer he wanted was as mean as a junkyard dog and twice as ugly. Finding such an attorney however had not been all that easy. For one thing he didn't have any money. For a second, the incident had occurred in the middle of the great depression. Thirdly because he, Morgan, wanted to do the unthinkable. In times when thousands upon thousands of men were out of work, he wanted to sue one of the few companies which were employing workers; Homestead Steel.

To the many lawyer doors to which he went the answers were always about the same. "What! Are you out of your mind! You must be insane! It's suicidal. Suing a giant like Homestead Steel. You can't win. Besides that they'll make an example out of you. They'll see to it that you never work in this town again; but... if you're that determined, you might try Frank Buckwilder. I'd say it's doubtful but he might be willing to take the case."

"Why Frank Buckwilder?"

"You mean you have never heard of Frank Buckwilder?"

"No, should I? What's so special about Frank Buckwilder?"

"My boy, do yourself a favor and learn something about the most eminent lawyer in Pittsburgh.

"Frank Buckwilder is so lily white and so revered by the community that not even the almighty Homestead Steel would dare to retaliate."

"What is he, God or something?"

"No, he's not God... but the two are probably on a first name basis. It would be my guess that God probably considers Frank a friend. He's the only man I know who has grace. But he's not a religious fanatic. No, Frank is just a rare human being that is an absolute gentleman; personified. He looks exactly the way a man of nobility should look. I'd guess he's probably in his late forties or early fifties, medium to tall in height, trim build with just a suggestion of maturing spread.

"He's never seen out when he doesn't look like he just stepped out of a fashion show. Always dressed in meticulous tailored-made virgin wool dark blue suits, starched white dress shirts, rose- colored sheen ties, the works. Has a full head of close cut wavy black hair, touched silver sideburns, sparkling blue eyes and unblemished olive skin. Single, never married, very wealthy, belongs to all the right social clubs, a patron of the arts; perfectly cosmopolitan. Highly sought after for all of the elite social functions; but can never be caught.

"But don't let that mislead you. He is one hell of a lawyer. Has a mind like a steel trap. When he's in court, he fights to win. If there were a lawyer in town who can whip the butt off of Homestead, I'd say he's your man.

"Ha, ha, ha, I was just thinking. Say you went to Frank and say he took your case and the two of you sued Homestead Steel, and say Homestead Steel decided to retaliate and attempt to smear Frank's name. Good God Almighty, do you know what would happen? Why there would be women by the hundreds, make that thousands, up in arms; Hell has no fury like women scorned, etc.

"Ha, ha, ha, that sure would be something to see. I tell you my boy, there are enough rich old widows in this town that are chasing Frank, Hell not just widows, every female socialite in Pittsburgh, if Homestead Steel even farted and it drifted over on Frank, goodbye steel mill! Ha, ha, ha. Hot damn that would be something to see. Damn, I hope ol' Frank takes your case. But in answer to your question, who is Frank Buckwilder?

"The best answer I can give you and the highest compliment I can pay Frank is that he is his own man.

"No one owns a piece of Frank Buckwilder. His soul is not for sale. It can't be bought; at any price. There's one other thing that might tell you about the man. One time when I was in his office, I saw a plaque he has on his wall that reads: '*The man who owns his own soul dwells in a lonely land.*' Now if you will excuse me."

There was a lot of eye contact the first time Morgan Smithfield and Frank Buckwilder talked: not confrontational eye contact but a searching by two men; each of the other. Certainly, there were introductory preliminaries. In better terms, a kind of instant spark or karma of sorts which materialized; that each man showed the world one face and kept the other to himself.

In rarity when two such men meet, a metaphysical imagery sometimes ignites. An inner revelation of one to the other is somehow known and understood; a transmission akin to men going into battle, the waiting moments just before the fight, in numbness they feel detached from their own bodies and they turn for an instant and look one to the other. They make direct eye contact and communicate a feeling of knowing; alone among many. Sometimes it helps; an instant bonding for the moment; an understanding and a wish of good luck.

Between Morgan and Frank there was a reserved eagerness on the part of each to make the acquaintance; but eagerness on each part held in check by caution. Caution giving way to certainty and a welcoming relief that at least for the moment there could be a relaxing of constraint. *Nevertheless, no sooner had it materialized than an unspoken paradox held the elation in reserve. Each could feel for the other but there could be no allowing the other to carry part of one's own load. For...that which is extended in goodwill will rob by virtue of its good intentions.* So the second time the two men talked, their respective feelings were held in check. The ordeal upon which they were about to embark held no allowances for compassion.

"Morgan," Frank asked, "let me see if I understand exactly what it is you want. You want to take Homestead Steel to court. Do you clearly understand that that means a trip to hell and back? If that's the case, let's be absolutely sure you can pay the freight. Let's have a clear understanding of what lies ahead".

"I already have a clear understanding, Frank. I got it from lying in a hospital bed for two months and damn near losing a leg. I've already traveled the road to hell, now I want to get paid for my trip. "So hear me on this Frank. They can't make it too tough. No matter what they've got, it's not going to be enough. So I guess I, we, can say Hello to Hell. I won't be a stranger."

So the necessary papers were filed with the Clerk of Court in and for the County of Allegheny. When the official notice of the lawsuit was served on Homestead Steel the reaction was predictable. PREPOSTEROUS! RIDICULOUS! INCONCEIVABLE! That a nonentity, a nonexistent nobody like Morgan Smithfield would have the audacity to challenge the hand that had fed him; the ungrateful wimp. Whining because he's been wronged! What if everyone who suffered a bruised fingernail decided to run out and get some two-bit lawyer? Homestead had no qualms about making him an example. To the end of squashing this gnat, the full resources of the Company would be brought to bear.

Frank Buckwilder would later say that the heat that was generated in court was hotter than the molting pig iron coming out of the blast furnace. Nevertheless, withstand the heat they did. Moreover, the red-hot coals over which they walked, holding the battle line where others would have buckled, welded a bond between the two men that would last a lifetime.

As Morgan now sat in the quietness of his office it all seemed so long ago. Something akin to a disorganized and jumbled nightmare. Wherein hordes of starving men had been begging for work. With outstretched arms their hands reaching for help through the strands of barbed wire blocking the closed factory gates while the big fat hideous faces of industry set up on the factory roof lines and sneeringly laughed.

In 1934 over 175,000 unemployed people were walking the streets of Pittsburgh.

That excess supply of labor allowed mills to reap the highest level of profits by keeping labor cost at the lowest possible level. At Homestead, the drive for profit was even more ruthless than in other mills. Men and equipment were run at 120% capacity; with standing orders of absolute minimum down time for maintenance and repairs. Morgan was a crane operator. The consequences in his case resulting in cables becoming frayed and tracks warped. It was a common occurrence for conveyer's belt lines to abruptly stop and for molting steel to find its way, not to a forging die, but on to attending workers.

Even death and injury were calibrated for maximum profits. It was more advantageous to pay for mishaps than to maintain safety. When a worker was killed if he had a widow she routinely received a take-it-or-leave-it lump sum payment of $1,500.00 for a release of all liability. Injured workers had their hospital bills paid and given a termination notice.

It was July hot in the afternoon when the tired, over worked cables on Morgan's crane could take no more. He was moving an overload of pig iron from the barge docks to the furnace when he heard a sharp cracking sound. He glanced up just in time to see the main cable starting to snap and unravel. In that split second he bolted enough to miss the direct fall and escaped certain death; but he could not elude the lashing whip. With his leg almost severed he fell mangled in blood to a cinder covered concrete floor.

Within minutes an emergency crew was on the site. Not for Morgan but to get the line back into production. With precision dispatch he was simply moved out of the way. In less than an hour new cables were brought in, threaded, tension tested, the debris cleared and another operator assigned. It was two hours before Morgan was finally taken to the Emergency Room at Allegheny Hospital. It would be two months before he left.

In those two months a Homestead attorneys would pay him two visits. The first visit was on the day after the accident wherein the attorney verified that Morgan's leg could probably be saved but he would never again be able to do manual labor and therefore would be of no further use to the Company. The second visit by the attorney was on the day Morgan was discharged.

The purpose of the second visit being to present Morgan with his job termination paper, and an offer of $500 to sign a release of liability. Morgan refused both.

When Frank Buckwilder filed suit on Morgan's behalf it was not an eventful item and certainly there was no mention in the *Post Gazette*. When Homestead Steel announced the contribution of a whole new wing to the Allegheny Hospital the news was on the front page. Not surprising then that when Morgan's case came to trial, hospital records could not be found.

A screen of smoke was blown up and access to critical medical records came face to face with a stonewall. In later times Morgan and Frank would ponder the case and frequently make the statement that, "You do what you have to do."

And what they had to do was deal with an unethical doctor on the hospital staff. On a verbal agreement of a twenty five per cent share of the gross settlement Dr. Daniel Owise would make sure that all of Morgan's records and x-rays along with damaging physicians' notes would become available.

On that note the case was won and won big, but in legal eyes it could be considered tainted. The taint pertained to the source of the hospital records. If it could ever be proven that the evidence from the hospital was obtained under methods of thievery, then there would be grounds for a mistrial. The hospital made it widely known that there would be no retribution against the person responsible for the leak. Homestead Steel made it widely known that they would be extremely grateful if the person would step forward.

In addition, if it could be shown that a practicing attorney had knowingly engaged in illegal dealings, then there may be grounds for being disbarred. All these after-trial items of subterfuge Dr. Daniel Owise kept neatly tucked away. Items he freely mention when he needed an unsavory favor from either Frank Buckwilder or Morgan Smithfield; but none of this was known to Jenny Craig as she showed up at the Stran that day to keep her rendezvous with Morgan.

"Hello! Anybody home! Knock, knock," came the sounds as she knocked on the outside entrance doors.

As Morgan was unlocking the door he looked out through the oval window and was struck by her youthful radiant beauty. Amazing he thought, that a woman with so much beauty should elect to spread it on the streets.

"Hello, my most lovely lady," he greeted as he opened the door.

"Hi handsome man. You look even better in the daylight, you know that?"

"I hear you," he replied as he closed the door and they moved to his office. "I'm in the mood to do some business Jenny, how about you?"

"About a million bucks worth," she commented. "I am so restless to burst out and conquer the world. There is so much in the sex field that I want to do. So much which needs to be done. Let me ask you Morgan, what are your expectations?"

Morgan didn't answer her question directly but responded with his mindset. "For right now, today?" he answered rhetorically. "For now, today, my thoughts seem to be focused on one word. If we looked it up in the dictionary it would be called character. It's on my mind because I have been thinking of a dear friend.

"Does," he paused as he was putting his feet on his desk and Jenny was taking a seat on the sofa, "it seem odd to you that I, we, should be discussing character in the same breath as selling a little loving? First though, let me ask, what is the professional word we want to use here?"

"Mine, or theirs?" she asked. "My professional words follow along the lines of beauty, a world of pleasure, a precious gift not to be wasted or soiled.

"Others call it whore, prostitute, hooker, selling snatch, spreading the legs, and I can give you a half dozen more. So by whatever name, the meaning is the same. I sell sex. I like it. It's what I'm intended to do. I can't worry too much about what it's called. If I were concerned about social approval, I would become a hypocritical bible thumper.

"I just happen to believe that the good I do by making men feel content is better than the guilty fire-and-damnation-you're-going-to-hell rhetoric which is bombarded on people by street corner bible screamers."

"Whew," Morgan released a sigh, "Jenny, what I was about to say, no longer needs to be said. I was about to use the word character in terms of saying let's believe in what we are doing. If we are going to do this I was going to say let's do it with dignity and respect."

"Thank you Morgan, for saying that."

"You are entirely welcome, but let me ask you, what do you have against God?"

"Against God!" she repeated. "Morgan you must be crazy. I don't have anything against God. I believe with all my heart and soul that He is out there; and He is with me every day, even as we sit here. Trust me Morgan, I have a strong belief in God. What I don't believe in are these self appointed screaming evangelists who get on the radio and scream about how we are all going to hell; molting burning spewing fire and brimstone hell. 'Yes Sir Folks, surely as I speak, your soul is being cast into everlasting hell... But wait, there is hope! Just send money. Yes Sir Folks, money is the way to salvation. The more you send the better your chances of entering the gates of heaven...' You get the picture."

"Just asking," Morgan held up his hand. "Now, would you like to hear some of my thoughts?"

"Yes, and whatever they are, I like them already."

"How can you be so sure?"

"Because," she said, "you, Morgan, are a man of character."

"Thank you again. But man cannot live by character alone. If he wants to survive in this ol' world he best include a great big helping of reality. Dreams are wonderful, but life is real."

"And?"

"And, our job is to change the packaging of spreading legs, to use one of your term, so that our dreams do not clash head on with reality. We can agree can't we that you don't think much of bible thumpers?"

"On that we can agree."

"To be sure Jenny and neither do I. But no matter how much you consider them to be hypocrites, you must admit that they can move through society without being hounded by the law."

"I'm listening," she replied in a questioning tone.

"So maybe a little bit of hypocrisy wouldn't be all the bad." Morgan then leaned back in his chair, raised his arms, and interlocked his fingers on the top of his head as he continued.

"If we really want to do this, then we have to do what we have to do."

"And what is it you are proposing that we have to do?"

"What we have to do is let society save face. It's been my experience that society is generally pretty tolerant. We the people have pretty much a live-and-let-live disposition until someone attempts to force an issue; and then the issue always loses."

"Morgan, remind me never to ask you the time. I would end up learning how to build a clock."

"O.K.," he laughed, "you're right. In a nut shell here's what I'm thinking. I think we have to do two things. One we have got to become mobile; get out of Pittsburgh. One of our problems is a simple matter of supply and demand.

"In Pittsburgh there is no shortage of hookers. A walk down Liberty

Street or out in the Strip District will confirm that. So I'm thinking that we go on the road. Go to where there is an ample demand but not so much supply; like over at Ft. McCaffey in Jacksburg. Big army base, lots of young GIs. Any thoughts so far?"

"Oh, yeah, sure. You think you're the first one to think of that. All of the girls along the strip have talked about going over to Ft. McCaffey. Great idea, bad pursuit, the Government isn't exactly sending out gold engraved invitations. And even if we could hang around over there, there is still the little matter of having a place."

"Packaging, Jenny. That's the other thing. It's all a matter of packaging," he responded as he rubbed an itch in the corner of one eye.

"I've been having thoughts about maybe getting some sort of a second hand passenger bus. The biggest we can find and giving it a complete overhaul. Rip out the existing interior and rebuilding it to our own specifications. Give ourselves a religious name, buy our way into the graces of the base commander and set up business."

A silence fell in the room when Morgan stopped talking. He was still rubbing at the itch in the corner of his eye and was surprised when he looked up to see Jenny with her mouth half opened just looking at him.

"You... you can do all that?" she asked in awe. "I mean, I, Morgan, it's... it would be fantastic!" she squealed. "I can't believe it." She jumped up from the sofa and moved to his side of the desk and grasped his hands in excitement.

"Do it, do it," she squeezed. "You do that and then stand back and watch me operate." She excitedly took his face in her hands. "How about a reward for the Big Boss Man," she said as she leaned over and gave him a teasing kiss and hugged his head to her no bra bosom.

The feel of her soft moist lips sent instant shivers into the depth of his manhood. As she pulled his face into her pomegranate size breast he felt the firmness of her hard young nipples and a thousand volts of electricity struck a sensation he had long assumed to be dead. At the same instant the fragrance of her intoxicating perfume filled his nostrils and emasculated his resolve to not get involved. The passageway to heaven was standing right before him; they're for the taking. Why fight it? Take it while the taking is good. Hell yes! He would do it and the consequences be damned

But, be it destiny or be it happenstance, it was a surrender which would live no longer than the blink of an eye. As he relaxed his resistance and allowed his head be buried deeper into the cleavage of her milk white mammary glands his body weight shifted slightly. A shift that pinched a raw nerve and a pain shot up from his leg; a searing reminder of how brutal the hurt could be. To have her and then loose her would be more than he could stand. His resistance instantly returned.

"Oh Boy! Morgan," she cooed. "You know what you have just done. I'm getting a tingle right in my nice moist crouch. Ooo, God, Ooo, damn, damn it's coming, uh, I could sure use a quickie, like right this minute. How about it? We never did use up that twenty buck you gave me, please?" she pleaded as she licked her wet tongue along his lips.

"Jenny, you're absolutely something," he laughed to mask his reserve, slightly pushed her back and hoped that the pain in his heart did not show.

"But not right now. It's almost matinee time and I have too much work to do. Maybe some other time." Words that hurt because it meant he would have to stand on his decision.

"Morgan, you don't know what you're missing. This one would have come packaged in a great big bundle of love."

"Some other time Jenny," he repeated as he rose up from his chair and escorted her to the door.

The storyteller paused and without effort let his mind become aware of the howling blizzard wind. With the self-reminder not to get bogged down he disciplined himself. The emphasis must remain on the search for broad clues that may have had a pronounced imprint on his moth... on Shelly Waters.

Two new names had come to the surface: Dr. Daniel Owise and Frank Buckwilder. The storyteller vaguely remembers hearing something about these two; especially the doctor. What was it he had heard? Owise was a conniving no good? Maybe it would be a lead worth following. As recalled, what he had heard happened along about...

Chapter 6

Dr. Daniel Owise tore open the square envelope and glanced at the gold embossed invitation to the Doctors Annual Charity Ball. *HA! Fat chance,* he thought. *Me getting together with you bunch of ass-holes. Don't hold your breath. I don't like any of you, none of you like me. You got no respect for me, I got no respect for you. So let's just keep it that way. You bunch of shit-heads have snubbed and mocked me for the last time.*

Without reading the particulars he crumpled the off-white card into a wad and threw it in the waste basket. The feeling was satisfying but short lived. As he sifted through the numerous advertisements and other junk mail on his desk his thoughts drifted back to the irritating invitation. It reminded him of where he was in life in comparison to most of his contemporaries. As he mentally contrasted the elaborate medical offices of other doctors to the ghetto facilities in which he was working he could feel blood rush to his face.

Look at the crap I have to work in, the thought caused him to clinch his jaw. *Dingy office, filthy floors and rusty needles. I'm a Doctor For Christ Shakes! Why is it I have to make a living in this shit?. By the damn someday I'll show'em who's who and what's what. All I need is one good break. Just one. Then we'll see.*

It was another Monday morning. The admission doors to the clinic had not yet opened and he was alone in his office; fueling his poor-me-itis. Holding a half cup of lukewarm coffee, he continued to glance around at his work facilities.

Dear the God, the thoughts kept going around and around, *crime infested neighborhood, junker building, mismatched furniture, dingy walls, poor lighting and rusted out plumbing. I hope to the Hell they're happy.*

Well they've got me for now but someday. Especially the Evaluation

Board over at Allegheny Hospital. Those snooty bastards, they never let anyone forget that I may have made some minor miscalls on a couple of my diagnosis. No Sir! They never miss a chance to smear me. I know what they say. They don't think that I know but I do. They like to call me Dr. Otherwise. Just wait...

"Good Morning Doctor Owise, time for our first patient," came the abrupt patronizing voice of his nurse as she stuck her head in his office door. Breathing a reluctant sigh he rose and started toward the half open door she was holding open.

"And a very good morning to you too Nurse Jane," he said as she stepped back to let him pass. "I see you are your usual sarcastic self this morning. What do we have to start with?"

"Looks like it's going to be another grandiose week, Doctor," she took up his step and followed.

"We're starting off with the usual. Our very first patient is an unwed pregnant woman."

"How far along?"

"Four, maybe five months. I'd guess she's around twenty five years old. This is her first visit. Welfare case. No husband. At least there's no man with her."

"No husband, no money," he commented. "We're really going to get rich off of this one."

"Be cynical if you like," she sniped, "but I doubt if it's going to do any good. You know the deal. You're sitting right on the verge of losing your privileges at Allegheny Hospital."

"I don't need to be reminded," he snapped back.

"Whoa. Don't get on my case," she responded as she was handing him the patient's chart. "You're the one who's charged with consistently making incorrect diagnosis."

"And," she proceeded to remind him, "it's the hospital, not me, who's on your case. You either spend a little time on the charity wagon and do a little doctoring of welfare cases or lose your privileges; right?"

"O.K. love of my life," he returned the barb. "Which exam room are we starting off with?"

"Ha, funny, like we had an untold number. Your royal Queen of England patient is in the end hall. Her name is Patricia Waters. Her mother is with her. And don't forget to greet them with your cheery hello when you enter."

"Funny."

"I thought you'd like it."

"Good morning all" he said indifferently as he entered the half open door to the examining room. "My name is Dr. Owise. I understand you're expecting, Mrs... Waters, is that right?", he ask in an apathetic tone as he glanced at her chart. "Is this your first visit to a doctor?"

"Uh, Yes. I guess I should have come sooner but..."

"Her husband's in the army, he tis," cut in Colleen as she moved slightly in front of Patricia.

"They only had a one night honey'moon a'fore he had to ship out for over'seas don't ye see. Such a short time to try and find 'appiness and now he's missing in act'ion don't ye know. But we've got her marriage license right here we do. Everything's proper and legal it tis."

"Yes, yes of course," he answered without looking in her direction. "I'm sure everything's fine ma'am, now let's see what we have here Mrs. Waters. If you will just lie back on the exam table and put your feet in the stirrups." Then without waiting he swung Patricia's feet up and began.

"Uh huh," he murmured as he pushed a cold steel dilator *sound* into her vagina and wiggled it from side to side. "Have you felt any movement?" he asked as he finished that part of the exam, pulled the dilator out and laid it on an adjacent tray. Without waiting for an answer he proceeded to pull her hospital gown further up, put his stethoscope to her mid-section, and listen.

"Good, Uh huh, O.K.," his tone more of a murmur than a conversation. "Now," he continued as he was removing the stethoscope from his ears, "let's see how your breast look."

And without any additional comment or waiting for her response he hastily reached up and opened the top of her hospital gown; a routine procedure on his part; a devastating occurrence on the part of Patricia

Waters.

This was only the second time in her adult life that anyone besides her mother had seen her oddity. She was instantly embarrassed and reactively threw her arms across herself just as her long dangling breast were exposed.

Dr. Owise in turn was caught totally by surprise. He was not expecting anything other than normal round firm breast of a young child bearing woman. When he caught the first glimpse he was taken back. A split second transitory silence followed and he also felt slightly embarrassed.

"It's..., it's a con'dition, Doctor," Colleen rushed in to break the silence. "Here I've got it written down on a piece of paper, I 'ave. It's called mammopendulopathy."

"I know what it is ma'am," he said as his composure returned. "It's just the first case I've ever seen. Nothing to be overly concerned about. That's why they call us doctors."

"But 'tis a CON-dition doc..."

"Ma'am... please. Would you just...! If you don't mind I AM the doctor. And I would like to continue with the examination of this patient; which I do understand is your daughter.

"Now," he turned back to Patricia, "Mrs. Waters, there's no need for panic or embarrassment here. Let's just proceed as usual shall we? I want you to just relax and answer my questions.

"What degree of touch sensation do you feel?" he asked as he picked up one of her breast and slightly rolled it in his hand. "For example does this feel normal when I squeeze. I mean does it feel like my hand?"

"Yes."

"Do you feel like you have full sensitivity. When I pinch the nipple can you feel that?"

"Yes."

"Do they ever hurt for no reason? Are they overly tender?"

"They're more tender now that I'm expecting and yes it hurts if you pinch too hard."

"But other than that, no continuous pain or anything like..."

"Ex'cuse me Doctor," Colleen again interrupted. "Her father, God rest his soul, took her to some special'ists he did. They said that what she's got it can't be fixed. That's what they told him."

"That may or may not be true... Mrs.???"

"O'Riley, Colleen O'Riley and this is me only daugh'ter."

"Yes, Mrs. O'Riley. Did you say you have been to a specialist? Could you tell me who?"

"It... 'twas a long time ago Doctor, don't yea know and fer the life of me soul I can't re'call," she embarrassingly lied.

As Colleen was speaking Owise started seeing things in a different light. A strange perception came over him of the low social order of this mother and daughter. In twisted thinking he measured their worth; *no money, no education, no breeding. They're nothing more than leaches living on society,* he mentally characterized. *What a waste of tax payer's money. If I was God I think I'd be tempted to cut'em up and start all over. Cut'em up.* The words struck a bell. *Hey, wait just a minute. This may not be all bad. A little cutting here and there.* The thought caused him to instantly take a different look at the two. And in a feeling of morbid superiority he experienced a sadistic adrenaline surge. *This is it. This is my big chance! I'll just give God a little helping hand. What He friged up, I'll fix up, and get myself a little recognition in the process.*

Ha! You snooty sons-a-bitches over at Allegheny General, this is where I rub your nose in it. I'm a gonna get my name in the medical books. This is a gold mine. Careful, don't bungle it, he controlled himself. *But just look at these two. Scum, they're nothing but welfare leaches. Nobody would give a damn if they live or die or anything else for that matter.*

"Uh, let me ask you Mrs. O'Riley," he came out of his thoughts and spoke in a tone of sincerity, "do you have an attorney or anyone to give you legal advise and could assist you in finding a way of getting corrective surgery?"

"Nary a soul do we 'ave, Doctor," she pleaded poverty in the belief that he would be charitable. "Not since the start of the depres'sion and 'tall. When me poor deceased 'usband lost all of our cap'i'tal. And of 'ourse with me poor son-in-law being missing in action and 'tall tis not been an easy lot, don't yea see."

"You say your husband is deceased?"

"Aye, that he is. The depres'sion don't yea know."

"And your son-in-law, you say he's in the Army and missing in action?"

"That's a fact and we got nobody. Me and me daugh'ter 'ere. It's rough, Doctor but we're not ones to comp'lain, we're not. But if yea can see the way in your heart to help..."

"Uh, well it might be possible for me to do a little something Mrs. O'Riley. I can't promise you anything right this minute. But let me check around and see what I can do.

"Patricia," he turned to Patricia as he rose from his chair, indicating the examination was over, "you and your baby both seem to be doing fine but I would like to see you again in a week."

With additional concluding words for her to eat lots of fruits and vegetables and to take a walk each day she was dismissed.

He then gave instructions to Nurse Jane that he would be busy for the rest of the day, would not take any more appointments, returned to his office and closed the door. He had no desire to do anything but think about this new found discovery. If he could develop a procedure for reconstructive surgery there was every reason to believe that it would catapult him into the annals of medical history. He even envisioned the procedure being called the *Owise Procedure of Reconstructive Breast Surgery; O P R B Surgery.*

With a lined writing tablet and a yellow lead pencil he leaned forward at his desk and started jotting down a list of thoughts. By his initial analysis there were four major factors, money, recognition, liability and lastly the actual operation, which would have to be addressed. First there had to be money; a lot of money. The cost of the operating room alone would be astronomical. Not to mention assisting surgeons, nurses, anesthesiologist, etc.

Secondly he had to make sure that he would get the recognition. Publicity would be the key factor in that aspect. If the case attracted a great deal of favorable public attention it would almost surely get noticed by leading medical schools and publishers of medical books.

Thirdly protection from liability; some safeguard if something went wrong. The possibility was strong that things may not turn out exactly as planned. In which case he wanted to make absolutely sure that he would not end up getting sued. If it turned out bad for Patricia that was one thing. She could simply go back to the Hill district and continue living on welfare. But for himself that was something else; he had to make damn sure that he would not end up on the short end.

To these three factors he formulated possible solutions. First, money could come in the form of a research grant from some medical school or university.

Secondly, the publicity and recognition would come if the procedure was successful and got published in medical journals.

And thirdly, protection from liability could be obtained by having both Patricia and Colleen sign iron clad release forms.

So what if the operation doesn't turn out exactly perfect, he rationalized. *They got no money, which means no lawyer, which means nobody else will give a shit. But hell, I can do it. That's the important thing. I can do it and it will turn out perfect.*

On that thought he dropped his pencil on the desk and leaned back in his chair. Interlocking his hands resting on the top of his head he started reflecting on item number four; on how the actual operation could be performed.

Item number four, the crux of the matter. What, he started trying to visualize, *would he have to do in order to turn a banana into a half grapefruit.* Bringing his chair back forward he started a sketch on the tablet, and then a second sketch, and then a third. Turning to a second page he sketched some more. And after a while he began to realize just how extremely complicated the procedure would be. *It just might be,* he started admitting to himself, *that I may have to have a little outside help.*

By the end of the day his thinking eventually drifted to the feeling that somehow the answer lies in applied mathematics. From that frame of mind his thoughts immediately raced to one of the greatest mathematicians in the world; and all it would take would be a little good-ol'-fashion blackmail. A smile came across his face as he started thinking about the squeeze he could apply. It had been just about a year back that a professor of mathematics out at Pitt University over in Oakland had traded a passing grade to a young co-ed in exchange for the right to ejaculate a load of his semen into her tender young vagina.

Unfortunately for the professor, an unintended sperm had gone along for the ride and ended up penetrating one of the co-ed's nice fertile eggs. And he, Owise, had taken care of that little unintended consequences by performing an abortion. On the telephone to Wolfgang Lutger the next day Owise called in his marker.

"Hello, Wolfgang, this is someone you haven't talked to in a long time; Dr. Owise... In the flesh... Fine, I'm doing fine. How about you? You doing O.K.? Good. And the young lady you brought over. She's doing O.K.? Uh huh. Of course. I understand.

"Listen, Wolfgang the reason I'm calling is I have a hypothetical problem. It's actually a medical problem but I think it's going to require some mathematical computations. And it occurred to me that you might be willing to give me a little assistance. I can't explain it to you over the phone but it's very important. And I was wondering if we could get together right away; say this evening after your last class.

"You don't have a problem with that do you, good? Now, we'll be needing to make some sketches and probably calculate some formulas and I was thinking that your classroom blackboard might be the best place. How about I run out to the campus tonight, say around seven o'clock. And... I do hope you don't have any ideas of fighting me on this Professor because if...? No? No problem? Good."

The meeting between the two men that night did not start with any preliminaries. "O.K. Wolfgang, here's the deal," Owise began as he entered the classroom and went directly to the blackboard. I am going to be doing some reconstructive surgery on a young woman's breast," he explained as he picked up the chalk and started drawing. "Now, what we have to start with are two tits which hang down like cucumbers like this," he drew a crude front profile showing the outline of the rib cage and two elongated U's. What I'm after is to go in and do some cutting and stitching and end up with two tits which will look like this," he drew a side profile of a half round circle with a nipple.

When he finished he dropped the chalk in the chalk rack, slightly dusted his hands, turned and looked in dead silence for a moment at the bewildered professor.

"So?" questioned a confused bearded immigrant Lutger as he looked at Owise over his thick black plastic reading glasses.

"So, to do the job is going to require some mathematical computation. That's where you come in. How do I turn a cucumber into a half grapefruit leaving the stem in the center?"

"But... You, what are you talking?" Lutger exclaimed. "What do you expect from me! I'm no doctor; or surgeon. What are you crazy? I'm a mathematician. I want no part of any such a hair brain scheme."

"You Are part of it WOLFGANG. Like it or not, you are part of it. You became part of it the night you brought that young co-ed down to my office in the middle of the night and I prematurely removed one of your off springs from her uterus. Do we understand each other?"

"But, what you are asking. It's impossible. What do I know about tissue composition, nerve ending, glandular structure, arteries, capillaries?"

"I'm not asking you to know anything about tissue, blood supply or nerve endings. You just work out the formula and an outline drawing as to where the incisions have to be made, stretched and stitched. I'll worry about shoving the meat around. O.K.!"

"But... I must protest. I have no idea of the tissue density. How am I suppose to know the composition of fat, the spreadability of tissue solids, I..."

"Look Wolfgang, for our purposes just assume the elongated tit is made out of model clay or whatever, air for all I care. What I want to know is just the necessary angles, incisions and separation points.

"Now you're suppose to be the man with the big gun in the mathematics field. I hear the Germans have some physicist by the name of Einstein that is supposed to be working on the idea of converting mass into energy.

"Surly you can come up with a way of solving something as simple as turning an elongated object into a half round ball. I don't know the exact dimension of her tits, I didn't take any measurements. But for now you can assume that each tit is roughly eight inches long and five inches in circumference. And one last word. I would like it by the middle of next week."

When Owise arrived at his office the next morning Wolfgang was in the waiting room. "MR. Owise," he said in a stiff greeting.

"Wolfgang..." Owise said coldly as the two moved into his office. "This is kind of unexpected. If you're here to protest, I have already told you my demands so don't expect to come in here poor mouthing about..."

"I'm not here poor mouthing or anything else, MR. Owise. I am here to give you what you requested. I was up all night but I did it. At least I believe I did it, at least mathematically it can be done. After that it's your problem. But no matter, when I give you this..., you and I are square on the board. What I am about to give you may bring some young woman some happiness and in that respect I hope it does. It may just as likely bring tragedy and heartache. I don't want to know either way. Also I don't want my name connected in any way. Do we have an agreement?"

"We have an agreement, now let's see what you've got."

"Good," said Wolfgang as he removed sheets of paper from his briefcase and spread them out on Owise's desk.

"First I will not release to you my computations. For one thing they are complex formulas which it is unlikely that you could decipher. The second thing is the testing. Since I will have no input or supervision into the actual testing I do not want to be bound by my theories.

"What I Have done is prepared profile sketches based upon my computations and that is all you are going to get. They are not to scale but should be fairly close. As you can see on the front profile the elongated breasts are illustrated in blue ink. Each reconstructed breast is represented by the enlarged round circle in dash black ink. And I have illustrated what I believe to be the best possible incisions by small x' lines.

"Notice that the nipple moves upward and in theory should end up at approximate center. Depending of course on how successful you will be in stretching the skin. As an added tool I have also included a side profile. The before breast is illustrated by the drooping 'U' lines hanging against her rib cage. I have superimposed the restructured projections in the form of an uplifted half circle with a nipple. Again, the incision lines are shown by x's.

"Do... you... have any questions?" he asked in a concluding curt tone as he stood up straight and removed his glasses. He then made direct eye contact to clearly establish that his marker was paid.

"If you do let's hear them now because when I go out that door..."

"Uh, No Professor. These are fine," Owise fought to contain his exuberance. "A little less than what I was hoping for but I believe I can make them do."

He desperately wanted to ask Wolfgang some additional questions. But to do so would mean getting snide remarks. So he elected to simply accept the data as gospel. In-so-far as he was concerned here was proof positive that it could be done and he was not going to cloud the issue. If the operation was successful it would bring him notoriety. If it wasn't he would just sweep it under the carpet and walk away.

"Everything's fine, just fine."

Wolfgang closed his briefcase and turned to leave. At the door he paused and half turned back to Owise. "Without mentioning any names or particulars I took the liberty of consulting some of my colleagues in the medical field.

"They advised me that the skin texture around the breast is fairly receptive to surgery. When it is done with professional skill the scars are not overly pronounced; again depending on the skills of the surgeon.

"Are You a good surgeon Dr. Owise?" he curtly asked, and left.

When Patricia and Colleen arrived for their scheduled appointment the following week Owise was ready. "Mrs. Waters, uh Patricia... may I call you by your first name? I may have some wonderful news. Uh, that is after your baby is born of course. But before too long after you deliver we may be in a position to do reconstructive surgery on your breast. Is that something you would like?"

"What? Uh, Well, I never thought about. I mean what does that mean? Does it mean you'll be cutting up my breast or something I..."

"Hush child," Colleen quickly admonished. "The Doctor here's a fine gentle'man. And what he wants is to be fix'ing what 'rong with ye. It may be the only chance we'll ever 'ave. I've heard with me own 'ars what these brill'iant young doctors can do these days. And Dr. Owise 'ere seems to 'ave tak'ing a liking to ye. Yea don't find that too often these days I tell ye. I'd like to hear what it tis he's think'ing."

"What I'm proposing Mrs. O'Riley," he spoke to Colleen as the one who would be making the decision, "is to reconstruct Patricia's breasts so that they are normal. Since your last office visit I've consulted with some of my colleagues and we believe it can be done with reasonably good results. In-so-far as we know it has never been attempted but that was before we had today's advanced technology; we now believe it's possible.

"The procedure will be very expensive but I think I can get the money in the form of a grant from a medical school or university. If we are successful it means we won't have to pay the money back. But to do it I have to work up what is called a Proposal. That means I have to put in writing what I hope to do and how I hope to do it.

"Now, I know that you probably find all of this very confusing. But if we can correct Patricia's problem I think you'll agree that the rewards will be well worth the effort.

"And as my good deed I will take care of all the details. If we succeed just think how fantastic we will all feel. I do however need for you to say that you would like to have it done.

"So now I am asking. Mrs. O'Riley is restructuring Mrs. Waters' breast something you would like for me to do?"

He watched as Colleen and Patricia looked at each other and could see their hesitation. "It's up to you," he quickly pressured. "You can go home and think it over if you like. But it's very unlikely that we will ever get this close again. The circumstances are such that I must have an answer now."

"Well Doctor," Colleen said sheepishly, "we don't want to be no bo'ther. If yea say ye can do it then we'll do it. I'm a pret'ty good judge of char'acter I am and I knowed right off that yea could be trusted."

"Good..." Owise moved aggressively. "I think you both have made a wise decision. Now there's no time like the present to get started. I have my camera here and the first thing we will need is some pictures. Mrs. Waters if you will be kind enough to take off your blouse and brassiere and stand here by the wall we can begin."

"But, you mean, Uh, take my cloths off. I couldn't. I, no...," Patricia protested.

"Come, come child," Colleen coerced. "Dear Baby don't yea see the doctor has to do what he 'as to do. Don't be bash'ful now. Take off ye top Dar'ling"

"That's fine," commented Owise as she removed her garments. "There are a couple of things which are going to be very important," he spoke as he was adjusting the floor light. "First we are going to need several close up shots. But we will also need some half body shots showing your full upper torso. Now in the half torso shots I want you to give me some very sad expressions. It won't hurt matters if we play on their sympathies a little.

"Good, a little more sad now, terrific, sad sad, frown. Good let me see you almost crying and slouch; lots of hollow chest slouching, good, slouch a little more. There, anyone who looks at these with even half a conscious will have to give us a grant," he finished.

"Mrs. O'Riley, Mrs. Waters that's about it for today. There is one last item which needs our attention. It's just a formality but I have prepared some forms for both of you to sign. Briefly they authorize three things. First these forms authorize me to proceed with the surgery in whatever capacity I think is necessary. Secondly you release me from all liability and thirdly all rights to the operation, including all notes and photographs are my sole property to do with as I please."

With a handed pen they signed, Owise kept all copies and concluded by saying. "Wonderful, I thank you very much. That's all we can do for now. From here on it's all up to me. Go home and I will keep you advised."

By the end of the week Daniel Owise had finished his Grant Proposals made several copies and the solicitations were in the mail to various universities. Included in each packet were a cover letter, the written proposal, copies of Wolfgang's sketches and profile pictures. He justified the proposed operation in the name of relieving mental suffering and the advancement of medical technology. In hopes of getting one fourth of the amount, he requested a grant of $155,000.00 as the minimum amount necessary to cover expenses. His final input was to ask that the procedure be known by his name. He felt good. Professional recognition would soon be coming his way and when it was all over he would be held in a lot higher esteem.

He resumed his normal practice and waited. Two weeks went by and then three. But no responses came. In the fifth week he did receive a call; not from a university but from Patricia.

"Hello, Dr. Owise this is Patricia Waters."

"Yes?"

"Dr. Owise, I hate to bother you but I don't know who else to call.

"What's wrong. Are you feeling morning sickness, abdominal pains, what?"

"No, it's not me I'm calling about. It's mother. I'm worried about her and I don't know what to do."

"What's wrong?"

"She seems to have just quit."

"Quit? Quit what?"

"Quit everything. Two weeks ago we both lost our jobs out at the shipyards. What happened was I was called up to the front office and terminated because of being pregnant. When I went to tell mother I had been fired a dreadful hurt came to her face and she just went into crying hysterics and carrying on like nothing I have ever seen. It was like... like the world had just come to an end or something. I guess something just snapped. She sank down to the floor and rolled around crying that she just couldn't take any more. It was just awful.

"Several supervisors came running over and when they couldn't get her to stop they told me to take her home and not to bring her back. When we got home she just sat down and since then she's been like a stranger staring off into space. It's got to where all she does all day is just sit; sit in her rocker. Sometimes she'll take to rocking and even talk to herself. And every now and then she'll laugh out loud. Why I don't know. I try talking to her but she doesn't seem to even know I'm in the house."

Owise contacted the Allegheny Welfare Department and the case was assigned to a social worker. Within the next month it was determined that Colleen had gone into regression, was no longer capable of taking care of herself and was put in a State sanitarium.

Patricia's own circumstances had also come to the attention of the social services and things had the potential of becoming troublesome. A case worker contacted Dr. Owise and asked for his input as to her well being.

This was sufficient for him to start becoming concerned. If the County assumed direct responsibility for Patricia's care then the prospects of surgery could be lost. At the very minimum the release of liability would no longer be binding. It was on this thought that he panicked and made an unsound decision. He elected to personally assume responsibility for Patricia. Without mention to anyone he hurriedly moved her out of her two room flat in the Hill District and into his own home.

But involvement was begetting more involvement. What started out as a minimum risk had moved into more dangerous territory. Becoming involved with a patient was professionally very dangerous. He was already on probation and any scandal involving a patient would mean his medical demise.

Still, he felt committed to his plan. If a grant would just come he could still pull it off. He was sure about that. Among the things in his favor was the lack of previous operations. That meant that there were no precedent by which his success or failure could be measured. He had to play it through; of that he was convinced. It just meant keeping a tight reign on everything.

He discontinued the services of his house maid and avoided all social activity. Patricia was given her own bedroom at the opposite end of the house and was forbidden to use the telephone or to go outside. But each day things grew more difficult for them both. He couldn't stand the presence of Patricia in his house and she could feel the resentment.

For Patricia she was alone for the first time in her life. She had no one to spend time with. No one to help make decisions and no one for company. She missed her mother and her worries grew about how she was going to support herself and her baby. She became more lonely and each day she cried a little more.

At the start of 1941 a dog-faced foot soldier in the U.S. Army was paid $21.00 per day; howbeit only one day per month. The cost of a brand new Fleetwood Cadillac was $1,500.00 and the price of gasoline was $00.11 cents a gallon. But none of that was on Owise's mind one morning in January when two men wearing expensive suits and business hats came to his office.

Dr. Daniel Owise's future was about to take an abrupt turn in totally unrelated ways and in circumstances he could never have imagined.

"Dr. Owise," came a slow, very heavy, Brooklyn accent from a short thick faced Sicilian as he pushed back his hat. "My name's Antonio Martignelli but youse can call me Knuckles and dis here's Angelo Scariano. Angelo he don't talk a whole lot cause he gets excited and den' he starts to slobber. Sooo, I'll be doing most of da speaking o' course if that's OK with youse. Now, youse name came to us by da way of some contacts wees has over at da Alleegainee Hospital see, and wees think da youse is jest da man we is looking fer.

"We knows youse is a v..ery busy man doctor, so we'll gets right to-da' point.

"We's... me and Angelo here, wees're here as bone-e-fied rep-re-sent-atives of the National Syndication of Radio Evangelist see. Those are da good people that preaches the word of God over da free air-way, see. Youse see, da radio lets us get da good lord's words to a lot of da fine believing folks ways out in the country; folks back in da hills so ta speak what wants to do right by our good Savior by sending in contributions, see. Now, in re'turn for der life'time pledge to support God's work we, at da syn-di-cation, promise to take care of 'em in their old age see and wees are in da process of finding us a doctor to put on our staff. Youse with me...? Good.

"Now, wees understand that youse is the type of doctor wees can work with so wees are here to make youse an offer youse can't refuse.

"We in da' Syndicate have this here new rev-a-lution-airy idea of combining the fields of Radio Evangelism and good holsum health care. A real first-class modern-istic hospital, see. Where's... good God—fear-ing old folks can come to ree-tire if they're sick and can't take care of dem-selves. It's-a-gonna-be a real first class operation see. Deese old folks who have contri'buted der life's savings and all, deese folks deserve the best, see.

"Of course now, we can't have folks who are still able to work coming in here to freeload don't yea see. And this is where youse is-gonna come in. Wees is-gonna need a good ad'min'istrator. It has to be a doctor so he can clearly certify that they are still able to care for themselves and dar-fore do not qualify and so we is here to-day to offer youse da job. Da pay is $25,000 a year. As we grow and ex'pand... naturally youse will have a staff of dem interns under youse. You can have youse own private office and youse own private sec're'tary and no-body will be giving youse any trouble, see.

"Now I guess dat's a-bout everything. Does youse think," Knuckles asked in a stern direct eye contact as he cracked the knuckles on his big calloused hands, "dat youse can accept da offer? Good..., very good...it makes me ex'treme'ly happy when 'nother man sees things my way. Dr. O'-wise, we will be in touch. A'ppre'ciate youse time. Now's youse don't bother with getting up to show us to da door, we can show our-selves out."

In the minutes, hours and days that followed, Owise became a man in a quandary. To be the administrator of a brand new hospital was a windfall beyond his wildest dreams. But by the same token he did not know what course of action to take regarding Patricia. He would still like to attempt the operation but his quest for a grant was not producing any results. He had sent out follow-up tickler letters but still no responses.

So for the time being he kept her on at his house and when she came due at the end of nine months he took her to a small privately owned hospital where he had privileges and personally delivered the baby. He took special steps to see that her breast did not get exposed and the delivery did not arouse any undue suspicion. She gave birth to a baby girl whom she named Shelly and the next day he quietly move mother and child back to his residence.

But the situation was now completely out of hand. In hindsight he was beginning to think the idea was insane. He lay awake nights wondering how he could have ended up with an unmarried woman and her child living in his house. Each day he eagerly waited for the mail and a letter that could possibly mean a grant. Finally the day came when he did get a letter. Not of his expectations, not from any university but a letter which expressed interest of a different nature. It came from Medico Enterprises; the publisher of the Encyclopedia of Rare and Unusual Genetic Birth Defects. In some round about way, unbeknown to him, pictures of Patricia's breast had come to their attention and they were interested in investigating the case.

An agent subsequently contacted Dr. Owise and related that it was customary for Medico to pay for all information and data used in their encyclopedia and arrangements were made for an inspection of Patricia's breast. Owise falsely advised Patricia that she was being examined by a team of reconstructive specialist. With clipboards in hand and guised as physicians wearing white coats, the Medico agents obtained what they came after.

In the initial stages they physically fondled and squeezed her breast for firmness, felt and pulled the nipples and observed the secreting milk. Measurements were also taken of both the length and circumference and after the physical manipulations were completed they compared the pictures from Owise.

When the examining was finally finished, Patricia was simply excused. With respect to the emotional aspects of the ordeal, the men felt no concern; Patricia hid away and cried.

Dr. Owise then received his negotiated compensation. For the sum of $5,000.00, Medico purchased full and exclusive rights including, but not limited to: (a.) all notes, sketches and photographs, including copies of consent and release of liability signed by Patricia, and (b.) all rights of publication.

Patricia Waters was never asked for her consent nor did she ever receive any compensation. When the next year's issue of the Encyclopedia of Rare and Unusual Genetic Birth Defects came out it contained three pages of photographs showing her breast; She had become a medical statistic.

The offer from the Syndicate of Radio Evangelist rapidly became Dr. Owise's one obsession and his desire for surgical fame came to an end. His fantasies now focused on being the head of a new hospital. He fantasized that the recognition which he had always sought would eventually arrive; it would just be from a different direction. His first problem was what to do about Patricia.

In fear of adverse publicity he was reluctant to put a destitute woman and her new born child out on the street. If it should reach the news media they would have a field day and the adverse publicity could have horrendous consequence. The violation of doctor-patient ethics is a serious offense. If it reached the attention of the State Licensing Board it would most likely cost him his license.

So, for the time being Patricia and Shelly were allowed to continue living in his house. But their presence never ceased to grate on his nerves. He viewed them as nothing more than street urchins and frequently expressed his disgust. At the slightest provocation he would unleash a tyrannical barrage of abuse; and was adamant that she keep herself and the baby out of sight. In raving threats he promised dire consequence if she should go out of the house and be seen by the neighbors. For the time being that was all he could do; for the time being.

*For the time being...*the storyteller mentally chastised those three words as he brought himself as he brought himself back to the present. It isn't God but circumstances that work in strange and mysterious ways.

For the storyteller some answers were beginning to materialize. One was the answer as to how the pictures of Patricia turned up in the encyclopedia..

But for every answer, there were always more questions. Such as the mobsters. How did they figure in all of this? On a larger note what kind of lasting imprint did Owise's behavior leave on Patricia and Shelly.

In pursuits of these and other answers the storyteller did a very unusual thing; he tried looking at the whole picture from a bird's eye view. He imagined himself levitating in a high ceiling room wherein two adults and one child were momentarily frozen in time. Patricia was holding Shelly and seated in a straight back chair. Dr. Owise was seated directly opposite and also in a straight back chair. This mental vision enable the storyteller to clearly see that the heavy burden of the world rested not with baby Shelly but on the shoulders of her mother, Patricia. No wonder there was a lasting motherly imprint

Of them all, who was the most profound; Owise, Morgan, Jenny, Frank, or others not yet known? At this juncture Morgan was beginning to surface as being the most dominant. Why would that be? At last recall, what was he doing? Something about Ft. McCaffey...

Chapter 7

The early morning sun was still half hidden in the eastern sky when Morgan pulled out of Pittsburgh for the 170 miles drive to Ft. McCaffey; the first step of his plan for Jenny. If not a first step then at least a first try. In fact of the matter he had no idea of what to expect. The only information he had going in was the base commander's name, Colonel Wainwright Bates.

He had never dealt with the military before but there was no reason to think that accessibility would be any more difficult than with other governmental bureaucrats and politicians. The principles which he had used in the past were simple enough. The first thing is to accept that you are on the asking side of the equation. Let the man who's in charge remain in charge, grovel just a touch, assure sincerity and show respect for both the man and his turf.

The prior week he had gone to a small printing shop around the corner from the Stran and placed a unique printing order. Working with the shop owner the two had designed a special style of stationery consisting of off-white matt paper embossed with a religious scene; an early morning, half hidden, sun ascending out of towering white clouds. Golden rays starting narrow at the rim of a half-obscured sun, widened as they cast outward and blended across the sheet in border stripes. A centered letterhead, also embossed in gold, simply read:

Benevolent Order of Youth For Christ
Pittsburgh, Pennsylvania

It was mid-day by the time Morgan pulled into the main gate at Ft. McCaffey, halted by an armed MP and questioned as to the nature of his business.

Morgan relating that he was affiliated with Youth for Christ, verified the name of the base commanding officer and requested a call from gate appointment.

Colonel Wainwright Bates had never liked the Army. For one thing he could never get uniforms which were small enough. For another, he had never received any degree of recognition or respect from his fellow officers. At 5 feet 6 inches and weighing only 135 pounds he barley pass the minimum requirements. Physically he had never measured up to the rough, tough, knuckle busting, beat'em up, stomp'em in, kick'em-when-they're-down military image.

When he joined the Army in 1912 he entered as a 2nd lieutenant with a degree in engineering. It was his expectations that he would build roads and bridges. But in 1914 when the first World War broke out he was assigned to combat infantry and shipped to France. And by his own admission, it was the seed which started the feud. He was a complete failure as a battlefield officer and after six months of mud, barbed wire and mustard gas he was taken out of the front lines. But least it be deemed that the Army rewards incompetents, he did not get to go home. Instead he was assigned to America's other war; the occupation of Haiti.

Supposedly the role of the United States in Haitian affairs at the time was one of peace keeping. A stabilizing force to end the years of internal strife wherein the Haitian people rebelled against their corrupt Government. It had all come to a head in 1915 when an angry mob stormed the Government palace and in mob hysteria roped and lynched President Vilbrun Guillaume Sam. Almost immediately thereafter the United States, under the guise of restoring order, seized the opportunity to invade Haiti. On July 28, 1915, 300 fully armed combat ready United States marines landed on the island, squelched the Haitian army, set up an American military government and stayed for some twenty years.

By 1919 when Wainwright Bates arrived on the scene the Marines had already killed and slaughtered thousands of Haitian and smoldering resentment burned against American military involvement.

In an attempt to improve relations, the United States initiated a massive public works program of building roads, sewers, and public schools.

The strategy and scope of the plan was simple. Military engineers would provide the know-how and Haitian semi-slave labor would do the work; some thirty thousand by best count. And in the best benevolence of the Army that was where Lieutenant Wainwright Bates was sent. In his opinion it was an insulting degrading assignment; deliberately intended to be beneath his stature, training, abilities and dignity. He may have been justified in his resentment but it brought him little satisfaction. He spent fifteen long years in stifling humidity, mosquitos infested swamps and blistering sun doing nothing but building roads about which no one gave a damn.

In 1934 President Roosevelt finally ordered the occupation ended. But by then the temperament of Bates was chiseled in stone; he nursed his sour disposition by hating everyone. He stayed on in the Army as a course of revenge. He had suffered irreversible skin and eye damage from the long exposure to the sun's ultra violet rays and he was determined that somebody was going to pay. His white sensitive skin was now perpetually red over his orange-peel pock marked face and he was almost blind without his thick steel-rim eye glasses. In reward, or apathy, through, the Army had brought him up through the promotional ranks and when he made Colonel he was given the job of base commander at Ft. McCaffey.

But none of this was known to Morgan as he waited his heel-cooling time in the outside waiting room. And when he was finally ushered into Bates's office, he entered with an extended hand; hoping to minimize his civilian status and immediately initiate friendly man to man relations.

"Colonel Bates, Sir," he spoke in his most folksy tone. "My name is Morgan Smithfield, same spelling as the Smithfield Bridge and Smithfield Street in downtown Pittsburgh." (Morgan nearly always made it known that the street name first appeared on the original town survey in 1784 and was actually named after an Indian trader named Devereux Smith; but this time that little tid bit was conveniently overlooked.)

"I surely do appreciate you granting me a few moments of your valuable time Colonel Bates, Sir. Like I say I'm from Pittsburgh. I drove over here this morning to talk with you in the name of our young men walking in the righteous path of our Holy Father and Savior who is watching over all of us."

Colonel Bates did not accept Morgan's extended hand. Instead he remained seated in his wooden, swivel chair behind his government issued wooden desk and looked up at Morgan with an icy steel cutting stare. Then slowly, while still holding his sneering look he leaned back, interlocked his fingers, brought his hands to rest on the top of his head and cast a piercing penetrating smirk. As the two men looked at each other there was a brief eye contact but Bates saw no need to hold it. Whether from military training or self discipline he had perfected a belittling, intimidating gawk which he now directed sternly at Morgan to be seated in the chair across the desk; then finally spoke.

"Mr. Smithfield...," he responded in a deliberately slow, concise, patronizing tone, "we..., here at Ft. McCaffey..., are always pleased to receive leaders in the community... who, Uh... take a personal interest in the moral's of our young fighting men.

"And having someone drive all the way over from Pittsburgh, why that's a special pleasure for me, because, I used to live in that fair city. As a matter of fact I went to Carnegie Institute of Technology. Graduated from dear ol' Carney in 1912.

"That was the year they changed the name from Carnegie Tech. Were you aware of that? I suppose all of that was before your time," he tapered off his voice in a patronizing tone. A stern silence followed as Morgan instantly picked up the military subservience of not speaking until there was a clear signal.

"You didn't mention Mr. Smithfield, and I do hope you will forgive me for asking, but the name Smithfield, is that 'the' Smithfield of such prominence in Pittsburgh?"

Hot damn!, Morgan quickly thought. *Hallelujah! He's for sale. He's lying. There is no Smithfield family in Pittsburgh; except mine. And mine was stolen a couple of generations back. When my ancestry came to this country as immigrants nobody could pronounce the Greek name Apostolopoulou. So they just adopted the name Smithfield and it has scared the hell out of people ever since.*

"Colonel Bates, Sir," Morgan carefully enunciated his response. "The good name of Smithfield has never endorsed, nor will it endorse any public endeavor. It is a time honored legacy to let any worthwhile cause rise or fall on its own merits and not be propped up by the strength of the family name.

"So you can see Sir, it would not be honorable of me to insinuate that there may be some strong Smithfield endorsement behind the Benevolent Order of Youth For Christ. No Sir, I am just out on my own doing the Lord's work. I...."

Morgan did not get to finish. Colonel Bates had established in his own mind that Morgan was more than likely backed by some strong measure of wealth. His next interest was to find out what it was he wanted. "Very fine folks, just the same; the Smithfields. Highly respected, very highly respected," Bates commented in southern drawl.

"One thing about the Smithfields though is they have always been very generous to the charitable organizations in Pittsburgh. Generosity, is that a common trait to the Smithfield name?"

Morgan felt a sigh of relief. A signal as big as a barn. He was home free; it was now just a matter of money and that was his game.

"Well, we here at the Youth for Christ do believe that the Good Lord helps those who help themselves. Yes Sir, Colonel Bates, Sir, we certainly do believe that. We in the Foundation believe that we can't just sit idly by and not provide a means for our young fighting men to help themselves."

"Just how much 'help' do you propose?" asked Bates. It was now Morgan's move and he played it with all the flare of a seasoned statesman holding an audience before the Crown Heads of Europe. He methodically opened his briefcase and cast an attentive look to the inside. Using the opened lid as a hide from Bates' eyes, Morgan cast a slight searching frown as he carefully fingered through several sheets of blank paper in an obvious search. Then, changing his expression to there-it-is he removed an eight by ten off-white envelope embossed at the borders with golden Sun rays.

Snapping the lid shut to his briefcase he then slightly leaned forward in his chair. Mimicking a second positive inspection of the envelope he looked up at the Colonel, smiled a slight smile and resumed talking as he held the envelope across the desk.

"Well Sir, I am just real pleased that we were able to bring the subject up. Because I did come prepared, Colonel Bates. Yes Sir I did do that. Right here in this Foundation envelope. See our logo, the Lord's own rays of sunshine descending down from Heaven?

"The Foundation has authorized me to make a cash contribution to FT. McCaffey. In the name of moral goodness I am prepared, this morning, to donate to the base in care of you the Commander, a sum of $1,000.00; to be spent in any way which you see fit. Now the foundation does not desire any self recognition Colonel Bates. I can't stress that too strongly.

"Our reward is just knowing that the young men on this base, those very same young men who will shortly be going into mortal combat, in the short time they have left before many of them will be going to their certain death, that they spend their little remaining time in the company of those who truly believe. Now this donation here is in cash and most certainly we do not expect a receipt."

A stark silence followed when Morgan stopped talking and there was no motion by Bates to reach out and accept the envelope still being held. In a touch of awkwardness Morgan lightly laid it on the desk.

Bates still had both hands interlocked and resting on his head. He slightly glanced at the embossed envelope. Then, without saying a word he swiveled his chair one half around to where he was facing his window and his back to Morgan. Putting one foot upon the window sill he slightly turned his brown high top riding boot from side to side. With an intent inspection, he lowered his interlocked hands, leaned slightly forward and fingered one of the pull-on straps. Concluding that it was O.K. he resumed leaning back, returned his locked fingers to the top of his head a while longer and finally spoke.

"It doesn't seem to me that you can buy much goodness for only a $1,000.00," came his unimpressed response.

"Ah, no Sir," Morgan quickly responded. "You are absolutely right on that account Colonel Bates, Sir. And I want to be quick to say that our concern for the moral inspiration of our patriotic youth is certainly in excess of a $1,000.00. Greatly in excess Colonel Bates, Sir.

"Also, I have some explanatory thoughts I'd like to share if I might. When I was driving over here this morning I swung through the town of Jacksburg 'bout 20 miles to the west of here.

"That's seems to be about the closest town around. I just wanted to see if there were any moral pitfalls over there to which these young men may be exposed.

"It seems to me like Jacksburg is the natural place that our young men would drift into on weekend passes. And Colonel, you will pardon me for saying this Sir. But there are just an awful lot of places down in the tenderloin district, along on 3rd and 4th Streets where temptation must surly lead out young men away from the righteous path."

Morgan was impulsively tempted to strengthen his pitch with preacher style bible-thumping words of the Lord's displeasure. But in wisdom he held his words in check and was relieved when the Colonel assumed the lead; howbeit in a different mode.

"Are you aware, Mr. Smithfield, that Ft. McCaffey is a basic-training installation?" he asked rhetorically. "Young men are sent here for sixteen weeks of basic military training and then they are shipped out. Most will be sent directly overseas. In effect this installation works on a sixteen-week rotation schedule. That means a new crop of recruits is processed through here every week.

"Now, for a lot of our young recruits, this is the first time they have ever been away from home. And an even larger percentage have never experienced a woman's intimate pleasures. What are your thoughts on that?"

"It pains me Colonel and that's a fact," responded Morgan. "The Youth for Christ certainly does understand the natural instincts of our young men. Yessir, we certainly do understand that. And one of the very things we have in mind is that they be provided the opportunity to associate with good wholesome Christian girls. Girls who themselves are believers. And we would like to initiate a program which would keep these fine young men from the evil clutches of those brothels over in Jacksburg.

"Now, as I was driving in this morning I noticed a small settlement about a mile or so up the road from here. Corbin Corners, I think they call it; crossroad service station, small grocery store, couple of old frame houses, clusters of eucalyptus trees along the road, this sort of thing. I also noticed a big metal quonset hut building which was standing there empty. I think it used to be a farm implements shop but I'm not sure.

"Anyway I stopped for gas and got to talking to the owner of the service station. Turns out he also owns the quonset hut, and he sure would like to have it rented.

"Now my thinking is that it could be fixed up along the lines of a Service Men's USO Club. A place for our men can go and have a soft drink, maybe one beer, write letters home or just relax.

"But the main thing we have in mind is to bring some good wholesome Christian girls over here every weekend from Pittsburgh for no other reason than to serve as hostess.

"The type of girls these young men will feel real good about. Now this would all be at our expense mind you. We in Youth for Christ certainly do not expect any funds or anything like that to come, in anyway, from the Base. No sir reee..."

"In what manner," Bates cut in, "do you propose to transport these young women over and back each week?"

"By bus. The Foundation has a bus which we use for Christian picnics and such. It's all fixed up real nice. We've modified the inside by removing all of the seats and installing mini berths along the lines of railroad car berths. Curtains and everything. That's just in case some of our girls should get tired while they are over here, then they'd have a place to lie down mind you."

"And," Bates responded instantly, "where do you propose to park this bus once you get it here?"

"Well, now I am pleased that you asked that question Colonel Bates, Sir. As I have said, we at Youth For Christ are not interested in attracting attention to ourselves. Like I say, our reward comes from just doing what the Lord intended.

"So I pretty much think that the bus should probably be parked around in back. That way it would be out of sight but still be sort of part of the building so to speak. That being the case we could then have a canopy and walkway between the bus and the back door of the hut so that there can be a free flow of traffic. There may be times when a young man would want to see the degree of traveling hardship which our wholesome girls endure to bring a little joy and comfort to the men in our armed services.

"Oh, and by the way Colonel Bates, Sir there is the possibility that we may take in a little money from the juke box, sale of soda pop, that occasional beer, and such. If we do, we would like for it to all go to Ft. McCaffey in your care Sir, cause we at Youth for Christ are nonprofit. So if you have no objections, whatever is left over after expenses each week we will see that it is delivered directly to you in one of our easily identifiable Youth For Christ envelopes."

Morgan felt that he was now at a stopping point. He waited to see if he had a sale. Colonel Bates showed no change of expression. With his back still to Morgan he leaned further back in his chair and put both feet up on the window sill.

Morgan continued to silently watch and hold in grovel-waiting while Colonel Bates timely brushed figments of lint from his uniform, reached up and pulled one ear slightly, sniffled his nose, interlocked his fingers and put his hands back resting on top of his head.

"Mr Smithfield," he finally said, "I am just real pleased that such a fine organization as yours has decided to take such a commendable interest in the morals and patriotism of our fighting men. I think that you would be interested in knowing that you have certainly helped me solve one of my major problems; and that is what to do about weekend passes. I don't mind too much if my young recruits go into Jacksburg through the middle of the month. Most of them do not have any money anyway at that time of the month so they can't get into too much trouble.

"It's the first of the month, on Army payday that worries me. Do you know how the system works? Each and every man gets paid in cash. The first of every month is payday. Pay lines form right here in front of Company Headquarters. And every man that steps up to the pay table gets $21.00.

"Now the simple fact is most of them are too young to know how to handle that much money. It always worries me when I see them leave out of here on payday weekend pass; heading for God knows where. Now if what you say is true, that your fine organization, Youth for Christ, that is the correct name isn't it?"

"Yes Sir, Colonel Bates, that sure is our name right enough."

"Good, I always like to make sure of names, anyway now that you tell me that the Youth for Christ is willing to put up some wholesome recreational facilities just a mile from the gate, why Mr. Smithfield that sure does take a load off of my mind."

With deliberate slowness Bates lowered his feet from the windowsill and swiveled his chair around to where he was again facing Morgan.

"From what you tell me," he was now speaking directly to Morgan, "I believe it would be in everyone's best interest if I took the authoritative step of modifying our liberty passes.

"It seems to me that our Country, these United States of America, could be well served by issuing passes on payday which limit the distance from the base to no more than two miles. This assumes of course that you will have your facilities in place in the not too distant future."

"Right away Colonel Bates, Sir, we can get on the details right away. And we will make you proud too, Sir. You can rest assured that everything will be top cabin. It is the very least we can do to support America's service men."

"Wonderful, very commendable. The change in pass policy will go into effect the first of next month."

Colonel Bates' face then turned expressionless and he offered no additional words. Morgan was being dismissed. A deal had been made. And when a deal is made it is essential that things move quickly. Morgan rose to his feet, slightly pushed the envelope toward the center of the desk and with expressions of appreciation put on his fedora and left.

Back in his car and passing through the gates leaving Ft. McCaffey, a young spit-and-polish MP threw Morgan a snappy salute which caused an emotional surge. He was touched by the caliber of America's young fighting men. He wanted in some way to show his appreciation. *Having their own whore house,* he thought, *should be some help.* He smiled at the touch of his own humor as he sped away from the gate. He had lots to do and was anxious to get started.

His first stop was at Corbin Corners Gas & Grocery where he arranged to lease the vacant quonset hut. When the elder Corbin received top dollar rent he reasoned that a little night time party noise would not bother anyone around there.

In Jacksburg he found a building contractor. Together they made an on-site inspection and Morgan gave instructions to clean up, paint up, light up, and install: bathrooms, bar counter, tables, chairs, booths, mood lights, juke box, and buff out a dance floor. And above all, he instructed, petition off an area for a Meditation Room and make sure it is outfitted with easy chairs, bibles, religious pictures, a small alter with cross and kneeling rail, candle holders and religious stationery.

He spent the night in Jacksburg and on his drive back to Pittsburgh the next day there was a lot on his mind.

The first order was to find a suitable bus and rehab it to their needs. Also it was important that he immediately get with Jenny and discuss an operating plan and how many girls she could get.

All the while, thoughts were wondering in his mind as to what he was getting into. He remembered something Frank Buckwilder had once said. 'Morgan,' Frank had commented, 'the major events in a person's life, be they good or be they bad, most usually start with the most insignificant beginnings. A chance meeting of someone in a bar, on the street, at a party, standing at a stop light...'. *How true* Morgan thought. *This had all started,* he recounted, *when a young hooker named*

Jenny made a pass at him, in the dead of night, on a deserted street, in the middle of a blinding snow storm.

Now he was about to become a woman runner. All because, he rationalized, he wanted to step forward and provide a reasonable means for young GIs to experience a good lay; which would be well and good except for one thing. There is the little matter of the law which is not quite so benevolent.

"No good deed," he utter as an expression of his reservations, "will go unpunished." Mind rambling was his by-product of driving alone.

As air noise whistled through the windows and the tires hummed on the macadam road he continued his 1939 black, four door Buick on toward Pittsburgh. In fickle thoughts he wavered back and forth; for and against.

Thoughts in favor of going ahead brought concerns about the law. Thoughts of forgetting the whole deal, brought feelings of guilt for failing to stand firm on his self-imposed commitment. *Either I do it or I don't,* he chides himself. *Don't be a gutless wonder. If you have any balls at all then quit worrying about your own sweet ass and do something for the boys; who by the way are going out to fight for that sweet ass.*

Then it happened, a different train of thought entered his mind. *What harm could possibly come from a young recruit getting a good fuck?* he asked himself; *but then maybe I don't know everything. If there were no laws, what would I feel. Just, in and of itself; is the selling and buying of pussy good, bad or don't make a damn bit of difference one way or the other?*

He had heard the term victimless crime. Meaning no person was actually hurt, only the law was broken. His mind's eye somehow narrowed the picture to just young GIs. "Here we have," he started arguing his point out loud as he drove, "boys which have grown from adolescence into manhood. Their bodies are fully matured but their minds and experiences are just developing.

"They're not even old enough to vote. But," he interjected, "they're sure as to hell just the right age to go out get themselves killed or maimed in a nice little capitalistic war.

"What that means is the American people are ordering them to go out and defend with their life a law which denies them the right to try a little growing up pussy. To me that's a real piss cutter".

He tried to comprehend the mind of a young soldier who has been blown apart by an artillery shell. *With his intestins hanging out, lying in his own blood waiting to die. All the things he would never get to experience. Surely a man has the right to experience the feel of a woman. Surely he is entitled to that much.*

By the time he reached Pittsburgh, Morgan was fully committed. He would do it and the law be damned. But, as he related to Jenny later that day at the Stran, it was going to be top cabin.

"Jenny," he started, "I think we have a deal. For better or worse we are now in business; or at least assume we are in business. That is if I can get my mind on straight. I want to hear from you, the one who is right there doing the humping, feeling and touching; and a young male body has just climbed out of your bed and headed off to war. Now just between you and me, the hard cold facts; that fantastic exciting fuck he has just had, are the long term effects going to be good or bad?

"What I am after," he continued, "what concerns me is, have I just set some innocent little shit on the wrong path in life? I just don't want something like that on my conscious."

Jenny felt a flush in her face. She didn't know how to express what he was looking for. To call sex a business seemed cold and impersonal; like calling nursing a business. It was something she did because it was what she was supposed to do. She had never thought it necessary to give it a consequential analysis. And yet she felt a responsibility to tell Morgan that selling sex does have warmth, depth and compassion. She experienced a touch of panic; a dryness in her throat and sweat on her forehead. She needed a few minutes.

"Uh, before I answer that," she commented, "maybe I had better run to the bathroom."

In the whimsical of human nature there are certain phenomenons in life, which trigger brief moments of brilliant thinking. For men, the phenomenon frequently strikes while they are shaving. For women, streaks of genius are prone to strike when they are taking a pee.

As Jenny sat on the toilet, she leaned back, closed her eyes and thought of Morgan's concerned about guilt. How could she tell him there was nothing to feel guilty about. As she sat there her hand reacted from habit as it slid down between her legs and found that tiny sensitive little nubble. The expected feeling of pleasure began as she slowly started to massage. Her legs opened wider and with her head tilted back and her eyes closed she drifted into a light trance. *Why is he so worried that something so pleasurable might cause a guilty feeling?* she thought as she continued to lightly massage.

She enjoyed her little plaything. It was part of her. She loved it, enjoyed it, was pleased with it, and to share it with others was all she really wanted out of life. *Beautiful, Oh Lord that's it. It's beautiful. Thank you Lord. That's it, beautiful. Morgan, you wonderful man worry no more.* The phenomenon of the toilet had provided an answer. *If sex is disbursed in a setting of beauty and compassion how can it possibly have a negative effect?*

As she rose she was moist but not dripping wet. She wore no panties, dabbed with tissue paper and brushed her dress down as she returned to his office.

"Morgan," she started talking as she sat down on the leather sofa. "What we will be doing, it's not like we just invented the idea. If a man wants sex he is going to find it; usually down on the tenderloin in dirt, filth, disease and crime. Not always the most pleasant of experiences. We both agree that ours will certainly be above that level. Ours will be the most relaxed, the most personal and most *beautiful* sex ever experienced.

"Sex has dignity if it is enjoyed in the manner it was intended; namely the expression of tender love. It is universally very beautiful and very satisfying. Your concerns stem form the dark side of sex. Wherein people start using it for purposes other than beauty; and that's when it has the potential to become harmful. They start using sex as an outlet for frustration, shortcomings and disappointments. In effect they start demanding something from sex which it cannot deliver.

"It is awfully easy to start believing that true happiness is measured in terms of harder, more intense orgasms. The mind is prone to fantasize about wilder and wilder sex. Fantasies to which there are no limits; multiple sex partners, oral sex, pain. It then becomes addictive and also dangerous." She paused to study his reactions. "Is," she asked, "something along those lines what you had in mind?"

Morgan did not respond and she watched as he adjusted his leg. She sensed his pain and asked how badly it hurt. "Let's go out in the lobby," he replied. "It helps if I move around."

Out in the lobby the majestic vastness of the Stran was bigger than life. Thick pile maroon carpet covered an area half the size of a football field. The towering walls were graced with huge murals of medieval castles, knights in armor holding a coat-of-arms in *Heraldry* (two lions rearing on hind legs holding a shield with their upper paws), banners waving, maidens on the castle ramparts looking to the distant hills; a blended theme of court, royal ball and chivalry.

Mood lighting accented decorative indoor plantings and a giant chandelier with a hundred lights hung from the rotunda dome. In the center back wall of the lobby was a massive snack bar; inclusive of an ornate candy case, silver soda fountain, aromatic hot popcorn, ice cream bars and candy. Patrons, with their treats move from the lobby to the main seating through either of two sets of polished brass doors; one set to each side.

For the lovers who prefer the balcony, access came from two spiraling stairways; one on each side of the lobby. Continuing thick maroon carpet and polished brass hand rails beckon those with a spirit of adventure to take the higher seating.

As Morgan and Jenny came out of his office they gravitated to a drinking fountain, then next to one of the large maroon sofas and dropped into the luxury feel of cool soft leather.

"Jenny, you were saying something about you and I both being in the same line of business?" She instantly realized this to be a fleeting opportunity to make the preciseness of her point.

"It all comes back to what you said earlier about packaging. If you want to sell something and have people feel good about the purchase it has to be dressed up bigger than life. The memories of beautiful sex should last long after the act is over.

"The absolute best example is this beautiful, gracious, theater. To enjoy a good movie, are all of these extravaganzas really necessary?" she asked rhetorically as she looked around.

"For those who come here, the answer is yes. But if all the viewer really wants is a place to kill some time then there are numerous less expensive places. Most of the movies which you show here can be seen in some of the cheaper theaters. It's just that the total experience will not be the same."

As Jenny was speaking, Morgan's attention changed from his original question to her enthusiasm. He felt himself smile over her exuberance; her belief that sex is a thing of perfect beauty, her desire to share, her interest in bringing good, it was unlike anything he had ever encountered.

"Jenny," he changed the subject, "I am just curious, I remember you saying once, you said you liked sex a lot, as often as ten times a day or so. As I sit here watching you, this is no reflection, just curious, do you ever get satisfied? I mean in terms of being at peace and content with the world and experience the feeling of what-a-wonderful-life mood?"

The instant change of subject was a surprise to Jenny. She had been very intense as she was talking and now all of a sudden she could relax. "Well, now," her voice went into purr as she squiggled slightly closer and initiated a playful advance by running her delicate soft forefinger lightly over Morgan's lips and tickled about his cheek, "do I detect a slight interest?"

"Jenny," Morgan said with a laugh as he took her playful hand into his, "you are really something. Your magnetism just seems to overpower everything else. The enthusiasm with which you want to do for others. I am just curious, at the end of a day, or night, when you are exhausted, what do you feel?"

"Then," she continued purring as she lightly nibbled on his neck, "my time is my own. And I am always looking for a big strong, handsome, mysterious, shaggy haired, mature man to take me in his arms and ravish my body. Ooooeee, I am getting one just thinking about..." but she was interrupted.

"Hey! Der!, Mr. Morgan," came an unexpected voice from across the lobby. And Jenny did not get to finish that she had never made love in a theater lobby and that the idea was exciting.

Jim Barkus, janitor, and all around handy man had just come out of the women's rest room when he spotted Morgan. "Mr. Morgan," he continued talking as he was approaching, "I needs to see yous for a minute when yous get the time."

"Well, now I don't know Jim," responded Morgan in a drawling tone as he turned his attention away from Jenny, slightly adjusted his seating on the sofa and cast a slight frown, "I'm awful busy right this very minute. Just lots of very important stuff going on here. You figure you're important enough to disrupt these high level talks that me and Miss Jenny here are conducting; we're a couple of mighty high level people you know?"

"Yeahsa," responded Jim in the drawl of a southern field hand, "I certainly do's thinks that. Cause if'n yous don't talk to me'ins, then you'ins am going to be in a heap of trouble."

Morgan smiled at Jim's match of witism. "Uh Huh. Well now we can't have a very important man like me getting into trouble. So I guess I had better cancel my appointment with the President. You think the President of these here United States will appreciate having a very important appointment canceled?"

"Yeahsa," responded Jim, "I already called and 'splained that you'ins has a stopped up sewer line and dem toilets dey ain't gonna be working by show time lessen we get some help huba huba. Da President assured me that taking care of toilets was a heap more important than any amount of Presidential business so he already canceled your important appointment."

"Sewer line! Damn." reacted Morgan, "Just what I needed. Well, it won't get fixed sitting here."

As they rose from the sofa, Jenny extended a handshake and Morgan accepted her small soft hand. "Here's to a beautiful partnership," she said as she pulled herself up against him. In response he released her handshake and, holding his weight on his cane in one hand he gave her a tight hug with the other; two bodies held together for the first time; a sensation neither expected. Her delicate small body fit so naturally up against his. The top of her hair came just to his nostrils and he took a deep breath.

It felt so heavenly soft and silky. He could feel the imprint of her firm nipple against his chest. But these tingling sensations were just preludes to that which radiated from between her legs.

She was not wearing panties and he could feel the tuft of soft pubic hair against his groin and the transmitted quivers induced an instant arousal. As their two bodies held pressed together his love muscle could feel the pulsation, like trimmers on a Richter scale. Just inside her legs was an active volcano; its life and power beyond limits.

Beyond limits, because in the presence of a volcanic eruption, man can but stand in awe, and witness humbled as molting lava spews upwards in search of the heavens, and the skies are shattered by the thunderous assault. But even erupting fire, hurled upward with incomprehendible force is no match against the endless sky; and the spewed lava falls smashing back to the ground to blend with its own kind and flow unchecked on its journey to the bottom of the sea; the ebb and flow of life.

And in similarity, the opposing forces of Heaven and Hell being constantly locked in mortal combat over the sexual energy between her legs; Heaven because of the unlimited good and beauty which it could do on earth; Hell to Morgan because in his own mind he realized it could never be his alone. Even if he should visit there, it would be just his visit among the many of others. That was the *whywith* it was put on earth in the first place: a gift from on high to the many.

Yet the sensation which he had just felt was instantly addictive. A twinge of goose bumps shivered through his body. *If only I was whole again; if only I was younger.* As their embraced relaxed, Jenny stood still while Morgan stepped back. They again looked into each other's eyes and a slight watering came to each. A fleeting pinnacle of heavenly bliss had been theirs to hold. A nino second when the soul of each forsook its own body to enter that of the other; only to be shattered by the brutal intrusion of an outside sound.

A voice in the form of Jim Barkus broke the trance. "Uh, I'm sorry about this Mr. Morgan but..."

"Yeah, Yeah, I know," he responded.

With a squeezing of hands and blurred vision there was a final look. Jenny flashed a dimpled smile and with the whispered words of "by for now" she left.

Morgan watched as she disappeared through the outside swinging doors. His last glimpse was of her round firm buns which fit skin tight against her dress.

He allowed himself one last fleeting thought of the nest between her legs and wondered, which force would win; would it bring peace on earth or torment from hell?

Without comment he then turned his attention to Jim Barkus. He was about to ask about the clogged sewer when he had a flash thought.

"Jim," he asked, "don't you work nights for the Westrail Bus Lines?"

"Yessa' I does that alright," he replied. "Been with'em for over fifteen years. Why?"

"What is it you do for 'em Jim? You a mechanic or something?"

"Kind of a jack of all trades. Whatever they wants I does. Grease monkey, spin wrenches, swab the deck, body repair, paint. Things being what they is today they can't get nobody to work. So when one of them big babies comes rolling into the yard me and a fellow named Jessrow, we jest take over and we tells the boss people what we needs. They jest tells us to go ahead and do's whatever we's thinks needs to be done..."

Here, the storyteller stopped. *Mother oh mother*, he thought. *What*

roads you rode. Mother, sweet mother how did your life and Morgan's life ever connect?

Chapter 8

When Morgan answered the telephone that Monday morning he recognized the other end. It was a voice he was not in the mood to deal with so he remained silent. Uncertain, the other voice responded again.

"Hello? Hello? Morgan...?"

Still Morgan held his pause, and then reluctantly answered.

"Yeah, Owise. What's on your mind?"

"Morgan,"the tone of Daniel Owise continued uncertainty. "I thought we had been disconnected."

"No such luck Daniel. I was hoping you would get the message that I'm not the least damn bit interested in talking to you."

"Uh Oh,"responded Owise in a tone of equal animosity. "I find that very interesting Morg ol' man considering that a few months back you sent one of your would-be pregnant girlfriends out to see me about a little sperm removal."

"Correction Maestro, I pointed her in your direction because I thought you could use a cash customer. At the time, I heard you were doing welfare. Not exactly the most prosperous line of work."

"Uh huh. And what else have you heard lately Morg ol' man. I mean even people who can't read sometimes get caught up in the latest news."

"Yeah, I heard the news, Shithead. The scuttlebutt is you got yourself head of some new hospital out in Mt. Lebanon. There must be no limit to the desperation of some people. To settle for a reject like..."

"That prize piece of news,"Owise cut in. "Did it happen to come from that un-pregnant young woman you sent to me for an abortion? By the way Morg, abortions are against the law; or didn't you know?"

"Yeah Dan, I know abortions are illegal. But I don't do abortions

Maestro. That's your line of work isn't it? My line of work is helping people in need.

"Which by the way includes medical doctors who are on probation over at Allegheny Hospital and have to do charity work. And unless I'm mistaken there's no law against trying to help borderline doctors."

"Really, Morgan I had no idea you would be all that jealous over my recent success."

"Dan would you mind telling me what the hell this call's all about. Too what do I owe this displeasure?"

"You know Morg it always makes me feel good to know that my calls are received in pleasure. I mean it requires such minimal effort on my part and if it brings happiness to those with a lesser degree of intellect then who am I to deny."

"That's another thing about you Owise, your repulsiveness is surpassed only by your arrogance. Let's stop the pissing contest. What's on your mind?" Owise took the shot without return and proceeded.

"Look, Morgan I would like to keep you entertained but I'm a busy man. Your information pipeline is correct. I have recently been appointed the director of, soon to be world famous, Mt. Lebanon Medical and Hospice Care Clinic and I would like for you to drop by and give it the once over. And while you are here we might even talk a little business; just for ol' times sake."

"Owise,"Morgan began in a slow pronounced tone, "I'll say this very slow so that there can be no misunderstanding. I am not, repeat am not, the least damn bit interested in seeing, knowing, touching, dealing or commenting on anything of which you may or may not be the director. Fact is, as I was coming to work this morning I happened to see a man on the street corner who was just about your double.

"He had two galvanized buckets setting there on the sidewalk. One was full of sewer and the other was empty. He spends his entire day emptying one bucket of shit into the other and then back again. And right at this moment I'm thinking I would much rather go down and watch his operation than to conduct an overview of your business. I know you need all the help you can get but I simply do not have the time or interest..."

"MORGAN,"responded Owise in a demanding tone. "You're not listening. I said, I think you should drop by; preferably this morning. You get my drift?"

An echoing quietness instantly followed and the only sound coming over the line was the static hum heard in each man's ear.

"You know... Owise, the way you say that,"Morgan again spoke in a slow deliberate tone with a pause for effect, "causes me to have second thoughts. I now believe that seeing you; sitting on your lazy conniving ass behind a fancy desk in that new clinic is something that a man should not pass up. All of a sudden there is nothing in the whole damn world that I had rather be doing. You get my drift? I tell you Daniel ol' Buddy my urge is uncontrollable. How would it be if I just dropped everything and headed out right now? I mean I'm on my way."

"Morgan,"replied Owise in equal curtness, "I'm glad you've come around to my way of thinking. I'll see you when you get here. In case you don't know the way just come out West Liberty Avenue to Castle Shannon Boulevard and turn left. Go about two miles to Mt. Lebanon Boulevard and take a right. You can't miss it." Click.

On his drive out to Mt. Lebanon, Morgan's adrenaline soared, his hands gripped the steering wheel, and he was impervious to the traffic and the city world around him. *Of all the arrogant bastards,* he kept thinking. *What a low life. Just call up and figure I'll jump. 'Well Daniel ol' boy the time has come to lay this dog to rest. And face to face is just the way to do it.'*

Things had changed since the days when Owise had him and Frank Buckwilder, as the saying goes, over a barrel. Morgan had money now and there was the ever lingering thought that some day he would square the deal. *A good face to face shouting match ought to do the job just fine.* When he turned off of Castle Shannon on to Mt. Lebanon there was no question as to what he was driving out to see. A few months earlier the area had all been undeveloped overgrowth land. Now it was a fully developed monument of greed masquerading as an angel of mercy. At first glance the complex gave the impression of a timeworn European cathedral and grounds; but not exactly. It took Morgan a second look to gradually grasp the total scheme. His immediate opinion was that some would-be-great architect had attempted to blend medieval design and modern construction; to the fucking up of both. Preeminence to the building front was a larger than life entrance.

Copied after the famed Abbey of Moutiers-St-Jean in Burgundy, France, the arched doorway with double wood fortress doors and enclave, towered some thirty feet. Marbled statues of biblical figures accented the massive front threshold and gothic architect. Inclusion of that design, Morgan assumed, was for the stamp of religious connotation. But then in oddity, the architect crossed over to modern design. The peculiarity was, for Morgan, totally baffling. The modern design aspect he supposed was to suggest the seal of modern medicine, modern hospital and modern care; all rolled into one. Even to his untrained eye the end results were an architectural debacle. On the north side an arcade walk bordered a groomed open courtyard. On the south side the wall was a flat face extension of smooth pearl white marble. *Landscaped grounds, curving walkways, bird bath and sitting benches on one side; banker thievery on the other* he summarized his thoughts. *A hell-of-a work of art.*

As he pulled into the parking area his assessment of the design was reinforced by the presence of a canopy covered handicap ramp leading from the parking lot to an imposing set of side-entrance double glass doors. *What a fucking abortion,* he thought again as he parked in the parking lot and made his way up the ramp. *It looks more like a bank than a hospital.* But for whatever were his first impressions, the moment he stepped inside the double glass doors he discovered there was more; much more. The interior of the building was even more ostentatious. The main corridor had high ceilings, art decorated walls and an off-white marble tiled floors; totally absent therefrom were any signs of wheel chairs, scurrying medical staff, doctors, nurses or administrators.

Good God, Morgan thought as he walked with cane assistance down the long empty corridor. Listening to the echoes of his own cane he searchingly made his was to a far back reception desk that was occupied by a bored sex queen receptionist. In an obvious surprised to be having a visitor she purred a patronizing inquiry as to the nature of Morgan's business. When advised that he was there at the personal invite of Dr. Owise she welcomed the opportunity to get up and provide Morgan with personal escort to Owise's private office.

"Why, gooo'od morning there Morg, ol' buddy,"Owise looked up and greeted Morgan from behind his desk without troubling to get up. "It's been a long time."

"Uh huh,"Morgan paused at the door as the receptionist left. Nice place you got here Maestro,"he pushed back his hat as he slightly looked around. "Mind if I inquire as to who's putting up all the front money?"his tone reflecting indifference as he walked on in and took a chair in front of Owise's desk.

"Oh, you know Morgan,"Owise answered with a snipe. "I have a friend who's a very good attorney. In fact of the matter he is what one might say a very well known attorney. And if one wants to get their hands on some money, I mean really big money just get this friend attorney of mine to sue some steel company and bingo... you get the mega bucks. You understand what I mean? If you want to get your hands on a lot of money Morg, you have to have a friend who is a good attorney. Law suits; that's where the money is."

The son-of-a-bitch, thought Morgan as his adrenaline pumped for a knock down-drag-out. *He never gives up.* "That good lawyer friend you're talking about, I hope his name is not Frank Buckwilder. Because unless you know something I don't know, I don't believe the feelings are mutual."

"Morgan,"Owise moved directly to business but with continued animosity, "the reason I wanted us to get together is I thought that you and I might be able to work out a little arrangement."

Morgan felt a twinge of satisfaction at the thought that the cards may have finally changed. Now it was Owise who apparently needed a favor. They looked directly at each other over the desk but both men deliberately avoided eye contact. In an intended overstep, Morgan showed his contempt by leaning back in his chair and patronizingly put his good foot on Owise's desk. Then, pretending that he was having difficulty, he hand lifted his mangled leg up. As he settled back, he formed a facial expression that spelled out that now it was time to talk. Putting his fingertips together in prayer fashion, he started slowly doing in and out movements of a spider doing pushups on a mirror. With deliberate slowness he looked at Owise and responded in a sinister tone. "O.K. Maestro, it's your nickel."

"Well... I'll say this,"replied Owise, "you do make it easy to get right to the point. Therefore, right to the point it is. I thought that since I had done you a good turn in the past Morg, you might want to return the favor."

Morgan's impulse was to let out a loud haw. Instead he carefully worded his response. "If that favor you are referring to is the one I am thinking of Dan my boy, I believe the obligation has been repaid many times over; if there ever was an obligation to repay."

Owise had not expected the tone or the denial and reacted too quickly. "Is that right, I'm not aware of any favors you have ever done for me,"he continued in an argumentative tone. "Maybe you would like to refresh my memory?"

"Haw!"this time Morgan did not attempt to contain his exuberance. "Owise, I shouldn't even dignify that remark with a response. But for openers I'll toss out just one of the little shittie you've pulled. I'm thinking about a little incident which happened not too long after our... yours, mine, and Franks, little lawsuit when things were still hotter than a doorknob on a steam room. As I recall it was along about then that you got your own fat ass involved in a little hit and run accident; remember that?

"According to the newspapers someone ran down a young woman and her child in a crosswalk and didn't stop. The police never did find out who did it. Odd though, the description of the car fit the model you were driving; remember? Remember how you called me in the middle of the night and put the pressure on me to hide your car; get it repaired on the QT. What was it you said? As I recall I believe you said that since I was street wise, whatever in the hell that means. I guess it means that doctors are entitled to run over women and children in crosswalks and not have to suffer the consequences." Morgan was on an adrenaline high and could not resist a one-two punch.

"And since we're on the subject, I believe it was along about the same time that you put the squeeze on Frank Buckwilder to improve your social standing. I believe it was on his abstaining from voting and thus not blocking, but in fact allowing, wasn't it that paved the way for you to be accepted into the elite of the elite Duquesne Club."

Morgan had expected a quick denial from Owise and was ready for a rebuff. But it didn't happen. The room became very quiet and Owise remained silent.

He had been twisting a pencil between his fingers and now stopped. Holding it up to the light, he squinted one eye and pretended a line-of-sight. Then as if he had reached a sudden decision he looked at Morgan and said, "Morgan I understand you now own the Stran Theater. Is that right? You know Morg I'm just real pleased about that. I think it's great. Just real great!

"Let me tell you," he continued looking squint eyed at his pencil point as he spoke, "I am really proud to be acquainted with the man who owns one of Pittsburgh's most famous landmarks. How's it going? Are you doing O.K.? I mean is the Stran giving you a pretty good income, you know, making any money?" He finished by looking straight at Morgan and expecting an answer

Morgan was caught by surprise but quickly answer. "It makes expenses," he replied. "Why? Is there some reason you have such a strong interest in how the Stran may or may not be doing?"

"Oh, I don't know. Curiosity I suppose. I was just wondering if it was making you a decent living or if you had to supplement your income in some way."

Morgan paused and shifted in his chair. Reaching with both hands he slowly moved his twisted leg from the desk and let it rest on the floor. Then, in one continuous motion he dropped his good leg, let it slam hard on the floor and leaned forward over the desk to where he could speak directly into Owise's face.

"Look you shithead, I get the feeling you are trying to say something so why don't you just spit it out. How come you're so damn interested in my livelihood all of a sudden?"

Throwing up his hands in defense, Owise mimicked a surprise and responded, "Hey, hold on ol' Buddy, don't be so sensitive. I was merely wondering if the world was treating you OK. It can be rough out there for a man with a bum leg and all. I mean I understand that sometimes we have to make it anyway that we can."

"And,"sniped Morgan, "what are some of the ways you say we all have to make it."

"Well, I was just wondering, that whore you sent to me for an illegal abortion, what was her name? Jenny? That's right isn't it? I believe that's what she told me. Anyway I was wondering Morg are you running whores now? Of course it don't bother me none you understand.

"But it would not look good in the papers and publicity and all if it were discovered that the owner of the famous Stran Theater was also running a "call-girl" ring. That's the word they like to use you know, 'ring'. It gives the story that sensational touch. Makes it sound ten times more scandalous. I don't have to tell you. You know how these damn modern-day reporters are. Once they get on a sensational story they don't stop until they dig up every last ounce of dirt they can find. After the whores, then there's the chance that our old lawsuit would turn up. Why Morg I tell you it would be a shame, just an absolute shame if the news media should keep sniffing around and dug up how the medical records of an old trial had been leaked out of the hospital. Tainted evidence I think they call it. Why, I tell you for a fact ol' buddy, something like that could flat ruin a man."

Morgan was surprised at how calm he remained but that belied his inner sensations. *God Damn it,* he thought. *A mistake. I made a big fucking mistake. Me and my God damned temper. I come running down here with my head up my ass without thinking... and this is what I get. I underestimated the son-of-a-bitch. OK calm down. Don't panic. Don't attempt to win the battle and lose the war. First things first. Make the son-of-a-bitch think he's got me. Let him drop his guard. Just one second, that's all I need.*

Owise kept looking steadfastly at Morgan and without moving his eyes he reached over and pressed the call button on his intercom. "Miss. Simmons," he said to the voice that responded, "I believe we are ready for coffee now. How about it Morg? Could you use a cup? I always like my mid-morning coffee, don't you?"

Morgan did not respond. For whatever reason Owise did not move in for the kill. Uh Ho, from Morgan's perspective, this time it was his mistake. It is absolutely critical to any kill-point that there be an immediate and decisive action. Otherwise, a diversion, no matter how slight amounts to a loss. In addition, the longer the diversion, the weaker becomes the point. In silence Morgan watched as a beautiful young woman, in a much too short nurse's starched white uniform, brought in a sterling silver ornate coffeepot on a matching tray and two silver inlaid white china cups with matching saucers.

Jesus, he thought, *high school. She's not old enough to even be out of high school. That just might cost maestro his ass.*

She had long flowing corn silk hair that dropped down over the side of her face as she bent over a little too low to serve coffee. Pouring for Owise first she deliberately bent over to allow him ample view down the front of her open collar dress to her braless firm young nipples.

She then gave Morgan the same view as she served his coffee and he was not embarrassed to look. As she leaned over he allowed himself a brief arousing look at her beautiful young firm evidence of womanhood. Her intended purpose completed, she flashed an innocent dimple smile at both men and turned for the door.

Morgan knew that Owise was watching him watch her and he obligingly prolonged the diversion. He accentuated a quick facial expression to imply an aching, lustful desire over her round firm buns and long shapely legs under her too short mini skirt. As she disappeared from the door he then bought some more time by looking down at his coffee. Holding the cup to his nose, he inhaled the aroma, took a sip, and pretended to savor the imported taste. It wasn't much but it put some distance from Owise's gut cutting point. Maybe a little more could be squeezed out.

"Nice. Jesus she is nice. What's her name?" he nodded to the door.

"Detrick," replied Owise, "Detrick Simmons. She sort of floated in with the building package."

"Is that part of the perks around here?" Morgan again nodded in her direction. "I mean, don't you think that maybe if you paid her a little more money she could afford to buy some longer skirts?"

"I thought," Owise, responded, "you might like that. Looks pretty good up along side that girl Jenny you got, don't you agree. Nice and young! Especially young. You get my drift... young?"

Owise was on a one-up-man-ship high. Morgan smiled just a hint from the corner of his mouth and nodded in slight agreement. It was the fuel Owise needed.

"Morg, how would you like something like that to play with every day? That would be O.K. wouldn't it? I mean YOU could handle something like that couldn't you Morg?" he patronized.

"Yeah, sure, I hear you Owise. We both know that something like that is sure as to hell going to happen."

Owise detected the skepticism and said, "No, really Morg, I mean it," he leaned slightly forward over his desk.

"If things work out the way I think, the sky's the limit. Among other things we can have an endless supply of scantly clad delectable sweet young things. Just take your pick. Just imagine how nice that would be; lounging around a big oversize swimming pool, letting some little cutie like Detrick hand feed you grapes and fan you with an Ostrich feather fan. Hey, Morg, now tell me you couldn't go for something like that. Tell me boy."

Morgan wanted to shake his head in disbelief but in better judgment he just played along. "And just where is this fountain of youth?" his tone indicating continued skepticism.

"So plentiful I can just reach up and pick'em right off of a tree like bananas." *Uh Oh*, he thought, *I may have overplayed.* But if he did it wasn't caught.

"In time," Owise responded. "In good time. Trust me on that. First though, I want to clear up the implication that the money for all of this may have come from your lawsuit. Morgan where I am going, the money I got from your lawsuit will not be a drop in the bucket." Morgan detected the shift in tone and followed by also speaking a little more serious.

"OK. Let's say I believe you. I don't suppose you're going to sit there with your bare face hanging out and tell me just where it is that you found this pot of gold?"

"Well, maybe some but not all. The situation is still in its formative stage so I can't afford to tell you too much."

Owise, Morgan thought, *you smug bastard you're losing your touch in your old age. You're getting careless. You're volunteering too much information. Just keep it coming. I'll get something yet*

"But,"Owise continued, "I assume that you 'did' notice the design of the building. Did you happen to notice the religious implications of the front entrance? Isn't that something? The party or parties with whom I am dealing brought the idea back from Europe.

"Would you believe that they went all the way to Europe for the express purpose of studying the architectural design of Notre Dame, the Louvre, the Abbey of Le Mont St-Michel and Moutiers-St-Jean, the cathedral of St-Julien and St-Etienne, all of those places."

Interest instantly swelled up within Morgan. He wanted to know who was behind this kind of money. He shifted in his chair so that he was again leaning slightly forward to Owise's face and responded.

"Well?"

"Well. What?"

"Well, what's the deal? Who in the hell is bankrolling this big ass operation you've got going on here?"he asked as he waved a circular motion around the room.

To that intrusion Owise suddenly became silent. He slowly leaned back in his chair and put his feet upon his desk. In apparent deep thought he looked at Morgan as he continued pushing a pencil end over end. Then with a tone of dead seriousness he shifted the conversation.

"Morgan I know that you don't like me. In fact detest would probably be a better word. All of this talking we're doing here like we were good buddy stuff is just one big pile of shit. I know it and you know it. I'm not buying it for one minute and neither are you.

"So we can dispense with the bullshit. It was fun but now I need to get to work and so do you. I am going to give you a little scoop on the deal. Not because I like you and for damn sure not because I trust you. I am going to do it because in this case, when I am talking to you I am actually talking to myself. I don't personally care about you one-way or the other. In my wildest dreams I can't believe that you would ever be in a position to damage me.

"But for what it's worth, I am going to be a big-somebody someday. Now, when I say big, I mean big like Carnegie big and MaGee big and Heinz big and Mellon big and the other big boys around town.

"And would you like to know why it is so important to me to be big? Well I'll tell you why. Revenge. Spelled R E V E N G E. Revenge on about three or four very specific assholes over at Allegheny General. For years I have put up with their mockery, patronizing and backstabbing.

"I'm a doctor. An MD. I get to put the initials MD after my name. Like me or not I have the right to be respected.

"And those low-life bastards, they choose not to, so that means war. Fine, they don't know that I intend to get their ass someday, but I know it.

"Now, to carry out this little fantasy, I need money; big money. If and when I get it I will use it

"Then and when, those certain people who belittled me, snickered at me, mocked me will know who is making them pay. If," he continued in a slow concise tone of emphasis, "the money grabbing boys over at the hospital don't want me, then the money grabbing boys in religion do."

As Owise finished, Morgan felt one thing. It was self-satisfying to know that he had not underestimated Owise twice. The situation was now up in the air. He had no idea which way it would go but he had gotten away from the 'whore-ring' point and wanted to keep it that way.

"Dan, I won't ask any further about the source of all this money but you did mention something about that monumental entrance to the front doors. All those trips to Europe, France. That's something I sure would like to know about?"

"Intimidation,"replied Owise. "Pure and simple intimidation. They don't think I know it but I do. It's designed so that the minute people see it they're intimidated. It's a tool which religion has used for hundreds of years to control people."

What...What in the Hell is he talking about? wondered Morgan. *Intimidation. Religious boys, the man must be crazy.* He was not cognizant of his own mannerism of raising his hands in prayer fashion and was holding them up to his lips. He felt a pressure to speak but was at a loss for words.

"Uh..."he was about to respond as he dropped his hands but the slight shift caused the two men to make an unintentional eye contact and the minute was gone. Gone. Whatever Morgan was about to say was gone. Owise had a cold calculating tone in his voice as he cut in.

"Ever hear of Radio Evangelism?"he questioned. "God's Hour of Talk, Old Time Faithful Guidance, The Lord Is Our Shepherd Hour and two or three others that I don't even know about.

"They're all owned by the same group; mobsters really. And it is impossible for me to sit here and tell you how much donation money is rolling in.

"I didn't have any idea myself until they approached me about setting up this hospital. I tell you in absolute sincerity Morg, these boys leave nothing to chance. Have you ever stopped to consider how many people listen to religion over the free airways?

"And how much egg and milk money, how many quarters, half dollars and faded dollar bills come in from every Country-Bumpkin hick across this land. Also how much money can be hid from taxes through a religious hospital? And that is all I am going to say."

A silence followed as Owise looked directly at Morgan and remained perfectly still. Morgan leaned back in his chair, locked his hands across his chest, took in a deep breath, held until the oxygen expired and then exhaled.

"Dan," he said with a slow enunciation, "I still do not know why in the Hell you wanted me to come out here. I suspect that this conversation didn't go exactly as you planned. It's possible that you brought me out here just to rub my nose in your newfound measure of shit; but I doubt it.

"What I suspect is, no wait. Let me hold that for just a minute. First I want to make one other thing absolutely clear. Earlier in this little ol' conversation you made the statement that we sure as to hell don't like each other. I damn well couldn't agree more. But in a couple of instances you have been kind enough to cut me a little slack so...in-even-measure I'll return the favor...

"Now, having said that, I will now say this. I would like to point out that I'm sitting here, in the very heart of your territory. If I were to analyze things I would say that that's one big ass mistake on your part. I don't know for sure yet that it's a mistake because I don't know what you have in mind. Maybe you feel you are on such strong footing that you can throw prudence to the wind.

"Now, again having said that, I'll say this. It will be a cold day in hell before I'll invite you into the Stran. I'd consider it a desecration of my most hallowed sanctuary. I think you're a king size asshole for the shit you've pulled. You're not a gentleman Dan. That's the reason you get no respect. You're self-serving and don't possess one damn shred of decency.

"Least you assume that I am overly compassionate let me emphasis this. I will always have a shot hanging in barrel just waiting for the day when I nail your ass. I don't know that I will ever get the opportunity to square the deal between us.

"But I am honorable enough to let you know that there will always be one in the chamber hanging with a hair trigger.

"Now, having said all of that in front of you, here is what I am now saying. I am going to let you win this round. I still don't know what in the hell you want. But if it's reasonable and legal it's your call. Now let's have it. What is it you want?"

All the while Morgan was talking Owise sat absolutely still and showed no emotions. A silence followed as the two men looked at each other. Then in an even, unemotional monotone Owise began to speak.

"O.K. Morg I assume that was your best shot. Now you let me say this, you've made things a lot damn easier. You went on record so I'll go on record. I appreciate you giving me the round. On behalf of the gentleman in me that you say I'm not let me say thanks.

"It eliminates the necessity of me having to resort to unpleasant gut-cutting threats. Now, using your words, having said all of that, those were the words you used weren't they; here is what I am now saying. I have some personal baggage from my past that I need to get rid of. I have a young woman by the name of Patricia Waters and her infant daughter named Shelly living in my house and I want them out.

"How they got there is none of your business. The fact of the matter is they are there and they are destitute. For obvious reasons I can't dump them out in the street. Those newspaper reporters I mention earlier would burn my ass and we both know it. That's where you come in Morg. You, my very good friend, you are going to take them off of my hands." ...

To the storyteller the past returned to the present. "Well I'll be damned," he blurted out the four words. "What a gold mine of information; the means where Morgan and Patricia came together. Thank you, Angel-of Compassion, that I might finally come to know that linkage."

Chapter 9

Office hours for Frank Buckwilder always started promptly at 8:30 A.M. and on this day his first client was Mr. & Mrs. Joseph Jason and the legal matter at hand was their Last Will and Testament. They had paused for a break while Mrs. Jason went to the washroom and was just returning.

"Now, Mr. & Mrs. Jason," Frank continued as she took her chair, "the substance of your Will thus far has been your real estate. This includes your residence where you currently reside, a summer home on the shores of Lake Champlain, NY and four vacant lots in Erie, Pennsylvania. All of which are now held in Joint Tenancy with right of survivor. After the demise of you both, all real property, in whatever situate, is to pass to your two children to share and share alike.

"The gender and names of your two children being (a.) your son Stanley Robert Jason, who is the eldest and (b.) your daughter Bernice Catherine Jason Lowindowski.

"It is your wish and testament not to put restrictions on how the two children shall divide the property. Further, it is your wish that in love between themselves and in honor of you, their loving parents, that the property division be fair and amiable. However, in absence of not being able to reach an amiable division the following stipulation will apply.

"On any item which falls in dispute, 'either child can', but 'one or the other child must', put a dollar value on their respective undivided one half interest. The other child then has the option of either buying that one half share for that dollar amount; or selling his or her one half share to the child setting the price for the like amount."

As he finished reading his notes he turned to the Jason's and asked, "Is this, in substance, an accurate depiction of what we have covered so far?"

Across his desk the Jason's were conferring when a knock was heard on his office door and his secretary, Nancy Evans, entered. "I am sorry to bother you Mr. Buckwilder, but there is a courier here standing behind me with a Special Delivery envelope. It looks very impressive and I thought you may wish to personally accept it."

Without hesitating he hand motioned the courier over to his desk and was handed a gold embossed, off white linen envelope. It was addressed simply: Frank Buckwilder, P.A., Grant Building. He glanced at the envelope, and then looking up gave both his secretary and the courier a small dismissal nod. Reaching for his letter opener he commented to the Jason's, "Would you excuse me for one moment? While you are discussing your thoughts I will attend to this small matter."

Inside the envelope was a single sheet of matching embossed paper upon which four lines of gold lettering were printed.

> *Laws are the rules governing the affairs of man*
> *And the practice of law is an honorable profession,*
> *But talk is the component for discovering the soul*
> *And search for truth is the fiber of a best friend*

He smiled a slight smile as he looked at and re-read the note. He then replaced the single page in the envelope, again noted the linen texture, and placed it in his top desk drawer.

"Now," he turned back, "Mr. & Mrs. Jason it looks like we're ready to continue. You seem to be in agreement on the disposition of your real estate holdings. So we can now move on to what we in the legal profession generally refer to as personal property and liquid assets," he spoke as he turned to a new page on his yellow legal pad.

"Your personal property includes such items as jewelry, china, silverware, furnishings, heirlooms, works of art, etc. Your liquid assets include such items as money on hand, bank accounts, negotiable instruments, treasury notes, stocks, bonds, etc. What are your wishes with respect to the distribution of these assets?"

"Well," responded Mr. Jason, "after we are gone whatever is left of course is to go to the kids. But we do have some questions."

"What we are not sure of,"cut in Mrs. Jason, "is how much we should help our children while we are still alive?

"You know,"she continued, "we have an awful lot of money in the bank. If we transfer everything over to our children now will we be able to save on probate charges, inheritance taxes and all of those kinds of charges?"

It was 12:00 noon by the time the first penciled draft was completed. The present session being over, a tentative date was set for the final draft. As the three rose, Frank came from behind his desk and escorted the Jason's to his office door where there was a final pause and a concluding exchange of parting cordiality.

Without watching their exit, Frank closed the door, returned to his desk and dropped into his high back, dark brown leather chair. Alone in the quiet of his office he sat for a while and pondered why he felt so unmotivated. The drafting of a will is not overly demanding but at times it can become energy sapping. At issue were two elements; money and greed. In the minds of these two gracious people, their whole reason for living will be fulfilled by leaving their children a substantial estate. And in their parental minds, their two offsprings were equally caring and unselfish.

It is inconceivable, he thought, *that this estate would ever be divided up in such a congenial and harmonious manner. If only the world was so perfect.*

For no particular reason other than to relax he felt it would be nice to have a little mid-day nip. In the absence of a demanding workload he reached in his bottom desk drawer and retrieved a bottle of twelve years old Royal Scottish Prime. The escaping aroma came to his nostrils as he poured a jigger and replaced the cap. His notion to have a drink was not so much the need for alcohol. It was fortification against the emotional conflict that he knew would probably come in writing up the final draft. He would once again be caught between two opposing choices. One choice being to advise these two noble people not to be so trusting of the love between their children. In the matters of writing a Will the disposition should be hard, cold and explicit. If not, in all likelihood there will be arguing and that would result in a high probability of a court battle. He recalled an age-old sayism of law, *the lawyer's dividend for that kind of good legal advice is to end up being detested by both parents and children.*

The other choice is for him to avoid being overly concerned about what may or may not happen between two offsprings at some future time. Simply accept the client's instructions and refrain from conjecturing the consequences. He knew in his on mind, *the dividend of that indifference is to end up detesting one's self.*

He held the jigger up in toast and lightly murmured,

"Ah my ol' friend Scotch. A conscience is the fiber of a good attorney. And a good conscience is the reason why attorneys need a good friend Scotch." He took a sip and waited for the reacting bite. Usually one jigger was his quota but as he looked out his window he could see it was a beautiful sun shinny day; why not, he suddenly reasoned, take a little time out and enjoy.

With a second jigger in hand he leaned back, put his feet up on the desk and fully intended to drift off into a pleasant daydream. But his mind was not so cooperative and before he knew it his thoughts had drifted back to the Jason's estate which was worth over ten million dollars; and almost assuredly a bitter fight in the making.

Shaking himself back to his notion of escaping, he realized that as long as he was in the office he would be thinking of work. What he should really do is erase all thoughts of law, office, and work. There are other aspects of life. To that end he proceeded. The second jigger finished he poured a third; and with that came the loosening of his tie. The world of glow was blossoming like the spring buds of a tree on the first warm day of spring. He leaned forward, clicked his intercom, and asked his secretary to telephone Morgan Smithfield.

Continuing to hold the switch down, he listened as Morgan's "Hello"came into the front office. "Hello. Mr. Smithfield,"Nancy started to respond, "please hold for Mr. Buckwil..."

"Hello, Morgan,"Frank cut in. "Listen, Morgan, the reason I called is, I keep getting these gold embossed envelopes from special delivery couriers. I was wondering if you ever got one. I think the one I just received is probably from the White House over in Washington. I sure don't think I know anyone in Pittsburgh who would send me something like this; gold lettering, linen paper and all. You sure wouldn't know anything about something like that would you?"

"Just a little class,"responded Morgan. "If one has it, it just comes out."

"Uh huh, and in some cases I know, its damn little and it stays out. What's the deal? You part owner in that little printing shop around the corner from the Stran? You must be trying to keep someone afloat or something."

"Would you believe,"replied Morgan, "that you just about hit the nail on the head about keeping someone afloat, but it's not the printing shop."

Frank detected the slight change of tone and waited.

"Lots of things are going on in my life Frank and I thought we might have a little get together. Beautiful warm day, stroll through the park, I might even ante up for a hot dog; course that offer don't include any soda pop you understand." The remark from Morgan and the glow from the Scotch came together at the exact same time.

"Ohooo,"Frank let out a mimicked sound that forewarned of the coming conversation. "Such barbaric vernacular that rolls from thy tongue. How'est thou do pain me, Morgan. Has thou'est no soul? Hark! I say, nay I pray, nay I beseech that I might commune with the Gods of Greek Mythology and deliver prose of velvet nectar fermented from the delicate dew imbued by the heavenly bodies; and you, you speak of soda pop?"

"Feelings, Morgan, my comrade-in-arms. Feelings! Yea, before the two of us, you and I, travel further upon this day's sojourn it is my considered opinion that a course in sensitivity is in order. Tell me my learned colleague, otherwise known in the better circles of rime, poetry and prose as Sir Morgan, have you ever been out to the Pepperdine Conservatory?"

"Uh..." Morgan paused. "You mean that big glass domed hot house out by Schenley Park where they grow all of them acres of flowers?"

It was a return that clearly established that the two were on a roll. The next barb-in-kind was now in Frank's court. In a sneering cringe that he knew could be heard over the phone he said,

"Oh that thunder be in my mouth would I have the Heavens roar in the pain of your decry, Morgan! You insensitive, callused, unemotional, anesthetized clod! To think that they shot a man like Lincoln and let you live.

"It is...not...a hot house...you incompetent reject from a steel mill slag pile. It's a Conservatory. A very special place in all the world where a man can go and commune with the wonders, nay say I, marvel, of foliage, greenery and verdure.

"A place where those of sensitive soul can stand in awe at the wonders of creation. To become captivated by the beautiful flowers and serenity which Nature bestows upon us. And to renew one's appreciation for life; free from the outside pugnacious antagonistic thorns in our daily living."

"CUT!"the storyteller reacted aloud to no one. "Hold up. Stop the cameras!"came his slang vernacular as his impulsiveness resounded to a room of a sleeping listener and the overtures of howling wind. "Wherewith comes this prose of 'commune with the wonders of creation, free from pugnaciousness...'? Who besides me, a storyteller, inherent with such ability and proficiency?

"This revelation I'll be damned, this lawyer, this Buckwilder, he's a word jockey; a wondrous, lovable, drunken jockey of word and prose. He is I; I am he. He was first, thence I be me. Mother Dear? Him, me? Impossible. Most assuredly not. Surely...not a lawyer.

"But... elsewhere... could my words have found their roots? On this finding, my quest I now speak 'seek not such answers this moment would have me ask, but stay thee on thy quest, the path of intent. At this moment don't ask...was it Frank Buckwilder? This is indeed a question for another time."

Then Morgan answered. "Naw, Frank, I've never been out there. I hear it's some kind of place though. Somebody was saying they have over two acres under glass. But Frank... I've seen flowers before. I know exactly what they look like."

"Morgan, you callused cold-hearted humanoid mechanical composition of intractable moving mass," Frank exhaled an exaggerated exasperation of hopelessness and said, "this afternoon, 1:30, main entrance, be there." With a slight satisfying smile over his rebuttal he was about to hang up when Morgan came back.

"Frank," he said in a mimicking tone. "Would you repeat that? I mean what did you say was the occasion?"

The question was an open invite for Frank to go for seconds; and go for seconds he did.

> "The occasion...?" he enunciated. "The occasion my friend, is that we pause for a while to visit a place where only the poet is licensed to dwell.
>
> "To walk among the wonders of Nature's creations. A realization that all plant life is but on loan from the heavens, sent to beautify our world that romance may bloom. From every flower the radiating fragrances are but Cupid arrows hurled forth in search of hearts young in boy and girl.
>
> "I ask you my close friend have you ever savored the flowers of the Orient? Where Geisha Girls in bright silk kimonos strum Oriental love songs and ply their docile charms? No?
>
> "Then enter with me into the Cherry Blossom Garden and linger for a while through the eyes of a

poet. Experience the tranquillity where the stars above are within easy reach and a tea house stands beneath a spreading Cherry Tree; where the reflection of Geisha Girls ripples in the clear cool waters of a gurgling fountain and fragrance of Cherry Blossom, moistened with dew, intoxicate the evening air. A lone cricket, perched under a full harvest moon, chirps his love call in the stillness of the night. This can all be yours my friend, if seen through the eyes of the poet.

"But least we be too presumptuous, the poet in you may be from another realm; from the land on the other side. In scrubbed white Holland, where fair skin milkmaids with sun drench faces walk in wooden shoes. In a land of turning windmills and windy blue skies, your love waits by a whitewashed garden wall. Love comes on starry nights to the hearts of those in two... who stroll hand in hand along earthen dikes, in the land that was stolen from the sea. Your waiting love is known by the symbol of her land; with braided blond hair for sturdiness, with full rosy cheeks for innocence and sparkling blue eyes to represent the heavens. Tulips in number about 10,000... some say more, but we will see, in the land of the Tulip Garden. This can all be yours my friend, if seen through the eyes of the poet.

"But... does not amour have many sides as well; even mystery and intrigue? Love also grows by candlelight, a glass of wine and a rose. Ours is a modern land, yours and mine dear Morgan, and women bid their own pursuit. Strapless gowns, some in red, most in black, low cut and usually without a back; a few with mink, more with pearls, all with fragrance in their hair. The Conservatory pays special tribute to the women of our land Morgan, which we will see at our next stop...10,000 roses in Baby Breath, in the Garden of the Rose.

"A rose is special, my friend, because it is an intriguing, flashing, exciting kind of love; found in romantic lounges on skyline boulevards, the Philharmonic and auld-langsyne at a New Year's Ball. They are prone to kiss and run away, these modern angels of the night.

"They are difficult to catch and even harder to hold. To hold her you must know her; to know her not... is to hold her not. It is a type of warped logic we have on our hands dear friend. A liken to the premise that 'happiness must be earned'.

"AH! But, I am told that the way can be found... if you can decipher the clues. Her gown may be mysterious black, calf length or more; and the dance you dance will be a waltz on a polished floor. Those not in black may be dressed in scarlet red, short and tantalizingly tight; and the dance will be a tango fire. This one touch not... unless your quest is a fiery flame.

"The saga of the romantic rose, my friend, is shrouded by many schemes; designed to test our limits. Once you are addicted you will be overcome with a strange sort of sadistic fixation not to leave until you know all of her.

"If your search stops short of finding all of the clues then you will find less than all of her.

"Tease and flirt, you will receive in plenty; a taste and then deny. Who is this goddess who beckons you? "Know you must... and so you embark upon a search for clues. Some you will find but there are always more... and more and more. Your search goes on and you cannot repent. Fatigue overcomes you but your journey has no end. All of her clues you must find.

"With hands in your pockets against the cold, your head bowed in torment and your collar turned against the wind, you will trudge on, Morgan, through rain and snow and gloom of night, sleep will cometh not, who she is... you must know.

"But, the more you know the more there is to know. Ah! HA! The scheme starts to unfold. Trickery is fair in the land of the rose, Morgan.

"The search for all of her clues is an endless pursuit. For she always holds something back. And that which you can know, is not all there is to know, and all there is to know cannot be known because she giveth not; the web keeps spinning and she holdeth you in mystery.

"Not withstanding if that is your choice, such a journey awaits you, should you dare to embark; through the eyes of a poet, my friend, in the Garden of the Rose."

Frank paused and downed the remaining shot of whiskey; the bite now more pleasing. Inhaling slightly he then continued.

"We travel, you and I, through this adventure land by pathways of exotic foliage; where greenery of every nature and design adorn the winding course of trestles and arches. We will become mesmerized by an ascending crescendo of intoxicating fragrance. Our euphoria will swell without limits through this walk which all-the-while leads to Nature's marriage temple; *la Café Ritz Élégant*. Where the lushness of a tropical isle and the succulence of French cuisine have been wed and await our presence in the *Tropical Forest Wing*; decorated for us by the Gods of twilight with the sounds of a calm surf, gently lapping below the evening stars of the South Pacific.

"Where wild orchard blend with plumage fern in a lagoon protected by the rocks of volcanic walls, clinging moss and spraying waterfalls; and French cuisine which is served with *café brûlot*.

"*Café brûlot let me repeat.* A drink made of coffee, sugar, spices, and orange peel blazed with brandy.

"If one must drink, and today my dear friend I must drink, then the Conservatory is the place. Among the splendor and surrounding of flowers and ebullient foliage; of exotic fern in misty spray, and clinging vines that decorate in green, romantic fragrance of honey suckle and gardenias, clean pure air oxygenated by gurgling fountains.

"HARK! What occasion you ask, the occasion my fellow mortal is the spirits of the soul that come out to dance with the spirits of the wine. I lend you my eyes my dearest friend that you too may witness barefoot virgins who dance in veils to mystify their innocence; in harem suits which teasingly show their round firm breast with up turned nipples and the softness of angel hair tucked delicately between their thighs.

"With white carnations adorning their hair, these young goddesses-of-love rush forth to the music of strumming harps and whispering violins.

"In splendor and grace they whirl and frolic across the cool marble floors. With innocent lips, sparkling eyes, youthful unblemished skin and alluring dimples they laugh as they near your reach, rise on tiptoe and then sway away.

"It is the pinnacle of poetry. Where a man without a country can defend a revolution. And women without love weep at what might have been. The Gods of Romance, of Beauty, of Eternal Youth, these are the reigning Crowns. The Gods of War, of Fire, of Hell and Damnation are forbidden entry.

"So come with me this afternoon Morgan and experience the search of a thousand poets in a land that can not be...in pain we know...not to be."

There was a silence as Frank Buckwilder stopped talking. His oratory finished, he reveled in his performance and his soul ascended to that fantasyland on a colossal stage where he bowed to repeated curtain calls.

"Frank?" Morgan curtailed his fantasy ovation by asking a one-word question.

"Yes, Morgan,"came a two word response.

"Frank,"Morgan spoke in a real world tone, "when you get back down to earth there is something I would really like to discuss."

"Morgan,"Frank returned.

"Yes Frank."

"Morgan... I am going to kill you."

In the moments that followed both men thought in silence. In Frank Buckwilder's mind, *a soul without poetry is like a violin without a bow. If beautiful music cannot be made then why the instrument. Morgan surely must be the luckiest man alive. His mind is not burdened with the searching for meaning.*

To him, Frank continued pondering, *such things make life unduly complicated. He simply goes about his daily living in doing for others. The wonderment of why, why do we live, to be; for Morgan there is no why.*

Morgan Smithfield found himself thinking. *Frank is the loneliest person alive. He's so brilliant he can't find anyone to talk too. Just being in his presence is to be intimidated by his intelligence. And if there was ever a person to whom I would trust with my life, it is Frank. But he tries so hard to tell me about something that can only exist in his own fantasies.*

At the appointed hour the two men met at the Conservatory and were walking toward the entrance when Frank remarked, "That elegant card which I received. It didn't make mention.

"But I assume Morgan, that there is something of rather importance on your mind".

They were blending in with other visitors and passing through the entrance doors and into the main lobby before Morgan responded.

"As a matter of fact I do have something very big on my mind. But it can wait until we find a place to talk."

They next passed through a second set of double doors and entered a biosphere of green. Morgan removed his fedora hat as he stared at a world that was light years away from his life on the street.

He felt an onus to speak but was embarrassed by his awe; so he remained silent. The two blended in with the other visitors and slowly moved along a velvet-roped corridors; coming to an exhibit, gazing in silence and then continuing on. The air was cool and oxygenated and the curving pathway wound past planters of nasturtiums, aubrietia, dianthus and lavenders. They passed into the Romantic Garden with its theme of intimacy; where the fragrances of honeysuckle and gardenias embraced the sound of a gurgling fountain and a path of slate stepping-stones led to a vine covered trellis and a lover's sitting bench.

It was first here that Morgan felt a stirring sensation and fantasized of being alone in the garden with a woman who had come into his life only the day before, Patricia Waters.

In turn the two men did indeed enter each of the Gardens of Cherry Blossoms, Tulips, and Roses. And in each case Morgan could feel what Frank had expressed.

In time they came to *la Café Ritz Élégant* and found a table with two chairs next to a cascading waterfall embraced by nebulous ferns. For Morgan the cool and tranquil setting was a much welcome stop to relieve the pain in his leg. For Frank it was the rendezvous point for his meeting with the Gods of distilled nectar.

From the French waiter, Morgan ordered a taster's assortment of *petites fours du beurre, madeleines, galette biscuits and macarons*. Frank ordered a *croissant croque-monsieur* and *café brûlot*. And then their bonding silence was broken.

"I tell you Morgan," Frank said as he took a long satisfying sip of the coffee and brandy, "the Gods may have created the earth but they gave loving birth to brandy." He savored the warm sensation as it lingered on his taste buds.

Either for theatrics or for self assurance he smacked his lips, lightly patted his stomach and then took another sip.

"Brandy, my man," he continued, "is uncaring in the morning, a loving Goddess at noon and the soul of passion at night."

Morgan had been waiting for an opportunity to speak and finally said, "Frank there is something we have to talk about. I...." But before he could finish Frank interrupted. "And talk we shall, my good friend talk we shall. All in good time. But what be our hurry. Time my friend, time.

"Time is like the gift of a young virgin. She brings us the fruits of her body, but if we do not praise it, relish it, pay homage to it, then she is hurt by the rejection and carries her gift away."

"Frank," Morgan asked, "why do you always talk like that?" As he looked at his friend he could feel moisture swell up in his eyes. It saddened him to realize that wherever Frank was, he could not be there with him. And where Frank was, was in the company of a man who had lived in another time, in the literary realm of Cyrano de Bergerac.

"My fellow man doeth ask in what tongue I deliver my prose. Is not friendship a priceless treasure, to be handled with none but the kindest touch?

"Expressions not haphazard or for granted taken. But in reverence, compelled am I of sounds that fall as a feather upon our binding link. For prose is the utterance of words in exultation. And a love of a lesser friend would bore a lesser prose.

"On this day my prose rises effortlessly as the intoxicating fragrance of honey suckle gently ascend to the heavens. The virtue of drink, and drink my dear friend does have virtue, is not the power it gives a mortal to be a poet on this day, but the fantasy that he will be one on the morrow..."

"Frank... Frank," blurted Morgan, "are you drunk?"

"Drunk? Nay. Nay say I; even the word is offensive. However and not withstanding, etc. etc. in light of my crumpled suit, my loosened askew tie and my moderately slurred speech I might admit to being slightly inebriated. Why?"

"Why?"

"Yes... my comrade. Why doeth thy ask?"

"The why is..."blurted out Morgan, "I'm thinking of getting married."

Then there was a quieting nothing. From those words, a silence fell on the presence of the two men. A silence on Morgan's part because he did not know what else to say. While across the table a silence came to Frank because of his first mind flash.

Marriage would mean that someone else would then be first in the life of his best friend. From that single moment of silence two things materialized. Morgan started feeling embarrassed because what he had just said was not true. Frank felt embarrassment because of the foolish role of a tipsy poet that he had been playing. When Morgan offered no additional comment, Frank's refinement and grace then assumed the lead.

"Morgan..."he spoke with decorum and dignity, "I had no idea that you were seeing anyone. Is it eminent; are congratulations in order?"

"No, no Frank,"Morgan felt reluctance over what he had just said, "nothing is in order, no order at all because what I just said, I'm embarrassed to say, is not exactly truthful."

Another awkwardness followed and again it was Frank's grace that emerged. "Sometimes Morgan, words do not always come out the way they are intended; nor do actions. I am now feeling that I have faulted you. Earlier in the day you passed to me a sign that you needed to talk and in my buffoon act I paid no heed."

The karma of the moment then dictated its own decorum as composure returned. "I am now of the desire that I would like to hear what it is you have to say."

"Frank,"Morgan then began, "I lied about getting married. That part was for shock effect." He then took a deep breath for the renewed energy he knew he would need to tell the story. As he exhaled he slightly shifted to where the two were looking directly at each other.

"Frank, I don't know exactly how to say this but I am either in possession of or, depending on the point of view, have on my hands a young woman and her baby child."

Frank looked very straight at Morgan and in a very slow tone remarked, "Would you care to relate to me exactly how much more shock effect you have?"

A slight smile became visible in the corner of Morgan's mouth at Frank's way with words. Then, in a you-are-not-going-to-believe-this tone, he answered.

"It appears that our ol' friend Daniel Owise had drifted back into our lives; at least back into mine. For reasons I don't care to explain right now Frank, I went over to see ol' buddy Owise yesterday with the intent of maybe settling up a few scores.

"Well it didn't work out exactly the way I planned. Not only did I not settle any scores but I ended up with a young woman and child on my hands."

At that statement the legal mind of Frank Buckwilder snapped like a steel trap and he cast a look at Morgan which said explain.

"Well,"Morgan started. "To make a long story short, the woman is someone Owise picked up, played with for awhile, ruined and then cast aside.

"And it seems that faith has decreed that I'm the one she was cast over to but I am not sure where in the hell to go from here."

For the next hour Morgan related to Frank the circumstances of Patricia Waters and her daughter Shelly.

"And,"Frank made a summarizing statement. "It was on Owise's insistence that you assumed responsibility for Mrs. Waters and her baby child?"

"Well in substance, yes. He was adamant that I take 'em and I did. But that wasn't the reason I did it. I don't give a fiddlers fart about that son-of-a-bitch. I would welcome a no holds bared session with him. Trust me, before all is said and done that little statement will be a fact of life.

"But right now I want you to know about Patricia and Shelly. I picked them both up bag and baggage yesterday. For the time being I have them housed in a little one bedroom walkup flat I own over on Wood Street".

"Wait, wait, back up a minute,"Frank quickly interjected. "Tell me exactly the circumstances of the meeting and why you agreed to his demands."

"Well here's how it goes according to his side of the story. How much of it is a lie I have no idea.

"But according to Owise, he was on duty at the Emergency Room one night when a lady arrived in labor and he delivered her baby. The delivery in and of it's self-posed no unusual circumstances. However, in the course of the events it was discovered that she had abnormal breast.

"Now this all may be a lie. At this point I don't know but from what he said the curiosity of the hospital staff over the mother's elongated breast caused a spectacle. Moreover, according to Owise's words he exercised a doctor's responsibility by shielding her from the malicious exposure. The first thing he did, as he tells it, was to take her to his home.

"From there the doctor in him became interested in the malformation of her breast. From a medical standpoint he felt that certain unconventional surgery might be possible to correct her breast.

"So he, Owise, invited Patricia and the baby, Shelly, to continue living in his home. And that's where they have lived until yesterday."

"So far,"said Frank I don't see anything wrong with that. I must be missing something here. To me that sounds more benevolent than self serving."

"What I've just told you,"replied Morgan "is the story according to Owise. In truth the bastard was bent on exploiting the situation. Not for a moment was he shielding her from the outside world he was isolating her for himself. He was having dreams of grandeur about medical recognition. He figured he could get in touch with some university, get a couple of grants, publish some pictures and get credit for pioneering a reconstructive surgery.

"His intentions were self serving all right. Make no mistake about that. Here let me show you a few pictures she was able to slip out."

Frank took a long look at the various poses of Patricia showing her elongated dangling breast. When he finally spoke, the grace in him was absolute. At issue was not the elongated breast that Nature had bequeathed to this beautiful, caring and loving young woman. The issue was an assault upon dignity; a trespass upon the bounds of human charity. Morgan could tell the extent to which he was offended.

"Did I understand you correctly that Owise, with malice aforethought, sold these photographs to the people who publish The Encyclopedia of Rare and Unusual Genetic Birth Defects?"

"That's my understanding."

"And without Mrs. Waters' knowledge or consent."

"You got it."

"And how much did he receive?"

"The word is $5,000.00; but we don't know for sure."

"And how much of that did Mrs. Waters receive?"

"None, not one thin dime."

"And, again, as for as you know did The Encyclopedia of Rare and Unusual Genetic Birth Defects obtain Mrs. Waters' consent to publish these pictures?"

"She signed some documents but she didn't know what she was signing,"said Morgan.

Frank appeared in deep thought as he continued to shuffle through and re-examine the photographs. Without looking up he finally spoke.

"At this point what is your interest in this woman and child?"

"Well,"Morgan began hesitatingly, "to understand it you would have had to of been there. I mean in the room and see it with your own eyes.

"Owise, the son-of-a-bitch, simply said to me that he had some baggage he had to get rid of. Before I could say go to hell, kiss my ass, or good-by, it happened. He simply reached over and pushed a button on his intercom. Next thing I know in comes an under age nurse with this woman and child.

"Frank it was the most pathetic sight I have ever seen. There they stood, Patricia holding that little baby. Bless her heart. Scared to death. It was the saddest damn thing I have ever seen in my life. I still don't know her age, probably around 24 to 26, but she might as well have been a 100. She had the saddest eyes. And there was our good ol' friend Owise, sitting behind his desk, feet up, smiling.

"Like he was proud that he could shuffle people around like cattle. God did I want to reach over and bust him one."

"So what happened then?"

"What happened, was that Owise looked at her, pointed to me and simply told her she was to go with me. No introduction, no explanation, just that she and the baby were to go with me.

"Well, along about then his short skirted nurse, Detrick Simmons, brought in an old beat up suitcase, set it on the floor and left."

"So," filled in Frank, "you then took Mrs. Waters and her daughter Shelly and left."

"Something like that," Morgan responded without giving any more details.

"And from there you took the two of them to where; the apartment on Wood Street?"

"Well, again you would have had to have been there. When we got in the car Patricia, Mrs. Waters, broke out crying so we didn't talk much. I didn't know what to do with 'em. I tried to find out if she had a place but she just kept on crying.

"I attempted to see if she had any friends or family but I couldn't get anything out of her. So after driving around for a while I just did what I had to do. I just sort of put the two of them in the unit, left the key on the kitchen table and in substance that's where we are."

"Is there any food in the apartment?"

"There is some, a bowl of fresh fruit, milk, cereal, coffee, not all that much. But I did leave her a little money"

While Morgan was talking Frank was again shuffling through the pictures.

"Amazing," he said without looking up, "the mysteries of nature. Tell me, do you know whether or not the mother can produce milk to breast feed the baby."

As Morgan answered his eyes were cast to the floor and his tone was in a manner of trying to recall details.

"It was an embarrassing type of situation," he started. "I felt uncomfortable looking at her so while we were driving I tried to keep my eyes straight ahead. However the baby did start to cry and out of the corner of my eye I noticed that she was breast-feeding. Now how much milk the mother can give, I can't say."

"But the baby did stop crying so I assume the shape of the breast has nothing to do with the production of milk."

"Amazing," Frank said again as he looked up from the pictures, "that Mother Nature in all of her wisdom will find a way. No matter what the circumstances the instincts of motherhood will prevail and the body will still produce milk; absolutely amazing."

Having said that, Frank abruptly shifted his point of issue. He had been watching Morgan's mannerism and was puzzled by the lack of more descriptive information. His experience in court had taught him the tremendous power of direct eye contact. Knowing that pressure can be felt in silence, Frank remained very quiet until Morgan turned to look.

He then forced eye contact and said, "Morgan, I get the feeling that you are not telling me everything."

"Frank. What?"

"Morgan... what's this what...?"

The attention to a concise point had resulted in an awkwardness that both men felt. From the pause, it appeared that Morgan was about to speak, but an approaching waiter broke the intensity.

"Pardon Messieurs, but it is closing time," he announced. "We close at 5:00 P.M."

With the check taken care off, the two rose from their chairs and

Morgan felt the pain of stiffness in his leg. He flexed it back and forth until he was sure of his step and then the two men started toward the exit. When they reached the parking lot Morgan again spoke.

"There is,"he began, "a thought I can share with you. At this point that's all it is; just a thought. No, that's not true either. It's more than a thought. It's something much more. Frank I'm standing here scared to death. When I looked at Patricia something came over me. All of a sudden nothing and I mean nothing in this whole damn world mattered except her and that baby.

"I don't think I've had two hours sleep. I can't explain it. The minute she came into Owise's office our eyes met; I have never felt anything like it. I can't get that look out of my mind. Her eyes looked like they had cried until there were no more tears. Well, something inside of me just clicked and for the first time in my entire life I think I felt love.

"I don't know if she could ever love a man with a twisted leg, but I am going to ask her. If she'll have me I'm going to ask her to be my wife."

To the storyteller, the word love that Morgan had used. The word had not turned up before. Not by Patricia's father, her mother, the marriage broker, her husband of a single night, by Owise; nobody. Why had that been? What about things from Patricia's perspective? Maybe it was time to bring her into focus. It might even be that she would emerge as the most important player.

Chapter 10

The very instant that Patricia O'Riley Waters laid eyes on Morgan Smithfield she knew he was a hood; a mobster. He looked like a hood, dressed like a hood, sweated like a hood, apparently had been shot up like a hood and certainly would kill like a hood. Her instincts told her if she wanted to stay alive she should not fight, not say anything and do as she was told. In her mind the thought simply did not exist that she had the right to do otherwise. The thought that did exist in her mind was that women can become the property of pimps, thugs, and the Mafia and be forced into prostitution.

Given the circumstance her impressions were understandable. Her transfer of ownership to Morgan in Owise's office left no doubt. When the order was given she frightfully cradled her baby tightly in her arms, obediently followed her new master out the door, walked across the parking lot, got into a big black mobster car and felt the door lock behind her. She was then whisked away, jockeyed through a maze of unknown streets and finally stashed in an obscure second story walk up; and in her mind, imprisoned.

Her first day and the ensuing night in the Wood Street apartment were long hours of agonizing fright; grappling with her apparent faith. Here she was, a young mother alone in the world with a month old child and no money, no relatives and no friends. As that first day started coming to an end and darkness began settling in, her senses told her to start bracing for what would probably happen as the night became pitch black. She would be raped. With her heart pounding she rechecked the doubled locks on the front door and rechecked all of the rooms, including the closets and under the bed. Then she sat down to wait. The fact that she did not find anyone in the flat did not make her feel any more secure. *Most likely,* she told herself, *there's a secret door. They do things like that to get you when you least expect it.* The hours did pass and the night did become pitch black and she maintained her vigilance; staying on guard as much as possible. Sitting in an over-stuffed armchair the slightest sound would bring instant tenseness and cause he hair on the back of her neck to bristle. Hour after hour she fought to stay awake; but her endurance gradually started reaching its limits. As exhaustion reached the collapsing point the temptation to give in became almost insurmountable. The cry for sleep, just a few peaceful moments of letting her eyes close would have been heavenly bliss.

Her mind determination increasingly eroded to the onset of hopelessness. Giving in would have been so simple. In an adjoining bedroom was the powerful lure of a double bed with fresh cool white sheets. Relief, serenity and peace could be hers if she would just quit fighting and go in and lie down. Somehow she was always able to jerk herself back to reality. She was not about to fall into that trap. *What if that man came back in the middle of the night to get her? Going to sleep in that bed would mean being vulnerable.* Not while she had a breath of life. *If I have nothing else,* she vowed, *I'll fight. No man is going to come in and buy me and make me his whoring slave.*

The best she could remember his name was Morgan, Morgan something field. Morgan Hatfield, maybe that was it. She couldn't remember that he had said anything or at least very little those first few moments. The chilling, sinister words that she remembered the most were those that had been spoken by Dr. Owise. For reason she didn't know why she had been summoned to his office. She had been ushered there by a nurse and as she unknowingly stood waiting she heard the words addressed to her 'You're to go with him.' At first she was simply confused. Go? Who? Go where? When she didn't move Owise's repeated his command in a much sterner voice. 'Didn't you hear me Mrs. Waters? I said you are to go with my associate here, Mr. Morgan ....field'.

The authoritative command in his voice the second time had caused her knees to almost buckle and she could hardly keep from dropping Shelly. She remembered her voice becoming speechless and she felt involuntary squirts of warm pee in her panties. In fear of being severely punished she somehow started moving toward the other man in the office who apparently had just bought her. *Oh God, please help me,* she had instantly prayed. *Where are we going? Am I going to be put in with other prostitutes? Oh God please, please help me.*

Him, with his shaggy hair, crumpled suit and gangster hat. If he's not a North side mobster then who is? It's common knowledge what they do to women. Oh God please!

Numbed with fear she had said nothing as they drove through traffic and when the car eventually stopped in front of the apartment she obediently got out. Following him up the steps she remembered the strong musty empty smell when they first entered. As she meekly stepped over the threshold she mustered up her first attempt to fight back. Holding Shelly tight in her arms she moved to the side of the door, held her back to the wall and refused to go in any further.

This is it. This is the first time, she remembered thinking as Morgan carried her tattered suitcase into the bedroom and opened up the drapes. *He'll be the first to rape me. First he'll wrestle Shelly away from me. Then he'll grab me, slap me around, rip my clothes off and then he'll do it. That's the way gangsters work. They've got to prove who's boss. He'll...*

Suddenly her awareness was snapped back from fantasy by a nighttime room sharp cracking sound. She instantly froze at the startling break in the silence brought on by temperature expansion and contraction of the walls. She set frozen still for a moment; and when nothing else happened she allowed herself to breathe a little easier. Slightly adjusting herself in the chair she resumed her thinking

I showed him, she thought. *I guess he got the message when I wouldn't go close to 'em or let him touch me. When he saw that I wasn't going to have anything to do with him he sure took off in a hurry; but he'll be back. Whenever he thinks I'm asleep he'll try to slip back in. He's just trying to wear me down. He knows that all he has to do is wait and eventually I won't be able to stay awake any longer. He thinks I'll eventually give up and go to bed. That's when he'll slip back in and do it. Well, this time he doesn't know whom he's dealing with.*

And so were her thoughts. All through the night she was up and down from the chair. Frequently going to the front window and checking the empty street; determined to stay on guard. During the earlier part of the evening she had held Shelly but gradually her strength gave out. At sometime in the darkened early morning hours her arms could take no more and reluctantly she turned the covers back and protectively laid Shelly in the double bed.

In the stillness she could hear her own sounds as she returned to the living room. Plopping back down in the chair she became overwhelmed and reached the end of emotional endurance.

"Mommy," she broke out in uncontrollable sobs.

"Mommy I can't take it anymore. Why has it always been us? You, me and now Shelly. Mommy they kick us and kick us and kick us.

"How can they do this? Why? Mommy forgive me if you can but how I do hate, hate, hate. I hate Poppy. The no-good coward, leaving us the way he did. How I wish he were here right now so I could tell him face to face.

"Mommy I know how hard we looked for me a husband but, Oh do I hate that prize of a man I married. Do I wish he were here right now, right this moment?

"Mommy, how I hate that slime Dr. Owise. Of all of them; he's a Doctor!"

As the night gradually dragged by Patricia's fury would subside only to resurface. Over and over she could see herself standing in Owise's office with Shelly in her arms and the total of her belonging in one frayed suitcase.

"Mommy I'm mad. I'm hurt and mad and I've had all of this I can put up with. I'm not going to take it anymore. The BASTARDS!" she cried.

"Damn them all. Damn, damn, damn. When morning comes, I'm going to do something about this. I'll show 'em Mommy, I'm going to..."

Going to do what? She knew there was nothing she could do; mostly because she simply didn't have the emotional strength. As the hours continued to pass the chair became moist from sweat, her dress stuck to her skin and her hip and knee joints ached. By first light of morning her hair hung in matted disarray on her forehead and down across her swollen cheeks. Her two-day dress was sweaty and wrinkled and she barely had the energy to move. In the quiet, still room she watched as darkness started to blend with dawn; and wasn't cognizant that her fingers were pulling and twisting a torn fragment of threads and frayed binding on the chair arm.

The circumstances of her life continued to spin around and around in her mind. By what dictates of faith was she here; all alone? To her it seemed like she should still be a young girl; not even old enough to have a baby.

That was something that was supposed to happen away in the future. *But look at me, look at how my life's going. I have a baby and no husband. Now I'm in the clutches of some gangster. I know he's going to force me become a whore. They can do things like that. If I don't do what they say they'll probably take Shelly away sell her to somebody.*

As the room grew lighter she rose from the stuffed chair and grimaced at the stiffness. Now that daylight was coming she would have to think of something. She picked up her purse, went to the kitchen table and emptied the contents. As she counted her meager resources a resurgence of tears filled her eyes. She had the total of twelve dollars and fifty-seven cents. Frantically she turned the purse upside down and shook, then searched the side pockets; nothing.

Hurriedly she ran to her frayed suitcase and looked in the inside elastic pocket on the back; two pair of panties and an old scarf but no money. Disheartened she returned to the kitchen.

"What am I going to do?"she sobbed aloud as she laid her head on her arms on the table, gave in to exhaustion, and drifted off to sleep. A short time later a knocking on the front door caused her to jerk up and as she listened it came again.

"Hello, anyone home. Hello. Did I awaken you?"

What? Where? Her groggy mind sprang to fear. *Who is it? What am I supposed to do? I'm not opening that door. That's a man's voice.*

What if there is more than one of 'em? What if he's come to get us or something? Again there came a knocking but this time her name was called.

"Hello, Mrs. Waters, are you OK? This is Morgan. I came by to see if you're all right. Can I talk with you?"

Cautiously she went to the door and opened it just a crack. Peeping out into the early morning light she saw the man who had brought her there.

"Good morning Mrs. Waters,"he said as he removed his hat and spoke through the cracked door. "I hope I didn't disturb you. I thought I would come by and check on how you're doing". When she remained absolutely still and made no motion to open the door, he continued.

"I know this must be very difficult for you Mrs. Waters. I'm as embarrassed as you are scared. I thought maybe if we could just talk. Just say hello. If there is anything, anything at all I can do for either you or the baby just tell me."

"Who are you?"she spoke in a tone that clearly signaled her suspicions. "Are you some kind of a gangster or mobster thug?"she asks, as she stood ready to throw her weight against the door. "What do you think you're going to do to me?"she attempted to sound threatening. "Because if you touch me..."

"No Ma'am,"Morgan slightly stepped back. "I'm not a gangster, or a criminal or anything like that Mrs. Waters. I'm just an ordinary citizen. An every day kind of man who, like you, has had some very bad dealings with Dr. Owise."

He paused slightly in hopes that his slow reassuring words would have some beneficial affect; swallowed and continued.

"It's a long story Mrs. Waters,"he straightened up his posture to show that he was being truthful.

"And... my dealings with Owise are not what's important. Right now what is important is you and the baby. Again, I know how scared you must be so let me explain something.

"How all of this came about was, I just happened to be in his office yesterday, the day we met. And he, Owise, simply asked if I was in a position to provide help to you and your baby," he lied.

Listening to his-self fabricating as he went along was causing Morgan to feel more embarrassed. He took a deep breath and swallowed just as the two looked directly at each other. There was a glimpse eye contact but no meaning surfaced. He waited an additional second to see if she wanted to say anything. When no words came he continued.

"Mrs. Waters I know you don't have any reason to trust me. But just let me say this. Anytime I can get someone away from the clutches of Daniel Owise I consider it a privilege. And that's about all there is to it."

"What do you want from me?" she attempted to sound argumentative. "You must want something so why don't you just go ahead and say it. Am I going to be your whoring property?"

Morgan felt a sharp cutting flinch at her suspicion but remained calm. "Mrs. Waters I know how frightened you must be. But if you will just let me talk to you for five minutes, I promise I'm not going to harm you. Then if you are still frightened, then I'll not be of any further bother. Now you can say no and I won't fight you. But if it's OK with you I'd like to come in."

Not knowing what else to do Patricia paused a final hesitation stepped back and slowly opened the door. Morgan braced his jake leg on his cane and entered. Inside they both stood for a moment and both felt equally awkward.

"Mrs. Waters," he took the initiative, "how about we sit down for a bit. This here ol' leg of mine seems to be acting up a might." He started towards the kitchen but noticed her purse and money on the table and instinctively turned back to the living room. As they seated, he on the sofa, she in the stuffed chair, he noticed that the outside door was still partially open and welcomed the suggested bit of her protection.

"Mrs. Waters," he repeated, "this is as unsettling for me as it is for you. I am hoping that if we talk, we can clear things up a little. The first thing I want to do, if I can, is to convince you that you are in good hands. Nothing is going to happen to you or your baby; not if I can help it. If you like living in this little place, you can stay here as long as you like. Make it your home. Whatever you like. No one will bother..."

"Who owns this?"she asked abruptly.

"I do Mrs. Waters. I own this place. I hope it's all right. If it's not, if you are afraid to stay here alone, anything like that then...."

"Oh, no,"she replied in her first unguarded tone. "The place is fine. It's just. How did this all happen? How did I end up here? Me, the baby, you Mr. Hatfield I..."

"Smithfield,"Morgan corrected. "My last name is Smithfield. But I would like it if you would call me Morgan."

Patricia looked but did not readily accept the informality. "Very well, Mr. Morgan". The sound of her own voice was causing her heart to race.

Should she be dropping her guard so quickly? How much resistance should she put up? How did it get shifted around to where she was the one doing the talking? She could feel dryness in her throat and her words sounded empty. It suddenly seemed so much easier to just confess and give in.

"Mr. Morgan,"a flood of tears swelled up in her eyes, "I'm all alone in this world. Can you understand that? That's my purse over there on the table. That's every last cent I have in the world. That's it, twelve dollars and fifty-seven cents"she spoke through tears.

But before she could completely break down and go into what he judged would be hysteria Morgan rushed in.

"NO! NO it's not Mrs. Waters. That is not all the money you have in the world; not by a long shot. Not if I can help it; if you'll let me.

"Now please, just please,"he spoke soothingly. "Mrs. Waters, why don't we do this? Why don't..."

"Patricia,"she said as she dabbed at her wet eyes. "As long as you own me you might as well call me by my first name."

Her words came as she wiped her eyes on the back of her hand and sought control. Morgan could feel the easing of tension and choose his words in the softest tone he could master.

"Patricia? Would you do me the favor of letting me put a little more money with what you have there on the table?" To his question, she started to gesture in opposition but he cut back in.

"No strings attached. Please, believe me when I say that it will be my pleasure. If you like I'll be happy to tell you why later.

"For right now though, just please do me the favor,"he talked as he was taking money from his wallet.

"What I have here is five one hundred dollar bills. It's not a lot but we'll let it do for now. I am going to just lay these down here along side your other money,"he rose and cautiously moved to the kitchen.

"Use it anyway you like; groceries, clothes for you and the baby. Or, for that matter, you can use it to leave; no strings attached. I am also leaving you my telephone number. I am the owner of the Stran Theater and I can be reached there anytime. If there is anything, and I mean exactly that, anything that you or the baby need I insist that you call.

"Next let me say this. If you feel that this is charity; or your dignity will not let you accept, I understand. If you want time to think it over I also understand.

"And again, if you want to take the money and leave, that is also OK. I said no strings attached and I mean it." He paused slightly as he shifted his weight to his good leg, supported one hand on his cane and stood fully erect.

"On the other hand, if you would like to stay, I assure you that you are most welcome. You can stay as long as you like; no charge; not one thin dime. Later on if you think that you would like to go to work or something I will see that you have a job. No strings attached.

"Now, Mrs. Waters, uh Patricia, I promised that I would not take more than five minutes and I believe that I have already overstayed. So for now I will say good-by and God bless."

He put his hat on at the door and was about to leave when he paused slightly to look back. Tears were again swelling up in her eyes and her voice was weak as she murmured, "Thank you."

He had an almost uncontrollable urge to reach out and grab her. To tell her she needs never to fear life again. At that moment though that was not the thing to do. Instead he gave her a little smile, gentlemanly touched the brim of his hat and departed. He hoped that his face was turned before she was able to see the emotions in his own eyes.

Patricia did continue on in the apartment but even Morgan's reassurance could not prevent her from being apprehensive and withdrawn. As inviting as it was she could not let her guard completely down and freely accept his help. In her mind she had to do something on her own; but what? For each positive idea that she came up with, her mind would find reasons why it wouldn't work. She sensed that help could be found through the telephone, but how. Several times she looked in the telephone directory under the heading Government but found only confusion. She had never realized that there were so many different kinds of governments; Borough Government, City Government, County Government, State Government and Federal Government. What do all of these people do? What's more, none of the department names sounded as if the function they did, whatever it was, fit her situation.

She wasn't even sure what the Federal Government did? What if she called and they admonished her. Should she call the City Police; there was no crime to report. She might even get in trouble for reporting something that wasn't a crime. All she could report was that she was in this apartment and did not know what to do. Besides, she reasoned, with all of the war news going on who would care about her.

So she did nothing. Morgan on the other hand attempted to do everything. He came by each morning and repeatedly called during the day; always inquiring as to how things were and offering his help.

Still Patricia could not open up; and so things went along. There was a small grocery store just around the corner where she went for daily groceries. Her first days of getting out were very difficult. Inside the apartment she was beginning to feel safe but going out still caused a sense of danger. The simple act of opening the door brought tightness to her stomach.

When the decision could no longer be delayed she would bundle up Shelly and brace for whatever might happen.

Holding the baby tightly to her chest, she would walk as fast as possible. Always walking to the inside of the sidewalk, staying close to the buildings and keeping her head down to avoid making eye contact with passing strangers.

Breathing a sense of relief in reaching the market, she stayed no longer than necessary, purchased only those items that were essential for the day and returned directly to the apartment. The remainder of each day was spent walking the floor. Restlessness and boredom were her companions but there was little indication that the situation would change; until one day; a day of a small first crack of a new dimension.

Totally by accident a book came into Patricia's life. An old forgotten book, that under different circumstances would not have remotely possessed a theme of future life influencing directions. Even given the existing circumstances it is incomprehensible that anything so insignificant as an old outdated book would lead to such extraordinary and far-reaching consequences.

It all started on an otherwise uneventful day when she returned from the store. She was putting the day's supply of groceries away in the kitchen cabinet when she rose up on her toes; reaching higher than usual, tips of her fingers felt a large book on the very top back shelf. A thick musty faded green book with a hard cover; corners frayed and pages stiff and crumbly. Taking it down she lightly blew off some of the dust and looked for the title. However, the wording on the front was too faded to be readable. Turning it and inspecting the binder back she could barley make out some gold lettering. By holding it at the best angle of light she was able to read: *"A Thousand and One Arabian Nights"*.

Without knowing why, her interest clicked. She had often heard the expression a 1,001 but never really knew from where it came. Curiously, she opened the book and started thumbing through the aging pages. As she browsed from one chapter to the next she started recognizing some of the titles from which movies had been made.

The first she recognized was *The Son of the Sheik* that she remembered had starred Rudolph Valentino in 1926, and *Arabian Nights* starring

Jon Hall and Maria Montez. There was another one, the one that everyone had talked so much about, *The Thief of Bagdad*, starring Douglas Fairbanks and his famous flying carpet.

Unconsciously, fantasies started coming to her as she pictured herself in the tales of romance in the mysterious sands of the Sahara Desert. Then, just as quickly, her interest subsided. She laid the book aside and continued putting away the groceries.

It was later in the day, at Shelly's nursing that she again remembered the book; thinking it might be a way of passing the time while her baby nursed. She got comfortable in the living room chair, reached inside her brassiere, took out one of her elongated breast, put the nipple in Shelly's eager little mouth, opened up the book and began to read.

The first tale was *Aladdin; or The Wonderful Lamp*. The first line on the first page started:

"It hath reached me, O King of the Age, that there dwelt in a city of the cities a man which was a tailor, withal a pauper and he had one son, Aladdin hight. Now this boy..."

Patricia continued to read that in the City of Bagdad, Princess Badr al-Budur, the daughter of the Sultan fell in love with Aladdin and rejected the attention of evil al-Talib; who was her father's choice.

In frustration al-Talib contacted his Evil Spirit and received instructions to go and search for a magic lamp hidden in a cave. It was not that easy however and when al-Talib could not get the lamp by trickery he hired Aladdin to do his evil bidding.

In due course Aladdin was successful enough in getting the lamp but the circumstance changed with respect to surrendering it to al-Talib. Realizing that al-Talib was going to use the magical powers for evil, Aladdin kept the lamp for himself; using it to acquire his own wealth wherein he then courted the Princess in grandeur.

Eventually however al-Talib did get the lamp and Aladdin again became a pauper. Meanwhile, Princess Badr al-Budur rejected all of al-Talib's wealth and professed all of her love only to Aladdin. Al-Talib became enraged over the rejection and was preparing to throw her to the lions when Aladdin and all of the Sultan soldiers arrived just in time to rescue her and save the lamp.

The loneliness in Patricia's life, having no one to talk to, seeking escape, reading these old stories with happy romantic endings started to create a stirring within; an unbefore experience of mating hormonal restlessness which settled into a latent sexual arousal. In the parts of the story where Aladdin and the Princess were madly in love she experienced a strange and exciting tingling in her panties.

In fantasy she became Princess Badr al-Budur and it was she who was rescued by Aladdin. The two of them, mounted on spirited Arabian ponies, would escape by fleeing out into the desert, across the distant horizon and disappear into the night. When they were finally safe in the middle of the vast desert quietness, beneath a galaxy of stars across the heavenly dark blue skies they would make love on the shimmering desert sands.

Completely immersed in her fantasy the milk that flowed from her breast to suckling Shelly became bonding love nectar to the eager lips of Aladdin. As their bodies came together and she was receiving him, a strange electrifying sensation came alive between her legs and she squeezed tight in response. Sensational new quivering pushed her harder and harder with each new encounter.

Addiction soon became her master and her relentless compulsion bordered on becoming a love slave to her fantasized lover.

With her eyes closed, her body rigid, and her mind concentrating she pushed harder and harder to receive him. Squeezing her legs tighter and tighter; her mind accelerated her fantasy faster and faster to an orgasmic pinnacle as she exploded, savored the brief ecstasy and then went limp. She had found the magic of self-intimacy and she would never again have to be alone.

Here, the storyteller paused and reviewed the circumstances and consequences of Patricia's life. The mental image of her seeking a degree of relief, the storyteller found both acceptable and understandable. Would any one of us here been any different? On a larger and more important note, it triggered a recollection. The night Shelly Waters was locked in jail, recalling what she had said to Morgan, that cause such of a stabbing pain; *'maybe my dream is to fly away with a handsome prince on a magic carpet to some far away land'*. *'Mother,'* the storyteller addressed her so. *'Dear mother,'* he formed the possible connection. *'Am I me because of your mother's imprint on you back then?'*

Each day Patricia read for longer periods of time. Each day she would suckle Shelly even more and savor her newly found pleasure. A world she did not know existed had opened up to her and she could at last find joy and contentment in being alone; and find joy she did; as many times a day as she liked; the world could stay on the outside and she would stay on the inside.

Nevertheless, change in the world is ever constant and just as often as not change can be instantaneous and unexpected. It was near the end of her fourth week in the apartment when Patricia was jolted from her world of fantasy to the reality of life.

Shelly became sick with high fever. It had started around four AM, when cries of gasping and throwing up pierced the quiet hours of predawn morning.

Inexperienced at doctoring, Patricia attempted to comfort her baby by holding and rocking. She dipped a folded diaper into cold water and applied a compress to her baby's forehead but it brought no apparent comfort. She walked the floor and attempted to provide either water or breast-feed but nothing helped. Little Shelly would not stop crying and her forehead continued getting warmer to the touch. By daylight Patricia knew she was in serious trouble. At 6:30 A.M. she dialed the telephone to the only person she knew.

"Hello".

"Mr. Morgan," Patricia sobbed, "I'm sorry to bother you this early in the morning but I don't know anyone else to call. It's about Shelly. She's very sick and I don't know what to do. Can you help me?"

No sooner had Patricia hung up than Morgan started dialing his telephone; asking for and receiving favors. From the first call he learned that the type of doctor he needed would be a pediatrician. The next thing he learned was who was the best. Finally, the thing that he needed the most. The personal words from that doctor to bring Patricia and Shelly immediately and come in through the side office door.

Morgan seldom attempted to walk with any hurry. But that morning the walk from the Stran to the parking garage was frustratingly slow. The time lost in his struggled walking however was more than made up as a 1939 black four door Buick sped out of the garage, headed toward Wood Street and gave no heed to either red lights or other traffic.

Leaving the car at the curb with the motor running he scrambled up the apartment steps and was greeted by Patricia at the door. As their eyes met there had been an instant communication that no explanation was necessary, no talk was necessary, no apologies were necessary. Nothing in the world mattered except getting to a doctor.

In that instant they, the two of them, planted the first seeds to becoming a team; each helping and complimenting the other. At the door Morgan gestured to take the baby, but they both quickly acknowledged his leg. Without embarrassment he stepped back, Patricia carried the baby down the steps and into the car. With the drive immediately underway there followed a few brief moments when they exchanged talk. Patricia started to make apologies for the inconvenience. Morgan emphatically assured that it was no trouble.

Dr. Freeman was waiting with the side door to his office open when they arrived. Immediately he took Shelly to the exam room and began; checking her eyes, breathing, temperature and asking Patricia questions. His diagnosis. The throwing up and diarrhea were probably brought on by a reaction to baby formula.

"How long have you been using the formula," he asked.

"Only yesterday," she answered apologetically. "It was something I picked up at the grocer.

"I normally nurse Shelly,"she went on to explain, "but my breast were becoming very sensitive so I thought I would try the formula."

"Are you able to produce sufficient milk?" Dr. Freeman asked.

"Oh heavens yes,"she felt slightly embarrassed at her quick answer. "Actually,"she clarified, "more than enough. That wasn't the problem. It's just that my nipples were becoming sore so I thought I would trade off."

"And is this the first time you have tried this formula?"

"Yes, it is. I just happen to see it and, like I say, I thought to give it a try. But I sure don't intend to ever do that again,"she atoned. "I have never been so scared in my life."

With Dr. Freeman's counsel that breast-feeding was actually the preferred method, Morgan settled the finances and obliged his own marker to Dr. Freeman. In concluding expressions of many thanks, Morgan then loaded Patricia and Shelly into his Buick and pulled away.

With the emergency of her baby out of the way, the stage curtain on the next act in the drama of their lives was about to call.

During the returning drive Shelly dropped off to sleep and for Patricia and Morgan the silence in the moving car became a slightly awkward companion. Patricia wanted to express her appreciation but she was afraid it would cause him embarrassment. Morgan on the other hand was deep in his own thoughts.

This woman and this child need a man to look after them. It's damn well not fair that they have to go it alone. It's about time I did something. Right now; while I have my nerve up. They need help and they need it now. To hell with waiting until the time is right. Acting on his resolve he turned right at the next traffic light.

On the south side of Pittsburgh, at the top of a steep switchback road, there is a street called Grand View Drive; which meanders along the edge of an overlooking cliff and provides panoramic views of the sprawling city. The scene is perfect for restaurants that capitalize on the stupendous views and *Café de la Belle Vue* exemplifies the pleasure of dining in such a setting.

Patricia took notice when Morgan nosed his car onto the first switchback. The steep grade put a strain on the car's engine and after the first switchback required a downshifting to second gear. It was at the third turn, as Morgan down shifted into low gear that she spoke.

"Excuse me Mr. Morgan, I was just wondering, this isn't the way we came...?"

Just as Patricia spoke the car reached a short level stretch of road and he shifted back into second. "I thought,"he answered as the gears changed, "that since Shelly seems to be doing OK that we might stop for breakfast. You haven't eaten have you?"

"Uh, No, now that you've mentioned. I'd even forgotten about eating."

"Well, that's kind of my thinking. And,"he paused slightly and asked rhetorically. "Would you like to know what else I am thinking? It looks like this is going to be one of those rare perfect days in the City of Pittsburgh; the kind of day that causes a person to be thankful. As for myself I'd like to show our thankfulness. I'd like for this to be an extra special day. So with your approval, I know a place up on Grand View Drive that is just about perfect for what I have in mind.

"The atmosphere may seem a little much for this early in the morning but the food is great and you can't beat the view. So how does it sound; OK?"

"Uh, Well, I..."

"Before you say anything, remember we have an awful lot to be thankful for. And lots of times in life when one good thing happen something else good will come along. And if something extra special should happen it would be a shame not to have it happen in an extra special place."

Patricia did not detect the hint. Her first reaction was surprise and her second thought was how she looked. "But I'm not dressed. I mean I look terrible. I've been up most of the night, I... I don't have any makeup on; my hair's a mess. And what about the baby? Will they let us in looking like this?"

"It's more than likely this time of morning that we will have the entire dining room to ourselves," he answered. "And in-so-far as how you look; you look fine. No wait, you look better than fine Patricia, you look beautiful; very beautiful.

"And you leave the getting in part to me. What's on my mind is to take the bull by the horns and be a little aggressive. I want some time for us. I know it's impulsive but I'm not going to apologize. The day is too beautiful and we have just been reminded of how precarious life can be. So I am hereby making the decision to relax for a little while and savor the beauty of what we have; you, me and Shelly in a beautiful world."

Patricia was slightly perplexed. She had been thinking in terms of what was appropriate and he was talking appreciation for life. Her mind did not grasp any hidden meaning and if this was what he wanted, she reasoned, then why not.

"OK, if you're sure? If they'll let us in with Shelly?"

By now they had reached the top grade and turned onto the curving ridgeline of Grandview Drive. The overview was so commanding that the conversation paused for a moment while the stupendous panoramic view captivated their attention.

"Patricia," Morgan then continued as they idled the car along, "this little place we're going to..."

"What kind of place Mr. Morgan? No wait, please I'm so sorry. I... I, do you think it would be all right if I just called you Morgan?"

Morgan fought hard to control his feelings over her words. He wanted to stop, he wanted to turn and hug her, he wanted to; but he didn't. He continued the discussion.

"What kind of place you ask? Well," he responded, "it's a restaurant, but it's a very unique kind of restaurant. Run by a Frenchman by the name of Pierre Dupré. Now ol' Pierre is a pretty smart operator. He is always open but he is always closed. How's that for a corker?

"Now what that means is this. Our man Pierre caters to the big money boys; multi-millionaires, steel mill barons, industrialists sort of people. The ones who like to throw their money around to impress people. You with me? Now he knows that one of the benefits of having money is being able to buy what the ordinary folks can't have. Nothing new about that. But what Pierre does is give them something really special. He lets them demand to be served in a restaurant that is closed.

"Now here's the way it works. Let's say you got lots and lots of them ol' greenbacks stuck in your back pocket and you're out and around town.

"Let's further suppose that you just happen to be down on 5th Avenue in front of the Mellon Bank about this time of the morning. You're passing the time by leaning on a parking meter when another greenbacker happens along. Now you don't really like this other greenbacker but that don't stop you from starting a little game of one-up-man-ship.

"So you pat each other on the back and do a little handshaking and decide that maybe a few refreshments are in order. So where do you go? To the royal elite Duquesne Club? Naw, too formal. William Penn Hotel? Huh Uh, never do. Too common. Nope, when you want to play one-up-man-ship in the money league there is only one place to go. And that's *Café de la Belle Vue.*

"Why? You ask. Because my dear Patricia, the *Café de la Belle Vue* is always closed. But don't forget now, you're a greenbacker. You got the mega bucks. So what you do is you and your friend just go right up and bang on the front door. And after you have rapped that big ol' brass door knocker loud enough to impress your one-up-man-ship friend then ol' Pierre comes and looks out at you through a little view door and in a huff tells you that he is closed and starts to slam the little square peek door shut

"But wait, then he recognizes you. With many apologies the big front door swings open. But you don't get to go right in; not just yet. Ol' Pierre comes out. Rushing around in a fuss he throws an arm around you, exclaims where have you been, why hasn't he seen you, and low and behold when the moment is just right you and your fellow greenbacker are ushered right on in. Even though he is closed, just for you he is open. How's that for some one-up-man-ship.

"Now I don't exactly have all of those mega bucks that his other patrons have. But what I do have is just about as good. See, there was a while back when he needed a little help with the Federal Immigration authorities in getting some of his family into this country. And immigration just happens to be one of my power bases. Ol' Pierre owes me big time for that one. I never thought I'd ever really call in that marker but I am. And I'm calling it today".

From the street there is little evidence that the *Café de la Belle Vue* is a Five Star restaurant. The front has no windows, is flat face weathered wood construction and is without design or statement. The entrance is a simple double door design with an un-ceremonial heavy brass latch. It has a faded canopy over a circular drive leading in from Grandview, but otherwise it is nondescript. Not even the restaurant sign provides a clue. Consisting of a small tarnished bronze plaque fastened mid-height to the wall adjacent to the doorjamb, it gives the impression of being an afterthought.

Morgan came to the circular drive, nosed the big black Buick in under the canopy and as expected there was no one in sight. As he was getting out of the car he commented, "You and the baby wait while I see if I can round up somebody."

The neighborhood was quiet at that hour of the morning and Shelly lay sleeping in the back seat. The only sound was Morgan's cane tapping on the cobblestones as he walked to the entrance and she watched as he banged the oversized doorknocker. Unexplainably, she seemed to notice him for the first time and studied him as he stood there in his wrinkled business suit, loose tie, collar unbuttoned, fedora hat and walking cane. Intuitively she tried to decide if he was handsome in a gangster fashion.

Momentarily the little view-door opened and then one of the double doors. She watched as he exchanged greetings with a short stocky man dressed in a meticulous dark blue suit and who looked as though he was indeed French. She couldn't hear what they were saying but she was still watching when Morgan turned slightly and pointed a finger toward the car. The man gave a quick look and nodded in agreement. The stocky man then put his arm around Morgan's shoulder and gesture they both go inside.

With Morgan out of sight Patricia became more aware of the silence and felt a little uneasy. Instinctively she locked the car doors and looked around the outside. Thankfully there were no lurking bodies to be seen. Now in a little more relaxed mode she again thought of Morgan and in a mind flash she pictured him as being a good protector. *After all he had provided her with a place to live, given her money and when Shelly got sick he was right there. Just like someone taking care of you is supposed to do.* She decided that it was nice having him. *Who knows,* she thought, *he doesn't have anyone and she doesn't have anyone. Maybe someday they might even become an adopted family.*

Shortly Morgan returned to the car for Patricia and Shelly and the three of them went inside. At the doorway a hatcheck girl wearing a skimpy white blouse with red bow tie, black mini skirt, black high heels pumps and black fishnet stockings greeted them. With loving oohs's and aha's she immediately took Shelly and carefully placed her on a make shift pad in back of the coat check counter.

On that signal an impeccably dressed waiter in a black tuxedo and red cumber band stiffly acknowledged their presence and nodded slightly that Patricia and Morgan should follow him.

As he was ushering them to a window-side table Patricia started feeling uncomfortably self-conscious. Walking past all of the empty tables with stiff white tablecloths and silverware settings, she felt like they were going to too much trouble for her. The formality of having her chair regimentally pulled out, inviting her to be seated and then nudged up to the table made her feel even more uncomfortable. As the waiter left, a water boy appeared and filled their drinking glasses with clinking ice water. And shortly thereafter the waiter reappeared with a heavily loaded serving cart and it was here that Morgan first spoke.

"Uh Patricia," he searched for an opener, "this food is all French and I don't know exactly what all we'll be getting. But here's what happened.

I told ol' Pierre that this is a very special occasion and I would leave it up to his best judgment."

And what Pierre judged best was a house specialty called 'The Eiffel Tower for Lovers'. The first things the waiter placed on the table were two crystal champagne glasses. Thence from a silver ice bucket he removed a bottle of Veuve Cliquet Champagne. Wrapped with a linen napkin, he displayed the label first to Morgan and then to Patricia. With Morgan's nod the cork was popped to a foamy overflow. Morgan tasted a sample, approved and their two glasses were then filled to two-thirds.

Both Morgan and Patricia continued to watch as additional servings came; the extent causing them both to feel inadequate. The 'Eiffel Tower for Lovers' consisted of four varieties of bread, *du pain grillé, du pain d'épices, du pain au chocolat, des croissants;* a silver tray of spreads, *cervelle de canut, tapenade, paté de campagne, de la confiture, du beurre;* one serving of fritters, *bugnes Lyonais;* two kinds of crêpes, *des crêpes de blé noir and des ficelles picardes;* two separate dishes of palate pleasing eggs, *des oeufs au cocotte, des oeufs brouillés au jambon,* one serving of house specialty potatoes, *gratin de pommes de terre aux truffes;* artichokes in cold sauce, *des artichauts froid à la sauce moutarde;* two world famous desserts, *un gendarme de St-Tropez, des poires à la beaujolaise* and hot french coffee, *café au lait.*

As his final officiate, the waiter presented to Patricia six long stem red roses in fragrant baby breath, arranged in a tall crystal receptacle and accentuated by a satin red bow and stringers. With a slight bend at the waist he executed a snap of his heels and withdrew.

A momentary quietness followed as Morgan looked at Patricia. She in turn was not looking at Morgan so much as she was looking bewildered. Morgan thought she looked embarrassed. He had a fleeting spark of panic that it may be too much; too out of place. But in a second instant he rebounded; telling himself that panic be damned, there is no one set, chiseled in stone, way of doing these things. *If some other man does something his way, fine and dandy. But I'm me and this is my way; right or wrong this is it. As bad as we got started it can't be any worse. For better or worse I'm playing this hand through to the finish.*

Slowly he picked up his glass of champagne and motioned for Patricia to do the same. As their eyes met their glasses clinked, slightly rose in toast and brought to their lips without yet speaking. This was her first taste of champagne and she tickled slightly at the frizzle bubbles going down. Not knowing what social graces were expected of her she just looked at Morgan. They both smiled and took a second sip.

If...there be Divine watchful eyes of Heavenly Faith, and if those Divine eyes be heavenly ascended they must have found the circumstances intriguing. What would the outcome be? This man and this woman, awkward in each other's presence, sharing a meal for the first time. Would the window-side table with its stupendous view be help or a hindrance? Would the ceremonial French breakfast set on white linen, christened by a vintage champagne, and complimented with a bouquet of fragrant red roses accomplish its intended purpose: or prove to be too overpowering. Heavenly Faith must have had no way of knowing because not even Morgan had any way of knowing. He only knew the hand had to be played. On their second glass of champagne he did his resolve; how-be-it, abruptly delivered.

"Patricia," he slightly lost words as he felt a rush of embarrassment, "will you marry me? I want you more than anything I have ever wanted in my life. I need you. I need Shelly. So I am asking you here and now, would you please be my wife."

To this proposal the observing eyes of Faith must have either cringed or watched in suspense. Because to this very same proposal a million thoughts of panics flashed through the mind of Patricia. Her very first thought was surprise that he was asking *her*. This was the sort of question which a man would normally first ask the woman's father, or uncle, or mother, or someone; but not her.

She shouldn't be addressing anything this significant on her own. At the very least there should be someone else there to help discuss the proposal. She certainly was not experienced or wise enough to make such a decision. That in turn caused her to become even tenser. All the words that the proposal implied; love, happiness, sickness, health, cherish, forsaking all others. None of these things even crossed her mind. Her first words reflected her panic.

"But, Mr. Morgan, Uh Morgan, don't you know? I'm already married. I assumed that you knew that. Surely you don't think that Shelly is illegitimate?" Morgan was staggered by the response.

"Oh No!"he gulped out his scared reaction. "No! A hundred times no, of course not Patricia. Certainly I don't think that Shelly is illegitimate. I know that you are legally married and that your husband deserted you. But that has absolutely nothing to do with my proposal. I want to marry you because I love you. Now, I have thought everything out. I have no doubt we can get you a divorce on the grounds of desertion. The thing is, I want you. And I am more than happy to take the whole package. Just the way everything is right now. If you will marry me I will adopt Shelly and we can give her my name. I will make us a good home and provide you with everything you will ever need. Now about the divorce, I have a good friend, Frank Buckwilder who is one hell of a good lawyer. I have no doubt that he can go into court on the grounds of des..."

"You mention the total package,"Patricia cut in. "You said you would take the package, just the way it is."

Morgan's mind flashed to her breast. Was that where her thoughts were? He froze at the insinuation. He could see what might be coming and was determined not to let the big picture be lost with a focus on the insignificant.

"Patricia,"he spoke in his most sincere tone, "the words I want you to hear are I love you and I want you to be my wife".

Over a beautiful breakfast in the most pleasant of surroundings two people sat. Two bodies apparently similar in nature and yet different of mind set. Morgan had wanted all of this to say,

Patricia I have come for you. You no longer need to walk alone. Follow me into my world and I will share with you all of my days. I will protect you and care for you in sickness and in health, I will love and honor you and forsaking all others I will cherish you and you alone... because there is nothing in the world I need more than you.

And Patricia thought,

I'm someplace but I don't know where. I feel strange. He's here with me but I don't know why? What is the real reason we are here? I don't belong in this kind of place. I like it. I like it a lot. I like him a lot. But I can't just give in. I'm not even supposed to be in a place like this. I don't know why but it's just not right.

Patricia could not give Morgan an answer of marriage because her mind could not comprehend what he was saying. The idea of her and Morgan being husband and wife simply did not register. The only person she had ever thought of being a wife too was her Arabian Prince who lived in the Sahara Desert. She couldn't betray him by marrying some other man. The short life she had spent with her young lover had been very wonderful and it was getting better every day. At first he had come to visit only once a day. But lately his visits had been increasing. And the more frequently he came to visit the more she enjoyed it. Someday she hoped he would come and never leave.

In Morgan's mind the failure was his own. He had blotched the job. Too much too soon. In rebound he guided the conversation to other aspects. Patricia needed a place and he had a place so it was settled that she would stay in the apartment for as long as she liked.

If she wanted to work, Morgan had a place. Whenever she was ready there would be a job waiting as cashier in the ticket cage at the Stran. If it would help matters she could bring Shelly to work. If she needed him, Morgan would be in his office just inside the lobby. The morning passed and somewhere amidst their talking their waiter appeared and asked, "Will there be anything else sir?"

A clear signal that the protocol time limit had elapsed; and acknowledged, as Morgan replied.

"No, everything has been very pleasant, just the last of the champagne and the check".

The waiter emptied the remaining champagne and presented the dinner check on a small ornate silver tray. Morgan glanced at the tab; reached for his wallet, laid out four fifty dollar bills and gave a slight wave. With the final moments at hand there was a brief silence as the two realized the end. Their eyes made contact and without breaking the gaze Morgan reached over and softly cradled her chin in his hand.

"Patricia before we leave let me say one more thing. I'm in a position in life where I am making more money than I ever thought possible. The more I make the more it seems to roll in. Sometimes I make deals with an almost indifference. They come, they are discussed, they are made and after they are concluded I feel alone again.

"I feel empty," he paused. "What I am trying to say is that making money is not what I had always thought it would be. Until I met you I was looking for something but I didn't know what. Then, the other day, the first time I saw you, you and little Shelly in Owise's office. I knew that you were what it would take to make my life complete. I need you and I want..." But Morgan did not get to finish.

She raised her small delicate hand up to his large stocky hand that was still holding under her chin and squeezed.

"Morgan you don't need me nearly as much as I need you. I need you because you have so much and I have nothing.

"You're all I have to keep something from happening to Shelly and me. Morgan you're all I've got, please don't turn me out."

If the storyteller had been reading a book, he would have slammed the pages shut in total aggravation of first the high upbeat, but then the down...a frig up. *These people*, the storyteller thought as the segment ended. I had rather investigate a triple ax murder case than try and figure out where they are headed. Nothing in any of their lives was ever simple. With this kind of linkage no wonder I'm frigged up in the head and everywhere else for that matter. At this point the only thing I can conclude is that Patricia fantasized about having a sex orgy with an Arabian prince while Shelly was nursing. I can't handle anymore. Where's that whore Jenny? Maybe her sex life is a little more conventional.

Chapter 11

In the world of sex-for-sale two things are generally predictable. When the sun comes up, men go to jobs and hookers go to bed. It was six o'clock in the morning in a different part of town from the Wood Street apartment and Jenny Craig had just settled into a tub of steaming hot water.

She was gradually leaning back and letting her body adjust to the too hot temperature. In another second or two she would slip all the way down and feel the final gush of steaming water come up to her neck; if... only the world was so perfect. In the real world the Gods of early morning pampering are not known to be in such harmony with the Gods of AT&T. Telephones are always more powerful by virtue of an electrical current. Moreover, it is more common than not that bathtub serenity will be shattered by the rude demands of an insensitive ringing.

"Hello," she answered. "Who ever you are go away," she spoke into a telephone being held out away from the tub by her dripping wet hand.

"Good Morning, Jenny this is Morgan."

"Morgan," her tone instantly changed. "Even this early in the morning you give me a tingle. You wouldn't happen to know why that is would you?"

"I hear you," he returned her glib and then asked. "Did I caught you at a bad moment?"

"Morgan, where you're concerned there are no bad moments; some are just more sex provoking than others, purrrr purrrr."

"Jenny," he feigned like he was a sexually exhausted lover. "Not this morning. I can't help you. I'm a delicate man. I don't have ten times in me; not today."

"Ten times? I, Morgan what on earth are you talking abou..."

"Remember you said you liked it as many as ten times a da..."

"Morgan, that's not funny. If you're not going to let me ravish your body then why'd you call?"

"Jenny, I'm just doing a little early morning what's-going-on catch up. One of the things I'm trying to stay on top of is that bus we are converting to Youth for Christ.

"I think you told me last week that we're running a little behind schedule. What I'm trying to do now is get clear picture of how far behind?"

"Hasn't,"she asks with a touch of surprise, "Jim Barkus been keeping you posted? I just assumed, I mean we've really been making headway Morgan. And, uh, since you're the one who's putting out the money I just assumed that..."

"Well, Jenny, you know,"he sighed slightly. "Yeah, Jim's been giving me a dab of the heavier stuff. From what he's told me he found a pretty good used one over at Westrail Bus Lines. Which, if I'm not mistaken we've completed payment. It's my guess that Jim must have a pretty good name over there cause according to what I hear the Westrail people are going out of their way to let you guys use work space at their maintenance terminal. I've given Jim whatever money he needs, but when I ask him how it's going he just pulls his ear a little and grunts `pretty good'.

"Now, I'm just wondering Jenny, you think you could turn on some of that soft sweet charm of yours and explain to me in a little more detail just what 'pretty good' means?"

"Morgan,"she soothed, "how come you're always so nice?"

"Uh..."

"OK, I know you're always busy, even this early so I'll be brief and talk fast; how's that. Me, Jim, and a crew of my girls have been working together almost every day for the past two weeks. Sweat equity if you will and in my opinion we've managed to accomplish quite a bit. If the final product turns out the way I think, it's going to be a real masterpiece; a one-of-a-kind rolling palace of amour. I get sexy just thinking about it. Even an ol' un-movable Rock of Gibraltar like you would get sexed up. Now here's where we stand.

"The first thing we did was gut everything out; nothing left but the steering wheel and dash board. Then came my input. I just sort of explained to Jim how I thought we should rebuild the inside. Mostly I talked and he listened. He doesn't say a lot, you know that? He just moves around a lot. I can make mention of something one minute, turn my head and the next thing I know he's gone.

"Then before I know it he's back with whatever; anything from a welding torch to a load of angle iron; just as unassuming as you please. Just like there wasn't anything to it. The next thing I know welding sparks are flying and sweat's a rolling.

"Before I could say squat he had the framework welded in for two rows of mini pullman berths; one row on each side of a center isle. All of that was just in the first week. It gets better. Then came the next step; padding and covering. That's where my girls and I came in. We gave ourselves the job of doing all the inside in sexy blue velvet with gold trim. Each berth will have a blue satin cover mattress, satin pillows, velvet drawstring curtains, the works.

"While we've been sewing and tacking, Jim's been working on a double wide bathroom across the back of the bus; gold trim faucets, vanity wash bowl, ggggger good stuff. And there you have it."

"Jesus, Jenny that sounds like it's really going to be something,"came Morgan's response in a tone that seemed to her was not as enthusiastic as she was expecting. "The times I've talked to Jim,"he continued, "he sure didn't paint the glowing exuberance that you describe. Maybe I should stroll over there and have my own look-see. You guys might be driving me into bankruptcy."

"But... but I thought it was what you wanted?"she was quick to indicate her scare.

"Just kidding Jenny, just kidding, spend the money. I'll get over to see it in a couple of days. I don't want you thinking I'm not interested Sweet Thing. Nothing like that. It's just that right now I'm pretty busy. I've got loads of stuff going on.

"I won't go into too many details but you might be interested in knowing that I'm thinking about doing a little expanding of my own; buying some more property. I'm thinking of buying the Underground Stage Playhouse on Sixth Street? You know the one; it's that basement walk down?"

"What! Why Morgan Smithfield,"she exclaimed. "You must be kidding! That's one of Pittsburgh's best-known landmarks. It's such a part of Pittsburgh that I don't think it has even ever occurred to me that someone might actually own it. I guess it seems like it's just always been there whenever any of us have an urge to take a little walk on the risqué side of life. Morgan, the thought of you and the Underground all in the same picture.

"That'll take some getting used to. However, tell me everything that's happened. And don't you dare leave out a single detail."

"Well, the story is we're still negotiating; pretty firm but nothing final. Just between you, the fence post, and me, however, I think I would really like to take a shot at the Underground. The trouble is the sellers also want me to buy the Palace Theater over in Oakland. And I'm not all that sure I want both of 'em; but we'll see."

"When..."she was about to ask, but was cut off.

"Listen Jenny I can't go into the details right now but I was wondering if you would do me a favor."

"Of course,"she answered with emphasis. "Name it handsome man and you got it."

"It's kind of unusual, actually it's two favors. First, do you remember Dr. Daniel Owise? He's the doctor that I sent you to when we thought you had a problem."

Jenny felt a touch of embarrassment at the mention but replied, "Hon, of course I remember."

"Good. Now here is what I'm thinking. I would like for you to think up some excuse to go back and see the shithead. Use anything from a toothache to an ingrown toenail. In this case he's not really my main interest. Well... he is; but just not right at this stage. The one I'm really interested in is a little short skirted, hard tit nurse working for him by the name of Detrick Simmons.

"And, what I'm really after is for you and Detrick to get acquainted. Work up a friendship if you can. As things progress maybe the two of you can even get to be buddies. Say, kind of slow at first. Talk boy talk, have a drink, whatever. The idea is to get to know her. I'll tell you why later."

As Morgan was talking a touch of jealousy ran through Jenny's mind and without thinking she asked, "Any particular interest you have in this girl; this Detrick? I mean it is OK if I ask isn't it?" There was a slight pause and then Morgan answered in a reassuring tone.

"No interest Jenny. She's all yours. I may have some thoughts latter but right now I simply want to have a set of eyes over in mine enemy's camp."

Jenny felt a sigh of relief and then in a little less inquisitive voice asked, "And the other?"

"What?"

"The other favor. You said you wanted two favors."

"Oh, Yeah. Jenny this is also something a little different. I don't think I ever told you but I own a little one bedroom flat over on Wood Street. It's right above Boxhimer's Dry Goods store..."His words did not end with a complete sentence but tapered off unfinished. Jenny detected the hesitancy and when Morgan did not continue talking she asked.

"Hello, hello, Morgan you still there?"

"Yeah, I'm still here,"he responded in a hesitating tone. "Listen, Jenny I don't know exactly how to handle this, but since the last time you and I saw each other my life has gotten a little more complicated. Again it all ties back to that shithead Owise. But to make a long story short I now have a young woman in that apartment. I think she's probably about your age, somewhere in her early to mid twenties.

"Anyway she's down on her luck. God love her, her back is so tight against the wall that she can't even breathe. Her name is Patricia, Patricia Waters and things are a mess. Through no fault of hers she got involved in a bad marriage, got pregnant, husband bolted and ran and now she has a baby; a little sucking baby girl and literally no place to go.

"I've given her a little money so she's OK in that respect, but what she desperately needs is the company of another woman."

As Jenny was holding the phone to her ear and silently listening to Morgan talk she experienced a roller coaster ride of feelings. When Morgan mentioned a young woman, she had felt jealousy; when he mentioned her being same age, she felt more resentment; when Morgan mentioned down on her luck, she felt a scheme, a ploy, a hard luck story; and when Morgan mentioned money, offense had swelled up as she pictured him falling for a sham.

Then, when he mentioned the need of another woman just to be a friend, her heart felt a touch of shame. An overpowering compulsion to rush to the aid of a fallen sister swelled up inside.

How could I have been so selfish? She thought. *I have to go immediately; immediately,* she inflicted her own self-sternness.

"Morgan,"she responded in a tone of deep compassion for a mother and child in trouble. "At this very moment there is nothing in the entire world more important than for me to answer the call of a sister in need. To me, as a woman, there is no greater calling than being both a woman and a mother.

"And I am touched that your thoughts turned to me. You have paid me the highest compliment; and I'll do my best to earn the honor. Yes, yes, yes, I'll go."

On the other end of the line Morgan was glad that they were not face-to-face. He would not want Jenny to see his emotional eyes. So he over compensated in his voice as he responded.

"Do whatever you need to do baby. Get her out of the house if you can. Maybe go shopping, lunch, drinks, take a taxi." Then to cover his apparent softness he quickly rebuffed, "But look for bargains now 'yea hear. Remember cheap cheap cheap."

Jenny arrived at Wood Street in a taxi loaded with three large sacks of groceries. Her shopping had been speedy but with thoughts of immediate needs. Included were milk, bread, potatoes, meat, seasonings, vegetables, baby diapers, baby oil, a rattler, soap, and a soft pink jumper suit. As the cab driver carried the sacks to the top of the steps Jenny was knocking on the door. Cradled in one arm she held a dozen long stem red roses. Her knock was answered with the door opening just a crack and a half-shielded face looking out from the darker inside.

"Mrs. Waters? Mrs. Waters my name is Jenny; Jenny Craig. I am a friend of Morgan Smithfield. May I visit your home?"

It was late in the evening when Jenny and Patricia stood at the apartment front door and the two said their good-bye. With a final little hug and an exchange of parting words Jenny stepped outside and started down the steps. The sun had already dropped behind the horizon and the warm twilight air was just beginning to feel like dew. A kaleidoscope of lavender and pale pink clouds painted the western sky, a coloring of purple hue hung near the lower horizon and a blending of darkness was starting to hang in the shadows.

As she was descending the flight of steps she fought to control her emotions. Control that she was able to hold until she reached the sidewalk, headed down Wood Street, walked past the shuttered shops and came to the corner. Pausing at the deserted intersection, she unsnapped her purse, searched for a hanky and slightly blew her nose. In the absence of street traffic she crossed with little thought of looking.

As she crossed the intersection and continued walking she started becoming cognizant of the soft twilight dew on her exposed skin, the eerie silence of the empty business district, the absence of traffic on Wood Street, the deep breath of air that she took in...and she let herself savor the wonderful moment.

Selfish or not she had found out that Patricia had no romantic interest in Morgan; and to have a new friend with the most beautiful baby; it was good to be young and alive. She could hear the sound of her high heels clicking on the sidewalk. She pictured how her round firm full buns and shapely calves must look from the back; heels snapping at the concrete and her hips swinging in a suggestive roll. She thought how arousing it would be to the eyes of a horny man and she started feeling wet. Click, click, clickied click.

She took another deep breath, threw her shoulders back, raised her chest high and stuck her hard firm nipples straight out. Click, click, click, click. She had the crown jewel of the universe right between her legs and dear God did she want to share it. A Yellow Cab cruised by and gave a slight touch of the horn. Without breaking her step she smiled and waved him on.

She came to the next corner and waited at the red light to cross. As she stepped from the concrete curb to the brick street her high heels felt slightly slippery. It sparked a feeling of being invincible and she welcomed the thrill of the icy feeling. She even scooted a little in play motion that she could skate across the street. Ecstatic, she exaggerated her walk to a slow rolling sexy swing of her hips and the click of her heels seemed even louder. She wanted to flaunt the world, and on an impulse she hustled a trick.

As luck, or destiny, would have it she was just coming upon the First State Bank building; fifteen stories high, set back from the street, massive concrete steps leading up to a towering column entrance. Glancing up to the top of the steps she saw a solitary gentleman just coming out of the massive street doors. It could have been almost any man but luck was running with her. His pedigree was well above average; he was a banker.

He was adjusting his hat as he unmindfully started down the wide tier of descending steps and started cutting diagonally across to the lower corner; putting his line of walk in the same general direction as hers.

Extremely distinguished looking, she judged him to be in his desirable fifties. He was wearing an impeccable dark blue three-piece suit, white starched shirt and a regimental dark blue and red stripe tie.

As the tangent of the two walkers started closing to the intersecting point the street lights flickered on and she could instantly see that his sideburns were salt and pepper and the years had been very methodical in molding his face with character lines. Heavy eyebrows over small crow's feet accentuated his deep set, sparkling blue eyes. He was tall and commanding. Not unduly large but a physique which would stand out in a crowd and the soft evening breeze carried a faint scent of his exotic cologne.

No matter where he was he would be noticed and maybe that was the reason for her impulse. The hair on her arms became electrified and her predatory senses sprang to life. Judging his distance she timed her walk so that they would come together just as he reached the bottom step. Sensing that she had not been noticed she softened the click of her heels held slightly to his blind side and then did it. Just as he took the last step onto the sidewalk she executed a flawless accidental bump. A slight collision and then an adjusting step to regain her balance.

"Uh, Oh, Excuse me, I'm sorry,"they both expressed their pardons in unison as they turned to each other. He was just in the breath of saying it was his fault, when she whispered in her sexiest tone, "Date mister? It's free, on the house."

To be jolted from banking thoughts to a proposition for a date struck Aspen Gerore McGee as hilarious; laughable. It felt good.

"My goodness,"he smiled in an air of pleasant surprise. "The world's oldest profession seems to have moved up town. Welcome to the financial district." The tone and demeanor signaled to Jenny that he might be receptive.

"Promotional duties,"she edged herself closer and purred in a May West impersonation. "We in the industry felt that we should upgrade." Aspen's smile broadened, and at her apparent invite he reached out and lightly touched her chin. She accommodatingly edged in a step closer and tilted her head up so that he was looking directly into her face.

"And,"he asked, "what grade-up are you?"

"Top grade,"she cooed. "U.S. Grade A Prime, number one cut. Would you like a free sample?"

Aspen's smile broke into a diminutive laugh. "How,"he questioned in mimic, "can I be sure of the grade?"

"Purrr,"she meowed. "I know all of the USDA meat inspectors by their first names."

"Interesting, and are you stamped?"

"Stamped?"she questioned.

"Hand stamped. A purple vile USDA stamp. If I'm correct I believe meat inspectors always stamp the meat that passes inspection. I don't suppose there would be such a stamp on that nice firm little bottom of yours?"

"Right cheek, capital letters,"she was quick to rebound.

"Extra ordinary,"he mimicked. "Most unusual. I would say that under these wartime conditions this is a rare treat. Most of our prime is being sent overseas. Are you telling me that you're the civilian allocation? Is that what you're telling me?"

"While the supply last,"she slipped her hands under his jacket lapels and pulled herself in closer. "If you don't trust the Government you can always conduct your own investigation." Aspen melted completely into a laugh as he put his arm around her shoulder and lightly hugged her body to his.

"Right now,"he said as his arm remained around her, "I'm thinking the government has overlooked a monumental natural resource. You seem to be the only thing around for which ration stamps are not required. But given time, they may ever decide..."he stopped short.

"So,"he then picked up again, "Miss. U.S. Grade A Prime do you happen to have any other name or is it just Miss Prime; or is it Mrs. Prime?"

Jenny paid no attention to the question. This had the makings of a perfect trick and she intended to turn on her full talents. The evening was quiet, inviting, relaxing and he was an unruffled extremely handsome man who appeared to be receptive. Her wonderful day was getting better. Squirming up closer under his hugging arm, she then guided it tighter around her shoulders. As she felt his squeeze intensify she straddled her legs over one of his and tightened down; suggestive but not overly firm. Holding the moment to peak perfection she then flexed her firm leg muscles and instantly locked down tight; impounding the sensation just long enough to let him feel the pulsation of her invitation to the Garden of Eden. Following through to annihilate any remaining resistance she took one of his hands and cupped it to her breast and then wrapped her arms around his mid-section. With her moist muff still straddling his leg she push it down firm, letting him feel the pulsation. In a momentary motionless body-intertwine, hormones surged and their two chemistries blended into perfect unity.

"The War Department is very adamant,"she cooed as the fragrance from his masculine cologne became even more intoxicating, "that the home front civilian men receive their fair share."

She had expected that her words would be followed by a clever return on his part and was puzzled when there was only silence. After an additional instant she loosened her seductive body hug at the same time as his hand relaxed from her breast. She looked to his face for an explanation. Their eyes made contact and to her interpretation a different type of message was being communicated. His eyes were doing the talking and they were saying, *Careful, be very careful. This is potentially very dangerous. It could lead to involvement. It's always easier to get into something than to get out. Stop now or assume there will be future consequences.*

But... it was too late. The page had already turned and the die cast. A flash of lighting had arched between them and formed a weld from which neither could escape. In silence they stood and Aspen ran his hand through her long flowing hair. In perfect cue she lowered her head so that it rested on his chest just below his chin. He gently gathered strands between his thumb and forefinger and lightly brought it to his nose and smelled the intoxicating fragrance of youth. With fingers spread he slowly plowed outward and watched as the strands of silk floated gently down. Then finger combed the locks that had fallen askew. As if on signal Jenny raised her eyes so that they were again gazing at each other. In cue to the next move he bent slightly down and very lightly touch his dry lips to her moist youthful mouth; and she responded by slightly opening her soft lips and returning a small touch of her moist tongue.

And at the bottom step of the towering First State Bank building, in the silent twilight, on a deserted downtown Pittsburgh street, destiny watched as two silhouettes stood oblivious to the rest of the world.

"Why,"came the first soft spoken words from Aspen, "may I ask do you have this uncontrollable desire to give such beautiful favors away for free?"

"Well,"she answered in a hesitant but truthful tone. "Up until about two seconds ago I was simply horny. I have had the most wonderful day. Quite by happenstance I have a new woman friend who has the most beautiful baby. We met, we talked I played with her baby, we went out to lunch, we gossiped and it was really the most delightful time.

"And... I was able to determine that she has no interest in a certain man of whom I won't mention. I... I guess when I left her place I was on such a high I just wanted to share it with someone. Well, not just anyone,"she turned the statement into a purr, "I felt so womanly I wanted it to be with an extra ordinary devilishly good looking man. And bingo, there you were."

"And that's it?"questioned Aspen. "You found a new woman friend with whom you can talk and that got you horny?"

"No... of course not. You're just being mean,"she smiled at the implication. "My being horny right at this particular moment wasn't one of those one-hundred per cent, I-need-some-hot-orgasm-sex-right-this-minute-or-I'll-explode- horny. It was more like one of those my-panties-are-wet-and-I-feel-so-good-I-want-to-share-it-with-someone-extra-extra-special hornies. You know what I mean?"

While she was talking Aspen was making a mental comparison between the magnitude of his business problems and the level of Jenny's explanation. *The simplicity of youth*, he thought. *How positively delightful is the simplicity of youth.* When she finished, Aspen made no effort to speak but instead mocked a little are-you-sure-you-are-OK look. Jenny knew he was mocking and accepted that she needed to clarify things a little.

"OK, maybe this will help. When I started out this morning I did so with the expectation that this other woman would cause me romance problems. But thankfully it didn't turn out that way." She then repeated her earlier statement.

"Without even discussing the issue, I was able to determine that she has absolutely no romantic interest in a certain man named Morgan."

As she concluded she gave him a look that indicated that anyone should now have a clear understanding.

"And may I assume that this man, this Morgan, is of very special interest to you?"

She felt a touch of embarrassment and did not respond immediately. On one hand she felt compelled to be truthful. On the other hand she felt a strong magnetism to the excitement of Aspen and she didn't want to lose him. Calculating in a tone and delivery that she hoped would convey the circumstances, she replied.

"Morgan? Yes, Morgan is of special interest to me. I hate to admit it but the attraction is probably all on my part. But that doesn't keep me from feeling the way I do. I haven't really known him that long. But just seeing him, or talking with him ignites an electrical charge in me. In some way or another he seems to be in back of my every thought. Always just out of reach. Yet we have never been together, never made love. Not even gone out on a date. Nor has he ever made any overtures to me.

"It's just that he's out there, in the outer zone of my life but as yet I do not know how or why or have any idea as to what will happen." Then in a change of tone she aggressively shifted the conversation back to the two of them.

"Now how about that date?" She flirtatiously put her arm inside of his, communicating the man leads and she would follow, and the two turned and started walking. They reached the street corner and were waiting to cross when Aspen commented.

"If you care to talk I have a couple of thoughts we can share." For Jenny it was a welcome remark because she had been searching for a way to keep their chemistry alive and block out thoughts of Morgan.

"You handsome man,"she quickly responded, "just being with you is talk enough for me but it might help me contain myself if I could savor your sexy voice. It might even prevent me from attacking you right here on the sidewalk and both of us getting arrested." Aspen grinned at her tease and then responded.

"I am thinking that we do not know each other's name and I keep wondering..."

At just that moment the light changed and they stepped from the curb. As they proceeded across the street she could feel the slippery bricks under her high heels and squeezed her interlocked arm firmer to his.

When they reached the curb on the other side and stepped back upon the sidewalk he continued. "I'm a reader; an avid reader. And I am thinking of something I once read; a poem actually, which reminds me of our situation."

"Someone," she asked surprised, "wrote a poem about the way we are?"

"Well, poem, prose, verses something along the same lines. It was a long time ago. I just happen to remember it."

"Can I hear it?"

"What? Hear it. Me? HA! Heavens no. I mean, I just remember the general theme. It was about a boy and a girl. They had just met. I don't remember why but they only had the one night. For some reason their lives would go their separate ways the next day."

"Are there any of the words you remember? I mean can you tell me why it reminds you of us?"

"To a large degree I know why it reminds me of us. But-in-so-far as remembering any of the words. You have no idea what you're asking. Me? Reciting poetry?"

"Could you try? Just for me; pleeeease."

The way she said please, the way they were both indifferent to the increasing darkness, an empty street corner, the sexual arousal of being together, he again surveyed her radiant youth. Truly he thought she is a vision of loveliness.

Youthful, perfect body radiant youth; why not? He thought as he impulsively cast off the yoke of prudence. *I'm just me. What's more I'm all I'll ever have. What's wrong with being a little foolish ever now and then? The past is past. If I'm ever going to have that new life there's no time like the present to start.* He took both of her hands in his and as they stood looking at each other he continued.

"OK but don't say you weren't warned. The best I can remember, it went something like this." He cleared his throat, thought for a moment and started.

"We know not each other's name, but what care we. Names are but garlands; calls by which mortals' answer in posture of the flesh.

"Our care this night, is of each other's soul wherein malice is forbidden,"he paused to think then continued.

"In, uh, in this perpetual moment, we, you and I, attach ourselves to the uninhibited wind.

"In the bliss of each other's perfection, and absence of each other's faults, unto one of us the other, we can sail to the land of endless love.

"In a land of twilight where the Gods of Love have decreed that the ingredients in twilight wine will be laughter, play and runaway,"he stopped again.

In silence she waited for an instance and then asked, "Is there more? It sounds so beautiful. Can you remember anything else?"

"I think,"he answered, "that it is better in my fantasy than in my recital."

"Please,"she pleaded, "tell me the rest, anything you can remember. It's so romantic."

"O---K---. If you're such a glutton for pain,"he elongated his words. "I'll tell you what. How about I recite what I can remember and then leave it up to you as to why I think it reminds me of us; deal?"

"Deal."

"In broad terms, the substance goes something like this.

"On the wings of innocence, we can reach for the moon and frolic among the stars; or walk feet in bare on moon beams across foamy waves.

"In the nude we can lie on a isolated beach, roll in the foam, and make love in the sand as the surf washes over our intertwined bodies.

"The night will live forever for in this land there is no tomorrow.

"There will only be the first rays of early light, cast like a cruel eviction notice upon the mountain side; that we must painfully depart this land of endless love.

"Ours then will be a return to the land of mortals, richer only by our memories and knowing that we once visited where only the Gods doeth dwell"

It was for Jenny a moment she would always remember. As she watched the beautiful rhetoric roll off the tongue of this mysterious man she was both awed by the delivery and frightened by the meaning.

He was asking her if this will be just a one-night stand or will it lead too much much more.

Not knowing what to say she awkwardly asked, "And the other? You said there were a couple of things you had on your mind. Can you tell me the other?"

They had resumed walking and as they meander arm in arm Aspen replied. "The other thought, my very lovely woman, is that we get to know each other's name. We will probably become involved. We will seek the rewards and pleasure of a fulfilling relationship.

"But with involvement will come commitment, inconvenience and to a very large extent the forfeiture of our freedom. My problems will become your problems and your problems will become mine. And the world which we both knew a few moments ago will be forever changed."

There were no witnesses to collaborate that moment. Words written on the wind cannot be chiseled in stone. But there is something greater and more enduring. It is a knowing which comes from within. A knowing that had already come to them both. It was now her decision and it came as they paused and again looked at each other. In the moment that their eyes met, Jenny was the first to speak. As she looked deeply into his and he into hers, she extended her hand in handshake and very, very softly said,

"Hello you most mysterious and attractive man, my name is Jenny; Jenny Craig."

As Aspen accepted her hand he gave his in return. "Hello my most beautiful and lovely Jenny Craig, my name is Aspen; Aspen Gerore McGee. And I am most delighted to make your acquaintance."

"Hey," the storyteller spoke out loud. "This Aspen character. I've heard about him. He got his tail in a crack over some big cattle deal. I remember way back, hearing the grown up's talk about how he damn near died out in some salt flat desert. Aspen, Aspen, normally I wouldn't think too much about any of this having any bearing on me but still one never knows. Wouldn't it be something if my ol' sweet Mama and Aspen???? Ha! What if I'm a banker and don't know it.

Chapter 12

Aspen McGee had not always lived in Pittsburgh. The only thing he had always been was a puppet banker and a sex-deprived husband. Either one, if not both, being sufficient to drive a man slowly to the brink of insanity. Slow insanity, which like the lines on a man's face, progress over time. In later times and by later accounts he would come to realize how dangerously close he had come to the edge.

If he had to pinpoint a precariously close moment, a moment which reflected a breaking point more than any other, it would be the day he moved to Pittsburgh and took up residency in his newly acquired penthouse. Purchased fully furnished he had moved in with suitcases in hand and still remembered those first few moments; when he knew he had finally escaped. No one was around. There were no voices, no talking, and no looking over his shoulder. Just the elevator ride up, the brass key in the door dead bolt and he was in; and then silence. Silence, which came with the clicking of the lock as the door closed behind him.

Letting his two pieces of leather luggage drop to the floor he made a quick tour from one room to the next in a second look-see at what he now owned. It looked better than he remembered. When he came to the massive master bedroom his feelings of freedom heightened as he looked at the expensive furnishings and the spacious floor plan that connected to a verandah. On an impulse he opened the outside French doors and instantly felt the fresh breeze rush in and bellow-out the sheer drapery panels.

Revolt, he thought. *Do something radical now; this instant. Kill the past and start the new. Go to the opposite end of the world. Do it. Let's make sure the break is clean. What would she find the most repulsive? Defy,* became his mind set as the panels bellowed up toward the ceiling and the coolness made him reflect on the moment.

Taking in a deep breath of the fresh outside air he expanded his chest until his lungs could hold no more and then released with a forceful exhale. *That breath,* he vowed, *was the last breath of the man I used to be and the first breath of the man I intend to become.*

Moving over to the foot of the king size bed he reached down and lightly felt the smoothness of the new quilted satin bedspread. Then as a measure of his revolt he flung himself backwards and landed in the middle of the bed, felt the bounce and lay there for a moment with his arms and legs outstretched spread-eagle. The satisfactions of that defying act lead him to scoot closer up to the headboard, his shoes then being completely on the bed. Reaching around his shoulder he pulled a pillow out from under the spread and bunched it up under his head. A moment of heaven came from the sensation of the privacy, the cool breeze, the quietness and the wide bed. Then, in the most ardent flaunting rebellious act he could think of he christened his new life.

With his eyes closed he reached down and unbuckled his belt, unbuttoned the top button of his trousers, unzipped the fly and squiggled his pants down below his pelvic. In a measure of contempt he had never known before, he reached down to his groin and took hold of his manhood. The sensation of doing it in broad daylight reconfirmed his newfound freedom and he squeezed it without any inhibitions. Foundling it with both hands he pulled, stretched and stroked it until it became erect. He had no need to open his eyes and look, he could feel it getting blistering hard, gored full of blood and standing straight up. As he fantasized about thrusting it into a receptive young vagina he savagely started masturbating. With tearing strokes he jammed his hand down again and again.

The pain of the dry tearing skin only heightened the pleasure; and as the pleasure heightened the intensity heightened until a torrent of semen exploded like a volcanic eruption, spewing whitish gobs of lava over his hand and belly. His years of suppressed sexual needs had finally been released and he instantly experienced a blissful feeling. With his hand of cupped semen resting on his mat of groin hair he relaxed and his love muscle started to go soft.

In the moments thereafter the semen that had ejaculated in thick consolidated gobs started to liquefy and he could feel it starting to ooze between his fingers onto his genitals.

As the next minute or two passed the liquefying process increased and the dripping sensation sparked an additional defiance to his deceased wife. Without opening his eyes he slid his hand off of his groin and let it fall on the bed, felt the shinny new bedspread and smiled as he wiped his hand dry. With his trousers unzipped and down, his flaccid muscle exposed and his shoes still on, he contentedly floated off to sleep.

Life had finally come to Aspen. At least in that moment in time, that had been his belief. It would later turn out that that belief would be grossly premature. Sooner than he had reason to expect he would discover that it takes more than a move to throw off the shackles of the past; especially when so much of the past would be a prominent part of his future.

The shackles to which he remained tied were rooted in a small town. Where he had grown up and married into the richest family in the community; a marriage that was opinioned by the community-elders that he was grossly beneath his wife.

In an attempt to rectify the situation the wife's family quickly made him a deacon in the ruling church. A new house was purchased in an acceptable neighborhood and his new father-in-law gave him a position as vice president in the family bank. These matters accomplished it was expected that the newly married couple would obediently settle into the community images and dictates.

By Aspens own analysis his life then became one of smiling nice, being married without screwing, controlling the masses with the threat of church damnation and stealing their savings at the bank.

His wife had been a strong willed, staunch puritan and her religious beliefs had completely dominated their lives. She was an overpowering advocate that pleasure was sinful and believed that sex should only be had for the conception of children. She steadfastly abstained from wearing makeup or jewelry and for their entire married life Aspen never saw her in the nude. They had borne no children and that had been the only real blessing of the marriage. As the years passed the wife's parents eventually died and she became the sole heir to the family fortune.

A manifestation that strengthen her level of dominance to tyrannical and when she died unexpectedly her dictatorial rule continued from the grave. Aspen did not get her money. He got the right to manage it.

Pursuant to the provisions of her Last Will and Testament her fortune was guarded by a pass-through arrangement. It would first pass to Aspen; '... in trust and under his exclusive control for so long as he shall live and thence to The Church of the Apostles'.

As is the normal course of such matters, there followed a legal battle between Aspen and the Church wherein the lawyers were the only winners. After lengthy and expensive proceedings an agreement was finally reached. Under the settlement terms, which the lawyers for both sides assured their respective clients was the best possible deal, Aspen would have full administrative and investment control over the estate. But, among other things, ...he must act at all times with prudence, exercise his best judgment in all investments, take whatever steps were necessary to preserve the estate and always exercise the highest degree of protection therein...

There was also a small subparagraph which gave Aspen the authority to move the funds ... from the existing banking facilities... if such move would be in the best interest of the fund...

The inclusion of that small subparagraph had materialized as the result of Church greed. In truth it was not anticipated that the estate would ever actually be moved from the bank of his deceased wife. Nevertheless, in the Churches' eyes the old guard would eventually pass. In the Elders' opinion the 'moving bank' provision in the settlement would serve as a deterrent to prevent a young guard from rebelling against Church control.

While Aspen had not revealed his feelings, he had been ecstatic with the provision. For the first time ever, he was able to secretly laugh at the self-serving interest of the Church. The closing negotiations between him and the church had been conducted in his lawyer's office. Crowded to capacity by power grabbing church officials, the suggestion about moving the funds had sparked an outbreak of conflicting opinions.

The ensuing arguing and shouting had inadvertently directed attention away from the document and in the confusion, the lawyers for the Church had neglected to put in one small provision.

There had been no stipulation as to where or how the funds could be moved; only that when in Aspen's judgment it would be in the best interest.

It was true that during the course of negotiations it had been mentioned that there was one particular bank on the other side of town that was always trying to get the account. Additionally, it may have even been implied that any movement of the funds would be to that one particular cross-town bank. However, implications are not a substitute for written specification.

The terms of the agreement went into binding agreement and the lack of specifics as to where the funds could be transferred went unnoticed. In the months following his wife's death, Aspen was overly diligent in his servitude to the Church. On Sundays he never missed early morning services and always strongly thanked the pastor for his personal condolences. He allowed himself to be patronized by his fellow deacons to be strong and returned the patronizing by fully agreeing that, "Yes it is certainly true that the Lord works in strange and mysterious ways".

In memory of his deceased wife he had a over sized mourning-reef hung on the front door of his residence with orders that it be changed ever three days. After appropriate time he returned to work but the Board of Directors had insisted on being exceedingly benevolent. Their collective opinion was that one of their vice presidents be given an extended period of mourning. With an eye toward public image, coupled with the reality of his deceased wife's estate being in Aspen's custody he was encouraged to get out of the office more; go to a park, sit and think, take all the time he needed.

That overly generous outpouring of benevolence made the Board of Directors feel good. It made Aspen feel good. The reason it made the

Board feel good was the confidence that Aspen would start to kneel. The reason it made Aspen feel good was the park that he went to was in Market Square; located in the center of Pittsburgh some three and a half hours drive away; where in fact he did think.

Thinking, not of kneeling but of reeling. He ask for and received an appointment with the president of the nearby First State Bank; a bank that very much liked his appearances, his banking credentials, and most of all the size of his trusteeship. He was wooed, wined, dined, and invited to joint their team. In a mutually satisfying arrangement, he would come on board as a Vice President.

His trusteeship would go on the bank's ledgers as baseline holding; which in turn would free up an equal amount of their funds. However at all times Aspen would retain sole control over management of the estate and all investments thereto. He would be provided a corner office on the top floor, secretarial services, and be accorded full VP privileges.

By Aspen's calculations the plan should work. The agreement with the Church had specifically said a transfer could be made to another bank. In that respect he felt safe in going to the First State Bank of Pittsburgh because it was fully chartered and subject to all Federal and State banking regulations.

With his secretive trips to Pittsburgh concluded Aspen's plan started moving in rapid succession. His first step was to cancel the standing order for the mourning reef. Next a For Sale sign appeared on the front lawn of his fashionable house. He continued reporting for work but his good morning greetings to his fellow bank employees were more reserved. He no longer lingered in the coffee room and was totally indifferent to the backlog of work on his desk.

Then one morning he came to the work earlier than usual, passed hurriedly through the empty lobby, went directly to his office and closed the door. When the clerical staff started arriving a little later they could hear the sound of desk drawers being opened and closed; followed by the static tearing of packing tape and packing boxes being stacked by the door.

Around mid-morning two men from Rapid Courier Company came through the bank front door pulling a loading dolly. Crossing the spacious lobby they went directly to Aspen's office and within fifteen minutes of their arrival all of his legal papers and personal effects were carted out and gone.

With briefcase in hand he closed his office door behind him and walked across the lobby. He had one more thing to do. He went to the Head Cashier and wrote out an Instrument of Demand for all moneys in his trust account totaling over $6,000,000.00 (Six Million) Dollars to be transferred in his name to the First State Bank of Pittsburgh. His move to Pittsburgh had been quick and uneventful. He simply packed a few personal things and left town. He had said no good-byes and had not looked back.

With the purchase of the penthouse and the settling into his new office, Aspen had expected an end to his life of being squeezed and smothered.

If faith would only go as planned. To his astonishment he had grossly underestimated the wrath of The Church of the Apostles. In the months thereafter the Church filed a blistering lawsuit. Charging, among other things, that Aspen's action constituted a breech of contract and asked the Court to set aside the transfer and ordered that the Trust be moved back to the Origin Base.

Aspen's defense attorneys argued that since the Negotiated Agreement did not stipulate where or when the trust could be transferred it was intended to be at the discretion of Aspen. The Church counter argued that the absence of a specific location of a transferring bank was an oversight; known to the Defendant Aspen and therefore a violation of good faith. Further, the Church argued that the move of the trust from its Origin Base violated the provision of the Negotiated Agreement wherein the Church had an implied right to monitor the safety of the investments and to audit the books.

After lengthy proceedings the Court handed down a decision wherein Aspen had been within his rights to move the trust. However the Court also ruled that Aspen was bound to show evidence that in all investments, he exercise a higher than ordinary degree of prudence.

It was that part of the judge's ruling that caused a knot materialized in Aspen's stomach. If at any time a case could be made that he was not exercising higher than ordinary prudence, there could be grounds by the Church to reopen the litigation and possibly force a move back to the bank of Origin Base.

The reason for Aspen's panic was an investment loan he had made before the court action was filed. A local Pittsburgh businessman, Clifford Acroe, had come to him for a short-term loan. Acroe was willing to pay 10% simple interest for a 60-day contract. The deal was to buy 6,000 head of prime Texas beef, transport them to the stockyards at Dodge City, Kansas, and sell them still on the hoof to the Army at wartime prices.

As collateral, Acroe had provided to Aspen an official Purchase Order signed by the Department of Defense that, upon delivery, guaranteed payment by the United States Government.

It was a cost-plus-contract and the plus equated 25%. On this basis Aspen felt secure in lending Clifford Acroe the sum of $360,000.00 (Three Hundred and Sixty Thousand Dollars). Now..., pursuant to the Court's ruling, that loan would have far reaching affects.

First and foremost, the personal freedom that Aspen had hoped for would be another while coming. The very first thing he had to do was to take whatever steps were necessary to prove that he was exercising prudence and diligence in protecting that loan.

Resultantly, the weeks immediately following the Court decision would be weeks unyielding. The next morning his first call was to Clifford Acroe only to learn that the deal had hit a devastating snag.

There was no rail transportation available to ship the cattle. Pursuant to provisions of the Federal Government's War Time Powers Act, all public transportation systems including air, rail and water, had been placed under Martial Law. All transportation space of whatever nature was allocated on a military priority basis. Troop shipments and war materials received top priority and all available transports were booked solid.

On learning this news Aspen felt a pot of hot molted lead in the center of his stomach. He had loaned out $360,000.00 and at that moment all he had was an apologetic borrower by the name of Clifford Acroe, a cattle rancher in West Texas whose name he did not know and 6,000 head of beef for which he had absolutely no chance of getting rail transportation.

Panic-stricken, he started looking for help. Closing himself inside of his office he started telephoning anyone who might be able to provide some assistance. He talked and re-talked with the Department of Defense, the Joint Chief of Staff, the United States Attorney General's Office and the Congressional Offices of Pittsburgh and Western Texas. For the next five days he feverishly explained and re-explained his dilemma and requested assistance; but to no avail. The military was having problems of its own; not the least being the matters of transportation.

At that very moment, a two star army general by the name of Waylin Hagg was personally overseeing a troop shipment from Grand Central Station in New York City on the east coast to Hunters Point Naval Ship Yards in San Francisco on the west coast. An event that eventually took a staggering fifty-two days under the most urgent wartime conditions.

It wasn't that beef for the Army was not a prime consideration. The Army desperately needed meat. But that did not change the circumstances. All transport resources were already choked to capacity.

In aspects other than transportation, the Government was anxious to be of full assistance to Aspen. So much so that the office of Joint Chief of Staff in Washington, D.C. insisted on assigning the matter to a liaison officer by the name of Captain Raymond Cornelio. Within his limits Captain Cornelio was to work with Aspen in securing whatever help was possible.

In the meantime Aspen had also made numerous calls to the cattle rancher, whose name he learned was Frank Delaney. Staying in touch by repetitive telephone calls, all three men (Aspen, Delaney and Cornelio) desperately tried to come up with some possible means of shipment. All attempts came up empty. No rail or truck transportation could be had. In the final analysis it boiled down to the fact that if the herd was to get to Dodge City it would have to walk. The same means by which cattle had been moved to market more than seventy years earlier; an overland cattle drive.

"A cattle drive," Aspen had said out loud. "IN THIS, THE YEAR OF OUR LORD, ONE THOUSAND NINE HUNDRED AND FORTY TWO AND NO/GOD DAMN SENSE, WITH ALL OF THIS COUNTRY'S TECHNOLOGY AND RAILROADS, HIGHWAYS, AIRPLANES, TRUCKS, BUSSES AND AUTOMOBILES; I GET TO MOVE CATTLE LIKE AN 1876 CATTLE DRIVE."

Frustrating as it was, payment had already been made. It was either move or lose. The onus was now completely his. Fanatically Aspen started trying to determine what all would be required. His time on the telephone continued but now the calls were mostly to Delaney. Stick by stick he started acquiring a rudimentary knowledge of the task ahead.

Taking each newly acquired bit of information and building, he moved ahead step by awkward step until he acquired a reasonable understanding of what would be involved.

He and rancher Delaney, talking over the telephone, each looking at identical maps, jointly laid out a tentative route. In broad, very broad parameters the drive would favor the least populated areas leading meanderingly from Texas to Kansas.

Starting in Van Horn heading generally northeasterly to Amarillo, turn slightly eastward for a short stretch and then back northeasterly and on into Dodge City. This meandering route was in effect the long side of a triangle and was broadly different from the old 'L' shaped Chisholm Trail of the 1800's; wherein cattle from Western Texas were first driven due east to Ft. Worth and then turned due north to Kansas.

With Delaney in Texas and Aspen in Pittsburgh connected by a humming telephone line the two men talked while each looked at their respective maps. Locating and marking landmarks here and explaining the drive rational there, a jagged line began to form. The initial leg of the drive would leave out of Van Horn and cross through the low, broken escarpments and sloping range country of the Apache Mountains for a distant of roughly 80 miles to the Pecos River; the first major watering hole and rest stop. Thence crossing the Pecos at a flood plain south of Oris the drive would continue on northeasterly roughly 15 to 20 miles, cross the state line into the southeast corner of New Mexico; and immediately face one of the most treacherous segments of the trip; the Malga Salt Flats.

The Malga leg would mean covering 60 miles of barren desolate sweltering crusty salt flats in a line-of-sight-travel toward an absolutely essential source of water at Comanche Wells; generally identifiable on the map as being slightly westerly of Eunice, New Mexico. After watering at Comanche Wells the drive would thence continue on northeasterly, crossing the New Mexico/Texas State Line and enter back into Texas at a point roughly 50 miles south of Plains.

From there the drive would head due north following the Texas side of the New Mexico/Texas State Line for a distance of roughly 150 miles. At a point north of Muleshoe, the drive would again swing northeast to a narrow passage between the southeast corner of Amarillo's produce truck farming community and the sharp escarpment headlands of Palo Duro Canyon.

Once at that point a difference kind of worry would start to materialize. Whereas in the early stages of the drive out of Western Texas, water or the scarcity of it would be a primary concern. Once into the Northern plain the possibility of too much water could become a serious problem. The spring rain runoff coming down from the higher elevations of northeastern New Mexico would be causing the water levels in all the drainage tributaries to start rising. Of major concern would be the crossing of Prairie Dog Town Fork Creek of the Red River.

Once past the water drainage confluence of Palo Duro Canyon the drive would continue northeasterly to Pampa and thence follow along and parallel to secondary State Road 70. With luck it wouldn't be necessary, but available if needed, the Highway 70 Bridge could be used to cross the Canadian River and thence continue directly on to Perryton.

At Perryton the drive would swing due north and head along the westerly side of North/South Highway 83 to the intersection of East/West U.S. 54. This would be a major highway crossing and all traffic would have to be stopped for an estimated six hours. Once across Highway 54 the drive would continue along the westerly side of Highway 83 north through open fields of spring wheat to the Cimarron River. At the Cimarron, there would be a second stopping of a major traffic artery. Law enforcement officials of whatever nature whether army, state of local would have to hold up traffic for another six or seven hours. The estimated time it would take to move 6,000 head of cattle, men and equipment upon the highway, guide over the bridge across the river and off on the other side. Once across the Cimarron it would then be straight drive over open wheat land for the last 50 miles into Dodge City. Delaney would provide all necessary riders, equipment, and supplies on a cost pass through basis. All of these matters were elements which Aspen and Delaney were able to put together.

But there was much more which would be necessary and that is where Captain Cornelio came in.

The first order of his business would be compliance with the quarantine laws in the four states of Texas, New Mexico, Oklahoma and Kansas. To that end Captain Cornelio swung into action and exercised his powerful authority under certain provisions of the WarTime Powers Act. To the degree necessary, he put top-level pressure on the top officials at the U.S. Department of Agriculture to immediately dispatch a crew of federal inspectors out to the TapRoot Ranch. Working around the clock if necessary each and every head of stock was to be run through a tick and disinfecting tank.

Next, Cornelio agreed that it would be in every one's best interest if Aspen personally went out to West Texas and took part in the actual drive. From Delaney's stand point, Aspen's presence as the lawful owner would go a long way in shouldering responsibility. From Aspen's standpoint taking part in the drive would serve as proof that he was exercising higher than ordinary prudence in protecting the loan.

On the highest of military priorities Cornelio put the pressure on the Air Force and made arrangements for Aspen to catch a Military Transport C-47 from Pittsburgh to Kelly Field outside of San Antonio, Texas. From there he would catch a second hop to an Army Air Corps Flight Training Field just outside of Midland, roughly 200 air miles to the west. From Midland, the situation was not as firm.

The Field Commander in Midland ran his base by the book and could not be bullied into a violation of military rules against carrying a civilian in a fighter plane; even if it was just a training flight. The Commander did say however that under certain circumstances, aircraft mechanics are authorized, and frequently do fly with the pilot for an in-flight mechanical evaluation of aircraft problems. Also it is was not uncommon that these small planes frequently had to make emergency landings on barren backcountry dirt roads in order to make repairs.

Finally, the Field Commander confirmed that he personally did not know all of the authorized aircraft mechanics at that training field. So if a mechanic did go up, he would assume he was authorized and had security clearance. And, the Commander further supposed, that if a civilian mechanic did go up with one of the young cadets, and if it became necessary to land, and if the mechanic did not see fit to reenter the plane, especially with an inexperience cadet, then he, the Field Commander assumed the civilian would take responsibility for his own well being and could not hold the Field Commander responsible.

Cornelio's next actions dealt in matters of Constitutional rights and law. The drive would be crossing over privately owned lands and there would be damages. While the Government could not be blocked from trespassing over whatever grounds it deemed necessary, the Government is legally bound to pay for any and all losses. To handle the matters of trespass and settlement of damages, three United States representatives would also join the drive. Two of these representatives would be Military Policemen dispatched from Ft. Bliss, Texas with the authority to exercise the appropriate provision of Marshal law.

Their orders were to ensure that the drive would not be hampered or held up for any reason; including their legal authority to stop and hold up traffic, permit the herd to move across or upon roads and bridges, to act in the name of the United States to halt and abate any confrontation and defend with arms if necessary the drive against all encroachments or impediments.

The third agent would be a U.S. Attorney, dispatched by the United States Department of Justice out of El Paso with War Time Authority to invoke whatever powers of Eminent Domain were necessary to acquire goods and services and to cross privately owned lands, with payments being authorized for and including damages to crops, destruction of top soil or roadways by hoof, cutting of fence lines, rights to water from whatever source including, riparian rights of streams, creeks, rivers and wells. Federal Tort Claim forms would be provided to all injured parties with on the spot assistance in filing a claim.

The intent of the Federal Government was clear; this cattle drive would go through. For that, Aspen was ever so thankful.

With all of the particulars exhaustively and tentatively worked out, there was only one thing left; the decision by Aspen as to whether to give it the finally go. In a tense three-way telephone conference call between Aspen, Delaney and Captain Cornelio, Cornelio put the question.

"Mr. McGee, it is now up to you. It has to be your decision. Is it a go or no go?" The time was 1:30 in the morning. Leaning forward over his desk Aspen's stomach was in a knot.

In the silence that followed he could hear the humming in the telephone line. His free hand wiped off the wetness on his brow. He was glad that the other two men could not see. Then surprised at the meekness of his own words he said, "I... I guess it's a go."

After he gave the decision and the three of them all exchanged concluding remarks, Aspen hung up the phone and sat for a long time. He felt weak from the strain and needed to grasp the magnitude of the decision he had just made.

He started looking back through the pages and pages of scribbled notes on his yellow legal pad and realized that he had to put them in some semblance of order. As exhausted as he was he would not let himself leave until he fashioned a list of the particulars that his banking eye could more easily understand.

Let's see, he started:

o date of drive	April 15, 1942
o cattle count	6,000 head
o distance of drive	630 miles
o miles per day	15
o days on the drive (estimated)	42
o number of riders (one rider per 300 head)	20
o Trail boss	1
o US Agents	3
o remuda (number of horses rotate per man)	192
o wranglers (remuda care takers)	2
o chuck wagons	2
o mules (4 per chuck wagon x 2)	8
o cooks	2
o food supplies: Beans	200 lbs
flour	600 lbs
salt pork	100 lbs
coffee	200 lbs
onions	50 lbs
potatoes	1,000 lbs
o condiments (salt,pepper,baking soda,lard, soap, matches, tobacco, etc.	100 lbs
o toilet paper	200 rolls
o water (gal's per day) men and stock	19,000

o Miscellaneous: ropes,rigging,bedrolls,guns, laterns,kerosene,axle grease,horseshoeing tools/supplies,first aid supplies,axes, wire cutters,utinsels,etc

The date was April 11th. The drive had to start no later than April 15th. This was calculated to be the best time for the cattle to graze on the new spring grass but any further delay would mean increased water run off; which would flood the rivers and arroyos to where crossing may not be possible. It was near 2:30 in the morning when he finally put on his jacket and with briefcase in hand started to leave his office.

At the door he turned out the light and then noticed the window drapes were still open. He went back and as he was pulling the draw cord he looked out over the lights of the silent city. He suddenly realized just how tired he was.

On an impulse he dropped his briefcase and sat back down in his swivel high back office chair. He pulled himself closer to the window and put his feet on the windowsill. For the first time he now had to face how awkward it was going to be for him to sit in a saddle for the next seven weeks. His riding experience was limited to training that he had received at equestrian school over 40 years ago. He did not even want to think of how saddle sore he was going to be. The quietness of the dark office with the city lights below caused him to have a flash back to the quietness he used to sense when he was alone inside the Apostle Church.

It was irony that he would sit in the silence of the empty church in order to think of a way of getting away from the church. And then he thought of his present circumstances. He thought of the responsibility of all those cattle, the men, horses and gear. Of the contract with the Army and the need of the beef to feed hungry troops. He thought of all the things that could go wrong. Quicksand and cattle drowning at river crossings. Losses to 'she' cattle dropping early calves. But those were not the worst.

Cattle are like any other creatures, man or beasts. They are comfortable in familiar surroundings. When removed from their home range they become fidgety.

Being subjected to days on end of prodding, goading and poking through choking blinding dust and going without water will incite their natural instincts to break and run. Tension will mount and the worst of all possible situations is a nighttime electrical storm; and for West Texas, springtime is the worst for lightning.

In his own moment of hopelessness Aspen murmured his own questioned, "How could all of this have happened? Lord what have I done that I have so offended thee".

Three days latter on April 14, on a lonely isolated barren dirt road roughly one hundred and fifty miles west to southwesterly of Midland, Texas, the first leg of the journey was completed. As the afternoon sun was descending low in the western sky, its color changing to a burning hue, the hum of a distant motor broke the silence of the Texas prairie. As the roar increased there could be seen on the eastern horizon a lone single engine airplane flying low over the unchanging terrain of mesquites bushes, creosote bush and rolling needle grass. A young cadet with a control stick in one hand and a terrain map in the other was worriedly looking over the side of the open cockpit; searching for identifying landmarks.

In the co-pilot's seat was a civilian who was also nervously looking over the side. Finally there appeared on the western horizon an intersecting point between a well-defined county line dirt road and a cut-off wagon trail. They both pointed in unison and nodded in agreement. The young cadet cautiously brought the AT-3 down to fifty feet and slowed the air speed. As they passed over the junction they could see a lone cowboy and two horses standing beneath a rustic timbered archway gate. From the open cockpit they waved and the cowboy acknowledged with a return wave of his hat.

As the plane went on past the pilot gently pulled back on the throttle stick, powered up and increased his altitude in preparation for landing. He made a wide circle and after carefully checking the road surface selected a landing stretch. He cautiously throttled down the engine and the aircraft slowly glided to a touchdown amid dirt, dust and chug holes. As they taxied past, Aspen caught a glimpse of the faded sign on the rustic gateway.

It read TapRoot Ranch. When the plane came to a stop the pilot turned and looked at Aspen.

There was an exchange of nodding as Aspen threw a flight bag over the side and jumped to the ground. With thumbs up sign the young cadet waved goodbye and taxied off. Aspen watched as he rose into the sky, circled and headed back into the eastern horizon.

The cowboy had mounted one of the horses and was trailing the other as he rode over. As he approached, Aspen was startled by his youth. He then received his first taste of West Texas with the young cowboy's greeting.

"Howdy, Partner. I sure hope your name be Mr. McGee. They call me Willie. Poppa Frank sent me to fetch you." Willie then turned to the empty horse.

"This here's your mount. Poppa didn't know how good you could ride so he thought for me to bring Palo." Aspen looked at the saddled horse and was startled by its beauty. It was a thoroughbred Palomino with long flowing white main and tail. A breed of horse generally used in show circles and for those who could afford them, usually ridden by women. His glance at the horse was broken as the cowboy continued.

"It's Momma Maude's mare. We call her Palo, short for Palomino. It's about twelve miles to the homestead, that's what we call the main house," Willie continued.

"Palo here's a pretty soft ride. I don't like her much myself. Too delicate. Every time I put a saddle on 'er I get the feeling something's gonna break.

"But it's a nice little lope going back. Little over an hour or so. Oh, and Poppa Frank said to be sure and say 'Welcome to the Tap Root Ranch'."

Here the storyteller experienced an unexpected feeling. He felt uncomfortable about his preconceived notion of bankers and love mistress. All the evidence pointed toward Aspen being an honorable man who stood fast against life's brutality and played out the hand that destiny had dealt him. In a mind flash he had a revelation; a *maybe* kind of revelation. *Maybe* he had been wrong. *Maybe* throughout his entire life he had focused on the wrong things. *Maybe* it wasn't what these players did so much as they really had no choice. Destiny had seen fit to cast each one with a certain role that intertwined with the dictates of the others. *Maybe* the wisdom that Shel...mother taught, wisdom never listened. Each in life must know who each is and each must know what each is supposed to be doing. What taketh it so long that I become me?

Chapter 13

With his eyes sheepishly half-opened that morning Morgan lay with one arm resting on his forehead and the other mindlessly doled on the empty side of his king size bed. The proclivity of his thoughts was that when a man opens his eyes in the morning he should have the softness of a woman to wake up to; but what he had was a half-empty bed. On this morning, like most mornings, he was lying in bed with an early morning sexual arousal; a semi stiffness that was more in need of a playful-snuggling-teasing partner than a mind exploding orgasm. He was thinking of Patricia.

But Patricia was not there and he knew it would be a long time before she would be there. *Maybe*, the thought crossed his mind, *I'll go see Jenny. Just one time wouldn't hurt anything.* The idea abruptly made him fully open his eyes. *NOPE*, he admonished himself. *That's not the way it works. I'll wait for Patricia. Surely I'm stronger than that. It's all so damn unnecessary*, his thoughts continued to swell. *Patricia over there and me over here. Everything I have ever wanted in a woman. And for what? What good is it doing me? Her mind has been so frigged up she may never come around. That bastard Owise*, he focused on someone to blame. *Maybe he didn't cause it all but he sure as to hell did more than his fair share.*

Nevertheless, he sought to calm himself, *at least now there is something. Before I didn't have anything. For the time being the only thing I can do is wait. If I can't do anything else I can stay busy. I'll make more damn money than I ever thought possible. If the day ever comes, those two people, Patricia and little Shelly are going to have everything they want.* In the mind of Morgan those were his wakening up thoughts.

A few blocks away in the mind of Jenny Craig there were different thoughts. Sitting at her kitchen table she was counting the money from her previous night's work. As she un-crumpled, segregated and stacked the receipts she assessed last night's wide range of sexual and emotional needs that had come to her door.

The stack of one dollar bills caused her to smile a matronly smile as she recalled the assortment of her many young Johns; those who were more than boys but not yet men. For some of these it had been their very first time; their demeanor being its own giveaway. Acting pretentious in hopes of conveying that it was all old hat, they would nervously undress, embarrassingly wait as she got in bed, then rush to get on top. In typical over anxious actions they would try to guide their own erection into her orifice and fumble away the moment. The simple electrifying thrill of an inexperience penis touching a moist vagina for the first time being sufficient to ignite an eruption. For these young Johns she hoped that their first experience with a woman had been a pleasant encounter and she wished them many happy returns.

However, where she felt an even greater gratification was in the husband category; especially the husbands to who time had brought lines to their face. She knew that most of the five's and all of the tens would have come from married men who daily shoulder the burdens of being a husband and a father. Men struggling at jobs of long hours and under pay; struggling with the demands of keeping a family housed, fed and clothed; struggling with medical bills, rent and utilities; bound by a strong sense of responsibility to family, church and country; and, a resolve to be a good man.

Given any single one of these husbands. Given any one set of responsibilities... it was not uncommon that he had to also live with a surging supply of seething hormones hanging heavy in his groin; the elements of worry, stress and exhaustion precluding the likelihood of his sexual craving being satisfied at home. The circumstances of such Johns confirmed to Jenny the very reason for her existence.

For most of them the price of her favors was a reluctant expenditure. Nevertheless, from their perspective, it bought more than an act of ejaculating an over supply of semen. It was a relief that helped them to continue facing the burdens of their duties and cares. To these hesitant

Johns she made sure their visits were rewarding; she did this because she knew how they felt. She had walked in their shoes.

When all of the one's, five's, and ten's were counted there remained two fifty-dollar bills; received from a time-withered lonely old man.

Money that his shaking hands had taken from a frayed snap coin purse, unfolded and awkwardly placed in her hand. Two crinkled pieces of cold impersonal paper which in his later years he had come to realize misrepresented the essence of life and which he now used with impunity to satisfy needs that a younger man would have no way of knowing or understanding.

She remembered how gratifying it had been to unhesitatingly surrender to his time honored years and to let him hold her with his stiff arthritic hands and feel her softness. Even now, this morning after, she could still sense his awkwardness as they lay in bed on the cool white sheets and she surrendered without resistance his need to gently pull her close. His frail arms squeezing her as if trying to mesh her youthful nude body inside of his. In full measure of compassion she became putty and let him put his nostrils to the top of her head and take in deep smells of her freshly washed velvet hair. As he nuzzled his sagging jowls about her face, neck and breast she conveyed her approval by stroking the back of his thinning silver hair. As they lay together in silence and his difficult breathing emitted small snorting sounds, she transmitted from herself to him all of her karma. And while the words were not spoken she knew that his memory had turned back the pages of his life and he lived for just a little while in earlier times. All in a night's work. All gratifying but with respect to total fulfillment, her own satisfaction was always lacking by one; Morgan.

Of all the men I held last night, she was thinking, *none of them were Morgan. Dear God how I could lov...* but her thoughts were interrupted by a knocking on the door. As she rose from the table she felt it would most likely be a young husband dropping by for a quickie before going on to work; a circumstance which she had rather not have because at that hour she did not look her best. With her hair askew, makeup faded and terry cloth robe wrinkled she turned the knob and as the door opened she let out a surprised gasp.

"Morgan!" she stammered. "What on earth. I mean I look a mess. Oh, I hate you for seeing me like...like this," she stepped back and motioned him in.

"Good morning gracious lady", he greeted her as he entered, removed his hat, and held it in the same hand with his cane.

"Baby," she pulled up to him with a hug. "This is just the sweetest thing. But why didn't you give me some warning? You're not being fair."

"Jenny, you look beautiful," he remarked as he returned her hug. "Maybe even more than beautiful; how about ravishing?"

"How about I not let you off the hook so easily," she defended as she hustled him toward an easy chair, took his hat and placed his feet on a hassock.

"Now! Mr. Mean Morgan," she said all in one breath as she whirled out to the kitchen and put on a pot of coffee. "You just make yourself comfortable and I will be right back. I have a major overhaul to do."

In the bedroom she rushed around in a state of goose pimples. *He's here. He's actually here. God I feel like I'm gonna pee my panties; cept I don't have any panties on. Oh please God I hope he's horny. I'll do anything. Just let it be that he came by for some loving. Pleeeease!*

As she hurriedly combed her hair and put on makeup she was thinking, *if I can get him in bed just one time I'm sure I can get him. Just once, pray pray pray.* The terry cloth robe she was wearing came off and dropped to the floor as she reached into the closet and retrieved a full length, expensive, special occasion, red satin robe. Taking one final look in the mirror, she gave her hair a last touch, pulled her boobs up high and thought, *OK Hon do your stuff. It's now or never.* She knew that the satin would cling tight against her firm round buns and show that she wasn't wearing any undies.

And it worked. As soon as she came back in, Morgan felt an instant arousal in his love muscle. With her hair pulled forward on one side slightly covering her eye and her perfume giving off a strong sexual scent she projected the image of being a forbidden woman. Which excited him. Which scared him. All of his life he had dreamed of a woman like her but in the back of his mind felt he could never have; a sex goddess that was somehow saintly. An instrument of heavenly sex that was created by some divine providence to service those men who were slated to be the most favored in life.

Those flashy, dashing, flamboyant men who were either extremely rich, extremely good-looking or extremely strong and therefore had first rights to screw the supreme choice of women. High society men in the upper class, bigger than life movie stars, famous athletes; but not him.

From somewhere out of his boyhood fantasies came embarrassing memories as to why these types of love queens existed. It was common knowledge among growing-up boys to be leery of such mythical supernatural goddesses. The sole purpose of these types of women, as everyone knew and talked on street corners and hangouts, was to dispense a level of sex that was profoundly superior to common women; and to touch it meant instant enslavement.

Once the fruit of these seductresses is sampled a man is hooked for life. His addiction to that immortal erotic artifice becomes his only reason for living. He becomes obsessed with the desire to screw that heavenly sent vagina to the end of the universe by slam banging his bristling manhood deeper and deeper into that sacred abyss. An uncontrollable craving takes over to get closer and closer to the very center of the opium pit. He pounds harder and harder. As he does those creamy white thighs start to spread wider and wider and that mesmerized passage gradually starts to open up bigger and bigger. As his slam-bang pounding continues his pelvic begins to sink in deeper and deeper; and it eventually gets to where only his upper chest and lower limbs remain sticking out. Then it happens.

A powerful vacuum that sucks him body and soul completely up inside that orifice moist cavern catches him. As the encompassing lips slam shut behind him he is spiraled across some supernatural metaphysical world to some forbidden queen's embellished throne room; to answer in her court. He falls from some twilight zone onto a polished marble floor in a dense fog. Then as the air gradually starts to clear she comes into view; the owner of that vagina. She is sitting on a golden throne with a scepter in her hand and a jeweled tiara on her head. Through the fog he can see her at the far end of the chambers on an ornate rostrum; lavishly decorated with maroon velvet lined walls. At her feet is a harem of male sex slaves. As he sees her, he sees that she is casting a stern look at him, her newest arrival.

Submissively he approaches and prostrates himself before her. If he proves to be worthy he will be permitted to become part of her harem...

"Hon, you just make yourself comfy and I'll be back in a minute", came the piercing words from Jenny that startled him back to the present. *Amazing*, he thought. *Simply amazing how much can flash through a man's mind in the split of a second.* As he watched Jenny out in the kitchen his sexual arousal softened. *Don't be tempted,* he told himself. *It will only bring you pain. If you reach for it, it won't happen. Even if it did it wouldn't be yours to own. At some point it would have to answer the call of its intended destiny. And to share with others; not to have the Garden of Eden unto thy self will hurt too damn much.* As she returned to the living room she had a cup and saucer in one hand and a pot of fresh brewed coffee in the other.

"I hope you drink yours black," she spoke in a purr as she started pouring. "Cause if you need cream we may have to improvise," she leaned over from the waist so that the top of her gown hung open and provided a close up view of her heavenly created mammary glands. His natural instincts bristled from the closeness to her exalted attributes and his hand slightly shook in taking the cup. For a splitting instant he felt sweat on his forehead and a flush of hate toward the forces of faith and the reminder of his twisted leg.

Why now? When I'm a damn cripple. Why not twenty years ago when maybe I could have handled her. Piss on you Faith. If you wouldn't give it to me then I'm not going to let you win now.

Her own coffee now in hand Jenny then settled in an adjacent easy chair and pretended innocence's as her slippery satin gown opened in front, parted across her knees and exposed the soft silky hair of her love triangle. Morgan looked and his vow against Faith instantly vanished. In a split second he saw her heaven. There it was. It was so close. Just to reach and touch. A lifetime of fantasies, always fantasies never expecting it to be more. Now at last there it was. He would do it. His mind raced with imagination of how it would be with him and her together in bed. Then, something unexpected happened. A clear and complete picture of his fantasy would not come into clear focus. He could visualize the two of them lying together under a clean white sheet.

He could even imagine how it would feel to softly caress her face, neck and to smell her soft hair. In his mind the image of her spreading her milk white unblemished legs and allowing him to pass through the golden-gate simply would not focus.

Jenny's own movements then did a strange thing. Pretending a touch of modesty she twisted in her chair and lightly flung her robe back over her crossed leg. Feeling embarrassed that she did so because he had been looking, a strange and unexpected sensation came over him. *It would hurt Patricia.*

In a sharp flash it seemed betrayal that he should even have been thinking such thoughts. Patricia did not have anyone but him. She was a lonely innocent woman standing alone without the abilities to battle the world. If he deserted her in favor of Jenny what would she do? Who could she turn too?

Jenny on the other hand did not need him; not to survive anyway. She was capable of standing against the world and taking whatever life threw against her. Between her legs must surely lay the supreme of all exultation. Personally bequeath by the heavenly Gods that mortals may have some inkling of heaven. For Morgan though he knew that heaven on earth could not be possessed. It could only sampled. Moreover, he would always be afraid of the moment when it would be taken away. Leaving him to come tumbling back down and hit the hard earth. It would be more pain than he could stand.

With Patricia, on the other hand, there were never any such thoughts or fear of consequences. His fantasies with her were always dressed in solid armor. He could easily picture her always standing slightly behind his protection; and he welcomed the opportunity to be her defender. With those firm reality thoughts he took a sip of coffee and as he lower his cup he commented.

"Jenny, I'm not sure why I came by this morning. You were just kind of on my mind. We haven't talked much for a while and I thought I'd run by for a look-see-chat." The unexpected nature of his words cut into her like a knife. Her response came with the realization that for her, love would not come this day.

"Things are going good Morgan," she concealed her pain. "Quite a few new things. I'm off the street now. I have also put on two new girls. One of them you know. Remember Detrick Simmons in Dr. Owise's office? Well I did as you suggested.

"I got an appointment with the Doctor and during the process Detrick and I did start talking.

"To make a long story short she is now working for me evenings and weekends. Now how about this, not only did I get Detrick but she brought a friend. Actually a super-doper friend would be more accurate. Her name is Donna.

"I call them the double D's and if you think Detrick looks young wait until you see Donna.

"She's actually twenty-one but honestly, she can be made up to look like a baby-doll; decked out in saddle oxford shoes, bobby socks, a mid-knee pleated skirt, hair in a pony tail.

"She can pass for thirteen; maybe even twelve. For the fun of it I've even thought of sending her down to the Stran sometime to see if she can get in on a half price ticket.

"Anyway the three of us are working out of here for now. We have thoughts of eventually getting a more prestigious place but that's just something in the future." As she paused for a sip of coffee, Morgan nodded in approval and then asked, "How about Ft. McCaffey? Any progress?"

"Oh Honey, progress! That's where I've been spending most of my daylight hours. As of this week the bus is ready to go; a real work of art. Velvet drapes all through the inside, including the windows and the mini berths. As a major attraction, two sparkling new toilets and a connecting vanity across the back.

"All new paint job. Base color baby blue to suggest wholesomeness and innocence, what else. In addition, something you in particular are going to love. Remember the design stationery that you had printed for the Benevolent Order of Youth for Christ? The biblical design with the sunrays shining down through towering white clouds?

"Well, Jim Barkus rounded up a friend who is very artistic and low and behold the very same golden rays of an early morning sun breaking through towering clouds are now painted on the sides and extend on to the back of the bus. Extra good stuff we've got going here."

"Jenny, you innocent looking little fart," he chose words which would accentuate his approval. "Aren't you something? I had no idea that you guys were doing such a bang up job.

"Absolutely great, that's just the type of thing I had in mind but never really expected to end up with. When do you anticipate your first run?"

Jenny pointed a finger to her with just a suggestion of cockiness and replied, "You are looking at a group that is ready to roll. There will be ten of us at first. In addition to Detrick and Donna I have seven other girls from the strip whom are willing to give it a trial run.

"This coming Friday as a matter of fact. Shooting for around noontime we will be leaving here with bells on and flags waving. Our thoughts are to arrive there early, cultivate some atmosphere and get the place ready for business. When those young recruits receive those liberty passes and start pouring out of the base gates we want to be right there to make sure they have the enjoyment of, quote 'wholesome girls'."

"You probably won't have too much setting up to do," Morgan tuned in. "I've been pretty much on top of my contractor over there and he tells me it is a done thing; juke box, paper lanterns, twisted crate paper stringers, polished dance floor, the whole works.

"Also," he continued, " the drinks, beer, cokes etc. everything you need is already in stock. Ol' man Corbin, he's the old fart that owns the place, is in for a little piece of the action. I think either he or his wife will be tending bar. The deal is he will be making his money from the monthly rent and a little pocket change for helping out. What's left over from the bar goes to Colonel Bates.

"You, me and the girls will be making ours from, well you know. Now, what I want to do Jenny is emphasize something. It's going to be your show all the way. Let's assume you own it, you run it. How you direct your girls to dress, act and behave is strictly your business but it would make me happy if I could give you a touch of my thoughts."

Jenny was overly anxious to assure Morgan that his suggestions were more than welcome as she responded, "Morgan, you know that you don't have to ask. Whatever you want is exactly what you will get. I have so much respect for your judgment; whatever you want is what I want. So fire away."

Morgan unhurriedly placed his cup and saucer on the coffee table and leaned back in his chair. For a transient moment he was searching in thought.

What he was about to say, he wanted to be sure that it was said with sincerity and that she would understand. He raised his eyes from gazing at the floor, slightly turned to where he was looking directly at her and began.

"Jenny I realize that we are in this to make money. That's all well and good, but that is not going to be the all-important, only reason. We have been over this before but I want to go over it again. There are certain things such as respect, dignity, grace, humility that I want us to use as our basis. Even in the sale of sex, or maybe I should say especially in the sale of sex, such qualities have a place.

"What I'm after is for you and the girls to recognize and understand what we are dealing with. Most of these young GIs will not be much over eighteen; a lot will be only fifteen and sixteen. Kids, just patriotic Goddamn kids. In order to get in the Army, they lie about their age and good ol' Uncle Sam doesn't ask a lot of questions. For most of 'em this is their first time away from home. After four short months of basic training they'll have a gun placed in their hands and get shipped out to fight in a war they know nothing about. Within a week from boot camp a lot of 'em will find themselves in the deadliest type of combat, in countries that they don't even know the name of. Some will not live a day. Others may be a little more lucky and only lose an arm or leg."

On that point Morgan paused, glanced down at his own leg and in a tormented tone said, "Though I'm not all that God damn sure just how much luckier.

"The point is," he continued, "a lot of these young men will be going into combat without ever having experienced the supreme pleasure of making love to a woman. That seems to me like our society and country is asking a little too damn much. In my mind I want to do what I can to level the playing field a little. Now, I know, and you know, that neither the law nor society will ever recognize prostitution with even the slightest degree of nobility. That aspect doesn't bother me one iota. We're not doing this for approval. What does matter is what we, meaning us, you, me everybody, how we feel. We've said it before. One way or another sex is going to be sold. If we don't someone else will.

"And, if it's the others, it will be done in a whole lot more damaging way. In fact that's exactly what's happening right now over in the skid row section of Jacksburg.

Let me relate the difference between them and us. In Jacksburg, GIs are getting knifed, mugged and robbed every night. When that ol' evening sun goes down at the end of each day the scabby ol' whores come out of the woodwork. With a nice dose of last night's unwashed semen dried between their legs and a cigarette hanging out of their mouth they parade along the sidewalks and hang out in doorways.

"Usually they are working for a pimp who pays off the local sheriff. In addition, every last one of them is sleazy, dirty, and diseased. In their mind that's all they have to be; flesh predators with wartime rights to belittle and badger young GIs into a quick hump.

"Without the slightest bit of compassion or understanding, they take the position that it is their job to intimidate young troopers, get their money and get them to hell back out on the street in the shortest time possible. Some of the whorehouses over there rush our young men through like cattle and even brag about how they can milk the semen out of so many men in an hour."

Morgan slightly shook his head to emphasize disgust. "Jenny, I want our operation to be on the opposite end of that spectrum. Your girls are to treat each of these young recruits as if he was their date for a high school prom. I know there has to be time limits, but I don't want that much of a limit. And above all, hear me on this, if you get a case where the young hero is obviously scared, feels completely alone and trying not to cry, that young man receives all the time and comfort you can provide.

"I don't care about the money. Just tell me how much you lost and I will personally make it up. If he needs a mother then be a mother. If he wants a high school sweetheart then match him up with someone who can convince him she will wait for his return.

"Jenny, no man should have to go into battle without a love waiting for him back home. If he wants a picture of her then he gets a picture. If he wants to write then he gets her address. Moreover, she is to answer. The need to feel loved is infinitely more important and will be infinitely remembered long after the pleasure of the insertion and the orgasm is forgotten."

Jenny watched as Morgan was talking and each of the things he said made her want to be more and more like him. Her thoughts of wanting to seduce him suddenly made her feel small. He had once said that character was the most precious commodity a person can own. To have it, stand by it and have nothing to do with people who put no value on it.

Now she was starting to understand his words and felt a glowing sensation at the thought of being a stand-in mother. She impulsively wanted to leave immediately and go see her kids.

"Now..." his emphasis brought her attention back, "what to wear? I have in mind that some of you dress exactly like the girl next door. Saddle Oxford shoes, white anklet socks, pleated mid-knee skirt, and ponytails. One corner of the club has been set up like a neighborhood soda fountain and you can take it from there. The picture we're reaching for is an old fashion booth, one soda with two straws.

"Also one other thing. Just in case the situation should arise, buy some of those little white bonnets that the Amish and Mennonite women wear. Maybe a couple of floor length gingham cotton dresses, etc. You know what to get. Understand where I am coming from on this. A certain number of these boys will have been brought up in very religious homes. I know that the Amish people do not believe in taking up arms but still, some of their young men are going against the elders and are joining up.

"It's a very touchy situation. If any of 'em happen to come to you it will most likely be their first experience. If you can, make the match with girls of their own image. No doubt they'll still have some guilt feeling when it's over. I just want it to be as soft as possible.

"When these poor little bastards are lying in a cold wet fox hole, in some foreign land, fighting a war they know nothing about, they are going to be lonely, lonely, lonely. Some of them will even break down and cry. Now there is not much we can do about all that. But if we give them a pleasant experience, we may be able to provide some of them with some memories which may help them along the way." Satisfied that Jenny understood his thoughts, Morgan then moved to other matters.

"Also I will probably see Jim Barkus before you do. He is going to be your driver and general overall protector. I would like for him to wear some sort of uniform.

"Maybe something in light gray trousers with blue strips running down the legs. In addition, make sure he has a matching bus driver's cap. Also, while you are out shopping, stop by the Quick Money PawnShop over on Ninth Street and pick up some sort of authoritative, law enforcement looking badge to pin on his shirt pocket.

"Lastly, I will give Jim an envelope for Colonel Bates. Before you do anything else make sure that the Colonel gets this donation. Above all else, it is not to go to anyone but the Colonel and it's not to be seen by anyone but him.

"Now," he emphasized a change of subject. "Now let's caught up on you. What's been going on? I hear you have a new boy friend." Jenny lifted her eyebrows and looked at Morgan in amazement.

"Morgan! If you're not something. How on? I mean, in this town news travels fast, that's all I can say. Is there nothing on the street that you don't know?"

Morgan smiled and reciprocated, "Don't be that way Jenny. My trouble is I like to gossip too damn much. It will probably be my damn downfall. The secret to gossip is to patronize your local newspaper stand. Best source of news in town. All for the price of a newspaper and a couple of bucks tip ever now and then."

Jenny shook her head in admission and commented, "I should have known you would know. I don't suppose anyone could do so much as even break wind on the streets of Pittsburgh without you knowing about it."

She then leaned back in her chair, cradled her coffee cup with both hands, and massaged it while she was thinking of how to answer. She wanted Morgan to know that she had found somebody but that he was not necessarily that somebody.

"Yes, I have found someone. I don't know if found is really the right word. We did meet. I do enjoy him and he seems to enjoy me. He's a mature man. His face has some lines but age makes no difference. He's a banker, a widower, no children. We enjoy making love but that's different from being in love. We have been going out to dinner and we talk a lot or I should say he talks more than I do but I enjoy listening.

"He married money, his wife or I guess I should say his deceased wife was an only child. Her family accumulated their wealth in coal mining. From what he tells me she was very religious. She never wore any make up and Aspen, that's his name Aspen, never saw her nude.

"Most of their married life was dominated by their church. My image is that it is some independent sect that seems to be prominent in rural Pennsylvania.

"Anyway after she died he wanted to get away, to start a new life so he came to Pittsburgh. And that seems to be just about it." Her ending statement indicating that she when she talked with Morgan she wanted to talk about something beside another man.

"Now," she concluded, "tell me what you have been up to. I hear you are getting to be Mr. Big Time in the theater business; two new ones on your list? And what about your lawyer friend Frank Buckwilder; have you seen him lately?" Jenny hoped that Morgan would not detect that she was asking a series of questions so that it would be a natural flow for her to ask one last question; when the timing was right she wanted to know about Patricia.

"As a matter of fact I have seen Frank recently. He helped me transfer title and handled the legal work on the two theaters."

"Well," Jenny complimented the conversation, "if you're in need of a lawyer I'd say that he's the one. I hear there are none better."

It was intended only as small talk but resulted in a spark of a different nature; a totally unexpected transition.

Their conversation came to a silent pause, a detected chemistry of awkwardness, and then a caution flag. For Jenny, there was a fright that she had unknowingly somehow touched a social discord. For Morgan it was embarrassing because he was just about to request a favor from Jenny. Awkwardly, her mention of grace and the name of Frank Buckwilder in the same breath collided head on with what he was about to ask.

"At the moment," he paused, "it's not a lawyer I need. Right now I'm in need of a different kind of favor." Relieved that there was no fault on her part, Jenny was quick to offer.

"Of course, Morgan. If there's anything that I can do, you know that's a standing offer."

He did not ask for the favor immediately. He first wanted her to know the sincerity of his need.

"It's extremely important to me Jenny. Normally it's something I would not think of asking. However, there is a hate inside of me that I can't control. No, that isn't truthful. The truth is I don't want to control it. I want that hate to grow and built up a little more each day.

"It pertains to Patricia and Shelly and how they have been wronged by Owise. I just don't think that I can ever let it slide. Someday I am going to even up the score and when I do I want the revenge to be as vile as possible." There was flush in Morgan's face as he finished and Jenny noticed the anxiety carried through to the clenched knuckles holding his cane.

"Morgan," she said very delicately, "Honey, what on earth? If I can, you know I will."

He swallowed at his loss of composure and then proceeded. "OK Jenny, it's important enough for me to ask. But if you feel like you can't or prefer not to, I will understand."

"Morgan, please!"

"Jenny, you mention something about your new girl, Donna. You say that she looks very young?"

"Unbelievable," answered Jenny.

"But she is of age? You're absolutely certain about that? There can be no mistake?" Jenny was pleased that she could be so positive. "I am sure, Baby. On that matter there is no mistake. I have a trade-favors-friend on the Pittsburgh PD. In exchange for my favors, he does me little favors. Little Donna already has a rap sheet. Not a long one but never the less a rap sheet. Prostitution mostly. On the street. About three years now."

A small relief smile came to Morgan. "Well well well, begging your pardon Mad'dam at my underestimating," his composure returning. Next question. You say she can be dressed up to look young?"

"No," answered Jenny. "What I said is that she already looks young; like a girl in her early teens. If you have in mind something younger, the answer is still yes. With a clean scrubbed face, no makeup, her long hair braided in side braids, tied with a bow, white short-sleeve school blouse, short little pleated skirt, white anklet socks and black patent leather shoes she would pass for preteen." At this point there was heightened attention in Morgan and unmindfully he was watching her eye to eye.

"And Detrick. Do you think you could persuade her to also dress up in girl clothes? Say the same type of short pleated skirt, anklet socks etc."

Hearing the question, Jenny reached out and took Morgan's one free hand in both of hers and pulled the two of them a little closer together. With a mimicking flirt on her brow and a slight disbelieving look in her eye she laughed a smiling little laugh.

"Why, Morgan," she purred, "aren't we full of surprises. Sweetheart, for you, you get the works. In addition, the pleasure will be all ours. The pinnacle of every young woman's dreams is to dress in bobby socks, wear a short skirt with no panties and play innocent." He felt an embarrassment at Jenny's implication but his mind was of a much more serious nature.

"Uh, that's fine Jenny. Appreciate the enthusiasm. However, this little scenario is not for me. This time it's all about someone else. What I have in mind is engaging in a little pornography picture taking".

As he finished, Morgan paused; waiting for her reaction; which didn't happen. Jenny's facial expression remained unchanged; as if waiting for him to continue with his request. At the lack of her comment, he felt the onus to go ahead and fill in.

"Is this something you can or would be willing to do?" he asked in an uncertain tone.

She in turn, seemed surprised at the limited request, and answered matter-of-factly. "Of course," she replied. "It's done every day." Then to reinforce her point she commented. "May I make mention of the staggering amount of wealth and money there is in this town."

Assuming his concerns were now calmed, she proceeded to the point. "Who do you want it done with and when?" He was amazed at her tone of insignificance. However, this was not his world and it was not appropriate to show his astonishment. He gave Jenny the name of Dr. Daniel Owise. He requested explicit poses. Good lighting, top quality facial shots of Owise in close-up sexual act, preferably oral sex, with two apparent under age girls.

His embarrassing request out of the way he wanted to immediately escape to the freedom of outside air. Shifting his body as an indication it was time to go he put on his fedora hat, rose from his chair and headed to the door.

Jenny, however, felt incomplete. She hungered for his attention, no matter how little, so she quickly revived their earlier conversation.

"You never did tell me," she spoke in a way that she hoped would encourage him to relax and perhaps stay for a while longer, "how is Frank Buckwilder doing?"

At that question Morgan paused, because it really was a welcome change of subject and he took a deep breath to heighten the relief. Then, in a tone that reflected melancholy he responded.

"I am not sure how Frank is doing. When we are together he is always exceptionally cordial and pleasant. However, as good a friends as we are, I never get the feeling that I really know him. He drinks a little more than I would like but I suppose we all do that. In addition, I do wish he would get out more.

"He's addicted to classical music and it goes in spells. At times he shuts himself in, drinks and listens to Mozart, Wagner, Strauss, whatever. He's also a devotee of the ballet and opera but right now there's only a limited amount of that in Pittsburgh. I sometimes think that Frank only really lives when he is off in his fantasy world of the arts. The rest of the time, who knows?"

At this point Morgan was feeling more comfortable about lingering for a while longer. He stepped slightly back from the door, shifted his weight to his good leg and, and as Jenny had hoped, he opened up. "Do you know which two theaters I purchased?" he asked.

"I think you mentioned, Morgan. One is the Palace over in Oakland and the other is the Underground on Sixth Street." Here Jenny paused slightly for effect. "Morgan," she went on to complete her response, "the Palace I can understand, but somehow I can't envision you in the live stage business."

"Damn if I can either Jenny but it's too late now. I've got it." Feeling that the visit was now going to be unmistakably over Jenny rushed in and asked the question she did not get to ask earlier.

"How are things with Patricia? How's she and the baby doing. Have you seen them lately?" She hoped that he wouldn't detect the series of questions that in fact were searching for any hint of love or no-love.

"As a matter of fact I was with her yesterday; just for a walk. We went down to Market Square and had some ice cream. I've talked her into going to work for me in the ticket cage.

"I'm hoping it will help. In truth she's not doing much better. She just refuses to come out of her shell. When I leave here I am going over to the Palace in Oakland and talk to the staff over there. They are all staying on, and there's a person over there I think will be good to train her. I hope it works out. She's lonely and if I'm truthful Jenny, I'm no less lonely."

By then they had edged out through the front door. He again put on his hat, adjusted the brim, and was turning to leave as she responded.

"Morgan, I," she fought to keep her emotions from showing. "Morgan," she purred with a flirting eye and a squeeze of his hand, "Let's hope the love you are searching for is closer than you think."

In silence, the storyteller took a deep breath. In flash points that were without beginning or end he traced his mind. In every story, truth, or fiction, there has to be a hero. Mothe...he was about to use the word mother but then changed to Shelly, Shelly his mind traced, who so influenced you that you so influenced me. All of this can't possible be just added up collectively... at least I don't think it can be collectively. There had to be a hero. That one single individual more than anyone else who fired and tempered your strength or; for that matter the villain who more than anyone else was responsible for your anti social... no wait, let's be blunt, your anti-social ways? Hell, let's say both.

It's possible that it could have been Owise but not to the full extent. There must be others? Now there's more; Morgan's two new theaters. What's the reason? In solitude the storyteller set with a fixed gaze out the icy covered window; impervious to the howling, blowing snow and wondered.

Chapter 14

When Morgan Smithfield purchased the Underground Theater he did so for reasons other than the prospects of making money. At the time, what he really wanted was the image and status of owning another one of Pittsburgh's famous landmarks. He was successful in his bidding; but for much more than he wanted to pay. In later times he would comment, "That little bit of fantasy flaunting cost me a lot of mega bucks."

When he first became interested in acquiring the Underground he figured he ought to be able to buy it for what it really was; a basement in a downtown retail building. The problem was that the owner wanted to sell it for what it really was; a theatrical name. Morgan had not been much interested in hearing the seller's pitch when they talked in terms of a going concern; that accounting principle of measuring value which holds that the worth of a property can be greater than the replacement cost.

In Morgan's thinking value should only relates to the cost of buying the nuts and bolts, sticks and stones and whatever else. The idea that something you can't see can have a cash value was, in his mind, a scheme concocted by accountants. A sham designed to intimidate those less skilled in the principles of crunching numbers. In the end he ended up paying most of their asking price because he wanted the property. However, that did not mean that he agreed with their pitch. To prove that he was right and theirs was nothing more than fluff he decided to make an on-the-back-of-an-envelope appraisal of what he had bought. His first step was to call an inventory meeting, to use newly acquired phraseology, of all the personnel connected with the theatrical operations. Meaning a gathering of stagehands, set designers, lighting and sound technicians, costume designers, actors, actresses and director.

He was unaware, but neither was he surprised, that collectively they all worked other jobs.

He had a vague image that theatrical people spent most of their non-performing day time hours in haphazard rehearsal throwing would-be temper tantrums and arguing about everything from stage conditions to interpretation of plots.

He further imaged that they spent their after-hours gathered in sleazy all night coffee-houses chain smoking cigarettes, flaunting conventionalism by wearing baggy unwashed wrinkled smelly clothes and all talking at the same time. Their general nature, in so far as he could tell, was to howl out woes of being misunderstood; which in their own minds justified their not being able to make it in the real world. That was what Morgan thought. That is what he did not care to become involved.

That which he did generally know was that the Underground was currently enjoying a flurry of popularity. A circumstance brought on, not so much from the particular type or nature of play productions, but from a twist in actor gender. The era being wartime conditions the military was getting first call on all of the country's young men. The pool of male actors in the Pittsburgh general area as well as elsewhere had dried up. To compensate for the shortage, women started acting in masculine roles. Unexpectedly, the depiction of women, especially younger women with large protruding breast, dressed in a men's clothing with theatrical facial hair and presumably male genitals sparked a wave of Underground sexual mystique. Overnight the Underground had become a trendy place that legitimized inquiring interest in sexual variations.

This was part of what Morgan had bought and that was fine with him. However, as the new owner of the Underground, he also inherited the reigning stage director Sidney Griffin; an unlikable individual who exemplified the sexual gradation being portrayed. At the young age of twenty-six, Sidney was the youngest person ever to be at the helm. He had held the position for six years and viewed the current popularity, reputation and vogue of the theater as being built in his own image.

Arrogant, temperamental, and obnoxious he considered the whole of the outside world subservient to the stage. He was contemptuous of anyone who placed monetary worth ahead of art and openly ridiculed the masses for their cumulative lack of sensitivity, sub-ordinate intellect and misplaced values. He detested Morgan before the two even met. It infuriates him that a common off-the-street neophyte with no other qualifications than deep pockets could just buy-in and become a paid up member.

If, as he unhesitatingly and profusely ranted, this new owner, Morgan something or another, wanted to really be a part of the theatrical world let him put funds in the hands of someone who knew how they could best be used; in short, contributions.

The greater the contribution the greater the proof of support. After that, the next matter would be a clear understanding of exactly who is, and who would remain, in charge. It immensely pleased Sidney Griffin to banish and exercise the power that went with being director; the final authority, the receptor of brown nosing and the caster of faiths. In his mind he intended to tell this new owner that he would not stand for his position being challenged. He would at all cost stand against art injustice. The unmitigated gall of it all that a house of drama could be passed around as if it was a discard. A hand-me down. From one pompous money lord to an equally repulsive near-do-well.

There was little doubt in Sidney's mind of his duty and responsibility to properly indoctrinate this new Morgan. As the Underground's new owner he instantly inherited a strong civic responsibility to align himself with and become a mentor of the thespian world. As a new bought-in member he was now obliged and responsible for promoting the arts and defending the propensity of actors and actresses.

As a starter kit Sidney had come to the meeting with a list of demands. Among the things that he wanted immediately were new lighting fixtures, new sound system, a new stage curtain and more money for props. All of which underscored Sidney's general position. And the first meeting between Morgan and Sidney chiseled in stone the forecast of things to come.

The very first thing that Morgan disliked about Sidney was his long cigarette holder. The second thing that he did not like was the apparent effort it took for Sidney to exhale; meaning the way he tilted his head back and blew smoke straight up in the air. And the third thing that Morgan did not like was the spurious manner in which Sidney attempted to take charge. Even before the meeting had fully got underway Sidney had started introducing the staff. And each introduction came with a curt insinuation that if Morgan had any social position at all in the community he would already recognize each of the actors and actresses; "... and of course allow me to introduce Miss Lillian Forthchild... certainly an introduction shouldn't really be necessary but assuming that you are not familiar with her many talents..."

The meeting was relatively short. Morgan spoke briefly with each individual and collectively expressed his appreciation for his or her efforts. In turn, so that they might get some feel of what to expect, he related that no major changes were planned. For the time being, he further related, his primary interest was that the Playhouse carry its self. As long as they were not loosing money but in fact were making at least some sort of a profit there probably wouldn't be too much interference on his part. With formalities concluded, Morgan dismissed everyone but asked that Sidney not leave. There was now the matter of establishing who was going to be the lead dog in the operation.

As the last of the technicians and cast went out the front door the animosity between the two instantly electrified. A silence set in and neither was willing to be the first to speak; but each prepared to face the other. Their movements echoed in the early morning quietness as Morgan casually took a seat in the front row, stretched out his twisted leg and adjusted his trousers. Sidney remained on his feet and profiled by pacing back and forth in the proscenium; the general open space between the front row seats and the stage. In the moments of testing, Morgan casually glanced around. When World War I was being fought in 1918 the Underground was already in existence. It was old, it was crude, it was ax cut rough hued interior; all of which gave it character and all of which made it the in-place in Pittsburgh to be seen.

With respect to its functional efficiency it was either too long for its width or too narrow for its length. There was only one possible floor plan; a single raked isle down the center with seats on each side. In addition, being a basement meant that it was always plagued with moisture and mildew. When it was filled to capacity there wasn't much of a noticeable odor but when it was empty it had an overpowering musty smell. The seats were spring equipped flip-up, upholstered with aged coarse red corduroy, now stained and threadbare. The lighting was circa late 1800's gaslights converted to electrical, hanging by extensions rods from the exposed crossbeams. The stage, steps and banisters were all wood construction; stained dark pine. The wall coverings were faded water stained murals of a classic Shakespearean Theater depicting 1600's royalty sitting in box seats. There was no band pit but there was a balcony; of sorts.

When the theater was first constructed a floating platform hung from the ceiling by iron extension bars. Situated about one third of the way back from the stage, a twelve by twenty deck had been installed as a lighting rostrum. Somewhere through the years it had been modified by the addition of a parapet wall and installing two rows of seats. Access was limited to a circular cast iron stair step and because of the inherent awkwardness it was seldom used for seating.

As Morgan casually glanced upward at the non-descript balcony he could not have known the monumental consequences that it would play in his not too distant future. As his attention drifted back down to floor level he started looking more closely at Sidney and noted his full head of dirty blond hair; oiled and slicked backed on the sides and cut to a ducktail in back. Its apparent social defiance made Morgan decide he had reached the end of his tolerance and he started to talk.

"Sidney," he commenced with a carefully picked tone, "I asked you to remain because I thought we should get to know a little bit about each other. Maybe you could start by telling me a little about your background; how you got started in show business, that sort of thing."

Blood vessels flexed in Sidney's face as he responded. "First of all, Mr. Smithfield, it is not show business as you so misguidedly refer too, but PERFORMING ARTS. And the way I got into the performing arts is by training as a ballet dancer from the time I was eight years old."

Morgan allowed his self a little indifferent smile as he responded, "You don't like me very much do you Sidney?"

Sidney was not expecting such an opening but he was thankful to be getting to the exact point. And to emphasize his contempt he answered Morgan's question with a question.

"How about you telling me, about Yourself, Mr. Smithfield. I am sure you must be a patron of the theater. But, it's just that I have never seen you at any of the social functions which are held by the Pittsburgh Conservancy for the Performing Arts." Without waiting for a response he continued.

"VERY much *the* in social, you know, formal attire, black tails and tie. Perhaps you have heard of some of our members; Carnegie, Mellons, Moorhead, Kaufmanns, you know the usual of Pittsburgh's elite." As Morgan watched the theatrics in Sidney's speech he wanted to laugh; but instead cast a puzzled look.

"Tell me Sidney, I can call you Sidney? Good. Tell me Sidney, how old are you. Around twenty-five or twenty-six I would guess. Is that about right?"

"Twenty six," snapped Sidney, "but what, may I ask, does that have to do with matters. Are you questioning my ability to manage this theater? May I remind...."

"Oh good heavens no, Sidney. Why I wouldn't question anything such as that. What I am wondering, and that's all it is you understand; just wondering. What I am wondering Sidney is why you are not in the army.

"In case you may have been away Sidney, this country had gotten itself involved in another little scrap. They seem to be calling this one World War II and I was just curious, how is it that you are here in Pittsburgh instead of the South Pacific fighting Japs."

"Uh Huh" responded unfazed Sidney. "Well you were correct in your first basic assumption Mr. Smithfield, I do not like you. Secondly, my not being in the military is my own personal business. And thirdly, if we are going to be working together, as apparently we must, then I ask that you not pry into my private life."

"But that's just the point," Morgan responded in a mocked tone of surprise at being misunderstood. "Here you are, asking me to lay out a great deal of money for all these proposed renovations. Now before I proceed with all of these changes I need to know that you and your enormous talent will remain on here. Why, you say in your own words that without you the Underground would fold in a week. Now I don't want to appear overly cautious but I am sure you understand. I mean are you scheduled to be drafted next week, do you have a deferment, political clout, what...?"

Sidney was not expecting this twist in their dialogue and was taken in by Morgan's apparent concern. The possibility that he had jumped to the wrong conclusions raced through his mind and he feared he might have jeopardized his chances of getting his requests.

In an attempt to amend the situation he instantly changed his demeanor. Exercising his acting experience he mimicked a surprised pause. Then in a tone that implied recognition of his mistake Sidney spoke in confidentiality.

"Mr. Smithfield," he said meekly, "I am not in the military because I am a different type of man."

It was difficult for Morgan not to smile. But instead he forced a questioned look and in a tone of concern he asked, "How do you mean that, Sidney. Surely it can't be that bad. You strike me as the finest kind of red blooded, all American, patriotic young man who would like nothing better than to serve his country."

At that point Sidney placed one hand under his chin, supported at the elbow with the other, and in implied feminine trait spoke.

"Mr. Smithfield, I think you know why I am not in the military."

Morgan felt a slight pleasure at being able to push the issue.

"Know what?" he responded as he pushed Sidney to come out with it.

"All right," rebutted Sidney with a slight huff, "if you insist, I'll say it. I'm homosexual. And certainly you are aware," he continued his huff, "that homosexuals are not allowed in the military."

A silence followed Sidney's admission. Morgan had established who would be working for whom and there was nothing more to be gained by furthering the issue. He respected that some people can have different sexual preference. In his own moral code, he considered the worth of a person based on their character and deeds and not with whom or how they engaged in sex. As the silence returned there manifested an unspoken acknowledgment that the meeting was over.

In preparation for his departure Morgan rose to his feet and braced on his cane. Methodically he put on his hat and adjusted the brim. As he turned to leave the two men made brief eye contact. Morgan slightly nodded and, aware that Sidney would be watching, raised his chest and widened his shoulders. With a solid commanding walk that left no question as to who would be in charge, he proceeded up the long racked isle and out the front door.

After the initial gathering Morgan did not give the Underground a great deal of attention. Intermittently he would drop by just to make his presence known. All in all he was satisfied. Revenue was above expectations and he was content with the status quo. With respect to Sidney's professed homosexuality there had been only one minor incident.

Roughly three months afterwards, a Federal Agent whose name was William Blate paid Morgan a visit. It had been mid-afternoon and Morgan was in his office at the Stran. Agent Blate had appeared and showed Morgan his identification. With formalities of apologies for the interruption, Blate advised that his purpose of business pertained to the matter of investigating one Sidney C. Griffin in the issue of his homosexuality. In strict formality the interview followed the lines of impersonal investigative procedures as Agent Blate explained.

"What we are trying to establish is whether Sidney C. Griffin is in fact a practicing homosexual to the exclusion of all other sexual practices." No mention was made or suggested that the claim may be a ploy as a way of dodging the draft. Morgan followed the strict code by asking and responding only to relevant matters.

"What," he asked, "might be some of the factors which would determine whether Sidney, or anyone for that matter, is, or is not a true, if I can use that word, homosexual?"

"One of the criteria which we use," responded Blate, "is whether the man in question has sexual relations with women. If it is known, or can be shown that the man in question engages in heterosexual relations, then it is assumed by the Government that he knowingly and deliberately is falsifying his status and would therefore be arrested and bound over for trial."

"What," Morgan asked, "is the penalty for such a conviction?"

"The United State Code is very explicit on this matter. In war time conditions the crime is a felony and is punishable by twenty years incarceration in a Federal Penitentiary."

Assuming nothing and implying nothing, Morgan then asked, "Am I, as a private citizen, bound by force of law to come forth with such information if it becomes known to me?"

A silence followed the question and Blate paused slightly before giving his answer. "Mr. Smithfield the very essence of why this country is engaged in this horrible war is the issue of freedom."

"Freedom for us as citizens, to unify and steadfastly vow that we as a Nation will never become subservient to an oppressive government; foreign or domestic.

"We're so adamant about our freedom that we are asking the flower of our young men to give their lives..."

Blate suddenly realized that he was getting too emotional and change his tone.

"No, Mr. Smithfield, neither you nor anyone else is required under penalty of law to come forth and disclose criminal acts. The exceptions of course are those among us who for various reasons are bound by sworn oath to uphold and enforce the law. I am held accountable by such an oath. If it comes to my attention, by whatever means, that law in which I am sworn to uphold is in violate then I am bound to come forward. However, you, Mr. Smithfield are under no such bound.

"The best the government can do is to appeal to your sense of patriotic duty. We ask that you help us to help you.

"This," Blate paused for emphasis, "is my country as well as yours. No one, myself included, enjoys the feeling of being a snitch. But the price of freedom is high and everyone, repeat everyone must help pay the cost."

With that statement, Morgan was silent for a moment and then responded, "I feel better for me having asked and I feel better for you having responded.

"For the dignity in which you handled the matter, I thank you. With respect to your investigation, I can reply that Mr. Griffin, in his position as my employee, related to me that he is a homosexual.

"However I have never seen him in any such activities, but neither do I have any knowledge of him having heterosexual sex."

A silence again followed and Blate sensed the dignity of the answer. He closed the top to his briefcase, snap the latches, and rose to leave. In parting amenities he said, "Mr. Smithfield here is my card. I am available any time; day or night. If you hear or see anything which you feel would be of interest, I ask that you put your feelings of repugnance aside. In the spirit of patriotism would you please give me a call?"

The storyteller wanted to think that nothing of importance could be assumed from this. But there was some unexplainable pull that was overpowering his mindset and forbid being pushed aside. Some metaphysical association connected the Underground Theater to something that happened; a tragedy. A mental picture shrouded by fog of a theater stage, an empty theater, a single spotlight and a dark shrouded balcony. He finally allowed the two clue words to come strongly into focus. A lead he could not escape or ignore... but not right now. To his self he sighs 'my weary twisted entangled trek gets no easier'.

Chapter 15

Two years later.

Jenny and Aspen are spending a Sunday morning in bed at Aspen's Penthouse. Their attraction to each other is still a composite of his being in his distinguished desirable fifties and her in her wild and free unblemished twenties; their relationship is still romantic and sexually driven. Love in a traditional sense of committing to each other has not yet arrived; but neither has the setting of 'roses and wine' departed. To Aspen the shameless uninhibited endless sex that the two enjoy continues to flaunt his departed wife's Puritanism. To Jenny, sex with Aspen is the pleasure for herself that she daily provides to others.

The morning started with chilled champagne in bed; followed by long, unhurried, emotionally endearing lovemaking; different than usual by Jenny being on top. For Aspen the position was effortless, intriguing, satisfying. His fulfillment came from keeping his eyes open and watching her radiant body, the beauty of her actions and her show of pleasure. On Jenny's part it was a time for her own ecstasy. Setting straddled on Aspen she closed her eyes as he entered. Adjusting to upright on her hind legs she started by moving her sensuous hands lightly over her own flat concave nude stomach and finger circling her navel. As her arousal heightened she fondled her breast and pinched the nipple between her thumb and forefinger. Shifting her position to exactness she then started slowly rocking her hips; slower at first and then increasing.

As her strokes quicken, her motions became more rhythmic and quickly accelerated to a frantic shaking until she reached an intense erotic orgasm; pausing, staying mounted, keeping her eyes closed, feeling his rod slip even deeper in her, brought on by her increased lubrication. In the glowing feeling which followed she opened her eyes, took a sip of champagne, savored the fizzles as she swallowed, and then started again.

Rhythmic rocking through orgasm after orgasm; and the early morning hours passed. As the peak of their sexual endurance gradually subsided, a let's-get-out-of-the-house mood set in and by mid-day they were out in one of Pittsburgh most popular show places; Schenley Park. Strolling and mingling they walked with index finger locked in index finger and generally followed the winding trails without talking.

Passing a flower vendor he bought her a pink carnation. Crossing over a small rainbow footbridge they paused for an embrace to the sound of babbling water. Stopping at a food vendor, they purchased hot dogs and cokes, ate on a shaded bench, people watched, and when the moment subsided they moved on.

Meandering off of the foot trails they climbed to the crest of an open grassy knoll that was perfect for lying in the sun. Stretched out on the grass with her head on his chest they gazed at fleecy clouds, smelled the crisp air, listened to the faint distant sounds of the city, and dozed. In times past, these being all the ingredients that would revive their sexual arousal. This time however there was something a little different. Different in the form of a mischievous urge on both their parts, along the lines of playful rubbing and wrestling in the nude on clean white sheets while holding in abeyance a second round of actual sex. Half ignited hormones that were influential enough for them to leave the park and return to the Penthouse.

However, the chemistry of the outside warm sun and fresh smelling grass was not the same back inside the bedroom. By 7:00 o'clock that evening the amount of effort required exceeded the level of pleasure received. Their mood of teasing gradually faded; replaced with passive reflection.

The French doors were open and a warm breeze intermittently bellowed out the sheer drapery panels. A bucket of fresh ice and a second bottle of Dom Pérignon remained almost untouched on Aspen's side of the bed and the only light from the otherwise unlit room came from the outside. Jenny was sitting up and leaning back on the headboard. Half covered by crumpled sheets she was gazing out the open doors while Aspen was lying motionless with one arm curled over his eyes.

"How you feel, Angel?" she asked in a melancholy tone.

"Lifeless, content, calm."

"That's it?" she lightly pretended surprise. "Just content? Calm? Jesus I must be losing my touch."

"Meaning?"

"Well," she attempted to purr little hints. "The words exuberant, exhilarated, splendor, ecstatic, anything along those lines would be a little more flattering."

"Those go without saying," he responded without too much emphasis and his arm still over his eyes.

"Uh," she now became a little more vocal, "I must be missing something here. Calm I hear. Splendor goes without saying. Hello. Are we in the same world? Aspen," she quickly justified her reaction. "I think I must be having a mood swing or else it's an after-sex let down."

"Care to maybe enlighten me?"

"Well, sex the way we've been having it all day. To me it is the most beautiful thing on earth. Intimate, pure, intrinsic, a man and a woman. A Heaven sent precious gift. The reason for living."

"Ah! Ha! Now we're getting somewhere," he rose up on his elbows to show he was getting into the conversation. "Love of mine, if you're looking for an argument you'll have to pick a different subject. Cause I couldn't agree more. So now where do we go?"

"Not us, me," she answered. "There's just something on my mind. Namely the people, no not the people, say some people, better still, a few people...maybe even a very few out there that do not see sex in the same beautiful light as you and I."

"Jenny, should I be getting worried here?" he raised further up. "Is there such a thing as sex insanity?"

"Aspen, let me ask you," she ignored his question. "How do you feel right this moment? Truthful answer now. How do you feel, really?

I'm not looking for a superficial at-peace-with-the-world type thing. I mean deep, really deep inside your soul. All the sex we've had, is it possible that really down deep maybe the sex we have had all day may in fact have been just an ounce shy of being perfect?

"I mean, I know it was perfect, but say just for the sake of discussion, would one more final tingle, would have done the trick...?"

"Who are we talking about here, you or me?"

"You. I'm just asking for a truthful answer. Would reaching for one more drop, a slightly harder concentration, a fraction deeper penetration, would it have been any more satisfying? Please just answer, it's important."

"Wheeze," he exhaled. "No talk? Just answer?"

"Just answer, please."

"OK Just answer it is. In answer to the first part of your question I'm in a hypnotic state. If you want to know why I'm in a hypnotic state I will tell you. I'm hypnotic because of the combined traces of our sex, the dried crusty semen all over my pecker hair, the feeling of your body, the smell of your sex juices, the licking and sucking on your nipples; God there is no greater Heaven on earth.

"In answer to the second part of your question about just one more tingle. The only thing I want from my soul right now is for it to provide an instant refill of my semen glands. My tongue still thirst but my supply of semen is exhausted. Baby the only other thing I could ask for is be able to grab hold of you and squeeze so hard that our two bodies and souls merged into one indistinguishable configuration of living sex.

"I trust that answers the second part. If you could just make direct contact to my soul's pecker then yes I assume that that would be better. Absent that my gracious woman, I am completely mesmerized."

She was looking at him as he finished and smiled at his humor. Reaching over she lightly licked his lips and then to his surprise forcefully ran her tongue deep into his mouth.

"Is," she asked when they finally came up for air, "that something along the lines you were thinking?"

"Just an eighth of an inch deeper," he responded. "Another eighth of an inch would have done it. But the real fact is there is still something on your mind. So...do I hear it or not?"

"It's something which kind of haunts me Aspen. It's a part of my business. Something which I don't like but feel obliged to do."

"Meaning what? Oral sex?"

"No of course not. That part I enjoy. Most of the time men just need straight sex. When oral sex is involved, more times than not it's the man who likes to start out by giving me oral sex then usually finishing with just man and woman insertion.

"There's always variations of course. Some men need to see how it feels just to touch and hold a woman other than their wife. Those are easy and very satisfying. I just surrender and let 'em explore. Sometimes a man needs to fight for it. Needs to prove he's a he-man. I don't enjoy it very much but it's OK Its something he needs or he wouldn't be asking. So I become a combative Amazon and then surrender." A slight rush came to her face as she realized how she was talking about her sexual exploits to her present lover.

"Aspen," she hesitated as she looked at him, "is all of this hurting you?"

He met her look and held for a second before he responded. "What? That you have sex? No Jenny. You're the cure for my hurt not the cause. I've told you before. There is a much more troubling Hell in my life; the clutches of which I am still trying to escape.

"You may recall that I was once shackled hand and foot to a woman that had no sex; with me or any other man. I'm still trying to get that out of my head."

"OK Honey, I just wanted to be sure."

"I'm sure. Now what's on your mind? Let's hear it."

"It's how some people degrade sex."

"Degrade, how?"

"Maybe it's not degrading to them but it is to me; especially when compared with what you and I have. It's probably better known as dominance and humiliation. It's a part of my job that I don't like."

"How," he asked with a slight hesitancy, "did we get from where we are to humiliation?"

"I don't know. It just flashed across my mind and now I can't get rid of it. It's funny. The usual routine for most of the tricks I do are with Johns who come in, get undressed, do it, get up, put on their clothes and leave. I don't even remember 'em. But the ones who are the worst..."

"Aspen," she abruptly changed the course of the topic, " is there any part of your business that you don't like?"

"Me? How'd I get involved in this?"

"Your work. What you do for a living. Doing what you know you're supposed to be doing. Anything about it that you really hate?"

"Well, hell yes. What's you think? That banking is all just one big bowl of cherries? There's lots of things about my work that I don't necessarily like; but I do 'em."

"Why?"

"Why? Because it's my job. That's why. It's what I do."

"Name one."

"One what?"

"One of the things that you don't like doing. Make it one of the most distasteful things you do because it's a part of what you do in life."

"Is this all leading somewhere?"

"Name one thing. I want to hear it."

"Hell, Jenny. Right here right now? I don't know. I guess one might be when I see little old widows insisting that they get themselves caught up in a money scam. They come in and want to draw out all their money to invest in some gold mine in Africa. Need I tell you more?"

"Meaning it's disgusting, but you go ahead and let them do it."

"Something like that."

"And do you think about it a lot?"

"Of course. Who wouldn't? You know what's going to happen. And yet..."

"And yet it's what they wanted."

"Jenny..."

"Aspen, what's on my mind is the same thing. God I, you, me most of the people in this ol' world think just plain ordinary sex is just wonderful. But there are those..."

"Those who what?"

"Those who lurk in the darkness. Those who are out of touch with sexual reality."

"I don't suppose you'd care to explain about this lurking in the darkness. You mean rape?"

"No, not rape. I mean that happens too. But my lurking, as I call it, is people who pay to be dominated and humiliated."

She paused, searched for her point and continued. "Some men, mostly men but also some women, can't get an orgasm any other way. And if that's what they want, what they have to have, I feel obliged to provide it. The circumstances usually run something like this.

"It's almost always after midnight. It seems that sexual humiliation is permitted only under a cloak of blackness; in those lonely hours when pain becomes overpowering.

"The caller will always be a solitary traveler. His or her pilgrimage shrouded in secrecy. But oddity of oddities, once inside my door will openly tell me who or what they are; as if to prove their qualifications for admission.

"Among those who come to me are a judge, a construction worker, a preacher, a business man, a closet homosexual, a postal worker, and a woman politician. The woman, for obvious reason, has become a kind of bonded friend.

"They're usually lonely souls for whom the night does not bring sleep. Say it's a man. He has no idea that his plight is seated in self-destruction. He only knows that in the end he cannot win. As the sleepless hours pass his torment continues until he reaches the breaking point and the need for relief is greater than the prudence of caution.

"So in desperation he dresses and leaves the sanctuary of his home and goes out into the perils of the empty streets. In a semblance of disguise he will usually wear a long black topcoat and black hat.

"With collar turned up and hat pulled down he prowls the lower side. He realizes the danger of being out alone and protects himself as much as he can by walking close to the store shadows; and watches carefully as he passes the pitch-black darkness of recessed doorways.

"As he comes to each intersection, or turns around a corner he hopes to see an outline of a female figure standing beneath a street light who can provide the relief he is seeking. But in the lonely hours long after midnight, or in the wintertime when the cold wind howls through the snow swirling streets, the silhouettes of spike heel shoes, short split skirts, and fishnet stockings do not venture out. In desperation his search continues until his path leads to my door.

"When I hear the knock, the hour tells me what to expect and I immediately prepare for the ritual. When I open the door, I open it abruptly, stare at him with cold piercing eyes, and administer a stern admonishment that he is late.

"He instantly feels a sigh of relief because he knows his search has ended. I domineeringly command him to instantly enter and he submissively obeys. Aspen you can pretty much visualize what goes on from there. Verbal assault, dog collar, threats of punishment, and then the demand they self ejaculate. Many plead for me to stand straddled over them as they lay on the floor and look directly up at my exposure." There was a brief silence when Jenny stopped talking. For Aspen he wasn't clear if she was finished talking. For Jenny she felt embarrassed for bringing that nature of sex into their relationship. In the silence that followed she waited to see if Aspen would comment. When no words came she followed an impulse to get a breath of fresh air. Swinging her legs over the side of the bed she lifted herself up moved across the floor to the French doors and went out on the verandah. As the cool night air engulfed her scantly clothed body she leaned against the parapet wall and gazed at the sprawling lights. From the bed Aspen watch without speaking. Waiting for a lingering moment he then rose, filled their two glasses with champagne, and joined her.

She turned and accepted her glass as he held it out but for the moment no words were exchanged. In unison they leaned against the coarse stucco waist high wall, lightly sipped and silently gazed at the sleeping city. Without looking she heard the sound when he deeply inhaled through his nose held the breath for a moment and slowly exhaled. She knew he was at a loss for words.

"Do you think me terrible?" she finally questioned.

"No. It's just. Hell I don't know what I think. I mean I don't think anything bad. I, Oh hell, drink." In search for time she took another sip of champagne and slowly let the bubbles ooze down. Resting her bare arms across the top of the wall she rolled the glass stem back and forth between the palms of her hands and finally asked, "Does it cause you to wonder why?"

"OK Why? Why do these few some people need something like that?"

"Because somewhere along the line they get to where they can't face the harsh work-a-day-world that is the substance of all life; working day in and day out, sleepless nights, worries about survival, responsibilities, job insecurity and so on. So they start looking for relief in sex. Somehow they start seeing it as easy way out.

"And before they know it, it becomes an addiction. They lose sight of the fact that sex can only do so much to make life pleasant. Aspen, sex is a reward for being happy; not a guaranteed formula for utopia. When it fails, they don't stop to question why. They just keep on trying to find kinkier and kinkier ways to achieve harder and harder orgasms. Like dope, they start needing a stronger and stronger fix. When this starts they're on a never-ending downward spiral. The world they are seeking doesn't exist. I... I just think it's a shame."

"And that's what you were thinking when all of this got started?" he asked.

"I know. I know. It's just such a contrast to what we enjoy. I just can't understand why they need it. That's all I'm saying."

She made a sweeping swing and said, "I'd like to bring them all up here; where it's real high and show 'em what you and I are looking at right this moment. That's the real world out there," she made another sweeping gesture to the city skyline.

"It's everyday people just trying to make it. It's a world of mostly hard work and very little play; of unemployment, sickness, injustice, cancer, hunger, corruption, kidney failure, crime, war, aggression, taxes, etc. etc.

"I'd like to make them see that the answer to their problems can't be found in despoiling themselves. I'd like to make them see that! God would I like to. But I can't. What they have to have, it's what I do."

Dinner that evening had been at a little Italian restaurant with red-checkered table clothes and sawdust on the floor; it was now later back at the Penthouse. Aspen was sitting in his favorite recliner with his hands resting interlocked on his head. Jenny half stretched out on the curved, pillow back sofa. Quietness hung in the air and each was in their separate thoughts.

"I think," he finally spoke, "I might take off work tomorrow."

"Oh? Just like that. No work?" she responded.

"Uh Huh, something just like that."

"You can do that?"

"I can do that," he continued. "Jenny, you know something? I must be about to have a mid-life crises."

"I hope is not something I said," she intended a pun. "I'm more into curing than causing."

"Jenny," he spoke back. "If you knew what is spinning around in my mind? Listen to this," he continued without finishing his sentences. "I mean the different things that are going around in my head right now. I've got sex, I've got God, I've got jerking off, I've got church and maybe a couple of other things all jumbled up in my mind to where I am as confused as a blind lesbian in a tuna factory."

"ASPEN!" she blurted out. "I can't believe you just said that. You, a dignified gentleman. A banker, a sharp dresser, a leader in the community, talking like..."

With her head tilted slightly she cast a disbelieving look in his direction and continued. "I mean, a blind lesbian in a tuna factor, God and jerking off in the same breath?

"REALLY Aspen. Don't you think maybe the combination is a little out of character? That last round of champagne must be having a delayed effect on you."

He returned her look, held for second and then defended his words. "Maybe I'm doing it on purpose. Maybe I've got so much stuff going around in my head I wanta say shit, fuck, jerk off."

His tone caused her to recoil slightly. "Uh, Aspen, I'm not nagging. I just, I mean where's this coming from...?"

"From that humiliation and dominance story you told about a John jerking off while looking up at your crouch. Well...not exactly, I mean the mind flash that I got, it probably was more like touching an old cord.

"But I didn't..."

"Jenny, you know what I once did?" he remained in control. "Something I did before I met you? I dropped my pants and jerked off right in there on that oversize size bed we've been screwing on. Pants down, shoes on and eyes closed I shot a cannon ball size load of cum all over that new bedspread; it cost me an equal size wad of greenbacks to have it dry cleaned, but I did it.

"And would you like to know why?" Aspen asked rhetorical. "God. That's why?"

"Oh Aspen! Surely, I can't believe..."

"Well of course it wasn't God personally. That's not what I meant. It was the Apostle Church and those damn stained glass windows that had always held me captive.

"It all started coming back to me earlier this evening, when you started talking about that dominance and humiliation stuff. While you were talking about that John lying on the floor looking up at your crouch, I was picturing it. And that's when I got to remembering why I did it; jerked off that is."

"But Aspen," she pushed her point, "you don't go around mixing your sex life with your religious life. IT'S just not done. HIS name is holy."

At those words Aspen cast his first-ever stern look at Jenny. She saw how intently he was looking and a surprised streak of cold chill caused her to feel tiny goose bumps.

"Uh, Aspen, maybe that didn't come out just right. What I mean is I'm just sur..."

"Do I get to finish? Good. Now, as I was saying, before I was interrupted. This no mixing of God and sex and Sunday morning that you mentioned? I'll take that to mean that we can screw all week and then run to some church and be sanctimonious on Sunday morning.

"That's the normal pattern isn't it? It's the way we were all raised. Keep the Sabbath holy. It's the way I used to think. Except in my case I didn't even get any of the weeklong screwing. The truth of the matter Jenny it doesn't happen to work that way. I..." His words ceased. He realized that his train of thought was becoming confusing.

"I'm getting ahead of myself. I need for you to understand something. Let's just back up a minute."

At that point the room became very quiet. The two were looking directly at each other but neither was attempting to force direct eye contact.

When the chemistry transmitted that the moment was right, Aspen started to speak. Talking slow, clearly pronouncing each individual word.

"Jenny, the picture of you standing straddled leg over some John..." he paused again for a split second as intensity hung in the air then continued. "Making that John look up at your crouch while he jerks off, it excited me." Taking in a breath, his tone still intense, his words slow, he continued.

"I felt an arousal in my pecker. It caused me to wonder if I would ever want to try it. And in truth Jenny," he passed into the role of confessor, "if I could do it without anybody ever finding out, I think I would like for us to try it."

The pause that followed indicated the onus was on Jenny to speak.

"Aspen, I, one minute it was God. The next minute..."

"BUT," he cut in to finish his point, "then, up comes that sex addiction thing you mentioned."

"But not God," she cut back in. "I didn't mention anything about God. That's not something I came up with."

"Well, yeah," Aspen fill in, "the God part, that's on me and it's really not so much sex as it is my screwed up mind. Actually up until this very moment I don't believe I ever dared to even think about God and sex in the same thought.

"But think about it. Why should the idea be so forbidden? God is life. Sex is life. The truth of the matter it depends of how each of us has been brain washed."

"Aspen, I..." At that instant she was interrupted by an outside intrusion. 'TOMBBB' The floor-to-ceiling Seth Thomas clock gonged out the time at 1:00 A.M.

"It seems to me," she continued after glancing at the clock, "that you're right on the verge of saying something but can't quite let yourself pass over. What? Sex is sinful or something?"

"Thank you Jenny, for opening that door," he said as he rose from his chair and started toward the kitchen. "It's a long and drawn out story," he continued talking as he took lunch meat, bread and other sandwich items out of the refrigerator.

"You wanna hear it?"

"If it's going to be that long then I had better go pee," she commented as she rose from the sofa.

"I'll take that as a yes," he replied as he started fixings two ham-on-rye sandwiches.

"I guess," he talked from the kitchen counter, "the best place to start is with a comparison of my relationship with God as of now and how it was up until a couple a years back.

"First I'll tell you how it used to be. Starting from when I was a child and for as long as I can remember I always approached God with a great reverence, as well it should be. The context I am referring to is each time I entered the church I, as do most other people, would bow my head, walk directly to my pew and feel an obedience to be seated and remain very quiet. I can remember that I always had the feeling that if I moved, then He might be offended. So, obediently I would sit very still, try not to let my breathing be heard, and pretend to be listening while the pastor gave his predictable sermon on the dire consequences of displeasing God.

"And that was always the substance. Be obedient. Bow down. Be meek. God is watching. He's always right there; ready to catch you in a sin. Ah! Ha! Gotcha. Now you punk you're gonna pay..."

Glancing up he looked in the direction of the bathroom and raised his voice slightly to make sure she could hear.

"In all of my life I don't think I ever heard any preacher, or anyone else for that matter, say anything about looking upon God as a living person; say a good 'ol boy, a best friend, just another member of the family. Someone you could talk to in a normal conversation. Maybe something like 'hey lets all get together and have a big ass church base-ball game; and God we would like for You to play shortstop'. Nope, nothing like that. Just bow down and make damn sure you please God or else your sweet ass is going to be cast into a fiery hell for ten billion years."

Aspen continued talking as a matter of conversation as he put the sandwiches and a slice of pickle on two plates. The sound of the toilet flushing echoed in the bathroom as Jenny came back in the kitchen, started making coffee and kept listening.

"You know the theme," he continued. "It's about the same in all religions. The question I could never understand though is what does God himself do? Now I knew I wasn't suppose to ask, but I always wondered exactly what it was that He did.

"In my mind's eye I used to see Him as a bigger than life Man sitting in a larger than life throne some place high up in the heavens. Like old Father Time, wrinkled and old with a long flowing beard. He's been dressed the same way for forty years. Every day there he is, sitting exactly like my last image of him.

"Oddly, I can never picture him quitting at the end of the day. He just keeps sitting there day in day out; always in the same long red velvet robe.

"He wears a gold crown, cocked over to the side of his head over a mat of uncombed white hair. And for as long as I can remember He has always looked bored and has never smiled. I even picture an endless spiraling stairway coming up from earth ascending through a thick layer of white clouds and ending right at the front of two big wide swinging gates; not gold but white. And there's always an endless line of poor, down trodden souls in tattered clothes climbing up those endless stairs, each waiting patiently for his turn to move forward.

"And for reasons I don't know why, I always picture a poor little ol' bald headed man and a taller hawk nose wife standing first in line. The man's head is bowed but the woman is looking straight at God, with an impatient look demanding an explanation as to why they are kept waiting.

"In the background there is an obscure mosaic of white fleece clouds and lightly swirling white fog but I can never see anything beyond that. Most importantly though, I cannot picture Him, God, ever turning anyone away. Everyone who approaches the gates gets in but I also have the mental picture of Him being bored to a fair-the-well.

"All he has to do all day long, day in and day out, is to sit there in that big oversize throne, look down at that endless stairway of people and routinely touch his hand to their heads. Once he touches them they seem to simply proceed on in and the next soul then steps up. Without even a smile, they pass on through, one after the other and fade somewhere into obscurity."

As he talked, Aspen took the sandwiches into the living room and Jenny followed carrying two cups of coffee.

"Don't you think," she said as she handed him one of the cups, "that your image of God probably comes from the pictures in religious books taught to you as a child?"

"Oh, I don't think there's any question. And to tell you the truth I don't really believe that sort of image. On the other hand neither can I tell you what an adult version of God would look like. In other words, I know the image I have is incorrect but neither do I have a replacement.

"But the image is not what troubles me. My question has always been why is it that God has to be so unreachable; why is there this great overpowering reverence of holier-than-thou between Him and people; stand in awe when you're in my presence, be respectful and on your best behavior?"

"Has anyone ever given any thought to the idea that maybe He would like to simply be treated no differently than anyone else? A next door neighbor that you go over and borrow his lawn mower?"

Eating as they talked, he took a bite of sandwich and washed it down with a swallow of coffee.

"Now remember," he looked back at Jenny as he finished swallowing, "when He's not sitting on the thrown, he's in that church. And that means sterile antiseptic image of stained glass windows, mournful organ music, a strict mandate of silence and the ever presence of statues with bowed heads all crowded into the small confines of four walls and a roof.

"Good God, Jenny," he unmindfully took another bite, repeated his coffee wash down and swallowed. With the entire world at His command why does He stay cooped up in such cramped quarters? Is He happy in there? Is this where He really wishes to be?

"Or, now get this, is this all something wherein man started dictating terms to God. In the name of religion, has man simply decided where God will live and serve; namely inside of a church. HA! Ever think about that. I build a church of some sort then send a second-class letter up to God and say 'Greetings My Good Man' your new residence is in a wood frame box that I just built and incidentally for which I get a tax deduction.

"Yes Sir, Mr. God I have decided this is where You will reside; that is if You wish to meet the people. And another thing, in order for my tax deduction to be in force You have to keep Your sweet butt right inside there and always be available for whenever a sinner may want to drop in and get a little quick dose of forgiveness."

As that statement ended, the need for a pause somehow materialized. Aspen aimlessly rose from the recliner, meandered over to the living room double French doors and started gazing out over the city. In the meantime Jenny picked up the sandwich dishes and empty coffee cups and moved to the kitchen sink.

"Aspen," she responded as she was rinsing out the cups, "I'm not very religious. I can't give you an answer. I don't even know what to say. I still get the feeling that you are trying to say something but it just won't come out."

As his gaze on the city lights gradually broke, he turned from the French doors and came back into the kitchen. Reaching in the refrigerator he took out a pitcher and poured a glass of water. Leaning against the cabinet counter he watched as she finished drying.

"Is," she asked as she folded the towel and turned to his face, "all of this for my benefit or yours?"

"...Mine," he delayed. "Of course. This whole rethinking about God is something that has just been screaming to get out of my head. Like it don't count unless someone else hears it."

"Then," she responded, "I have only two thoughts. One, if you have something which needs to be said, it's probably now or never. Secondly, I would feel hurt if you felt that you could not talk to me."

"OK Jenny, That makes it easy. What I want to do is tell someone special, someone like you, about an experience that has given me a completely different perspective about life and my relationship with God. Let's sit down and get comfortable. Remember that heard of cattle out in Texas..."

The storyteller sat cognizant of his own breathing. He took in a deep breath for renewed energy. All of these people, he thought. Each separate-one of them, in their own way, has borne the burdens of life. Each separate-one lays testament that life without burden does not exist. Each separate-one appears to have stood their ground. Each appears to have become stronger. None have crumbled. Of theirs, surely I can learn.

The storyteller then looked at his sleeping listener friend. A friend of timeworn bond. A friend seldom from sight. A comrade in arms against the mortal plague of loneliness. A friend so pronounced as the two being one. As he watched his sleeping affection, there came without warning an unexpected thought. A thought he would never have thought possible. A thought inconceivable.

The body that was spread out there on the spring worn sofa was that of a simpleton. A simple simpleton. Thence to the storyteller came seeds unfamiliar to realize. Of his mind's thirst for self, came his own searching question, 'Is this the best I can do?'

Chapter 16

"OK, handsome man," were Jenny's words as she returned to the curved sofa and watched as Aspen sat back down in his recliner, "let's hear it. What it is you've been trying so hard to say?"

"A few months back," he started directly and right to the point as if delivering an opening argument. "Actually it's been better than two years... before you and I even met," he clarified. "Somehow the twist and turns of life ended me up on a cattle ranch in West Texas. I won't cloud the issue with lengthy details right now but in substance, I was part of an operation that drove 6,000 head of cattle overland from Van Horn, Texas to Dodge City, Kansas."

"Uh," she interrupted. "Aspen, am I missing something here? Ten minutes ago it was God and sex, then God and church and now God and a cattle drive. You think maybe that's not a little odd?"

"Of course it's odd. I'll agree that the concept of God and cattle in the same context doesn't seem like a normal association. In this particular situation however there was a powerful third ingredient; namely money. If you think that all sounds loony, wait until you hear the ending.

"Now, that third ingredient? What we had, meaning me, was a three hundred and sixty thousand dollar investment, a contract with the military, a worldwide war raging out of control, the army needing meat for troops and no available rail transportation.

"Mix them all together in the form of a cattle drive and I ended up with a new religious experience; an entirely new perspective about God and his relationship with people. In the mist of all this, if I had to pinpoint the exact source it would be a cattle rancher by the name of Frank Delaney.

"Now, to have a good understanding of where I am coming from you need to know a little something about the man and the circumstances.

"Poppa Frank, as he is affectingly called, is a stocky sort of man and a blueprint of a Texas cattle rancher, personified. Scuffed cowboy boots, faded half worn out Levi's, belt line hanging just below a slight pot, Stetson hat, deep squinted eyes and weather beaten lines across a leathery face.

"He is a self reliant, rawhide and leather, don't rest until the work is done, kind of man who stands against the wind and Hell would freeze over before he would quit. I don't know his age exactly. In fact I would be surprised if any one knows his age, exactly. By the best estimates he is somewhere around sixty.

"If this brings to mind an image of an old man forget it. Trust me when I tell you he is anything but old. What he is, is a gent who forges ahead in life one solid determined step by solid determined step. He neither expects nor hopes for an easy break. If there was ever a mortal soul forged from molting steel right out of a Pittsburgh blast furnace and shipped out to the barren brutal plains of West Texas to be tested it surly must be Poppa Frank.

"I followed him in the saddle for forty four days and over six hundred miles across parched alkaline plains, lightning storms, stampeding cattle and watched him wear down men half his age.

"Where he originally came from no one knows for sure but there is a legend of sorts. Along about 1905, as the story goes, he and another young buck named Jess Marks left the Oklahoma Territory and headed for Texas. All that either one had was their mount, a Winchester rifle, a side of hog back, and one hell of a backbone. It took them a couple of week riding through hostile Comanche territory until they came to what has become known as the Texas High Plains; an uninhabited million square miles of cactus, sagebrush, mesquite, needle grass, creosote bush and rattle snakes.

"When they reached the Pecos River they camped on the south side in a bend for a few days, and it was there that they divided up the state of Texas. Jess Marks turned south toward the Big Bend country and Poppa Frank continued on West toward the watershed range of the

Guadalupe Mountains.

"To make a long story short, he carved out 100,000 acres or so of raw prairie, put his brand on it and started raising cattle.

"Somewhere along the way he acquired a wife and sired eight kids. But eight kids are not enough to run a 100,000 acres ranch.

"So, as the herd grew, cowhands started drifting in and through the years it developed into a pretty prosperous operation.

"But then in 1939 Hitler invaded Poland, started World War II and most of Poppy Frank's hired hands and his oldest son went off to fight. Well that left the 'ol boy pretty short handed and he had to take up his own slack. He started spending weeks at a time in the saddle. And being out on the prairie like that means being away from every living soul for days on end.

"Well, it seems that somewhere out there, as he tells it, he ran across God." At this point Aspen paused, looked directly at Jenny and commented, "We're now getting to the part you're interested in...God right?" Then without waiting for a response he continued.

"The phrase 'running across God out on the prairie' may be a little off base but it'll do for now. Actually, as the story goes, Poppy Frank figured that God had simply been out roaming around sightseeing, instead of working like he should have been, and had gotten Himself lost. God would never admit it of course, but that's what Poppa Frank claims.

"In actuality it really didn't make a no never mind as to how God did happen to be out there. The bottom line is, it wasn't Poppa Frank's nature for anybody, God or man, not to be working; or as he says 'earning their keep'. Anyway the two of 'em, God and Poppy Frank, hooked up and started riding trail together, got to talking, and the rest is history. Poppa Frank started teaching God the cattle business and God took to it like a duck to water.

"God's working part really got started in a peculiar sort of way. There were times in those days when at the end of the day poor 'ol Poppy Frank would be so tired he would rein up, unsaddle his mount, throw a bed roll on the ground and just drop. Well, it's not the smartest thing in the world to just drop a bedroll on the ground without first checking the area for rattlesnakes. So one night Frank asked God to attend to the matter of clearing the camp. From that time on, the matter of snakes in camp just disappeared and Poppa Frank sure did like the results.

"He figured since God did such a good job with snake clearing He was responsible enough to assume bigger jobs.

"So before long God's work assignment began to expand. Little things at first, like riding down to the end of a gully and checking for strays.

"Well, God would take off in a dust raising gallop, search out the gully and report back in record time.

"If the gully was empty they would move on. In Poppa Frank's words, God had the makings of a top hand and it just turned into one of those perfect partnerships. God was more than happy for the work and Frank appreciated his efforts; which included everything from punching cattle to busting bronco to mending fences.

"The only thing, as I understand, God's only short coming was his lack of self-confidence. He never did feel confident enough to go out on his own. He always wanted someone to go with him. Well, that seemed reasonable enough to Poppa Frank so he just made it a practice to always send out doubles.

"When he was sending a man out he would say, 'Jake, I want you to take God and the two of you ride over and check the fence line from windmill #36 to Warren Lake.' Alternatively, Poppa Frank might say to one of his sons, 'Willie put a saddle on the gray and take enough grub for three days. Take God and the two of you work the range east of Dry Fork Creek. And listen Willie, I don't want you two out fart'en around. I'm not sending you two out there to jerk off, shoot rabbits, or look for Indian arrowheads. Just ride the fence line, push all of the strays back in with the main herd and I want to see both of you back here in three days; four at the most. We got a damn site more work that has to get done'."

By this time Jenny was having trouble keeping up. Shifting slightly on the sofa she pulled her silk robe over her legs and remarked.

"Uh, wait, Aspen. Tell me again. How did you happen to get involved in all of this?"

"What?" he was slightly surprised by her question?

"You and God Aspen? I mean I'm not sure I follow", her tone relating that she was lost.

He took a deep breath, deliberately held it, looked directly at her in a disbelief head shaking manner and exhaled. "It's not supposed to make sense," he chided. "Remember, I've just spent this entire day humping my brains out."

"Oh Aspen don't be silly. Would you get back to your point?"

"Point?" his tone implying a mimicked surprise then responded.

"The point being that I had made an investment loan on some cattle and then had to protect my investment. If that investment had failed then there would have been a pretty good chance that The Church of the Apostles would have gone back into court and I would have lost control of six million dollars.

"So I went out to Texas to oversee my investment. And Jenny I never dreamed there was so much land in the world.

"I had never seen a country where you could see until the land just run out of sight. If there was ever a natural place where God would want to roam, it would have to be out on that prairie. When I compare the freedom out there with the suffocating quarters of a church...I start to wander about the actual where-abouts that God is likely to be.

"Out there, it seems to me, He would find a feeling of being able to breathe. An exciting inspiration to do something. To build, work the land, fight the elements. Meaningful work. When they say it is a place where you can breathe it means just that. Just the mental picture makes me want to fill my lungs until they burn," Aspen paused for a moment to decide how he wanted to proceed.

"It was," he finally continued, "the most unbelievable event of my life.

"I arrived at The TapRoot Ranch around six or seven o'clock in the evening on April 14th, spent the night in a bunk house and got rousted out of the bunk at three o'clock the next morning. Two hours later, around five or so, I was in the mist of a sea of bellowing cattle, shaggy looking cowboys, a remuda of trail horses, chuck wagons, riders, and before I even knew where I was supposed to be, the order called out you could hear for a country mile, HEAD'EM UP-and-MOVE'EM OUT.

"That unleashed a torrent of cowboy yells and the drive was under way. Like a military order, it set in motion more energy than I will ever hope to see in a lifetime. A kind of momentum started with everyone following the man in front of them. A wave of cattle, riders, chuck wagons, and horses began moving in a northerly direction and stretched out as far as the eye could see. But that is getting way ahead of the story."

Aspen pushed his lounge chair upright and went to the refrigerator for another glass of water. Standing with the door open he took a long swig, then had a change of mind and took the glass with him.

"I tell you Jenny, I could write a book about that experience. I might do it too.

"I only met Poppa Frank for a few minutes the night I got in. We shook hands and exchanged greetings but right at the moment he was one busy feller. He hooked me up with his foreman, Snakey Ramsey and I proceeded to get outfitted for the trail.

"First damn thing I learned about cowpokes is they don't talk much and they don't accept you until you have proven your worth. No exceptions. Course there are other things I learned too, like they always have a half smoked, roll your own, Bull Durham cigarette hanging out of the corner of their mouth. And they always light it by striking a kitchen match across the cheek of their ass."

As Aspen was talking he was moving from the kitchen back to his chair. He had on a terry cloth robe and was bare footed. His steel gray hair was askew and the absence of shoes made him appear shorter. The remark about cowboys striking a match on the cheek of their ass came out just as he walked passed Jenny and a smile came across her face. She never grew tired of his distinguished looks but at that particular moment she could not help laughing at the thought of Aspen trying to strike a kitchen match across the right cheek of his lily white behind.

Aspen glanced her way at the slight laugh but paid it no mind. He returned to his chair but this time he did not lean back. Instead he crossed his legs, took another drink of water and continued.

"As I was saying, first thing you learn about cowboys is they don't talk much. When we were introduced, Snakey and I shook hands and then without saying a word he turned and started toward the corral and I'm left just standing there. When he had taken about ten steps or so he turned and looked back in a look that implied 'well are you coming or not?' It took about a tenth of a second for me to realize that I was supposed to follow. I rushed to catch up and fifteen minutes later I was outfitted with a bedroll, chaps, spurs, a few other items and pointed to the bunkhouse.

"Later that night, when no one else was around, another feller, Jake Marlow, kind of eased up to me a little. He fixed me up with a Stetson hat and a pair of cowboy boots.

"At first I was reluctant to figured that these were something that I really needed but Jake informed me that both the boots and hat are life and death working tools to a cowboy.

"The hat protects from the soaring heat and when things get tough it is also used to hold drinking water for your horse. And the heels on cowboy boots are designed to prevent the foot from slipping all the way through the stirrups; in which case if a horse bolts and runs, meaning with a man's foot slipped all the way through the stirrup, then it's a pretty damn sure thing that he is going to get dragged to death.

"Lots of other things I learned too; like the temperament of cattle and the history of cattle drives. A trail drive is a living hell. In the old days when the big ranchers used to bring cattle up from Texas on the ol' Chisholm Trail, it was a measure of being a real man to make a trail drive. Once a drive started there was no turning back. "Under the very best of conditions it meant 14 to 16 hours a day in the saddle seven days a week for 60 to 90 days.

"The worst of times meant cattle plagues, drought, alkali watering hole, quicksand at the river crossings, prairie fires, Indians, roving bands of cattle rustlers and the ever present danger of the cattle stampeding.

I didn't know this but there is no discernible way to determine when cattle will bolt into a stampede. None. One minute they may be calm the next stampeding. And something else. Once they have broken into a stampede and they have run the course, that doesn't mean that they are through for a while. Not by a long shot. They may bolt and run again at any moment. And then even a third time.

"But back to the old days, the pay was usually a dollar a day and grub. If you got sick you had to keep riding; there was no place else to go. If you got wounded in an Indian fight you had to find strength to keep moving. Your only hope of surviving was to keep riding because there wasn't any room in the chuck wagon. And many a poor soul didn't make it. If you got wounded or sick and couldn't go on, it was considered lucky if you died at night in your sleep.

"Those that died during the day usually just dropped from the saddle. But the death of a single cowhand didn't mean the drive would stop. The cattle had to keep moving so one or two of the other hands would drop back to take care of the burial.

"Usually the dead person would be buried in a shallow grave dug out by a skinning knife or spur; covered over by loose dirt and left. Sometimes a close friend might fashion a cross with dead limbs from a mesquite bush and if he knew how to write he might have scribbled a note saying who he was. But most of the time the dead man's horse was simply unsaddled and turned back in with remuda and the drive kept moving.

"So any cowboy who had made a drive and lived was accorded high respect. Back home he got recognition around the bunkhouse. Younger pups called him mister, let him water his horse first at the watering trough and people in town bought him drinks at the saloon.

"The trouble..." Aspen's story was abruptly startled by the chiming of the Seth Thomas clock. 'Tombbb, Tombbb, Tombbb,' vibrating across the spacious, modern décor living room.

Reactively, both he and Jenny glanced at the clock. Almost in unison they expressed their surprise that it was 3:00 A.M. and Aspen was the first to follow through on the note.

"Tell me most beautiful one, has Seth Thomas, that insatiably glutton of time, broken my captive audience hold?"

Jenny's mind was never quite as quick as Aspen's and she did not instantly connect to his jester. "What," she glanced to his eyes? Aspen caught the questioned look and quickly returned.

"Am I running this into the ground?" he asked. "Too much, too little, enough for one night, what?" he ended with a question.

"End?" Her wit instantly catching up with the one she had just missed. "You dare! Here you have me out on some cattle baron's ranch in West Texas and just because it happens to be three o'clock in the morning you have thoughts about just leaving me there. How dare you! How do you expect me to get back? I tell you, some people.

"There's a real measure of true love for you," she mimicked. "A man takes you half way across the country and then decides it's too much trouble to bring you back."

"It's not that it's so much trouble," he continued the wit match, "it's the mode of transportation. Here I am, traveling all around the country all night in this damn stiff back chair. Suffering from stiff bones and tired head, and it is starting to affect my memory."

Putting his hand to his forehead he mimicked absent minded. "I forget, where was I? I can't seem to remember, my mind is foggy. No wait. I am beginning to see something. A place. A place to lay my head. It is foggy, but there is some definition now, valley? Yes, valleys and peaks. Mountain meadow? No, no. Something much softer. Color creamy. Yes, creamy and pink. Creamy with a pink center. A hard firm pink center that sticks out about a half inch. Like a nipple. That's it; a nipple. The picture is clear now. If only there were two beautiful, creamy breasts with hard inviting nipples on which to lay my weary head I am sure I could continue.

"A revitalization of my memory by the sweet nectar which flows form the succulent taste of a moist nipple in my mouth."

Where Jenny was slow at first she now held her own. "Aspen, I didn't want to mention this," she replied, "but all the time you have been talking about all those young cowboys I have been thinking about starry nights, and all those blankets on the ground. Just imagine, an army of young ball-bearing studs spread out on that wide-open prairie. And me, a nude, nighttime Yellow Rose of Texas, with so many needing my services.

"I have been thinking about it so much my mind is having a vision. Yes, blanket, ground." She held her hand up to her forehead. "A blanket, ground, wide open spaces, warm nights, starry skies. More vision is coming. Yes, that's it. Pillows, blanket, floor."

With that she bolted to the bedroom and quickly striped the bed. She dashed back into the living room and with a swing of her arms a fleece blanket settled to the floor. With a pounce she grabbed Aspen and they frolicked in a fall to the blanket. She nuzzled his head to the cleavage in her breast, held tight and yelled.

"Take me, you wild cowboy you. Ravish my body, force your sun parched lips against my soft breast, be rough and clumsy, bite hard, let me feel the beast in you, let me smell the sweat on your chest and the feel of power in your wild savage hands. I must have the raw, bristled, brute force of your hard lean cock deep inside my surrender vagina. TAKE ME BACK TO TEXAS."

Aspen was perplexed between laughing or diving in at her request; obligingly he elected on the latter. Anxiously he began to taste her nipples and was attempting to maneuver himself between her legs.

"But she resisted by closing them tight and sighed, "NO, NO, NO, not yet. First I must know. WHAT HAPPENED NEXT?"

At that, Aspen raised his head from under the tension of her arm and looked up. She was lying firmly outstretch on her back and had a fixed stare. With a chiseled exaggerated smile she held perfectly still and looked straight up at the ceiling.

"W h a t h a p p e n e d next," he remarked in a spaced out disbelief manner, "is that everybody in the whole DAMN world is crazy. Including some women that I know who have a fantasy about getting laid on a cowboy's blanket."

"Oh please," she purred as she shifted herself up on her elbows, "I am serious. I am spellbound by your adventure. You are a good storyteller so don't stop now."

Aspen reached for one of the bed pillows and positioned it underneath his chest. With the tip of his tongue he teased one of her nipples. He then took a soft nibble, felt a shivering tingle flow through his body, and then yielded to her request.

"OK, if you insist on being such a glutton for punishment, who am I to deny. Where was I," he asked feigning absent-mindedness.

"You were saying something about trouble," answered Jenny.

"Oh yeah, OK. What I was about to explain is that cowboys in 1942 are not quite the same as they were in 1876. When the news got out that there was going to be a 6,000 head modern day cattle drive, every available cowboy in West Texas wanted to get in. Some drove as far as 200 miles, truck and trailer and brought their own mounts to volunteer. Now this sounds well and good. A nice supply of eager young heroes' anxious to get in on a final chapter of history, but it don't work quite that way.

"Cowboys are the most competitive, temperamental, opinionated, independent, combative breed of men on the face of the earth and a successful cattle drive depends on a proven crew.

"And to have a proven crew you have to have men who have tested each other. And the very first test is usually a pretty good round of fist'y cuffs.

"Now a fist fight may or may not last very long but it is for damn sure that any new man on the job is going to be tested; at least two or three times and maybe by the whole damn crew. So what you have here is not one new man but a whole new crew. Can you imagine what in the hell is in store? After the fights comes the checking out as to how well he can ride, bust broncos, brand cattle, go without water, etc. Under normal circumstances it would be awfully poor judgment on the part of a trail boss to mix a flock of new men together and start out on an unknown trail 600 mile long.

"But like I say, the war got first call on most of the old hands at the TapRoot Ranch and Poppa Frank got what was left. Moreover, what was left was a skeleton crew of six riders that sort of defies description.

"He had, as he called them, three hard headed, shaggy looking, anvil-breaking, miss the ground if they fell on it, know-no-fear, tobacco chewing, would rather fight than eat, sons by the names of Gene, Willie and Jerry.

"He also had a leather and raw hide, thin as a rail, raw boned, six foot six, hard knuckled, weather beaten foreman named Snakey Ramsey. A red face, bushy beard, stocky no-nonsense, bull moose of a man named Bill Porter. A baby face, smooth skin, out-of-place, don't talk much, grins a lot, nicest guy named Jake Marlow. And... about 200 volunteer cowboys camped out around the corral wanting to be picked for the drive.

"By Poppa Frank's calculation he would need a total of twenty riders or 14 additional men; not including wrangler and cooks which were being borrowed from an adjacent ranch.

"What," Jenny interrupted, "about God? Was he part of the crew?"

"What?"

"You were talking about God being considered as just another hand. Was he included in the selection?"

Aspen cast a slightly disdainful look at her for her again having interrupted his train of thought and then answered.

"He was included all right. You can bet your boots on that; just not in the way you might think. Now if I can continue. As I was saying, with more volunteers coming in each day, the growing numbers increased the odds of any one individual being selected so each hopeful cowboy had a built in resentfulness of the other.

"Well on the late afternoon of April 14th, a couple of hours before I got there, the selections were made and from what I heard it was a pretty emotional situation. The way it was told to me the picture looked something like this.

"Here we have 6,000 head of prime Texas beef already rounded up and holding in a nearby canyon. It was that time in the afternoon when it is evident that the sun is on the downward slide and starting to take on an orange hue."

"Everyone is getting more anxious. Some have been camped out around the corral for three days. They know the waiting is about over. In the backdrop of a big orange hued sun, every soul on the ranch is gathered in the huge corral. The entire top fence rail is lined with seated cowboys. All of 'em perched shoulder to shoulder. Nobody is saying much and most are trying to contain their nervousness by smoking a roll-your-own Bull Durham cigarette.

"There are also cowboys seated on the edge of the watering trough, saddle racks, and bails of hay. They have been milling around most of the day. Some have spent their time sharpening and re-sharpening that ever-present Buck pocketknife. Others moved from one small group to another. They gravitated from the stock pens to the windmill, take a drink of water, turn to leave, nod to the next feller behind and meander on.

"Well along about four o'clock Poppa Frank comes out of the big twelve bedrooms ranch house and briefly pauses next to the weathered wood railing on the huge back porch. Tucked up under one arm is a crumpled brown paper sack. He looks out to the corral at all the men who are looking at him. Some he knows; some he has just met. He considers them all to be good friends. By his code, the mark of friendship is to never have to say no to another feller. But he knows that in this case, that is not going to be possible. He hopes that when the selection is over there will be no ill will.

"He pulls his hat down close to his eyes and briefly looks at the sun. Then with the paper sack still tucked up under his arm and both hands in his pockets he descends the three wood steps and with his head slightly looking down he starts toward the corral. He walks with a type of reluctance, looking at his scuffed boots as he moves across the barren red clay.

"About halfway he stopped, reached down and picks up something, possibly a rusty horseshoe nail, gave it a brief once over, flipped it away and continued on.

"As he enters through the corral gate he is the center of attention. Like the starting moments of a stage play, as the curtain starts to raise all talking stops. The only sounds are the occasional snort snickering of nearby saddles ponies, the mixed bellowing of the cattle in the distant box canyon and the crunching sound of his boots walking across dried crusty cow manure. Tenseness hangs in the air. To a man, each of these young cowboys desperately wants to be a part of this final page in history. And each knows that the odds of being picked are roughly 1 in 14.

" Poppa Frank is not used to giving speeches. He is nervous and his first words probably show it as he starts.

"'Howdy men.'" He is surprised at how shallow his voice is and he clears his throat. Then in a more forceful tone he continues.

"'Boys, I'm not too long on words. Wish that I were. Because I need all of the words I can get to express my appreciation for all of you being here. I shore am touched by the number of you fine fellers who have turned out to help me in a crisis like this.

"'As most of you know, I have been ranching in these parts now on thirty odd years which is way before most of you were born.

"'Some of you I have helped bring into this world; and others I know about. For those of you who I don't know, it is a pretty good bet that I know your folks. And I would just like to say that I look upon all of you like I do my own sons.'

"He is becoming less tense now and the crowd is becoming more at ease. 'Fact is,' he continued, 'a lot of you are probably a hell of a lot better all-around cowboys than those three misfits I call my own. Hell I'd be happy to trade any day of the week.'

"A laugh rises from the crowd. The atmosphere is a little more relaxed. Frank pauses for an instant and glances around at the many faces seated on the corral fence.

"'I see Curt Bailey,' he motions, 'over there on the south rail. For those of you who may not know, Curt was awarded All Around Top Cowboy last year at the Cheyenne National Rodeo. Stand up Curt and say howdy.' At that Curt Bailey stands up and gives a wave and the crowd returns applause.

"'I also see Wayne Marks over there. Wayne's been riding the rodeo circuit since he was 14. He won the Junior Cowboy Award in Ft.

Worth when he was 16. His dad, Jess Marks and I grew up together in the Oklahoma Territory. We first rode out here together back in 1904,1905 somewhere around there.'

"It now begins to appear that Frank was making small talk to avoid getting down to the actual selection process. He probably felt that the more recognition he could spread around the less disappointment would come to those who were not selected.

"At that particular instant he could see that the crowd was searching for a look at Wayne, and that gave him the chance to continue his own glancing about.

"'And I suppose,' he continues, 'that every man here knows Bobby Boy Warren. Bobby Boy, his brother Sonny and the two Sheldon boys had a hell of a shoot out with the Texas Rangers a few years back. It happened just north of here over in the Guadalupe Mountains.'

"'Outnumbered 10 to 1 they held out for three days and three nights and wore out every Winchester they had. The story goes that they fired so damn hard and fast that the rifle barrels got so hot the guns wouldn't shoot. They didn't have any drinking water left so they had no way of cooling down their firepower. To keep from having to give up the fight they pissed on their rifle barrel to cool it off enough to keep firing.

"'Bobby Boy and the two Sheldon boys got shot up pretty bad but so did one hell of a lot of Texas Rangers. After three days and nights word came down from the Governor's office to call a truce.

"'Now I can't speak for the rest of you but it makes me proud to know that men with that kind of guts and steel want to saddle up and ride a trail with me. Fellers, that shore makes me proud.'

"With that, a round of yells and whistles went up as every cowboy in the crowd identified with the idea of being one's own man.

"'For those of you who may be new to the area, 'Poppy Frank continued, 'the fight broke out over water rights.'

"'There was a group of big money boys in State Capitol down in Austin who got in next to the Governor and decided to steal a little range water.

"'They proposed to build a dam on the West Fork on Mesquite

Canyon and divert the water to the Pecos River and then take it out again down stream to be used for irrigation farming.

"'The only problem with that little thieving, stealing scheme is the water from Mesquite Canyon feeds the South Slope of the Guadalupe Range and the water rights had already been dedicated to the Rocking W Ranch.

"'Well, to this day the Texas Rangers won't admit that they got their butts whipped but there never was a dam built and the Rocking W still has its water rights.' As Poppa Frank finished, a second round of yells and whistles roared out as the group sanctioned their approval."

"Frank goes on to mention a few more names but the thrust of the gathering is now at hand. A silence simply starts to materialize which signals that the time has come.

"'Men,' Frank commences, 'I know that this has been a good chance to be among your fellow cowboys, catch up on a little grab- ass and I have even tooted a few horns.'"

"'But that is not why we are here. The reason we are here is to drive 6,000 head of beef from here to Dodge City, Kansas. Now I know that some of you see this as a final page in history. And it may well be.

"'That will be for the history books to decide. One thing is for sure. The story has been picked up by the news media and is being blown a way to the hell out of proportion.

"'It is being hailed on the National News as a great patriotic undertaking. An example of the war efforts being made by this country to feed our fighting troops.

"'All that means to me is one hell of a lot more pressure to make sure we come through. Now hear me out, if we are not successful it will go down in history as one big ass folly. And I have no doubt that it would become known as Frank Delaney's Folly.'"

"Frank pauses again, searching in his mind for his next wording. Standing there, in the middle of a dusty corral, his weight shifted to one side, both hands in his pockets, sort of slouched forward a bit, he looks at the ground for a moment then raises his head and starts to speak.

"'Now when I hear that word folly I always think of a little incident back in 1849 known as Jayhawkers Folly.

"For those of you who may not be acquainted with that bit of history it happened on the old Salt Lake to Los Angeles Trail. A group of immigrants was trying to get to California in a wagon train that lacked discipline, leadership and common cause.

"'Well, when you have a situation where everyone is thinking of their own interest, you have the makings of a disaster and that is exactly what happened.

"'It wasn't long before the different factions started fighting and the train broke up. All of the unmarried men, who called themselves Jayhawkers, left the married men, wives and children and headed out on their own. This is where history comes in.

"'The wisdom of their plan was born out by the fact that they got themselves out into a barren alkaline salt flat and all but a couple 'em died in a little place that is now called Death Valley.

"'I tell you this because we will be heading across stretches of alkaline flats that are as bad as any place on earth. There is a 60 mile stretch after we cross the Pecos that is as dry as the hubs of Hell. There's not a man here that doesn't know about the Malga Salt Flats.

"'I don't like it one damn bit that we have to do it. But I believe it is better than the alternative. Which is to leave here and head due east until we hit the outskirts of FT. Worth. There we could swing due north and follow whatever remnants are left of the Old Chisholm Trail.

"'That route has been tried and proven but it also would throw us into a lot of heavily populated areas and add about 300 more miles to the drive. By my calculation that's too heavy a price to pay for following the known.

"'What I propose is to take as straight a line as possible which will be like taking the long side of a triangle. It also means crossing the Malga Flats and toughening it out.

"'In about five days after we leave out of here we should be crossing the Pecos. I have in mind to hold up for a day or so at the Pecos, get the stock watered and take a little breather. But when we leave the

Pecos that will be the last water until we reach Comanche Wells over by Eunice, New Mexico.

"'What I want, is to get to Comanche Wells in two days. That means doubling our normal pace.'

"Frank paused a moment to let that sink in; doubling the pace over the hottest part of the drive. Not a whisper stirred from the crowd.

"Seeing that every man there understood the agonizing hell ahead, he continued. 'Now there are two ways we can look at it. You can picture in your minds the misery and torment of 110 degrees heat, breathing alkaline dust and sitting in a saddle twenty hours straight; or, you can picture in your mind the sweet beauty of a four-hour rest stop each night.

"'As for myself, I prefer to think of the rewards at the end of the day. Whichever way you choose, when we hit there, just remember Death Valley and keep moving.

"'Now for those of you who have never moved a large herd, there are definite techniques and procedures. At the front of the column is the first point man, most of the time that will be me. I will be as far as two to three miles or so out in front but only to lay out the trail'.

"'The rest of the time I will be up and down the line. Next back will be two second point men; one on each side of the lead steer. Their job is to keep the nose of that lead steer right on the crack of my ass. After a few days he should become accustom to the direction and the point job gets a little easier.

"'Next back behind the point slots comes the swing men. Your job is to keep the front of the herd in tight. I can't over stress the importance of keeping the front in a good grouping and tight formation. It will probably take five or six days before the character of the drive is developed. Until that happens you will have to kick, ride up against and lay a lariat across the nose of many an obstinate steer. Once the herd becomes accustomed to the movement, holding a formation becomes a little easier. But make no mistake about it. The lead steer and the other up front steers are usually the most obnoxious and meanest of the lot. That's why they're the leaders.

"'So the working scope of the swing slot will be only a hundred to three hundred yards back and forth from the point.'

"'Now let's move to the back of the herd. I want four drag riders. The job does not need a lot of explanation. It will be the hardest and the dirtiest work on the drive.

"There will never be a time when you will not be eating dust and at times it will be so thick that you won't be able to see a steer ten feet away. And in that respect let me give you something to think about.'

"'When you're on drag if you don't like all of that dirt and dust, neither do the cattle that are at the ass end of the drive.

"'Their natural instincts tell them to get to the hell over to the side to where they can breathe. So it will be OK to have some spread in the rear. Just make sure it doesn't get too wide and strung out.

"'The same few steers are likely to account for the majority of your work. So if you have to, lay some rope across their backside.

"'And that's about it. The rest of the crew will be riding flank. The best I can determine we will be strung out a little over four maybe five miles from lead steer to drag. With six flank riders on each side that means that each man is going to be in charge of damn near one mile of moving cattle. The riding is going to be tough, long and mean. Each of you will wear out two horses a day and the flank riders will most likely wear out three. All the positions will be rotated every day so that the shit work will pretty much be spread out fairly even. At night we bunch the herd up and organize a three men, rotating night watch. Two riders will outer circle in one direction and the third will counter circle. Each nightshift on this drive is the same as it was in the late 1800's. Rotate ever two hours and those who are caught in the sunrise shift will not get a break from the start of the day's drive.'

"There was a pause as Frank stopped talking, went over to the windmill and got a drink of water. The cowboys also used the pause to shift, push back their hats, stretch, take out a sack of Bull Durham tobacco, roll and light a cigarette.

"As Frank returned to the center of the corral he removed his hat, wiped his forehead on his shirt sleeve, held his hat up as a shield, looked at the sun, gauged the time and then continued.

"'Men,' he commences in a much sterner tone, 'I want to cover one final aspect. Being a cowboy means cattle is your business; it is my business; it is our business. It means that everything a cow or steer does is our business. How and when they eat, graze, water, when they are content and when they are uneasy. To a large degree cattle are a lot like people.

"'They generally know where they belong and are accustomed to their familiar surrounds. They are also accustomed to seeing and are reassured by the presents of cowboys. Moreover, they are like people with respect to fear of the unknown.

"'When they get out of their own territory they start to feel uneasy and fear starts to set in. Tension can sometimes become so tight you can feel it in the air. Your job is to keep the lid on. That's when you'll have to have a little more patience. When you yell, yell in a tone that doesn't reflect panic. In addition, when you are on night watch, it's part of the job to sing a little tune. It helps to pass the time and it's a comforting sound to the cattle. It also seems best if all three nightriders have no objections to harmonizing in on the same tune. It provides a sense of unity.'

"Frank stopped talking at that point to study the two hundred faces which surround him. He takes a crumpled red bandanna out of his rear pocket, removes his hat with the other hand and wipes the sweat from his forehead.

"Then, as if it was the only thing of importance, he carefully wipes the sweat from the inside hat sweat band. It is his way of letting everyone know that he is not prone to making snap decisions.

"As he replaces his hat and bandanna he gradually turns and makes eye contact with as many of the men as possible. It is intended that the moment-in-time stand still.

"'What I am about to say now,' he slowly continues, 'I want to make sure that every man here understands. It is my duty to tell you that in spite of everything we do, the odds are heavy that we will have at least one and possibly several massive stampedes.'

"A silence followed before he again started to speak. 'Now I know,' he continues, 'that most of you have never experienced a stampede. Cattle are not prone to run when they are on their home range. So I will give you a few particulars. Flash storms are a prime potential. Electrical storms at night are almost a guarantee of a run.

"'But don't get the idea it takes something that big. When a herd is skittish it can be anything; a coyote's yell or a nightrider lighting a cigarette.

"'There will be no warning and the oddity of all oddities is that cattle on stampede do not bellow. The one consistency is that they will always follow the leader.'

"'He pauses as he prepares to make his next statement. And before it is even said, every man there knows what is coming. What must be done to stop a stampede. No man made a sound.

"They are all modern day cowboys. They have all heard horror stories about what can happen to a rider if his horse stumbles in front of stampeding cattle; but none have ever witnessed a stampede.

"Now they are being told if they take the job, it is a danger they will most likely have to face.

"'Men,' Frank starts as the last measure of his orientation, 'for those of you who have not brought your own side arm, there will be a supply of six guns in the chuck wagons. In the most likely event that we do have a stampede there is only one way we'll be able to get it stopped. Some any one of you... me included...any one of us has got to get... to the lead steer.

"'You Must,' he stressed the word, 'you must get right in next to... and ride rubbing right flat up against him. That's when you are going to need a six-gun; if you don't have a six-gun a rifle will do. But you'll be riding dead out, blind and having to lean over in your saddle to where your gun hand is right next to the face of that lead steer. When you are in that slot you start firing; not at the steer but into the ground.

"'The object is for the flash fire of the gun power to be right next to his eye. The flash fire, plus the ear busting sound will cause him to veer off.

"'Your job is to veer right with and stay right on 'em. Stay right up against him and keep firing. Make sure each shot is right next to his eye. If you empty your six-gun use your Winchester but don't let up. He will keep veering off until he eventually makes a circle and comes right up on the ass of the last steer. That's what we're after.

"'Now, if you have not heard anything else listen to this. When a run breaks, the closest man in a saddle is the man responsible for the lead. I'll repeat that so that there is no misunderstanding.

"'A run can break in any direction; toward a canyon or toward the open prairie. When cattle break they have no sense of direction. "And the closest man in a saddle is the man responsible for the lead. There can be no hesitation.

"'Spur and spur hard. The quicker to that lead steer, the quicker the hit the better the chances. Now one final thought. When you're right up against him and rubbing sides, stay light, and stay leaned all the way over in your saddle; right down by the lead steer's head; if you can do it.'

"That sentence ended with a pause and the seriousness in the air signaled that there would be something coming. Frank inhaled a full breath of air, felt his rib cage expand, held it until it burned, let it out with a force and then continued.

"'Sit as light and loose in the saddle as you can. If your horse hits a prairie dog hole or stumbles, and you see he's going down, try to throw yourself on the back of that lead steer.

"'With any kind of luck you may be able to grab his horns and ride him bare-back until another rider can move in and pick you up. It's been done. And some men have been fortunate enough to make it out alive. Others...many others have not been so lucky.'

"There is an additional pause and then Frank concludes, 'Let's hope that it doesn't happen to us.'"

"In the middle of his last sentence, Poppa Frank feels a surge of blood rush to his leathery face. He suddenly realizes that he had committed a social blunder. In his intent to make the perils fully known, he has over stepped the lines of code.

"No cowboy wants to be told how to do his job. To talk further would only compound the infraction. There is no need to point out that there is no rank, age, or favoritism of riders in a cattle stampede. The lead man is whoever is there at the moment and everyone knows that whatever has to be done would be done. Nor is there any need to point out what will happen if a horse stumbles and falls in the path of 6,000 head of stampeding cattle.

"Frank's only thought is to finish the business at hand. 'I think,' he continues, 'that I have said enough about that side of the operation.

"'It's now appropriate to add a little balance by reflecting on the positive. I believe, as do most of you, that this drive will probably be the final page in cattle drive history.

"'Time and circumstances have bestowed upon us this rare opportunity to be the ones to write the final page. It will be something we can all tell our grandchildren.

"'But on a more important note we will be doing a job which needs to be done. And if any of this beef gets to the bellies of our men in combat then we will have done a patriotic service for our country.'

"'Having said that, I think it is time to determine which of us will be selected for this bit of history. I have taken a count and if I am correct there are 203 of you who want the job. I wish I could take you all but I can't. I only need 14 additional riders. So before we go any further I wish to express my appreciation to all of you who have volunteered. I know that many of you have traveled a long distance at a cost of time and money. I want to take this moment to express my appreciation.'

"With that Frank reaches down and picks up the paper sack that he brought out from the ranch house. 'Now,' he continues, 'what I have here is a large size brown paper sack that is going to be passed around. Inside are small folded pieces of paper; each with a number from 1 to 203.

"'There should be one square for each man. As the sack is passed, take a square and pass it on. When you are all through I am going to call out random numbers which come to my mind.'

"With that he hands the sack to the first cowboy and leaves the corral. In a short time he returns and asks whether everyone has a number. When that is affirmed he unceremoniously announces.

"'Men, I would like for the following hands to sign on with me for the purpose of driving 6,000 head of cattle from Van Horn, Texas to Dodge City, Kansas: Nos. 22, 14, 196, 89, 33, 202, 57, 112, 46, 166, 9, 171, 136 and 100. I would like those men to report to my foreman Snakey Ramsey to sign on and get their work orders.

"'The rest of you I would again like to express my appreciation. You are welcome to stay on here as long as you like. There are empty bunks in the bunkhouse and we have plenty of grub. I would like to visit with each one of you but I am planning on pulling out of here at 4 o'clock in the morning. So right now if you will excuse me, I'm sure you'll understand if I have to keep moving.'"

Aspen paused as he finished the part of the story that happened before he arrived. In the time-line of events, his own participation was now at hand; and it was a moment torn between impatience and timing.

On one hand he was anxious to share with Jenny the advents that became turning points of his life. He wanted to narrate his story in colorful dialogue and portray in detail the men, the cattle and the Texas plains. He wanted to recount cliff hanging episodes and the suspenseful ending.

On the other hand, the mood for story telling had changed. In the silence of the moment it was coincidental that Seth Thomas again announces its presence by Tombbb, Tombbb, Tombbb, Tombbb, 4:00 A.M.

Without comment, both Aspen and Jenny knew that this was an appropriate ending place. His episodes on the Texas prairie must be left for another day. For now, the situation would be concluded under etiquette and protocol of eastern breeding. Jenny was the first to speak.

In a tone implying sleepiness, a yawning mouth and sleep suggesting stretch she asked, "Then what happened?"

Aspen was thankful for her signal. "What happened", he replied.

"Was an adventure which will take time to tell. And the mood in me tells me not now."

Jenny's answer complimented his; but she also raised an unexpected question.

"I have mixed feeling," she responded. "I am sleepy so I will yield to sleep on one condition. Give me a hint. What is the substance of this change with God in your life?"

Aspen had been lying flat on the floor but when Jenny finished he rose up into a sitting, knee prop position He paused with his hands draped half over, half around his knees. His head was slightly tilted forward with his eyes staring at the floor; as if a crystal ball was occupying the space between his legs. His voice delivered as if a sequence was unfolding inside the crystal ball and he was announcing the event.

"The substance of my change," he spoke in a voice that was slightly uneven as if waiting for the fog to become more clear "Is," followed by another slight pause, "there is no way in this ol' world that The Church of The Apostles is ever, going to get, that six million dollars.

"I am personally going to see to it that it is put to uses other than going to an antiseptic, stained glass monument to hypocrisy. Wherever it does go, however it is spent, it will be out in the air, out in the streets. I have thoughts of doing like Poppa Frank does; give God a job.

"Something along the lines of giving God and a helper, a sack full of money every morning. Telling the two of them to hit the bricks. Their orders will be to go out and see that poor people get some grub for their bellies; and not to come back until the sack is empty."

Then with a pronounced, "And something else Jenny. I have come to the belief that you and I have not yet met 'the' person; that rebel, that challenger of corruption, that street fighter, that he-or-she-Bobby-Boy-Warren of Pittsburgh, around whom ours lives will eventually be centered."

To the storyteller, new thinking was starting to evolve. From a bygone youth came unlistened words from Shelly. *In life she had taught there are those who kneel and there are those who live by the words they feel.* In his searching of all her plights, the storyteller spoke to the early morning darkness of the room. "Mother of mine," his voice audible only slightly above the whistling wind, "I believe mine eyes are beginning to see."

Chapter 17

The year was 1944. The age of Shelly Waters was three. In that year her age, combined with certain unorthodox happenings, intersected in a time line that would influence the course and direction of her adult life. In the analogy of these influences, some have said that the two intersecting experiences were simply happenstance. In the opinion of others however, the events, be they complicated and twisted were in fact destiny; the avenue by which she was molded into the preordained purpose of her adult life.

As the calendar that year turned the opening months, mother and daughter, Patricia and Shelly, were living reasonably well in Morgan's flat on Wood Street. Patricia had been working in the ticket cage at the Stran for almost two years and was developing some semblance of a normal life; semblance to the degree that she had roots to a home and worked regular hours. Nevertheless, she was still unduly reclusive. At the end of her work shift each day, she and Shelly would routinely head straight home with diversions only for groceries and other essentials.

Patricia still showed no signs of opening up to Morgan. She still had no friends other than an occasional visit from Jenny. She still bestowed all of her affection on Shelly, still held and rocked Shelly, still nursed Shelly even though she had long since ceased to produce milk and she still kissed Shelly directly on the mouth. On Shelly's part, this was her mother; the only other person besides Morgan that she knew.

On Morgan's part the year brought him the title of Daddy Morgan. While Patricia was reclusive, little Shelly had no such inhibitions. And the lap of Morgan was her first order of affection as she and Patricia arrived at the Stran each day. And the softness of an innocent child with sparkling blue eyes, rosy cheeks and glistening blond fine silk hair brought a brightness to his life which he never thought possible.

Whereas Patricia showed no interest in opening up her heart, little Shelly gave her's freely.

Between she and Morgan there were large daily helpings of hugs, kisses and lap sitting. The Stran became a second home for Shelly, and like a bear cub her curiosity knew no bounds. She would inquisitively climb over, under, in and out of every nook, cranny and doorway.

She had a free rein to wander from the ticket cage into the lobby, Morgan's office, up into the balcony and within limitations had rights to the refreshment stand. Given the frame of things at the start of that year, it would have been reasonable to conjecture that in time Patricia would come out of her shell. That in time she would open up to Morgan, they would get married, Morgan would adopt Shelly and they would become an all-American family. Certainly there was nothing on the horizon to indicate otherwise; not at the start of that year.

However, in fact of the matter a mid-1944 business deal on Morgan's part <u>and</u> a 1941 past year happenstance on Patricia's part would come crashing head-on like two steam locomotives; the impacting consequence of which could never have been foreseen.

The substance of the collision was two independent, stand-alone factions. One faction was the fable book *A Thousand And One Arabian Nights* read by Patricia in 1941. The second faction was the purchase of the movie version of *A Thousand And One Arabian Nights* by Morgan in 1944.

Patricia had read the book and discovered her self-intimacy at a time when she was at her lowest point. Morgan, at a time when he was at his highest point, acquired the 1920's film series *A Thousand And One Arabian Nights*. The dividend of that unorthodox amalgamation was something that Shelly was far too young to have control over but non-the-less-she was influenced. In later years, as she grew into adulthood it would be the yardstick by which she would search for and eventually measure love.

By best recollection the time line started along in midyear; the advent being Morgan acquiring ownership to the Palace Theater out in Oakland. Among the items that had been included in his purchase price was an inventory of the old Arabian Nights film series. Most of the movies in the collection were more than twenty years old, out of date and had little value except in a nostalgia sense.

In context of the era, reminiscence from the 1920's when the *Thousand and One Nights* craze had swept through the nation's movie houses and that distant land of fiery romance had captivated America.

Glorified by Hollywood, the Sahara Desert was fantasized as a land of mysterious forbidden love and boundless sex amidst beautiful slave girls in sheer harem suits. Bagdad was immortalized as the city of enchantment, sorcery and magic. Sword fights, desert oasis, horseback rides across endless sand and, that most memorable of all, the flying carpet. Add to that, the depictions of dazzling Arabian palaces, gurgling fountains, luscious young women wearing face veils and spacious marble- floor bedrooms with sheer drapery panels which bellowed out from the cross ventilation of warm desert winds.

All were glorified as a perfect setting for a hero to sweep his princess away and soar into the heavens on the magical powers of a fringed ornamental carpet; all of which Patricia had first read and imagined. In the book however she only had the benefits of word descriptions; but the film version...the film vividly depicted the most seductive aspect of all. Beautiful warm clear nights with a big full moon shinning down on the endless shimmering sands of the Sahara.

All of which, by 1944 standards had little potential as a main feature draw at a movie house. But Morgan felt the collection might have some profit producing possibilities if they were promoted as part of a double feature package. He moved the inventory from Oakland over to the Stran with the intent of running the series as a bonus mid-night draw; that decision appears to have been ground zero.

On the first night Morgan started showing the silent films, Patricia attended the initial showing out of little more than curiosity. At the midnight hour, patronage was light, the majority of the seats were empty, and the balcony had been roped closed to the public.

In time sequence, the main feature had ended a few moments earlier and a short intermission was in progress. Patricia had taken Shelly by the hand and the two had proceeded through the double swinging doors. Pausing briefly to adjust to the light, she indifferently viewed the vast number of vacant seats.

For no reason other than openness she selected seating that allowed space from the scattering of other patrons. As she and Shelly set looking around and waiting for the showing to start she had no frame of mind other than curiosity.

She could not have known that in a few minutes hence certain life changing forces were about to unfold. In a few moments hence she would be catapulted from her world of boredom into a realm of self-administered sex. *And for Shelly, a mother's imprint on the mind of her child was about to be forever and irreversibly stamped. The nature of such begets the question why*??

Why, and for what reason did the things that happened next happen? Who but the Philosophers can be held to answer?

When the first reel started to roll and the scenes of the Sahara Desert started revealing its mystical splendor Patricia was instantly seized by an overpowering force of tingling sexual arousal. In a nino-second her memories flashed back some three years to the time she first discovered self-intimacy. A time when she was with a newborn child, alone in a strange apartment, the accidental finding of the *Arabian Nights* stories in an old green book and the self-administered sexual pleasure that the stories had brought.

Pleasure that had come to her at a time when it was desperately needed but with the passage of time the intensity thereof had lessened; and printed words on crumbly pages had drifted into obscurity. Now, totally unexpected, she was seeing on a giant silver screen that which she had only fantasized back then; and her dormant womanhood arousal started stirring. The hero that she had only envisioned in the book was now there, bigger than life and looking even more handsome than she had pictured.

Forgotten desires started to awaken and as the erotica on the screen became more suggestive the tingling in her crouch became more intense. Shifting and turning in her seat she fought to keep her composure but to no end. The surge of hormones was too powerful. She and self-intimacy would again become friends. Hoping that none of the other patrons would notice, she carefully slid her hand inside the waistband of her slacks and panties.

Her first touch of her flaccid clitoris felt strangely foreign and insensitive. But as her finger searched for and found that sensitive point, tingles of electricity came to life.

Quiescent sensations burst forth like an unexpected thundercloud releasing a torrent of rain on a spring day. Warm rain falling from the heavens on a drought stricken valley and the barren fields were quick to respond. As moisture brings softness to a parched land so was the happening in her womanhood.

With a few quick strokes of her finger a deluge of her feminine juices saturated the fringes of her pubic hair. Then nothing. It was over, like a downpour that suddenly ends; the promise had been exciting but the results were not fulfilling. Her first climax had ended too quickly. While enjoyable for an instant it had not been emotionally explosive. There had been no sensation of foreplay, the fantasy of deep mouth kissing, the arousal of her nipples or the intensity of squeezing her lover in a powerful hug as she sank her fingers into his back. She had been too tense; too cognizant of other patrons.

Nevertheless, she had once again tasted the nectar and she left the movie that first night with a hunger; a hunger that would eventually become almost unmanageable. In the days that followed, her craving for stronger more emotionally intense climaxes would unknowingly lead her into forbidden sexual tenets. Caught up in an overpowering craving she was pulled into pagan acts of self-intimacy that would be cast like chiseled stone into the impressionable mind of Shelly.

The first step on that path happened shortly after the initial showing. Patricia asked Morgan to let her change her working hours in the ticket cage from days to evening. The change made attending the midnight showings much more accessible. It was customary for Morgan to be gone at that hour and the theater ushers always roped off and closed the balcony; but no such barrier applied to Patricia. Each midnight as the opening scenes of the Arabian Nights era started to flicker across the screen, she and Shelly would be hidden away in the highest part of the otherwise empty balcony. Taking the darkest isle seat, she would lift Shelly into her lap, get ready, and wait.

As the projector whirled, and the movie credits came to an end, her trip would begin. Her imagination of boundless sex was heighten by the opening erotic scenes of scantly clad slave girls in harem suits lounging among throw pillows on the cool marble floors of a desert citadel.

Ruling monarchs and royalty languished on satin cushions and ate grapes from the feeding hands of ravishing young beauties as dark tan male servants fanned huge ostrich-feather fans. Then would come her hero. There he was. Her Arab Prince wearing a white turban with a large inset ruby. His tan hard trim body clad only in an open vest and lounging pants.

His perfect features and dark sparkling eyes coming to life as the camera zoomed in for facial close-ups. And for the next ninety minutes the real world of Patricia Waters was left behind as she rushed to her lover's side and lived his conflicts, fought his sword fights, eluded the chases of ruthless solders and narrowly escaped death by jumping over city walls. Her heart would flinch with piercing pain when his odds became overwhelming; but then came his triumphs and she and her lover would sail away on his magical flying carpet. And her pull into pageantry would propel.

In her fantasies it was she and not princess Badr al-Budur that was beside her lover as the two looked down on the lights of Bagdad. As the carpet sailed across the desert sands she fantasized herself rolling over on her back and her scant harem suit coming off at the waist and her lover finding his way into her eager receptacle. With her knees pulled up and her legs spread wide his golden tan love muscle would enter her craving womanhood. All the while the warm desert breeze swirled her long hair as his eager mouth found her hard firm nipples.

Shrouded in the security of the balcony darkness, she would unbutton her blouse, reach her hand inside, slide up her brassiere, uncoil one of her long breast and bring it out. Intuitively Shelly would take the placid nipple in her soft little mouth and snuggle up to the only person she had ever known. In proxy, Patricia would run her fingers through her lover's soft baby hair as she held him close. With her other hand inside the elastic waistband of her panties she would massage her aroused nubile and gazed at the stars on the screen as they traveled across the galaxies. The majestic beauty of the heavens intensifying a thousand folds as their mutual orgasm exploded and hurled electrifying charges across the universe. And night after night she traveled to her lover's land; and her pagan acts multiplied.

Caught up in her own passion for harder and harder orgasms she unmindfully started squeezing Shelly closer and whispering, "Suck baby, suck harder. That's it baby. Harder, suck, suck, suck. These quivering vibrations were received by Shelly's baby teeth and sharp biting would follow. As Patricia felt the cutting sting, her normally placid breast would swell firm hard and become elongated.

As her arousal reached greater heights electrical charges intensified in a signal for Shelly to bite even harder. For Shelly, the harder bites triggered a subconscious premature twinge; absent of any mortal input but born of nature's basis primitive instincts to promulgate. A tiny arousal had electrified in her panties. An impressionable first time tingling...that in her lifetime...would never be unlearned.

And in a self-fulfilling prophesy, Patricia's passion would at times become so intense that her baby's sharp little teeth would cross over from euphoria to a cutting pain. Instantly answered by a quick slapping pop of Patricia's hand across Shelly's head; and though being a signal, such poppings were not signals to stop. To the contrary, sexual pain begets sexual pain. And the flinch Patricia felt in the first case was welcomed in the second and subsequent harder bites; being answered each time by a slightly more intense pop... crescendo the numeral times that followed; to perfection if there was a sharp bite at the instant of orgasm.

The supreme moment in Patricia's ecstasy reaching its explosive zenith if she could successfully orchestrate the fantasy of she and her lover locked in deep embrace at the moment the screen cast a big full moon on the endless simmering sands in rhythm with her rapid strokes and the sharp pain of Shelly's biting. Happen it did...in numbers. And in just as many numbers there was the aftermath. The sensations, while boundless in ecstasy, lasted but a few short seconds and then, as with all orgasm, the utopia subsides as quickly as it arrives. As the movie reached its end, the house lights would abruptly come on.

Where there had been security of darkness an instant before there was now stark defenselessness against brightness and a feeling of exposure and guilt. Quickly removing Shelly from her lap she would return her exposed breast to the security of her blouse and hurriedly hand brush the wrinkles from her clothes.

Getting to their feet, the two would descend the balcony to the main floor. On any one such night Patricia would feel embarrassed as they mingled in with other departing patrons and cross the lobby. Without making eye contact she would nod goodnight to the last usher and, holding tiny hand in mother's hand, they would exit out into the damp night air.

The city lights were generally always bright but the street would usually be empty as they walked without talking the few short blocks to the apartment.

Nevertheless, pagan pleasures once tasted are apt to return to haunt the mortal soul. That which was originally conceived under a cloak of darkness is known to reemerge when darkness again returns. Not uncommon would it be that back in the apartment, when they were again alone in their shared double bed, under the security of bed covers in the quiet night, Patricia's guilt would gradually subside. Replaced by loving holding and baby talking to her child.

"Da wus fun Mommie. Shelee like. Da we do when we watch-en da man on da fly-en carpet.

"Did you like it Baby?"

"Uh huh, it wus fun Mommie. We do dat som mor?"

"We'll see."

"Mommie why da men in pictre fite wih ech otter?"

"Well Baby it's because the Sultan, their king, is an evil man."

"Wat da king Mommie?"

"Honey the king is the ruler."

"Wat da rul mean?"

"It means that he tries to tell everyone what to do. He steals all of the people's money so that they have to go hungry."

"Why king do dat?"

"Because he uses people Honey. He don't care about them he just uses them."

"Dat why men in pictre fite?"

"Yes Honey, the prince and princess fight the bad old king because they know that what he is doing is bad. So they stand up to him. They refuse to let him push them around. And when they win all the people are happy."

"Whe you win yu happie?'

"Very happy honey?"

"Dat when you fly away on mgic carpt?'

"Uh huh, Just me and my prince."

"Pince suc you mlk do dat make him strng so he can fite?"

"That's my love, Honey. I'm giving him my love."

"Mommie yu a pincess?"

"Uh huh, Baby in our dreams, your Mommie is a princess and she fights at the side of her prince. You like?"

"Yesss yesss, Shelee lov Mommie, we see her som mor."

"Well, maybe, if you're good. Maybe tomorrow night?"

"An da next, pleas..."

"And the next."

"An da next"

"And the next. Every night for as long as we like. Now snuggle over here closer to me and let Mommie hold you and go to sleep."

If Patricia said nothing more, little Shelly would yawned in pre-sleep, and say "Goo nite Mommie, I luv you."

Sometimes she would say other words. "Mommie," her tone requesting attention. "Yes Honey," Patricia would answer. "Mommie, you all i gots in da hol worl."

Patricia's eyes would slightly water as she hugged her only child and in their natural pattern Shelly's mouth would come to suckle one of her elongated breast. The child, feeling secure in cradled arms, the mother, pretending to be holding her lover the two would drop off to sleep.

Such were the starting perimeters of the Arabian Nights era; but not the ending. When it originally started Patricia had been overjoyed with her new found pleasure. A ray of sunshine had finally broken through the bleak clouds of loneliness. They were moments of pleasure and she waited anxiously for each succeeding night.

As with all things however, moments of high must be followed by moments of low. After an unknown while, her orgasms were becoming less fulfilling and much more arduous. Little by little strong misgivings were starting to surface and overpowering guilty feelings were beginning to materialize as to what she was doing with her child. But if Patricia felt guilty, when Morgan discovered what was going on he felt even more so.

In the beginning he had not known what was happening and had been pleased with Patricia's unexpected interest in the silent films. The thought had even occurred to him that eventually she might even take an active pursuit in the theater business.

At first when she kept requesting reruns of the flying carpet series Morgan was pleased. But in time her repetitious request for the same film started causing suspicion. When the understanding of what was happening finally came to his light it brought a gut clinching staggering guilt.

The emotional swell-up which he flashed within caused a surging teeth grinding, gut anger of such intensity that it triggered a fighting resolve. The whole damn shenanigans had gone on too long. Enough is enough. Right, wrong, or someplace in between, right then he was going to force some understanding between him and Patricia. Just as flowing water can wear away stone, he had clung to the idea that in time she would come to him in her own right. Now time had run out. For better or worse he was going to start taking control. A new chapter in their life was about to be opened.

As a means of crowding his way into her world he simply firmly took her by the hand, led her to the car, started driving and started buying. In a forced togetherness he insisted that she go with him on shopping sprees. The first thing they did was to completely refurbished the apartment; new furniture, new decorations, new linens, new house wares.

The initial firm step had increased their talking and discussions but the avenue to her heart still remained closed. He next turned his attention to her wardrobe and together they spent hours at Kaufmann's, Horne's and the leading women's apparel shops along Grant Street; it helped but didn't cure. It had brought some brightness to her face, a stronger straighter posture, the exchange of hand squeezing and her arm inside of his as they walked.

Underneath, however, she continued to harbor the feeling that even though he was buying all of these things for her, somehow they were not fully hers. Bundles and packages from children's shops and loads of new toys had brought squeals, neck hugging and kisses from Shelly but only appreciative squeezing and light kissing from her mother.

He made reservations at dinner clubs that had the best bands and entertainment. Sitting at a choice table and receiving special service, the winds of romance would sometimes tease if not caress their moments. The progression of food from appetizers, to entrée complimented by vintage wine to dessert followed by after dinner liquor would usually bring a peaceful feeling.

Nevertheless, dinners drift gently to an end and as the dinner hour ticked by, moods of the evening change. The clearing of tables and the wiping of crumbs from white tablecloths send a signal to the band to strikes up dance floor music. For Morgan and Patricia the change in music tempo came a harsh reminder; the world of dance requires fully functional legs.

Music that spawns laughter and gaiety to others guest of the evening brings awkwardness to Morgan and silence to Patricia. They linger at the table for a while and alternate between glancing at each other and watching couples on the dance floor. The remaining wine is nursed until the last swallow but then it is over. There is nothing left to build on. With the tab paid, they rise from the table without comment. Morgan supporting on his cane they make their way past the other patrons and leave. The shooting stars of their possible love would once again burn out, flicker and die; the remains being left at the table to be hurriedly cleared by the food handlers and discarded with other waste.

As dinner after dinner faltered, Morgan began to realize that some other avenue had to be explored. It was in that time frame that a major social event was about to come to Pittsburgh; the first time presentation of the ballet Swan Lake. On the hearing of that news, a fantasy came to him of how it would feel to attend such a celebrated event. It was something for which he had always felt a yearning but never pursued. A mixed image of something he wanted to do but a feeling that he didn't belong. With Patricia in the picture however it became more plausible as he pictured a formal evening among the elite and wealthy. Himself in a black tuxedo and Patricia in a beautiful gown; they would be the handsomest couple in Pittsburgh.

It settled in his mind. Attending the performance of Swan Lake would be perfect. Hyped by the news media, as being the aristocratic event of the year it would be a social to top all socials.

Tickets were clamored after with the royal elite of Pittsburgh having first call and the near elite secondary. All other could expect no possibility. Morgan did not consider him to be in either category, but he did have something which neither the cream elite nor near elite had. He had favor markers out to most of the ordinary, everyday people who worked behind the scenes to put the production on; including those who metered out the tickets.

When opening night arrived he had two seats, second row, center isle at the Nixon Theater; that architectural wonder which was once proclaimed by world-renown Senator George T. Oliver as "the world's most perfect playhouse". For the evening Patricia wore a full-length formal gown of high-cut satin green, dangling diamond earrings, choker necklace, a diamond tiara crowning her swept back hair and long white gloves.

Lights, celebrities, flash bulbs, Pittsburgh's social elite; for her these all equated the attending of a royal ball. She was spellbound at being among the opening night crowd and it was in the lobby of the colossal theater that she experienced a fleeting sensation that sent shivers through her body.

It happened just after she and Morgan had worked their way through the crowd from the street and into the lobby. Caught up in the excitement she was standing slightly aside while Morgan dealt with the ticket-taker and usher. As she looked at him in his formal black tie and tails, with his too much jet black shaggy hair falling around his collar and his dominating eyebrows complimenting his heavy mustache, deep set sparkling blue eyes and character lines running across his masculine face, she was struck by his being gangster like handsome.

With that came a fleeting revelation, a blinding flash that there he was, her knight, her dream, her life. Impulsively she stepped up closer to his side and ran her arm through his. Instantly she wanted to tell him; to tell the world she had finally found love. She felt proud to be by his side and in a flash of divine rebirth she felt the urge to become his wife. As they were being ushered down the isle of the massive, capacity packed theater to their plush maroon velvet seats, she was overcome with pride. With her chest high in a posture of dignity she held the arm of her man who walks with the aid of a silver-handled cane.

Looking back this had been the pinnacle of events that, some three weeks earlier, had started with the unexpected arrival of a new fur coat. It happened one morning when a dignified, black delivery van with uniformed driver stopped in front of the apartment. There was a knock on the door. When she answered, a distinguished, formally attired gentleman who announced that he was from Lord Barrenoff's House of Furriers greeted her.

It was his pleasure he informed Patricia that his purpose of business was to fill an order placed by a Mr. Morgan Smithfield

Having properly presented his credentials and verifying Patricia's identity, he clapped his hands to a waiting attendant. And from the back of the delivery van came two racks of full-length mink coats.

"But... but... there... there must be some mistake," she had exclaimed; her look and response clearly showing her complete surprise.

"No mistake Madam, I assure you it is a legitimate order," he stiffly answered as he directed the bringing in of the two racks.

"But, but a fur coat for me? Why?" her tone attempting to show her point. "Those are for rich women, I mean, I wouldn't know what to do with one. I..."

"*Madam. Please!* I must insist that you allow me to proceed. Forgive me if I sound rude but Lord Barrenoff's House of Furriers is not in the posture of making mistakes. Now if you will be so kind as to stand here in the middle of the room where the light is good we can proceed.

"In," the Conciliar proceeded in charge, "looking at the color of your hair, complexion and general stature I suggest we start with this Autumn Leaves model. If you will, would you be so kind as to slip in your arm. Good now the other, good. Now, would you walk to the door and back..."

"Are? Are you absolutely sure this is really for me. My very own?" she meekly attempted one last time.

"*Madam! For the last time!*

From the many that were tried, a selection was made which she was told 'her beauty most complimented'; natural deep brown in color, mid-calf length, cuffed sleeves and upturned collar. While she stood still, came the final hand-under-chin stand-back look, the final turn around assessment, the concluding approval nod and it was done.

For Lord Barrenoff's House of Furriers it was just another sale as the delivery van loaded and pulled away. For Patricia Waters it was an unimaginable experience equating the passing through a new-life time zone.

In such a context there are sometime moments in, as well there should be, that are the pinnacle of a sweeping change.

Things that can only be described as *epiphany, a sudden flash of recognition, blind faith, maturing, can never go home again* or *simple destiny.* By whatever name it will usually happen once in everyone's life. For men in combat the moment is apt to be in the face of a horrifying death and they instantly change from rogues to Christian believers and pray to a God they previously mocked. For parents of young children the moment may come when a neighborhood fireman risks his own life to retrieve a child from a burning building and they instantly reassess life's priorities.

For a shy and bashful schoolgirl the moment may come when she is asked for a date by the high school football hero; and her self-esteem instantly soars.

For Patricia Waters such a pinnacle-moment came when it dawned on her that she was to be the actual owner of an expensive mink coat. Not one that she would be permitted to wear but actually belonged to someone else. No such stigma, just a brand new glorious mink coat that was all hers; mink, lining and buttons all hers. She owned something of value and she was worthy. A quantum leap in her self-esteem garnered that she was as good as anyone else. In that flash she cast off her shackles of always being docile. As the door closed behind the departing furrier her life-change moment spiraled to its zenith.

The feel of the coat was as natural as if nature had intended it to be there. It was where it belonged. As she felt the cool silk lining and the soft seductive mink against her face and neck she whirled around the room. *It's mine! It's really mine!* she cried to herself. *I'm rich. I'm rich. I own something valuable and it's mine. I'm as good as anyone else. I don't have to hide out in a dark theater night after night anymore. Oh thank you, thank You God for finally setting me free. No more stepping aside for rich snotty women. No more letting 'em go ahead of me at the store check out register. Oh God! I never realized how good it could feel.*

She ran to the bathroom for a look in the vanity mirror and her feelings further electrified. From the bathroom she ran to the bedroom to the larger mirror on the dresser. By stepping back she could turn and get a side view. With the collar upturned and pulled around her face she hugged herself with both arms and continued her ecstatic thoughts. *Look at me. I'm beautiful. Oh damn, Oh gosh, that's me in there, it's really me.*

The feelings of self-worth which she was having were telling her that she could conquer the world; indescribable feelings. Feelings she had never before experienced in her lifetime. As would happen, however, before they could even take hold they would be tested.

At that very moment there came a knocking on the front door. A knocking she had to answer; which of her persons would be the one to answer; the old or the new? Waiting on the other side was Morgan in a 'just-happened-by' pretense.

"Morgan!" her new self squealed as he entered and she excitedly stepped back and made a big sweeping whirl. "I love it! You wonderful man."

Coming full turn she then rushed up and frantically gave him a hard hug and her first intense full mouth moist kiss.

"Morgan," she exclaimed again, "it's beautiful. Oh it's absolutely gorgeous. Oh God is it beautiful. I know I shouldn't ask. Moreover, no matter what I don't care. It's mine and that's all I care, but why? What's the occasion?"

Morgan felt a glow in her joy, dumfounded by her out of character actions and was frightened it would slip away if he did not answer exactly right.

"Well... " His tone drawled and nonchalant, "It's not really all that big of a deal. But, there's a little shindig coming to town that I thought we might take in. That's of course if it suites' your mind? If fin' it does, why we'll just have to have something respectable for you to wear."

"Shin-dig, new mink coat, Morgan," she cast an unsure look she had once seen in a movie, "what are you trying to surprise me with?" Then came a cautious moment of her relapsing into the old.

"Will it mean people, crowds of people? You know I'm not good at that sort of thi..."

"Uh. Trish now don't you get excited. It'll be OK. A few people here and there. Just enough for me to show the world how beautiful you are.

The way I see things it won't be a matter of you fitting in with them. The deal will be whether they will fit in with you. Now here's..."

"Morgan! It doesn't matter! From this moment on I AM GOING TO BE ME! That kiss I just gave you? Come here and get inside of this coat," she interrupted him as she opened the coat out wide and stepped up close.

As Eve must have felt in the Garden of Eden the birth of Patricia's womanhood exploded to life in that moment. In a blinding flash she felt like a total woman. A woman in her glory, free of inhibitions and her Arab Prince was right there; hers for the taking. Her mouth found his hungry lips and they locked in a deep mouth, moist lip searching embrace. "Tell me we are going to fly away?" she whispered as she let up.

"Well, Uh. I," he stammered at her out of character behavior, "Baby I, Uh, I don't know too much about flying away but what I have in mind may be the next best thing."

"And?"

"And, it's a little thing that's coming to town called Swan Lake. That's a ballet. And I was wondering. If you're not doing anything I thought we might give it a little shot.

"Course if it's a little too tame for a sophisticated woman like you there's a cute little co-ed usher down at the Stran that I might be able to persuade..."

"YOU DARE!" her different character continued to surprise him. "OH! No! Morgan Smithfield! This coat and me. We're definitely your Swan Lake date.

"But," she followed up with a hesitant tone indicating slight panic, "Morgan I have to tell you that I know nothing, absolutely nothing about the ballet. I don't even..."

"Neither do I," he rushed in his reassurance; but then modified the statement. "Well, maybe a little; at least about this particular one. The reason is that, it is the one which has always floated around in my someday dreams. Swan Lake is supposed to be the most romantic of all ballets. And it is the one I want us to see together."

"But what's it about? I mean how is it romantic?"

"Well, as I understand it," he answered, "the story goes something like this."

As he prepared to tell the story he picked up a kitchen chair and turned it backward so that his arms were folded across the back. He stretched his twisted leg out to the side and as he settled. Patricia still wearing her fur coat dropped into the easy chair.

"The thing about a ballet," he started, "is you may, or may not always be able to follow the story. However, that's not important. The idea is the beauty of the dance. The trick is to identify with the dancers as they move across the stage." As he was talking he felt an embarrassment. He, a man with one bad leg, was describing dance steps. So, with a shifting of tone and switching to characters he became a little more comfortable.

"As I understand it," he continued, "Swan Lake is a four act play that goes something like this. The principle players are a young hero by the name of Prince Siegfried, Siegfried's mother, breath-takingly beautiful Queen of the Swans Odette, an evil sorcerer named Von Rotbart, and Von Rotbart's tricky daughter Odile.

"The setting opens in the garden of Prince Siegfried's castle. It is his twenty-first birthday and a party is celebrating it. There are a lot of people standing around drinking and generally having fun and Siegfried is right in there celebrating with the rest. After drinking all day and into the evening he and the boys are getting a little out of control.

"Siegfried's mother starts to become a little concerned and reminds him that tomorrow night his birthday will be celebrated by a formal ball. All of the young ladies of the land will be there and he will have to choose a bride.

"Now right at that particular moment Siegfried is not really too interested in discussing the matter. So to get away from mother, he and his buddies decide to go hunting for swan at a nearby lake. Now back in those days swans were not held in as high esteem as they are today, but back to the story.

"Down at this particular lake a little sorcery has been going on."

Here, Morgan starts slipping into the vogue of orator. On the pretense of adjusting his leg he pauses and then continues.

"At sometime in the past there was this beautiful young maiden and, evidently this evil sorcerer by the name of Von Rotbart tried to put the move on her.

"At this point I can't say that I know much about that part. We don't know exactly what happened but we can assume that she rejected him because he turned around and made her into a swan. I am not exactly sure about that part either, but the story goes that she had to live down at the lake and her name is Odette, Queen of the Swans.

"Like I say I don't know the full particulars about how she happened to get turned into a swan but anyway that's the case.

"Actually she's only a part-time swam. Between the hours of midnight and sunrise she emerges back to herself of being a beautiful maiden. And if during that brief time she should happen to find a man who will love her, marry her and never ever be unfaithful then the spell will be broken."

Morgan again paused with a look, that maybe this part was getting too complicated and that he shouldn't explain anymore. Patricia in turn looked at him and with the palm of her hands turned up in mimic and asked, "OK, so then what happens?" Satisfied with her encouragement he continued.

"OK, so now we have Siegfried and the boys heading for the lake. Well it must be after midnight when they arrived because Odette is at the side of the lake in her natural form of a woman.

"Siegfried sees her and instantly falls in love. He holds his hand to his heart and vows that he will always love her, will marry her, and never be unfaithful. He tells Odette that he has just come of age and if she will come to the ball tomorrow night he will marry her. Ah, but few things in life are ever that simple; there is a catch."

At this point Morgan can tell that Patricia is listening to his every word and he elects to heighten her interest by again pausing. Pretending to adjust the bind in his trousers he shuffles slightly when she cuts in.

"What catch?" she urged impatiently. "What kind of catch?" Pleased with his maneuver he said in a tone indicating explanation, "The catch is Odette cannot come to the ball until she is married and Siegfried cannot get married until she comes to the ball.

"Now right here, this is another part about which I am a little fuzzy. Even though they can't get married right at that moment Siegfried goes ahead and vows his fidelity.

"He also vows vengeance against Von Rotbart but Odette warns him to be careful. She says that Von Rotbart is full of trickery and if he can connive Siegfried into being unfaithful then it will cause her certain death."

Morgan stops for a minute as he notices a look of question in Patricia's face. "I know it's not perfectly clear, but don't worry about it," he gestured, "It gets better. The thing is just picturing all of this in the beauty of the ballet.

"Now we are up to the next night at the ball and it is time for the grand event. Siegfried's mother has rounded up six beautiful women from which Siegfried is to choose a bride. In actuality though all he can think of is Odette. Picture if you will the general setting of the ball. Castle ballroom, lots of people, everybody talking, laughing, drinking, and making hoopee. Then suddenly a tall bearded knight appears at the castle door and steps in out of the night. As the crowd becomes silent, he announces that he has brought his daughter Odile to be considered for marriage.

"Siegfried is beside himself. Though she is wearing a vale he is sure that Odile is actually Odette.

"But of course this is not the case. Odile has simply been made up to look like Odette in a trick by Von Rotbart to get Siegfried to be unfaithful.

"And it works. By shrewd manipulation Von Rotbart gets Siegfried to promise his love to Odile. Siegfried swears an oath of fidelity and at that moment there is a crash of thunder. The ballroom darkens. Odette screams above the thunder. Both Von Rotbart and Odile laugh a hideous, screeching laugh.

"Siegfried sees through their hideous trick and turns and sees helpless Odette in the background knowing that she will shortly die. She quickly runs back to the lake to meet her faith and Siegfried rushes to her. She tells him that only in her death will she be free to love. And then, Siegfried follows her into the lake and drowns himself."

There is a silence when Morgan finishes. Patricia was captivated by the description and is startled by the abrupt ending.

"Is that it," she asked with a surprised look. "They just die?" "Of course not," replied Morgan with a mischievous grin. "In the end, good overcomes evil. They triumph and live in perpetual love."

"Then why did you stop?" she asked. "Tell me the ending." Morgan glanced a sideways look as if he had just been asked a forbidden favor and responded, "Oh no, I'm afraid I can't do that pretty woman. To find out the ending you will just have to join me in attending the performance."

By all accounts the performance of Swan Lake on that opening night was flawless and superb. Anticipation throughout Pittsburgh had been building for weeks and the day finally arrived. First on the scene were spectators; many of who had arrived early in the afternoon in order to lay claim to the best gawking spot. At dusk the bright glittering lights on the marquee were turned on and young ushers dressed in tuxedos could be seen scurried about the entrance.

Then came the first patrons, usually by taxi. As the minutes ticked away the crowd thickened, traffic increased and the tempo intensified. Next came limousines, usually rented. Next, when the time was appropriate, large black private limousines began to arrive driven by chauffeurs who obediently held car doors open for Pittsburgh's social elite.

The flair increased as the traffic backed up. Evening gowns became more elaborate, the jewelry more ostentatious and both spectators and photographers clamored toward arriving socialites. The ushers quicken their steps as they stiffly moved patrons down the isles to their seats and then ran back. Patrons who were among the first to be seated started to feel restless; repeatedly looked at their program and tried not to look obvious as they glanced about. Standing up to adjust one's seat was acceptable and a perfect time to cast an upward looks at the box seats. Holding the decision, whether to go to the rest room one more time before curtain call.

As the house filled, the noise level increased and there were certain ones whose talking could be heard above others. Then the moment arrived; the dimming of the lights and the audience became silent. A spotlight came on and cast a bright beam on the stage curtains. The band conductor entered from the side stage, walked to the center, and took a small bow. The audience applauded as he stepped to the podium.

In formal account he then raised his arms, held, and came down in a strong downbeat. The overture started, and the curtain rose. The presentation of Swan Lake was underway.

For Morgan and Patricia the ballet was more than just a momentous experience. It was an evening of the most exquisite pleasure. Almost immediately after the performance started they, as did everyone, left the real life world and became mesmerized in a time zone of grace and beauty. A soul penetrating kinesthetic experience as they mentally assisted each dancer through difficult movements. They gasped as dancers leaped through the air, and they became tense when a ballerina was held overhead with one hand.

It was a flawless performance in which Patricia became so caught up in the movements that she never once flashed back. Her lack of understanding about the story did not deter her from grasping the spirit. For her, the beauty had been in the purity. For Morgan the experience was no less rewarding. From the corner of his eye he had watched her as if a child taking her first bicycle ride. Anxious to share but holding himself from being overly helpful.

At first he had attempted to keep her abreast of the play by whispering explanations. However, it soon became apparent that it wasn't necessary. Her experience was fulfilling on its own right. As the first act came to an end he attempted some comments but it was apparent that no real discussion was necessary.

She was enjoying and he was pleased. The real discussion did not take place until their rented limousine had chauffeured them back at the apartment. Their formal evening clothes now rumpled and wet from perspiration, they each nursed a late night glass of champagne as they set next to each other on the sofa and talked.

"Tell me my beautiful ballerina, did you understand the story?"

"Understand?" her tone implied an emphasis. "On what I saw or on what I felt? Morgan Smithfield... you most wonderful man, I don't have the words to express my thrill. To think, I finally visited the world of the elegant. Me, Patricia Waters, a nobody, from a two room flat in the Hill district. Uneducated, unsophisticated me, I was there. Morgan it's the world I have always dreamed of but never really knew that it was reachable.

"Its made me see; made me realize. People can leave their own bodies and be whatever graceful creature they want to be."

At the moment Morgan did not pay any significance to what she was saying. He simply continued. "Naw, now Trish, I can't just set here and pass over the story bit,

"There has to be a story. For example, what did you think of the scene where the sun was coming up and Odette had to return to a swan and die? Remember how the ballerina rose up on her point, then dropped slowly to the stage. She came to rest on her left knee, with her right leg stretch out in front.

"Then, how she brought her face down to her right knee and extended her arms all the way forward like enclosing wings. Couldn't you just picture a swan?"

Patricia was watching how Morgan was almost talking to himself. She felt the tiredness from the evening and knew she could not match his strength in conversation so she just let him talk.

"And how about the ending?" he continued rhetorically. "Remember how I wouldn't tell you the ending before. Well now I can.

"You see the key is in Siegfried's death. Even though he professed fidelity to Odile it was not the truth.

"The key word here is truth. When he died for Odette that was proof of his true fidelity and ultimately the cause of Von Rotbart's downfall.

"When ol' Von Rotbart sees that he has lost, he dies. That in turn makes way for the lovers. The last scene was a magical barge, a boat, on which the two lovers were then free to sail away to a land of perpetual love."

He paused and when Patricia did express additional agreement he was puzzled. "So what do you think?" he asked inquiringly. She paused for a second longer and then answered in a context he was not expecting.

"Morgan," she started, "to me the entire ballet was the most beautiful thing I have ever witnessed.

"It's as if I have experienced a new religion. I have been born again, only not in church but in the world where I belong."

Morgan looked at her and then retraced his thoughts back to her comment about not caring about the story as such.

"I seem to get the feeling," he said slowly, "that you are trying to tell me something Trish, may I ask what?"

It was here that Patricia released all of her rebirth emotions. Without warning she burst forth. "Oh Morgan," she blurted almost in tears. "Can't you see? I have found my kingdom. The land where I belong. I can travel to all the wonders of the world and I must go. I must, I must, I must" she lightly pounded the bed with a closed fist. Morgan was almost frightened by the unexpected.

"Trish," he asked in a very very slow tone. "Am I hearing what I think I am hearing? Are you telling me," his very slow tone continuing, "that you want to become a ballet dancer?"

"Oh, Morgan," she burst back to his question, "can I? Please? Please say yes. It's what I want. I know it. I know it's what I am supposed to be."

They talked long into the night, that night. The difficulties in what she was seeking. Ballet dancing is usually started at age seven or eight. Where would there be a school that would take an adult. Did she realize the torturous training her mature muscles would have to endure? None of which discouraged her. As the night ended Morgan promised her, her dream.

Mother dearest of our times, the bell I wish to unring. You cared, you shared, you told of measures three: man against man, man against the elements, man against himself. Your service at the helm thence passed to me for other measures beyond those three; answers to war, defects of birth, restraint of government power and so many more. Answers when I find of these, then I will find unto me.

Chapter 18

The next morning when the rays of dawn cast the first hint of light through the bedroom window Patricia was already awake. Lying in the double bed beside Morgan she watched the retreating darkness slowly let his face become more visible. As he slept on the indented pillow his hair was matted and his mouth slightly open. Teasingly she reached over and lightly ran the tip of her index finger along his lower lip. It felt dry. In an edict of tenderness she touched her finger to her mouth and then lightly caressed his lip with a touch of her saliva. He twitched but his eyes did not open. She remembered how intoxicating his lips had felt the night before. She hadn't thought that anything so coarse looking could feel so soft.

Their sex had been frantic on both their parts; exhausting, clamoring, scrambling, sweat covered beautiful. Even more than that, it had been an expression, a surrendering, a mating in the wildness; and if she was truthful to a much larger degree on her part than his; and now she wanted more; much more. Within her soul were trimmers of a hormone volcano on the verge of erupting.

As the room grew gradually lighter she sat up in bed and gently pushed all the bed covers off except the top sheet. This she hand held up and fanned so that it billowed then drifted down and lightly settled. Snuggling her soft nude self up against his sleeping body she gently slid her hand down to his manhood and felt his source of life; and his eyes gently opened.

The hand which was beneath the sheet then moved up to his matted hair and held his face to her wet moist mouth with the intent of ingesting his tongue. Her smooth vibrant skin then meshed tightly against his and for the very first time in his life he experienced an erection which was born, not of lust, but the divinity of unconditional love. After their covenant was consummated, there came the anointing rituals. Two tightly held bodies now bound together by a single soul lying together in embrace.

In the natural order of their unity his masculinity assumed its rightful place as the leader of their lives.

Words returned that he had spoken to himself a long time ago. *The thing I have to look for is need. She must need me to look after her, to care for and protect her.* Now, as they lay there his body half on top, he protected her from his weight by positioning between her spread legs and supporting himself on one elbow. In an ecstasy he had dreamed of hundreds of times he caressed her face, nibbled softly on her lips and smelled her soft hair; love had gently settled into his arms and he vowed to never let it go.

His maimed leg made no difference, her breast made no difference. Theirs was the world at the end of the rainbow; a love whose birth rose up from the shoes of a ballerina. A union preordained to the premise that first, last and foremost a ballerina she would become. In shoes that are made of satin fabric, held on the feet by thin ankle straps, and designed for point, her life henceforth would be to whirl. Wherever there was beauty-and-grace-in-whirling their quest would take them. Their voyage had begun.

With the early morning sun just starting to grace the taller buildings of Pittsburgh, Morgan kissed Patricia at the apartment door and headed for his office at the Stran. He was impatient for the business day to begin. He had arrangements to make, dance schools to call and instructors to meet. Patricia's exuberance was no less restless as she swooped Shelly up, whirled her around the room, and fell across the unmade bed. Lying on her back she repeatedly raised her child up at arm length and then dropped her down in laughter.

In a pause to caught their breath Shelly asked, "Mommie... hypie?"

"Yes, Baby Doll, Mommie is very happy. Happier than she has ever been in her whole life."

"Why dat Mommie, why yu soo hypie?"

"Because Baby, remember how we have always dreamed about those romantic castles in far away lands? Where the women wear beautiful gowns and dance in beautiful ballrooms? Well Sweetie Pie, someday we will travel to all those places."

"And fly wy inn da skyy?"

"Yes, Sweetheart and even fly on a magic carpet."

"Wenn Mommie goo wy in skyy?"

"Someday Baby, someday."

"Shelee goo too?"

"Yes Baby, Mommie would never leave you."

"Shelee lik fly-en on mgic car-pet."

From habit Shelly reached her little hand inside her mother's robe as she asked, "Can weee pla fly-en mgic car-pet noww?"

A strange sensation suddenly came over Patricia and she quickly reacted by taking her child's hand in hers, moving it away and saying, "Honey, we can't do that any more. You're getting too old for that. Sweetheart you're going on four now."

"Nooo, Shelee notts too ol'. Wee play, pease, Mommie."

"No Baby, we have got to stop. We will soon be going to other lands and they won't allow us to do that there."

"Why da Mommie?"

"Because, just because."

The mannerism in which Morgan usually used the telephone was to lean forward in his office chair as he dialed and then lean back to talk. As the rings started to ring he would habitually put his good leg upon his desk. With the receiver to his ear he was impatiently listening to ring, ring, ring. He glanced at the clock. *Nine thirty,* he noted.

What the Hell time do dance schools normally open? Half the day is gone. They must make a hell of a lot of money that they can be so damn independent. Maybe I should put in....

"Hello," came the receptionist on the other end, "Lefèvre School of Ballet Repertory"

"Hello, Yes, my name is Smithfield, Morgan Smithfield, I would like to see how you go about getting a student enrolled in ballet classes."

"Just a moment please."

"Hey wait," he rushed to keep from being put on hold. "What I'm after is to see about some ballet lessons. Can you people down there maybe give me a little help?"

There followed a short silence, then the continuing words of the receptionist. "Just a moment Sir. You'll need to speak with Madame Lefèvre. I'll see if she is available."

There was a pause and then the receptionist came back on, "Hello, Sir, what did you say is your name?"

"Smithfield, just like in the street Smithfield, look could I please talk with the owner or whoever..."

"One moment please.

"Hello, Hello Mr. Smithfield, sorry to keep you waiting. This is Madame Lefèvre secretary again. Madame Lefèvre asks who may have referred you?"

"What? Referred? What are you talking about? Me, Morgan Smithfield, spelled S M I T H F I E L D, owner, and operator of the Stran Theater, spelled S T R A N. I referred me. Now may I please speak to whoever is in charge I would like to see about getting a student into one of your classes."

There was another pause and then Morgan heard a new voice. "Hello, this is Madame Lefèvre, how may I help you?"

Shit, he thought, *just what I need, an accent speaking foreigner.*

"Yes," he answered without indicating his irritation, "I'm calling to make inquiry about getting a student in one of your classes. How would I go about that?"

"Uh, I see, yes. But of course. May I ask Monsieur Smithfield, do you have any references?"

"Yes Ma'am! Mrs. Lefèvre," quipped Morgan, "I am pleased to inform you that I do have references. The best references there are.

"Now here's what you do. You get a pencil and a piece of paper and write these down. The first reference is Mr. U.S. Greenback, the second is Mr. Fifty Dollar-Benjamin Franklin, and the third is Mr. One Hundred Dollar-Ulysses S. Grant. Best references available. Now I don't know which one of them foreign countries you came from but over here those are pretty good references.

"You may have seen their picture around on some of that good ol' American currency that all you foreigners are so damn anxious to get your hands on. Now, can we talk a little about why I called?"

"Certainly Monsieur, it's just that..."

"Tell me about your school," he cut in. "That's what I'm really interested in. What kind of credentials you people got down there?"

"I can a'ssure you Monsieur Smithfield that we have the highest credentials. When our students graduate from here they are qualified to proceed directly to the American Ballet Theater."

"Do you," he moved to his point, "have an opening for a new student?"

"Well, possibly Monsieur. The normal procedure is to audition for acceptance. We will be forming some new classes in the near future."

"Perhaps we could include one more student. May I ask, how old is the child and is it a boy or a girl?"

The question was sharp, unexpected and Morgan's response reflected his state of impatience.

"The it, if I can use your term, is a female and she is not a child she is a grown young woman."

There followed a dead silence and Morgan wondered if something had happened. He was about to respond with an inquiring hello when the voice on the other end came back.

"Hello? Monsieur Smithfield, are you there?"

"I'm here," he replied, "what..."

"Monsieur Smithfield did I understand you to say this person you are inquiring about is a grown woman?"

"That's right, Mrs. Lefèvre, she's a grown, healthy woman; in her mid-twenties. Now, here's the deal. She's very anxious to learn and I am sure you will find her easy to work with. I..."

"Monsieur Smithfield," cut in her sharp voice, "is this some kind of a joke. If so I fail to see the humor. Now if you will excuse me I...."

"Hey! No, wait. Just a gol darn minute," he rushed in. "This sure as to hell, excuseee my French, is no joke Mrs. Lefèvre. What would make you think that I have nothing better to do than sit around and call in telephone jokes?"

There was another pause on the other end of the line and Morgan hoped that some degree of composure was materializing.

"Monsieur Smithfield," came the voice of Madame Lefèvre that seemed to Morgan to be in earnest. "How much do you know about ballet?"

"Little, very little," he returned in a tone that he hoped would convey his appreciation for her change in manner.

"Monsieur Smithfield," she continued. "I have no idea of your circumstances, but let me just give you some thoughts. To be a ballet dancer, students usually start when they are around ten years old; some as young as eight.

"They are required to work through a graded system and we may be talking as much as three years before we even allow them to put on pointed shoes.

"Then, there is a period of twelve to fifteen years of ridged very strenuous training. I, I somehow get the feeling that you are earnest in your search but I must tell you that what you are attempting is impossible. At least we cannot handle your request and I would be surprised if you can find any school that can. I wish you success, now if you will excuse me I am very busy," click.

That was call number one. Call number two was no different, nor was call number three, or number four, or the many others until the day drew to an end. As he sat in the quiet of his office he remembered the plaque on Frank Buckwilder's desk. *Truly,* he thought, *few things in life are as they seem.*

The uncomplicated nature of the idea that he had started out with in the early morning gradually transformed through the day as he developed a greater understanding. After talking to so many different people his attitude changed from demanding to requesting; and he became more proficient at describing what he wanted. He acknowledged that Patricia was starting very late and yes the situation was very unusual. Certainly he let it be known that he had no illusions of her becoming a great ballerina.

He wanted her to take lessons, he would relate, as a form of therapy and self-improvement; a means of opening up new doors, setting goals and building self-confidence. Nevertheless, in spite of his change in tactics he could not find a school that would take her. They all expressed encouragement of his objectives but his pursuit was wrong. The muscles of a mature person, he was repeatedly told, simple would not respond to the demands. There would be a strong probability, not possibility but probability the word was stressed, that both the joints and muscles would suffer irreparable damage.

Most of the schools had suggested that Patricia could find fulfillment in simply taking classes in ballet appreciation. Morgan respected their suggestion but knew differently. Simply learning about ballet would not be sufficient. There would be no substitute for physically experiencing the purity of the dance.

He was leaning back in his office chair as his attention drifted back to the yellow pencil which he was unmindfully turning end over end. Tomorrow he thought, he would try again.

The next day Morgan did try again. In desperation he altered his approach to pleading with the schools to give Patricia a chance and strongly expressed that money was no problem. Still there were no takers. Sitting alone in the stillness of his office he realized that he had now exhausted all normal channels. He had only one card left. Reluctantly, he resolved to make the play.

He remembered that Sidney Griffin, his theater manager over at the Underground had once been a student of the ballet. The working relations between he and Sidney had never improved to any significant degree but for his part it hadn't mattered one way or the other. Profits from the Underground were running better than expected and beyond that he had little concern. However, that frame of mind was before Swan

Lake. Now there was a greater and more important component. For the wide latitude and free reign he had extended to Sidney's insolence he was going to call the marker; and he hoped the situation would not be unpleasant.

The two men did not shake hands the following morning when they arrived at their scheduled meeting in front of the Underground. As Sidney was unlocking the door, Morgan nodded.

"Morning Sidney, I appreciate you giving me a few moments."

"No problem Mr. Smithfield," Sidney responded in a cool tone, "stage rehearsals start in an hour anyway." Morgan made a mental note of the coolness and the emphasis on the last name.

With the door unlocked and the lights switched on, the two gravitated without comment down the center isle. Sidney did not extend an invite to use the back stage office and Morgan did not insist. It was plain that Sidney viewed the office as his territory and Morgan respected the common ground of the outer theater. That was the nature of their relationship at the outset and the pattern had not changed in their few subsequent meetings.

Morgan took his usual front row seat next to the isle and Sidney took his usual standing position in the proscenium; the open area which separates the stage from the seats. Morgan knew there were two ways in which he could approach his request. One, he could open with small talk, thence move into complimenting Sidney on doing a good job.

If that approach appeared to be working, additional rewards could be hinted and then guide the conversation toward Sidney teaching Patricia. The second approach would be to go directly into the request of asking Sidney to train Patricia as a ballet dancer. Having made the request, he would then let Sidney stipulate his demands for taking the assignment.

As it turned out, it was resentfulness on the part of Sidney that in fact forced the tone of the meeting. With a pretense of indignation he commented.

"Could I ask, Mr. Smithfield, what is the purpose of this meeting?" Morgan again detected the last name basis and decided to follow suit.

In demeanor for demeanor he started.

"The purpose Mr. Griffin is I have a personal request. As I recall from one of our prior meetings, you have a strong background in ballet." Sidney had no idea of what was coming but he grasped the opportunity to bolster his importance.

"That is exactly right Mr. Smithfield," he said in an icy tone. "I believe I told you that I started ballet lessons when I was eight years old; two years younger than the normal age. I have danced professionally and I have been a teacher. For a time I was a member if the Corps De Ballet in France where I shared the lead performance."

"Excellent! Sidney," Morgan seized the moment. " I mean if I heard you right. You did say that you have been a teacher; at some point in your past you have been a teacher?"

This sharp cut-in by Morgan surprised Sidney. He had mentioned the point of teaching only as a small bolstering factor and certainly had not intended that it should be equated with his other credential. His sense of suspicion instantly flared and his response equally guarded.

"Mr. Smithfield I also said I started taking ballet lessons at age eight and have danced with..."

"But you have been a teacher? You do know how to teach?"

"Is, that all that is of interest to you?"

"Right now Sidney the answer is yes. At this particular moment I am extremely interested in your teaching abilities and I'm happy to tell you exactly why. There is someone I want you start instructing."

Sidney was not expecting anything of this nature. His reaction was to make facial expressions of indignation and then outcry disbelief. "WHAT...teach? Me? Teach some snot nose kid? Are you out of your mind?"

From Sidney's demeanor he must have felt his response chiseled in stone his position. If so he was about to be in for a jolt. Morgan wasn't fazed in the slightest. In a very blunt and overpowering voice he continued.

"Here's the deal Mr. Griffin," he reverted back to last name basis to clearly signal that he meant business. "I have an adult woman, a personal friend, mid-twenties whom I want to start taking lessons. Now... I have already heard all of the outcries about her being too old. And I've been told no less than a dozen times that her joints will not stand up under the strain.

"I am also aware that she will not have exceptional balance and that it will be extremely awkward learning. So save all of your pseudo gestures of outrage bullshit." With the ending of his statement Morgan faced Sidney in a stare down and then continued.

"In substance Sidney, IT IS going to happen." He paused for an instant to see if he was going to be challenged. When none came he continued.

"Now... I have a couple of ways we can go about this. Most of it depends on you. The choice is really Most of it depends on you. The choice is really yours. One of the things you can do is blow a lot of huff and pretend great insult and indignation. In which case, Mr. Sidney Griffin, that feminize ass of yours is fired, out the door, hit the bricks.

"Simple as that. Goodbye, gone, end of story. Don't call me I'll call you.

"Or... the other option is we can see if the two of us can't work something out."

At this point there was no doubt as to who was in control, but to avoid overkill Morgan paused as a courtesy for Sidney to respond. When he remained silent, Morgan continued but in a little softer tone.

"Good, now Sidney if we can, I would like to discuss this like two gentlemen. You give a little; I'll give a lot.

"First let me stress again that lessons for Patricia are something that is important to me; very important. So much so that I guarantee I'll make it worth your time.

"I'll get back to the worth while bit in a moment. First though, here is what I want. I want you to take the job and I want you to start immediately. Start tomorrow if you can. Today would be even better. Her name is Patricia Waters and she is extremely important to me. I can't stress that enough. I am aware of the physical torture that she will be going through. I have already mentioned that. So in that context you do not have to worry about me getting unduly upset."

It was a natural moment to pause and the two men looked at each other in silence. Morgan searched Sidney's eyes for adversity but could get no reading. Feeling that a degree of decorum was materializing, he softened his tone to show his intent to be a gentleman and continued on a first name basis.

"Sidney in hopes that we can work together I will tell you that I understand what I am asking. If I were in your shoes I would probably feel exactly the same way that you do. I know that her muscles will have to be stretched and trained; that she will have aches and pains.

"And I already know that there will be times when she will be so sore that she can't move. That's all fine and good; no problem. I understand that these will be the necessary birth pains of being a born-late ballerina.

"But," he continued, "I want to also express my concerns. This is a new hope in the life of Patricia and she will be hanging on by a very very thin thread.

"Please do not do anything to discourage, hamper or traumatize that new hope. Be firm but careful; avoid injuries to the joints if possible. And always, always talk encouragement."

At that point Morgan paused and shifted in a manner to continue showing that his stern argumentative posture had subsided. He again made eye contact with Sidney and again could not get a clear signal. No refusal, no hate, no agreement, no understanding; nothing. Just a clear blank.

OK, he thought. *Let's see what we've got.* As a preface to his next step Morgan lifted up his posture, put one elbow on the seat arm, slightly moved his leg and took a noticeably deep breath.

He purposely paused a place-to-start, brought the hand of his leaning elbow up to his chin and started.

"Sidney," his tone implying this was now on a man-to-man level, "if you'll do this for me it would mean a lot. Now I know that you can't be forced to take the job. I'm well aware of that. I also know that even if you do, you will teach as you please. What I'm hoping is that we can get our heads together. If we can do that it might turn out to be something that will be pleasing to both of us.

"But pleasing us is not the point. Patricia is the point. She's the one I want pleased. Even more than pleased. What I want, what I would dearly like, is for it to be a mesmerizing experience. You do that and you will make me one happy man. I want her to experience the heart and soul of ballet; not just the steps and moves. I am hoping for her to experience the grace, the beauty, and the purity. Uh... well, Sidney I'm sure you know what I'm saying.

"Now, having said what I would like to happen, it is time to say what I am willing to pay. First let me apologize for my earlier manner of talking.

"It's not something I enjoy. I just thought it was necessary that I be understood. Maybe on a softer note I can convince you that I am not all that bad. Let's talk about the Underground. Do you think you would be interested in being the new owner?"

An instant quickness flashed across Sidney's face. His first impulse was to gulp but then guarded himself with an acid response.

"Really Mr. Smithfield! What kind of question is that?" he sniped. "Of course I would be interested. Who wouldn't? I have only put in six years of my life here. Built it up to the best theater in town. Now! I just know that out of the goodness of your heart you are going to sign it over to me. Really, Mr. Smithfield, please give me some credit..."

Morgan liked the answer. He also knew that suspicion could cloud the issue and the point of it all could be misalign so he decided to lay out the deal.

"Sidney," he started, "here's what I'm thinking. I know how important the Underground is to you. To me, it's no longer that big of a deal. When I first bought it I wanted the status symbol but now, it's just an investment; nothing more.

"Patricia Waters on the other hand is very important to me. You want the Underground; I want her to learn ballet.

"It seems to me that both of our dreams are in your hands. How you handle the situation is up to you."

There was a tinge of arrogance in Sidney as he asked, "Are you saying that if I teach this woman, what's her name, Patricia Waters, if I teach her to dance ballet, the Underground is mine?"

"That's exactly what I'm saying," responded Morgan and then continued. "Now I know you have a lot of questions. In addition, a lot of what-ifs, as well you should have. Moreover, all of those what-ifs will be answered; but not right now. I'm not in the mood to spend all day convincing you I'm a straight shooter. I'm more interested in getting started. So here's what I'm willing to do. The hourly wage around town is about a dollar twenty cents to a dollar seventy five cents an hour." At this point Morgan leaned back in his seat and gestured in a manner that he meant what he said.

"I am willing to pay you twenty bucks an hour for as many hours as you want to put in. That kind of offer ought to make it damn clear that you will be well paid for your time. I'll pay you cash in hand or put the money in a bank in your name; whichever you prefer.

"Then if things work out and you hold up your end of the bargain we can then start talking about you becoming the new owner of the Underground. At the end of three years or so you can have your choice of all money and no Underground or the Underground by itself. I'm not interested in trying to screw you."

The next step was up to Sidney. Morgan felt that there was an easing of tensions and was prepared to respond favorably to any question. His mind was set on assuring Sidney that he would honor the terms of the agreement. He expected innuendoes of suspicion and distrust. That is not what happened.

"Tell me, Mr. Smithfield," Sidney started, "what is the particular reason that this Patricia Waters needs these ballet lessons so badly?"

It was a direction that Morgan had not anticipated and he answered without thinking.

"I am hoping they will be a kind of therapy."

"And," asked Sidney, "what are the circumstances which require that she have this therapy?"

Morgan was momentarily perplexed. On one hand he was reluctant to divulge Patricia's oddity but on the other hand the tone of Sidney's voice had a suggestion of sincerity. He quickly decided that if he were going to err, he would gamble on the side of understanding. Therefore, he prefaced his answer with a foundation statement.

"Sidney, remember how you once confided in me that you were not in the army because you were a different type of man."

Sidney did not speak but acknowledged the statement with a slight nod. Accepting the nod as an answer Morgan continued.

"Well Patricia is a different type of woman and because she is, she has had a terrible life. My reason for being here is to level out her playing field. And it's my sincerest belief that if you will accept my offer, I feel that all three of us, you, me, Patricia, all of us will have much happier lives."

Sidney had backed up against the stage and was standing in a leaning back stance with his arms crossed.

"Since you know how I happen to be a different type of man," he answered in an implying tone, "I think it is only fair that I know how Mrs. Waters is a different type of woman."

Morgan again gambled on compassion and hoped he could lay the groundwork for a possible bond between Patricia and Sidney.

"She was born with a birth defect. She has elongated breast. Instead of being round and firm they hang down and dangle like long cucumbers with a nipple."

He unmindfully made a thumb-to-finger circle with each hand and brought them to his chest in a gesture describing her breast.

Damn, damn, God-damn-it, he instantly thought. *Me and my big mouth. Why in the Hell did I have to over explain?*

In the silence that followed Morgan could feel his resentment. And he could feel more blood rush to his face when Sidney caught him further off balance by taking a couple of steps forward, sticking out his hand and accepting the deal.

"OK I'll do it; with one stipulation. You are to stay completely out of the Underground. That means no watching, no offering suggestions, no visiting, no dropping in unexpectedly, nothing."

The conclusion was sudden. It seemed to Morgan that there should be more; but there it was. Sidney standing in front of him with his hand out.

With the aid of his cane he rose and extended his hand. It was the first time Morgan had ever physically touched Sidney. As they shook hands a danger flare went off. An instant caution shot through his body and an uneasy feeling stirred within.

The handshake lacked sincerity and firmness. Sidney showed no emotions or expressed assurances of cooperation.

The meeting was simply terminated with Sidney saying, "We'll start tomorrow. Tell Mrs. Waters to report to the Underground at ten o'clock sharp."

With a dropping of the hands Sidney stepped back to leaning on the stage. Morgan made one final little nod, turned and made his way out the front. Outside his exuberance overshadowed his caution. He freely let his fantasies intensify as he made his way back to the Stran. His determination had paid off. Patricia was in. Her journey to the land of grace and beauty was underway. Her new world was waiting. How well she would do was not important. He felt good. Then as a momentary, wide-open unlimited fantasy he pictured Patricia as an accomplished ballerina. Somewhere in ballerina land she would someday perform before a capacity crowd; decked out in her classical tutu on opening night; center stage spotlight. He smiled as he fantasized how she would spellbind the crowd with her pirouette sur le cou-de-pied; whirls in number across the floor; a fantasy that walked with him back to the Stran.

Nevertheless, as he was unlocking the front door, the world of reality came back into focus. The feel of the brass key in the dead bolt caused his thoughts to flash back to the arrangements. Strange that Sidney Griffin was so agreeable. No cry of protest, no temper tantrums, counter offer, or clarifying questions; just agreement to the terms and the meeting terminated.

Morgan attempted to control his suspicions by rationalizing. *There's no need to worry. All we are talking about are dance lessons. If they work, they work. If they don't, they don't. What could go wrong?*

An inscription by the author's husband.

In the theme of the author's writing, I believe her blueprint was to first write just the saga of Shelly Waters. While I never knew, I can now picture that having completed Shelly's saga, the author returned to the story beginning and added in the emotions of the storyteller. The power of this second tool, namely the storyteller's hunt for his identity, actually challenging the central theme.

Sadly, the author passed away before the storyteller found his journey's end and I believe she would be saddened to have it die with her. Speaking from what I feel, I believe that she would want it finished. Knowing that she is watching as I write this, she is touched by my leaving the door open. Meaning somewhere out there in the wilderness, there must be a voice that will take up the storyteller's quest; that his journeys not go unfulfilled

Chapter 19

When Patricia arrived at the Underground for her first ballet lesson the next morning the front doors were unlocked but not open; and a wonder of what-to-do flashed through her mind. She had expected that her first meeting with Sidney Griffin would be out front. Attentively she opened one of the double entrance doors, entered the chilly, stale, empty lobby and searched for some semblance of an office; but nothing was discernible.

Still uncertain, she proceeded though the second set of doors into the main theater. The lights were on but as she looked out over the rows of empty seats she still could not see anyone. Awareness flashed to her of the contrast between the stark quietness of being inside and the bright sunshine outside. Age had taken its toll on everything inside; including the house lighting. Some of the fixtures were little more then exposed incandescent bulbs hanging from exposed crossbeams. The wall murals, which contributed character under more subdued lighting, showed heavy water stains; and there was a pungent musty smell in the air.

Not knowing what to do, or not to do, she started slowly walking down the raked aisle toward the stage and could hear her own footsteps on the threadbare carpet-over-concrete. She had no purse but was carrying a gym satchel containing workout clothes. When she reached the area in the aisle where the suspended balcony blocked out direct lighting she paused and attempted to make her presence known.

"Hello! Hello! Anyone here?" she called out; her voice echoing against the flat walls; still there was only silence. Passing on under the suspended balcony she repeated her greeting as she neared the empty stage.

"HELLO! YOO-HOO, is there anyone back there?" and still

there was no response. Feeling that there must have been some misunderstanding she was turning to leave when Sidney Griffin emerged from the side stage curtain.

"Mrs. Waters?" he asked in a piercing tone as he walked out on the creaking stage floor.

"Yes," she responded as she turned back around and glanced up to the stage, "I hope I'm on tim..."

"Yes, yes quite," he cut in as he came to the front of the stage and look down. With both arms crossed in front he stood in a defiant stance and cast a patronizing sneer. "Now, that you are here," he exaggerated his snip, "if you will be so kind as to come up on the stage we can begin."

Patricia felt blood rush to her face at the unexpected inflection but said nothing as she rushed to step up the short flight of stage steps.

"I brought my workout clothes," she attempted to establish greetings. "I didn't know just what we would be doing on the first day. Whether we would just be getting acquainted or..."

"We will be training on the first day Mrs. Waters. That is why we are here, isn't it?" came his cutting response.

"Well, yes uh, I just didn't... All Morgan told me was to meet you here."

"And," he continued to snip, "now that you are here, we have work to do."

Thereafter, the mode of those belittling introductory moments further intensified as Sidney and Patricia started their working relationship.

"Mrs. Waters," he started, "I think you should be aware that I am totally against what you are attempting. I think it is silly and a waste of time for us both. But, be that as it may, I made an agreement with Mr. Smithfield and I will try to keep my end of the bargain."

The insinuation was cutting to Patricia but she had the strange sensation that Morgan was standing right beside her and he would be furious if she allowed herself to be abused. With the feeling of his strength, it was one of the few times in her life she attempted to defend herself.

"Mr. Griffin, is there some reason why we can't be friends? I assure you that I want to work with you. I, uh, from what Morgan tells me, you are our best hope. So believe me when I say that I am really very grateful and I will do whatever you want. But, couldn't it also be enjoyable?"

Without waiting, Sidney adamantly rebutted, "Mrs. Waters, you simply do not understand do you? What you are proposing will be anything but enjoyable.

"If you have any thoughts of this being pleasant or even mildly discomforting you're going to be in for a big surprise. It's obvious that you have no idea of the magnitude of what you are asking. The pain, the suffering the torn ligaments..."

He paused, slightly inhaled for effect and then continued.

"Mrs. Waters you will be asking your body to do something which is completely foreign to human nature. You will be asking it to whirl, leap, raise on point, leg extension, sustain airborne, balance..."

He paused again in a head shaking gesture to emphasize the hopelessness and then finished.

"In the name of being a ballerina, you will be asking your body, not only to do these things but to do them with ease, confidence, force, freedom and expression."

At that point he was not looking at Patricia but staring off into space. As he finished he turned to her face in order that she might respond but when she said nothing he continued.

"Are you aware," he asked, "that students usually start ballet lessons when they are around eight to ten years old?" Then, as if he again realized what was ahead he emphasized.

"Your bones, your muscles and ligaments. They are already fully-grown and matured. They will have to be torn down and retrained. The probability of injury is a hundred percent. I don't even know if they can take..."

For the first time Patricia sensed that Sidney, while hateful, was also sincere in his concerns. It was clearly a job that he did not want. She did not respond to his comments because it was imperative that he did take the job; so she stood in silence as the drama continued.

At her failure to comment, Sidney threw up his hands in a hopeless gesture and turned to pacing. For the moment, he was not saying anything; just pacing, not in thought but in futility. As Patricia watched, the scene made her feel like some lower ranking military officer standing before a higher authority and being reprimanded. The only thing she could do was to remain silent while he ranted and raved at the idiotic notion.

The absurdity of it all caused her to have a slight smile. Which made even worse, the horrible, devastating comment that was about to come.

Abruptly, and without warning, Sidney turned and said, "Morgan tells me you have long dangling tits that hang down like cucumbers. According to him he wants you to have ballet lessons as a form of therapy. Is that what's driving you to embark upon this insane notion?"

The piercing hurt which shot through Patricia had no bounds. Instant degradation flushed to her face in crimson red and her open hands rushed to her mouth. She attempted to cry out but her voice would not respond. A river of tears instantly flooded her eyes, spilled over and streamed down her cheeks. Agony and shock were forged in her face. Sidney may have flinched at the degree of hurt because he continued.

"That is what Morgan told me about you Mrs. Waters." Without waiting he kept talking.

"Now, I'm just wondering what he told you about me. Did he just happen to tell you that I am a homosexual? Though I suspect the word he would have used is cocksucker."

At the sound of those words, the searing agony in Patricia transferred to blinding animal rage. A subconscious reckoning that the enemy also had a weakness; which triggered an explosive impulse to attack. The urge swelled up in her to claw out his throat. To claw and sink her teeth into his neck until blood flowed from the juggler vein and then to stand back in satisfaction as lifeblood drained from his body out upon the stage floor. Since he had so ruthlessly cast dispersions about her very personal condition why should he not suffer equal degradation.

In her most vile thoughts she wanted to scream back in retribution, *And ARE YOU A COCKSUCKER Mr. Griffin?* But the revenge that flushed within her could not exceed the bounds of her dignity.

All she could say was, "You must hate me very much to want to hurt me so." From those words came a fleeting moment. A realm in human behavior which surfaced one time only and which she would never see again; the despicable Sidney Griffin dissipated into an emotional collapse; a fleeting capitulation.

A notion somewhere in the corners of his own mind that living was just too difficult. The rewards for continuing to live were not worth the fight for survival. In words which seemed detached from his own body Sidney said, "No, Mrs. Waters, I do not hate *you*," with emphasis on you.

"I hate the world." Then, as quickly as his emotions had softened his anger re-appeared.

"I hate the world. I hate the world of superficial, unimaginative people with imbecilic, retarded moronic souls who reject art as their nourishment to life and turn instead to materialistic, self serving pleasure seeking."

As Sidney was talking, the rage in Patricia momentarily subsided. She momentarily realized that he himself was in torment. *Is*, she wondered, *his reason for hurting me, is so that he will have company for his own hurt. But why? Why such hurt? What must have happened in his childhood, or even in his adulthood?* Abruptly her thoughts were interrupted as he called her name.

"Mrs. Waters I tell you these things because henceforth neither of us will have the luxury of dwelling on what's wrong with ourselves. From this moment forward... your hanging tits, as with my cocksucking, must... yes MUST, pass into oblivion.

"You cannot think of it because it does not exist.

"You cannot use it as a crutch because it does not exist.

"You cannot ever, ever think of what is wrong with you.

"You can only do one thing. Pray for the strength to go on.

"In the weeks to come the going will be difficult and trying. I will give you my best teaching but you cannot look to me for encouragement or moral support. I've... I've got my own problems."

There was a pause as he lit a cigarette. Then in the comraderie gesture of a combat soldier in a foxhole offering a drag to his buddy, he held the cigarette to Patricia.

She shook her head in waving it away but commented, "I do not smoke Mr. Griffin but may I ask, what is that awful smell".

Sidney took a deep drag, held his breath until the oxygen expired before he finally exhaled, smiled and answered.

"Its called marijuana Mrs. Waters. Otherwise known as pot; very legal in Mexico; very illegal in Pittsburgh.

"Maybe not so illegal over at good ol' Pitt University in Oakland. Lots of it floating around the campus."

He took another long drag, sucked it in deep, again held, finally exhaling, snuffed out the butt with his fingers, put the roach in his pants pocket, stepped back and transformed into an instructor.

"Mrs. Waters it seems we have concluded our formalities. Let us get to the matter of learning ballet.

"We will now be leaving the front stage. Our business on this day begins in back. I will say this here. The trip to the back is but a few short steps. But returning to the front center stage on a performing night will be a long and arduous journey."

As Sidney then turned Patricia followed. "Back stage," he continued as he walked, "we have a long wood barre which is attached to the back wall. Not a rail Mrs. Waters but a barre, please remember the term. It is exactly three feet and two inches high and roughly six inches from the wall. In the weeks and months to come it will become both your best friend and your worst enemy."

Here he looked at Patricia to reinforce his point and enunciated the words, "*to, the exclusion, of, everything else.*" Then as if he remembered something, he backed up.

"But before we start with the barre, we start with the mind. An understanding of exactly what it is we want to accomplish; correction, make that dedicate. To what it is we intend to be so dedicated; to be so accomplished.

"Suppose we start with a question and an answer. The question being what is ballet? Easy to ask; difficult to answer. I'll give you my interpretation.

"Ballet, Mrs. Waters, is a blending of the physical and the spiritual. The underlying essence, the very reason for its existence is the purity of grace.

"Grace, Mrs. Waters. That degree of *grace* which dwells beneath a hundred tons of molten volcanic rock and through which you must enter and return; the only place where it can be found.

"A place to which you must journey in order to bring back unity of mind, body and soul presented in a form unparalleled by any other movement of man.

"Grace which is so revered that it becomes the quintessence of beauty. Nay, it is even more than that. Grace is the very doctrine by which all other forms of beauty are measured.

"AND, Mrs. Waters the very nucleus towards which all the other parts of the ballet are directed; the theater, stage, setting, costumes, plot; especially the plot.

"Even when the plot is a tragedy, a hurt, a sadness, it must be delivered in a form of grace and beauty.

"Think, accept, and believe that art is the where-with-all of man's true communications.

"When it is done correctly, the stage becomes the center of man's universe; that kingdom in the twilight zone to which all souls desire to ascend.

"And, Mrs. Waters, the whirling-in-chains of the ballerina's pointe shoes holds the boarding pass.

"Through an invisible metaphysical connection from the viewer in their seats in the audience to the ballerina's body on the stage, your followers will become captivated in your quest."

Here Sidney paused to prepare his final delivery. He slightly straightened up and induced a noticeable flexed in his rib cage. Following that he made a fist in one hand and held it with the other to show a circle of strength and inhaled a full capacity of air. With sternness in his face he then emphasized,

"And... this above all else, Mrs. Waters. Your body will explode with a feeling of authority. When you are there you will experience the utopia of being in total command.

"There will materialize in you a sensation that you have the power to capture the souls from the audience for the purpose of doing your own bidding.

"You will know when they are yours. They will willingly and obediently forsake the safety and security of their seats and join you in your fight against evil. When you are good enough, when you possess the power, they will unhesitatingly join with you in rebelling against being wronged, to rise up with you against oppression, to stand fast with you against tyranny; and lastly to join in your triumphs and bask in your glory."

The power of Sidney's words held Patricia in awe. His dominance so overwhelming she felt unworthy to embark upon such a course. So intense was her perception that beads of perspiration formed on her forehead. When he made his final pause she had anticipated a silence so extreme that her own breathing would be an intrusion.

But there was more. "And, for better or worse, Mrs. Waters, happiness can only be yours when the souls of others gladly and willingly surrender to your spell.

"Forsaking their own bodies they come for the purpose of protecting you, their high princess; fighting your battles as their battles, to the extent that no matter what the outcome, nothing more could have been done.

"Then, either in victory or defeat, soaked in perspiration and drained of energy they release themselves 'from' you. Their exhausted selves return to the bodies that remained in the audience seats.

"In short Mrs. Waters you will be preparing your body for the occupancy of other souls. In order to be worthy of that honor, you will endure untold weeks, months and years of preparation.

"Ahead of you are sweat, strain and suffering. You will feel it insurmountable. And yet if you *believe,* you *will* go on."

"So great is that honor that you can never prepare your body enough.'

From Sidney's words, there unfolded within Patricia the clearing of a heavy fog and before her lay a glittering milky way. A now clear understanding of her life's quest; the price of passage being extracted in sweat, pain and tears. Her feelings of revulsion toward this man turned to awe.

Surely, she thought, *he has been there and has paid his dues. He knows the price of passage because he has made the voyage. I will pay no less and will ask for no reduced fare. There can be no other way. Through this door I must pass and follow my star.*

In that split instant, Patricia resolved to always cast her eyes upon the very best in Sidney's teachings and to shield herself from the abuse. From that resolve, she found strength. She straightened up her posture, threw her shoulders back and held her head high. Such was her thinking as the two embarked.

In the days and weeks to come she allowed herself no mind of her own. When Sidney would yell, rave or berate it was not her to whom he was talking. It was a detached life form that had to be molded without mercy. So surrendered was her mind that anything other than what he said was inconceivable. That his words might be other than gospel simple did not register.

But... few things in life are as they are perceived. And that which she perceived and that which would happen were diabolically opposing. The words that Sidney delivered were words pure in truth. Words that he had been taught from birth and pressed to him from age eight. Words that on this day, he blatantly stood in the shoes of Brutus and betrayed.

In his initial thought process... he may have felt a twinge or a momentary surge to dream his own impossible dream.

To take Patricia by the hand and lead her to that distant star; and through her to live himself again. A fleeting surge of adrenaline, as it were, to challenge the invincible foe, and to fight on when his arms were too weary. So spontaneous was that surge that his oratory would have made Shakespeare applaud.

That was the split moment before. But fantasies aside, in terms of months and years, unemotional analysis clearly revealed the insurmountable. As his oratory fantasy dissipated, reality returned and in his own mind he knew that he could not, would not, ever allow such an unworthy as Patricia to penetrate the sanctity of the ballet. He there on resolved that his teaching of her would have no true intent, purpose, discipline or honor.

In a further dimension, Sidney conceived how Patricia could be developed into an instrument of revenge; spawned out of his own disappointment of having traveled the journey and failed to be rewarded. His years of training had resulted in nothing more than bit parts and the viewing audiences had never accepted him as a creditable dancer. However, that would all develop in the future. On this, their first day the deed got underway.

"Now, Mrs. Waters," he started their first lesson, "there are five and only five basic positions in ballet..."

At eleven o'clock on that same morning, Morgan sat in his office and nervously watched the hands on the clock tick by. Since early morning when he said goodbye to Patricia at the apartment he had tried to mentally project how her first day would go. By around eight o'clock he imagined, she and Shelly would be having breakfast. By prior arrangements Shelly would be left with Jenny.

At nine o'clock or so, he figured, mother and daughter would be arriving at Jenny's flat and some allowances had to be made for small talk and gossip.

Probably he figured, Patricia *would be on time and get to the Underground by a quarter to ten or so.* And ten o'clock for Patricia became ten o'clock for him. When he figured she would be starting her first lesson he pictured his own body feeling her initial stretching. He wished he could be there and somehow be the one to endure the pain while she started first learning; wishful thinking which made him more restless.

He rose from his desk and moved around the theater. First out into the empty lobby but the vast open area made him feel lonely. Thinking that perhaps some outside air would be a better choice he opened the swinging double doors and was greeted by the early morning sounds of the city. The air in the alcove was still cool and moist. For something to do he decided to check the ticket cage. He reached in his pocket and brought out a bulky set of keys.

With support on his cane he unlocked and turned the latch. As the door opened the lingering fragrances of Patricia's perfume radiated out and filled his nostrils. He savored the moment and imagined that if she were there at that instant how soft she would be to embrace.

Returning to his office he shuffled papers on his desk until the clock on the wall finally chimed eleven times. Allowing for travel time, he conjectured he would have to remain calm for at least another twenty minutes.

When she gets back to the Stran I can't appear overly anxious he thought. He tried to decide which position would appear the less obvious. First he assembled some papers on the top of his desk and pulled his chair up close and looked down in pretense of deep concentration. Better still, maybe talking on the telephone would look more natural. In a practice run he picked up the phone and pretending that she had just walked in mumbled some final words and hung up. Looking around he had another thought. It would be much better if both of them could sit on the same side of the desk. He hurriedly pulled one of the guest chairs around next to his.

Then, at that moment it happened. His reactions flinched as he heard a knock on the door, a "Yoo-Hoo" and in she came. Dressed in black ballet tights, white blouse knotted at the waist, bandanna wrapped around her hair, carrying a satchel on her shoulder, make-up and perspiration streaks on her face she rushed in, dropped the bag, bounded across the floor and threw herself into his lap.

With her mouth open, her lips moist, her soul ecstatic, she planted on his receptive open mouth a tongue kiss of her lifetime. Followed by numerous tight squeezes she rapidly showered him with delirious small kisses about his face and neck, her wet lips leaving a trail of saliva, and a second long deep kiss on the mouth.

"Oh Morgan, it was wonderful; absolutely the most beautiful thing. I feel like I am finally alive, free, I can breathe," she pronouncedly exclaimed as she impulsively ran her hands into his full head of matted hair and pulled his lips to hers and gave him another deep, open mouth uttering kiss.

Then, as rapidly as her exuberance had exploded she settled down; quietness came and their emotions turned to silently looking directly at each other.

"My goodness," he remarked attempting to hide the wetness in his eyes, "such enthusiasm. Maybe I'd better go back over there and do some more investigating. I thought it was a ballet class. I didn't know it was an emotional supermarket. Tell me my most wonderful one, how did it go? Do I have a future ballerina in my lap?"

Patricia did not know how hard Morgan had looked for an instructor. Therefore, speaking from what she knew, she wanted to convey to Morgan her instant love for the ballet but also her mixed experience.

"It was," she started, "both harsh and beautiful." She paused as she searched for tactful words. "It was harsh because Sidney seems to have a split personality. One minute he can be so inspiring and the next minute a type of hate for which he shows no remorse; a sadistic pleasure from causing pain and void of compassion. Next minute he can convey the most beautiful and elegant meaning of ballet. Add to that he has his own unique way of painting the most inspirational rewards for being dedicated."

When Patricia used the words hurt and pain Morgan's thoughts flashed to his prior conversation with the other ballet instructors wherein they had all forewarned; for an adult to undertake ballet would be physical torture. He also knew that Sidney was their only possible instructor. So speaking from what he knew he expressed a tone of understanding but determination.

"Baby, it doesn't matter about the hurt and pain. Each ache is only a brick of gold on the highway of beautiful tomorrow's."

Patricia misconstrued this to mean that if she did not continue with Sidney, Morgan would be greatly disappointed and she resolved that no matter what, she would endure. With a resurgence of exuberance, she straightened up in Morgan's lap and related the elements of beauty and grace that had come to her from the very first session.

But the descriptive words of grace and beauty did not convey the actions that actually happened; on the day next and the next, and the next. The training that had started out on an intimidating note eventually graduated to fiendish sadistic.

The first week Sidney had taught with a tone of demanded submission. "Mrs. Water, when I tell you something I expect you to remember. Do you understand me? First remember grace and beauty delivered in a flawless rhythm. The five basic steps are...."

The second and third weeks he taught in a tone of hopelessness, trying and taxing. "No, no, no Mrs. Waters, when I ask you to do the *demi-plié* I mean a partial bending of the knees! A full bend of the knees is a *grand-plié*. What does it take for you to learn?"

On weeks twelve to fifteen Sidney taught in a tone of relentlessness. "Mrs. Waters I am not concerned that your muscles ache and hurt. You were apprised of the circumstances. I am highly disappointed with our progress."

And so it progressed. On his more ruthless days he would scream, "Mrs. Waters you imbecilic incompetent, *movements at the barre are comprised of demi-plié, grand-plié, battement, round de jambe, relevé! Movement at the center will be working with the arms. Do I make myself clear?*"

On his less ruthless days it was because he smoked marijuana; which usually resulted in more than just putrid air. He was apt to spend most of their training time talking in a rambling stupor.

"Mrs. Waters," he asked on one such occasion, "what is it you really hope to achieve by putting yourself through this rigorous torture? I mean really?"

Patricia's aching body was thankful for the pause and welcomed the time to just talk. He was sitting down and leaning back in a straight back chair with one foot propped up on the training barre.

She correctly assumed that he was not in the mood to teach so she allowed herself the luxury of sitting flat on the floor, knees pulled up and leaning back against the wall.

"What I really hope to achieve, Mr. Griffin are the things which you told me on the very first day."

"You mean about being able to whirl across the floor and captivate an audience?"

"That, Mr. Griffin, and more, much much more. I have a lifetime of dreams I have to pursue."

Sidney pulled a drag deep into his lungs, held and then exhaled.

"Do you really believe," he asked, "all that jargon about dreams?" Patricia was sitting with her eyes closed and her head tilted back against the wall. She did not move as she answered. "We all have dreams, Mr. Griffin. Without dreams there would be nothing."

Perhaps because she was lost in her own thought she paid no mind to his response.

"I am inclined to suggest Mrs. Waters that your dreams would become much more realistic if you shared a joint of this grass."

"Not me, Mr. Griffin," she answered with her eyes still closed and her head still tilted back.

"I intend to follow my star to the end of the universe. And it will be on my own wings. I don't need the crutch of dope."

The remark cut Sidney. His offer to share a drag had been in friendship and she dared to decline. The rejection instantly provoked revenge. *You sassy bitch. That'll cost you dearly.*

"Patricia," he cunningly used her first name. "Let me ask you," his voice in a tone which suggested that he possessed some highly forbidden, guarded secret, "would it give you that much of a thrill to just go ahead and start whirling across the floor to an audience? I mean much sooner than we had anticipated?"

His ploy worked because she caught his suggestive tone and immediately responded. She opened her eyes, looked at him in a clearly receptive glance and answered.

"Of course Mr. Griffin, more than anything else in the world, but why are we even discussing the matter. We both know that it will be years before that will be possible."

"Maybe yes, maybe no," he countered. "I'm the instructor. I'm the one who decides what is our best course of action."

Patricia felt a tremble of delight at the prospect of altering the routine of grueling practice.

"Could I ask what you are thinking?"

Sidney experienced a ripple of satisfaction in playing with her hopes. Before he answered he took another drag of marijuana and basked in the hallucinating glow.

"Well, don't get overly excited Patricia, but there may be a remote possibility, very remote mind you, but if you are good, practice really hard and do just as I say, then we may be able to move you ahead a little."

In her mind the suggestion meant more than a little. It meant a lot and her attention became more intense as she believed he was about to share a major turn of events; an inaccurate assumption on her part.

Sidney deceptively changed the subject. "Are you sure you won't try a drag of this?" he asked as he again held out the marijuana joint. Then, knowing she would refuse he continued, "You really ought to go with me over to Oakland sometime.

"My ol' fraternity brothers, Phi Smia Delta, over at Pitt U, they have some mighty good pot parties."

Changes that occur in everyone's life usually start with the most insignificant beginnings. With respect to the lives of Sidney and Patricia this conversation bore the seeds of change wherein three things happened. For one thing Sidney started smoking more and more marijuana and most of the time he was in a hypnotic trance. In the weeks to come he took to hanging out more at his old fraternity house and became a sort of cult guru to the younger students. He made mockery and goading against being serious about education. Under his influence most of the fraternity members started cutting class and holding daylong pot parties. Secondly, Sidney approached Morgan about taking cash payments for Patricia's lessons instead of accepting an interest in the Underground. Thirdly, he persuaded Morgan that it would be in Patricia's best interest to increase her training to two hours per day; to which Morgan agreed. But it would prove to be a tragic decision; perpetuated by his given word not to interfere. Thereafter Patricia's sessions did increase, the teaching fees doubled and each Friday morning Sidney dropped by Morgan's office and picked up his money. Morgan always paid and made no comment.

By his resolve not to interfere he further contributed to the mistake. Almost immediately, it was apparent that Patricia had stepped out of the realm of acceptability and into the pains of Hell. Overnight she became a physical and emotional wreck. Where she once bounced into his office and shared the day's lesson she now dragged in and sought only rest and quite.

In looking back, Morgan recognized the reasons for his mistake. At that particular time he was heavily involved in a new business venture; the building of a new colossal size, all modern drive-in restaurant in the North Hills section of Pittsburgh.

He envisioned it to be in partnership with another woman he once could have loved; Jenny Craig, if she could be persuaded.

"Jenny," he had started, "if you are interested I think the timing is right to build a modern first class drive-in restaurant. Now here's my thinking. I want a big modern round building with circular parking on all sides. This war we are in right now will be over before too long and the boys will be coming home.

"Now, I don't know very much about a lot of things but there is one thing that I am pretty damn sure about and that is America has fallen in love with the automobile. There's going to be a lot of young ball bearing hero's coming back and the first thing they are going to want is a car. Thereafter they are going to be out cruising and back-seat top-down loving. In my thinking a big drive-in coke and hamburger place will be a natural."

Jenny as always was receptive to Morgan's ideas but she was also sure that there were additional considerations. "Of course I would be interested," she responded. "But why me?" she probed. Morgan was glad that she was the one who raised the question.

"I have been thinking," he replied, "that it would be a natural compliment to your present profession. If there are times when the commercial loving business is slow and maybe some of your girls are falling a little behind, they may be able to pick up a little supplemental income from car hoping.

"And on the other hand, if your main business keeps growing, young trainee carhops may be a potential source for professional work."

Once initiated, the idea grew and in that time frame Morgan and Jenny were in constant company. Their relationship stayed completely on business however because they both realized the circumstances. Morgan's only romantic interest now was Patricia. And while Morgan could see that Patricia was in agony from over training he still could not bring himself to act; not immediately. Eventually something did click which caused him to see a red flag.

It was happenstance that on one Friday morning Jenny was entering Morgan's office just as Sidney was leaving. Morgan noticed that as they saw each other, they exchanged startled glances and then Sidney seemed to rush on past. As Jenny turned to Morgan she could see his look of question.

"Is Sidney someone you know?" he asked.

To anyone else, Jenny would not have answered but with Morgan, she had no secrets.

"Very well," she responded. "He seems to be one of those men who has an insatiable appetite for sex. Remember my two star girls, Donna and Detrick? Well he not only likes one, he likes them both and both means at the same time. He's been one of my steady customers for a long time. It used to be that he only came in ever now and then. But lately he's been coming in almost every day. I don't know where it's coming from but he seems to have a good supply of money."

An animal instinct triggered inside of Morgan. But the code

between he and Jenny would not permit him to quarry the matter. So, as if it was of no importance, he pulled himself up to his desk and started arranging the papers that they would be discussing. With the engineer's blue-line drawing of the proposed building laid out he pointed to some particular feature in pretense of calling Jenny's attention to a construction matter.

Then, without explanation or implied obligation and in an insignificant tone he said, "If there are any pictures available of Mr. Griffin's encounters with Donna and Detrick I would be interested."

"Consider it done," she responded in an equally unimportant tone and without looking up.

From there, Morgan started additional investigating the circumstances between Patricia and Sidney. Bits and pieces started to surface that were not in tune. Sidney's life had been a series of tragic circumstances. Since childhood he had been led to believe that the ballet was an honor; entrusted in the hands of a chosen few. It was the golden avenue by which the masses could escape the drudgery of their daily lives and visit the land of fantasy. For that respite the masses would be forever thankful to ballet dancers. Not in reality had it turned out that way.

The honor that was supposed to come never came. It was supposed to be there but it wasn't. Sidney had never even came close to making it to the top.

His disappointment and frustration had eventually turned to rage and under the hypnotic effects of marijuana he started fantasizing about getting revenge. A means of showing them all. Even as Morgan was investigating the mode continued.

"Mrs. Waters," Sidney announced one morning amidst the haze of putrid smoke that permeated through the back stage, "I have been thinking that someday you and I might do our own ballet. Wouldn't that be something? I will write it and you can dance it. As a matter of fact I already have some thoughts.

"A ballet that has lots of what you do best; whirls in chain. How about we go ahead, starting today we concentrate on your whirls?

"Remember the type of slippers we are wearing, *techniques slippers*. No *pointe shoes* for at least two years.

"Remember the term *tour chainé* pronounced toor-sheh-Nay meaning turn in chain?

"Or *chainés papillon* pronounced she-Nay pa-pee-Yawn meaning chains like a butterfly?

"Now, in three-four time, arms extended out to the side, turn one and two and three and four; to the music.

"Good, keep going, all the way out to center stage and then hold in circles. Remember on your toes but not on pointe, just a little ball of the foot spring; good, bravo, keep going, very important keep your arms extended straight out to the side, whirl, keep going, two and three and four; stay in step with the music. As the crescendo increases, increase you whirls.

"The chains-in-butterfly that will be our specialty. Over and over we will practice. Chains-in-butterfly, arms fully extended, straight out to the sides as you whirl faster and faster.

"Bravo, Mrs. Waters, bravo. Our very own Butterfly Ballet Mrs. Waters. Think about it."

Chapter 20

Friday nights for Jenny Craig were always her busiest. For Aspen McGee, Jenny's busy times were the times he reserved for the pleasure of his own company. On that Friday night he was late getting away from work and slightly flustered over the inconvenience. Declining an offer by his fellow banking colleagues to meet at a club for cocktails he left his office and drove directly home. With briefcase in hand, his work week finished, he inserted a brass key into a Yale lock and welcomed himself into the silent, rambling plush of his penthouse.

The sound of the door latch closing behind him signaled that he was fortified, at least for a while, against the outside world. His interest for the evening being a light dinner and a glass of vintage wine; followed by classical music and a good thick book. By eight thirty he was in his pajamas, Mozart hung softly in the background, he was leaning back in his favorite recliner, a snifter of brandy was on his armchair table and he had entered the realm of Count Lev Nikolayevich Tolstoi's *War and Peace*.

Evening hours flow quickly in such pleasure and at a little after eleven the onset of peaceful drowsiness set-in. He was fond of reading himself to sleep. He enjoyed the sedate feeling of a book gently dropping from his hands into his lap, feeling the slight disturbance and then proceeding to bed without fully waking up. For Aspen the sayim that 'tranquility can come in through the keyhole of a Yale lock but annoyance can bust down the door' required no proof.

On that night, tranquility arrived on scheduled in the form of a deep peaceful sleep. Annoyance arrived at sometime around three AM in the form of an ear-piercing ring of a bedside telephone.

Muttering his aggravation Aspen answered with a reserved, "Hello?"

"Hello, Aspen this is Jenny. I...know I must have awaken you?"

"Jenny." His tone immediately changed. "No, no it's OK. I...uh just wasn't expecting. Where are you? I thought you were supposed to be over at Ft. McCaffey this weekend?"

"I was Aspen, or I should say I still am. But we seem to have gotten involved in a little situation here."

Reactively he sat upright and his voice instantly reflected his concern. "Jenny, what happened? Are you hurt, are you OK? What's wrong?"

"No, no I'm not hurt Aspen. I'm OK in that respect so there's no panic. But I'm afraid we're in a little jam."

"What Baby? Where are you? Your voice sounds reserved. Have you been crying?" A pause followed before she responded.

"Well, it's a little embarrassing Aspen but I seem to have gotten myself and all of the girls arrested."

"What!" he stammered. "Arrested! Jenny what are you talking about? Where?"

"ASPen," she cut in, "don't panic. It's not like our lives are in any danger. We're OK. We just happen to all be arrested and in the county jail in Jacksburg. It happened a few hours ago."

"What...? Jenny? On what... charge? How? All eleven of you?

"I'm afraid so Aspen. The whole crew."

"But... What happened?"

"What happened was the County Sheriff and a load of his deputies just barged in on us, loaded us all in cars and brought us into jail. I'm sorry to call you at this hour Aspen. I just didn't know anyone else to call. I didn't want to bother Morgan right now after what he is going through."

"No, no, it's OK Jenny, I want you to call me. Now tell me what's happened so far?"

"Well so far we are all just being held in jail. One deputy wanted to know who was in charge and when I responded he told me I could make one phone call."

"Have they formally told you of the charges?"

"Uh, well Aspen, I'm not very good at these things so I don't know what formal means. When they busted in on us they simply said that we were all under arrest for prostitution in violation of some State Code."

"OK," he responded. "Now, listen carefully. I don't know how much time they will allow you so we'll have to talk fast.

"First, I don't know if you can get away with it, but if they start booking procedures, reading the charges against you, number of counts, etc., tell them that you do not want to be booked until you have a lawyer present.

"Secondly, if they start to fingerprint you, same thing. It may work. Especially on the fingerprints, just keep your hand closed. Again, tell them that you are not refusing to cooperate; you just want to wait until your attorney is present. On this end I'll call Frank Buckwilder as soon as we hang up.

"Knowing Frank, it'll be OK. Unless something goes wrong we should be over there by ten o'clock in the morning. Don't say anything and don't sign anything."

Aspen had been talking rapidly in expectation of being cut off. When it appeared that they had more time he continued.

"Do you know the name of the sheriff and whether he was there in on the raid?"

Jenny was surprised by the question. To her it didn't matter, a sheriff is a sheriff, and if they say you are under arrest then you are under arrest.

"Aspen, I don't know how I can find that out. I am standing here in a sort of open lobby area by the front desk and talking on a wall phone. There's a deputy sheriff of some sort working behind the desk, do you want me to ask him?"

"No! No, don't give anything away. Now listen, can you remember how many officers were in on the arrest?"

After a silence, "Five, I'm pretty sure there were five because there were four cars and there were two officers in the front seat of the car in which I was riding."

"Can you tell me if one of them was tall, scrounge looking, sort of hunch-back, with yellow dingy teeth. He's mostly bald but what hair he does have is probably shaggy and he would be wearing a worn-out slouchy western hat; sickening grin, has bad breath and chews on a matchstick? Answer yes or no."

"Uh...uh... yes. That description seems to fit the sheriff on the passenger side of the car they put me in but how did you kn...?"

"Sorry Ma'am, time's up. Sorry, time's up lady," came the intruding voice of the attending deputy as he came from behind the desk to escort her back to the cell.

"Aspen, I have to go."

"OK. Look don't worry, we should be over there by ten or ten thirty o'cl..." Click.

It was a few minutes before seven o'clock the next morning when Aspen's steel gray 1941 four doors Cadillac headed out of Pittsburgh and the level of talk between he and Frank was mostly one or two word sentences. "Morning Frank." "Morning Aspen." "Ready?" "Yeah." "Got everything?" "I believe so." "All set?" "Let's do it."

The sky was overcast, traffic at that hour was light, and the transition from sleep to being fully awake was not quite complete.

The mood was one of heading the car down the road, nursing a cup of hot coffee and squirming into their seat pattern. Frank had brought along the morning newspaper and by the time they had reached the outskirts of Pittsburgh he was settled and scanning the front page as he asked, "How far to Jacksburg?"

Aspen glanced at Frank and the upheld newspaper being read through reading glasses and had the mind flash of, *if this isn't something. He sure seems overly concerned about our problem*; but still, he responded to the question with demeanor.

"Roughly three hours, give or take. We'll most likely get there in time enough but I don't know if we can get much taken care of on a Saturday," his tone slightly resentful that he did not have Franks full attention. Frank was responding with a spread newspaper across his lap.

Aspen casually glanced, as Frank tore out three separate articles, each roughly a quarter page in size and put the jagged pieces in the top pocket of his brief case.

"Aspen," he asked rhetorically without looking up as he continued reading, "can you believe how these modern day Radio Evangelism are taking over this country and saturating the free airwaves?"

Frank's off-hand remark about radio preaching touched a sensitive nerve in Aspen on two accounts. With respect to their immediate problem of Jenny in jail it didn't seem to Aspen that Frank was overly concerned. On a more pronounced note the account that sparked a latent revulsion was the mention of airway bible thumping.

Aspen had assumed that his and Frank's driving time would be spent discussing Jenny's problems. It hadn't occurred to him that long past religious troubles would again flair up. When it did the spark caused an instant flushing of his face and his knuckles tightening around the steering wheel. He needed to say something.

"Interesting," he spoke a single word sentence in a tone that invited a response.

"What?" Frank lowered the paper and looked at Aspen over his reading glasses. "What's interesting?"

"Your comment. That remark you made about the radio evangelist; about how they're taking over the airways."

"Oh, Yeah, it's something," he answered in a tone of no importance as he raised the newspaper back up and continued reading. As the shuffling sound of the moving paper quieted down, Aspen again spoke.

"It just caught my interest," he said; indicating that he did not want to drop the subject.

Frank again lowered the paper and responded. "You interested?" his tone showing that he had picked up on the drift. Twisting to where he was looking over at Aspen he finished the remark. "Interested in what? Evangelism or religion?"

"Neither, both. Hell I don't know. Slavery, control, scare tactics, God and man. Are you a religious man, Frank? I mean, is it something that's important to you?"

A dead silence followed as Frank, with his black half-rim reading glasses on the bridge of his nose held a solitary stare at Aspen; who in turn could feel his face flush as he continued to look straight ahead through the windshield.

With deliberate slowness Frank folded the pages of the newspaper, half turned and tossed it in the rear seat. Continuing, he removed his reading glasses and put them in his coat pocket.

"Aspen," he said as he raised up to adjust his seating and pull his trousers loose from the bind in his crouch, "base on the tone of your comment I am going to say something.

"It is my guess that your religious experiences and my religious experiences have been very different. Now I can't comment on yours so let me confine my remarks to just mine.

"God has a place in my life. I attend church..."

"What church do you belong too, Frank?" Aspen interrupted and then became fluster at his rudeness.

"I'm sorry Frank. That didn't come out right. It was rude. I, apologize."

It was a moment where the gracious character of Frank Buckwilder reflected his breeding and composure.

"Aspen, I sense there is something you're searching for. Sometimes these things are awkward so in answer to your question I am a Methodist. If you are wondering why, I will also answer that. It is based on the doctrines of free grace and individual responsibility.

"There is a serenity about the Methodist religion which I find very comforting. In substance a quiet and gracious sanctity that permits me to visit God in a most beautiful setting.

"Our visits, God and mine, are extremely uplifting. We talk and visit. I find comfort in expressing my appreciation for the world He has given us; life, beauty, freedom.

"I never go to Him with my troubles. My burdens in life are mine to solve. Besides, it would be unthinkable to soil the few blissful moments we have together by discussing my troubles.

"I ask nothing more of God than He be there and I am extremely content with our relationship."

There was no more for Frank to say. His position on religion was there for Aspen to consider in whatever way he chose. The atmosphere at the moment suggested that a silence would follow but to Frank's surprise, Aspen continued.

"It sounds like the concept of your faith is to simply bring you and God together so that you can find your own relationship." Frank was surprised by Aspen's statement but felt it was actually a question.

"*Our own relationship*, I have never thought of it in just those terms Aspen, but I would say it is a fair interpretation."

"Would you say that all of the big religions are about the same Frank? I mean do they just simply want to bring people and God together for the pleasure of both? I mean, say the Catholics, Baptist, Amish?"

"Aspen, I can't answer that. All the religious people I know seem to be pretty happy with their faith.

"To some degree most Christian faiths are all different, but in a lot of respects they are all pretty much the same; meaning a close personal relationship with God."

"But the Church itself. What does it do? Is that the function and purpose of the Church; to just act as the place where God and a person can come together?"

"Yes, I suppose; if that is the point-of-the-pin you are after. All of the big organized established religions, if I can use those two terms, have the common thread of having a house of worship. They also have the common thread of serenity and grace because it is generally accepted that reverence of God should be in a quiet, tranquil setting.

"Now, Aspen is there something specific? Talking religion is something which I ordinarily shy away from."

"You're right Frank. I'm embarrassed. It's not a subject I usually touch. Again, I apologize. The thing that riles me is the hypocrites who use religion as a means of controlling people."

"Meaning?

"Meaning for one, the church which I used to attend. Meaning for two, all of the radio evangelist you mentioned who spew out over the air waves their scare crap of God casting people into everlasting hell."

"Aspen," Frank spoke in a charitable tone, "I hardly think you can put the two in the same category. It's common knowledge what the radio people are doing. It's a big new deal, propaganda. Mind control of the masses. It's a business. They're in it strictly for the money.

"It should be illegal the way they get their hooks into people, especially older folks, and drain them dry. But there is no law against it. In fact they are actually protected by the freedom of religion and the freedom of speech provisions of the United States Constitution. So the thing to do is just ignore it"

"All the same it galls me."

"Aspen, accept it. Accept also that it will get worse. Radio is still young; fifteen-eighteen years old. According to the story, a young Westinghouse engineer by the name of Frank Conrad sent out the first radio musical broadcast. Young Frank had built himself a small transmitter in his garage back in 1916 and discovered he could talk out over the air.

"Well before long people would give him messages to send, etc. Then one day he simply put his microphone in front of his phonograph and bingo the birth of a new industry.

"Now, more to the matters at hand. Aspen, when we were on the phone this morning you said something about knowing the Sheriff over in Jacksburg?"

"Buck Wilson, Sheriff Buck Wilson," responded Aspen. "He's been the sheriff in that county for twenty five years; no good scum, sorry as they come."

Frank turned and looked at Aspen for continued explanation.

"I used to live in Jacksburg, Frank. I never told anyone especially Jenny but that's where I came from when I moved to Pittsburgh."

The legal mind of Frank Buckwilder instantly shifted. His casual watching of the countryside as they drove in silence did not reflect the cunning of his mind as he registered this information. Switching to a mannerism of courtroom decorum he asked the question.

"Is it reasonable to assume that you have a working knowledge about the circumstances with which we are dealing?"

"You mean do I know the town politics?" retorted Aspen. "Yeah, Frank, I know the town politics. Trust me. I know the town politics."

"I trust you," answered Frank, "but I could sure use a summery. If you can, how about just a broad picture."

Looking for a starting place, Aspen inhaled a deep breath and began. "It's what everyone in town calls an arrangement. In substance, Buck Wilson is in charge of graft and the Church is in charge of fleecing the law abiding. I used to..."

"What church is that?" cut in Frank. Is there only one Church in town?"

Aspen was caught off guard at the difference in the level he was starting at and the level of Frank's interest. Slightly taken back he retracted to answer the question. "For all practical purposes, yes there is only one Church; The Apostle Church.

"And believe me when I say it controls the town of Jacksburg. It controls everything from the bank to the law; it controls the town.

"I used to be a Deacon in the Apostle Church and I was also a Vice President at the Bank.

"Once a month good ol' Sheriff Buck Wilson would come into my office to make a Church contribution. If the contributions were good then the Church was not overly concerned about how the law was enforced. Meaning hookers, pinball machines, poolrooms, and illegal gambling down along the tenderloin on 3rd and 4th Streets.

"Yes sir, it's what the town, meaning the Apostle Church, called an arrangement.

"Come election time Mr. Law and Order Wilson gets the Church's reelection endorsement and low and behold, Buck is good for another four years."

"So," murmured Frank, "Jenny's little operation is not so much a moral concern to the town as an infringement on territory. Very interesting."

"In truth, I don't really understand what is going on," said Aspen. "It's got to be something bigger than that.

"Jenny's operation is not cutting into the tenderloin network that much. So I'm surprised about them busting her; I don't know.

"It's possible I suppose that it could be like you just said. Maybe they are just trying to control their territory. But I'm awfully suspicious. I think it's going to turn out to be much deeper than that. My guess is that in some way or another the bottom line is going to be control. The Church has a strangulation hold on everything and everybody in Jacksburg.

"You want a job, belong to the Church. Need a building permit, belong to the Church. Start a new business, belong to the Church."

There was a momentary pause as Aspen finished. Both men were in thought, and the silence amplified the sound of the tires singing on the macadam road as the car wheeled on. A legal chemistry continued to formulate as Frank now started to assess the broad circumstances.

"What," he finally asked in a slow methodical tone, "do we have?"

Aspen had already conjectured what he thought would be their best defense and was ready with a reply.

"The best I can come up with are three possibilities, maybe four. The first is entirely in your field; purely technical aspects of the law.

"Meaning what are the charges, what do they have in the way of evidence, any witnesses who are willing to testify, etc.

"The second is entirely in my field. I have in mind to go see Bishop 'Back Wall'; actually his name is Walback but people call him Back Wall because he tries to keep everyone's back right to the wall.

"I still have six million dollars that he would like very very much to get his hands on. So I may be able to wrangle some clout from that angle.

"Thirdly, I am thinking about the aspect of one Government power, meaning Jacksburg/Hensley County, running up against another Government power, meaning the United States Military.

"It just might be possible that our patriotic Colonel Bates over at Ft. McCaffey may be in a position to flex a little muscle.

"I figure he won't like the loss of that little contribution which Jenny sends his way every week."

As Aspen was finishing, the traffic was bunching up behind a slow moving truck. Slowing down he waited until on coming traffic was clear and then passed. Once around the truck and back to normal speed, Frank asked, "And the fourth? You said there was a possible fourth."

"The fourth," Aspen said in a very reluctant tone, "could get very, very messy. A dooms day possibility if it appears they intend to go for maximum jail time and some heavy fines."

Frank was massaging his face with both hands while Aspen talked. The increased circulation was soothing and if truth were known he had indulged in a might too much distilled spirits the night before.

As he continued massaging he considered what he had just heard. It was helpful that Aspen understood the harsh realities of life. The unity of their minds sparked a touch of comraderie.

"If you care to say it, I care to hear it," he responded.

"Well," Aspen started, "my thinking is we should be prepared for a worst case scenario. So here's what we've got. A few years back, Martha Wilson, who at the time was Buck Wilson's wife, died a very mysterious death. Mysterious, meaning it gets nice and messy. Ol' Buck had gotten himself involved with a young whore down on 3rd Street. And before long she starts putting the squeeze on him to divorce his wife and marry her.

"The only problem is the Church of the Apostles doesn't take kindly to divorce. So to make a long story short, Martha Wilson conveniently died.

"You got it, she died one day and was buried the next; no Coroner's inquest, no autopsy, nothing; just a rush rush burial. The local gossip was that she had been poisoned but nobody was ever strong enough to stand up against City Hall.

"I was a Deacon in the Church during that period and I know of what I speak. My very own wife at the time was adamant that there not be a town scandal. So I personally was responsible for some of the quick shuffle." Aspen paused and took another deep breath. He did not like telling the details but it was necessary so he continued.

"It all started early one morning when Buck supposedly woke up and found her dead. He called a Church controlled doctor who diagnosed that she died from a heart attack.

"She was pronounced dead by the doctor at the scene, taken to the local mortuary, prepared for burial, put in a casket and delivered directly to the Church on the same day.

"And flowers, too many flowers, given by unknowns. Far in excess of what would normally be expected; arrived by delivery van and filled up the Church that same evening.

"Services were held the next morning and by one o'clock she was in the ground."

Aspen did not have the opportunity to elaborate further on the story. The outskirts of Jacksburg started materializing with cut- rate service stations, wrecking yards and billboards coming into view. The morning had passed faster than either he or Frank realized.

It was barely ten o'clock and they were already entering the city limits. Frank felt a need to at least get a feeling of the situation if it came down to having to do battle with the Church.

"What is the extent you would be prepared to go on this underlying control we may have to fight?"

Aspen took a breath and slowed the car as they approached a red light. "I have already thought of that," he replied. "And the bottom line is this. I love Jenny and I hate them. I have six million dollars that they consider their money and I really don't give a shit. For all I care we spent the whole six million.

"They have a newspaper editor here in Jacksburg by the name of William Offhill who nobody likes; including me. Nevertheless, I do respect ol' Will and I think he has some respect for me.

"Of course the reason nobody likes him is he can't be bought. His disposition is that there isn't a single person in Jacksburg that's worth a tinker's damn. Ask him and he will tell you in minute that every last person in town is obsessed with greed and larceny.

"His greatest pleasure in life is publishing news which proves he is right. If there is anyone in town that the Church does not own I suppose it is Will Offhill. And I think he would move Heaven and Earth to get at something like this."

As they started getting closer to downtown the traffic became more congested. Aspen worked his way through a few more red lights and they finally came to the Court House Square; the center of City and County Government. He jockeyed around the block, finally nosed into a parking place and turned off the ignition. There was a brief silence then Frank finally spoke.

"Listen, Aspen there are formalities which must be followed in these matters. The big propaganda in the legal field is that all lawyers are Fellow Officers of the Court.

"Given that, decorum and dignity is to be accorded to all fellow lawyers and government officials in general.

"I am bound by protocol to introduce myself and establish that I am the representing attorney. There has to be a shaking of hands and cordial small talk; time honored traditions.

"It is all hypocritical of course. No lawyer likes it but we all have to do it. It's how the game is played. Now since they know you, it might be in our best interest if I take it from here. I am thinking that you may have some other business; maybe go out and check over Jenny's bus."

"Say no more Frank. From here on in it's your show. I'll get us a couple of rooms out at the Jacksburg Motor Lodge. If we miss connection take a cab and I'll catch you there. Good luck."

With a quick handshake, Aspen backed out and drove off. Frank was standing on the sidewalk and watched for a minute as the gray Cadillac blended in with the traffic.

He then straightened his posture, corrected his jacket, adjusted his tie and became a lawyer.

Ascending the wide concrete steps, passing past the towering white pillars and through the massive double doors he entered the Hensley County Court House.

Inside he walked down the wide marble hall checking the names on the various department doors. Finally he came to a door with the title County Jail. Inside he introduced who he was and stated his business to the on-duty deputy jailer; and without being further questioned was escorted back to the holding cells. Jenny and the girls appeared none the worse-for-wear and Frank was pleased to hear that they had not been fingerprinted or booked. *Strange*, he thought; but he did not ask why. A further piece of luck fell into play when he discovered that the district attorney was in his office. *Unusual,* he thought. *Saturday and all. Why?*

When Frank entered the DA's office that morning he borrowed upon the famous line spoken by Sir Henry Morton Stanley as he stepped off of the launch and extended his hand to Dr. David Livingstone. With his hand outstretched but not overly pronounced he moved across the room as the district attorney rose from his desk. As their hands accepted each other Frank said, "Mr. Rodney Stomey I presume."

"In the flesh, and you would be the Honorable Frank Buckwilder; a pleasure. Sit down Mr. Buckwilder, make yourself comfortable."

Protocol followed with small talk as Frank put his briefcase on the floor and accepted the chair. *Amazing,* he thought. *They were waiting for me; but why?* As the amenities between Rodney Stomey and Frank Buckwilder settled down to the matters at hand, they were silently joined by another figured who entered from a side door to the office; a man in a dark suit. Frank gave a natural quick glance but returned his attention to talking with the DA. The side figure quietly took a seat at an obscure desk and pretended to be working.

"Mr. Stomey," Frank finally reached the point, "we seem to have a little confused situation here this morning which I am sure we can straighten out with a minimum of red tape.

"It appears that your extra ordinary fine law enforcement authorities here in Hensley County have made a serious mistake.

"Through some grave unfortunate circumstances they arrested a group of fine upstanding girls from our religious organization, the Benevolent Order of Youth for Christ.

"Naturally we are highly indignant about the incident. But we understand that mistakes can happen so if it pleases you, we would like to have them released immediately and without any adverse publicity or fanfare."

Rodney Stomey leaned back in his chair. He would have enjoyed putting his feet up on his desk but that would be rude at this stage. Instead he interlocked his fingers across his midsection and smiled a little smile.

"Oh, I wouldn't think that our very proud and noble officers would make that sort of a mistake Mr. Buckwilder. I am sure that you, as legal representative for the Benevolent Order of Youth for Christ, are simply not aware of all the circumstances."

Frank liked the way the events were unfolding. His first impression was that Stomey knows the routine.

"Well, of course that is entirely possible. So why don't you tell me the particulars that would cause your Sheriff to take such harsh steps as to disrupt a religious function? Here we have these wholesome young women with solid religious beliefs, donating their time to providing social amenities to this country's young fighting men and they end up getting arrested.

"Now Mr. Stomey that smacks dead onto freedom of religion."

"Oh, I hardly think prostitution is a function of religion Mr. Buckwilder."

"Come, come now Mr. Stomey, surely you can't be serious, prostitution? Really... Mr. Stomey. On what do you base such preposterous allegations?"

"Oh we have been watching Miss. Craig's operation for quite sometime; young GIs coming and going."

"And," Frank cut in, "because young recruits have been seen entering and leaving the Social Hall you assume that our young women are prostitutes?"

"Look, Frank, I am not prepared to..."

"Since you have been watching, as you say, the situation, do they do anything else besides this alleged prostitution?"

Not cognizant that he was now on the defensive, Stomey asked, "What do you mean; do they do anything else?"

Frank felt good as the first punch landed. Based on this first skirmish, Stomey knows his protocol but little else.

"Well in terms of prostitution, what does that really mean. I mean, when I hear the word prostitution I am thinking of, say like some of the whores that you have here in Jacksburg standing out on the sidewalk down on 3rd Street.

"In the way of an example, say a young GI is walking along, one of the whores down there puts the proposition to him, he pays her the money, they go inside, have a little sex, he's up and out of there.

"Now that is what comes to my mind when you say prostitution. Would you say that that is a good broad generalization?"

Stomey was still leaning back with his hands interlocked across his midsection. He felt on the defensive but was fighting to keep it from showing. He did not answer immediately but pretended to be studying the question. Then in a tone that he hoped would reflect both sincerity and an absence of undue hostility he conceded.

"Well, OK For the sake of argument I'll concede that that's a reasonable description. But what's your point."

Frank could not believe his own ears. That the District Attorney of Hensley County would sit there and agree in effect that the town of Jacksburg had whores.

"You ask what the point is. The point is prima facie evidence; which as lawyers we both know means just on the face of it.

"Now," Frank continued, "from what we have just said, there is no evidence that a sex act with any of our religious girls actually did take place. But, based on prima facie evidence, a law enforcement officer could reasonably assume that a sex act did take place and therefore it would be proper to make an arrest. Would you say, Mr. Stomey, that that is a fair analysis?"

"Absolutely," Stomey said with emphasis as he unlocked his fingers and leaned forward. "Frank you yourself have just made our very point. An Officer does not have to see the actual insertion to conclude that a sex act has taken place."

Frank contained his exuberance at Stomey's forceful reply. The thought flashed through his mind as to how some lawyers ever get through law school.

"So what you are telling me, Mr. Stomey..."

"Rodney, call me Rodney or Rod," Stomey cut in. "We're not as formal out here in the country as you big city lawyers."

Frank continued to be amazed. Where was this man's mind? He is more concerned with his good-ol'-boy country image than with the point.

"Very well, Rodney. You certainly are a gentleman. Now, what you are telling me is that a whore down on 3rd street is a whore; but surely you can't compare the circumstance of a whore down on 3rd Street with the Bible Center operated by our Miss. Craig."

At this point there was a scooting of a chair by the figure in the dark suit at the far side of the office. There was also a pause as Stomey started to realize there may be a danger signal here and to be careful in his rebuttal.

Frank turned his eyes just enough to detect the figure but Stomey did not notice the noise.

"Let me ask you Mr. Stomey, uh Rodney," Frank continued on the assertive, "have you ever visited our fine religious establishment?"

"Well, no," responded Stomey. "But that's not necessary on my part Frank... you as a lawyer know that. Sheriff Wilson has filled me in with the details and you can't fool ol' Bucko Wilson.

"If he says your girls are engaged in prostitution then that's good enough for me," Stomey finished with assertiveness. Frank allowed him the courtesy to bask in his smugness and simply switched points.

"Can you tell me at this time Mr. Stomey," Frank now using the last name as a signal that the fun was over, "how many counts are my girls going to be charged with?"

"Eleven counts," answered Stomey feeling that he was now on the offensive. "Eleven girls, eleven counts."

"Meaning," Frank asked in a clarifying tone, "one count against each girl?"

"Why certainly," he cast a questionable look at Frank. "What do you think; we're going to pile all eleven counts on just one girl and the rest walk free?

"Boy, Mr. Buckwilder, you big city lawyers. You're really something. We don't do things like that around here," he again leaned back.

"So what you are telling me," mused Frank in a leading tone, "is that you have eleven witnesses who are prepared to come forward and individually testify that each one had a sex act with each girl."

It was apparent that the control was again back in Frank's hands as he continued.

"It would surprise me Mr. Stomey if, during wartime conditions such as these, that you could persuade the United States War Department to go to all the trouble and expense of yanking eleven men out of front line combat and bringing them all the way back to Hensley County just to testify at a trial of prostitution."

Stomey's face flushed red at the apparent mocking by Frank. He shifted from leaning back to forcefully coming forward and slapping one hand on the desk.

"I can assure you Mr. Buckwilder," he boisterously said, "that Sheriff Buck Wilson is highly thought of in this town and I can get a conviction based on his testimony."

Frank mocked surprised at Stomey's sudden change of demeanor and in a tone implying clarification played his next card.

"Why no. Absolutely nothing along those lines Mr. Stomey. I wouldn't think of questioning the integrity of your County government. What I am saying Mr. Stomey, is this. Pretend for a moment that you are on the jury. And here I am as defense lawyer.

"Now we have already described the typical circumstances of a street whore remember, you agreed to the broad picture.

"Now it's going to be my job to contrast the scene of Jacksburg street whores to the religious setting of our social hall maintained by the Benevolent Order of Youth for Christ.

"Permit me if you will to go on because in court, of course, I will have all the time I need. If the jury should choose to go out for an on-site inspection they would find our establishment is just like a hometown corner drug store.

"Juke box, dance floor, balloons and paper stringers hanging from the ceiling, soda fountain, prayer room with bible, non-alcoholic beverages, and above all that, our wholesome girls dressed in high school skirts and saddle oxford shoes, sitting with groups around a table talking and laughing like young folks do. Not to mention...."

Frank's delivery was abruptly interrupted by a knocking on the outside office door and there entered a young secretary.

"Excuse me Mr. Stomey I hate to interrupt, but I have an urgent call for Mr. Buckwilder."

She turned her attention to Frank and said, "It's from your office Mr. Buckwilder, your secretary Nancy Evans, she says it's very important. You can take it at my desk."

Frank excused himself and followed the young secretary but was extremely perplexed. He had not told Nancy he was leaving town. How did she know where he was and what could possible be the nature of an emergency call to this number. Without showing any expression he answered the phone knowing that extension phones were probably listening in.

"Hello," he answered without expression.

"Hello. Hello Mr. Buckwilder, this is Nancy."

"Yes Nancy," he said without surprise or question.

"Mr. Buckwilder, you asked me to keep you up to date. Your client from West Texas called to tell you that he is en route and will be in Pittsburgh when you get here."

"Good," responded Frank. "Nancy, I appreciate you calling. I know you will do this anyway but I will mention, can you be sure and take care of the lodging arrangements. See about getting a room at the William Penn Hotel?"

"Everything will be taken care of Mr. Buckwilder, see you when you get back."

As he hung up the phone he felt a glow of pride at Nancy's cunning in not giving anything away. Nevertheless, the call itself had only created more mystery. What client from West Texas? He didn't have any client in West Texas or any other part of Texas for that matter. 'He will be in Pittsburgh when I get there?' He could not imagine who it might be.

Frank returned to Rodney Stomey's office and as he entered was surprised to find another man standing at his desk talking in low tones. Who? Where... then he looked; it was the dark figure from the far end of the office. As he took his chair he looked in question at the new man on the other side of the desk. A look that put the onus on Stomey for an introduction and he quickly moved to protocol.

"Uh, Mr. Buckwilder," he said. "Mr. Buckwilder, I would like for you to meet an associate of mine, Mr. Walback. Mr. Walback meet Mr. Buckwilder."

As the two men shook hands the thought flashed through Frank's mind. *Interesting. Very interesting. Is this the Bishop Walback that Aspen spoke about? Why had he not been introduced as Bishop instead of Mr. Walback? The plot thickens. What is the extent of his interest?*

Bishop Walback was tall and thin with slumping posture that reflected his age of mid sixty. He was bald on top with long hair on the sides being an oily gray and slicked back to his collar line. He wore cold steel bifocal glasses and his face gave the impression that it had been assembled from a series of mismatched parts and undoubtedly accounted for his disposition.

Nothing seemed to match or fit. The profile of his head resembled an oversized light bulb. He had a small chin of sorts but rather than protruding outward it blended downward into his neck. His mouth was small and discernible only by his tightly drawn lips. Frank could not tell whether he had any teeth. His eyes were cold, without expression and in perpetual squint. All these features centered around a big hawk nose so that the total composite resembled one long continuation of skin which started at the back of his bald hairline and ended at his protruding Adams apple.

Bishop Walback wore a sagging wrinkled black suit with dandruff on the shoulders. His shirt was a droopy black, buttoned up to the top at a clergymen's stained white collar. As the two men shook hands,

Walback tilted his head back in order to get a better look at Frank through the bifocals; and two protruding oversized nostrils suffocated by matted clogged hair was the greeting.

"Mr. Buckwilder," Walback started. "Mr. Stomey tells me you're from Pittsburgh. Welcome to Jacksburg. We take pride in extending our hospitality. Did you come over by yourself, any friends, or family with you? Can we assist you with sleeping accommodation?"

"No," dodged Frank, "I think I'm in pretty good shape, but I do appreciate your generous offer."

"Not at all. We here in Jacksburg always try to make sure that everyone has a pleasant stay. How was the drive over, tiring anyone come with you to help drive?"

"Oh, you know traveling these days," Frank answered a question with a question."

It was instantly apparent that Walback had assumed the authority on the other side of the desk. Moreover, it was even more apparent that Walback was going to be a formidable foe.

"We used to have a banker here in Jacksburg who deserted us sometime back and moved to Pittsburgh," he continued. "Finest fellow you'd ever want to meet. We sure did hate to lose him." His tone was cold, calculating and without emotion. He was laying groundwork. His expressionless eyes staring through cold, steel rimmed glasses signaled that he was used to having his way.

"You may have heard of him," continued Walback. "His name is Aspen McGee. We understand that he went to another bank over in Pittsburgh." The sentence ended with an implication for Frank to respond.

Frank opened very lightly. He leaned to the side of his chair with one leg crossed. He rested his weight on one arm of the chair and lightly pulled on his chin with the other. Frowning an uncertain look as if searching his mind he slowly commented, "I... I don't know; seems like I may have seen that name in the newspapers, but..."

"If," Walback sneered, "we can cut through the bullshit Mr. Buckwilder let's get down to brass tacks. Since you and McGee are such good friends we thought that he might have come over from Pittsburgh with you."

The tone and context of the comment had been intended as a smashing gut punch; but for Frank it was child's play. His years in court had matched him against some of the best and his response reflected his genius.

"Why Mr. Walback, may I ask, why would you assume that this... this Mr. McGee would be traveling with me to Jacksburg?"

There followed a momentary silence. The two men were locked in eye-to-eye gaze. The callous, vengeful eyes of Walback saying *'the fun and games is over you stuck-up city lawyer. You frig with me baby and you'll suffer the consequences.*

The soft blue eyes of Frank saying, *Walback, not in a dozen lifetimes would I ever want to be as miserable as you. Go ahead you hypocritical S O B, throw your best punch. Get to the gut cutting. Let's see what you've got.* Then the silence was broken.

"We thought Mr. McGee might be coming over with you because we also know that he is living with Miss Jenny Craig; who as you know is the ring leader of this bunch of whores."

Frank did not flinch. The cold searching look of Walback detected no change in Frank's eyes as the charge was blasted. Frank showed no anger, no hostility, and no outrage.

What did happen was Frank's mind exploded. *BINGO! JACKPOT! BRASS RING! I'll be damned. Walback you son-of-a-bitch you gave your hand away. So that's what this is all about.*

They don't want Jenny and the girls at all. They want Aspen. Now it all becomes clear. It's all a clever scheme to get Aspen back into Hensley County.

Once he's back in the County he gets arrested and they charge him with running prostitution. Tried and convicted would mean five to ten years in prison. I'll be damned, Frank continued thinking. *What a calculated devious scheme by the Apostle Church.*

They want to make an example out of anyone who tries to run. By getting Aspen convicted and locked behind bars the Church would have grounds to reopen litigation and strip him of his trusteeship of the six million dollars.

Frank's adrenaline surged as he comprehended the level of stakes. He uncrossed his leg, straightened up in his chair and took a fortifying deep breath as he prepared to respond to Walback's allegations.

"Oh, surely now, Mr. Walback, an important man likes Mr. Aspen McGee? Certainly you don't think he would have time for a small time, plain Jane attorney like me." It was a line of talk that would buy time to think in light of this new revelation.

"What, with him being famous for his cattle drive from West Texas to Dodge..." Frank abruptly paused. *Cattle drive. West Texas. Client from West Texas.*

Well I'll be doubled damned. That's what the call from Nancy was all about. Somehow Aspen found out and got to the hell out of Jacksburg. He's sitting high and dry in Pittsburgh right now. That sly ol' fox. God I could give him a hug.

Frank allowed himself the pleasure of a broad smile and a minuscule fantasy.

When this is all over, he fantasized; *it would be a happy moment to find just Aspen and me enjoying a little comraderie. Just man to man playing a good game of draw poker; with all the trimmings. Trimmings meaning a very dignified occasion of two gentlemen dressed in formal attire at a man's club; black tie and tux. Seated at a hexagon mahogany poker table with a flawless bright green felt cover and a center overhead Tiffany swag lamp complete with a matching turn-of-the-century massive ornate pool table.*

Two gentlemen of social standing, he thought. *Convened for the evening in a masculine mahogany paneled room. Thick pile brown carpet, heavy wood carved, straight back Captain's chairs in deep brown leather; a knight's suit of armor with lance standing in one corner and two crossed swords on the wall along with two good Havana cigars and a bottle Napoleon Brandy. Complete with a covey of beautiful long hair, long legs young women with low cut blouses showing their bulging firm bosoms. Wearing mini skirts with fish net black stockings and high heel pumps and standing behind a fully stocked bar ready to light a cigar or freshen up a drink.*

The perfect setting to experience the pleasures of a keen sharp perceptive mind. Not in the context of predator and prey or competitiveness, but the exhilaration of matching wits. The fruits of pleasure that flourish from mind challenge. Each hand of poker providing new clues. That which comes from studying body language or facial expression, leaning forward, leaning back, nursing the cards, shuffling the hand, verbal one-upmanship disguising a bluff. All blended with the tang of brandy being swirled in a crystal snifter.

Frank breathed in deep. He felt the surge of air flowing in through his nostrils and filling his lungs to capacity. He held his expanded chest until the oxygen exhausted and then exhaled with a readiness to fight. *God,* he thought, *there could be a moment of Heaven on earth.* Bringing his thoughts back to the present, he continued.

"You'll pardon me Mr. Walback," he shifted into his smooth courtroom decorum, "if I feel it's worth making mention of Mr. McGee's prominence.

"Why, you know the man is actually famous. You are aware, aren't you that he received national recognition for his part in that now famous cattle drive.

"Nation wide coverage on radio, newsreels, newspapers, all the news media about his call above and beyond one's duty to support the war effort.

"I'm sure you must have read about how he left the comforts of his plush office and went out and spent over six weeks riding horseback in scorching heat and dust in order to help get six thousand head of cattle to market so our fighting troop would have food to eat.

"He was even called up to Washington and received a Meritorious Award from the War Department as an example of how this country needs to pull together in these terrible times of war."

Walback's mind was quick to catch Frank's drift and counter with a panic assault. "Very commendable," he said. "Wouldn't it be something if the American people knew that Aspen-the-Great-American-Hero was actually a whore runner."

Now, thought Frank. *Walback you unscrupulous gob of spit, it's time for your juggler vein.*

"I'm pleased that we are getting back to the matters at hand Mr. Walback. I appreciate you getting us back on course cause we do need to get this matter settled."

At that point Frank rose from his chair and pretended to be brushing the wrinkles from his 100% virgin wool, pin stripe suit. In a mannerism which reflected years of successful courtroom experience, Frank straightened his tie, checked his cuff links, and moved a couple of steps back from his chair to force a distance profile.

Clearly establishing that the time was his and that Walback and Stomey's protocol was to listen. He pretended to be starting when he cast an intimidating glance at the loose dandruff on the shoulders of Walback's suit. When he was sure that Walback caught his direct stare, he then looked at his own suit shoulders and gave them a light brush of his hand as if brushing off lint. With movement that reflected solid confidence, he then reached down for his briefcase, placed it on the corner of Stomey's desk and clicked the latch.

In a preparatory look he slightly pulled out the three ragged edged newspaper articles. Looking at them, he held one apart for a moment, let a slight smile come to the corner of his mouth, started to put it back, glanced at the other two one more time for a recheck, appeared satisfied, returned all three to the lid pocket, closed the briefcase and set it behind his chair.

"Now gentlemen," he commenced, "if my summary of the matter is correct, you are presently holding eleven young women in your jail. Fine, Christian, wholesome girls whom the Church has sent to Ft. McCaffey to entertain our troops as they are preparing to go off to war and fight for our Country.

"You are planning on charging these innocent young women with the outlandish, preposterous crime of prostitution.

"We of course will plead innocent. Among the character witness whom we will be using in court will be the Right Honorable Aspen

Gerore McGee who has recently been decorated by the President of the United States, President Franklin Delano Roosevelt, with our Nation's highest civilian metal. The story carried in all of the papers"

Here he paused for a moment to reflect a deepening of thought, but his mannerism clearly implied that he was not through.

"Now, as I understand the situation, you are not prepared to produce eleven witnesses, meaning eleven young GIs who would have to be taken out of front line combat and at government expense shipped back here in order to testify at the trial.

"If I am correct you will be relying solely upon the testimony of Sheriff Buck Wilson." At this point he again paused for effect, placed one hand on the back of his chair, glanced slightly up at the ceiling as if trying to decide how to best present his next point, deeply inhaled and continued.

"Gentlemen," he spoke in a tone of a request, "with your indulgence I would like to diverge here for just a moment. Just for a second if I may, and then we will certainly get back to the matters at hand.

"But I have always been fascinated by mysterious deaths; a fixation with unsolved mysteries. I suppose it's nothing more than a fantasy on my part of wanting to be a hero. But gentlemen I have always had the desire to wade into some high profile unsolved murder case and expose some blatant criminal wrong doing."

As he finished Frank pretended to be staring off into the distance; then brought himself back.

"Gentlemen, I'm getting way off the track. I'm well aware of that. What brought it all about is a bit of confusion in my mind. It is a little thing but I am hoping you can clarify something for me.

"Your Sheriff Wilson that you are going to be using as your most reliable and truthful witness; there was something in the newspapers but I would like to be sure. Is he the same Sheriff Buck Wilson whose wife died of a mysterious death a while back? The same death where the body has never been exhumed and analyzed for traces of poison or anything of that nature?"

Frank had laid his bomb and now he needed to get out of the way.

He quickly fended a need to go relieve himself.

"Gentlemen, Uh! Goodness. I am slightly embarrassed here. I hope you will excuse me. I am embarrassed that this should happen at this critical moment, but is there a rest room around?"

Slightly fidgeting he continued, "These unexpected urges, I suppose they just come with age." When he had received directions to the rest room, he picked up his brief case and commented as he was leaving,

"This may take a few minutes. I have some pills here in my case that I always carry with me. It takes a few minutes for them to work."

When Frank returned to the DAs office fifteen minutes later he was wiping his face with a handkerchief he had lightly wet in the wash basin and was startled by a deputy sheriff who was walking out the door just as he entered. Walback and Stomey had their heads close together and were talking in low tones. As the meeting came back to order, Walback was the first to speak.

"I'll get right to the point Mr. Buckwilder. My learned colleague and I have come to the opinion that we are not going to prosecute this case.

"NOT that we don't believe that we are right, MIND YOU. Your girls, as you call them are nothing but a bunch of whores.

"But we do concede the importance at this time for this Nation to have heroes. While we see Aspen McGee as a whore running propaganda hero, to the Nation he is none-the-less a hero and we will not tarnish that image.

"So in the name of patriotism, you might say, we are dropping the charges. I, uh I mean Mr. Stomey has just instructed the jailer to release all of your whores and bring them to the front for dismissal. So you and all of your whoring group will be free to leave in just a few minutes."

Frank was flabbergasted by this unexpected turn of events. Still, the moment required the highest degree of composure. He looked directly at Walback, smiled just a suggestion of a smile, nodded his head in understanding, and relaxed his posture. The next move was extremely important; express appreciation with dignity and execute the final protocol. Always allow your opponent to save face.

"Why, that's a wonderful news gentleman. Just wonderful. Moreover, I certainly agree with you that in these wartime conditions it is imperative that we all forget our differences and pull together as a Nation. In appreciation for your gracious gesture I will instruct my clients to be on their very best behavior.

"And that brings to my mind another little matter which has been bothering me for quite some time. In reviewing our records a while back I discovered that we had completely neglected to get a business permit when we set up our Youth for Christ Social Hall.

"I don't see how it could have been overlooked. Apparently it was just an oversight but I do want to rectify the situation.

"Now, today being Saturday and all I know the Court House is officially closed and I am wondering.

"Do you think it would be possible for either of you fine gentlemen to do me the favor and save me the time and money of having to make another long trip over here.

"It would be a great favor to me if I could just leave enough money with you to cover the cost of the customary Permit Fees."

He spoke as he slightly sat down on the edge of his chair and opened his briefcase. Then mocking a slight surprise he continued.

"Well I'll be. You know something else, gentlemen. I am just a mess today. I'll be hanged if I didn't go right off and forget my checkbook.

"But I do have a little cash which I always carry with me; in cases of emergency you understand," he spoke without looking up.

"Now I know that Business Permits cost quite a bit; what with processing and all.

"So if it's OK with you," he removed the money from his case as he looked up at both Stomey and Walback, "I have fifteen, one hundred dollar bills here. I will consider it a great favor if you will allow me to leave it with you. I trust it will be sufficient to cover the permit cost."

Neither Walback nor Stomey moved or responded. Frank eased the money on to the outer corner of Stomey's desk and without further eye contact, snapped his briefcase shut.

Knowing there was nothing more to say he rose to leave. He had almost reached the door when he paused for one final remark.

"Oh, and by the way, in reviewing our records, the Benevolent Order of Youth for Christ has scheduled the continuation of these weekly socials for another six months.

"At the end of that time, our funding for these trips will be exhausted and we will not be able to come back to Hensley County. Does this seem amenable to you two fine gentlemen?"

Now anxious to conclude the matter, Walback nodded a slight nod to Stomey. Stomey rose from his chair but remained behind his desk; making no gesture to escort Frank to the door.

"In view of all that we have discussed, Mr. Buckwilder, I believe we can tolerate the situation for another six months."

At the door Frank paused and nodded a slight nod, moved into the hall and closed the door. There was no parting handshake.

Chapter 21

Getting released from the slammer has its own time-honored code; never yell until you are out of hearing distance of the jailer. Under the watchful eye of three deputy sheriffs the cell door to the Hensley County Jail was opened and Jenny Craig and her ten girls were escorted through the halls and out the main entrance of the Courthouse. On the front steps they were released to the custody of Frank Buckwilder.

There had been no parting words from the deputies to Frank; though there was an exchange of looks and slight nods. With Frank as the father image they all maintained a strict decorum, gathered in a small tight group and remained silent while waiting for Jim Barkus to bring the bus. As they stood together their faces had no expressions but the fingers of their dangling hands searched for and interlocked with each other to mutually signal their stifled jubilance.

Within a few moments Jim pulled the big powder blue bus around in front and parked at the curb. Still maintaining their composure, they boarded in silence and mostly stood in the aisle rather than taking seats. With the door closed the big engine revved up, black smoke belched from the exhaust pipe and the bus slowly eased out. The wide rubber tires gave off a spongy feeling as the first block of traffic passed, then the second block of traffic passed; and then went their silence.

"YEA! FREEDOM! FREEDOM!" up went a wave of yells. "Hip! Hip! HOORAY! Hip! Hip! HOORAY," came repeated cheers as their frenzy exploded. "We won! We won!" their restraint completely dissipating as they all crowded the aisle and talked at the same time. "It's party TIME! Drinks all AROUND!" yelled Jenny, even while Jim was still nosing through downtown traffic. To the sounds of continued yells Jenny wiggled through the standing bodies to a built-in ice cooler and retrieved the first bottle of champagne. Handing out cocktail glasses she popped the first cork and began pouring fizzing bubbles into the cluster of waiting hands, filling and sloshing without caring. As soon as the first round was gulped down the glasses were refilled. This time numerous hands raised in toasts of cheer and thence a show of their appreciation to the man who had made it possible.

To Frank Buckwilder came an onslaught of young feminine attention in the form of wet moist kisses and a smothering of firm tits being hugged into his face. The weight of eleven women all attempting to sit in his lap at the same time held him captive in his seat as young lips with smeared lipstick repeatedly kissed and nibbled about his face. His response was to mimic objections and faintly fend off the insisting affections. But inside, the touch of so many beautiful women felt incredibly wonderful and it required considerable effort for him to hold his propriety in check.

Not to say that his mind and thought process did not momentarily reflect on all this lavish affection as 'yesterday's witness to prophesy'.

His poetry, that day at Pepperdine Conservatory with Morgan had just come to pass. To his mind this onslaught of heavenly attention was proof positive that a man's greatest fantasies are seeped in the arms and lips of beautiful women; and the fantasized setting of an ornate ballrooms, classical music, formal attire, and graceful waltzes are but compliments to a reachable rainbow.

Eventually however the celebrating tempo did start to settle down and then questions started being asked as to how he did it; and his modesty proved to be a perfect escape. For all of their prodding as to what happened all he would say was that he just got lucky and that the real credit belonged to Aspen and his status as a National hero; and the bus rolled on to Pittsburgh.

It was the next morning, in Aspen's penthouse before Jenny was to get a full understanding of Frank's words. Over a light breakfast of toast and coffee, she and Aspen were discussing the experience. To one of her specific queries, Aspen responded, "How did I find out they were actually after me and I got my sweet little baby pink butt out of Jacksburg?" he rephrased the question.

"Luck," he first said. "Pure and simple, sweet happenstance luck." He then started providing details. "After I let Frank out at the County Courthouse I headed out to the Jacksburg Motor Lodge. On the way I happened to be passing a service station that was owned by an ol' friend and I simply whipped in for gas.

"His name is Bat Lancy and he owns City Texaco. Bat and I have known each other and been good friends for twenty years. In fact he had been sweet on my deceased wife back when they were both in high school. It never worked out, partly because Bat wouldn't cotton down to the Church.

"There were some other reasons of course but the manner in which the Church tried to play dictator was the biggie. It was sufficient to break them up and Bat has held a grudge against the Church ever since, and that's about it."

"Well," Jenny asked in a why-are-you-stopping tone.

"Well," Aspen accepted the implication that he would have to continue, "I saw Bat at the pumps just as I was pulling in. I greeted him as an old friend but his handshake was hesitant; sort of standoffish and his demeanor was almost ghostly. Like something was very wrong. And, as it turned out, something indeed was very wrong.

"Bat has never been one to carry gossip. He is just a solid, straight arrow type of guy who doesn't lie, cheat, steal or get into other people's business.

"So the circumstances were out of his character but he finally broke the ice by asking. 'Aspen,' he asked in a tone which was clearly awkward, 'what brings you back to Jacksburg?'

"Of course I detected the signal that something was not quite right so I was cautious in my reply. 'Just an overnighter, Bat.' I answered. 'I have a little business down at the County Courthouse and I'll be leaving in the morning.'

"Well to make a long story short, there were a few more questions of whether I still had any close friends in the Church. When Bat was convinced that I was totally in the dark he unloaded. I guess it must have been town gossip, about how if the Church is to maintain dictatorial control they cannot afford to let anyone escape.

"Anyway Bat used the words, 'they're out to get you Aspen. You're walking smack into a trap. You'll be arrested the minute you walk into the Courthouse.'"

Aspen paused to indicate that the story was about over and in a concluding tone he said, "The rest is history. I filled my tank with gas, gave ol' Bat my appreciation's and got my behind out of Jacksburg. But I'll tell you one thing, I owe ol' Bat, and I owe him big time."

In an attempt to taper things off Aspen commented, "Now you have the whole story. Frank has told you his part and I have told you mine."

But Jenny would not be so easily denied. "Why," she asked, "did Frank pay them the fifteen hundred dollars."

Aspen again felt that this was all going to be too long and too difficult. Still, when he looked at Jenny, she looked so young and innocent. She had no idea of the workings of the world.

This must be, he thought, *how it is to raise a kid. Trying to teach them some semblance of the real world and hope they can survive.* He supposed he would have to go on.

He was still looking for a starting point when he rose from his chair and went to the liquor cabinet. What the hell, it was Sunday and a drink at that particular moment would hit the spot. Holding the door open with one hand he slowly looked at the assortment of bottles and could see nothing of interest.

Damn, he made the mental remark; *I can't even make up my mind about what kind of booze to drink.* From habit he reached for a half-filled bottle of Canadian Blend. On the rocks, he had a sip at the wet bar and experienced the familiar tangy sensation as he returned to his easy chair.

Maybe, he thought, *it wouldn't be too bad. Staying in for the day. No going out. It's nice and quiet. Maybe a few drinks. Caught up on a little loving; sounds pretty good.*

Reclining in his chair, he set the drink on the side table leaned back and threw one arm L shaped up over his head. Jenny was on the sofa in her favorite position of half sitting up with her legs stretched out. They were looking at each other but not in eye contact.

"Jenny," he started, "the reason for the fifteen hundred dollar payment is protection; pure and simple. Frank bought you the right to continue operating for another six months.

"After that you will have to decide whether you want to buy another six months or pull out. My guess is you will be better off pulling out. The smart thing to do is to build yourself a strong political base here in Pittsburgh. Money and power go hand in hand. It takes money to make money and it takes power to hold it. The first step is to start making contributions to all the public elections. Now... here are some strong words of advice.

"Do not, repeat, do not trouble yourself with the smoke, fluff and talk of the different candidates. Politics are not your concern. You don't particularly care who wins; you simply donate to all sides."

Aspen could detect that this sort of talk was foreign. It was the first time any of their discussions had drifted to such a serious side of their relationship and to a degree he already didn't like it.

"Jenny, in a way getting thrown in the slammer is the best thing that could have happened. It shows you just how unforgiving and precarious life can be. In this case you received benefit of the experience without having to pay too heavy of a price.

"I'm hoping it will make you realize just how easy it is to get caught up in what I call 'life will get your ass'. And for those unfortunate people who do get caught up, they always lose. It then becomes just a matter of degree. If you are lucky, as in this case, the toll will be reasonably light; if you are lucky.

"But understand that it could have been catastrophic. If Frank had been less skillful, if they had called his bluff; if hardball had been the name of the game, the outcome would have been much different. What if they had been determined to make you an example? The end results could have been prison time. The point is, power. It can either save you or it can wash you away like an outgoing tide."

When Aspen finished he expected Jenny to comment. To show some sign that she comprehended what he was saying; and to indicate an element of thankfulness for the lesson. But when he looked at her, she simply looked back and he felt a tinge of exasperation. Didn't she comprehend what he was saying? Was she resentful that he was lecturing?

Youth, he thought, *the belief that it can't happen to them.* He reached for his drink, took a big swig, swished it a couple of times and let it ooze down his throat. The bite seemed to compliment his feeling that he was proper in stressing these things. It gave him a renewed surge to continue.

"Jenny," he started again, "in my business as a banker I am in a position to know the forces of change which are and which will be affecting our lives.

"The advent of radio only a few years back was a quantum leap toward influencing public opinion and mass mind control. Comes radio and with it comes the ability to influence thousands of people without getting out of the studio and presto, comes air wave religion and there is now an industry with mind bending powers unheard of in the history of man.

"Would you be surprised to learn that some of the steel mills right here in Pittsburgh are backers of some of these Radio Evangelist. Experimental, they call it. A cheap way of controlling the workers; fear God and obey your master. One's master, of course being the steel mills. The next big talk is a thing called television. In a matter of five or six years you will be able to see movies from a box the size of an orange crate sitting right in your own living room," his words tapered off as he finished.

Spoken without emphasis, he had been watching Jenny and realized that the mind spread between the two of them was too broad. He rattled the ice in his near empty glass and was pondering the thought of a refill when she started to respond.

"Aspen I realize, or think I realize, what you are saying. I should be more cautious. And I agree. But Aspen that is nothing new in my business. I give favors to the police all the time. It's just understood in my business, so unless I am missing something...?"

Aspen took a deep breath, held it and searched for direction. He had started something that was getting out of control. The thing to do now was to lightly close the subject and decide later whether the matter should be continued.

"The thing is Jenny," he exhaled in a manner that implied finishing up, "because of radio and the forthcoming television, air-wave-religion of hell-fire-and-damnation is on the rise.

"Now, the hell-and-damnation boys have got to have something to attack. Surprise, surprise your profession, not just you but the whole profession of whoring, my very loving woman is exactly the one that they will be hitting the hardest.

"If you expect to survive there best be some well laid plans toward building a strong political power base and now is the time to start; end of story."

The character of their conversation had clearly become unappealing; too much gloom and doom. Almost in unison they agreed to change the subject. Aspen reckoned that some good classical music, a bottle of rosé wine, nudity on the carpet, an array of pillows and soft unhurried loving would be a good choice.

Jenny's ideas on the other hand sought the enjoyment of Aspen's story telling. So she lightly brushed aside his suggestions of afternoon lovemaking.

"I want to know," she declared, "about you being a such a hero. I had no idea."

Aspen looked at her in a questionable manner and asked, "Don't you ever read the papers?" Jenny returned his expression with a tilt of her head, implying wait just a sweetheart-minute and said, "I am one of those people who works nights and sleeps days, remember?"

"Now I am not real sure," Aspen jested, "if that's a sufficient answer to wave off my notion about loving. It seems to me that if you work in the dark you should be able to read in the dark."

"I'm going to read you in the dark," she barbed. "Now tell me what happened on that cattle drive that created such national fan fair."

"What happened," Aspen jested, "was a photographer took a close-up picture of my face right next to a steer's face and everyone agreed that the steer was better looking."

"Aspen, you're dead meat," she countered. "The doors to the vault are closed and sealed for the duration. Call it my contribution to the war effort."

"Jenny," he exclaimed in mocked disbelief, "that's cruel and unusual punishment; specifically forbidden by the Constitution of the United States."

"No jury would convict me," she refuted. "Now tell the cattle drive story or suffer."

Aspen then brought his chair forward from the leaned back position and rose to his feet. With empty drink glass in hand he spoke as he returned to the bar.

"Jenny, you must be crazy. We're in a position to make history. We could be the very first documented case of two people actually screwing themselves to death. Think about it. We would be discovered locked in final embrace with happy smiles on our faces and become national heroes; the ultimate in that great final moment of glory.

"A clear understanding would go out to all of our young men in uniform as to what it is exactly that they are fighting for."

"ASPen," she emphasized loud then tapered to normal, "I'll put it this way. If, purr, you will tell me a story, purr, I'll be good and go to bed."

A grin came across his face that then turn to a small laugh. "Damn, Jenny you do have a way with words; you know that?" His slight laugh then led him into his response. "O.K., you want a story, how about the Three Bears?"

Jenny remained silent and just looked. "No? Then how about Golden Locks," he teased.

"Cattle drive," she retorted.

Feeling slightly intoxicated he playfully reached down and grabbed his own crouch and said, "I've got your cattle drive right here."

"Uh Huh," she replied in mocked chilling tone, "then why don't you take it to market. I'm sure you'll get a good price per pound."

Aspen released his crouch and shook his head. "O.K., cattle drive. If that's what you want, but you got any idea how long this is going to take to tell..." Then, without waiting for her input, he started.

"If I am going to do this, and it seems like I can't get out of it, I hope I can tell it in such a way that you visualize the complete picture; the dust, confusion, fear, sweat, success; make you feel proud; and finally leave you exhausted at the end. This is the last time I want to ride this trail."

The room then became quiet as he searched for a place to begin. "I guess the way to start is first things first," he commenced.

"Four A.M. on the Tap Root Ranch brings one hell of a breakfast. Momma Maude, the four daughters, Betty, Ina Lee, Theresa and Shannon and the two cooks who would be making the drive have all been up since about three in the morning. It was still pitch dark when the grub bell rattled. And of course that brought every sleepy eyed cowboy on the place rushing to get in line. And grub like you would not believe starts being piled on oversized tin plates.

"Three eggs, sunny side up, a six ounce T-bone steak, a heavy spoon of mashed potatoes covered with white gravy, pancakes with hot syrup; and black coffee in a big tin cup.

"Eating was done outside of course; wherever a cowboy could find a place to sit. No one is talking much. There is an urgent need to eat in a hurry, grab a second cup of coffee and get ready to ride. No one wants to be a straggler. Poppa Frank eats last.

"And when he finishes, he simply gets up, put his empty plate on the edge of the back porch, gives Momma Maude a hug and they exchange words to be careful.

"Poppa Frank then heads for the corral. First thing he does is drain his bladder on a fence post. Shaking it dry, he then mounts an already saddled big red roan, takes out his pocket knife, cut a big chew of Red Tag Tinsley chewing tobacco, kicks his boots hard against the stirrups, adjusts his hat, and with a wad of tobacco in his cheek, gives a nod to his foreman Snakey Ramsey.

"And that's when all hell broke loose. Snakey stood up in his saddle, cupped both hands to his mouth and let out a blood curdling yell to 'HEAD'EM UP AND MOVE'EM OUT'.

"And, with that, came a flotilla of cowboy war hoops, rebel yells and a mountain of rolling beef leaving out of Van Horn, Texas and headed for Dodge City, Kansas."

Aspen paused and took a deep breath. He knew that before Jenny could truly experience the drive she had to have a good mental picture of the size.

"OK Jenny let's suppose we put you on a little Pinto pony and let you ride along with me. That way you can see for yourself what we got. First off, my initial mount; a big bay with black mane and tail. You may recall that I had met a fellow named Jake Marlow. Well, God bless Jake's heart. He must have known that I would be going through hell because he singled me out a good soft ride.

"I really didn't realize it was happening at the time but the unspoken language of 'facial expression' is a big thing with cowboys. I'll tell you what I mean. It was the first few minutes just after breakfast and I was feeling out of place to a fare-the-well. And that's when Jake came by and gave me a nudge.

"He didn't say a word mind you, just nodded to where his mount, a sorrel and the bay stood unsaddled and reined to a hitching rail. I latched on to his message and trailed along behind him to the saddle shed; and still without saying a word he picked up his own saddle and nodded me. I was hesitant as to which one to pick but he nodded me to a big Mexican wide leather job. And after we saddled our mounts, he gave me a parting nod that he had no more time and moved on."

Aspen paused for effect and then asked, "You with me so far? Good. Now remember, I only got in there the night before, had maybe five hours of restless sleep in a strange bunk house; up at three in the morning and I was as lost as a poor soul in Hell.

"So now at least I am feeling a little better. I have a saddled horse and I figure I will follow the others as we go along. But going along is a lot easier said than done.

"Jenny, I tell you I was not prepared for what happened when that yell went out. The first rays of light were just starting to streak across the eastern sky and, like I said, I arrived in there late the night before so I had not really had a good look at the cattle. But that changed when I mounted up and started riding on out.

"My first good look was staggering; an endless ocean of restless, pawing, horn goring, bellowing, cattle trying to break out of a box canyon. At about the same time, I just happened to look off to the northeast and there goes Snakey Ramsey, taking the lead.

"Then, like clock work, two point men start forming a line. Everywhere I looked cowboys were yelling, swinging lariats and shoving cattle. Somehow a line started taking shape and little by little we started moving. I was lucky enough to start out on the upwind side so I was not eating dust right off.

"Now, let me pause right here and say something. Jenny, as good as that cattle drive ended, the beginning was an absolute hell. I don't want to get too far ahead of the story, but be prepared for some hard times.

"At first, I knew that the best thing I could do was stay out of the way. So mostly I rode out on a wide flank. Naturally, we started out on TapRoot land, which was fairly good range. It had the normal flora of range grass, prickly pairs, scattered mesquites and dry gullies but overall it was pretty good land.

"But there were a lot of other things which were not so good. The men had not yet forged into a working crew and it wasn't long before yelling and bickering started breaking out. As one cowboy would whip a steer or two into the line, four or five head would break out. Then would come cussing and shouting at each other as to who should be holding the line in and who should be punching in.

"For whatever picture you are imagining right now, the situation was worse. By nine o'clock or so on that first morning I was convinced it was hopeless. I could just see my three hundred and sixty thousand dollars going straight down the drain.

"And if I am truthful I was starting to worry about Poppa Frank. He had not yet set himself as the advanced lead man.

"On that first day he was up and down that line like a mother hen.

Yelling out orders, whirling his mount, hitting a dead gallop, cutting off strays and working in a dead run. He cut back and forth across that cattle line like a zigzag sewing machine. I would lose sight of him as he went over a rise but before long he would be back in a dead run.

"By ten o'clock in the morning his khaki shirt was soaking wet with sweat and he had worn out the first of three horses for the day."

Aspen now needed to move the story along. He looked at Jenny and a smile came to his face. He decided it was time she shared a laugh.

"I just thought of something," he said. "Maybe I'll let you savor a little of the colorful side. We were still only about six or eight miles out and I was still feeling awful useless. I wanted to help but had no idea of what I should or could be doing. Well, I just happened to look toward the front and off to the left flank and I noticed Poppa Frank had reined up on an overlooking knoll.

"Damn if he didn't remind me of an old Indian Chief up on a hill overlooking a herd of grazing buffalo. On an impulse I thought this would be a good chance to get acquainted. So I touched the spurs to my mount, kicked up a little lope and rode on over. He must have noticed me coming but he didn't make any motion until I rode right up. I was actually hesitant as what to call him; Poppa Frank, Frank or Mr. Delaney.

"'Morning Frank,' I said before I knew it. He had been leaning slightly across his saddle horn but as I reined in he straightened up and nodded, 'Morning ASper.'

"I caught the modified pronunciation of my name but paid it no mind. Having acknowledged me, he then looked back at the herd. And from that vantage point the situation looked even worse

"A cloud of dust, extending as for as the eye could see, of break-and-run cattle, being prodded along by an unproven crew, at a ratio of 300 head of stock per man; and Poppa Frank already looked tired.

"Wheee, I just took a deep breath. There was nothing I could do but look. I still felt a little awkward so I followed his lead and we just sat there a minute or two before he finally spoke.

"'If...' he finally said, 'that doesn't look like the ass end of Ol' Miss

Fortune.'"

At this point Aspen paused a storyteller's pause for emphasis. When he knew that Jenny was with him he continued.

"Now it's just my bet that Poppa Frank has started many a conversation with those words because they sure got my attention. He could tell by my look that some explanation was necessary and before I could ask he started.

"'ASper,' he asked, 'have you ever used the word misfortune? Like, whenever there has been a tragedy or bad luck some people are prone to say *it was just a terrible misfortune.* You don't hear the expression too much out here on the prairie but whenever I am around city folks I hear it a lot. City folks seem to misfortune this and misfortune that. Now I have never really got a proper handle on misfortunes but it appears that certain misfortunes can be a lot worse than others.

"'And judging from my limited knowledge I would say that what we got down there,' he nodded his head at the cattle, 'is the real royal ass-end-of-Ol'-Miss-Fortune.'"

Jenny smiled as she tried to picture the two of them reined up side by side on the top of a knoll. But then Aspen brought her attention back as he continued.

"Well the description seemed pretty fitting to me so I just went with the flow. Good thing too because along about then Ol' Miss Fortune decided to play another hand. This one involved that cowboys-testing-each-other situation I mentioned earlier. Poppa Frank and I both watched as one of the young MP's a young kid from Iowa named Kobrinski came galloping up the hill.

"I have to pause here and tell you Jenny if he wasn't a fine looking young hero. All decked out in freshly starched and pressed combat fatigues.

"His waxed helmet-liner with the MP insignia across the front shinning and glistening in the sun; an oversized MP band on his right arm and a .45 caliber automatic pistol strapped to his side.

"And ride; damn if he couldn't ride. Anyway that young trooper came galloping up that hill in a no nonsense manner right up to where we were sitting and abruptly stop directly in front of Poppy Frank.

"Sitting tall in the saddle with his shoulders thrown back and his eyes straight ahead he threw up a snappy salute and said, 'SIR, PFC KOBRINSKI, REQUESTING PERMISSION TO SPEAK, SIR.'"

There was an unexpected break in the story flow and Jenny looked at Aspen and could tell he was trying to hide an emotional chock up; and she instantly knew. Aspen was back on that hill in West Texas.

"Well," he finally continued, "it was awkward protocol for Poppa Frank so he just nodded.

"'SIR,' Kobrinski started, 'I am not sure what are my duties, SIR? A fight broke out in the rear ranks, Sir; what are your instructions? SIR.'

"'Who was it?' asked Poppa Frank. Kobrinski's face turned embarrassing red as he hesitated and then answered. 'SIR, it was one of your sons, SIR, and another cowboy whom I don't know, Sir.'

"'Which son?' Frank asked. 'SIR, the one you call Willie, SIR.'

"'How did it go?'

"'SIR, it was in very thick dust, but I would say about six or seven punches each and some ground wrestling.'

"'And?' asked Poppy Frank.

"'Sir, I would call it about square on the board, SIR; one has a swollen eye and the other has a busted lip, SIR.'" Then as if he realized he had been daydreaming Aspen returned his look to Jenny.

"Jenny," he continued, "it was a scene I will always remember. Out on the high wind swept plains of West Texas, an old man with time weathered lines, wearing a cowboy's uniform of a sweat stained hat, a long sleeve khaki shirt, Levi's pants, time worn spurs, and the brand of raw hide and leather seared across his soul.

"And, sitting eye to eye and horse to horse, awaiting orders, an Iowa corn fed young man in a stiff Military Police uniform; unblemished skin of youth, fuzz on his face, nineteen years old sitting there stiff as a military board, tall in the saddle.

"A wetness came to the eyes of Poppa Frank as he looked at the promise in the young man before him. Then, in the most unexpected thing I have ever experienced, Poppa Frank turned directly to me and nodded a slight sideways nod at the young soldier.

"And in a choked cowboy drawl, he said, 'By God ASper just look at that. Damn if a son like that wouldn't make a man proud. If ever there was a cut of a man, there's one right there', Frank continued.

"That's what we raise in this Country Asper. Now you look at that and tell me...how in the hell do the Goddamn Japs figure they stand a chance.'

"Having broke the emotions, Poppa Frank then turned to Kobrinski and with a knowing look, replied, 'Don't worry too much about the fights young Trooper, there'll be more.'

"With that the young trooper whirled and rode away, and Poppa Frank made one more amazing comment.

"'ASper,' he said, 'I'm a little worried. I haven't seen God all day. I hope to the hell he didn't beg off on me. I sure am counting on him. He's one of my best hands.'"

Aspen paused and sipped his drink. He was savoring that part of the story. But then he heard the ice clink in Jenny's glass as she was taking a sip and realized he had a lot more to tell. She finished sipping as he did and was waiting for him to continue. He felt a slight pleasure that she had become so engrossed.

"The rest of the day," he continued, "was about like the morning. The only thing different, we started to notice one particular steer goring and fighting his way to the front.

"On that particular day, and that is the only day I can attest too, that one damn steer would hook a horn into anything or anybody that got in his way; from cattle to cowpokes.

"And in a couple of more days he had worked his way to the lead point and as it turned out he took the herd all the way to Dodge City. It was kind of funny. As I watched him horning his way through, it struck me that he had a message. I got the feeling that if he could have talked he would have said 'that this was one hell-of-a-frigged up operation; and to get to the hell out of the way and let someone take over who knows what-the-hell is going on'.

"Now, here is the best part. A couple of days later I was to learn that the steer's name was Bolivar Bag-Ass; and he had been raised from birth as a pet by son Willie.

"And according to Poppa Frank, Bolivar and son Willie were back to back personalities. The two would fight with anything and anybody on the ranch. Find a fight and one of them would be in it. And when they couldn't find anyone else to fight with they would fight with each other."

Jenny grinned at the story and Aspen felt it was a good place to break. He rose and proceeded to the bathroom and Jenny moved to the kitchen. When he returned she had set out the makings for sandwiches.

"Turkey or corn beef?" she asked. Aspen parked on a stool on the opposite side of the counter and responded, "Corn beef, lot of mustard and maybe a cold beer."

"So," Jenny responded as she proceeded with preparations, "you must have finally made it through the first day."

"Barcly," he answered, "just barely. But yes, along about 4 o'clock we reached a little meadow that Poppa Frank had planned as the first day's stop.

"Good place. Good grass for afternoon grazing and a creek for water. Along about dusk the stock started bedding down and the trail ended for the day."

He shifted on the stool and tried to decide how much detail to tell. About how it was, that God may not have been around helping with the herd during the day but there was a reason. He had gone on ahead to make preparations for the first night. With evening chuck out of the way, the cowboys all fed and the cattle bedded down, tranquillity materialized that could only be known to a Texas prairie at night; as the tiredness of the day begged to be answered with sleep. There was a picture Aspen could paint about sleeping out on the ground, and gazing up at the stars so clear and bright one felt like you could just reach up and hold one in your hand. The wonderment of a big full moon hanging just above; how it was so clear and bright you could almost reach up and touch it. Along in the quiet of the night, the sound of a lonesome coyote could be heard as he howled out his call on a distant hill. Using a saddle for a pillow and smelling the smell of leather. All of this blended to the fragrance of the prairie mesquite, the cool night air, the sound of crickets chirping. One knew that God had been very busy that day in his welcoming preparation. And for all of His perfect work, every cowboy was thankful for the sweetness of that night.

But these were all things Aspen could tell to Jenny in the years to come. So in response to her urging, he simply commented that the first night had been a welcomed stop. And to keep the story moving he turned to the events of the next morning. Word spread through camp that the cattle drive story was being picked up by the Associated Press and would become National news.

"During the night," he started, "a newspaper reporter by the name of Gates Standwick from Associated Press rode into camp. The next morning the first thing Gates did was to hunt down Poppa Frank and asked to cover the story. But Poppa Frank dodged the issue.

"He pleaded wrong person and pointed Gates to me. Since I was the one who had put up the money Frank reckoned, I should be in charge of press coverage."

Aspen paused as he took a large bite of corn beef sandwich and washed it down with a swallow of beer. Jenny had opted for cottage cheese and fruit.

"Later that morning Gates and I met but it was a quick 'Hi-By' type of thing. I forget the reason but I was in a hurry at the moment; but back to the events.

"Our next... major milestone was the Pecos River some 70 miles across uninhabited escarpment and undulating, rolling prairie. Poppa Frank had laid out a river crossing a few miles south of the little town of Oria; where the Pecos fans out onto a flood plain and the banks have an easy slope.

"From that first night in the meadow, it took us four hot, dry, dusty, days to reach the Pecos. By now the cattle were adapting to trail driving pretty well but the crew was still unorganized and sure as to hell not yet welded. Everything was still a pretty much self-interest-first type of situation. Every man there was suffering but he was suffering to himself. There was a pronounced absence of camaraderie and morale was already starting to sag. For the most part the operation was just going along under its own momentum."

Aspen paused for another bite of sandwich and swallow of beer. He hoped that Jenny could visualize the magnitude of cattle, cowboys, horses and chuck wagons all engulfed in a trail of rolling dust five miles long.

"The first fracture in that zombie-like situation," he continued, "came when we were about ten miles out from the river. Dry desert winds are prone to shift directions back and forth. And when the shift came out of the East the wind started bringing faint smells of water from the Pecos.

"When that happened the reaction of the livestock was almost instantaneous. Their heads started rising, their mooing and bellowing increased, their nostrils flared and the pace quickened.

"Our job then immediately changed from prodding them along to holding them back. All of a sudden the most dangerous part now fell on the point riders as they tried to keep the lead steers from breaking into a run. But try as they did, in the end it was hopeless. As we got closer the smell of water grew stronger and the rear cattle commenced pushing the front.

"By the time we got within a mile of the West bank the herd broke into a run. The momentum was so strong that when the lead steers hit the water they were pushed right on across to the other side and had to turn around and come back in. I tell you Jenny," his voice now in remembering, "that was something to see.

"But anyway, we reached the Pecos late in the afternoon and by all standards the crossing had not been too bad. By dark the herd, the remuda and the chuck wagons were all across and a semblance of camp had been established.

"Once watered, the livestock moved out along a low lying flood plain where the river was prone to overflow its banks and had created a mile or so of grassland meadow. The crew now had a feel of what to expect and it was a good point of reckoning. The decision was made for a one-day rest stop that gave everyone a little walking around time and a chance to shore up their gear.

"For Poppa Frank it was a time for assessment. The real hardships were still ahead and he was not pleased with the outlook. For one thing, the spring rains that should have been normal for this time of year had not come and he was getting concerned about watering holes. Just a few miles beyond the Pecos River lay the Malga Salt Flats; sixty miles of barren alkaline desert and Poppa Frank had serious doubts as to whether the crew, given the state of morale, could or would make it.

"That evening he mingled among the hands searching for a semblance of unity. Giving everybody a word here and a barb there, he paused and joshed a word of wit with Bobby Boy Warren and dropped a word with Kurt Bailey. But the answers he got back were hollow and carried no feeling.

"Moving to the next circle he jeered a little about drugstore cowboys, but he also made a mental note that Bobby Warren and John Sheldon who had fought the Texas Rangers together were now at different saddle circles.

"As he passed by the next saddle circle he also noticed that Wayne Marks was not present; probably out walking the prairie preferring his own company. And when he, Poppa Frank, finally returned to his own bedroll by the chuck wagon he had a troubled mind. There was not yet enough molten steel in this crew to withstand the onslaught of the Malga Flats. He had one day to mold the crew or risk losing everything.

"When he finally dropped off to sleep that night he had a plan; with God's help it might work. The next morning just before sunrise four men rode out of camp. The first to ride out was the United States Attorney. When he left camp he headed his mount away from the first rays of early morning light that were painting the eastern sky; and with a touch of his spurs galloped off into the darkness to the northwest.

"His instructions were to ride into Carlsbad, New Mexico some fifty miles up the Pecos River. He was to exercise the powers vested in him by the United States Government pursuant to the 'War Time Powers

Act' and any other vested sovereign authority so needed.

"His assignment was to take ownership of three, open bed wagons and secure three good teams of mules. Next he was to acquire any and all available 55 gallon water barrels. Hopefully there would be enough to fully load all three wagons.

"And finally, hire three mule skinners and fill all of the barrels with fresh drinking water. On the third day hence, the wagons were to leave out of Carlsbad at sunrise and drive in a southeasterly direction across the Malga Salt Flats until they intersected with the drive.

"Gates Standwick was the second man to ride out of camp that morning. As he saddled up, he glanced at the same thin ribbons of red streaks across the dark eastern sky. Then with a last sip of hot black coffee, he mounted up and pointed his roan north to the nearest telephone; the General Store in Oria.

"Nobody knew the purpose of Gates' trip; but Gates knew. When that isolated, remote store opened at 6:00 o'clock on that April morning his first dispatch went out over the only telephone wire in the area. And... on the morning next... news of the cattle drive was on the front pages of newspapers across the Nation; including the Eunice Globe, in the little town of Eunice, New Mexico some seventy-five miles northeast.

"Gates did America proud in his story. He used words of God and Country; and of American patriotism. He tied to the spirit of the American frontier some sixty and seventy years earlier; of self reliance, sweat and toil which had made America great. He told of our life on the trail, of dust, sweat and thirst gladly endured in the spirit of getting meat to America's fighting men.

"And Gates closed his first dispatch with the comment that he was proud to be among men of such fortitude and unyielding commitment.

"The next to ride out that morning were the two MP's and when they left camp they turned south with instructions to ride into Pecos, Texas which lay 35 miles down river. In Pecos their instructions were to make three stops. First, they were to stop at Wexford's Saddle and Leather Shop on Alamo Street. Tell Sam Wexford they have been sent by Frank Delaney. Request that he stop whatever he is doing and fill an order; two, double stitched, deep well, 'saddle flag-holsters'; one left-side mount and one right-side mount.

"The second stop for the two MP's was the County Court House with instructions to go see Judge Carl Yates. In his courtroom, Judge Yates had two large flags crossed hatched on the wall behind his desk. One was the United States of America Flag; the other was the Lone Star Flag for the State of Texas. Judge Yates declared a thirty-minute recess in his court proceeding and received our two young men in his chambers. They again identified themselves as being there on behalf of Frank Delaney and needed a favor. With a proud to be of service, Judge Yates personally removed the flags from the wall behind his desk.

"Awkwardly but with emotions he first rolled the American Flag around the five foot guide-on staff and handed it to PFC Kobrinski. Judge Yates then rolled up the Texas Flag and handed it PFC Antonio Garcia whose hometown was Lamesa, Texas.

"With expressions of appreciation and accepting a message to Frank of good luck and God speed, the MP's gave a stiff snappy salute, made a heel to toe military about face and with flags in hand they left.

"They had one more stop to make and one more borrow to ask. The Pecos Post of the American Legion had a polished brass bugle ceremonially kept stored in a black leather case lined in red velvet. Carl Price is the Post Commander. He and Poppa Frank fought together in World War One, back in 1918. Both had been wounded in the Argonne Forest in northern France and lay for three days in a bombed out field of tangled barbed wire, mud, artillery fire and mustard gas and damn near lost their lives together. With a touch of emotion Post Commander Carl Price placed the bugle in the hands of the two young MP's returned their military salute and sent a message of 'God and Country, bring our boys home alive, Frank'."

Aspen took another bite of his sandwich, but this time his chewing was a little slower. He was thinking that the events of the story were not coming together exactly right. In order for Jenny to fully experience what happened he needed to back up a bit. As he washed down a swallow of beer, the backup place came to him.

"First though, let me back up a bit. I happened to be standing there and I saw and heard this. As Poppa Frank was giving the two MP's their final instructions he got choked up a bit. A wetness came to his eyes at least it looked like wetness to me. Anyway he choked up for just a second but then went right on.

"'Men,' Poppa Frank reckoned, 'if you two young heroes ride hard you should be getting back into camp from Pecos along about sundown. In fact it would be greatly appreciated if you make damn sure that you come riding in just about sundown.'

"He then told them what he had in mind about the manner in which they would be returning. Off to the south of camp was the declining face of a long sloping grassland hill, free of mesquite and creosote bush. Any riders coming down off of that slope in a flat out gallop in a cloud of dust could be seen for ten miles. I think the way Poppa Frank put it was 'that he'd like to see two horses coming down that long slope with their nostrils flaring, their head down, their tail up, their ears back and their legs opening and closing like a jack knife.'

"On some things Poppa Frank could be pretty descriptive. On other things he sort of left it up to one's own imagination. At the moment I didn't know what was going on but I soon figured it out when I heard the rest of his instructions.

"'Troopers,' he said as he stood between the two and put his arms around each of their young shoulders, 'along about the time when that ol' sun starts going down it shore would do my ol' heart good if I could cast my eyes to the south and see the pride of America's manhood returning from Pecos.

"'I can just picture it now. Here in camp, the first thing anyone will hear will be a faint sound and the first thing anyone will see will be a small cloud of dust high up on the crest of that ridge. Now whoever sees you first will tell somebody else and within a minute or two the whole camp will be looking; and we will all be trying to figure out what's going on.' Everything will be happening pretty fast.

"'While we are looking up at you, you will be picking up speed coming down that long slope and then pretty soon we will be able to make you two out; and that's the moment we're shooting for.'

"'There you'll be, sitting tall in the saddle, with shoulders back, head high, eyes stern ahead, riding two abreast with flags unfurled and flapping hard against the wind; the American flag on the right, Texas on the left, coming down off of that hill in the ride of your life. Now... for the bugle. Do us all proud Troops. This will be your sound. Give me lungs and lots of it.

"'With the mouth piece of that bugle pushed hard against your lips the thing I want coming out is the sound of a cavalry charge...and I'm looking for a charge that can be heard for ten miles.'

"'The horses you'll be riding are two of the best three year old stallions we've got. I might as well tell you now they gonna be hard to hold on the bit.

"'God knows they've been bred to run and they'll probably fight you all the way to Pecos and most of the way back. But when you start down the face of that south slope give'em their head. Don't hold anything back; even give'em a spur if you feel like it. I want to see hell-bent-for-leather, nostrils flaring, eyes wild, and hoofs pounding.

"'And now... for the purpose... of all this. If you will Troopers, listen to my thinking. You, me, all of us. We've come to this land at a later page in history. Other young men in uniform rode this country long before us and they staked first claim; and... the ghost of those men do not relinquish the reins easily.

"'The time to realize this is when you are out riding alone. A good time to think and take the time to rein in your horse and stop on the top of a lonely hill and sit for a while and look out over that endless prairie.

"'If you listen you can always hear the sound of pounding hoofs; of wild eyes horse with flared nostrils carrying fighting men of another time. To this very day the spirit of young troopers just about your age but in another era still thunder across the sky; their destiny forged in the manner they died; their last full measure was given as they answered the final call, the call of a bugle sounding out a cavalry charge.

"'Troops,' Frank says in an emotional tone, 'I now have a strong need to hear the sound of that charge. I need to see a bugle glistening in the last rays of the sun.

"'And I need to see you, America's next generation, coming on strong; knowing that you gladly assume what those who have gone on before now hand you. The souls of America's fighting men past now become forged in your souls. Let them be proud. Let them see those flags unfurled and waving.

"'With love of God and unyielding fight for County, sound that bugle. Come down off of that slope in the spirit of those before you.

"'And when you reach camp, your ride is not over. Ride hard and circle the full camp; from front to back, circle proud so that every man here is brought to understand they can no longer think of themselves. From here on in the crew and the drive must come first.

"'And when you have finished your circle, if you will, end up with me at the head of the drive. I will be mounted and waiting; and I will be honored if you would rein up, one on each side.'"

Aspen stopped talking at this point and Jenny felt the onus to speak. But Aspen was lost in a silent gaze and did not hear her the first time; so she spoke a second. "Aspen," she repeated with more emphasis, "that was so touching. Just look at these emotional tears in my eyes."

"What?" He responded as he recaptured his own attention. "Heart touching," she reiterated, "the vivid picture of those two young MP's riding into camp like that."

"Yeah," Aspen answered in a very slow tapered off tone and then took a breath, "it was something all right. I was there and I can tell you that it was very emotional. But as touching as that was, something more emotional was about to happen.

"Something more?" she asked in a surprised, questioned voice. "What could possible be more dramatic?"

"Well," Aspen continued, "when those two young bucks came down that south slope you could hear the sound of that bugle for ten miles, they came down right on cue; just as the sun was sinking on the Western horizon.

"Poppa Frank's dream was realized right enough as they come riding into camp two abreast. Those two flags unfurled and flapping hard against the wind as they circled the camp.

"And when it was over a type of strangeness settled in; a quiet uneasiness that no one in the camp would look directly into the eyes of another. After the first few minutes they all gradually got back to doing his own business but things were not the same. They would pass each other polite enough, but somehow their hats were pulled close to their eyes and they seemed to nod with their heads slightly down. Control of one's emotions is a very big thing with cowboys.

"And later on that same night, when the cattle were bedded, the camp swallowed up by endless miles of rolling range, the moon in full color looking down at the tiny spot amongst the vastness of the land, the silence was once again pierced.

"Up on the slope of that very same southern hill, the silhouette of a lone soldier mounted on a dark stallion could be seen sitting with a bugle to his lips.

"And from the lips of an Iowa, corn fed farm boy came the slow, long, lonesome sound of military taps; the end of day.

"When the call ended and the quietness of the night returned every cowboy knew that he was where he belonged. And within each of them there was a resolve that henceforth personal considerations would be cast aside.

"No demand would be too hard and no hardship too great to stop the movement of the heard to Dodge City."

The next words that Aspen said came out of nowhere and must have had meaning only to him.

"And the last taps and the last cavalry charge in Texas had been sounded."

He probably did not even realize that he had again stopped talking. There was a gloss of wetness in his eyes as he remained lost in his own thoughts.

Jenny touched a tissue to her eyes and finally spoke. "Aspen that was so touching and so spell binding. But I haven't moved for an hour and

I have got to go pee.

"Another five minutes and I would have wet my panties," she spoke as she rushed to the bathroom. Aspen followed her and half set against the vanity while waiting his turn. As her pressure released she unmindfully continued talking.

"I have been hanging onto every word and living every dusty mile," she said. "I'm exhausted, totally exhausted from having to help get those cattle to market. How much further do we have to go?"

Jenny's words gave him a satisfying feeling but he also knew that the story could not go on forever. Still, there were certain things that almost demanded to be told.

"It was," he responded as she got up from the toilet and he took his turn, "a piece of history. A living, real life page in history."

As she moved past, Aspen raised the lid and continued, "But you are right Jenny. It is getting too long but the next leg of the drive simply cannot go untold."

Finishing his relief he turned as she was at the vanity and he smelled the faint fragrance of her perfume. In reflex his arm went around her, she surrendered and they lightly embraced.

"How about it," he asked in a suggested change of interest. "I hereby renew my offer for us to screw our brains out the rest of the afternoon."

She gave him a light peck on the cheek and responded, "Sorry, I'm too tired. I have been on the back of a horse for five days and I am just now leaving the Pecos River.

"Only I don't know where I am going. So I guess you just better keep on talking or we may never get to market."

Out in the living room Aspen leaned back in his chair, took a swallow of cold beer and began.

"Well, the first thing I want to mention is the effect of those flags and that bugle. The next morning the camp atmosphere was a 180-degree from the night before; instant congeniality.

"The first place it showed up was at the chuck wagon. Men already waiting in the chow line invited others to move in ahead. A politeness at the water barrel, one man getting a dipper of water would hand it to another before he drank. I tell you Jenny it was a peculiar situation. All of a sudden there was a brotherhood and nothing else mattered. And it was a damn good thing too because we were about to embark on four days of hell the likes of which I never want to go through again."

Here he paused to determine exactly how he wanted to start. Then, as if he remembered a very important point, continued.

"Well, we broke camp an hour earlier the next morning and as Snakey Ramsey took the point, guess who was on his flanks?

"Riding three abreast were our two flag carrying MP's and good Ol' Snake; a real sight. Damn if it wasn't."

"They played it to the hilt, too. Heading off to the Northeast in a nice little gallop. Well, the enthusiasm just kept picking up momentum as the cowboys mounted and started the herd moving.

"A new excitement was in the air and a restlessness to get moving. The cattle had already been herded into the Pecos for a final forced drinking and the crew had all forced drank and filled their canteens to the brim.

"Poppa Frank asked me to be seen ridding with him and we were ready, or thought we were ready to tackle the Malga Salt flats.

"But Jenny believe me when I tell you that what we thought and what we got were two different things. At that point all we had, or at least all I had was a mental picture of what was out there.

"But about six to eight miles out from the Pecos River the reality started becoming evident; a thinning of vegetation and patches of white crust mingled the sand.

"And then there it was. A blistering flat land-plane of crusty, barren white salt as far as the eye could see. It was around ten o'clock and the sun was just beginning to get hot."

"The cattle sensed what was happening and started to balk and shy back. The lead steers, including Bolivar, started trying to turn back to the Pecos.

"Ironically, it was the momentum of the back herd which forced them to continue. But it wasn't easy. The riders on point and swing had their hands full simply maintaining a tight line.

"And the very first thing to happen was the force of all those pounding hoofs started pulverizing the crusty alkali and turned the place into a rolling cloud of salt dust."

Aspen did not like remembering the burning of raw salt sweat. Subconsciously he touched the crease lines in his neck, elbows and armpits where salt had collected and before it was all over the skin would ooze blood. And yet, it was a first hand experience of how brutal life can be.

As he picked up the story he could still feel the burning salt in his eyes and the rawness and ooze bleeding in his groin caused by four long days and nights he and the others sat in the saddle.

"By noon," he moved along, "the temperature had risen to 100 degrees. The cattle were bellowing and a type of panic was beginning to show. The realities of our circumstances were now being driven home.

"Poppa Frank called for a rest stop and the drive came to a halt. But it was an uneasy halt. There was a very real awareness that the cattle were becoming prime to stampede.

"Everyone could feel the tenseness and the men who dismounted to stretch, did so with caution and without any sudden moves. After an hour or so, Poppa Frank decided that it would be better to keep moving so we started on."

"But God what a plight. Our trek across those flats had barely started and we were already burning up. The critical element was control; slow and easy. And that within itself was a paradox. At a time when we needed to move fast we couldn't. Any yells or prodding would have set the whole six thousand head in a stampede.

"So we just followed our instincts and moved at a steady, zombie like pace. All of us pretty much lost in our own thoughts.

"If the others thought the way I did, and I am sure they must have, you start to feel awfully insecure. There is a frightening loss of self-confidence that you may not be able to make it.

"A kind of self prayer sets in to please don't let yourself be the one who buckles first. As a gauge of your endurance you watch the sun as it moves across the sky and cuss at how slow it moves; knowing that sundown will bring some cooling relief.

"Finally that ol' sun grudgingly moved along and reluctantly dropped below that western horizon and we stopped to rest; if you could call it that. In actuality it felt worse while we were resting than when we were moving. We had been in the saddle for sixteen hours; our joints had gone into a type of paralysis and when we dismounted our knees buckled.

"We had not covered nearly as much ground as we needed to cover and it seemed like stopping was a waste of time. So with a bite of grub, some black coffee and a refill of our canteens from the water barrels, we mounted up and pushed on through the night.

"At day break the next morning we ate breakfast on the move. The chuck wagons were staying out on the flank a couple of hundred yards, rolling along on the upwind side.

"As we could we took turns of riding over for a bite of cold beans and corn bread; but God bless those cooks because they did manage to have piping hot coffee. And by the time the sun started to break we had been in the saddle for twenty-four hours.

"On through the next day the routine was about the same. The cattle were becoming zombie like so the threat of turning back was no longer a problem.

"From habit, we continuously looked at the distant horizon; searching for any gauge of progress. With hats pulled down low over our eyes there was nothing to do but continue on; looking at either the white barren ground at our feet or the distant, ever distant skyline for any silhouette of life or change.

"It was along about four o'clock on the second day when we started noticing a slight dark blue line just on the very edge of the northern horizon.

"In an hour or so it grew and told of heavy weather moving in. A wave of optimism spread among us. Maybe, just maybe a rain shower would break.

"But that was not to be. Whatever moisture there was in those clouds had already been dropped on the rangelands up in the northern panhandle of Texas. What we got was a living-hell in the form of an electrical storm.

"It first started with lightning flashes off on the distant horizon. We watched, as it kept moving closer, and by nightfall thick clouds blocked out the sky.

"We began to smell electricity and as night became pitch black, the distant flashes of lightning were becoming more intense and were starting to light up the sky like day.

"We were then faced with a crucial decision. Whether to round up the cattle in a holding pattern as a means of containment or to keep driving and trust to luck.

"By having the herd bunched up there may be a better chance against stampeding. On the other hand, valuable time would be lost and there was no guarantee it would work. In what must have been a hard, hard decision, Poppa Frank he decided we would keep moving.

"By ten o'clock that night hell itself had swallowed us up. What had first been ground to sky single streaks of flash lightning grew into split jagged forks of lightning and blues fizzling arcs.

"The air was so electrified that the hair on our neck and arms stood up. And like nothing I even knew could exist, balls of blue fire flashed and rolled across the ground and then swished out. There was a strong putrid smell and our mouth tasted like burnt sulfur.

"But that still wasn't the worst. It was like we were in a vacuum of a million volts of unorganized electrical charges; the air around us became filled with blue streaks sparking and dying, sizzling and rolling in a blue light on the horns of cattle and the metal in our horse bridles."

"Zooming-swish' blue sparks flashed, igniting and swirling out. The sweat moisture in a man's hat was enough to attract a sizzling spark and leave the taste of burnt sulfur.

"And there wasn't a damn thing we could do but hold a tight ass and keep moving; praying that we wouldn't get hit by an organized bolt and praying that the cattle wouldn't bolt and run.

"Around eleven o'clock Poppa Frank sent a rider around to collect any guns, knives or spurs that anybody wanted to put in the chuck wagon. A few article of metal went but no one wanted to part with either his spurs or guns.

"Tension, holding a tight ass, flinching at every move, knowing that a stampede could break at any moment. We all hugged in close to the herd to keep as tight a line as possible and that probably helped.

"When a steer became panicky and tried to break out, there was usually a cowpoke right there to nudge it back in. Always as quiet as possible; no hollering or yelling just quiet nudging; hour by hour moving slowly onward and being ever ready for a run.

"By one o'clock in the morning it looked like the worst was over. The sizzling blue lights on men's hats and on the cattle's horns started to subside and it appeared that the storm had moved on through.

"When it got to where we could breath again Poppa Frank held up his hand and signaled a rest stop. And a welcomed stop it was but we will never know whether or not that was the best of all possible decisions.

"As the drive slowed and came to a halt, we all started to dismount and damn near couldn't stand on our own two feet. We had to hang on to the saddle for support until the circulation came back to our joints. Finally being able to take a step or two we started gaining our footing, began clustering around each other and making small talk.

"I don't smoke but most of the men lit up a shaky roll-your-own cigarette. Our attention to the herd slacked off for the moment; but that moment was all it took..."

Aspen felt a touch of embarrassment at that statement. The words had not come right. They implied that the crew was momentarily lax and inattentive; which was certainly not the case.

The case was a colossal streak of lightning that flashed across the sky and lit up brighter than day; instantly followed by a clap of thunder that cracked like dynamite. And in that second, when everyone's guard was down, the cattle bolted.

"What I mean Jenny," Aspen changed the sentence, "is that in a single instant, lightning flashed, thunder clapped and the cattle bolted into a stampede."

Aspen felt tightness as the telling of this part started to unfold. He and a few other hands had been standing in the exact path of the onslaught and had experienced the terrifying fear of looking directly into the faces of the oncoming cattle.

For a split second he froze, but then recovered. Holding a tight rein on his uneasy horse, he swung up into the saddle and escaped serious injury or death by becoming mixed in and moving along with the moving mass.

He wanted Jenny to share that experience; not in terms of hero, but in terms of peril and life threatening circumstances. So in a tone and mannerism reflecting the dangers, he continued.

"Jenny, picture if you will a group of exhausted cowboys trying to get their legs back with the help of a welcomed cigarette and 'wham' a fiery hell comes out of nowhere and shatters the earth; instant panic.

"Most of us had gravitated over to the left flank. And as luck would have it that was the direction of the bolt.

"Somehow I managed to get mounted but I was totally engulfed in shoulder to shoulder cattle. At that point they were just moving in mass confusion and had not yet reached a full run. That's probably the only thing that saved me.

"But I was helpless to do anything but move along with the flow. My horse showed some frenzy but he didn't rare-up and attempt to throw me or anything. He did throw his head up and jerk hard on the reins a few times attempting to loosen my hold and get some slack of his own but instinctively he just kept pace and at that point we were not suffering too much.

"Mostly we were just being squeezed. But I knew I had to get out fast or six thousand sets of horns would likely be ripping both the horse and me apart. I'm not that good of a rider and I knew that if my horse went down, not even God could help."

"I don't know how far I rode along mixed in with the cattle. I do know the speed was picking up and from out of somewhere I heard my name being called. At the moment I was awfully busy but I quickly glanced off to my right. The sky was still being lit up with intermittent streaks of lightning and as I turned I saw Snakey Ramsey riding about a hundred yards over to the side.

"'ASPEN,' he was hollering, 'GET YOUR FEET UP OUT OF THE STIRRUPS, GET YOUR FEET UP ON THE SADDLE, SIT ON YOUR LEGS!'

"Of course I jerked both legs up, but at that instant an awareness flashed through my mind. I couldn't believe how clear I could hear Snakey's words. And then it came to me. The herd was not bellowing as they ran. Not a sound except the collective sound of stampeding hoofs and of course the hollering of the cowboys. Later I was to learn that that is just a peculiarity that stampeding cattle do not bellow.

"But not to get away from the story. My horse somehow pawed, pushed, shoved and I kicked steers in the head with my boot heel until we made our way to the outside and broke free.

"In retrospect, the cattle were not what you would call vicious or combative. When we were shoving and crowding our way out, the temperament of the cattle, in a way, bordered on politeness because they didn't try to fight back or anything.

"When I would kick one in the head he would flinch sideways and slack off whatever he could, give way and let us through. Like I say it wasn't that they were intent on goring or maiming.

"It was a case where each steer on his own was simply trying to stay out of the way of the ones behind and they were all caught up in the momentum.

"So, now I am out in the open and all is OK; right? Wrong. In about two seconds I see just how big of a problem we've really got. We are now in a full-scale stampede. That means six thousand sets of pounding hoofs are running blind-leading-the-blind across those salt flats and twenty seven saddle weary riders, including Gates Standwick the MP's and everyone else except the cooks, riding flat out blind toward one thing; to reach that lead steer and force a turn into a circle.

"And lightning, the thing which had sparked the stampede was now the only source of light. As each streak shot across the sky we could all get a quick assessment of what was going on.

"It was from the light of one big streak that I first made out a lone rider running dead out and holding his horse solid against the side of the lead steer.

"From there on in we all kept looking and with each flash streak trying to make out what was happening. We could hear gunshots but they didn't sound like a handgun; more like a Winchester.

"Sometimes the lightning flashes were so short you couldn't see much but a couple of times I was able to make out that lead rider was swinging a rifle down across the face of the lead steer.

"I didn't know it at the time but I was to learn later that he splintered the gun apart and finally just let it drop. I wondered what happened because the next flash it looked like he was flogging a lariat across the steer's face and horns. But nothing was helping.

"Neither the steer nor rider was giving in. With every flash of light we could see it was a dead heat standoff with rider and steer holding together like the hubs of hell in a dead out test of wills.

"Over to my back side I could feel more riders moving up. It was Poppa Frank and son Jerry. As they were passing me I heard Frank shout, 'WHO IS IT? WHO'S ON THE POINT?' Jerry stood up in his saddle and in the next streak of lightning he could see the horse's distinctive brown and white markings.

"There was only one horse with those colors. Still on the run and standing tall in the saddle Jerry cupped his hand to his mouth and shouted back, 'ITS THE PINTO, POPPA, THE PINTO, IT'S WILLIE.'"

Silence followed as Aspen stopped talking. He could feel beads of sweat on his forehead. His mouth was dry as he looked at his half filled bottle of beer.

He wanted a drink but something more fiery and stronger than beer. He rose, went to the liquor cabinet, got an opened bottle of Scotch and a glass; no ice, no water. He poured two fingers, held the glass to Jenny and understood when she shook her head. He then tossed down the stiff shot, felt the soothing burn, grimaced the muscles in his face and continued.

"I can only guess what must have flashed through Frank's mind but I saw both him and Jerry instantly spur a hard spur and a slap of leather rein across their horses.

"In reflex I also spurred hard and followed. I don't know what I could have done but I spurred. Running dead out and at times running blind, the white ground was flashing beneath me; I decided it was better to not look down.

"A prairie dog hole would have seemed like a bottomless pit but there was nothing else we could do. We closed in to fifty yards or so from the lead and with every flash of lightning we could see Willie leaning low on the side of his saddle and flogging that lariat.

"Then came this colossal lightning streak which lit up the sky and held the brightness for what seemed like minutes."

Aspen stopped again and Jenny watched as he simply leaned against the kitchen counter. Sweat was breaking out on his forehead and she could tell he was having difficult with his words. He was a man reliving fear. She watched as he poured another drink, brought the glass to his mouth and downed a second shot. Then in a tone that reflected that the story must go on, he continued.

"And then," he started in a tone which reflected hopelessness, "in that instant luck played out. It happened; the Pinto went down. It could have been a washout, a prairie dog hole, a stumble, no one knows. But in a flash, horse and rider just dropped from sight.

"We could see the immediate commotion of cattle starting to pile up behind the horse's carcass which in turn was causing a piling up of more cattle as the back momentum kept pushing.

"Frank, Jerry, myself and a couple of others reined up at the outside line and I heard Frank utter, 'Oh My God, No' And I wouldn't even know how to describe the pain and hurt he must have felt.

"As for myself there was a feeling of utter senselessness. First I felt a sharp senseless cutting hurt, then instant rage and I started to cuss the heavens. 'How about some God damn fucking light,' I remember thinking.

"'Where in the hell is all of that God damn lightning when we need some.' But none came. All we could do was impatiently sat reined up at the side, watch the stampeding cattle continue to jump over the horse's carcass and wish for light, but still none came; and still none came.

"By now two or three more men had reined up and we just kept watching the cattle leaping over and pushing their way around that pile of flesh. God if we could only have some light.

"Then, after what seemed like eternity it happened. Another flash lit up the sky. And the miracle of God unfolded before us.

"In that flash we instinctively glance to the front and caught a glimpse of the lead steer, and made out what we thought was Willie, hanging, dangling onto the side of his neck.

"Son-of-a-bitch! The little tow headed bastard. As his horse went down he must have bulldogged off and caught the steer by the neck, we don't know; but God love'im there he was."

Aspen paused and inhaled a well-deserved deep breath. In the shared experience Jenny also experienced a relief, at least he was alive.

Aspen rolled the empty whiskey glass between his thumb and forefinger and pondered having another drink. Feeling relieved he decided not just yet and continued.

"Now I know," he said in a welcomed tone of humor, "what they mean when I hear the word bullheaded. That steer was not giving in and neither was Willie. Crazy, absolutely crazy. Both of 'em totally Goddamn fucking insane.

"The steer wouldn't quit running and Willie wouldn't turn lose. There he was bouncing, grabbing, and fighting every step of the way. One of his arms was draped at the armpit over the top of the steer's neck and it looked like he might even be biting in with his teeth; but he was hanging on.

"I don't need to mention that in a hair of a cat's ass we spurred the hell out of our mounts. I don't know about the rest but I no longer gave a shit about myself. I just wanted to get that little hard headed shit-ass out of there; but wanting and doing were sure as to hell gonna be two different things.

"As lightning flashed we could see him throw one of his legs up over the steer's neck a little and set his spur as a anchor point.

"But then with the next flash we could see him slipping back down to almost on the underside and about to lose his grip.

"Back and forth, he would throw his leg up and it would slid back down, kick it back up, try to set his spur as an anchor, lose it and slide back down.

"And all the time the steer running in a dead out run with Willie dangling on the side of his neck. Can you imagine what would have happened if they had of hit a gully or escarpment..."

Aspen left the sentence unfinished. With a surprise change of mood he decided maybe he would have another drink. He again held the glass to Jenny, she again shook her head. He tossed half a slug down and toyed with the jigger between his thumb and finger.

"Things then started to happen," he continued, "which I will remember all my life. In the luck department, son Jerry was riding a horse called Covered Wagon.

"One of the biggest horses I have ever seen. He was one half Clydesdale, stood fifteen, maybe sixteen hands high and weighed twelve, thirteen hundred pounds.

"If there was ever a horse meant to shove through cattle it was Covered Wagon because that is exactly what happened. It had turned dark again after the last lightning flash but I could make out the silhouette of Jerry and Covered Wagon cutting their way into the middle of the herd.

"In a dead out run, the cattle were now spacing out a little and Jerry was mingling, cutting and moving on up to the front.

"As it happened the weight of Willie had caused the front steer to start falling back and other steers were filling in the lead and that helped some because Jerry did not have to get right out on the point. For the most part we were all riding night blind but luck gave us another flash or two and we could see Jerry working his way up.

"Over to my side Poppa Frank was galloping right next to the herd sideline and I could hear him hollering, 'GET IN THERE GOD, GIVE'EM A HAND, GOOD JOB; STAY IN THERE JEROME. GOD, REMEMBER WHAT I'VE TAUGHT YOU.

STAY IN TIGHT, CROWD'EM; KEEP CROWDING; HOLD'EM STEADY GOD, DO LIKE YOU'VE BEEN TAUGHT HOLD'ER STEADY.'"

Aspen became so overly excited in mimicking the yelling that he spilled the remnants of his drink on the counter. He paused, gave it a brush wipe with the back of his hand and continued.

"Well, along about that time it would have helped if Mother Nature could have been a little more compassionate. A few streaks of light across the sky would sure as to hell been appreciated.

"But it wasn't happening and I was again cussing the darkness. Finally, after what seemed like eternity, another streak did come, a big one that lit up like day, but this time Willie was not in sight.

"My panic thought was that he must have gone down. But the little bastard, he must be indestructible, because the light held long enough for us to see just the soles of his boots sticking up, just above the steer's shoulders and he had both feet locked around each other.

"Of all the, don't ask me how but he was still hanging on. He had slid all the way down under the steer's neck and was riding upside down, dangling underneath with his arms and legs wrapped and locked around the steer's neck.

"God what a sight. Frank kept hollering for God and Jerry to hang in there. And they must have been listening because what happened next will never, ever on this green earth be seen again.

"By now Jerry had nudged Covered Wagon right up against the steer and was leaning over low in his saddle trying to grab hold of something; anything or anyway of catching Willie.

"And making a blind bouncing sweeping grasp in the dark, damn if he didn't hit that once-in-a-life jackpot; the strongest possible place.

"He grabbed inside the waist band of Willie's Levi's and got a hand full of pants and that ever present two inch wide western belt."

At this point, Aspen shifted his tone. He did not want Jenny to jump to the conclusion that things were now in hand. Because things in hand they were not. He wanted her to feel all of the exasperation that in fact followed.

In his now looking back, Aspen experienced a feeling toward Willie that any parent goes through when a kid is in danger of losing his life and then is rescued. A feeling that now-that-you're-safe-you-little-bastard I'm going to kill you. So he started talking in a way that he knew Jenny would detect the change of concern.

"Now Jerry knows that this is as good as it is going to get; there isn't going to be any seconds. So here we are, all the rest of us riding along the sideline.

"Jerry is leaned all the way over in the saddle and holding his saddle horn with one hand and holding Willie by the waist belt with the other and running dead out blind.

"We could see Jerry gripping that saddle horn, anchoring himself in the saddle and getting ready for the weight when he makes the pull. We can even hear him yelling to get ready.

"But Willie doesn't see things quite that way. Oh hell no! Nothing that simple. No sir, not just yet. Not until we determine who's running this little dog and pony show. God if I could have just killed. First we determine whose the boss.

"And the way to establish who's the head-shed of this little rescue operation is to have a little argument while you happen to be running blind, in front of a wild stampede, in the middle of a lightning storm; perfectly understandable.

"The minor bit of difference we had here," he underscores, "centered around Willie and his hat; and which would be saved first, him or his hat.

"Don't ask me how but he still had it on; pulled down hard over his head and ears. Even today I shake my head at him being able to hang on under that raging steer and still keeping it on.

"Anyway, Jerry has him in a once-in-a-lifetime grip and we should be ready for the big pull up, right? Wrong. Like I say, what we need first is a little something to break up the monotony and boredom.

"Something to pass the time. A man's hat is always good for a few words. Willie wants Jerry to release his miraculous hold on the Levi's and first take the hat.

"Jerry gives his response by yelling, 'WILLIE, YOU GOD-DAMN IDIOT IF YOU DON'T GET YOUR ASS UP HERE RIGHT GOD-DAMN NOW POPPA FRANK IS GONNA PUT SCARS ON YOUR ASS YOU'LL TOTE TO THE BONE YARD'

"Now I suspect, just suspect mind you, that Willie may have heard those words before because the prospect of a good ass kicking didn't seem to worry him too much.

"I suspect, just suspect mind you, that what worried him more was the prospect of losing his hat because we could all hear the two of them yelling.

"JERRY YOU GOD-DAMN NEW-HIRE, NEAR-DO-WELL, PISS POOR EXCUSE FOR A COWBOY, TAKE MY HAT FIRST. HELL, WE AIN'T GOING ANYWHERE. WE GOT ALL GODDAMN DAY.

"'WILLIE, YOU SHIT-HEAD I'M NOT TURNING LOOSE, GET YOUR GOD DAMN ASS UP HERE RIGHT-GOD-DAMN-NOW.

"'JERRY, YOU ASS HOLE IF I LOSE MY HAT I AM GOING TO KNOCK A FART OUT OF YOU THAT'LL WHISTLE LIKE A LONG LOST FREIGHT TRAIN.

"'WILLIE, IF WE EVER GET OUT OF THIS I AM GOING TO START A DOUBLE SIZE BOOT FACTORY RIGHT SQUARE IN YOUR ASS. YOU CALL THAT REJECTED RAG A HAT? IT WOULDN'T MAKE A WART ON A HAT'S ASS, NOW....'"

"ASPEN!" Jenny yelled with a holler, "I AM GOING TO KILL YOU IF YOU DON'T STOP TRYING TO DRIVE ME CRAZY! Just tell me what happened. Did Willie get saved or not?"

Aspen was startled, but then grinned, laughed and moved around the counter.

"Jenny," he changed the mood by joking as he moseyed toward the double French doors and went out on the verandah, "just thought you might like to know a little something about the mentality of cowboys; in case you ever start thinking about trading in a middle age Pittsburgh banker for a West Texas cowboy."

"As far as I know, there's not much of a market for dead banker," Jenny retorted as she moved outside and brought her arms to rest on top of the parapet wall.

"You're right, Jenny, I am getting a little too emotional. But I would like for you to look at this twitch in my right eye. You see that? That twitch wasn't there before I went to Texas. Now what I want to know is who is going to pay for that. Here I am branded for life, a twitch in my eye and a jerking of my neck and right shoulder now I think that somebody should have to pay..."

"So just tell me what happened," quarried a peeved Jenny.

"Damn, you're the crowning glory of compassion Jenny, you know that," he sneered back. "Well, what happened is Willie finally saw it Jerry's way. With a big shouted NOW he unlocked his legs, Jerry pulled and in one sweeping motion he swung up on the side of Covered Wagon. Another heave and he was all the way up. His hat came off, landed beneath pounding hoofs and don't even ask about the consequence."

Aspen looked up at the Pittsburgh sky, noted that it was clouding over and decided to return inside. Jenny followed and, as a change of seating, they both dropped on the sofa.

"Well to continue, Jerry and Willie worked their way over to our side as Frank, I and three or four others pulled in to help.

"In the meantime the rest of the crew was still in the chase. The last point we saw, Snakey had taken the lead. He was still carrying his Winchester and over the horizon we could hear gunfire and knew that he was probably firing along side the head of the lead steer. Eventually he got a turn started and along about three o'clock in the morning we had one giant size circle and things finally quieted down."

"By our best estimates we had run fifteen to eighteen miles and the aftermath did not look good. We did a backtrack search to make sure everyone was accounted for and by wild-eyed-guess we probably lost fifteen to twenty head which had stumbled and gotten trampled.

"The pinto horse of course and according to Willie the worst loss was his hat. Everyone was sweaty, salt covered and exhausted. One of the chuck wagons got knocked over, which we up righted. But both of the water barrels on that rig were lost which meant that our water supply had been cut in half.

"And Poppa Frank now had to make another painfully critical decision. Whether to turn back to the Pecos and recoup; or continue on and tough it out.

"The crew was tired, worn out, thirsty; and this time the waving of the American Flag by two young MP's was not going to be enough.

"He made his way through camp, talked with the men and came to a decision. We would rest until first light and then start on and not stop until we reached water. We had now been in the saddle for forty-five hours.

"Without much talk all the men unsaddled their present mounts and turned them back into the remuda. Each of 'em then singled out a fresh mount, threw on a loose saddle in case of another run, then holding rein in hand lay flat on alkali salt for even a few moments of sleep.

"Everyone that is except Gates Standwick. For Gates, his work could not wait. I didn't realize it at the time but Gates had been out on the flank popping camera flash bulbs the entire run. Now, the story had to get to press.

"At four A.M. he saddled a fresh mount and headed the fifty miles to Carlsbad, New Mexico. That same afternoon, newspapers across the Nation, including the little town of Eunice, carried front-page pictures of lightning splitting across the sky and riders in a full gallop trying to force a turn.

"Gates' write-up gave a full accounting of the stampede, the blinding perils and the heroic deeds of the cowboys trying to get the drive across the salt flats and to market. He ended with a personal message to all of America's fighting men to 'just hold on. Our Country is giving every ounce of support as fast as we can.' "Gates' dispatch of course ignited across the country like wild fire. I tell you Jenny, by now the whole damn world must have known about us. Except of course...us, meaning me and the rest of the crew, out in the middle of that salt desert. We had no way of knowing about all the notoriety. But apparently even

Tokyo Rose somehow got wind of it. I don't know if you remember who Tokyo Rose was or not but she was the female Jap radio announcer who was so famous for broadcasting demoralizing propaganda out over the airways in the South Pacific.

"How's that or a piss cutter? Japs in Japan knowing about us. Like I say, we only found out about all this later.

"But is seems that sweet Miss Tokyo Rose spread her version of propaganda out to America's outnumber, war torn troops over the nightly air waves. 'Dear American GI tonight I bring you the broadcast news that your own countrymen have again illustrated inept and inability to rescue you from the horrible swamps and mosquitoes. This time American incompetence has been illustrated by a group of pathetic cattle ranchers who drove ten thousand head of beef cattle out onto a salt flats desert and allowed them to go without water until they suffered the painful death of dehydration and all ten thousand head dropped dead. This very same beef that could be feeding American military forces in the Pacific is now bloated with flies and is feed for the buzzards. As far as the eye can see there is nothing but white bleached carcasses. You poor American GI's. Why do you insist on fighting when the food you were promised is now lying dead by the thousands in Texas salt flats? Give up, surrender your arms and the Japanese Imperial Army will give you warm food and a warm bed. Something your own weak and demented people cannot give you'."

"Now," Morgan paused and repeated. "Jenny, let me pause for a minute and tell you something about that little bit of Jap propaganda. What that little bit of bullshit did was piss America off. And of all the people it pissed off, nothing nowhere, no how like the people in the little town of Eunice, New Mexico.

"A little later on I'll be covering more about Eunice. But for now I'll just say that Eunice is really little more than a small framing community on the far-side rim of the salt flats. Pretty much what one might imagine. Not much to get excited about under normal circumstance, certainly not much in the way of national significance. But the words 'demented' and 'weak' from Tokyo Rose simply did not set too well with them folks.

"For the moment though, their emotions are not what I have on my mind. At this point my purpose in all this is to point out the degree of worldwide attention, even in Japan. Everything else I'll cover later. Right now my concern is to not get the cart before the horse. I'll just say that the Eunice outrage flared beyond any degree of normal sanity.

"In less than an hour every living soul for miles around, men, women, children, school kids, merchants, farmers, teachers...any and everybody had congregated in the center of town; all milling around the court house square with the town fathers huddled on the top of the court house steps. And in less than an hour thereafter, their contribution to the war effort was underway. Working in the unison of a well oiled machine, nonstop, around the clock, without expected pay or appreciation, every living soul gave their all. And the end product of what that all was, was a dry creek bed on the outskirts of town which they dammed up, filled with water from every available source, and formed a meandering mile long water ditch filled with ten feet of water."

A brief silence then followed as Morgan paused to collect his thought. He was not then looking directly toward Jenny but set with his head slouched in a slightly downward gaze. "Uh..." an unsure utterance came out. And then as the words he wanted formed, he started. "Jenny..." speaking as he turned directly back to her, "setting here, the way we are right now, I expect it's fairly easy for you to picture in your own mind, what that man-made watering hole must have looked liked. That being the case, then the next picture in your mind would be the assumption that everything was going to work out hunky dory. Don't even think it," he emphasized. "There was just too much hell between the salt flat crossing and that life saving watering hole. So for now let's get back to the story.

"Around five o'clock that morning two additional men rode out of camp. The first to ride out was Frank's son Gene. His instructions were to ride north to northwest on a scouting trip an estimated thirty five miles or so in a direction which should, with luck, intersect with the United States Attorney and the three wagons of water.

"If the attorney had been able to obtained the wagons and if Gene could make an early intersection, they would turn the water barrel train due south and at least there would be water for men and horses.

"The next man to ride out was Jake Marlow. Jake was to ride the forty miles or so east to northeast to Comanche Wells and check on the conditions of stock water.

"The rest of us drank our fill of hot black coffee, tighten our saddle cinch and mounted up. Making allowances for an hour or so of uneasy sleep, we had been in the saddle over forty-eight hours, had crossed an estimated thirty-five miles of the flats and then lost roughly fifteen to the westerly stampede.

"By now the behavior of the drive had taken on a zombie like trance. The cattle moved without temperament, commotion or ruckus and the crew moved in a mechanical pace along the outer flanks.

"There was little or no talking and a kind of hypnotic stupor hung in the air. Every two hours there was a rotation of the drag rider, as the drive kept moving. By noon on the third day the temperature was up to 100 degrees and no relief in sight.

"All day we just kept moving, east to northeast. Ever moving toward a horizon that never seems to get any closer. The salt dust was relentless in finding new places on the body to burn.

"At about four o'clock we spotted a small silhouette on the horizon off to our left. As it grew we could make it out. It was son Gene returning with the water train.

"With orders to keep the herd moving, Poppa Frank spurred and rode out, waving both hands in a motion for the wagons not to come any closer.

"It was crucial that the herd not get a smell of the water. The U.S. Attorney had filled the orders almost exactly. Instead of three wagons he commandeered four, each carrying fifteen barrels holding fifty-five gallons each; or allowing for losses, roughly three thousand gallons. Not nearly enough for the cattle but more than enough for men and horses.

"Leaving stern instructions to keep the water wagons down wind,

Frank and Gene returned to the drive and started a system of riders going out. In groups of two's and three's, men and horses rode out, watered up, washed off some of the salt, stretched their legs, savored a relaxed cigarette and then returned. At that point the water was not wasted but neither was it rationed. Not at that point.

"At nine o'clock that night the drive stopped for an hour rest. The chuck wagon that had lost its water barrels in the stampede moved out to the water train and replaced its water supply. A small campfire was started and five gallons of coffee made. By one's and two's the crew moved out for coffee and a cigarette. Around ten o'clock the order went out and we started moving again.

"Around ten thirty that night, Jake Marlow rode back in. He, and we, had now been in the saddle over sixty-six hours. But as bad a shape as the crew was in, Jake was worse.

"Even in darkness we could tell that he was moving on sheer guts; tired, thirsty, saddle weary and on a horse sweated down. From the time he left the drive that morning at five o'clock, man and horse had covered over a hundred miles.

"And for that torturous ride he had only bad news to report. There was no water. Comanche Wells were dry. The snowfall in the Southern Rockies including the *Sangre de Cristo* and *San Juan Mountains* had been light that year and the underground aquifers did not get replenished; and the secondary water supply of spring rains had not come.

"For the first time in remembered history, Comanche Wells, that great prairie oasis which had served Texas cattle men since the mid 1800's now had only dust to offer.

"Jake arrived at the Wells around ten o'clock that morning. In horror he grudgingly walked his horse down into the shallow bone-dry lake. He could feel the parched cracked mud crunch under the hoofs of his horse.

"His life and his world instantly blurred into a cosmos of being detached from his own body, of head shaking, of telling himself No, No, No.

"From childhood, every person who lives on the Texas prairie learns the life-critical importance of water. Water, always the first concern on which all other matters of prairie livelihood are centered.

"The cowboy and the cow can endure almost any hardship except this. Without water at this point Jake knew it was all over.

"The cattle had nothing left. Death by dehydration would start within a matter of hours.

"If the momentum of the drive should stop, the cattle would not start again. They would simply stand until they drop and then wait; once down they would never get up.

"Jake knew the country and in a state of panic he knew there were only two other possible sources of water.

"One was Escarpment Springs; a fluke ravine in the prairie formation some twenty-five mile due east toward the little town of Andrews, Texas.

"If there was water at Escarpment Spring, the cattle could still be saved. By ridding hard, there was still time; but riding that hard brought a high probability of his horse dropping dead beneath him. He would have to gauge close; if there was water at Escarpment Spring it had to be done. It would be close but he had to take the risk.

"The only alternative lay not to the east but due north, roughly fifty miles towards the oil boom town of Hobbs, New Mexico and water supplied by artesian wells. A fluke water supply created by man.

"In the course of drilling for oil, an elongated zone of impermeable strata had been penetrated and hydrostatic pressure forced ground water to swell to the surface from the holes drilled for oil.

"The probability of water at these wells was stronger but the distance was further. The weaker stock, especially the she cattle and calves would start dropping early and the overall loss factor could run as high as fifty percent.

"Jake's mind could not accept the picture of a cattle drive trudging across the salt flats leaving a string of carcasses in its wake.

"In what he prayed would be the right decision, Jake Marlow spurred his horse into an energy sapping lope and headed east.

"Three hours later he arrived to face the consequences of his decision;

an empty dry ravine.

"He first started to feel the pangs of consternation about a half a mile out, when he could see no birds or wildlife breaking to run.

"Refusing to panic he held his agony until he again rode his horse over a small rise and descended down into the sun parched, cracked crusty mud.

"In the depth of his despair all he could do was pound his fist on his saddle horn and in a cracked voice of hopelessness said, 'it's not fair.'

"He now had to carry the news back with no alternative but to turn the drive north. And that which he refused to picture earlier he now had to accept; a trail of dead, bloated cattle strung out across a fifty mile stretch of alkali salt. It was the lowest ebb of his life.

"When he left camp that morning Jake took only one canteen of water; the expectation being that he would refill at Comanche Wells. By the time he reached Escarpment Springs his mouth was too dry to even spit.

"But his horse came first. He removed his Stetson hat and poured in what was remaining; about half a canteen and held it for his horse to drink. With trembling hands he then rolled a Bull Durham cigarette, struck a kitchen match across the cheek of his Levi's, mounted up and turned west.

"Poppa Frank was riding point when he saw the silhouette of Jake Marlow coming in. When they met, Jake turned and the two rode point together for a long ways.

"When they parted Jake did not return to the herd but rode out to the water wagon, a mile out of wind on the outer flank."

"Frank continued on the point. He had no need to look back. He knew that men and cattle were now void of perception or feelings. In zombie file they moved because others moved. One step at a time, when one step means only that another step must follow.

"And yet, they now had to give more. Their steps, taken one at a time, now had to add up to an additional fifty miles. How much, he did know, could flesh and bones endure?

"Frank never felt so alone. After awhile he asked to have Gates

Standwick come up, and the crew could see the two men out on the point riding side by side.

"At midnight Poppa Frank called a halt and signaled for a full crew meeting at the water wagons. The cattle were not going anywhere. With very little comment the crew meandered in, waited their turn for a cup of hot coffee, rolled a cigarette and clustered behind the rear water wagon. When everyone was settled Poppa Frank proceeded with his arduous task.

"'Men,' he started, 'Jake Marlow rode in awhile ago and the news he brings is not good. In fact I would say the news is PISS POOR.

"'This is one of those times in life when I wish I was better with words, but I'm not; so I'll just tell you what I have to tell you.

"We got no water. None. For the first time in history Comanche Wells is bone dry. So is Escarpment Springs.

"'Now I don't have to tell you what that means. We have just been handed a second dose of pure hell,' he went on without stopping.

"'Our only option now is the artesian wells over by Hobbs.' On that point he did stop. He could not see the men's faces but he didn't have too. Fifty miles. Another fifty miles. He could feel the despair. But that was not the time for pity. Pity would only make things worse. So with a command of steel he brought authority back into his voice and proceeded.

"'I am not going to dwell on the circumstances,' he continued. 'We are facing almost impossible odds. But sometimes it helps if we know there are others who are suffering even worse hell.

"'I thought it might help a little if Gates Standwick would bring us up to date on the war news. Gate what can you tell us?'

"'Gentlemen,' Gates nodded at the group of exhausted men sitting on crusted alkali in the middle of night, 'the war news continues to be as bad as it can get. All of our bases in the South Pacific are falling like flies.

"'The Japanese have now captured Iwo Jima, Saipan, Guam, Wake Island; most of Micronesia. The list goes on and on.

"'Right now, even as we sit here, Guadalcanal is being shelled around the clock and is not expected to hold more than a few more days.

"'Our men are fighting under the most God awful swamp infested deplorable conditions. They are fighting in hand-to-hand combat without food, water or ammunition.

"'Luzon, Bataan, Cavite are all gone. On Wake Island our troops were so ill equipped that the Japanese aircraft could fly higher than our anti-aircraft guns could shoot.'

"Gates paused as he looked at the crouched gathering of tired young men. He felt a lump in his throat. He was not accustomed to giving speeches. But they had to give more. To stop meant to die.

"They had to be made aware, so he continued, 'Even tonight as we sit here thousands of young American men, your age most of them, some may even be your brothers, are fighting in hot, humid, mosquito infested islands in the Philippine, trying to buy us some time.

"'There is no hope for reinforcements and they know it. They have been pushed back into the jungles and many of them are living like rats. They stay alive by eating raw snakes or monkeys or anything else they can get. But the one thing that they have not done... is quit.

"'Gentlemen, I have just mentioned on how many of these sweltering islands the American flag has been ripped down by the cowardly hands of the Japs and been replaced the Japanese Rising Sun.

"'But there is something else you are entitled to know. Every time our flag, that red white and blue banner of freedom has fallen, it has been defended to the last man; and that last man looked right into barrel of a blazing Japanese gun and fired his one last shot.

"'That shot, that one last shot, somehow, somewhere bought one of our other boys some precious time; maybe even someone you know.'

"A deathly silence followed as Gates paused and then continued. "'Now, we all know what lies ahead of us. I know Mr. Delaney is going to ask you not to quit but to give that last full measure. You will be tempted to just accept hopelessness, we all will. Before you do I ask you to take just one more step; just one more. It might help to remember what our troops are going through; hiding and living in jungle swamps and foliage so thick you can't see another man ten feet away, weather so humid you can't breath, mosquitoes so thick they clog up your nose, water so infested it is undrinkable without adding nausea chlorine pills, fighting with outdated guns...

"'Men, our battle here is no less important than the ones being fought in deadly combat. If we all keep pulling together we can make it. And I have no doubt that you will; as for myself I am proud to be a part of such measure of men.

"'If you reach the point where you think there is no more to give, just remember one thing. You are at least one measure ahead of our boys fighting in the swamps and jungles. They have no hope that even their bodies will be found; they do not even have the option of dying on American soil.'

"Gates stopped short. He felt embarrassed over what he almost said. There was silence, no more needed to be said so he just nodded back to Frank.

"The silence lingered another second and then Frank started. 'Men, by my estimates we can expect to lose fifty percent of the herd. They have now gone seventy-two hours without water.

"'By noon tomorrow the weaker stock will start to drop. Some will just stop walking and stand still, others will stumble and not even try to get up.'

"Frank waited before he could finish. 'And when that happens, what has to be done must be done. When one falls, there is no need to let it suffer. For those of you who don't have your own hand gun there are some extras in the chuck wagon.'

"His words came out in a choked tone. A picture to horrendous to even think about. They may have to face the ordeal tomorrow but not tonight. A few of the men rose and walked away; leading, instead of riding their horses back to the herd. With one last drink of water, everyone singled back out along the line, Poppa Frank rode back out to the point and gave the order; 'let's head 'em due North.'"

At that point, Aspen quit talking. Telling the story continued to trigger the pain and strain that he had endured and he now wanted to change the subject.

But Jenny spoke up in a tone that forced him to continue. "Oh, Aspen," she exclaimed in a frown of anguish, "how horrible. Dear God please, tell me it didn't happen!" Her tender feeling moved aspen but he felt he had to let her experience the horrors of life.

"It was," he picked back up "a living, dying reality of life. A test of one's will to live or surrender and die. What Frank said about the cattle stopping and refusing to move was already starting.

"When we resumed the drive it was harder than hell to get the herd started again. It took a lot of yelling, pushing and prodding but eventually we got some momentum going.

"But from then on there could be no more stopping. Whatever stamina the cattle had left was what they would have to go on. The duration of life was now measured in steps." As that statement ended Aspen paused to remember the next sequence.

"Poppa Frank moved the chuck wagons and the water wagon an extra half mile out. He could not risk a sudden shift in the wind that might bring the smell of water to the herd.

"But other than that we just kept moving in what was the longest night of my life. Finally, when it seemed like it would never come, traces of thin red lines started streaking across the eastern sky.

"Just the sight of daylight brought some renewed hope. We continued to alternate going out to the chuck wagon for coffee and a bite of cold beans.

"At five A.M. on that third day we had been in the saddle for nearly eighty hours. By eight o'clock that morning the limits of our endurance were becoming more and more evident. The she stock, as they call the cows and calves were falling further and further behind. Some were starting to lose their equilibrium and stepping side ways."

He again looked at Jenny and could see she was grieved to tears. "Oh Aspen," she sobbed, "please, please tell me it didn't happen. What a horrible thing," she put a tissue to her eyes.

It was difficult for him to continue to describe the explicit details but he had a reason. Life has no bounds in its measure of harshness. In his role of storyteller, he hoped it would stir within Jenny a realization that there is never a time in anyone's life when just the simple function of living is not precarious. There is no answer as to why a tragedy will happen to some and not to others. If there is a great Master Plan, it can never be comprehended or understood. And in life, staying alive is the first priority.

He watched as the tears streamed down her cheeks and finally, in a comforting tone, he said,

"Dry thy tears my little Flower. Because somewhere, there must be a Master Plan. And that Mater Plan decreed that on that day and on that cattle drive there would be no disaster."

"WHAT?" she cried out in question, "Aspen don't fib to me. I can take it, but please, don't lie just to protect my feelings."

"No fib, Jenny," he felt a surge of relief at now being able to tell the ending.

"In life the unexpected will happen, truly the unexpected. And no, it wasn't rain that save us. Mother Nature was not so compassionate as to alter her weather plans.

"No, something much more dramatic. As it happened the source of our deliverance came, indirectly, from one of our very own; none other than Gates Standwick.

"His news reports about our plight were being read across the Nation; which included the people in the little town of Eunice. Hallelujah for newspapers and the people who read them; especially in Eunice. The people in that little town knew that both Comanche Wells and Escarpment Springs were bone dry.

"During the time frame when Gates' first report hit the papers they knew that we probably would not make it without their help; and this last great cattle drive was not going to end in a catastrophe from lack of help on their part.

"As soon as they became aware, community spirit swelled up and those wonderful people started sacrificing their own well being for us. Without thinking of themselves, that little town rolled up its sleeves and built us a reservoir.

"That's what I said, a man made watering hole. Long and narrow so that thousands of stock could water at once. Here's how and what happened.

"Just on the outskirts of town there was a dry gully bed. And these people moved in with earth moving equipment, scooped up the sides, dammed up the creek mouth and made a trench over a mile long.

"Next they ran a make shift pipeline from the municipal water well and drained in the first hundred thousand gallons of their town drinking water.

"Tank trucks from construction companies were volunteered and water started coming in from outlying private wells. Everyone from whatever source was bringing in water; barrels, buckets, tankers, you name it.

"All the time the town pumps were pumping. And pump they did, around the clock. To the extent that water to the community was rationed to an hour in the morning and an hour in the evening."

Aspen was elated to be telling this part. For Jenny to share with him the moments of coming back from depths of despair and the feeling of exhilaration.

"There is so much that I can tell about us and them coming together; their search team riding across the salt flats to find us; our explosive jubilation at the surprised news; the speed with which it flashed through our ranks.

"The turning of the herd and the arrival at the water; townspeople, cattle drive people, cattle and horses all rushing at each other."

"So much, I can still see the community all turned out, the cheering as we arrived, the proud, emotions, everywhere tears of happiness, uncontrolled feelings. So much, but first let me get back to what actually happened.

"As I mentioned, it was along about ten o'clock that morning when we actually started to accept the reality of what was going to happen. The best we could hope for now was that no human life would be lost.

"Truly our darkest hour and it seems that that was when divine providence stepped in. Why it was so ordained, we will never know but it was just about then that we noticed something moving on the eastern horizon.

"One cowboy noticed it first then others. At first we all assumed it was a mirage. But it kept getting a little bigger and appeared to be coming our way.

"And sure enough it was. It continued to get bigger until we could finally make it out to be a group of men on horseback; a scouting party out from Eunice.

"They were waving hats and yelling all excited over finding us. Frank and I rode out and were greeted with the unbelievable news that a lake holding ample fresh cool water was only ten miles away. Fresh cool water ready and waiting."

"Wait," Aspen exclaimed, "before I get too excited I have got to tell you how we damn near missed each other. You see the towns people didn't know two things; one that the stampede had thrown us way off course and secondly that during the night we had turned due north.

"They had been out since five o'clock that morning searching in the area where they thought we should be, fifteen to twenty miles to the east.

"When they couldn't find us they second guessed what might have happened and split their forces, one group heading toward Escarpment Springs and the other group, the ones who intersected us on the trail, headed North. As of that meet-up there were only ten miles between us and life saving water.

"But there was one last problem; turning six thousand head of cattle which were in a state of zombieism. Some of the stock were starting to go blind and simply would not respond to a kick, shove or yell. The cohesion of the herd was gone and the turning of one steer had no effect on the next.

"We were all riding right in the middle of the herd a kicking and a shoving but nothing was happening. Some of the steers would turn to avoid being hit with a lariat but then just stand there.

"Don't ask me why, but there had to be one final last agonizing moment of despair. We were weak as kittens ourselves and literally did not have the physical strength to go on shoving and pushing cattle that would not respond.

"Well, in the end it was true leadership that again saved the day. It was Poppa Frank who came through.

"How he got the idea I don't know but he signaled for the water wagons to be brought up to the point.

"When we got them up on the wind side some of the men got on the wagons and started splashing the water barrels.

"The smell of that water was instantaneous and the lead steers started coming to life and moving as best they could towards the wagons. We then started the wagons rolling and kept them just out of reach.

"Also, Poppa Frank did one other thing. The two MP's with flags in hand jumped upon the water wagons. They dunked the flags in the open barrels and then held them up to wave in the wind.

"Hot Damn, cheers went up you could hear for ten miles. Now we had a system; the water trailers rolling just out in front, men splashing and our flag boys dunking and waving. The smell of that water reached all the way to the back of the heard and we just kept rolling, dunking and waving.

"Life returned to the stock and the drive picked up momentum. I think it must have been the fastest ten miles of the trip and by noon a stampede of cattle, men and horses plunged head on into that elongated pond of water. God bless the citizens of Eunice."

As Aspen finished he exhaled a long breath of air and looked at Jenny and she looked at him. In reflex of relief they both broke out laughing.

"Aspen," she blurted in a short spasm of tears mixed with laughter, "you shithead, you knew all along that we were not going to lose the herd.

"Why'd you make me suffer so? I hate you."

"I know," he responded, "but look how good you now feel."

"Don't try to justify," she quipped. "I will have revenge. You are going to pay and pay big. Even now I am having this strange vision."

"Yes, I see this strange, sex starved man just after he has crossed the desert and wanting relief. But for his own good he will have to suffer.

He will feel better for it."

"Don't be that way," he teased. "Such cruelty, to a man starving in the desert," he sighed in a mocked breath.

"Remember, I am not just any man coming out of the desert, I am a National hero."

"Oh! Yeah! That's right. Now that you mentioned it," she picked up. "Where did all the hero stuff come from?"

Aspen felt a touch of embarrassment. That meant talking about him and so in an attempt to avoid the matter he responded, "You don't really want to hear about all that?"

"Yes, I really want to hear about all that."

"Now?"

"Yes, now."

"How about later?"

"How about now!"

"Well, OK," he started, "it's a long story. I could write a book. But for now, how about we just touch a few of the highlights? OK."

"First things first. First, the hell part was over. And starting at Eunice it turned from a cattle drive... are you ready for this, a Nation wide campaign to sell United States War Bonds.

"Can you believe that? By what stretch of the imagination would something like that happen?

"But I am sitting here telling you that it did happen and what should have been a normal every day run of the mill cattle drive turned into a National saga. That's the power of publicity.

"How, you ask? Simple. First we already had one reporter from Associated Press. Well at Eunice a reporter from United Press International came on board to start covering the story for the other national news network.

"So now we have two national reporters sending out daily accounts of our heroic efforts.

"The War Department picked up on the story and pounced on the publicity to sell War Bonds.

"In the next couple of days the Army flies in staff writers for the official military news paper, Stars & Strips and a whole entourage of men, jeeps, cameras and publicity banners.

"But wait, it doesn't stop there. Newsreel people from Movie Tone News also rushed to the scene. So what we now have is a traveling conglomerate that defies description.

"We figured there must be one publicity man for each steer." Aspen smiled at remembering the trek of that caravan. Spread out over five miles long cutting a swath across open prairie, farm lands, roads and towns."

"Even theatrics, especially theatrics, entered the picture. A movie director from God knows what movie company turns up.

"Dressed in riding pants, high top boots, black beret, ascot, long cigarette holder and eye monocle; Hollywood had come to the West Texas prairie.

"From that minute on any semblance of real life cattle driving disappeared; replaced by glitz.

"Poppa Frank and I now rode out on the point. We were flanked on each side by the flag carrying M.P. with Snakey Ramsey and the U.S. Attorney next behind.

"Each morning before breakfast we were pampered by make up people dusting powder on our face. And one time I remember, Poppa Frank expressed his thoughts about all of this by looking the make-up person right in the eye, and letting a FART you could hear a mile.

"Every man on the drive now strapped on a gun and wore a dust scarf around his neck. And tripods of cameras were grinding away everywhere we looked.

"Aerial Newsreel planes flew low over head. And it became a 'general order' that the MP's would play that bugle at reveille each morning and taps each night.

"The original travel route which Poppa Frank first laid out was changed. Where we had originally planned to shy away from towns and populated areas; the publicity crew convinced us to become more accessible to the people.

"On coaching from the War Department we started swinging the drive in closer to towns and communities. The Government publicity crews would travel ahead of us and set up for the business of selling War Bonds.

"With flags and banners waving and loud speakers playing the Stars and Strips Forever, a caravan of jeeps would entered every little town along the way; always circling the courthouse square.

"Military publicity personnel with bull horns blasting told the gathering crowds about our passing cattle drive and hyped up support for a turnout.

"At the bigger towns the War Bond People were able to get the schools to close for the day and have the high school bands turnout and play as we passed by.

"Business establishments closed their door in the middle of the day and entire communities in cars, trucks and busses came out to witness the event.

"The 'Buy War Bonds' people set up tents, complete with folding tables, banners, American flags, marching music and Uncle Sam Wants You posters.

"The operation was repeated time after time all along our route. Thousands upon thousands of people turned out to see this last page in cattle drive history.

"As we passed, High School bands usually played the National Anthem and the War Bond people used bull horns to hype the crowds into supporting the war effort."

Aspen realized he was repeating himself but still there were certain things that needed to be mentioned before the picture would be complete.

"In movie houses from coast to coast, that big ol' silver screen brought the scene to millions of people.

"Their favorite was to show the silhouette of a young MP sitting on a lone stallion blowing a bugle at taps on a mesquite covered hill backed dropped by the biggest brightest full moon in Texas as trail weary cowboys and six thousand head of Hereford cattle bedded down for the night.

"And then the next morning the same silhouette of an MP playing reveille just as thin streaks of red traced across the morning sky; bringing the symbol of America's patriotic war effort to life."

Aspen looked at Jenny to see if she could picture any of this. But then concluded it didn't matter. What happened happened and he went on with the story.

"So now we got a trail drive which, for publicity purposes, has taken on the flavor of the old West. In the spirit of the frontier we got cowboys, cavalry and settlers. But history is not quite duplicated.

"Somebody realizes that we need some Indians. In the old days when cattle men drove their herds north from Texas to the rail heads at Abilene and Dodge City they had to cross the Indian Territory; in what is now the State of Oklahoma.

"Well, back then the Indians discovered that they could extract a bounty for crossing their Territorial lands. So back in those days, when a drive was coming, it became the practice for a band of braves dressed in war paint to ride out and put the arm on the trail boss for a few head of beef."

"And seldom did a trail drive get through without payment. If the Trail Boss refused to turn over a few head, the Indians simply went into war yelling commotion, stampeded the herd and drove off any strays in the confusion.

"So, to duplicate history someone concludes that what we needed was a band of war painted Indians. Well it all came together up the trail aways. History reenacted."

"It happened up in the northern part of Texas in the area known as the Panhandle which was once the tribal lands of the Comanche Indians.

"In the rolling plain just south of Palo Duro Canyon, we were making our way north with intent of swinging just slightly to the west and around the Canyon headlands.

"It was about midday, the weather beautiful, good sun but not too hot, cool breeze, perfect for filming.

"As we were approaching the staging area where this Indian attack was going to take place we could see the outline of open tents, outdoor portable bleachers and rows of parked cars off in the background.

"Then exactly like it must have happened in 1865, in a cloud of dust a band of Comanche Indians came riding up over the rise.

"At the first sound of the Indian war cries, all of our cowboys grabbed their fire arms in preparation for battle but Poppa Frank held up his hand to hold steady.

"The Indian Chief, riding out in front was wearing a war bonnet and the braves all wore war paint. In a thunderous roar they came riding in amid war cries and waving tomahawks.

"To give a good show they made a number of wide flanking circles before finally coming to a stop in a cloud of dust with ponies rearing up on their hind legs in wild eyed commotion.

"Then on queue, Frank and I rode out for a pow wow. I tried to look stern and stonewall; indicating that Frank would do the bargaining.

"He was well acquainted with the Comanches and even knew their sign language. So it was all really pretty realistic to watch.

"For benefit of the Newsreels, the Chief and Frank reined their horsed up nose to nose and sat face to face exactly like it must have happened.

"The Chief started the barter in sign language demanding one steer for each brave as he held up one finger and then made a wide sweeping motion toward all the braves sitting in back.

"Frank stood up in his saddle, looked past the Chief at the number of braves, lowered back down and shook his head to signify too much."

"In sign language he cupped his arms to indicate the holding of a papoose and then held up one finger. Frank was offering one steer for each brave who had a wife and family."

"Back and forth, they negotiated until an agreement was reached of one steer for the married braves and a half steer for the unmarried braves.

"Each of the two then held a close fist to his heart and the negotiations were over.

"With cheers of approval from the hundreds of spectators, Frank then made a signal to Snakey. Some of the boys then cut out twenty head and pointed them toward open range.

"The closing scenes showed the young bucks circling the prize several times and then stampeding off over the rise; and Uncle Sam sold another million dollars worth of war bonds."

"After that," Aspen continued, "the drive was one continuous picture taking routine. The little town of Pampa, Texas closed the schools, the school band played and the Mayor presented Willie with a '4-X Beaver-Stetson' hat to replace the one lost in the stampede.

"From there we just kept moving. We entered into Oklahoma and the open wheat lands following along the eastside of Highway 83 and on into Kansas; and a major milestone.

"The morale was already high but crossing the Oklahoma/Kansas State line made the adrenaline surge. The smell of success was in the air.

"We had only a hundred and twenty five miles to go and the terrain was nice rolling wheat fields. The weather was perfect and Poppa Frank slowed the drive to six miles a day to let the cattle regain some of their weight by gazing on the tender spring wheat.

"Everything was going along perfect except for one thing. Mother Nature wanted to make sure that She was not forgotten in this little final page of history.

"As a guarantee of her remembrance, she handed us one more little scenario in the form of the Cimarron River.

"Runoff from Kansas spring rains had raised the water level to near flood stage and a ford crossing was not possible. And so there we were. Us and six thousand head of cattle on one side, Dodge City on the other."

"But once again the people came to our aid; this time the citizens of Kansas in the name of the Kansas State Highway Department.

"Authorization came down that we could drive the cattle across the mile long bridge on State Highway 56. This meant among other things that traffic on a major highway would be held up for at least six to eight hours.

"But even this had a final barb. The cattle did not like the feel of walking on concrete and the lead steers refused to cross.

"Imagine that, to come this far, to be so close and the cattle refusing to cross the final link.

"Well, a lot of huddle talking took place between Poppa Frank, the News Media, the United States Attorney, the Kansas State Highway Officials and I suspect some telephone calls to the Governor's Office at the State Capital.

"But a solution finally emerged. If the cattle did not like the feel of walking on asphalt and concrete, then the asphalt and concrete would be made to feel like dirt.

"There was a lot of chatter talk back and forth on two-way car radios and before long an endless caravan of earth moving equipment and dump trucks started arriving on the scene.

"Wheels started turning like a well oiled machine and it wasn't long before a two mile stretch of the road leading up to and over the bridge was covered with six to eight inches of dirt.

"When it looked sufficiently camouflaged, Poppa Frank threw a lariat around the horns of Bolivar and saddle pulled him across the bridge and the rest of the herd began to follow. Six hours later the last steer crossed over and we were back in business."

Aspen was tired of talking. It was tempting to end the story. Jenny would feel that the drive was a success and anything after the bridge would be anticlimactic. But that was not the way it ended. The ending made it all worthwhile and it was important that Jenny shared the joy. So without comment he simple went on.

"After the bridge, we knew that we were home. A feeling of accomplishment settled over us. The twelve-day drive on into Dodge City and the Santa Fe Stock Yards were the most pleasant days.

"The pace was slow, the weather was perfect and the crew basked in pride and comraderie. Every man had pulled his weight, every man had stayed to the finish and ever man had measured up.

"Strangers when they came together, they had forged into a team, accepted the challenge, endured the hardships and completed the mission.

"The final page in cattle drive history had been written. They would be going home knowing that they had measured up to those who had gone before. No other reward was necessary.

"But that was not quite the way it ended. If you want a real happy ending, ask Hollywood; Hollywood knows that *an ending with happiness* is not the same as *a happy ending*.

"The women of the Nation are entitled to recognition for their contributions. Before the Nation can be truly proud, it must be proud of both its men and its women.

"While none of us out there on the trail knew anything about it the Nation was about to be truly proud.

"Under orders of Top Washington Priority, Two DC-3 Military Cargo Transport planes were dispatched from Kelly Field to Midland, Texas. And there the rest of the story was loaded on.

"The publicity people for the War Department were coming home with their Sunday punch; the grand finally. This drive was going out in a flame of glory. Starting on the Dodge City outskirts.

"And what a final flame of glory it was. A full scale, Dodge City, rooting tooting, horns blowing, drums banging, flags waving, parade of marching bands, military drill teams, baton twirling short skirts majorette, fire trucks, military hardware, forty head of prime beef, one chuck wagon and our crew of gun toting cowboys passing down Second Avenue on the east side of Wright Park to the Arkansas River and turning West to the Fair Grounds and a big United States of America style outdoors speech giving, War Bond Selling Bar-B-Q."

"At the front of the parade, embarrassed to be there, but nodding to the cheering crowds, rode Poppa Frank on a big high stepping bay with flowing black mane and tail.

"By his side rode the gracious Queen of the Tap Root Ranch, Momma Maude. Wearing a baby blue western ensemble of riding pants and blouse studded with rhinestones which matched her sparkling eyes and rosy cheeks she sat on the back of prancing Palo; her pride and glory pure bred Palomino with flowing white mane and tail.

"Next back, riding four abreast, dressed in tight fitting Levi's, stove pipe cowboy boots, jingling Mexican spurs, open collar, western cut, bosom bulging, blouses unsnapped to just legal, rode the four daughters, Betty Jo, InaLee, Theresa and Shannon.

"Next back, riding four abreast were sons Gene, Willie and Jerry with a fourth saddle being empty, but draped with an American flag for son Tommy who could not be there. He was killed fighting the Japanese on Wake Island December 23, 1941.

"From there on back," Aspen spoke with a tone of winding down, "there were just too many to mention.

"After the three sons and the empty saddle; next back, riding in a brass polished surrey being pulled by a glistening red roan gelding were the Governor of Kansas, Payne Ratner and the Mayor of Dodge City, Z. Arthur Nevins.

"Next back riding four abreast, flanked each on an outside were the two flag bearing MP's with me and Snakey Ramsey in the middle; so on and so forth and Uncle Sam sold another ten million dollars worth of War Bonds.

"A few weeks later Poppa Frank and I were called up to Washington D.C. and in a ceremony by President Franklin Delano Roosevelt we each received a Civilian Meritorious Service Award. And that, my very lovely and desirable Jenny, is how the cattle drive ended. A hero I am not. But the press and war bond sales needed someone. I just happened to be there.

Chapter 22

The unfair circumstances of his life continued to prey on the mind of Sidney Griffin. His youthful dream of being a *Danseur étoile, premier,* the highest rank in the cadre of the Paris Opera for a male dancer, had passed into oblivion. Instead, faith had seen fit to cast him into the menial role of teaching one lone, awkward, inept day dreamer adult female student.

He increasingly turned to smoking marijuana and spending more of his time in the company of his old fraternity, Phi Smia Delta. His frustration grew on a daily basis and as the weeks continued to pass, his relationship with Patricia turned more and more contemptuous. It finally reached the point where he simply did more talking and very little teaching. Talking not in a normal conversational sense but deliberate patronizing; a manipulation which Patricia failed to recognize.

"Tell me, Patricia," he ask one morning when they were doing nothing more than sitting idly on the stage floor. "Do you agree that grace, beauty and love are all things in the world?"

"Of course," she quickly responded. "You know it's something of which I have dreamed all of my life and I feel so fortunate that we can share our thoughts."

Sidney shook his head in disbelief. *This woman,* he thought, *is mentally retarded. Doesn't anyone know this but me?*

"On the contrary my dear Patricia, it is I who is blessed with good fortune. Just talking to you seems to make things so much more clear. Tell me again what it is you want to do someday," he baited as the two remained sitting with their legs pulled up and leaning back against a wall.

"My dreams, you mean? Oh, there are so many," she answered as her head was tilted back and her eyes were looking toward the ceiling. "But the dream I like the most takes place in a beautiful castle in a setting of royalty. It's in some foreign, way-off land and I can't really make out the country.

"But that's not important. What's important is the elegance of a huge ballroom. Especially the high dome ceiling, the marble floors and the gold ornate crystal chandeliers.

"It is crowded with prestigious people all standing around talking in small groups. All the men are tall, dark and distinguished; some are dressed in dashing regimental uniforms and some in tuxedos.

"The women are all wearing full length satin gowns adorned with expensive jewelry. The evening is perfect; a warm summer night with a slight breeze and not too humid.

"I pretend that I am Anistisha Vaganova, grand niece of Agrippina Vaganova the greatest Russian ballet teacher of all times. On this night I will give the greatest performance of my career; a special engagement for the Crown Heads of Europe.

"It is the moments before I make my appearance. I am dressed in a white tutu and my makeup has been applied. My attendants and I are waiting in a small foyer off the end of the ballroom.

"On the other end of the ballroom, my lover is standing by a set of giant double doors which lead out onto a marble terrace. He is tall and handsome; dressed in a white military uniform with gold braid on his shoulders.

"On the toes of my ballet slippers I must run to him where we will dance the night away. As I first reach my beloved we fall into each other's arms and gladly surrender to our heart's call to dance. Our whirls will first take us around the ballroom where we are the center of attention. Eventually we seek our own company and move to the seclusion of the terrace and dance beneath the stars.

"But before any of this can happen the dance of ballet will extract its payment in the form of strife, danger and fright. The onus is on me and I must pass through a dark and perilous passage. The dance I will perform will represent three factions. Courage and purity, I am grace and he is love.

"In my fantasy I can see myself as it is getting closer to the time to go on. Out in the ballroom an orchestra is seated in one corner and waiting. The music had not yet started. Preparations have been delayed and the guests are restless as they mingle and exchange social amenities. More minutes tick by and the noise level increases.

"Then, just at the perfect moment the air is pierced by a thunderous drum roll; all talking quickly ceases.

"Those guests who are congregated in the center of the room intuitively move to the sides and there is a dead silence as all eyes turn to see my entrance.

"Then it happens. I enter, pause slightly on *'sur la pointe'*, glance at the guests, and then go into my whirl in *chains papillon,* cascading across the floor. Already the sweat is forming on my forehead at knowing what I must now pass through.

"Each *pirouette* brings me closer to his embrace. The expanse between us is wide and treacherous. There is a foggy swamp that I must cross. Darkness descends, a thick haze sets in and I become confused. Lightning flashes and I know that if I fall into the murky water I will be lost. Evil demons with fiery eyes, hideous screams, and claw shaped hands seek to grab me; but I escape their clutches.

"I must keep whirling. My one true love is waiting for us to be together; it all depends on me. He is helpless to come to my rescue because he is bound by mortal.

"There is more danger as I *chain papillon;* more lightning flashes, tangled woods block my path, the way is dark and foggy but I continue on, and on. I am becoming weary. I get lost in the pitch-black darkness. I stumble. More lightning flashes but on I go until at last, long last I come to a clearing; where my beloved waits and my quest is ended. Exhausted and weary I raise up on point one more time.

"Then I fall into his waiting arms and we unite; grace, beauty and love; three in purity. I will have given my best performance and the guests will recognize it as they give me un-ending applause. I take my many bows, the ball begins, and gaiety reigns until dawn."

Dear God, thought Sidney, *the mind of a twelve year old in a grown woman's body.* He took another deep drag of marijuana and his mind drifted into hallucination. Images of Patricia whirling around like some great ballerina with her exposed tits flopping out brought insidious fantasy laughter. A delusion started unfolding of a way he could cast revenge against the world and at the same time immortalize him to his fraternity brothers. In continued mockery he fueled her fantasy.

"Don't stop, Patricia," he baited, "I have never heard anything so beautiful. I can vividly picture your destiny. Your triangle of grace, beauty and love must be united or there is nothing." He paused as if in deep thought and then in a hesitant tone continued.

"Patricia you have no idea how your fantasy excites me. I can hardly believe I am saying this, but I will. I am going to propose something I never thought possible."

"What?" she asked anxiously. "Is it something to do with me?"

"Once, a long time ago," he ignored her question, "I saw a one-act ballet. I don't remember the name but I do remember one particular scene that was absolutely beautiful.

"It was," he continued, "the unfolding of a beautiful butterfly from its cocoon and I have always dreamed of duplicating that scene."

Patricia unsuspectingly followed the lure and quickly asked, "What is it Sidney? What are you thinking? Tell me you're thinking what I hope you're thinking."

"Well," he led in a mocked uncertainty, "it's kind of hard to explain but basically the ballerina was suppose to be a cocoon. Her upper body was completely wrapped in a long roll of sheer white cloth that represented the cocoon. Supposedly one end of the cloth was attached to a tree.

"In actuality another member of the cast was just holding the loose end. Anyway, the ballerina left the tree and whirled in chains, *chains papillon,* unwinding as she whirled out across the stage and when she came to the end of the cloth she emerged as a beautiful butterfly.

"To help the audience's imagination there was a small set of wings on her back which sprang open at the end of the cloth. And it was really very touching as she did a fluttering bouncing zigzag routine in celebration of her new freedom and flew away."

He paused, looked to the ceiling with a coy smirk, and waited for Patricia's reaction. It was crucial that she is the one to take the initiative; that she be the one to make the suggestion.

"Oh Sidney, let's do it!" she took his bait. "We can do it. I know we can. It would be so beautiful and it would be such good experience."

Terrific, he thought, *absolutely beautiful.* By allowing himself a controlled smile he was able to choke back a rancorous laugh. He savored the moment by slowly snuffing out his joint, rolling the residue between his thumb and forefinger and forming an expression that maybe he had jumped too quickly; better to wait.

"I will do whatever you say," she reinforced. "Just let me try, please."

His compulsion to break out laughing was almost uncontrollable. Reactively he hid the smirk on his face by putting a hand in front of his mouth and pretending further skepticism.

"Please."

"Well," he drawled, "the Underground will be closed for the rest of the month so it would be an opportune time. If you're sure?"

"Oh, yes, yes. I'm sure, please."

"Well, OK! It's a deal," he sealed the hoax by pretending excitement and squeezing her hands in his.

"Now here's the deal," he spoke as they were getting up from sitting on the floor. "We'll start right now, this very moment and practice every day for the rest of the week.

"Then, on Saturday night, you can get off work can't you? Good, on Saturday night we'll come down and give you the benefit of a nighttime dress rehearsal."

Patricia was ecstatic with the rapid change of events and did not completely understand about the dress rehearsal. All her mind could picture was a ballerina dressed in a tutu, whirling across the floor and turning into a butterfly.

It was difficult for Sidney to continue hiding his hideous humor. He turned away, stifled a laugh and then forced a normal look on his face.

"OK," came his words," let's get started. When we leave today I will stop by a fabric shop and pick up a bolt of white sheer cloth.

"We will be needing it for dress rehearsal. Now, for our first position stand here at the edge of the stage," he instructed as he switched on the music and moved into the next phase of his connivance.

"Patricia, as of now pretend that you are wound up like a cocoon. I'll make like I'm holding the anchor end and as I count to the music you start whirling. You know the routine. We've practiced it almost everyday.

"It's going to be just a little different this time however because I want you to hold your arms to your sides until I yell the end of the cloth and then let your arms swing outward.

"Doing it this way should help you to learn balance. OK. Let's get started. Here we go; to the music. Whirl, 1 and 2 and 3 and 4.

"That's it, on the ball of your toes, keep moving, arms to the side for now; whirl 1 and 2 and 3 and 4. Keep moving, with grace and beauty on across the floor, keep moving out, out across the floor. Remember you are unwinding; grace and beauty."

The remainder of the week was practice and more practice. "Whirl harder," he coached. "Be ready for the end of the cloth. That's the instant when you'll go into your hardest whirls. When the final wrap of cloth comes off throw your arms straight out and continue to hold them straight out as you whirl. Stay in the center of the stage. Stay center stage.

"Arms straight out like they are wings and whirl harder, harder. Make your arms fly on the wind.

"Use your own momentum to make the arms stand straight out. Faster, faster, catch the wind. Arms extended like the letter T. Picture the whirl and remember grace and beauty."

The pride in Patricia exploded that week. Her whirls were done in flats and not in pointe shoes but that did not hamper the spring on the ball of her feet. As each day passed she became more excited and for the first time in her life she started experimenting with make-up. To add to the spirit of dress rehearsal she planned her own surprise.

The following Saturday with Shelly in the care of Jenny, she spent most of the afternoon applying face makeup. That which she had played at as a young girl now came to life in real. First she meticulously applied a foundation base accentuating high cheekbones. Then she used a black marker to make her eyes appear large and upward slanted.

Next she put on long false eyelashes, drew a black line back from the corner of her eyes, and applied a light pink blush to her cheeks. For eye shadows she used pink, blue and silver. As a final affect she put on bright red lipstick and exaggerated the outline of her lips. After all made-up had been applied and retouched, she still had time on her hands and impatiently paced the floor, watched the clock and did practice whirls.

Finally dusk started to settle. She gave a final look in the mirror, made one last blot to her lipstick, adjusted her knotted blouse and turned up her collar; time to go.

It was slightly after seven when she arrived at the Underground. The front door was unlocked and as she entered she was startled to see that the seating area was pitch dark. The only lights that were on were the stage lights. She felt a degree of caution as she proceeded down the silent eerie aisle. There was a heavy odor in the air that she thought familiar but paid no mind.

Just as she was passing under the suspended balcony Sidney came out from behind the stage curtain.

"Welcome Ballerina," he called from the stage. "My compliments Madame on the makeup; very nice surprise. Stupendous. You have my complete approval."

It was the first time he had ever expressed any degree of approval and she quickened her pace to further please him. As she lightly bounced up the stage steps he continued the charade.

"Ah, here we are at last Ballerina," he reached out and took both of her hands in his. "After all the months of practice you're finally ready. Are you just a tiny bit stage frightened?"

In slight hesitancy she answered, "A little I think. It looks so different at night. I never realized before, but the stage lights shine directly into the performer's eyes. How do you know if there is anyone out in the audience?"

"Did you see anyone in the audience as you came in?" Sidney responded with a question?

"No, but that's not what I meant. I was just wondering how you know..."

"Such concerns," he interrupted. "Really, Patricia you are now on the stage and you must learn to think stage.

"First learn to speak up so that you can be clearly heard. Now in a louder tone, Patricia do you have something you wish to share with the world?"

"Yes I..."

"Louder, Patricia, I can't hear you."

"Yes I do," she exclaimed in a much stronger voice.

"Something you are very proud of?"

"With all of my heart," she answered.

"And what is it that you are proud of?"

"Grace and beauty,"

"Two names," joined in Sidney. "Are we to understand that one name would not convey all that you want to show us?"

"How can you have one without the other?" she asked; pleased with her reply.

An atmosphere of stage decorum was developing and she liked the feeling as she spoke out to a pretended audience.

"So one is Grace and the other is Beauty. Are you proud of your grace and beauty?"

"More than anything else in the world."

"Has anyone ever seen this side of you before?"

"No, never."

"And tonight will be your premier showing. Are you ready?"

"Yes, yes I am."

"Very well my Ballerina it is time. Let's go back stage and prepare."

It was here; in the dressing room that she encountered her first stark shock.

"Patricia," Sidney started apologetic. "I'm sorry I neglected to tell you to wear a skin tight blouse. It's my fault I know, but we can't do this in the loose blouse you have on. You will have to remove your brassiere and blouse."

Hot blood instantly rushed to her face as she felt the embarrassment and spontaneously raised her hands to her breast.

"Uh, but Mr. Griffin," she stammered, "I don't understand. What, why? No, no I could never..."

"Oh, for heaven's sake," he responded in an intimidating hot temper.

"Don't be so childish Patricia. This is art. It is the *art* we are interested in; not some sexual interest in your bare bosoms."

"Now if you can't see the difference then perhaps we should call the whole thing off," he finished in a threatening tone.

Patricia, flushed and intimidated, tried once more for understanding but Sidney became even more overbearing. He explained in impatient tones that of course in the actual ballet she would be wearing a skintight body suit. He again offered a half apology for not having told her earlier, but then continued reprimanding her for being so sensitive.

Finally she conceded to taking off both her blouse and brassiere but only if he would turn his back until she could wrap herself in at least the first few turns of the cloth.

In a mocked disbelief he threw up his hands, agreed and turned. Nervously she unwrapped a few feet of cloth and let the rest of the bolt drop to the floor.

In a clumsy maneuver she held the loose end under her chin and awkwardly removed first her blouse and then her brassiere. Embarrassingly she hurriedly wrapped the first few feet of cloth around her exposed, long dangling breast. Her modesty saved, she sheepishly responded that Sidney could now turn around.

With matters now fully under his control, he became much more cordial. Picking up the bolt he instructed her to turn while he fed and between the two of them they continued the body wrap. All the while he fueled her imagination of the grace and beauty upon which she was about to embark.

"Think of the audience reaction," he fueled, "when a common cocoon unfolds into a beautiful fluttering butterfly."

Finally wrapped in the likeness of a mummy from her neck to her waist the time had come. Standing just inside the curtain, her nervousness grows. Should she be doing this? She felt panic at being confined. Stage fright. She shouldn't be here. It was too late, the music started and she had to begin. Holding his end of the cloth she heard Sidney's command.

"NOW ballerina, DANCE. Dance ballerina. Whirl thee across the land."

Obediently, she stepped out on the stage and picked up the rhythm. Almost instantly her fears subsided as she whirled, 1 and 2 and 3 and 4. Excitement surged through her as she moved outwardly toward center stage.

"Whirl ballerina. Whirl to your destiny," he coached from the side. "Whirl, 1 and 2 and 3 and 4. Concentrate! You're not concentrating! Keep time to the music! Faster!"

The world she had waited for had finally arrived. With her eyes closed, she became lost in her dream and paid no heed when suddenly the stage lighting went off and a single spot light came on and shown down from the balcony. She was in the center of the only light in the house as she moved across the stage. In the wings, Sidney continued to coach.

"Whirl beautiful ballerina, whirl."

And whirl she did. Her adrenaline surged. Her rhythm was prefect. Each rise on the ball of her foot gave her stronger momentum and the unwound cloth stretched out longer as she moved further across stage. She began to feel the increase of freedom with each unravel.

Then it happens. The last wrap came loose and fell lightly to the floor. She was free. She sensed the coolness of the stage air upon her bare skin. She felt a renewed surge to obey Sidney's continuing commands.

"Whirl, faster, faster. Make your arms stand out like wings. Around the stage, around the stage," he coaxed.

"Faster, make your arms fly out, out to the wind."

She continued to whirl with all her strength and the spot light from the balcony kept her in center. In exact however, the focus of the spot light was not on the swing of her outstretch arms, but on the outward swing of her exposed elongated breast. Like long tentacles they answered the law of centrifugal force and stood straight out. Tentacles that were directly linked to her shy, exposed, delicate soul.

The dance continued longer than any of her practice. She could feel her energy starting to play out and was thankful when Sidney's calls began to taper off. As the tempo slowed she gradually wound down and came to a halt.

In half nude exposure, her breast dropped to their normal position, her head slightly bowed, she stood in heavy breathing with her hands on her hips facing the front of the stage.

The music had stopped and for a few seconds there was a dead silence; broken only by the sound of her heavy breathing echoing across the stage. However, that all changed in the next split second.

As unexpected as a thunderous clap of lightning on a clear summer day the spot light went off, the house lights flashed on and the atmosphere was violently shattered by voices raining down from the balcony. Voices in the name of fraternity Phi-Smia-Delta; young college men dressed in their blue blazer jackets, white shirts and regimental stripped ties heralding down yells of Hurrah! Hip! Hip! Hurrah! And bravos. Cheers of Encores, Encore! Herald down; from their place of despicable ambush in the balcony.

By the compliments of Sidney Griffin the full fraternity had just been given a show. In stark horror Patricia turned and looked upward at the assembly of drunken young men holding up beer bottles, leaning over the balcony parapet, clapping their hands and hollering down.

Blood instantly surged to Patricia's face as she was overcome by shame. Reactively she drew up her arms to cover her breast and for a split second stood in frozen panic. Thence rushing to escape she ran to the back of the stage and frantically pawed at the pleated curtain but could not find an opening.

In the same moment that she was trying to flee, Sidney rushed out on the stage. With his arms motioning upward he encourages more applause from his rowdy fraternity brothers. Responding to their increased yells and cheers of approval he bowed and mimicked acceptance for a great performance.

As they commenced staggering down the circular stairway from their place of hiding, Patricia's panic was to flee. In the side dressing room she hysterically put on her blouse and her trembling hands buttoned mismatched holes. Clutching her bra in disgrace she half stumbled down the stage steps. With her head bowed down to avoid eye contact she ran up the center aisle, out the front door and into the night.

In less than an hour, word of the heinous deed reached Morgan Smithfield. He was in his office at the Stran and his wrath was a wrath unknown to man; instant, insane, volcanic and without bounds or redemption.

Rage seared through his body as he verbally cast their abominable soul into eternal hell and damnation.

"May they burn in everlasting fire; the loathing despicable scum of spittoon wash."

Trembling and quivering he wielded his cane with a smashing blow across the top of his desk. Saliva sputtered and drained from the corners of his mouth as his vengeance raged. Stumbling and shoving he stammered back and forth in his office.

Another swing of his cane came smashing across a desk light as it shatters to pieces and strewed across the floor. Palpitations flushed his face and neck as he again slammed his cane at his desk and chair.

"To a man they will pay. Thou empathetic illiterate dregs of human dignity," he raved.

Jim Barkus had been working in back when word came of Patricia's ordeal. He now stood silently in Morgan's office as rage continued to flair. It was a scene that any man, in any lifetime, could live without. Finally the settling word came.

"OK Jim," flustered Morgan with as much composure as he could muster. "Let's go after'em. I want'em and I want'em bad.

"So let's hit the bricks. That means right now. Put the word out. You know what has to be done.

"Start with my main man. Six feet six, two hundred eighty pound black man 'Gimmie' at the newsstand. I want him leading the pack.

"From there round up as many men you need; and when you have all the men you need, then double it.

"I want this town covered like the morning dew. Call in every marker I have ever put out for the last ten years if you have to; but I want them found and I want them found tonight."

In a slow enunciated vengeance he continued, "The bastards who are responsible for this are going to wish they had never been born.

"Jim," Morgan looked Jim Barkus straight in the eye. "Understand what I am saying. I don't want just that despicable gob of coughed up slime, Sidney Griffin.

"I want every last soul in that theater. So put out the search. Every marker I am owed in this town, no matter where, no matter what, is hereby due and payable."

"THAT MEANS HERE AND NOW. End of story." Morgan paused and in self thought said. "And God help those who don't make payment."

When Jim Barkus left the Stran, his first stop was the corner newsstand. LeRoy 'Gimmie' Jones had already heard and was quickly closing.

The day's receipts were hurriedly dropped in a nearby bank night deposit box and the two of them hit the nightlife streets of the City.

Starting in the area along Liberty Avenue they stopped at every bar, club and brothel. They talked to every hooker in every doorway and they put out the call on Morgan's markers. In chain reaction those-in-turn put out the marker call and within the hour the streets were prowling.

From Liberty Avenue, Jim and LeRoy turned east on Seventh Street and then up Bedford to the Hill District. At every bar and club, when the two entered the room became instantly silent. The drinking ceased, dancing ended and the band stopped playing.

The story spread and inquiries put out. Does anyone know anything;

if not, go and look? As Jim and Gimmie would leave, there came a quick finishing up of counter drinks and a departing of patrons. The dragnet expanded.

It was an off duty policeman by the name of Hugo Zambrowski who thought to stop in at Jenny Craig's place. At sometime around 1:00 AM Morgan's telephone rang. Jenny was on the other end.

"Morgan," she said, "this is Jenny. I just heard. Is there anything I can do?"

With the loss of his desk light, Morgan had been sitting in the dark. He was glad that Jenny could not see the wetness in his eyes. In an appreciative tone he thanked her for calling and then added, "Jenny, if you can I would appreciate it if you would go over to the apartment on Wood Street and be with Patricia.

"She's in pretty bad shape right now. I know it's Saturday night and all..."

"Of course, Morgan, say no more. I'm leaving right now," she cut in.

"But first, Morgan," she continued, "I don't know if there is any connection but I thought to tell you.

"About an hour or so ago there was a group of fraternity boys over here from Pitt University. They were drunk and disorderly so my doorman refused them entry.

"There may be some connection but I don't know. I was with a patron at the moment, but I did hear the disturbance.

"Like I say, I..."

Morgan did not wait but cut in.

"Do you know who they may have been, anything at all, any of your girls know them? It's important Jenny."

Jenny felt her face blush at the suggestion that she didn't comprehend the seriousness but she made no comment.

She simply responded, "Just a moment, hang on, don't go way. I'll be right back."

Morgan leaned back in his chair with his good leg on the desk. He held the phone to his ear and as he was waiting he pinched his thumb and forefinger across his eyes.

Wetness came out and he rolled his moist thumb and forefinger together. His office door was slightly ajar and some weak light was intruding from the lobby.

Otherwise he was alone and he had never felt so alone. He was about to pinch his eyes again when Jenny returned.

"Morgan," she came back, "I don't know if there is any connection but one of the girls here is a part time actress.

"She doesn't know Sidney Griffin real well but she seems to recall that he belonged to a fraternity which goes by the name of Phi Simma Delta, Phi Smia Delta; something like that."

"She's pretty sure about the Phi and Delta part of the name but she's not too sure about the middle name except it starts with an 'S'.

"It's a group that's into dramatics, theater, acting, that sort of thing... uh just a moment...

"Hello, Morgan, she thinks its Phi Smia Delta. She thinks they have a fraternity house someplace along fraternity row over in Oakland." Morgan thanked Jenny for her help and also thanked her for going to be with Patricia.

It was around 2:00 AM when Jim Barkus and LeRoy 'Gimmie' Jones got back to the Stran. With his own key Jim let himself in through the outside door and went across the lobby to Morgan's office.

He couldn't see Morgan at first but he knew he was there. In words as slow and unexcitable as possible Jim related his findings. First, there was some news about the marijuana. A pusher up in the Hill District had put out three bags along about 6:30 P.M. to a fraternity group from over at Pitt.

"What did the group look like," asked Morgan.

"From the way he described, they must be a group of piss ass preppies," Jim answered. "All matching coats, hair oiled down, faggy talk. The pusher's with me. He's just outside if you want to talk to him." Morgan wave his hand no. When there was no follow up comment, Jim continued.

"The other thing is I have about thirty or forty men outside waiting. What do you want I should tell them?"

In spite of his hurting rage, Morgan was touched. A call of comraderie had gone out and it had been answered; in the middle of the night.

A short emotional feeling swelled up, a tiny wetness came to his eyes and a slight hurting smile touched his face.

"First," he responded, "express my appreciation; would you do that for me. By rights I should, but at the moment...

"Just tell each one of them I am much obliged. And make sure they know I mean it. When you're all done, ask Gimmie if he will stay and let the rest go; and again express my sincerest thanks.

"I have a pretty good idea now of what we are dealing with and I don't think we will be needing all that much muscle. I'm pretty sure the three of us, you me and Gimmie can handle it."

Over at Pitt University in Oakland there is a street named Bigelow Boulevard. It is an older neighborhood of single-family dwellings. In a style of the 20's most of the structures are wood frame, have large front porches and full-length oval glass in the front doors.

The houses are mostly two stories with the bedrooms upstairs and parlor, living room, dining room and kitchen downstairs. In its day the neighborhood was upper middle class and very prestigious. That was a long time ago. Now the houses have all been converted to student housing and the street is known as Fraternity Row.

It was shortly after 4:00 AM as Morgan, Jim Barkus and Gimmie Jones slowly idled a black 1939 Buick along the street. Silently edging along from house to house with a powerful spot light searching for the fraternity sign of each house; reading the name and then moving on.

It was toward the northwesterly end that the light came to rest on the one for which they were searching. There, hanging from the front porch was a faded, slightly askew sign with the words Phi-Smia-Delta.

At that pre-dawn hour the neighborhood was ghostly quiet. Early morning dew was just starting to cover the sidewalks and an eeriness reflected up from the streetlights. The silence was first broken by the parallel parking; then there could be heard the closing of three car door and steps on the concrete walk.

The next infraction of the silence was the shattering of glass as the big iron callused fist of Gimmie Jones smashed through the large oval glass of the front door. Reaching through, he quickly found the inside night latch, turned and unlocked the door and barged inside.

The light switch next to the inside door was found and the living room was immediately illuminated. With the speed of light Gimmie pounced across the living room and up the stairs two steps at a time to the second floor; followed on his tail by Jim Barkus.

Morgan's moves were not so rapid. He cautiously pulled his leg over the fragment of broken glass and was careful to place his cane on the solid floor. By the time he got completely inside, both Gimmie and Jim had disappeared into bedrooms and were out of sight.

Nevertheless, their sounds could be heard. Loud commotions were coming from the upstairs bedrooms. From what Morgan could determine doors were being smashed in.

As he looked around he surveyed the habitat of student living. College pendant flags and various movie posters were tacked to the walls. A life-size picture of Ann Sheridan and John Litel were at the top of the stairs.

The living room was semi partitioned off between a study zone and lounging area. The larger portion of the room, adjacent to the parlor side, was furnished with a large oval table and several straight back chairs. Study zone, he conjectured as he noticed the various textbooks and scattered writing paper.

The lounging portion of the living room was directly at the bottom of the stairs; a corner affair which had some semblance of a formal sitting area. In circular arrangement were three over stuffed easy chairs centered by a small wood coffee table. Easy chairs, as it turned out have some fall absorbing qualities. In the movies there are frequent scenes where suitcases are flung from the top of stairs and tumble smash landing on the floor below. Morgan had never seen a body thrown. Not up until then.

At the top of the stairs stood the monstrous body of Gimmie Jones.

Under his huge powerful black right arm he had a bear hug around the waist of a jockey clad yelling, kicking, screaming young man. Under his huge powerful left black arm Gimmie had a bear hug around the jockey-shorts clad waist of a second yelling, kicking, screaming young man.

The right arm was first in flight. As the body was unleashed it sailed airborne halfway down the stairs before it hit, bounced and came to rest at the bottom on one of the easy chairs. It was happenstance that the first body served as cushion for the flight of the second.

As Gimmie darted back to the bedrooms for seconds, Gentleman Jim Barkus stepped up to the head of the stairs; how-beit with only one young body in hand. And how-beit the young man's descent down the stairs was propelled, not by an airborne fling, but by the lifting power of a size ten boot; the bouncing, smashing, tumbling results at the bottom were none-the-less the same.

When it was over, the full house of twelve Phi Smia Delta fraternity brothers were in some stage of piled up arms, legs and bodies on the floor at the foot of the stairs. Some were moaning, some were sobbing, some were silent.

None were whistling, applauding, shouting, yelling, or cheering the whirling breast of Patricia Waters.

As the pile of young men lay crumpled in the corner, the powerful bodies of Gimmie and Jim stood looking on. Gimmie then glanced over at Morgan and Morgan gave a slight nod. On signal, Gimmie let out a roaring command and the room fell silent. All eyes now turned on Morgan. There was about to be thunder on the throne.

The woman of his life, the only woman he would ever love had been violated; and violated in the most despicable despising manner and now the guilty were going to pay. He had arrived with a ferocious appetite for searing revenge; a craving that could only be satisfied by the smashing and mangling of bodies.

But somewhere in the melodrama before him, his vengeful adrenaline went limp. With fire in his eyes, Morgan looked at the huddled young torsos. They, in turn, were simply just looking back. As he surveyed the pile of shaking young flesh, his vengefulness turned to a different kind of anger.

THERE WASN'T ENOUGH MEAT HERE! For the type of revenge he wanted there had to be an army of he-men. He wanted the entire football team, or the boxing team; some mean motherfuckers that could put up a fight. He wanted a clash of Titans where the earth would shake when a towering giant fist smashed into one of their faces. There had to be busting and shattering and hurling of bodies; the splintering and breaking of bones and furniture smashed to the end of a devastated war zone. When that army of Goliath's lay in a shattered, blood splattered pile he could walk out the door a revenged man.

How could he be so cheated. These, these scrawny, scared, insignificant collection of dippers, graduated to wearing jockey shorts.

He shook his head in apathy as he looked at the lot of them. Scared and shaking little bastards. For most of them it was probably their first time away from home, caught up in a violence they didn't even understand. A sense of what's-the-use came over him. *Poor little bastards,* he thought, *in a year, two at the most they will all be sleeping in mud, sleet and cold in a foxhole somewhere in Germany.*

Still, he would hold court. There had to be some retribution. He exhaled a tension relieving breath, removed his fedora hat and laid it on the large table. Awkwardly, he then drew up one of the straight back chairs and seated himself in front of the group. With deliberate slowness he ran his fingers back through his hair and slightly pointed his cane for Gimmie and Jim to stand aside.

"Now, boys," he started, "how about we establish the order of this little party. The first thing I want is for all of you to get your skinny little asses up on your feet. The second thing I want is for you to all line up here in front of me. I know most of you don't have any balls but at least pretend you do. DO IT!"

As they hurriedly obeyed his command he again felt cheated at the collection of meek thin bodies standing before him. But what had to be done would be done.

"Good. That's better," he commented as a line formed. "Now, let's talk about that little episode that went on down at the Underground earlier this evening." He paused to let them experience the dread of what was coming.

"Let's do some talking, shall we. The first thing I want to know is whose bright idea was this?" At first there was only silence to his question. That silence was quickly shattered, however, by his bellowing demand that someone speak up. Instantly, all twelve were talking at once. Morgan looked at Gimmie and Gimmie gave a roaring command to quiet down.

"OK," sighed Morgan. "We can't have everyone talking at once. Who is the leader here?" Intuitively all the young eyes turned to a tall, lanky young man who had raised his hand.

"Good," said Morgan, "now what's your name?"

"Jeffery."

"Jeffery what?"

"Jeffery Carotin, Sir."

"All right Jeffery Carotin, now suppose you tell how you came up with the bright idea that it would be so much fun for all of you to go down to the Underground and hide like rats in balcony while a little girl was goaded into humiliating herself?"

"Uh...well..."

"Speak up Jeffery! Speak up. Come come. You weren't so damn shy when you were hiding up in that loft. Speak up!"

"Well, Sir uh, it just kind of got started."

"It just got started! What? You were all just sitting around here bored and decided it would be great sport to go out and goat some innocent young woman into humiliating herself.

"Jeffery is that what you are telling me?"

"No sir. That wasn't the way it was at all, Sir."

"Then what are you telling me, Jeffery!"

"Well, I guess it all started when Sidney started hanging around here. It used to be that he would only drop by every now and then.

"But a couple of months ago he started coming by more and more.

At first he told us he was in the area because he was trying to get a job with the Oakland Playhouse.

"But I guess that didn't work out because he stopped talking about it.

"Then he would just come by to hang out. He had some pot and none of us had ever tried it so we did. Then it was more and more. It got to where we would light up everyday."

Jeffery paused as if not wanting to incriminate himself anymore than necessary. To Morgan, Jeffery had said all that was necessary.

His revenge against the fraternity had subsided but there was still a scorn to be dealt.

"This Sidney you speak of. Does he have a last name?"

"Yes Sir, its Griffin, Sidney Griffin."

"And why did you happen to get involved with this Sidney Griffin?"

"Uh, well he was a former fraternity brother, he was older and..."

"And you thought it was cool to have an older brother hanging around teaching you the facts of life?"

"Yes sir, I guess that's about it."

"Tell me Jeffery, how old are you?"

"Eighteen."

"Eighteen," he repeated in a tone of hopelessness.

"How about the rest of you?" he turned to the rest of the group.

"Anyone in here over eighteen?" Silence. Morgan then forced eye contact with each one.

"Just because Jeffery is doing the talking don't mean I am not going to get some of your butts too," he admonished.

"Didn't any of your mothers ever teach you anything about respecting other people's feeling?"

"Yes sir," responded several meek replies from the back.

"Yes sir, but you didn't learn very well did you?"

"No sir," came several answers. Morgan paused and cast a stern intimidating look of disgust at the group.

"So now you've come away to college, all grown up, and somebody a little older comes along and you think what he has to say is a lot more cool than what your mothers taught you; IS THAT WHAT YOU ARE TELLING ME?" he raised his voice rhetorically.

"NO SIR," came several redemptive replies.

"Well I am older and I am going to teach you something about respect for other people; in particular I am going to teach you to have respect for other people who may be a little different."

Morgan looked at Gimmie and motioned.

"Gimmie," Morgan started, "how much do you weigh?"

"Bout two ninety."

"And how tall are you?"

"About six eight."

"And what is the color of your skin?"

"It be black Mr. Morgan."

"What is the size of your arms?"

"Eighteen inches."

Morgan was now sitting straight up in his chair with both hands resting on the top of his cane. With piercing eyes firmly glued on the group he continued.

"Gracious, two hundred and ninety pounds, seven foot, black skin, eighteen inch arms. Would you consider yourself maybe a little different than the young men here in this group?"

Gimmie knew that no answer was necessary so he remained silent.

"I see," said Morgan as he continued staring at the students.

"Tell me Gimmie, where did you get the name 'Gimmie'?"

"Had it a long time."

"I know that, but where did you get it?"

"When I wus younger I got in the habit of saying to people 'gimmie a dollar, gimmie fifty cents'."

"So that sort of became your handle."

"About it."

"OK, so that makes you even a little more different. Now what if some of these young men decided to make sport out of mocking you; because you happen to be a little different.

"Tell me Gimmie, do you think you could do something about that?"

"Yes sur," announced Gimmie in a stern tone, "I certainly does believe I could handle dat little matter."

"But the lady which they goaded and humiliated tonight; she doesn't quite have your physical strength does she?"

"No sur, she shore do not."

"Does that upset you?"

"Yes sur, it does, it upsets me a lot."

"How about it," Morgan asked the group, "does anyone back there think it would be great sport to maybe poke a little mockery at our different friend Gimmie?" Silence.

"Well suppose that Gimmie became so upset he could not control himself. What if he decided that a mockery on that lady is a mockery on him? Do you still think it would be as much fun?"

"I see," he responded to the silence.

After another long stern look, Morgan signaled that the admonishment was over. He rose from his chair, picked up his fedora and was preparing to leave when Jeffery spoke up.

"Sir... excuse me sir," he said as he held up his hand, "...can I say something?" Surprised, Morgan turned and responded.

"What is it Jeffery?"

"Well sir, I would just like to say on behalf of myself and the fraternity. Sir, we are very very sorry for what we did. If there is some way we can make it up...

"Would you please tell the lady how sorry we are?"

Morgan couldn't help but notice how small and shinny he looked. Standing there in his under shorts with his hair askew and traces of dried blood out of his nose and mouth. Frightened but willing to step forward and accept responsibility for his acts.

The war clouds across Europe were getting darker every day. In a year the faith of our Nation will rest in his hands. Thank you God for giving America such fine young men.

A spark of charity ignited in Morgan and he was instantly sorry for his forceful actions. They are just boys he thought. He was about to extend forgiveness when Jeffery continued.

"If it had not been for that stupid Sidney and his stupid girl friend and her stupid kid..."

"What did you say!" exclaimed Morgan. Jeffery was startled by the outburst but started to repeat himself.

"I said we are sorr..."

"No, no, I mean about Sidney. What you said about Sidney's girl friend and kid."

"That's when it all started," Jeffery started explaining.

"We were doing just fine until they started coming around. First they wanted us to just baby sit while they went out dancing or whatever. Then came the pot. None of us smoked until they started bringing the stuff around.

"Him and his big ideas. He even told us how to dodge the draft. First this and then that. It just got out of control. But starting from right now, no more pot, no more booze and no more stupid Sidney."

Morgan was very careful how he worded his next question.

"I don't suppose you would happen to know where Sidney lives?" Without hesitation Jeffery replied.

"You mean where he keeps his skinny girl friend and her spoiled, snot nose kid? Yeah, we've all been out there several times. They like for us to all sit around and get high on pot while they put on sex shows for us to watch. It's over on the North side. Spring Hill Apartments on Lappe Street."

The closing of three car doors pierced the silent damp air for a second time on that early morning just before dawn as the three returned to the Buick. There was still no talking as Jim and Gimmie loaded in front and Morgan sat in back.

As Jim Barkus pulled the car away from the curb, Morgan took his hat off and laid it beside him on the seat. It was now after five AM. In the predawn light he put both hands up to his face and massaged back and forth. As the car nosed down the wide empty street they pass a garbage truck and the clanging of empty cans. Evidence that in a short time the city would be coming to life.

A little further down the street the silence in the car was very reservingly broken when Gimmie turn from the front passenger's side and glanced back at Morgan. In an unsure tone he placidly asked Morgan if they would be paying a visit to Sidney.

Morgan did not respond immediately. In deep thought he was gazing out the window. Gimmie continued watching and could see the strain in Morgan's face as streaks of early morning light flashed in between shadows of the giant Oak trees they were passing along the boulevard.

Without breaking his gaze Morgan finally responded in a tone which reflected a larger measurement. In a setting aside of personal vengeance for the obligation of a higher responsibility he said, "No, not tonight Gimmie."

Then as if explaining his decision he continued, "What good would it do?"

"Mess up his face a little, break a few ribs. For what? The son-of-a-bitch would be back on the street in a week.

"No, our friend Sidney is the type of slime which represents the scum of the earth. If it had not been Patricia it would have been someone else. He's a leech on society. A self-serving-taker and never a giver. He finds more pleasure in destruction than in contributing.

"No, what I have in mind is for the good of society. My contribution, you might say, to the war effort. So for now, let's just call it a night. And you, both of you, my gracious friends, I thank you."

Back in his office Morgan was thankful for the silence. He sat leaning back in his chair, pondered the string of events and watched the clock. Finally it was time for the workday to begin; 8:15 the time when the business world comes alive.

It was time for him to make two very important calls. With the telephone held to his ear he could hear the ringing sound of Jenny's phone on the other end.

"Hello," came a cautious feminine voice.

"Hello, Jenny this is Morgan. I just took a chance. I didn't know if you were home yet or still with Patricia."

"I just walked in Morgan. I've been over there most of the night. We made it through. It was terrible but things have now quieted down a bit and she seems to be doing a little better. Right now she's sleeping. She finally dropped off about an hour ago.

"I have Shelly with me and we are going to try and catch a few winks ourselves.

"Morgan," she instantly felt embarrassed at the start of her comment because she knew it was not necessary, "you may want to go over to the apartment a little latter this morning.

"I think she would like to see you. She's hurt pretty bad and it's going to take a while."

"I know," responded Morgan. "Don't worry, I'll be there when she wakes up."

"But right now I have a more pressing matter.

"Let me ask you, Jenny do you happen to remember awhile back that I made mention of pictures of Sidney having sex with your two girls; Detrick and Donna?

"I am embarrassed to ask, but did you, uh did it happen to happen?"

There was a silence and then Jenny not being quite sure asked, "You mean with Sidney and the two girls?"

"Yes."

"Yes, I have them. A full role in color already developed."

"Jenny, could you possibly get them ready. There may be someone coming by to pick them up?" Without any further inquiry or questions she simply answered.

"Of course."

"Thanks, Jenny. You know how much all of this is appreciated."

She could detect the strain and hurt he was suffering and tears came to her eyes. A compulsion came over her that she bit hard on her lip to control. As she felt the instant tearing of tissue she bit harder to keep from saying, *I love you Morgan.*

Instead there were just the words "Yes Morgan, By By" as she put the receiver back on the cradle.

Morgan had one more call to make. From his desk drawer he took out the business card of United States Federal Agent, William Blate.

When the phone was answered, Morgan asked for a Mr. Blate. "Speaking," came the reply.

"Mr. Blate you may not remember me, my name is Morgan, Morgan Smithfield."

"Of course Mr. Smithfield, you are the owner of the Stran. How can I help you?"

"Mr. Blate, you once asked me in the name of patriotic duty..."

"Of course. We are not interested in personal feeling Mr. Smithfield. The business we do is in the name of the people."

"May I ask," inquired Morgan, "what is the penalty for intentionally and premeditatedly dodging the draft; in particular dodging the draft under the guise of being a homosexual?"

"Uh, Mr. Smithfield is this something we should be discussing over the phone? Uh, if you would care to come to my off..."

"Mr. Blate, I am aware of the awkwardness of this but if you have no objection I prefer that we make this as brief as possible."

Agent Blate's many years of law enforcement told him of the tenseness on the other end. In a calming voice without emphasis or qualifications he replied in the simplest context.

"These are war time conditions Mr. Smithfield. The maximum penalty is execution by firing squad. Now having said that, most of the sentences have been 20 years at hard labor in a Federal Penitentiary without possibility of parole."

"What is the maximum penalty for possession, sale and distribution of marijuana and for contributing to the delinquency of minors?" There was a pause before Blate answered.

"Mr. Smithfield," he again inquired, "should we be discussing this over the phone. I will be happy to meet you...."

"No, No Mr. Blate. Please, I would like for this to be taking place under more pleasant circumstances but I am simply too overwrought. And I want to do it right now. First, assuming a worst case scenario, what is the time on the marijuana and the delinquency charges."

Morgan could hear a deep breath intake on the other end.

"Mr. Smithfield, I..."

"Roughly, how much?"

"Well the Federal Statutes call for a maximum of twenty ye..."

"Would they run concurrently or consecutively, I mean first one would have to be served before the second one starts?"

"Consecutively, first one then the other," came the answer.

"Mr. Blate the address on your card. Is it still your correct address?"

"Yes, certainly, but..."

"Mr. Blate you will be receiving some pictures delivered to you by one of my people. Whoever it is will not know anything so don't even ask. He or she will simply be making the delivery.

"The pictures themselves are self explanatory. I understand that the Sidney Griffin that you came to me about can be found in the Spring Hill Apartments on Lappe Street over on the north side.

"Now, you will be needing some collaborating witness. First, you may contact Miss Jenny Craig. You can reach her through me.

"Next I would like to talk to you about a fraternity and in particular I want to talk about cutting a deal. You get something if you give something."

Blate cautiously asked, "What is it you want?"

"The deal is this. You get their testimony if you give me your word that they go unharmed.

"By that I mean no charges, no record, no blemishes. To make this perfectly clear, I mean you can have their testimony only if they come away lily white."

Morgan could hear a clearing of the throat and then, "Mr. Smithfield, I, there is no..."

"LILY WHITE!!! Mr. Blate. Your word! I will not jeopardize the lives of these young men just to get one worthless slime like Sidney Griffin."

There was another small pause and then Blate started.

"You didn't let me finish Mr. Smithfield. I was about to say that there is no way I would ever jeopardize the lives of your young people.

"Now having said that I will hereby reinforce it. You have my solemn word Mr. Smithfield. On that I stand. I swear on my oath that no harm will come to these young men."

Morgan felt a touch of embarrassment, but he also felt good that he made absolutely certain about the point. Then he said, "Mr. Blate you may find it fruitful if you will talk to the fraternity Phi Smia Delta over at Pitt."

When they hung up Morgan felt a relief of tension and his energy drained. *The matter,* he thought, *has been squared, and we both have lost.*

Now Morgan was tired. He moved over to the sofa, unlaced his shoes, and stretched out. Before he felt up to going to Patricia he needed a few minutes of sleep.

With a crunched throw pillow under his head he listened to the silence. As he closed his eyes he pondered. *Beauty, grace, love, purity, fulfillment. How could a man like Sidney Griffin so promote these virtues in his daily vocabulary, and in his life still have such a vile disposition?*

He remembered again the plaque on Frank Buckwilder's desk; *truly, few things in life are as they seem.*

Chapter 23

The night of the hideous Underground cocoon dance did not end with the coming of dawn; consequences in life, once set in motion, generally direct their own destiny. Morgan knew and accepted the pattern of expanding rings from a pebble tossed in a pond of water. To his life would come additional consequence rings; of that his mind automatically accepted. Moreover, the odds were that they would all be bad. In his present need of a buffer against coming tomorrows, his mind planted seeds of a somewhere Garden of Eden; a longing free of smoke, congestion, noise and unsavory people. As he drifted off to sleep came a dream of distant hills, painted in purple, on a far away line of sky.

When the sounds of the city came to life the next morning Morgan woke with a startle on his office sofa. How long had he slept? He glanced at the wall clock, ten thirty; two hours. *Damn, damn. He had to get to Patricia. She may already be awake and alone.*

Feeling the aches and pains of the night as he stood up, he quickly unbuckled his belt, unbuttoned the top of his trousers, unzipped his fly and tucked in his wrinkled shirt. With his pants and shirt half-presentable he squirmed into his crumple jacket. His tie was loose and crooked but no matter. He ran his fingers through his thick mop of coarse black hair and with a little spit smoothed back the sides. Grabbing his hat he immediately started for the door and once again experienced the pangs of aggravation as he tried to get his leg to move faster. Outside he flagged a taxi with instructions to the driver to please hurry.

As the cab stopped in front of the apartment he scrambled out and immediately felt the morning air on his body sweat as he pulled his leg up the front steps. How could he face her? What could he say? There was dryness in his mouth and he was nervous as he knocked on the door.

"Patricia! It's me, Morgan. Baby are you in there?" he called as he continued to knock. "Patricia!" he called as he used his own key to let himself in. "Patricia? It's me, Morgan. Baby are you OK? His voice echoing in the empty living room as he closed the door behind him. Without hesitating he went directly to the bedroom.

Sprawled out across the double bed there she laid, fully clothed on top of the bedspread in a deep sleep. She was lying half on her stomach, half on her side with her face breathing into a semi-crunched up pillow. One arm was L shaped outward, the other was half buried under her body and her long hair fell skewed about her face

Morgan approached the bedside and for a moment watched as the only sounds were her breathing. Struck by her innocent and peaceful serenity he reached down and gently touched her hair. She made no stir. With his thumb and forefinger he lifted the skewed strands away from her cheek and let them fall to her back. It was then that the extent of her pain became evident. The anguish of total despair was chiseled into her face. Her normal creamy complexion was blotched with puffy redness and dried tear stains. He stood silently and looked for a long time. How vulnerable and faultless she appeared; a loving soul who had never on this earth caused harmed another living soul. As he watched her breathing, her pain became his pain and he wanted to assume her heartache; to take over her hurt and make it his hurt. A wish he could not be granted. In helplessness he straightened up, adjusted his twisted leg and slightly stepped back. Glancing around he looked for a place where he could sit and wait. He wanted to be by her side when she woke. He remembered there was a small make-up chair in the bathroom where she sometimes sat to apply night cream and brush her hair. It was in the course of getting that chair that he discovered the reason for her deep sleep. On the edge of the vanity was a small, brown prescription bottle. Snatching it up he immediately examined the label.

Damon Pharmacy, 346 Forbes St.,
Pittsburgh, Pennsylvania
Doctor: Daniel Owise, MD

#16372 05/1/41; 20 count
Seconal: 1 ½ grains/ capsule
Take one capsule at bedtime for sleep

In an instant frantic he removed the lid and looked inside. Six capsu... no wait seven, seven capsules. His hands trembling from panic he again looked at the number and date; 20 count, seven remaining, dated 05/1/41; over three years old.

Wheee, he breathed a sigh of relief. It was not a current prescription. Probably it was one that she had gotten when Shelly was born; thank God. *If she had been determined to do something drastic,* he reasoned, *she most likely would have taken the entire bottle.*

My ol' friend Dr. Owise, you sorry scum, he thought as he slightly rolled the bottle between his thumb and forefinger, *it seems you are back in my life again. Now what to do? Take the bottle and keep it away from her? Alternatively, put it back to avoid suspicion.* Reluctantly, he put it back.

The first days following the Underground calamity were the lowest ebb of both Patricia's and Morgan's lives. Low for Patricia because of her having suffered ordeal. Low for Morgan because he was powerless to help. The soul and spirit inside of her had simply curled up and died; leaving an empty shell void of any function other than the motions of living. The new-life Patricia that she had enjoyed for a brief moment was gone; never to return. She now dwelled in the life of the old Patricia and existed in an abyss where there was darkness but no hurt. She had no need to talk because there were no feelings, wishes, desires or dreams to express.

Morgan lived in a world of extended reaching; every hour of every day trying to reach out to her. Sadly, his extended hand could only grasp the fog in which she lived.

When it became necessary for him to go out of the apartment on business matters he did so with reluctance and returned as quickly as possible. During those first days they moved about the apartment in a meaningless function of existing; from the kitchen, to the bath, to the living room. If the two happen to move at each other she would step to the side of Morgan and never to him. In the close confines of the small apartment he frequently tried to gather her in a loving squeeze or hug but to no avail.

The body he was attempting to hug would go limp. She would turn her face to the side to avoid eye contact and simply let her arms dangled in none resistance.

It hurt Morgan to be rebuff but he kept his feelings in check. *In time,* he would tell himself. *It will just take time.* As an outlet and to take up the void he increasingly paid more attention to Shelly. Because of his leg he spent most of the time sitting in the big easy chair; and she playfully started climbing up into his lap. He found saintliness in her baby softness and remembered the baby game of hand clapping paddy-cake-man.

A game connected bonding started materializing as they clapped hand-in-hand "paddy-cake, paddy-cake, baker man..."; once never being enough. If he indicated a stopping she would squeal more, more.

"Hey now," he would frequently challenge. "Hold on here just a Pittsburgh minute. You're dealing with a very important man here.

"And a very important man like me can't afford to be a push over; no sir, not by a long shot. A very important man has to be tough and he has to make sure he gets paid for his efforts. This paddy-cake man business takes a powerful lot of work and I don't seem to be getting any hugging and kissing for my effort. Now what do you think we ought to do about that? A man can't stay in business if he works for free now can he?"

Shelly would then make payment of a hug and a tiny kiss and the game would start over again. Initially Patricia was indifferent. Most of the time she simply lay by herself on the bed. The sounds of clapping hands, the singing words paddy-cake, paddy-cake, baker-man, Shelly's squeals, and Morgan's laughter however carried to the bedroom in an unexpected way. The sound of happiness to a mind in depression tends to kindle resentment and she reacted by taking Shelly to herself.

"Come baby, it's time for our bath. Would you like to take a bath with Mommie?" As the next ring of consequence came into existence, Morgan adjusted by waiting until Patricia was sleeping to play with little Shelly. He began to notice a pattern that in the afternoon she would start becoming drowsy and lie down. On a hunch each day he would quietly go to the bathroom and check the bottle of sleeping pills. Six, then five and then four and the time of Patricia's sleeping became a time for Morgan and Shelly.

"Why Mommieee sleeppping so much?"

"Honey, your mother has been through a very bad experience and she is trying to heal her hurt."

"Whatttt kinnnd of hurttt? "

"Well, Sweetheart, she was hurt very deep by some mean ol' college boys."

"Whyyy dayyy hurt Mommieee?"

"Well, Baby, your mother was born a little different from other women and these college kids were very cruel and made fun of her and it hurt her very much."

"Dayyy laughhh attt Mommieee?"

"Yes, Honey, but they could not have known how much it hurt. They were just having fun. Sometimes though having fun can hurt people very much. So, when you get older, always remember how much it hurts if you make fun of someone."

"Whoo dattt colleggg boysss?"

"College boys are just kids who have grown up and gone away to school. College is school."

"Sheleee no likeee colleggg."

"Oh, Sweetie it's not the college, it's the young people who don't think about what they are doing."

"Sheleee no likeee colleggg."

"You mustn't say that Baby, I know that you don't understand now but when you grow up you'll be going away to college just like all the other kids."

"No! Not Sheleee, I neverrr go dat colleggg. I hateee dat theyy hurt Mommieee."

In one of Patricia's sleep times and with Shelly in his lap, Morgan called his office.

"Wat dat you dooing dat tel phonnee?"

"Why I am going to call my office and make some big decisions. An important man like me has to make important decisions on the telephone. That's how people know you're important."

"Tan Sheleee make portanttt cissionsss on tel phonnee?"

"Well, now I don't know. You have to be a really important person to make an important call on the telephone. Are you a very important person?"

"Yesss! Yesss! Sheleee bery portanttt personnn. Can tlk on dat tel phonnee."

"You're sure now, you're sure I can trust you when you tell me you are really, really important?"

"Uh huh, releeey portant, pleaseee."

"Well, since it had been established that you, Shelly Waters, are a dyed-in-the-wool, documented, bona fide important person, then I think it is time that you made an important call.

"It sure don't do no good to be a very important person if you can't make some ' portant decisions. Now suppose we call up my general manager and you tell him some orders. Would you like that?"

"Yesss, yesss, Sheleee talkkk phoneee, pleaseee."

"You're sure now, that you are very important?"

"Yesss, Sheleee, BERRY portant".

"Well I think you are too. OK, the first thing we have to do is dial. Now here's what you have to do. First, give me your finger, here we go, put it in this hole, see that? That's a number three, now pull it all the way around until it stops. Now we need to pull a six. Can you show me a six? Good, now pull

"Now let it go, see how it goes back. OK now a four, then six again.

"Now, listen, hear it ring. Hear that? It's ringing on the other end."

"Hello, Hello, Stran Theater." After that, Shelly and Morgan would frequently call the Stran and Shelly would always say, "Disss is 'bery portant phonee calll".

The diversion of games with Shelly however was only shallow camouflage over the heaviness of his mind. For a brief time in their lives, Patricia had opened up and come to him. She had showered him with affection and his life had been exalted. Then, in a heartbeat, it had all come crashing down.

Why? Why is life for some so natural, while for others it is so precarious; what so profit life that it be so brutal?

For Patricia, there were her own but equal thoughts. *Why?* She kept asking. *Why me? What is my sin that I must suffer so?*

Somewhere it came to Morgan that answers, if any there were, lie in getting away, and he made the decision that they were going to get out of that apartment.

In the darkness before dawn a morning later with only a minimum amount of preparation, Morgan, Patricia and Shelly loaded into his big four doors black 1939 Buick.

"Shouldn't we be taking some food or extra clothes?" Patricia reluctantly inquired even as she gave in over her own objections.

"Whatever we need," Morgan answered reassuringly, "someone will already have when we get there."

Possibly for reasons of delaying the first step of venturing out she non-the-less packed a few things in a small suitcase and as they were going out the door, she grabbed Shelly's favorite blanket. With the apartment door locked and the car loaded Morgan started the engine, edged out from the curb and they got underway. Maneuvering through a maze of dew covered, overcast checkerboard streets they headed south to southeast until they intersected with U.S. Highway 40, and then turned easterly toward the foothills of the Allegheny Mountains.

By mid-morning the smoked clogged skies over Pittsburgh had given way to crisp blue horizons and brisk clean air. Steel mills, coal barges and slag piles were replaced with farmsteads, fence lines and fresh mowed fields. The traffic-free macadam road in its endless pursuit wove through rolling terrain and the crest of each new hill brought a higher panoramic view of pristine meadows, grazing livestock and a distant mountainous skyline. The vigorous air of the countryside gradually chipped away at the melancholy of Patricia. Little by little her tenseness started to subside and a feeling of guarded serenity began to surface; and then something unexpected happened.

An awareness of Pennsylvania's history started to materialize. First brought on by noticing the still present massive four-foot-high obelisk Highway 40 Concrete Mile-Markers that were put in place at the time of original survey by George Washington. Once the first mile marker was notice, looking then started to see the second and then the next; and being the person to first see each next obelisk monuments became a victory win; as the Buck wheeled along on war-time gas rationing.

From mile marker monuments the car-game gradually grew to include other historical bronze commemorative plaques; some of which they would pull over to the side of the road and read.

At a restored historical road-toll house they pulled over and stopped. In getting out of the car Morgan unassumingly lifted little Shelly and attempted to walk and carried her. The sight of Morgan's struggling re-triggered Patricia's hurt. She quickly reached for Shelly with a cold comment that it would be safer if she carried her child. Without protesting Morgan simply surrendered; *time,* he thought as he felt the release. *God please heal with time.*

Back in the car the feeling of the open road relaxed Morgan to take off his fedora hat and toss it in the rear seat; where it would remain for the rest of the trip. As the foothills of the Allegheny Mountains continued to rise, he pushed the heavy smooth ride of the Buick on eastward on the two lane-winding road. As they topped the crest of each new hill the panoramic view became further than the one before; and the declining road of each higher crest being steeper and longer than the one before. It was near mid-day when they started down an unusually lengthy decline. After hugging the downhill curving pattern in due time the horizon opened up and the road dropped into a small rural community; where the terrain widened into a valley; and they decided it was a good place to stop.

Pulling into the gravel and dirt driveway of a Gulf Service Station/ General Store they were greeted by two gasoline pump sentinels. One ethyl, one regular, which stood with their tanks made of glass perched precariously on top of one-arm levers where gasoline first had to be pumped to the top of the glass tank and then gravity fed through a hose to the car tank. Leaving the car doors un-locked, windows down, in the driveway the first thing they did was to walk around in back where relief was found in the manner of two wooden outhouses.

With nature abated they entered the store and browsed through the aisles of general merchandise, hardware and food goods. In total they bought ten gallons of gasoline @ fifteen cents per gallon plus ration stamps, six bottles of Coca-Cola in hour-glass green bottles, three cans of Vienna sausages, one loaf of Holsum bread, a jar of pickles, 1 lb. of baloney, mayonnaise, one spreading knife, napkins, potato chips and three Baby-Ruth candy bars. Back in the car they continued driving eastward until they came to a roadside pull-off and a gurgling fresh mountain stream.

Under a warm mid-day sun and a soft cross breeze they ate a picnic lunch on the out cropping rocks worn smooth over time by flowing, gushing, white foamy water. Their mood continued to become more relaxed and small talk increased in the scenic beauty and tranquillity. With the picnic over and the drive continued, the chemistry of Morgan and Patricia gradually started blending to frequently looking at each other, exchanging faint smiles and gazing at the wondrous outdoors.

A second ring of consequence had started with the rediscovery of the bigger outside world. A world of renewed awareness of open land, bounty from the fields, fragrance of pine trees, and a beckon to a more docile life style; a renewed state of mind where time is measured, not by a clock, but by the sinking sun. Nearing sundown, they pulled into and spent the night at a motor lodge in Gettysburg.

The next morning, they did what all visitors to Gettysburg do. They toured the Gettysburg National Military Park and Cemetery; a remembrance place where the insane senseless waste of human life had one of its finest hours; a place in history where two American armies ran up against each other. The Confederate Army, 75,000 strong under the command of General Robert E. Lee and the Union force 88,000 strong under the command of General George Gordon Meade.

In three days of slaughter fighting, the Confederate Army suffered 28,000 casualties including 3,155 dead, 5,425 missing and 18,735 wounded. The U.S. Army of the Potomac had 23,000 casualties counting 3,000 plus dead, 5,365 missing and 14,529 wounded.

The most remembered event being when General Lee gave the order for his troops under the command of Longstreet make a frontal assault up a rolling hill through the center of the Union lines in hopes of dividing their forces. When Lee gave the order to his second-in-command, General Longstreet was reluctant but saw to its execution in what has become known as Pickett's Charge. A name begotten because of the combined commands of Pettigrew, Trimble and Pickett headed across an open field into the point blank range of field artillery and the full line of Union forces to the most massive human butchery in American history. Two thousand acres have been set aside as a memorial to that carnage.

In an atmosphere that always hangs heavy in the air, both Morgan and Patricia toured the grounds in silence. Each was thinking of their individual plight in relation to this massive butchery. For Patricia there were silent feelings of anger that men in such numbers would abandon the responsibility of their homes, wives and children for the pursuit of such an idiotic cause.

She personally felt the loneliness, the despair, the hopelessness of the forsaken loved ones who had been left back home to fend for themselves. *Men men men,* she cursed their contemptuous souls, *in the name of glory they show total disregard for the consequences of their actions in killing and being killed. And double the curse on the commanders who stand safely in the background and give the orders.*

For Morgan the chapter of Gettysburg reflected a different perception; the unexpected question of the evolutionary order of man. Without expectation, his mind sought out reasons as to why; why all of this. What good did it do? What did they hope to prove? If to him the whole idea was senseless, than surely those whom were responsible would have known better. And yet, they did it. What if...just maybe what if the overall direction of man is guided by the species of 'man as a whole' and not individuals who direct the course? That would mean that the men who are standing there at that time and place are simply pawns in the actions of the species.

In the time element of mere seconds, and without his being cognizant, Morgan's kept racing on the issue of why. In circumstances where a species has natural predators, a safeguard system against over-population is held in check by natural losses. Man on the other hand has no natural predators to keep the population in check. It then becomes a self-fulfilling prophecy for man's self to do that which must be done. If man did not kill himself off, then the world would long ago have become so overpopulated that there would be insufficient resources to sustain life; and the whole of the species would have been endangered.

Morgan abruptly brought back his self-awareness. He found no comfort in allowing the scope of man's plight to become his own responsibility. He had a life of his own to manage

When Morgan, Patricia and Shelly left Gettysburg the next day they headed north toward Lancaster; the heart of Amish country and a dramatic contrast in 'reverence' to mother earth. At Gettysburg, man had seen fit to use the land as a carnage arena. In Lancaster the Amish believe that the intentional taking of a life is abominable. These docile gracious, isolated people whose lives are guided by a strict separation from worldly influences.

A conservative people, they adhere to old-world ways of men wearing beards and 18th century clothing. Their purpose for living is preordained and is for reasons other than pleasure.

They farm the land with great reverence and refuse to use motorized machinery, vehicles or electricity. As Morgan's black Buick followed the narrow macadam road past the rich fertile fields of picture perfect crops, they entered a realm of different serenity. The atmosphere communicates a respect for quietness; and to all whom enter there... a desire to stop along the road and touch the rich loamy soil; and to compliment Mother Earth on her beauty. A respect is fostered to be overly courteous and considerate.

On the roads of Lancaster County, horse drawn carriages are the main mode of family transportation. High wheeled buggies of black-covered-canvas carry men, women and children moving in time with their destiny to the rhythm of a single horse clopping a rhythmic gait; people whose march in life is to the beat of a different drummer. In approaching these buggies from behind, Morgan would slow the big black Buick down to an idle, hang back in respect, then pass in cordiality. There was no compulsion to hurry in this quiet land.

At noon they ate lunch at a farmstead restaurant in an atmosphere of wholesome home style cooking served by rosy cheeks girls wearing floor length dresses with white aprons and net weave small white bonnets. That night they slept in a motor court lighted by kerosene lamp. In the quietness of the night when the lamps were turned out and Shelly slept, Morgan and Patricia shared thoughts of the day. How different were these people. It would be inconceivable that they would cast dispersions upon a human that was born with or suffered any degree of abnormality. In lingering talk they contrasted the destiny of Gettysburg and the manner in which the Amish choose to utilize the land.

A comparison which put their own state of mind in a different perspective and they went to sleep in each other's arms; closer now than the days before.

From Lancaster they drove to Erie, PA. The next few days they spent on the shores of beautiful Presque Isle; a spectacular peninsula of ecological phenomenon that juts out into the waters of Lake Erie. On an isolated beach they had spread Shelly's blanket on the sandy shoreline and bask in the warm sun. As sand castles formed in the hands of their child, Morgan and Patricia gazed out at the source of all life; water... in its endless, ever-endless docile waves lapping upon the sand.

In a rare phenomenon, out of the vastness of Lake Erie there came to Patricia an unexplainable chemistry from the water; the mother of all life. A silent feeling shared only between she and the intuitive soul of Mother Water; as the two became lost unto themselves on the warm sun-drenched sand they communicated in their own privacy. In metaphysical realms they talked to each other, Patricia and Mother Water; they communicate the wonderment of life and what it means. Without spoken words, there materialized in Patricia a realization of fulfillment, of contentment, of serenity and of purpose. The first purpose of woman is to bring forth life. This silent message Mother Water brought to Patricia. A woman is first a mother, then mother to child in order next to man.

A fleeting instant...or was it longer...and time had simply stood still, they bonded in sisterhood, the one on the shore understanding the message by the one in the water.

Then, once understood the communications were just as quickly over. Mother Water returned to her home in the blue and Patricia's attention came back to her child and man. She then reached out and smoothed a small area of sand and with her index finger wrote the words *Patricia Smithfield and Shelly Smithfield*. Turning back to Morgan, a tiny smile came to her face. Holding their eyes in contact she then spoke to Shelly. "Baby Doll... why don't you see if you can persuade Daddy Morgan to go and buy us some ice cream."

The following day started their drive back home. And somewhere in the time zone following the setting sun, between Lake Erie and Pittsburgh, when Shelly was asleep in the back seat and their own talking had subsided, she turned to Morgan and looked at his face in the soft light cast by the dashboard.

"When we get back," she alluded to the feeling brought to her by Mother Water, "maybe its time... maybe we could... maybe...maybe I'll stop working before too much longer."

With the road to themselves, the big 1939 black Buick sped on through the night with high beams brightly showing the way. Out before them lay an open road and to their silence came the hum of tires upon the macadam as the miles passed and their royal coach carried them homeward toward a new life.

Hope upon hope, were the thoughts in Morgan's mind as he drove in silence. *A frail patch has formed over the gaping crevice. And for that dear God I am heavenly thankful. Hope and prayer that life brings forth no more harm or hurt. Prayer to God, do not let this frail stitching falter but let it grow in strength. Grant my prayer in the name of love and benevolence. For I fear there is not enough strength left nor would her will-to-live be strong enough to withstand another on slough.*

Chapter 24

In the Allegheny Mountains of Central and Western Pennsylvania the autumn leaves make their début early; fashion designer Mother Nature usually schedules her fall showings around mid-October.

This year for the first time Morgan and Patricia attended most of the performances; in the mode of being inseparable they took scenic drives, they had picnic lunches, they walked in the wilderness and they felt humbled by Mother Nature's grandeur. To see the best of nature's painted landscape meant traveling the winding miles out beyond the realm of urban influence. By daybreak each morning Morgan's black 1939 Buick would already be on the road. By the time the first clearly definable red streaks of dawn painted the eastern sky they had uncapped a thermos. Each with a cup of hot coffee in hand they jointly welcome the first rays of sun coming in through the on-looking windshield.

For them it was a time when their days were balmy content and endless. The beginning of each new day starting where the prior day left off; which had been taken up from that day prior. Somewhere along these wandering miles a joint fantasy had materialized; a dream of finding some secret place they could call their own. In their shared thinking their best chances of such a hide-a-way would come from getting off of the main highway and driving the secondary back roads. Preferably those which were dirt and graveled but little used; where the hillsides were more densely vegetated and where Mother Nature could give a full showing of her stupendous colors.

In search of this quest their daily pilgrimage increasingly headed them toward an easterly thin purple line cast upon the horizon and told of far distant hills; hills that called to those in love seeking a hide-a-way nest in the wilderness. On such an obscure winding back road with the car speed slowed to an idle they rounded a bend and came upon a setting.

The composite being one that only God could have painted. His lead-in creation first being a meandering small stream of clear babbling snow water flowing in its wandering route along the road edge. The front-face of a gently sloping hill of unspoiled flora traversing up to a rounded crest; crowned with a majestic Elm Tree. When the paint strokes His Master portrait were complete He then embellished the frame. A natural widening of the road; that chariots passing in review are afforded a place of linger.

It was mid-morning of a perfect day as Morgan and Patricia pulled to the side, turned the ignition, and succumbed to the hypnotic of what their eyes beheld. In silence they set side by side stirring only for a better view as their hands searched across the seat one to the other. In code used for the first time, a squeezing that communicated their unspoken unison that this was the place. Sealed with an exchange of smiles and a front seat hug, each turned to their door, stepped out of the car and felt for the first time the invitation of the road surface beneath their feet.

Taking a blanket, a hot thermos and each other's hand the two started exploring. Crossing the babbling stream came by natural stepping-stones that were accommodating to the degree of an ice cold drink of pure mountain water. The flora was plentiful but not thicket and beckoned zigzag trail finding. The slope to the crest was challenging but possible. Morgan used his cane for balance and Patricia assisted with the difficult steps. Together they climbed to the summit for a look-see. And what they saw was magnificent beyond their dreams; dreams with an unlimited view.

As virgin as God had left it, there were no harsh or defacing scars left by prior man across the rolling face; and they wondered why? There were no signs of prior tire cuts defacing the road surface and they wondered why. Standing as they were at the very peak, it readily becoming apparent that there were additional particulars about this hill that set it apart. At the higher elevation line above the natural ground cover, the apron was rolling grassland, absent of trees save one; the picture perfect Elm standing at the very crown. Standing as it was, in the posture of a stately Queen this lone Elm stood in vigilance over her domain.

From her choice vantage, she kept a watchful eye over a vast expanse of rolling apron that blended into the lower consolidated foliage.

Perfectly dress in her leaves of autumn gold, Miss Elm beckoned visitors to come and share her unexcelled view. An invite which Morgan and Patricia enthusiastically accepted. In a moment in time when rush or hurry had no place, Morgan spread the blanket. In leadership and dominant of the relationship he adjusted his recline leg, dropped down to a setting position and extended his hand to Patricia. As she also came to a setting position she tilting her head over and rested on his shoulder. For the initial few moments they simply gazed in silence; captivated by the unparalleled beauty in the valley below. Then gradually their silence gave way as each started pointing out to the other the endless array of blends and colors.

Euphoric in their setting, the thermos was again uncapped and they shared another cup of steaming coffee; in two they sipped, savored and then stretched out on the blanket and lapsed once more into a quiet peaceful lull. Patricia readjusting slightly to get a better half-doze view brought her head to rest on Morgan's chest. In the silence of the land, soothed by the warmth of the autumn sun and the tranquil pleasures of touching, they drifted off into a light sleep and succumbed to their separate dreams.

At sometime later, near mid-noon Patricia half woke and through the narrow lids of her partially closed eyes she again gazed at the array of golden leaves cast against the clear blue sky. Gently adjusting her head on Morgan's chest she spoke without expecting a response.

"A penny for your thoughts."

A pause drifted by before he responded.

"Daydreams," he answered in dozing affection, "I'm just kind of daydreaming."

"Daydreaming?" she asked with a still sleepy question. "What kind of daydreaming?"

"Oh wild, nonsensical personal fantasy type daydreams. Kind of silly but pleasant."

"So?" she indicated innocent inquiry. "Tell me, please."

Morgan feigned a slight laugh at thinking of how he would ever describe the wild dimensions of his fantasizing.

"It is," he spoke in a tone-of-talking to himself, "amazing how rapidly one's mind can conger up a fantasy and then how fast it can jump from one situation to another." He paused in search of words that would reflect the nonsensical trail.

"They jump with lightning speed from here to there and who knows where. What starts here is next over there and then somewhere else," his explanation implying that dreams can never be accurately described.

Describe or not, the manner of his talking caused Patricia to feel a stirring sensation. An electrical charge of positive electricity tingled the soft hair on her arms. Not for want of sex but from the thought of a new realm into which she could possibly pass; an instant thought she had of how it would be to leave her own body and enter his. A feeling that if she could merge herself into his fantasies then unimaginable voyages would be theirs for the taking.

In her own instant fantasy, if they merged together they could frolic in unlimited bounds; in and out of dreams wherever they pleased. Hand in hand, side-by-side they could sail, soar, wade, or walk; roll in powder puff clouds or stroll in green valleys; explore castles in Spain or make love in the moonlight on shimmering desert sands. In whimsical jester she persisted in her want to enter into this new land. To her own surprise she blurted out words she had never used before.

"I never told you this," she spoke in rebuttal, "but I am really, really very fast and I can move as fast as any ol' daydream." Then to reinforce her jest, she charmed.

"Would you like to try me? I am really super, super fast at jumping around. Please," she begged.

Morgan was both surprised and pleased with her playful lure. After her now in the past night of horror he had come to assume that laughter and tease would no longer be a gift of her character. And this tiny breakthrough was a spark he wanted to encourage. In a manner suggesting reluctance, he responded.

"Well, I don't know now. When you start dealing with a man's fantasies you are dealing with some pretty powerful stuff."

She slightly turned her head so that his sideways glance could see her face and without saying a word simply puckered out her bottom lip and held a look of pouting. The power of a pouting lip; brought a small laugh and he playfully surrendered.

"OK, you win," he started.

"But this here fantasy is not just any ol' fantasy. No sir, it's a very complicated fantasy. For want of a better description I'll call it the sisterhood of women and trees. And essentially it's been a sort of leap frog series of pictures which have jumped about at their own free will, but it does border on prose."

"You mean something like a poem or sonnet?" she asked, pleased that she was getting her way.

"No," he slowly replied. "If I wasn't a man, cause 'he-men' don't do this sort of thing, I suppose you could call it romantic. If it was a woman, then it could probably be considered romantic, or at least I think it would probably romantic; but not in the sense of poetry. In my way of thinking a poem has to use words that rhyme. Now the way I see poems, rhythm and rhyme generally take precedent over substance; credibility suffers at the expense of verse and the relevance of the story becomes secondary.

"No," he paused for emphasis, "if I am going to tell this, and I am not sure that I can, I have thoughts of talking in terms of pictures. What my mind's eye sees and how it all seems to related to our own lives."

"And," Patricia spoke in a way that made it easy for him to continue, "what is it of the sisterhood between woman and trees that you think to tell me?"

"Actually, it's of men, women and trees," he said implying he might as well get started.

"But if I do tell it, do I get to talk romantic?"

"Ohooo Of course," she purred.

"Really romantic," he teases.

"Uhooo Yes, really romantic," her tone now hinting that you-are-trying-me.

"Really, really romantic..."

"Morgan!"

"OK," he grinned. "Just checking. It all started while I was half gazing at one of those young sapling tree lower down on the hill," he made a nodding gesture.

"And from there my mind jumped to this beautiful fully mature perfectly shaped tree that we are laying here under. Then somehow or another I started comparing the two in terms of a life line; or say youth and maturity if you will."

He slightly turned and glanced at her tentative eyes and when she did not say anything he continued.

"Words can never describe a picture, but in my mind's eye the comparison of that young sapling and this towering Elm jumped to a similar analysis of women; or actually girls, women, old men, young men, maturity men and it all traveled something like this.

"In this daydream the scene starts in early spring as the snows of winter are starting to melt and the cycle of new life begins. Young mothers give birth to new baby girls and Earth gives life to new sapling trees.

"In some sort of a forest setting, the proud young mothers with their youthful figures are in dress-up fashion, including high heels to show their shapely legs, and are pushing baby strollers along a cleared winding path through the middle of mature trees where young saplings have sprang up.

"It's almost as if it's a warm Easter morning and women-mothers and tree-mothers, all dressed in their Sunday best are out for a stroll and as they pass they pause to compare each other's babies.

"Then somehow in this fantasy the multiplicities of the many women-mothers become just one mother. And the picture is then just the one mother on this path in the forest at the dawning of a new day. As the rays of a rising sun are just beginning to cast streams of light through the trees she is pushing her stroller easterly; into the early morning sun. Then I see a tired homeless old man coming from the opposite direction. Moving slowly down the same path, shuffling westerly away from the sun.

"From his silhouette she can tell he is short stature, has a full matted beard, is stooped and weather beaten from enduring the miseries of a hard cold homeless winter. He has on layers of tattered dirty clothes that tell of sleeping on the ground.

"As he gets a little closer it can be made out that he is wearing a black cap with an upturned bill and untied ear flaps. Shaggy matted hair is falling around his collar and blends into his beard. Half gloves without fingers show his stiff thick fingers and his squinted eyes water at the strain of trying to see.

"He is nearing the end of life, this old man coming away from the sun toward the stroller; which carries the beginning of life and heading to the sun. Shuffling along the freshly cleared path in his shaggy clothes, he has no place to go. His time is short and he is seeking only a warm dry place until the end.

"At this point, the fantasy narrows to just the baby in the stroller and a young sapling tree. Somehow the two, the baby and the sapling, blend into just one; and the baby sort of becomes the body for both.

"And the baby's mind quickly realizes that it, the baby, is just starting out on life's journey. A natural realization that it is just entering the path. In an intended faith the first person that the baby meets is life's end. They meet; the end and the beginning, they pause and look one to the other. As they look face to face there is a meeting of their eyes.

"As the infant baby-tree looks upward the old man looks down. With fingers coarse and stiff he reaches down and lightly touches the baby's delicate new skin and feels the celestial softness. Then he reaches to the tender branches of the sapling tree. To his nostrils of matted hair, he brings a branch of blossoms and smells the fragrance of spring. In this fleeting moment they bond, this life beginning and this life ending. Then, with a nod of understanding and a watering of eyes they pass.

"The cycle cannot be stopped as time moves on; even to the land of cherry trees the blossoms soon will fall and from the baby the smell of freshness will fade.

"In this same time frame there is an earlier generation of young boys passing from adolescence into young men. Their interest is not yet centered in maturing young girls or new growth trees but in adventure. With developing firm bodies, sun drenched skin and unruly wind blown hair they have a need to test the elements. When the winter snows start to melt their eyes turn to the highland and answer the call of chilling spring. Clad in knee length shorts and new hiking boots they strap on bulging backpacks and set out to explore virgin forest, drink from gushing snow melting streams and swim nude in ice cold mountain lakes. To prove their manhood they scale towering cliffs, seek the thrill of danger and sleep alone in primitive lands.

"But theirs is also a time in flight and soon there will be a different call; seasons on the mountain must also be left behind; for on the low lands, the young girls and young trees have now grown and become the call of young men's interest.

"As spring blends to summer, fresh sprouting saplings mature and branch into exciting full bodies. Fresh and young, our feminine trees with their shapely figures strut their stuff. Sassy and defiant, they challenge the summer breezes to test the vigor and spunk of their flexible young limbs. Young girls with budding firm nipples dress up in their first pair of nylon hose and high heel shoes and parade the boardwalk with shapely firm legs. All of our young maidens and our tender trees have become sisters in the flower of womanhood; full of life, flighty and seeking excitement.

"And the time has come for the young men with their tight firm bodies to abandon their pursuit of mountain adventure. In search of romance, chivalry and nobility they rush to the charms of waiting young virgins. Somehow the many young men become just one, but then, the one is still they. And under the inviting firm branches of maturing trees, these young men find their first love and carry her away to the land of Camelot where they romance her under bright starry nights and cool evening air.

"In pursuit of their love they dance with her in black tuxedo to the sound of violins as they whirl away the nights on marble gardens in Morocco and Spain. They mortgage their souls to bring her trinkets of gold, precious stones and vintage wines. In vain they plead that she will never ever go away.

"But time moves swiftly in youthful love and summer matures so quickly. A change is stirring within our maiden tree and, in mystery she doesn't know why; she glances to the distant north, searching for what she does not know."

"And as summer slips away, the beg of young men that she must never go away is lost to a stronger call.

"The days of autumn are coming and her time now must pass to an older man; a man of maturity, experienced and understanding. Such men were also thinner once; as they went off to war. In the supreme test of courage they endured the horror of deadly combat, long freezing sunless winters, bomb craters, tangled barbed wire and mine fields. Through endless nights they huddled together in cold as cannons roared and flashes lit up the smoke filled skies.

"Life had been measured in minutes then, as they watched their comrades die. But, because some single one of them stood strong, they all stood strong; pulling strength from one another they held fast, these young men with their thin firm bodies and ever present dreams of returning home to the waiting arms of the young women they left behind.

"Without flinch they stood before the mighty foe, in resolve that the God given right to be free, would forever be. But that was way back then, when he went off to war.

"His body is thicker now and his wind blown hair is thinning. He walks with a slower pace and the lines on his face tell of the trying hardships that he has endured.

"In search of solitude he returns to the primitive lands; whence once he found adventure when he was thin.

"In Autumn, he walks with upturned collar amongst trees with painted leaves. For this manner of man now find his beauty in women of maturity. To his eye she is in the zenith of desire. She is sexually appealing not for the caliber of her sexual favors but in the manner and poise in which they are dispensed.

"Alone in the forest he sits in solitude and watches with arousal as our tree of maturity softly and unhurriedly releases the leaves from her up-stretched arms and they float lazily down; like feminine garments which come to rest on a carpeted floor. In unhurried time he finds excitement more in the suggestion than in the quest. The leaves go first from her higher branches, slowly next will be her bosom cleavage. In crescendo, his attention is heightened as the center of her life is held for the last.

"She is careful to hold his attention, this mature tree of autumn for she knows that he is the final man of her life. The one that all the others have prepared her for. For she was also younger back then; and life had been lived for the times. But maturity has brought wisdom and moon beams have faded with the light of dawn."

"Now she willingly surrenders her quest for castles in Spain to the next generation of restless young virgins; and our mature woman passes not from something but to something; this her man of Autumn.

"Somewhere there is an empty home in need of warmth and love; a fireplace eager for a roaring flame and embers glow, and laughter of family giggling and gaiety to enrich the place where happiness dwells. There is a final bonding, of our woman and our tree; firewood on the forest floor offered up by trees of past and gathered up by women of present, accepted with blessings, gathered in Autumn to keep her house of winter warm. The winds of winter..."

Morgan paused here; as if he suddenly realized how far the trail had taken him. He gazed at the picture in his mind of the endless expanse out before him and realized there was no end. On whatever road he was traveling, it was time to turn back.

There would be other chapters for other times. For now it was better if he did not go on. His absence of talking introduced serenity as both he and Patricia lingered peacefully in their own inner world of emotional peace. The mid-afternoon sun was now hanging with a red hue in the brisk western sky as they still lay quietly on their outspread blanket.

A gust of wind rattled the trees and a torrent of golden leaves came cascading down. Squirrels and chipmunks could be heard scurrying through the leaves in search of acorns. Somewhere in the distances a lone black crow caw-cawed its call.

Morgan felt a slight embarrassment at his fantasy description; Patricia fought to keep her emotions in check. She adjusted her head up closer on his shoulder and reached over his chest to his other free arm. With a slight tug she pulled it across herself and nudged that he should squeeze her tighter. Morgan squeezed and buried his nostrils into her soft shinny hair. He searched for words, but then surrendered to silence and simply continued his holding. It was sometime after when the chemistry of their hugging lessened and it was Patricia who broke the silence.

"Morgan," she began, "that was so beautiful. How wonderful it would be if I could see the world through your eyes." She reactively put her hand to her elongated breast in calling attention.

"Through your eyes I can see that these do not matter. If only I could rid this terrible complex, and truly believe that they really do not matter.

"I have tried, but it's so very very hard. Every time I look in a mirror, or put on my bra. They are always there; the last thing when I go to bed at night and the first thing when I wake up in the morning. It's...".

She paused in decision. Then shifting to a mode of fighting back she blurted out, not to Morgan, but to the world.

"Only the foolish would think that milk is the only thing which flows from a woman's breast." As soon as the words came out she realized it seemed out of character but she wanted to salvage some semblance of the point. Therefore, she softened her tone but still made reference to the only example of which she could think.

"So far... my precious little Shelly seems to be the only person alive who has discovered that."

Morgan placed his free hand on her hair and his chemistry transmitted a consoling signal. Then, in a more natural tone she continued.

"For the first time, I have no hesitation in seeing us as one, you and me, forever side by side; in family totally complete man, woman and child. And my breasts are not any different than those of other women.

"Whatever they are, they are. But they are not all of me," she whispered in a pleading tone. "Please help me to always remember that."

Then in a change of decorum, she rose up on one elbow and looked into Morgan's eyes. They held each other deep in gaze and in words no one else would ever know she said, "I am so thankful that you're my man of autumn."

They talked of a home, Morgan and Patricia; and the things it must be. From Morgan came the words that it must be in a very prestigious neighborhood. One characterized by stately homes, tree lined streets and dignified residence; a neighborhood of nobility, integrity and grace.

Certainly it would have to be a solid house, built of stone, with a strong gable roof and massive front porch. Most important it would have to be a large house; as large as any house in the neighborhood.

It would also have to have a large circular driveway framed by two strong towering Oak trees, no wait, Elms, make that Elm trees, to let everyone know that the people who live in this house are solid and stable.

From Patricia came the input that there must be plenty of bedrooms for family to come; possible three or four. And most important of all there must be a massive fireplace that can handle a large roaring fire. A center place where all the family can gather in warmth and security and lock out all harm on cold winter nights.

That autumn passed for Morgan and Patricia and with the last of the leaves, they returned to their duties at the Stran. The work pattern was altered so that Patricia would only work in the afternoons. With her own money there were things she wanted to bring to their new home. In a more protective mode now, Morgan insisted that she and Shelly be home early and not on the streets late at night.

As October drifted into November the days became shorter and the north winds started to gust through the downtown streets. The ticket cage at the Stran however had benefit of the warm afternoon sun that added to Patricia's new smile and she found pleasure in sharing her sparkle with the theater patrons.

Shelly was nearing four and in a state of perpetual motion between Patricia in the ticket cage and Morgan in his office. In particular she was attracted to the telephone and constantly pestered to use it. Morgan in turn let her toy with the phone to nurture their closeness.

"A busy man like myself," he would mimic, "needs a secretary to take care of the important phone calls around here. Now I wonder who I could get to help me with such an important job."

"Me," she would squeal, "I tan answer *ever* call coming to dis office; peease."

"You sure you are grown up enough? You really have to be grown up you know. People are not likely to think much of this operation if they think we are not all grown up."

"I pleately gown upp," she said frowning that he should even ask.

"Well then, you should be able to tell me all of our telephone numbers. I don't suppose you are that grown up are you?"

"I kneww alll themm before I growed up," she responded with her tiny hands resting on her hips.

"Well now, that's pretty good because I am getting kind of old and old people are sometimes forgetful. For the life of me I can't remember all of the numbers around here, you think you could help me remember?"

"Menn," she stamped her tiny foot, "I swear I don't know what wee going to doo withh youu.

"Da numberr heree is 3-646."

"And da numberr dat partment is 3-928."

"Is that a fact," said Morgan acting surprised. "Well what about the number out in the ticket cage. What's that number?"

"Dat number iss easiest of all. Seee justt watch my fingerss. First 3 den 6 den 5 den 4."

"Well, that seems pretty grown up to me, but how do I know that you can dial a telephone. If I needed for you to make a very important call you think you know how to dial?"

"I, *can* dial with thiss finger," she stuck up the index finger on her right hand for Morgan to see.

"Well now, if I have a telephone secretary on my payroll I guess I better put her to dialing right away. I can't have any of my employees sitting around not working.

"I see by looking at my very important gold watch that it's getting about time for something to eat. An important man like me likes to have a little snack in the afternoon.

"I don't suppose you could dial the pizza place and have a pizza sent over? Now be sure and tell them that this is a very important call."

Pittsburgh is a city where cold cutting winds lurk in the narrow, sunless streets of the towering office buildings. As November drifts into December, downtown becomes the bellwether that winter is on the horizon. Freezing winds sneak down from Canada and seek out these sunless byways; waiting in ambush for shoppers who venture away from the sun warmed sides of the streets. To the pleasure of winter's hideous nature, unsuspecting pedestrians who turn around blind corners are instantly hit with a blast of bone chilling air. Arrogant, ruthless, and defiant these early winds are advanced scouting parties for the conquering forces to come. They have been sent down to test the strength of the weakening Sun.

In the eternal battle between cold and warm, the Arctic is preparing to launch its winter offensive.

Rested and rearmed, the cold is impatient to begin the invasion. In a few short weeks the Sun, now weakened by months of field duty, will be overrun and forced to a southerly retreat. For the time being a last stand battle is being waged. The Sun's forces are clustered in southern exposed pockets of resistance that the early winds have not yet been able to overrun. And downtown shoppers scurry to the storefronts that face the south. The Stran Theater with its massive overhanging marquee and southern alcove is a warming box where pedestrians whip in for a respite.

But... in the balance of life... when all who pass flock in for protection, that which brings good...will also bring evil; and to the lives of Patricia and Morgan, evil came. It was on such a day in early December when, without warning a disastrous page from Patricia's past reappeared; and that, which was destined from the very beginning, now came in demand of restitution.

In the form of a short fat man, the vicious cold cutting razor of life assaulted the warmth of Patricia's ticket cage. She first noticed his presence as he stood in the Stran alcove, near the poster window displays. He was holding a large open book and his head nodded up and down as he looked back and forth from her to the book. Her first glimpse of him was thwarted when a patron approached the cage and purchased a ticket. Then as she returned her look, her eyes and the eyes of the short stocky man made a glimpse contact and there flashed a danger signal. Instantly, he closed the book and turned in pretense of watching the street.

Patricia's focus had not been on the book he was holding but on his stature and decorum. He was a short, stocky, overweight man wearing clothes that represented some place other than Pittsburgh. He wasn't conveniently visible but she observed that underneath a tattered sport jacket he had on a long sleeve white shirt with a dirty collar, a wrinkled red tie that was loosely pushed to the side and soiled with tobacco juice. His trousers were checkerboard black and white, baggy and he had a potbelly that hung over his sagging belt line.

As she watched, she noted that he was chewing on a soggy unlit cigar and he was pretending to be concerned with the weather.

The large book was tucked under one arm and his hands were shoved into his trouser pockets. He had black, greasy, glued down hair and was wearing a black bowler hat. It seemed to Patricia that he did not actually have a neck and his oversized head was attached directly to his rounded shoulders. His out of character image was further evidenced by the collar of his wrinkled black topcoat being only partially turned up and covered with flakes of dandruff.

Their unexpected eye contact had cause Patricia and the fat man to enter a momentary time warp wherein there was no protocol on either. In a bid for nonchalant the out of character man attempted to light his soggy cigar and the smell of putrid smoked drifted into her cage. Using her hand as a fan she was waving off the smell when a patron stepped up to the window for the purpose of buying a ticket. The time factor of selling the ticket and making change was brief but when Patricia's view was again clear the fat man had disappeared.

It was the next day when the two would actually come face to face. This time it happened at the ticket cage. The chilling winds of the previous day had retreated and the Sun had reclaimed some of its lost ground. Topcoats were not needed but a few shoppers and pedestrians were seen to be on the cautious side. A kind of thankfulness hung in the air and the matinee at the Stran was experiencing a good attendance. A sizable crowd had lined up at the cage and Patricia was unusually busy. In her normal routine she was going about the business of greeting each patron with a smile, accepted their money, making change and issuing the tickets. The lengthy line was moving without incident when the ticket machine abruptly jammed. For a brief moment she lowered her head to look under the counter and gave the dispenser a jolting hit. When she rose back up she was startled to be looking directly into the face of the fat man. They made direct contact and a feeling of panic ignited, as she looked at his cold, colorless, eerie eyes.

He was standing arrogantly close to the cage with his face almost against the glass. His purplish, blood vessel lips were inches away from the round voice opening and she could smell the mixture of foul breath and putrid cigar smoke. The dandruff from his hair was mixed with sweat and collected in the wrinkles on his neck. Two days growth of beard covered his sagging jowls and blended into his black bowler hat that he had pulled down tight on his forehead. Without any pretense the fat man held eye contact to the point of rudeness. Then, when there was a blink he continued his rudeness by blatantly staring at her bust line.

It was Patricia who forced the issue by curtly asking, "May I help you sir!" He made no sound but simply held up the first finger on his right hand.

Patricia, slightly startled at the short grubby finger with the dirty nail, interpreted by asking, "One adult?"

The fat man nodded and laid the money on the counter. Without further words, she transacted the money and pushed the change and ticket through the window. As he turned to enter the theater she noticed that in his left hand he was carrying a canvas satchel. It was bulging to capacity and the protruding outlines indicated there was something heavy on the inside; something with straight lines, possibly a large book.

When all the patrons were finally ticketed, it became necessary for Patricia to refill the ticket machine. The fat man was still on her mind but there were other matters that first needed attention. Stepping off of her elevated chair she squatted down out of sight. Inside her cage, with her head under the counter she was not able to see. But no more than a few minutes passed before the fat man came out of the theater and disappeared into the street.

It was a week later when the fat man's presence resurfaced. It came in the form of a telephone call from the law offices of Buckwilder, Lower, Bishop & Mills. Shirley Lower was making the call as Patricia answered.

"Hello, Stran Theater."

"Hello, is this Patricia? Patricia Waters?" Shirley inquired.

Patricia, slightly surprised because she could not imagine who might be calling, cautiously answered, "Yes. Yes it is."

"Mrs. Waters, you don't know me but my name is Shirley Lower. I am an attorney in the law office with Frank Buckwilder. Do you recognize the name of Mr. Buckwilder?"

"Why yes, of course, he's Morgan's best friend."

"Friend and attorney," established Shirley. "Normally Mr. Buckwilder would be the one making this call; either to you or to Mr. Smithfield, possibly both.

"But Mr. Buckwilder is out of town for the time being and I am responding on his behalf."

"What responding?" asked Patricia. "I don't have any legal dealings."

"Well, to tell you the truth Mrs. Waters we are not sure ourselves. Permit me to explain; or should say ask.

"Have you ever had any dealings with the Law Firm of Denning, Denning and Cope?"

"Uh, no not that I can think of," responded Patricia.

"Could," inquired Shirley, "they have been the ones who handled your father's legal affairs? Possibly is the law firm which probated the family estate?"

"Not to my knowledge, but then I was not very involved. Mother handled most of those matters, so I can't say for sure one way or the other."

"Can you think of any reason why a prestigious law firm like Denning, Denning and Cope would be wanting to reach you? Have you had any contact with your husband or do you know his where about?"

"NO!" screamed Patricia. "IS HE GOING TO TRY AND GET SHELLY? IS THAT WHAT THIS IS ALL ABOUT?"

"No, No, Mrs. Waters, please, now don't get excited. We don't know anything like that. Now please, please Mrs. Waters just settle down I don't want to frighten you. I am just asking."

"And I am telling! They are not about to get Shelly!"

On the other end Shirley Lower felt a flush of embarrassment at Patricia's anxiety.

"Please don't panic Mrs. Waters. Nothing had been said in any way pertaining to Shelly. All I can tell you is what I know.

"Early this morning I received a call from Bob Denning. His law office is in our same building and we all know each other on a first name basis.

"Bob knows that Frank Buckwilder is Morgan Smithfield's attorney and that you and Morgan have a relationship.

"As a professional courtesy Bob Denning called our office and advised that he has a need to contact you. He didn't have to do that. He could have simply contacted you directly but as a courtesy he called us.

"He would not however reveal what it pertained too. Are you with me so far?" Shirley asked.

"I, well what does he want? What did he say?" responded a frightened Patricia.

"Again, Mrs. Waters, Bob Denning did not disclose to me the nature of his business. He was merely exercising professional courtesy.

"In substance it means that he has a need to contact you for some legal matter. If you wish to have us present as your attorney then we will be happy to represent you. If you do not wish to have an attorney then that is fine. But the critical element at this point is that you be fully advised." Still on the other end Shirley paused and felt she should further clarify the point.

"To make sure that I haven't over frightened you, Mrs. Water, let me explain. An attorney by the name of Bob Denning wishes to contact you. If you would like for me to be present I will be happy to be there.

"I have no idea of the reason. It may be nothing. It may be something. He is not at liberty to discuss your matters with me unless you so authorize.

"It may be matters pertaining to your father's estate. It may be something pertaining to your husband. It might be that he wants to get a legal divorce; or have your marriage annulled.

"What I am saying is don't jump to conclusions because at this point we don't know.

"But I do know Bob Denning and I know that he is a very ethical attorney. I can't picture that he would be a party to anything of a dubious nature."

On her end of the line Patricia remained silent. Shirley felt that the panic had been held in check but she wasn't sure. In a cautious but controlled voice she asked, "Mrs. Waters would you like for me to contact Morgan? Is this something you would like?" There was a long silence before Patricia answered.

"Miss Shirley," she paused in apparent fear, "I'm not sure. I, I'm afraid that it might be something which I do not want known to Morgan. What do you think?"

"Mrs. Waters, I can't advise you in that respect. It's whatever makes you feel the most comfortable. If you like I will be happy to go with you for the first meeting.

"We can at least find out what this is all about and then decide if you want to include Morgan." In a shaky unsure tone Patricia asked Shirley to proceed.

It was 9:00 A.M. the next morning when Shirley, Patricia and Shelly entered the prestigious law firm of Denning, Denning and Cope. Greeted by the receptionist they were immediately ushered into the office of Bob Denning.

"Shirley," greeted Bob as he rose from his desk and met them at the door, "how nice of you to come," he offered his handshake.

"Bob," responded Shirley as she accepted his hand and looked at Patricia.

"Bob Denning, may I introduce Patricia Waters; Patricia this is Bob Denning, *attorney extra ordinaire*."

"Mrs. Waters, a pleasure. I hope we haven't been too unnerving on you. Please, won't you all have a seat."

Additional protocol and social amenities followed but then Shirley brought the point of business to hand.

"Bob," Shirley commenced, "we are wondering. What do you have for us?" Bob Denning paused before he answered.

"Shirley, Mrs. Waters, our linkage in this matter stems from a telephone call we received by a law firm in Lakeland, Florida.

They have a business proposal for Mrs. Waters and have asked that we act on their behalf.

"In effect, we are stand-in attorneys."

"What sort of business proposal," inquired Shirley?

"Unfortunately," said Bob, "their field representative is late. He was supposed to be here at 8:30 this morning but as you can see he is not present."

Shirley noted that Bob Denning had not answered her question and it flashed a caution sign.

"I am not sure I understand Bob. How does some sort of field representative figure into this? Who is offering what? Is it the Florida law firm who is making the proposal and what is it they are proposing?"

"No Shirley, the law firm in Florida is acting in no other capacity other than legal counsel. They have simply asked that their Client in the mode of a field representative be the one to personally make the offer.

"Our role, in substance, is to provide a meeting place and if an agreement is reached with Mrs. Waters, then we will prepare any necessary legal documents."

"But what is the offer?" pushed Shirley. "We are here, we are waiting, and you have certainly caused Mrs. Waters and her daughter Shelly no small amount of anxiety. If I am permitted, Bob, I am surprised. This isn't like you."

Bob Denning felt a flow of blood rush to his face and wondered if it showed. Then, recovering with the poise and polish of a master statesman he spoke in elegant measure.

"Yes, of course, Miss. Lower and you Mrs. Waters. You are absolutely correct. I have made a social error and beg your pardon.

"The truth is I find myself in a bit of embarrassment. I agreed to this assignment as a bit of legal courtesy.

"Offering my office, as it were, to a fellow lawyer. At the moment it seemed to be no more than providing a meeting place.

"Now I am beginning to feel concerned. In truth I have not yet met the Field Representative.

"As I mentioned he was supposed to be here at 8:30. I had planned the extra half hour to be used as interview time.

"Certainly the onus is on me to be informed and fully aware of his proposal. However, I am sorry to tell you that I am dreadfully in the dark. It has something to do with traveling; some sort of job with a year's contract. But I..." His secretary abruptly cut off Bob Denning as she entered his office.

"Excuse me, Mr. Denning. There is a gentleman here. I believe he is expected. Would..." The secretary did not get to finish as Gabrielle Wabacle pushed his way past the door and entered. His rude manners fitting exactly the dirty, smelly disdainful state of his personal appearances.

Smelling of alcohol and cigar smoke he had neither bathed nor shaved. He was wearing the same soiled white shirt, crumpled red tie, black and white checkered trousers and black bowler hat; the very same fat man which Patricia had seen at the ticket cage.

"Howdy, people," he rudely announced.

"My name's Gabe and sorry about being a little late. But if it weren't too much of an inconvenience to you it sure was worth it to me," his opening remarks were delivered with a sneered grin. He mimicked smacking his purplish lips and continued his explanation.

"I was out on the town a little bit last night and damn if I didn't run across this cute little filly down on Market Street," he gave a little tee hee.

"Young and cute if you know what I mean," he paused with a snide grin and then continued.

"Well sir, ha, ha, one thing led to another and you know how it is. We sure didn't want to turn loose of each other this morning. But, we all have to make sacrifices so here I am."

The propriety of the office was overwhelmed by his obnoxious presence and Bob Denning rushed to establish some semblance of decorum.

"Mr. Wabacle," he forcefully said, "there seems to have been some misunderstanding here.

"I agreed to stand as counsel in your business proposal but I will not tolerate your foul vernacular. It is offensive to these fine people, to me and to my office."

"Gees," replied Gabe in a tone of rationalization. "What's with all the uppity crap? We're all adults here. Don't tell me you's have never run around the mill a few times."

"No, Mr. Wabacle," resounded Bob as he moved from his desk and stood between Gabe and Patricia and Shirley.

"We are not all adults here. In case you haven't noticed there is a child present. But that's beside the point.

"The point is we do not wish to talk about or engage in antics at the sewer level.

"Now, may I ask you SIR, what company do you represent and what is the nature of your business."

At that point, Gabe's tone turned from tee-hee slurring to who- do-you-think-you're talking too, stepped back from Bob Denning and gave him an up and down look of contempt.

"Look Mr. Hot Shot Lawyer, don't look down your nose at me. I am here to make a business offer; you got that?"

"Mr. WABACLE, I will repeat my question," Bob burrowed in. "WHO DO YOU WORK FOR, WHAT IS THE NAME OF THIS COMPANY YOU ARE SUPPOSED TO REPRESENT."

"NOT suppose," answered Gabe. "There is no supposing about it I DO.

"I am an Official Field Representative for Bannum Brothers' Circus and Carnival out of Lakeland, Florida.

"My JOB, SIR," Gabe boisterously proclaimed, "is to find people we can use in our show.

"And I am here to make that lady right over there," he pointed to Patricia, "a bona fide offer of a one year contract to joint the carnival."

"Me," spoke up Patricia. "Why on earth do you want me? How could I possibly be of interest to you? The only thing I know how to do is to sell tickets. Surely you don't expect us to believe that ticket sellers are that much in demand..."

Gabe moved slightly to the side of Bob and in a direct line-of-sight with Patricia said, "Ticket selling? Who said anything about selling tickets? What are you, crazy or something?"

He then abruptly reached down and removed a book from his black canvas satchel. It was the *Encyclopedia of Rare & Unusual Genetic Birth*

Defects.

He hurriedly opened it to the pictures which Dr. Daniel Owise had submitted showing Patricia and her elongated breast.

"This is you with the foot long tits isn't it?" he asks in a blatant lunatic voice.

"That's what we want. We want them weird looking tits in our freak show.

"Now here's the deal," his talking had become so aggressive that droplets of spit spewed out as he attempted to move past Bob so that he could talk directly to Patricia.

"Now here's the deal," he repeated. "We can bill you as our center attraction in the freak show.

"Give you lots of publicity. Paint a new giant mural on the front of the tent. Maybe we could show you as a mysterious wolf woman; half woman, half wolf.

"Found in deepest darkest Africa. Show you on a queen's thrown, nude from the waist up.

"Sitting there in an jungle temple with them long animal tits hanging down.

"As a back drop we can show a pack of fang-snarling saliva dripping wolves there to protect you. And at your feet a bunch of hungry wolf pups anxiously jumping up wanting to suck."

Gabe Wabacle was talking so loud and boisterous that he had not heard the instant objective voice of Bob Denning. He paused just long enough to take a deep breath and then continued his assault.

"Now I can make it all happen; trust me on dat. This here half wolf half woman thing, that's just one thought, you understand. The big boys in the front office will likely have other ideas.

"But that's a no never mind on your part. Promoting you is our business and we have lots of people down in Florida who handle those matters.

"Now the thing for you to know is that it will be an easy job; nothing to it. Easy money.

"All you have to do is just sit inside the tent, nude from the waist up and let people pass by and look at them long dangling tits.

"We are willing to pay good money, just awfully good money for what you will be expected to do; and don't worry about any pornography charges.

"We think we know how to get around that problem. Now, I am here to do business Mrs. Waters. Today, right now I can give you a year's contract to start…"

"SIR," shouted Bob Denning, "You uncouth clod. How dare you be so vile and degrading? You despicable foul wretched excuse for a human being. I order you to shut your mouth."

In a reflex of rage Bob sprang up against Gabe and forced his outraged face into blearing direct eye contact. A non-violent man, he is unaware that his fists are clenched as he continues.

"Who do you think you are that you can spew your repugnant sewage on decent propriety people, you repulsive swine? Remove yourself from my office at once or I will have you thrown out."

"What!" recoiled Gage? "HEY, What'd I say? All I am doing is offering Miss Long Tits there some easy money…"

"OUT YOU LOATHSOME HEINOUS COIL OF VENOM," Bob shouted to the point where he himself was spewing spittle.

"DAMN YOUR UNCONSCIONABLE SOUL," he bellowed as he shoved Gabe toward the door.

Shirley Lower jumped to her feet in Patricia's defense and joined in with Bob Denning as he continued shouting, "OUT! YOU LOATHSOME SCOUNDREL."

"OK, OK," conceded Gabe as he held up his hands feigning no more argument.

"All right already, I'm leaving. Boy you try to do some people a favor," he mumbled in leaving.

The entire incident had lasted no more than a minute or two. The consequences would reach beyond the lives of all those present. The instant effects were searing, unbearable pain which stabbed and cut through every fiber in Patricia's body and soul.

A piercing anguish erupted inside with the violent swelling of a volcano as tears burst forth in uncontrollable wailing.

In haste Shirley gathered Patricia and Shelly and proceeded to leave. Repeated apologies by Bob Denning were politely accepted but the urgency was to leave. It was unbelievable that anything so repugnant could have happened. Outside on the street she supported Patricia with one hand and hailed a taxi with the other and accompanied them back to the Wood Street apartment.

It was while they were in the cab that Shirley witnessed just how strong was the bond between Shelly and Patricia. Shelly's little mind realized that something was dreadfully wrong and sought the security of her mother's lap; something she had grown away from in recent months. With her head nestled against her mother's breast she softly said, "Don't cry Mommie. Dat meannn circuss mann. I haate dat circuss. Shelliee take care of you Mommieee."

Finally within the security of the apartment, a kind of tense quietness settled in. Shirley spent the remainder of the day and for whatever good she poured out words of comfort. Several times during the afternoon Bob Denning called with expressions of apology. He felt totally responsible that the vulgarity of the incident had defiled and besmirched the grace and character not only of Patricia but his own life.

For Patricia the hurt could not be undone and the hours that followed unraveled into one onslaught of anguish after another. Eventually she became so exhausted her eyes would no longer produce tears and the desire to continue living simply slipped away.

At sometime along in the late afternoon, when she had reached the limits of hurt, there materialized a sort of transcendental experience; an unexplained feeling of relief, a heavy burden was lifted off of her shoulders and it was instantly easier to breathe. In a strange metamorphosis the hurt started to subside and the reason for her existence rose up as if ascending out of the fog. There it was, all of a sudden it was all so clear. She was what she was. How could she have ever expected to be anything more than what she was intended to be?

A joke. Her life was intended to be a joke. An object of humorous ridicule. An example for others to see, ogles, laugh at and realize but not really accept that it could have happen to them. Her mind was clearer now; and to think of all the years she had spent fighting to the contrary. Everything now seemed so simple. Either be a joke or be nothing. One cannot fight one's intended purpose in life.

How stupid that she could not see in herself what others had seen all along. Her father, her husband, Dr. Daniel Owise, Sidney Griffin, the fraternity Phi Smia Delta and lastly, Gabrielle Wabacle; theirs was the truth. The assurance by Morgan that she could have a normal life was nothing more than wishful thinking. He stands alone in his vision 'that it matters not'. God bless this wonderful man. But it was hopeless from the start. Now it is senseless to continue.

When the circle of people in Patricia's life received word of what happened in Bob Denning's office, rage was expressed over the incident and condolences poured out to Patricia.

The word reached Morgan out in the North Hills at the construction site of his new drive in restaurant and he immediately rushed to Patricia. The next was Frank Buckwilder who cut his trip short and returned home the same day. Jenny Craig and Aspen McGee were together when they received the call by Morgan. In grief and anguish they hurried to Patricia's side.

In grace she accepted all their charity but in actual concern the issue no longer mattered. Shortly she would be leaving. The troubles of this life no longer mattered. Her objective now became one of secrecy. For a while it would be necessary to continue her normal pattern in life. In a show of strength she maintained her composure and steadfastly asserted to everyone that there was no crisis. As convincing evidence she related that she simply considered the source and she felt a victory when those around her started to indicate a sigh of relief. The next day, with eyes dry and her smile happy she continued her duties at the Stran.

Morgan however was not totally convinced. There lingered in his mind an element of suspicion and he was ever watchful but not intrusive.

Several times each day he would leave his office and amble out to the ticket cage. In light humor or jest he would give Patricia a squeeze or touch. In her masquerade, she responded by returning a light touching kiss or a hand squeeze and flashed reassuring smile.

But in her own privacy, the last days in the ticket cage were spent making travel preparations. She now watched the passing pedestrians in a different context. She wondered how long it would be before some of them would be making the same trip; or for that matter if any of them would be traveling at the same time. In a stronger sense her watching was a final backward glance. This had been her life's destiny; the people and streets of Pittsburgh. She wondered if there was a reason. Why her? Why here and now? Was she a small part player in some great overall mosaic portrait? A contributing building block to some larger design that would have an influence on the lives of all of these people; she wondered.

She pondered the season, Christmas. Would she soon be learning the truth? She watched as shoppers scurried pass with Christmas gifts and wondered if that was what it was all about; the giving of gifts in order to satisfy a self imposed obligation rather than the promoted notion of pleasure being derived from simply giving. The Christmas carols that were in the air brought sadness rather than joy. These she had always loved and in particular when 'Oh Holy Night' was played a tear would come to her eyes.

She sat in the cage each day and continued to work as the time shortened and on December 23, she asked Morgan to watch Shelly and left the apartment early that morning. Supposedly to do some last minute Christmas shopping and insisted she would be at work for the afternoon matinee.

At show time she was in her cage, appeared perfectly normal and Morgan breathed a sigh of relief; but in the back of his mind he could not help but feel that it was all a facade. Sooner or later it would crack and they would have to come to terms with her hurt. For the moment however it looked as though they would make it through Christmas.

Morgan did not go to the apartment on the night of December 23.

There had been an emergency at the Stran. At 10:36 P.M. an electrical fire broke out and the Theater had to be evacuated. The Fire Department responded immediately and the blaze quickly extinguished but that did not end the danger. Electrical fires are prone to smolder and hot wiring is apt to lie concealed in the building walls. As a precaution, Morgan and the projector operator had stayed all night and took turns at fire watch.

He was still asleep on his office sofa when the telephone rang the next morning. The time was 8:30 A.M. The date was December 24, 1944. Shelly Waters was on the other end of the line.

"Helloo, Daddyy Morgann," she spoke with a fright in her voice, "diss iss a very importantt phonee calll. Mommiee iss sleepingg and won't wake upp."

When Morgan arrived at the apartment little Shelly was at the front door waiting. Patricia was lying across the bed in her final sleep. On the kitchen table was an empty prescription bottle. He grabbed it and fanatically read the label.

> *Damon Pharmacy, 346 Forbes St.,*
> *Pittsburgh, Pennsylvania*
> *Doctor: Daniel Owise, M.D.;*
>
> *#24944 12/23/1944; 20 count*
> *Seconal: 1 1/2 grains/ capsule*
> *Take one capsule at bedtime for sleep*

"Damn! Damn! Damn! God be Damn You Daniel Owise. Damn Your Unconscionable Soul!"

To be the one to make the discovery, to be the one to search for life signs by touching, shaking and shouting, to realize there is no life, the disbelief and rechecking to make sure, the loss of contact with one's own body, suddenly realizing that a part of one's own life is gone, a split second before there was whole, a split second after there is loss: these minutes are human trauma absolute. There, in stark reality, without any warning or preconditioning.

For Morgan Smithfield the emotional results were to pass into a fog of three, intertwined emotional milieu. The first was instant pain; a piercing pain stabbing directly into the heart. A pain so intense it possessed the ability to burst. It caused incoherence, a shortness of breath and hesitancy in speech. Then, with a mustering of strength there surfaced an emotion of rage; an explosive desire to seek out and painfully destroy whoever was responsible.

Then thirdly, the emotional demand for accountability; a direct confrontation with the Great Master Plan. With raised clenched hand, he looked to the Heavens and demanded an answer.

"What so profit Thee?" he wailed to the Creator. "That her death is better than the good which we could have done if we had been allowed to live out our lives together?" To his demand there came no answer.

On December 25, 1944 a Courier Truck delivered two Christmas presents to the apartment on Wood Street. One was a small package addressed to Shelly; wrapped in delicate white paper with a gold bow and trim. Inside the box, nestled on a bed of cotton and white satin, were two small porcelain figurines. One of the figurines was a fairy tale princess. She was dressed in a white flowing gown, had long blond hair, sparkling blue eyes and tiny pink lips for only one true love. The other figurine was a tall and handsome fairy tale prince dressed in a white military uniform with gold braid. He had dark hair, a tiny mustache and was wearing a gold turban.

On the gift note Patricia had written:

To: *My Darling Shelly,*
   Let these serve in remembrance of our wonderful dreams. They were all we ever really had. Have a good life my precious and may you find love. Mother loves you more than you will ever know.

The other gift was for Morgan. It was a potted plant; a sapling Elm Tree. A tree that was awkwardly wrapped in gold Christmas foil with an attached hand written note.

To: *Morgan,*
  You most wonderful man. Please plant this by my sister Elm tree on our far-away hill. Tell her I will see her soon. Goodbye my love, I am thankful that you were my man in autumn.

━━━▷◆◁━━━

As the City of Pittsburgh learned that the love of Morgan Smithfield had died and the City of Pittsburgh showed its respects. On a cold snowy day at the end of December in 1944 a lone funeral was held in Allegheny Cemetery. And not since the days of prohibition and gangster funerals had so many fresh cut flowers been brought to a single grave; flowers from every walk of life and every part of Pittsburgh. They came from downtown, they came from the districts, and they came from the outlying suburbs.

They came and they came: From the down town streets of Duquesne, Penn and Liberty on the West Side; Wood, Smithfield, Grant, 4th, 5th and 6th in center; North Ave, Ohio Street and Tripoli on the North Side; Beford, Webster, and Wylie up in the Hill District to the northeast; Grand View Ave up on Mt. Washington; East Carson on the lower South Side; further outlying communities of Homestead, West Mifflin, Dormont, Crafton, Carnegie, McKees Rock, Wilkinsburg and Duquesne.

Black limousines and floral delivery vans started arriving at the Allegheny Cemetery in early morning, in possession of such numbers as to created a waited turn. And the following day a newspaper reporter and columnist for the Pittsburgh Daily News wrote a City wide commentary;

'In our sorrow for Morgan Smithfield: This was not the funeral of a President, or a Governor or some political power boss. This was a funeral of the people, those among us who mind the store six days a week, who sweep the sidewalks in front of the store in the morning and roll up the street awnings at night, those among us who have lost a job or suffered ill health and had to borrow a dollar until we could get back on our feet, those among us whose means of surviving is a strong back and callous hands, those among us who look at their fellow worker and know that each in turn is fighting every day just to stay alive.

'All of these among us know Morgan Smithfield. We each know that if we are ever in need, he is a man we can turn too. He gives of his self and he gives of his wealth and he so gives without asking explanation; he know not of a turn away. To Morgan...from all of us...our highest respects. We do this because Morgan Smithfield is one of us, and his loss is our loss and we mourned the passing of the only woman ever to enter his life, and for all of us who mourn, we herein say the words, 'Good-by Patricia and may God Speed."

By Morgan's specific wishes, Patricia's funeral was private; attended only by those directly in her life. Three men, a woman and a child stood by the grave.

Appropriately, the adults were dressed in black. The child, in a knowing wish of the mother, was dressed in white. For her final goodbye, Shelly wore a knee length white wool dress trimmed in small pink flowers at the neck and sleeves, calf-length white socks, white shoes and white gloves. She was kept warm by a calf-length white cloak with a fur-trimmed hood.

At the graveside she stood with those who would now be her guardians. Jenny Craig stood holding her tiny hand on the left and Morgan Smithfield held her hand on the right. Aspen McGee and Frank Buckwilder stood in silence.

Patricia's eulogy and parting blessings were delivered by Father O'Conner of the Crafton Parish. He spoke knowingly of a woman who had an abundance of love to give, and was hurt by there being so few takers.

As the eulogy was being delivered there were thoughts on their minds; these four adults whose life Patricia had touched.

Morgan Smithfield had thoughts of anger and his wrath was directed at the highest possible power. *Damn You God!* He vowed in silence.

Damn You! Damn You! Damn You! You have reached the lowest of the low. You welshed on the deal. I trusted You. I trusted You completely. I thought we had a deal. It would have been good for her and me and You know it. Patricia and I would have made a good family. We would have given You good children. Made You proud. But Hell No! That wasn't good enough for You. And I don't want any crap about You needing her more. Just stay to the Hell out of my sight God and don't ever come around expecting another deal.

Literature in classics beholds stories of love, tragedy, death and pain; and Frank Buckwilder was a scholar of the Classics. Certainly, Shakespeare had many times presented his central character as a soul in torment. But today, as Frank stood at the grave of an innocent young woman he studied the bereave look on his best friend's face, and pondered the senselessness of it all.

That something of such beauty should bequeath the gift of so much pain; but even conceding 'that to love is to pain' who decrees that the measure of love be paid in exact, by equal amounts of pain. More still, why is it chiseled in stone 'that to love is to pain'. Why must there be a price extracted at all. Especially for something that is essential to the natural order of life. All things being equal then why aren't there a payment-in-pain for breathing, or seeing, or hearing.

Frank knew that these were questions without answers and he put them aside. He felt relieved that he would never hurt so much. But later after they had left the grave and he was home alone, he experienced an overriding sensation of being cheated; that his life had never brought him such an intense love.

As Jenny Craig stood by Patricia's grave, she felt grief for the loss of her friend. Their lives had crossed for the betterment of both. In a woman's world they had shopped together, laughed, gossiped and shared lunches. Jenny had loved Patricia as a circle in her life. Unto herself however, Jenny Craig cursed Patricia for dying.

Damn you Patricia for doing this to me. How could you be so selfish? Her thoughts swelled up. *How dare you be so damn inconsiderate; I hate you, I hate you. It's not fair. What you have done has caused Morgan to be lost to me forever. You Hear Me! He's lost to me forever. You knew that in the back of my mind I had always dreamed that someday he might be mine.*

Aspen McGee had not known Patricia as the others had, yet she had touched his life. As he stood by her grave, there was a statement on his mind. A 'statement' that he had made to Jenny a long time ago; the exact words he was trying to recall. Word by word the statement returned: *'we have not yet met the person who will have the greatest impact on our lives'.*

And as they all stood for the eulogy on that cold December day, his eyes kept drifting to little Shelly; bundled up all in white, as if destiny intended that she should standout. With each passing word of the eulogy, Aspen could not help but watch the celestial face of Shelly; the words of his statement kept returning; and he wondered.

Continued in Book Two

Chapter 25

Mobster Bugsy Siegel never had much personal interest in religion. What he did have was a lot of interest in the amount of money that religion could bring in; especially airwave religion. A newspaper reporter once ask Bugsy what he enjoyed most to which he replied a 'Thompson Sub-Machine gun. But that is getting ahead of the story.

During the 1920's the crime syndicate in New York City was run by five families: the Masserias, the Castellammareses, the Mineos, the Reinas and the Profacis; all of whom would have agreed with Siegel's comment. With great proficiency and the efficiency of the Thompson, all five families went about the daily business of killing off each other; and in even larger numbers, innocent bystanders.

Gunned down shootings were common occurrences in restaurants, fish markets, and barbershops. Drive-by machine gun strafings were carried out with impunity on crowded down town streets as storefront plate glass windows were shattered with resounding effects. Territorial boundaries became public knowledge in sections of Little Sicily, the Lower East Side and along Delancey Street where Meyer Lansky and Bugsy Siegel were establishing themselves as mob overlords. Names such as Peter 'Cluch Hand' Morello, Vito Bonventre, Maranzano and Dutch Schultz were simply considered a part of the everyday world and to the public at large that was just the way things were.

Given time, however, tolerances of things change. In New York City the first seeds of a backlash probably started when a then unknown upstart by the name of Lucky Luciano killed mob leader Masseria in April of 1931. Meanwhile in the city of Chicago things were not any better. Well-known mobster Al Capone was doing battle with the Weiss-Moran gang and the notoriety that surfaced was just as bloody.

Typical was the story of a young up-start named Toney Accardo who battered one of Capone's men to death with a baseball bat and earned the name Joe Batters.

On Valentine's Day in 1929 an event occurred which would forever immortalize February 14th; the day of hearts and flowers. A crew of the Moran gang was loading illegal whiskey in a warehouse on Chicago's north side when four of Capone's men, posing as police officers, busted in at gun point and ordered them all up against a brick wall. Then, with the same erstwhile Thompson submachine gun efficiency, mowed them down in what would become known as the Valentine's Day Massacre.

Thereafter Capone started putting his own people in City Government; including City Mayor. He became so blatant that he personally stole the election by stuffing the ballot box with the name he wanted. Once the new mayor was sworn in Capone then called him out on the courthouse steps and slapped him around in full public view to leave no doubt about who was running the town.

The news media, how-be-it self-serving, were aligning on the side of the law. Newspapers in both New York and Chicago scandalized the abhorrence of unabated murder and showed bloody close-up pictures of innocent men, women and children in both cities who were unfortunate enough to get caught in reckless crossfire. Hard hitting columnist daily printed loathing articles and refused to be intimidated by mob threats. Little by little the tide of public indignation started building. As blatant killings kept on the rampaged, citizen outcry kept gaining momentum and eventually whatever measure of tolerance the public had for mob acceptance turned to despicable contempt. Still the warlords showed little concern. The Mob had long known that power and immunity could easily be bought. From the cop on the street, to the precinct captain, to the mayor, to the governor, any political figure could be bought. It was just a matter of price.

Then came a turn of events. The Federal Government stepped in and started assuming a stronger law enforcement role. Things started to change and the pendulum slowly came to the end of its upswing. For all of the mob's buying power, Federal Agents were a different breed. With the arrival of Federal agents, came one additional component; a jury box which could not be intimidated.

The combined power of these two forces first surfaced when a young hotshot United States Prosecuting Attorney by the name of Thomas E. Dewey got a simple federal conviction. While it was a relatively minor case, it was sufficient to start an avalanche. His ease of conviction on his first case prompted Dewey to start a more aggressive program of brining in small time hoodlums; and he was amazed that he could ask for and got maximum sentences on the flimsiest of evidence.

While some of the first cases may have been petty, they received out of proportion publicity; the crime pendulum had reached its zenith and had just started its downward swing. Prosecution momentum on the other hand was on the upswing. As conviction after conviction was won, Dewey's fame grew. In the eyes of the public he was the great messiah. In his own eyes however, he never lost sight of the reason; that the jury box represented the public; the public was fed up; the jury box was the only avenue the public had to fight back.

Shrewdly, Dewey played on the mob's repugnant image and with great oratory skills swayed jury after jury to verdicts of guilty; in some cases guilty simply by association.

At about the same time a Federal Judge by the name of Samuel Seabury was about to get revenge. Years earlier as a then young lawyer, Seabury had been owned by the Mafia but had been cast out as being an insignificant. In revenge he rode the tide of change with a vengeance. Every case that came before his bench he handed down the maximum sentence and made sure that every case received maximum publicity. What Judge Seabury started, other Federal Judges followed suit. Resultantly, almost overnight State Judges likewise began to meter out maximum penalty.

As Thomas Dewey's conviction reputation grew so did his ambition and he eventually set his sights on the Underworld's undisputed number one kingpin overlord; Lucky Luciano. This time Dewey was acting as Special Prosecutor for the State and in a case that took two years to develop he charged Luciano with ninety counts of compulsory prostitution. If convicted on all accounts Luciano faced 2,000 years in prison. After months of legal maneuvering, evidence gathering, and witness interviewing by teams of State and Federal agents, all of the pieces were finally in place. The soon to be famous case of State of New York v. Charles Luciano, (and eight others) came to trial on May 13, 1936 in the New York State Supreme Court in downtown Manhattan.

The presiding Judge was Philip J. McCook; a stern moralist and no friend to crime. On May 29, 1936 after three weeks of testimony and over sixty witnesses Dewey rested his case against Luciano and his co-defendants. Then came the presentation of Luciano's defense, which with cross-examination lasted until June 6, 1936.

The jury of twelve men and two alternates retired to the jury chambers at 10:30 PM on a Saturday evening. After only ten minutes in the jury room a vote was taken and the count stood at eleven to one for conviction. By the next morning a verdict was reached and at 5:30 AM Sunday June 7, 1936 the courtroom was called to order and the verdict was read: "Guilty on all counts."

It then came time for Judge McCook to pronounce sentencing and he bore his duty as though speaking directly for God. In a courtroom packed with reporters he orchestrated the proceedings to the highest level of suspense. Starting with those lesser charged and ascending to the more severe, one by one the defendants were brought before the bench.

In dry sobering words Judge McCook dished out admonishment in terms of their loathsome, repugnant deeds; words of offensive and nauseating to the morals of God-fearing, law-abiding people who strive to build a better society. With the passing of each defendant the suspense heightened and then it was time.

Lucky Luciano was brought before the bench. The courtroom became deathly silent and all eyes watched as Judge McCook looked down in scorn on the man standing before him. Holding the scene to its pinnacle, he slowly broke the silence by clearing his throat and began to speak.

"Mr. Luciano," he started in a decisive monotone with emphasis on Mr., "the lifetime of deeds that you have done, or caused to be done, loathsome, foul and repugnant. That God Almighty should put such a scoundrel as you on the face of this earth is inconceivable.

"Your entire life had been a leech on society without concern for consequence. Now you stand before this court for atonement. I find no pleasure in dispensing your punishment but it is a duty which I gladly accept."

Then Judge McCook pronounced Luciano's sentence. As the words echoed through the chambers a deathly silence hung in the air for some additional seconds; and then pandemonium broke loose as reporters bolted over chairs and benches in rushing to telephones.

While not in such an exact order, the next edition of newspapers all across the nation, as part of the story, provided the following tabulation:

> Al Weiner: two to four years
> David Marcus: three to six years
> Jack Ellenstein: four to eight years
> Ralph Ligguri: seven to fourteen years
> Abe Wahrman: fifteen to thirty years
> Tom Pennichio: twenty to thirty five years
> James Frederico: twenty to thirty five years
> David Betillo: twenty five to forty years
> Lucky Luciano: thirty to fifty years

Anticlimactic from there, all of the prisoners started serving their sentences with little notice except one. Lucky Luciano continued to hold public attention; being first sent to New York State Prison on June 18, 1936. Coincidentally, attention remained high in this same time frame for Thomas Dewey who sought to capitalize on his popularity by running for governor; and oddity of all oddities the two separate circumstances unfolded in a truth-is-stranger-than-fiction phenomenon.

To run a successful campaign Dewey needed money; a lot of money.

And in a strange turn of events Luciano contributed over two million dollars to get the very man who had sent him to prison, Thomas E. Dewey, elected Governor of the State of New York so... that he, Lucky, could get paroled. Moreover, it worked. Dewey got elected and on January 3, 1946 after serving less than ten years, Governor Dewey announced that Lucky Luciano would be freed on the condition that he is deported back to the place of his birth, Sicily. However, again that is drifting away from the story.

For the people of New York the incarceration of the mob members came like a breath of pure fresh air. It fostered a renewed faith in the American system of justice and a feeling that in the end good will always prevail over evil.

Organized crime on the other hand was thrown into a state of chaos. Overnight the Mafia had been striped of its untouchable image and the undeniable fact was the underworld and the American people were now at war; a war that the mob could not win.

The Warlords finally conceded that something had to be done to improve their public image and regain some semblance of acceptability. But that time was not quite yet. It took one additional bloody incident to blow the lid off of the power keg; another gangland shooting. Only this time it happened in Pittsburgh instead of New York.

On a summer night in 1938 Pete "Smirkie" Gulsik was in a round booth in a dimly lit back corner of the Coppa Capri nightclub on Pittsburgh's North side. He had spent most of the evening fondling a young 18-year-old blond hooker by the name of Babs who had just opted to become one of his girls. On the part of Babs her agreement with Smirkie meant getting one of the more profitable corners on North Park Street. It wasn't the 100% corner but a mid-block corner that fronted on a dark alley. The alley was the prize that she was seeking. An almost guarantee of the class of Johns who swing in off of the street, keep the car engine running, unzip their pants and get a quick, front seat, five dollar blow job; five dollars being only half of the going price for a full sexual encounter. By Babs' calculations, however, she could make more money. She could turn a blow job trick in roughly two minutes, three at the most and be right back on the corner. By working on simplicity and volume she should be able to more than double her receipts.

On the part of Smirkie, he had proven once again that his trademark, a snarled upturned lip and a casting look, could intimidate people; proof that you can get something for nothing.

He had successfully bargained off a corner that he did not own for an agreed cut of 25 percent of her take. To seal the agreement Smirkie insisted on a free sample.

Accommodatingly, Babs slid under the table and unzipped his trousers, while he was raising one leg up in the rounded booth. Placing one arm up on the back of the seat he squirmed to exact position and then pretended to look out at the haze of cigarette smoke hanging over the dance floor.

Three or four couples were hanging on to each other in a slow dance called rubbing-off sex. The music was coming from a bored lack luster five-piece band that was tired and wanted to go home. All in all a perfect setting for the perfect type of sex which he liked.

As Babs reached inside his trousers and initiated the preliminaries he closed his eyes. A tingling sensation ignited at the first touch of her moist lips. As she pulled his semi erection completely out of his zipper his arousal heightened. With the onset of her fast oral stroking she brought him to a rapid explosive climax. True to her talents, in less than two minutes she surfaced from under the table. Dabbing her mouth with a handkerchief as she stood up, she then brushed the wrinkles out of her dress and bid goodnight.

Alone in the booth Smirkie casually zipped up his trousers, tossed down the last of his drink, watched as Babs cut across the dance floor and noted that she did not look back as she went out. He glanced at the wall clock and from habit then checked his own pocket watch; 1:53 AM not much action left for the night. He stretched, yawned, looked up toward the front bar and nodded to a short stocky man sitting on the end stool; a signal that it was time to leave.

As Smirkie scooted around the booth and rose to his feet the stocky, no-neck man meandered over to the front doors and waited. Smirkie in turn had one more card to play. A game of one-upmanship was at hand. As he walked passed the long empty bar he cast a defiant, upturned-lip-smirk at the two bartenders. Then in a continued show of animosity, he paused just inside the entrance doors and took a cigar from his vest pocket. In a no-hurry stance he peeled off the cellophane wrapper, licked down the sides with moist spit, bit off and spit out the tip and shoved it into his bulging right cheek.

Knowing that the two resentful bartenders were watching he then adjusted his jacket and slightly straightened his back to reflect a parting contempt. Feeling he had sufficiently conveyed his impertinence he then nodded to No-Neck. On cue the door was opened and the two men stepped out into the quiet deserted street; now covered with early morning dew that reflected streaks of pink and green from the Club neon marquee.

The cool night air was a welcome change from the smoke filled room inside. The silence of the street was slightly disturbed by the passing of a lone car; a big black Packard loaded with people. A type of vehicle that brought an instant tenseness to Smirkie but when it passed and the quietness returned he experienced a feeling of relief. He inhaled a deep breath, stuck out his chest, hooked his thumbs inside his vest sleeves, and lightly strummed his fingers. He had showed them that Pete "Smirkie" Gulsik fears no man. He gave another nod for his car and watched as his man disappeared around the corner.

Smirkie then did two things that he should not have done. First he took out a kitchen match, struck it on the building wall and proceeded to light his cigar. Secondly he assumed that the sound of an approaching vehicle was his own car. The bright flame of the kitchen match made a perfect target. And the car, which in fact was not his, started spitting out a hail of Thompson sub-machine gun bullets.

In less than a second, the elaborate neon sign of the Coppa Capri fell under a hail of bullets. Neon smoke filled the air and the big plate glass front windows shattered like thunder. Tires screamed as the get-away car rounded the corner and Smirkie Gulsik fell to the concrete in a pool of his own blood. Godfather Smirkie of the West Side Gulsik

Family had been warned before; he should not come up to the North side unless he was invited.

When the police and ambulance arrived he was alive but unconscious. Rushed to the Allegheny Hospital he was put on a gurney, wheeled into one of the Emergency room cubicles and assigned a waiting number. From somewhere out of his unconsciousness, the blurring lights of the ceiling began to come to his eyes. And it was here that he discovered that he was not really a very good Mafia man; he went into cold fear that he might die. In panic he yelled, shouted and screamed to attract attention. The first to respond was an on-duty male nurse who came through the curtains, took one look and left. It was a few minutes later that the attending Emergency Room physician came in.

"Hello, Mr. Gulsik," he said as he unceremoniously came through the curtain and rapidly pulled back the blood soaked sheet. "I'm Dr. Owise. Let's see what we have here."

Smirkie Gulsik did not die but he remained in the hospital for several weeks. In the first few days his fear of dying was so intense that he fought to keep from going to sleep. He trusted no one but Dr. Daniel Owise and would accept no other physician. Since Owise seldom received such solicitations he accepted Smirkie's request as a compliment. At the end of his shifts in the Emergency Room he would always take the time to visit Gulsik before going off duty.

It was near the third week when Owise received a surprise as he arrived home late one night. At the front door he routinely checked his mailbox and found a bulky sealed envelope without any address; either return or mail. In curiosity he tore open one end and the contents therein would seal his destiny; the first fruits of Mafia money had been delivered.

Smirkie in turn passed the long days in the hospital by listening to the radio and developing an interest in what he called the Radio Religion Boys. After eight weeks he was finally able to go home but the stay would cost him over fifty thousand dollars. He was astonished that so much money could change hands without the use of a gun. For weeks thereafter he thought of only two things; radio religion and the way hospitals could legally gouge people. Both seemed to be an easy way to make money; certainly better than being gunned down in the streets. Eventually these thoughts would find their way into the Mafia coffers.

In the spring of 1939 the top warlords of organized crime called a nationwide meeting. The word went out to assemble in Pittsburgh, Pennsylvania where operation New Face was to be implemented. The era of violence had come to an end and the era of white-collar crime was being ushered in.

The first order of business was to announce new directives on guns. Effective immediately any person caught using a gun, except for personal protection or otherwise highly justifiable circumstance, would be severely admonished; meaning stripped of all standings and banished from the syndicate. Henceforth there would be no more prostitution, drugs, pinball machines, extortion, protection rackets, or any similar acts of direct injury perpetrated upon individuals. The new era would operate within the framework of the law and engage in activities that were acceptable to society.

The shift would now be to gambling casinos, manipulating the stock market, labor unions, race tracts, professional sports, and other highly visible enterprises. Lawyers would replace hit men and anyone who could not or would not bend to the new rules was out. Gambling would be taken out of back alleys and put in the best casinos money could build and would operate strictly on the odds in favor of the house; meaning that for every dollar which crosses a table ten to fifteen per cent goes to the house. The first targeted areas were Nevada, Atlantic City and Havana. The convention lasted for three grueling days and was nearing completion when the lingering consequences of Smirkie's shooting experience would actually materialize.

As the meeting was winding down the chairman inquired if anyone cared to offer any additional worthwhile contributions. Expecting none he was about to gavel the meeting closed when to everyone's surprise, even his own, Smirkie Gulsik rose to his feet with the suggestion that the syndicate should also get into radio religion and hospitals. In a clamor of gaff haw and ridicule outburst, Smirkie held to his proposals and ultimately was able to convince the ruling fathers that a vast fortune could be fleeced from the public; and it fit the new criteria exactly. The airwaves were free and people feel good about sending in their donation to fight the devil's sinful deeds. Lastly, there were the benefits of a money laundering operations. In following the new guidelines, Smirkie further felt that the hospitals should also have a religious theme and built on the same scale of grandeur as gambling casinos.

As a gesture to the Host City the ruling fathers put the matter to a vote. Mostly because Pittsburgh was the host city, a slim majority approved an experimental program; to be established in Pittsburgh.

An allocation of five million dollars was made available with the stern admonishment that the Pittsburgh Godfather would be held responsible for its success. With the proposal now a reality it wasn't long thereafter that the same architects who designed and built the Copacabana in New York City, the Casino Royal in Atlantic City, the Riviera Hotel and Casino in Havana, and the Flamingo Casino in Las Vegas came to Pittsburgh. In due time the Hospital of Abbey Moutiers-St.Jean was built out in Mt. Lebanon and one Dr. Daniel Owise was invited to drop by.

For the radio religion portion, the syndicate first turned to a voice which Gulsik had heard while he was lying in the hospital; Jeri Swagart who supposedly was somewhere down in Texas; Ivan, Ervin, Vining, something like that.

On a hot sweltering day in July a black 1938 Packard model 1608 twelve cylinder, limited addition four-door convertible with Pennsylvania license plates entered the City limits of Vining. At a Gulf Service Station they stopped for gas, made inquiries, ask questions and directions. With the convertible top back, two men with Pittsburgh accents paid for a full tank, thanked the attendant with ten dollars for his time and headed across town.

The conspicuous presence of two hoods in a sleek aristocratic Packard convertible did not exactly blend in with the character of a small Texas town. Nevertheless, if they had any concerns about avoiding attention it wasn't evident. They made no pretense as they crept along South Houston Street checking the house numbers. Eventually they came to the number 1142; a pre 1920's run-down wood frame structure with peeling paint and torn window screens. The slow moving Packard pulled to the curb and stopped. A sleeping dog laying on the porch of the house next door raised up and woofed a single bark and then dropped back down.

Otherwise the street was quiet as the two men in double-breasted business suits remained in the convertible for a moment and listened. From the slightly opened front door, vocal pain muffled sounds were being drowned out by louder feminine voices. In a precautionary check before getting out, each man methodically felt inside the armpit of his jacket for the reassurance of a shoulder holster; old habits being stronger than new rules... and expulsion threats to the contrary.

Each man then reached in the back seat and retrieved his dark blue hat and without comment left the car, walked up the cracked sidewalk, stepped up the rickety wood steps to a large dilapidated unpainted wood porch and knocked a hard knock on the sagging screen door.

The whiling sounds from inside abruptly ceases but there was no answer. A second hard knocking produced results. From behind the slightly ajar front door the face of a young woman with long black hair appeared.

Heavily painted with rouge and lipstick the rest of her body was not visible. It didn't have to be. The two men from Pittsburgh knew in an instant she was a whore.

"Yeah," she responded with a surly look through the sagging screen.

"Jeri Swagart?" came a raspy question with a Pittsburgh accent; which contrasted sharply with her southern drawl.

"So! " she answered, still keeping herself concealed behind the slightly opened door.

"Jereei Swagart!" pronounced the raspy Pittsburgh accent. "Is dis da place wheres' dis hot shot Swag'art lives'?"

"Who Wants To Know?" countered the painted face in what she hoped was a stern sounding tone.

"Me' see! I wants to knows," answered raspy Pittsburgh as he grabbed opened the sagging screen door and both men pushed their way inside. The door lady was dressed only in a scant G-string, fishnet stockings and black high heel shoes. Across the room was a second lady with equally long black hair, fishnet stockings and high heels and looked to be a twin.

"Sw'gart'?" saliva corner mouth raspy demanded, as he looked down at the nude young man on his all fours with a dog collar around his neck.

"Is youse or is youse not, da one's and only Jeri Jerk- Nut Swag'art?" he repeated as he pushing his hat back, stood leg spread and flat foot.

"I'm looking fors da Pussy Face Jer 'Shithead' Swag'art' dat does the rad'io free air preaching. Is da youse?"

The second twin whore who had been standing with her crotch straddle over Swagart's face quickly moved back as Pittsburgh ruthlessly took over.

In a scared quivering voice Jeri Swagart spoke as he was getting to his feet.

"Hey Fellow, just who in the hell do you think you are?" his weak vulnerable voice almost cracking. "How, how dare you break into a man's house..."

"Shuts youse pissing face and answer da ques'tion," demanded Pittsburgh. "For da last times', Jeeeri' Swag'art and no's otter Swag'art or not!"

"Yeah. I'M SWAGART," answered Jeri in a short surge of lungpower. "So what?"

"Soo's get youse clothes on," ordered Pittsburgh one. "Wee'ze are going ta be doing some migh-ty im-por-tant business."

"And youse," Pittsburgh number two bellowed at the two hookers, "here's a twenty spot fer each of youse. Say goodbye to your boy friend. Keep youse mouth shut. Takes' the moneys and run; you savvy?"

Without wasting time in getting dressed the whores grabbed their clothes and scrambled out the door in their G strings, fishnet stockings, high-heel and darted across the barren front yard to an old rusty Ford park at the curb.

"Mis'ter Swagart," said Pittsburgh as he cracked his knuckles and dropped full weight down on the sagging sofa; paused slightly for intimidation, stared an icy stare and again cracked the knuckles on his giant calloused hands,

"Wees 're here to makes youse an offer youse can't refuse. Youse is going to become ones of da most cel'e'brated radio religion boys in da coun'try."

In less than an hour a sleek black Packard, limited addition, four door convertible with matching leather upholster, wide white wall tires, the top up, carrying three men pulled out of Vining, Texas and headed toward Pittsburgh. The two men in the front seat alternated in turning and speaking to the man in back; Pittsburgh on the right doing most of the talking.

"Let's hear youse say "SSSweet JJJesus," he turned to Swagart. "Goes on' say it. Lis'ten to dis Al," he nudged the driver.

"Uh, really fellows," stammered Swagart. " Here? Right here? Now?"

"Ah, come on Reverend, dis aint no time ta be shy. One time. Let's hears youse says it with feel'ings," egged on Pittsburgh on the right front seat.

"Al," Pittsburgh right turns to the driver, "youse has gots to hear dis guy. Goes a'head Rev, says it. Let's hear youse say SSSweet JJJJesus."

In the back seat sweat broke out on Swagart's forehead as he mentally tensed himself up and then came the words, *"Dear dear Sweeet-ate Jeeesus."*

"Hey! Hey, did ye hear dat Al? Didja hear it. Wus I rights on da mon'ey or not? Does weze have our'selves a boy or what?"

"Now, here's da deal Rev.," he remained half turned as he spoke into the back seat. "We's don't wants youse to concern youse-self about what's youse will be preaching.

"Everything's al'ready been thought out for youse. From here on in, youse is ta con'sider youse-self a crusader against da smut in Hollywood," he paused to relight a half smoked cigar, puffed several big puffs of smelly smoke and then continued.

"Youse see, Rev'erend," he goaded Swagart as he turned further around and laid one arm upon the seat back, "everyone knows da peoples in dis country has to al' ways got to have some big pissing crisis to dwell on; you'se understand what I'm saying? Good. Lets me puts it dis ways.

"Heaven fur'bid dat there isn't some threat to man'kind going on. A good war is just fine, youse understand? It gives everybody some'n to focus on. Da trouble is, it's gonna be another year or two befores we'ens gonna have any kind of a good war going. Now we's in Pittsburgh can't afford ta wait that longs. Youse with me?"

"Well, yeah..." Swagart was about to answer but was cut off.

"Good," interrupted Pittsburgh. "Now, we's has it on good au'thor'ity that God-in-Heaven, in his infi'-nite wisdom, is ex-tremely dis-pleased da so many googie-goodie two shoes peoples here in dese United States of America keeps picking on da likes of us mis'under'stood hard-working peoples; also da us hard working peoples is unfairly referred to as da mob," he ended the sentence with a stern stare at Swagart.

"Nows," he continued without breaking the stare that left no doubt that he meant business. "Wes happen to knows fer a fact dat God would be lots more pleased if da attention of dis country wus focused on da filth that's being pumped out by some of da big money hungry un'scrup'ulous movie studios in Hollywood. Dat's wheres youse will be focus'ing; ya understans?

"Maybes in time da good Lord-in-Heaven will sees His way clear for youse to get back to da damnation of whores; buts dat's down da line, youse understand."

"Uh," Swagart started to respond but was cut off.

"As I wus saying," Pittsburgh continued in a voice that was ice pick chilling, "I'll ex'plain it to youes like dis. It's time the at'tention of dis Nation wus directed in some other di'rection.

"It's what God wants and youse has been chosen. We's know fur a fact dat it's very offensive to God dat there is so much lewd and sug-ges-tive sex in da movies.

"It's cor-rup-ting the morals of our youths. We's ex'pect that youse and God work'ing together and da donations from the good and right-eous people of dis country can bring dis scandalous sit'u'ation outs in da open."

The situation explained it was accepted and radio religion moved to its next step. On the road from Vining, Texas to Pittsburgh, Pennsylvania the radio broadcast program "Hour of Decency" was born.

In August of 1940 a second radio voice in the name of Jimmy "Holy Jim" Baker also became syndicate property. His assigned mission was to create support for the hospital by bringing the elderly and infirm to God's House of Healing.

And *praise the Lord* he brought with him his own ideas of building up a radio congregation who would send in contributions toward buying into a fully paid up retirement slot in the church sponsored retirement home; right next door to the hospital where medical help would be readily available. By his calculations the long-term venture could easily bring in over a hundred million dollars.

In the realm of biblical teachings, there is an ancient Jewish proverb that says, 'the reason the world is round is so that we cannot see too far down the road'. The three most prominent elements that influence the course of any individual life are likely to be the evolution of times, world events and 'where-one-was-when'.

In the life of Shelly Waters, the three preordained factors came together in the form of the great depression, the rise of the motion picture as a means of fighting loneliness and the growing attempt to *control the country's morals* through the use of radio, the movie industry and other mass media.

Chapter 26

Sixteen years later.

Once when Shelly Waters was a young girl, Frank Buckwilder had talked to her, as he frequently did, in a father daughter bonding. It had been at a time in her restless youth when she was anxious for love and anxious for maturity to arrive.

"Shelly," Frank most always called her by name when he was intent on fatherly guidance.

"Loving someone is not the same as being in love. In the same vein, growing to maturity in order to simply live is not the same as guiding, managing and discovering one's purpose of life. Before you seek to find love first seek to know life. I call it possession and purpose. If you have life, that's possession. The possession of life in turn, comes with an inherent responsibility of purpose; meaning what we are supposes to be doing. The two cannot be separated. Others are responsible for giving you life; you are responsible for giving that life purpose. Possible the most difficult choice one can face; you, me, everybody.

"There are always a few among us of course, for which the combination of life and purpose comes easy. By in large however, in far greater numbers, finding one's intended reason for living comes slowly and is usually born out of pain, strife and great difficulty; but... when it does finally come it has far greater worth."

Frank having said that he then paused. There was one additional part, to what he termed the blessed trinity. What happens if one does not? In order for there to be a trinity, a third leaf is necessary.

"Shelly," he started without undue hesitation. "Think in numbers of the whole human race. A few seem to be relatively happy. Those are the ones to which possession and purpose came easy.

"In greater numbers are the ones, who through pains and strife finally arrived.

"The vast majority of the day-to-day world around us however is comprised of people who live without purpose and do little more than occupy space; the owner's of these lives pass on through without ever having known a reason for living

"In a fatherly manner I can tell you these things; but my input ends with the telling. Thereafter the awesome burden of self-determination must be born by you alone; you and your own soul."

As Shelly Waters sat in the Pittsburgh jail on that October night in the autumn of 1960 she became lost in the pages of her life. As the hours dragged by her thoughts unmindfully drifted from her mother to other facets. In a nonsensical pattern she started remembering.

If this isn't just hunkie dorie, she focused on herself. *Some life, some purpose. Me sitting on my can in the county jail; again.* She shook her head. *Where have all the years gone?* She thought rhetorically. *Yesterday I was a child now I'm here.* Somewhere in her wondering mind she started thinking about her three best friends, Celia Clair, Lillian and Laura; and she felt a flush at what their reaction would be when they learned that she had collided with the law again.

She knew where they probably were; attending a formal ball at the ultra swanky Hilton Hotel located in the City's newly developed renaissance Gateway Center. A gala fund raising extravaganza being given in honor of Richard Milhous Nixon who was in town campaigning for a second term as President.

Hosted by Pittsburgh's most prominent Republican families the affair was by invitation only; to which she and her three friends had been invited and were expected to attend. *However,* she thought, *I managed to dodge that little bit of agony.*

While she had grown up in the circles of Pittsburgh's socially elite she had no taste for stiff social protocol; the pressure of having an acceptable escort, the boredom of standing around in an uncomfortable full length evening gown, being scrutinized by the elders. All the things that she disliked; or at least the reasons she used for avoidance.

Within her mind though, she knew it ran deeper. Her friends and she were growing apart, and it was difficult to accept. In earlier times of their growing up years they had been inseparable. From first grade to their teens their motto had been one-for-all and all-for-one and called themselves the Four Queens; from the deck of cards.

Celia Clair was blessed with the combined attributes of outstanding beauty and dripping honey sweetness; endowments that gave her the power to break young men's hearts and it was natural that she fell heir to the Queen of Hearts.

Lillian's mold in life followed that of her mother's image; cuddly plump, her natural inclination was to dispense her favors more freely to young suitors who graced her with gifts of jewelry; endowments which associated exactly with the Queen of Diamonds.

Laura reached her puberty earlier than the others and her young sexual hormone clock started in overtime. She was always horny and allowed that one lover would never be enough for her and when she wanted to get rid of a man she would just screw him to death and then bury him; reason enough for her to be the Queen of Spades.

And Shelly, because of her natural strength and protector of the group became the Queen of Clubs.

But that had all been in their younger years when the main interest was ruckus rousing. Eventually their lives moved past that phase; replaced by a preoccupation with sex; how to get, how to do it and who was the best; and for the first time Shelly did not feel in unity with the other three.

Sitting there in jail, the contrast echoed loud and clear, 'Hey! 'Hey! You'se. Stop that snoring and let's a person get some sleep'. Words being herald by some unknown inmate at some other unknown. As she remained sitting on the jail floor her mind wandered back to the ballroom where she knew the other three would be in the mist of things. Glitzy would be the theme and snobbery would be the scheme; crowded dance floor, strewn balloons, paper stringers and confetti, big band music and everybody watching everybody; and from that mental picture a smile came to her face at what she had dodged.

In earlier times when she and the other three were frequently compelled to attend such formal affairs they would deliberately flirt with older married men, flaunt their bosom cleavage and generally flaunt the rules of protocol.

Now here in the middle of the night, in the stark reality, on a concrete floor in the cold damp atmosphere, amidst the crowding of other inmates she thought of her friends; but yet... she didn't want to see them.

Not because she was in the slammer while they in turn were most likely promenading themselves with a little more reserved decorum. Since it was a Presidential affair she knew that their display of dignity, if that were in fact what they were doing, would be nothing more than a mocking facade; which would be shared in continuous laughter the next day.

Her reasons for avoidance were strictly of her own accord and probably not even detected by the other three. It was always a given, that with the passing of growing years there was bound to be small differences here and there. Thus far there had never been anything to a degree of causing a separation of ways. If and when it did happen she reasoned, it would probably stem from the womanly difference in the way youthful sex was being experienced. What the other three felt is not what she felt; the notice thereof being more on her part than theirs.

Outwardly she didn't feel that it was she who was doing anything drastically different. In so far as she could tell her romances were pretty much on par with theirs. On most of her dates she expected and often times did engage in foreplay, kissing, breast fondling and sometimes sexual intercourse. But for her it never amounted to anything more than being pleasant.

The other three in turn gave glowing accounts and descriptive details of euphoric, cataclysmic, earth shattering sex. So, wherein was the difference? She had had only one date that seemed to have some of the passion that the others described. But the reason for her experience had come, not from the advances of her lover, but from the seeds of her infancy.

The incident had happened, to a large degree, because of youthful date boredom. She and her date had been looking for something different to do and on happenstance opted to go to a vintage film theater. Located on the sleazy side of town it was an old rundown decaying building that was marginally able to stay in business by showing old silent pictures. Debris and wind blown litter swirled under the sagging marquee. The only attendant on duty was the ticket seller who tore their tickets in half directly in the ticket cage; there was no usher nor was the concession stand in operation.

As she and her date entered through the double swinging doors into the main seating area she was struck by an instant pungent smell. On the first whiff it wasn't too overpowering but as they took their seats she smelled again and this time it was much stronger.

She had smelled that smell before and it triggered an unexplainable sexual tingle. Moreover, that was only part of the perception. The sensation was followed by a strange sexual stirring from the combination of dim lights, a silent film on the screen and the vast number of empty seats; a subconscious picture surfaced from out of her past. In her conscious thoughts the idea that such unromantic surroundings could be sexually stimulating seemed silly and she attempted to push them aside; but the twitching spark in her panties would not die. As they sat and silently watched the movie she was drawn to taking in deeper smells through her nose and experiencing increased sensations and by the time the feature ended she was on fire.

After the show they drove in his convertible up to Grand View Drive, parked, put the top down and overlooked the City. In their usual sequence of petting he had put his arm around her and started with the preliminaries. On her part it was too little and too slow. She was jittery and antsy and after a few unsettling moments she went on the offensive.

Grabbing him in a bear hug, she pulled him over on top as she spread her legs and fell back in the seat. Instantly receptive to her aggressiveness he quickly unbuckle his trousers and opened up his fly.

With anxious hands he started removing her panties as she squirmed with impatience; but his progress wasn't fast enough. Without waiting she fervently reached down, took hold of his engorged love muscle, pushed her own panties aside and guided it into her throbbing vagina; animalisticly expecting that his first full thrusting penetrating stroke would cause her to explode with an orgasm.

However, it didn't happen; the throbbing volcanic single stroke penetration she need for gushing satisfaction. Nor did any of the following rapid hunching. Shaking with frenzy, her mind turned back to the putrid smell of the theater and she sniffed in deep air through her nose as she pulled his face to her breast. With her eyes closed she hugged him tight with both arms, pushed her naked hips up more forcefully and concentrated harder as he increased his stroking.

"I'm cumin," she murmured. "Don't stop. I'm almost there. Almost, almost. Push!" her murmurs turning to commands. "Harder push harder! ANOTHER FRACTION!" she ordered as she desperately pushed to bring herself to an orgasm.

In frustrations, as each savage thrusting drive neared the crucial pinnacle her concentration would snap and retreat back into hiding. In no more than a minute or two they had slid almost completely off of the seat and onto the floorboard. Without losing the insertion their bodies stayed glued one to the other as they squirmed back upon the seat.

As he was realigning for a better foothold he cause a skip. And that single skip in rhythm had caused her to open her eyes and in so doing she looked directly upward at a spellbinding midnight blue sky that was ablaze with a million stars.

Next in that split instant an electrical charge flashed through her mind of a big wide silver theater screen showing a starry desert night. She again sucked in deep air through her nose and this time the remembered smell was strong and pronounced of a dark empty theater with its rows of empty seats; and it triggered an uncontrollable quivering in her lips.

In instant reflex her legs went into a squeezing clamp around his waist and her mouth went into hysteria. She insanely grabbed her lover's full head of hair with both hands. Pulling his lips smashing to hers she forced his mouth open wide and sucked the full length of his tongue into her mouth.

As her nude thighs clamped tighter, a million volts of white hot passion arked through her body, her vagina pulsated gushing juices, and she bit down ferociously into her lover's fully ingested tongue.

Like an astronomical flash of lightning at night that lights up the sky bright as day and then disappears, her orgasm electrified her across the ends of the universe and then ended just as instantaneously. Releasing her teeth, her lover instantly screamed in pain and fought to break free.

As they quickly squirmed out of their prone position and became upright the damage that her biting had done was instantly apparent. He was unable to fully retract his tongue, blood was gushing out, and he yelled in jabbering agony. As rapidly as possible she took the steering wheel and they rushed to the Emergency Room at Allegheny Hospital.

As she sat in the waiting room she felt ashamed and embarrassed over her loss of control. *But why,* she kept justifying to herself, *didn't he pop me a hard one when I was biting? That would have been the natural thing to do. I know if he had of just popped me a fast one I would have let up.*

The incident had been so brutal that it had never happened again. Nevertheless, the orgasmic electrifying feeling remained with her. For days thereafter the craving would not go away and she couldn't keep from clenching her jaws. To prevent damage to her teeth she constantly chewed on kitchen matches and tooth picks until they splintered. Yet she could not bring herself to reveal the incident to her three girlfriends. She knew they would never understand. In their minds the only normal orgasm was an intercourse orgasm; anything along the lines of biting a man's tongue until it bled would be viewed as cannibalistic. In the years to come she would little by little come to understand her actions. But this night was not yet that night.

For the present she simply accepted the fact that her three friends were probably normal and she was different. Different, if for no other aspect than they each had only one father and one mother. In comparison she had had the benefit of three fathers and two mothers.

After Patricia's death it fell natural that Jenny would assume the role of mother. A blessing so great it must have been intentionally and meticulously engineered and carefully orchestrated into the great master plan.

It started at Patricia's graveside on that cold December day. Jenny had reached down and gathered Shelly into her arms and by that act, there came to earth the second life by Immaculate Conception; in as much as Shelly was born to Jenny.

In the passing years, all things humanly possible flowed from Jenny to Shelly. Things of love, attention, teaching; balanced with the discipline to not over smother but allow youth to experience its own achievements as well as mistakes and learn thereby. Shelly was never sheltered from sex but neither was she introduced to it. Instead she was taught about it. She was taught that it is natural that sex can occur without the element of love. On the other hand, for love to grow to its fullest bloom it must be anointed with the blended sex fluids of both man and woman. That she learned from Jenny.

From Morgan, Shelly received the love that should have gone to her mother. She became an everyday part of his life. The spectrum ranged from Morgan routinely dropping by Jenny's each morning to frequently having her in the afternoon. The pages of Shelly's growing up life were filled with playing around the Stran.

To Morgan there was a natural bonding by her sitting in his lap and writing at his desk. As growing years passed the two would drive together to the beach at Presque Isle and walk through the woods in autumn with her little girl's fingers curled to the calloused index finger of his giant hand. He told her stories over and over of the brief times he and Patricia shared; and with each telling, the memories grew.

When it had come time for school it drifted logically to Frank Buckwilder. In 1945 the Paragon Preparatory Academy was Pittsburgh's most exclusive private school. Admissions were contingent upon social standing and sternly screened by an interviewing committee. In the fall of that year Paragon received a record number of six hundred and thirty applications. Of that total, one hundred and fifty were accepted; most of which was mega money. Most, but not all.

Among those accepted were Celia Clair Frick, granddaughter of Rutherford Henry Frick; a multi multi millionaire financier, philanthropist and close associate to Andrew Carnegie. Lillian Forsythe, daughter of William Jason Forsythe; of Forsythe Steel, Forsythe Plate Glass and North Atlantic Shipping Lines. Laura Cochran, the only child of John Cochran; sole heir to the Cochran Conglomerate, Ltd. of oil, steel, newspapers, and banking. And, Shelly Waters, orphan under the guardianship of Frank Buckwilder; attorney at law, bachelor...and intensely sought after by the school's founder, Miss Lillian Carver. On their first day in school these four fresh faces, all dressed in white, had found instant acceptance in each other.

They immediately bonding into playmates, became inseparable and would forged lifelong ties. Whatever the other three had in the way of extravagant privileged indulgence so had Shelly...in the nature of Frank Buckwilder; including Saturday morning equestrian classes, tennis, swimming and summer camp.

Thus the seed of Michael O'Riley, the coal miner in a business suit would finally mingle with the seeds of wealth. This time the forces of destiny were aligned on the outside of money. For Celia, Lillian, Laura and Shelly the next generation was underway.

To any outsider, the mismatched physical anatomy of the four being of such as to question whether or not it was a destiny joke. The only common physical characteristic among the four was that there was no common characteristic. Tall, short, fat, thin, shy and rebellious. Laura for example could never make a decision, would mature to over six feet in height, have poor eyesight, and wear thick horn rim glasses. Lillian's growth would copy her mother's exactly. In her maturing years she would develop big high chest boobs and become overweight. Celia would blossom into a radiant woman but of such innocent mind she never realized her own beauty. Shelly would become equally beautiful but rebellious and had no trouble or hesitation in making instant decisions. Hers was a natural trait that would cast her as the group leader and protector.

As the years past the pattern would intertwine them into almost inseparable lives.

In 1946 Morgan and Jenny went into a joint business venture. The building boom of the post war era was getting underway, building supplies were becoming available and together they built the North Hills Drive-in Restaurant; and for Shelly and her friends it would become a hamburger-and-milkshake hangout.

In late 1947 Frank Buckwilder curtailed his law practice to spend more time with Shelly and over the following years would strongly influence her life in the realms of social graces of elegance, poise, etiquette's and protocol. In later years he taught her about art, philosophy and beauty; of law and justice and the price one must sometimes pay for fighting for that which is right.

Through Aspen Gerore McGee she learned of banking matters. In the mid 1940's Aspen's fight with the Apostle Church would again breakout. He went back into court to contest the legal restriction which limited his right to make investment decisions; arguing that he was a person of high moral and ethical fiber as demonstrated by the extra ordinary degree of concern he endured in protecting the investment in the cattle drive.

On the basis of his exemplary efforts to exercise prudence, combined with the basic premise that to invest is to take risk, the court removed all restriction on his right to invest.

In 1949 when Shelly was eight years old Aspen struck the first of many blows to the Apostle Church by paying an 'investment' price of two million dollars for the Citadel Hotel and then leasing it to Jenny for one dollar per year. Located two blocks from the County Government Complex it was the most luxurious, ornate and debonair small hotel in Pittsburgh and soon became Pittsburgh's most fashionable and elite brothel; with penthouse living quarters for Jenny and Shelly.

In 1950 when she was ten Shelly attended a social tea at the 144-room mansion of Henry Clay Frick. She was accompanied to the function by Mother Jenny; who carried herself tall, held her cup of tea with her pinky finger extended and met for the first time the wives whose husbands she had been servicing for years.

In 1951 Shelly discontinued equestrian classes, choosing instead to spend Saturday mornings with Poppy Frank Buckwilder. Together they explored the sites and sounds of Pittsburgh; including the Pepperdine Conservatory, Heinz Hall for the Performing Arts, the Buhl Planetarium, art showings, the Museum of Natural History and in particular the Carnegie Library where Shelly would someday return many times on her own.

In the same time frame of 1951 Morgan Smithfield did not believe that the advent of television would ever develop into a major media and certainly would never be a threat to the movie industry and considered it a wise investment when he purchased a chain of five additional theaters. Thereafter, when Shelly and Morgan were together the time was usually spent in the matters of theaters.

In 1954 when Shelly and her three schoolmates, Celia Clair, Lillian, and Laura were all in their early teens the first of Shelly's many fights broke out. The four had started hanging out on Saturday afternoons at North Hills Ice Skating Rink and were just learning to skate. For Shelly, skating came natural and in short time she was accomplished. Not so for the other three; their progress was much slower; especially Celia Clair and Laura.

Celia Clair had not yet started to develop and was small, thin and lacked physical strength. Falling and then falling again even as she was attempting to scramble up, her poor backside was taking an unmerciful beating. Where Celia was simply small and lacked physical strength, Laura was tall and ungainly. Her wobbly legs would alternate between knocking in at the knees and flying outward as she fell out of control her backside.

All of this had not gone unnoticed by a gang of boy skaters who did what boys of that age always do; they decided to have fun at the girl's expense. They singled out Celia Clair and Laura as objects of heckling. Circling around and about they would veer in close at racing speed and call out "Mutt and Jeff" as they passed by.

It was a field day for that particular group and their youthful mischief gained momentum as they skated in circles closer and closer around the terribly embarrassed Celia and Laura.

Both girls had succeeded in getting to the sideline and were holding on to a support rail when Shelly and Lillian skated up. On the other side of the rink the jeering was continuing as "Mutt, Mutt" and "Jeff, Jeff" were being gangly shouted in their direction; and it was here that the defender in Shelly made its debut. Whirling around on the ice she bounded into a sprinting stride across the ice. Gaining momentum as she went, she shot across the rink at full speed and plunged head on into the entire crowd.

Most scattered but not all. She hit a fifteen-year-old boy dead center and the two went sliding across the rink in a tangled heap. As they came to a slippery stop Shelly was on top but she could feel his weight about to push her aside.

Within the next instant numerous skaters moved in and the fight was stopped. There was some aftermath jeering which Shelly answered in like kind, but for the day the incident was over. Fights among teenagers however are prone to continue and throughout the following school week the young man vowed face-saving retaliation. Word quickly spread and the following Saturday afternoon the second episode would be played out. When Shelly and her friends arrived at the skating rink a mixed group of youths were waiting outside. When Celia Clair heard the calls of "Mutt, Mutt" she wanted to leave. The same held for Laura as they called "Jeff, Jeff, here Jeff Jeff," but it only riled Shelly. The teachings of Poppa Frank Buckwilder were about to be tested.

At first it was just face-to-face shouting between she and the dishonored youth as the crowd looked on. In all probability it would not have escalated but he overstepped the bounds by poking his finger in her chest and shouted for her to take her beanpole, skinny friends and leave.

In reflex she threw a punch with a direct hit to the nose and his blood started spurting out. A second youth, in actuality a misunderstood good samaritan, jumped in between the two with the intent of stopping the fight. Except reflex stepped in and Shelly threw another punch; this one connecting with the Samaritan's nose. His good intentions thwarted, he angrily grabbed her in a bear hug and threw her across the scrubby trampled lawn. As she scooted half sideways across the grass she could feel the dirt dig into her mouth.

As she stopped sliding he was again misunderstood. His intentions were to help her up but the hand he extended was met by a clamping set of teeth; which instantly brought his other hand popping across her head.

The stars she saw was sufficient for her to concede it was an overmatch. From somewhere a man in a uniform broke through the crowd, pulled the two apart and with scolding words of admonishment order the crowd disbursed.

Shelly had not been proud of the fight. In truth she was embarrassed that she had acted so unlady like. While she did not know it then, the pattern of her later life had just been forged. In a mood of enough trouble for one day the foursome did not remain at the skating rink but went downtown to Kaufman's Department Store.

Standing at the free samples counter of the cosmetic department she and the other three attempted to repair the scuffing damage. In typical teenage fashion they tested samples of perfume, put on lipstick looking in a cosmetic mirror, giggled and caused each other embarrassment.

From there they stopped at the magazine rack and browsed through Hollywood magazines and ooed and awed at pictures of movie idol, James Dean.

Outside on 5th Avenue they mingled in the Saturday afternoon crowds and yelled back at good-looking guys in hot wheels cruising the streets. It was fun to have finally started their growing-up years; but somehow Shelly did not feel that she had the right to laugh as loud and freely as the others.

In late summer of the same year there was another change. Jenny Craig bought a house and she and Shelly moved out of the Citadel. It all came about in a moment of happenstance when Frank Buckwilder telephoned Morgan Smithfield. There was a rare opportunity to buy a highly desirable property out in Squirrel Hill at a distress price.

The owner had died and the estate was being hit with heavy estate taxes. The heirs all lived in Europe and had no interest in coming to America. The property was put up for sale but it had to be an all cash transaction. Within the hour Jenny, Morgan and Frank made an inspection and under the encouragement of Morgan and Frank, Jenny made a cash offer which was accepted. A week later, in a mahogany paneled room with a long oval table and high back executive chairs the closing took place. In a brief paper signing Jenny presented a cashier's check and received the keys.

She remembered experiencing a strange sensation that there should be something more; more than just getting a set of keys. To own this beautiful home was the fulfillment of a life long dream. That it should happen by simple pass a piece of paper did not seem enough. As she put the key into the front door and entered, those thoughts immediately went away. A smell of musk combined with the odor of luxurious carpet filled her nostrils. She breathed in deep and thought to herself, *this moment, it belongs to Shelly and me.*

"Welcome to your new home, correction, our new home," Jenny had said to Shelly as they entered the broad spacious living room. "It took a long time getting here but we finally made it."

"Oh, Wow," said Shelly as she and Jenny glanced about and gave each other a loving hug. "I love it, I love it, imagine living in a mansion in Squirrel Hill."

"Well," replied Jenny, "it's not what you would call a mansion, but it will do until one comes along. Let's explore and see what we've got."

Excitedly, they took each other's hand and started to look. Their tour took them through five bedrooms, three baths, a formal living room, a formal dining room, a smoking room, a large kitchen and dining area.

The furnishings were elaborate with the level of each room exceeding the fashion of the last. Maroon velvet drapes with gold rope braid adorned the windows and the dividing arch between the formal living room and the formal dining room.

Gold and crystal chandeliers suspended from the ceiling and works of art hung throughout. The living room was furnished with floral patterned silk covered chairs, sofa and a settee. The formal dinning room was furnished with a long mahogany table, twelve high back Royal Palace chairs and a matching floor-to-ceiling, diamond leaded glass hutch. Chippendale chairs were tastefully located in selected room corners and in the hallways.

On the second floor each bedroom outdid the first. As the two explored first one and then the next they frequently squeezed each other's hands and then Shelly excitedly asked, "Which one is going to be mine?"

"You mean for your very own?" Jenny mimicked. "Gracious now, I don't know about that, I will have to really give this some serious thought. Let's see here. I received some very strict house rules when I got the key.

"And I remember that the instructions said that young ladies who are permitted to pick their own bed room have to be extra extra special. Is that anyone we know?"

"You bet your sweet War Bonds," exclaimed Shelly as she returned the tease. "Me, myself, and I. Right here," she pointed her finger to her chest.

"Three for the price of one. And all three of us are super duper, world wide, monumental, royal flush extra ordinary special."

"Goodness," responded Jenny, "then I had better fix you up with an extra special bedroom with frilly curtains, teddy bears, silky bed spreads and such. Otherwise I might get evicted for not following the instructions," and they hugged.

That night they were preparing a special celebration dinner when in casual talk Shelly asked, "How do you suppose the neighbors will react when they find out you are a Madam? I mean will they boo us, or hate us or what?"

"Well, Sweetheart," Jenny spoke without showing any surprise as she continued to toss the salad, "I suppose it will be the same as if I was a lawyer, a dentist or garbage collector. I assume there will be some who will hate us, some who do not care one way or the other and some who will be very appreciative to have us as good neighbors. Why? Are you scared or ashamed?"

Shelly was putting plates on the table as she responded. "No, I'm not scared and I don't see anything to be ashamed of. I've lived with you and the rest of the girls all my life.

"I know everything that's going on and as far as I am concerned, fine. It's just now, realizing that we are going to be living in a house like other people, all of a sudden I feel older and I want to talk."

She had been setting dishes on table as she was talking and as she returned from the dinning room to the kitchen she found Jenny looking at her. Their eyes made direct contact and silently signaled this was an important moment. Jenny stopped mixing the salad, briefly wiped her hand on a drying towel, extended her open arms out to Shelly and they gave each other a warm hug.

"Honey," Jenny continued as she stood back slightly but continued to hold Shelly by the shoulders, "what I am about to say I hope you will always remember. You can always talk to me. Day or night or anytime in between. Talk to me Honey and it doesn't matter about what." The words brought a slight watering to Shelly's eyes.

"Well now," Jenny continued as she slightly brushed away a small tear, "I believe you have grown up right before my eyes and I didn't even see it.

"Maybe instead of a pink and white bedspread and frilly curtains for your room I should be thinking in terms of movie star posters, cosmetics and mini high heels?"

"Oh pleeease Mother Jenny, nothing like that. I see men come in and out of the Citadel rooms all the time," she paused in search for words and then continued.

"I'm not old enough to know the right words but what I am asking is why do you and the other girls do what you do and why do men come there. I mean if they have a wife why do they come to you?

"Isn't it supposed to be that boys grow into men and girls grow into women and they get married and get all the sex they need from each other?"

Jenny proceeded with setting the table in a normal manner but to herself she said, '*Please dear God. Please let me handle this exactly right*'.

"Honey," she turned to Shelly and spoke without too much emphasis, "as you grow older you'll learn that life is very difficult. I don't want to get too involved right now but I will say this. The men who come to me are usually very good men. Most are hard working and dearly care about their homes and families.

"It's just that sometimes the pressures of the world become too unbearable and they need a moment to themselves. The reassurance of just feeling another woman.

"Honey its really very complicated, but from my perspective I simply feel that it doesn't make a good man bad. I don't look at it as him having extramarital sex. I see him as having a need that in his own way he has to satisfy; and if I can do that I feel better for it.

"Each of us has only one life to live Sweetheart. So live it for you. And the thing which I want you to remember the most is this, the one single thing which has ruined more lives than all other things combined, is worrying about what someone else might think."

For their first meal Jenny and Shelly sat down to table with a stiff white linen tablecloth and matching napkins rolled in a silver napkin ring. Two ornamental silver candleholders held two long smooth candles, flickering in compliment to the soft atmosphere of the turned down chandelier. They had before them a tossed salad of fresh sliced tomatoes, crisp green lettuce, sliced red onions and shredded carrots.

For their entrée they had pork chops seared for one minute in a hot skillet and then sautéed in white wine to medium well, homemade potato salad with half sliced boiled eggs, carrots, diced apples, raisins stirred in a wine sauce, creamed corn and hot rolls.

The glassware was lead-based crystal, ornamental etched diamond cut, stemmed goblets and water glasses. Complementing the glassware were white Sheffield England plates with a silver border and a horn-of-plenty wheat stalk embossed in the center.

As they sat down, they lightly bowed and Jenny said a little prayer.

"Dear Lord please believe me when I tell you that tonight I am ever so thankful for all that is before me." She lightly touched her napkin to her eyes, looked at Shelly and said, "My most wonderful child how much I love you." They touched their wineglasses in toast, took a sip and started eating.

Probably because of the new surroundings, the getting used to settling in, a pause accompanied their first few bites. Not hesitating so much as a slight feeling of awkwardness Shelly then asked, "Mother Jenny can I say something?"

"Of course," responded Jenny. The child in Shelly could be seen in her eyes but the maturity in her was to be found in her words.

"I have wanted to tell you this for a long time," she started. "Actually it's two things. First I want to say that I love you very much. Then I want to say that I love my mother even more.

"There is no time when I am not thinking about her and how I wish that she had not died. I know that thinking about her will not bring her back but I can't help myself.

"It's just that I remember over and over the things which we used to do. In a way I am scared because I am always thinking 'mother if you were here you could tell me what to do or not do' on things. But I also thank God that He sent you as her stand in."

Jenny reached over to touch Shelly's hand. In a response gesture it was Shelly who reacted. She grasped Jenny's hand and with the squeeze of a young girl's touch it went to her lips as she said, "Next to my real mom no one could ever hope for anyone better than you."

What then followed were silent moments as precious as life. It was a pinnacle when no words needed to be said. The heart of each was in the emotions of these moments.

The feeling was far too blessed to leave. Any word, any other thought, any sound would have been like a lance piercing the heart of an angel.

Thereafter they dined without talking; substituting loving glances and soft smiles. After the meal was finished and the dishes washed Jenny looked at Shelly and said, "I have been thinking, how would you like to sleep with me tonight?" It was the perfect gesture to a perfect evening and that night the two shared a bed for the first time in a long time.

When the lights were finally out and the quietness of the room settled in, there seemed to be a need to talk.

"I am pleased," started Jenny, "that you remember your mother. I have often wondered how much you remember. You were not yet quite four years old when she..."

"Died," continued Shelly. Jenny was silent and Shelly went ahead.

"It's OK, I'm not hurt by using the word. We are all going to die.

"What I don't understand is why so much love should die and all around me I see hate that is alive. Did you know my mother?"

"I knew her," said Jenny. "She was my friend and I knew her but I never knew what was deep inside. I don't think there was anyone who really knew your mother. I remember how she used to hold you and shower you with love, hugs and kisses."

"And let me breast feed," said Shelly. The comment caught Jenny completely by surprise. She swallowed and was panicky searching for exactly the right response when Shelly continued.

"I didn't know it then but I do now. It wasn't right for me to still be breast-feeding past the age of three. I think about it everyday and I need to talk about it."

"Sweetheart," responded Jenny, "I am right here and here I will be for as long as you want to talk. All night, all day, a week, a month, there is nothing more important in my life than you."

As if she knew this, Shelly's voice did not change and under the cloak of the silent darkness she continued.

"Do you know what we used to do? I mean almost every night after mother closed the ticket cage.

"Did you know that we used to go inside and watch the last show? We liked to be by ourselves so we would go high up in balcony to the back row where there wasn't anyone else.

"I can still remember the long flight of stairs leading up and how my little short legs could hardly reach the next step and mother would hold me by the hand and sort of help pull me up.

"Then, when we got to the very top row and looked down, it seemed like the screen was a million miles away. It was always real dark up there and until our eyes adjusted we couldn't see but we always managed to end up in the very top row where there was no one else behind us.

"Sometimes there would be some lovers scattered down on the lower floor kissing and hugging but we were always lucky enough to have the balcony all to ourselves.

"I would sit in mother's lap and she would cradle me and open up her blouse and I would take out her breast and nurse. I wasn't getting any milk or anything, but even today I can still remember how I couldn't wait.

"I remember how it felt to first reach my hand inside her brazier and feel the soft skin. Her breasts were very long and she just sort of curled them up inside of the brassiere cup.

"And the instant when I would take it out and put the nipple in my mouth there was a feeling I don't know how to describe. I kind of wanted to pee but that is not exactly right either.

"It got to where the thought was always on my mind. Somehow I started realizing that when the last show started we could do it. I was always real good so that there wouldn't be any trouble or anything and we could hurry up and get started."

Then, without explanation Shelly stopped talking and a silence fell on the room. Jenny didn't have to reach over and feel, she knew; the lonely little girl beside her had tears in her eyes.

With pronounced softness, she asked, "Honey, do you mean to tell me that after all these years you can still remember how it felt?"

"Yes," Shelly responded meekly. "I can still remember wanting to get as much of her breast in my mouth as I could and then to hug her real hard.

"It seemed that if I could just get all of her breast in my mouth then I was all hers and she was all mine."

There was a pause and again Jenny spoke. "Do you want me to talk?" she asked.

Again as if Jenny hadn't said anything Shelly continued. "I remember when I had all of her breast in my mouth I could not keep from biting. Sometimes I would bite too hard and mother would pop me a little on the head and I would let up.

"But then somehow my pee sensation would just seemed to pass and I would quit sucking and start watching the movie. Mother would put her breast back in her blouse and we would stay until the movie closed."

Then with a change, perhaps as in the change from when she would stop sucking and start watching, Shelly asked, "Would you like to know which movie I remember the most?

"It was Aladdin's Magic Carpet. About this handsome Arabian Prince in the Sahara Desert and he had this magic carpet.

"At night when the moon was full and stars were bright he would take his beautiful princess and they would fly up in the heavens with the wind blowing through her hair.

"They could look down and see the moonlight shinning on rippling desert sand. They were so much in love and they lived happily ever after. We must have seen that movie 50 times."

Shelly had no way of knowing the pain that shot through Jenny at the mention of Aladdin's Magic Carpet.

An instant flinch hit Jenny. The mention of that movie caused a splitting flash back.

Morgan. He must have known, she thought. *He would have had to of known. Why else would he have shown that film so often? After a while everybody in town had seen it.*

That poor wonderful man, how tormented he must have been; to have known what was happening and not knowing what else to do.

Whatever sleep there was in Jenny's eyes before, was now gone. The renewed memory of herself, of Morgan and of Shelly's mother, Patricia was instantly vivid in her mind and she silently cursed.

What a waste, she thought. *A waste of happiness in all three of our lives. I wish I hadn't remembered.*

Damn, damn, damn, she said again to herself. *Isn't there one single thing right in the whole damn world? I wanted Morgan but couldn't have him, Morgan wanted Patricia but couldn't have her and Patricia just wanted to feel like a normal everyday woman but the world wouldn't let her. Why is...* but her thoughts were interrupted by the sound of Shelly's voice.

"Mother Jenny," Shelly asked in a hesitating tone. "Yes Baby," Jenny answered in soothing tone as she instantly realized how terrible had been her thoughts.

"Jenny," Shelly asked in the same hesitating tone, "can I feel your breast?"

Jenny lay so still she could hear her own breathing. The starkness of the question had cut through to her heart. Her anger of a moment ago now turned to shame. Sealed in her mind by the knowing that in their lifetimes this moment would never again be experienced.

Without speaking another word there came from Jenny the natural guidance of reaching down and finding Shelly's hand. Giving it a reassuring squeeze and then gently bringing it up to the neck line of her night gown and held it there as her free hand unbuttoned the front.

Then with the same softness, guided the inquiring hand onto her breast. The touch of the child's fingers on her nipple ignited a fleeting feeling of clairvoyance; in that instance, she felt herself become Patricia, and this was her baby.

Without conversation Shelly's fingers first touched the nipple and in circular motion massaged the rubbery module to firmness. Her inquiring hand lightly opened and closed around the total breast; to experience the size, roundness and firmness of the full breast; her fingers traced the outline where the breast and chest cage come together.

Her hand then moved to the other breast where her quest was repeated. Then with a final touch she pulled back her hand and let it fall across her forehead.

A moment of silence followed and then Shelly said, "I am tired now" and with exchange of "goodnight" each adjusted in bed and became lost in their own thoughts.

In the minds of these two women there were equal but totally different reflections. For Jenny there had been the urge to grasp Shelly's hand and force it to squeeze harder; to convey that a woman's breast are a fountain of love; a flow of love which can be heightened by the chemistry of firm squeezing. She had wanted to hug Shelly to her body and say, *it doesn't hurt Baby, it feels good. Squeeze and experience the depth of my love.*

In the mind of Shelly there was a comparison to her mother. And a pondering of worth and desire. *Why is a woman with round full breast worthy of being loved while a woman with elongated dangling breast is not?*

In the spring of 1955 Frank Buckwilder took Shelly on a tour of Europe. In Greece he taught her about Ancient Greece as being the cradle of democracy, philosophy and mythology.

"Democracy," he had explained, "comes from the Greek word *démokratia* meaning common people and delineates government by the people as exercised directly or through elected officials."

At Shelly's tender age, his words had little meaning as they stood on the grounds of a restored 'agora'; a market place in ancient Greece customarily used for popular assembly. However, in later years his words would become profoundly meaningful.

"In Greek Philosophy," he had also related, "pleasure seeking is a myth; it does not exist. Pleasure, at least lasting pleasure, has to be earned. The only true happiness in life stems from achieving, of building, of dedication, of being all that one can be.

"The greatest voyage on earth," he spoke while sitting on a fallen stone in the Temple of Zeus, "is the voyage of looking within one's own mind, to explore one's own limits and then going beyond.

"In Greek Mythology," he continued to teach, "for beauty to exist there must be two things. It must be shared with someone you love and it must be interpreted with words, not of the tongue, but feelings so intense they can only dwell in one's soul."

At the temple of Aphrodite his words took on meaning as he shared with her the origin of her beauty.

"The eye of the beholder," he had explained, "should not look at the statue of marble, be that beauty within itself, but look at the Goddess of Love therein.

"There you will see a beauty which radiates the softness of morning dew as it glistens on the peddles of a firm red rose.

"Testimony to her innocence sparkles from her soft unblemished face of milk white skin and rosy cheeks.

"Envision her hair as being shinny black as it flows in the wind and she frequently pushes it back as she looks at her suitors with eyes that glisten in the light of a heavenly moon.

"She was so perfect and so delicate," Frank went on to describe, "because she was made from just the foam of the crystal clear green waters of the Aegean Sea."

The mental picture of the Gods and lovers triggered Shelly's romantic fantasies. She imagined how it must have been to have frolicked around the heaven and wished that she could have lived back then; to have been Aphrodite, dressed in a white flowing thin gown and being Zeus's loving mistress; and how they would have made love among the stars.

In Paris they went to the top of the Eiffel Tower and were awed by the stupendous view. Frank pointed out the beauty of things when viewed from afar; but beauty is almost always tarnished or lost if the beholder insists upon looking too closely.

They visited the Museum of the Louvre and as they passed through the lengthy corridors of master paintings Frank shared his thoughts on man's expressions on canvas; in pursuit of dreams which come not to life in real.

In 1957 when she was sixteen Shelly had an out-of-body experience; brought on by an automobile drag race which went bad. For Christmas that year Lillian Forsythe received a brand new Chevrolet black convertible with a white top and red upholster. It was shortly thereafter when the four friends were violating the Paragon Academy curfew by being out at three in the morning.

Cruising the streets of Pittsburgh with the top back at that hour the streets were mostly deserted. Shelly and Laura were riding in back; sitting not in the seat but upon the back boot.

They were stopped at a red light to the entrance of Mile-Long Bridge when a 1957 Ford Fairlane 500 with three Pitt football players pulled up along side.

At the prospect of male attention Laura slid down in the seat to hide her height but Shelly remained up on the boot. Ford against Chevrolet rivalry instantly flared as each car heckled the other and bragged about their own. With engines revving and tail pipes rapping they ragged each other while waiting for the light to turn green. In a flash the two cars bolted, tires screamed, rubber burned and the race was on.

In the first two hundred yards the automatic transmission of the Ford started loosing ground to the stick shift of the Chevy.

Shelly was still sitting up on the boot with the wind blowing through her long hair and Lillian's foot was flat down on the accelerator. Topping out second gear she speed shifted into third, the tires screamed and the gap between the two cars kept widening. Shelly, still high up on the back boot, turned half around and was waving a flaunting wave; but there was an accident waiting to happen.

The left front tire of the Chevy became entrenched in a trolley car track and Lillian was not that good of a driver.

Instead of letting the car correct it's on course she fought the steering wheel and when the tire broke out she over-steered. The car went out of control, fish tailed and smashed head-on into the concrete bridge wall.

The impact caused the three girls who were sitting down to slam body and head into crumpled seats and dash board but Shelly was catapulted completely over the windshield, over the bridge parapet and was headed for the dark murky water of the Monongahela River.

She was not yet in panic but she instinctively knew the impact would be like hitting concrete and that in one half of a second she may die. Then suddenly her falling stopped; stopped completely, suspended in mid-air.

She looked at the bridge and could see her three friends slammed against the crumpled front dash and windshield; their heads down with their arms thrown up in front of their faces.

But they were not moving, she was not moving, neither of the two cars was moving, nothing was moving and there was ghostly silence.

Then she heard a voice. From out of the deathly silence there came a voice. Clear, almost crystal clear; like the tapping ring from a crystal glass. She was hearing words that were pronounced with precise diction but very soothing; instantly comforting. She was not alone. There was someone right next to her.

"There, there my little one," said the voice. "Why are we in such a hurry to injure ourselves. Perhaps we could talk about it before things go any further."

Still she was not moving; that is to say she was not falling but she could turn and look around.

"What's happening?" she asked of the voice. "Why am I just floating? Am I dead? I didn't feel anything. I..."

"All in good time little Princess. No, you are not dead, you may get wet in a little while; but no, you are not dead."

"But who are you? Everything is so quiet. How can I talk to you but can't see you. How come I am just floating here? I..."

"So many questions from one so young," the voice responded and then continued. "Would you like to see me? To talk to me?"

"But, how can we keep staying here?" she asked again in a tone becoming more frightened.

"I'm scared. I don't want to be here," she started crying. "I'm afraid of dying.

"I haven't even started to live. Please, please, whoever you are," she begged as tears were streaming down her cheeks, "I just want to be home in my bed."

"There, there little one. We have all the time in the world. First things first. First let's do away with you being scared. Tell me if you are feeling a little more relaxed."

"I, strange. I'm feeling strange. It's, I feel so peaceful," came her response. "How did you..."

"Now for the matter of time," the voice cut in. "Trust me when I say we have an hour, a year, two thousand years; as long as we like. So just relax, feel safe. There is no time."

"But who are you?" she asked. "How come I can talk to you but can't see you?"

"Ah, that's my fault, I'm not thinking; sorry little one. I forgot for a moment that mortals have a need to see some sort of life form. In heaven there are no bodies. I..."

"Are you GOD?" she gasped.

"First," He set about his intent without answering her question, "let me take on a form you can relate to. Since you are white, Caucasian how about a fatherly wise old man with beard and a full head of shaggy gray-white hair dressed in a robe sitting here beside you on a cloud. How's this?" God materialized Himself as He finished.

"GOD," she again grasped. "Why me, why here. How did..."

"Why did I catch you?" he finished her question. "I just happened to be in the neighborhood. Everybody and everything has to be somewhere. For now I just happened to be here."

"Oh dear God, my, my most heavenly Father, there is so much I would like to ask but, but I don't know where to start. I feel like You must be so busy and that I should hurry..."

"My little Princess, listen to Me. I repeat. There is no time limit. Time as you understand it is something so complicated it is beyond mortal comprehension.

"It all relates to distance, space, life beginning and life ending and so much more. So for now let's just talk. We have as long as we need."

"God I love You, I feel close to You but I'm only sixteen. I don't know what to talk about. All I know is I am supposed to bow down to You."

"And you feel that if you were a little older you would be more wiser, is that it?"

"Well, yes. I guess that would. I mean older people are supposed to be smarter."

"OK my very nervous one, how about we just move your mind up the age-line to what you will know when you are about forty. How does that feel?"

"God," she immediately asked in the most adult way, "is there really a heaven and hell?"

"Shelly, that's such a radical jump. We've just this instant met. Maybe it would be better if we just sit here and get relaxed in each other's company. Before we get into things like life after death.

"Maybe we could just talk a little about living; to understand heaven you first need to become a little more aware about life.

"But heaven," she responded without realizing that it sounded like arguing, "from everything I have ever heard, I mean ever since I was just a child, the idea is to just make it to heaven; once you get there you've got it made."

When He didn't answer immediately she looked directly at His face. It seemed to her that she saw a faint smile and that He might even be questioning His wisdom of moving her mind-line up; at least He seemed to be thinking about something and in no hurry to respond. She didn't know whether Gods actually breathe in air or not but if her perceptions were correct He seemed to inhale a deep breath before He responded.

"Shelly," His voice reflecting that He would let her have her way, "to enter heaven, or as you say, go to heaven, you must first live through your conflicts."

"Conflicts?" without thinking she cut in with a question. "How did conflicts get into this? What's that got to do with getting into heaven? I mean...?"

This time God did not smile but neither did He frown; not yet. What He did do was to slightly shake His head and think to Himself, *Uh OH... This one has the makings of being really something. It should be very very interesting to watch this little tiger grow into adulthood.*

"I..."

"...Don't understand?" He finished her question for her. "Conflict it's a term used here on earth, meaning challenges which human life must endure in order to live and survive."

"You mean," she asked in a questioning tone, "all the thousands and thousands of everyday problems we all have to watch out for just to live?

Is that the big deal?"

The choice of her words caused Him to cringe. *Is*, he instantly thought, *'big deal' the talk that kids are using today.*

He wasn't used to being questioned. It caused Him to feel defensive. All of a sudden it was she and not Him who was directing the conversation. The questioning of His wisdom was causing a streak of annoyance. *Well, I'll be, if this isn't something,* He thought. *New hires; They're all alike. As soon as they get on board they start running the show. I'll never learn; try to do something for someone; proof again that no good deed will go unpunished. I can just imagine what the consequences might be on heaven IF she ever gets there.*

"Conflicts! Shelly!" He pronounced the two words with emphasis, "of which there are only Three." The last word He also emphasized to make sure she understood it was important. The surprised look on her face indicated that He might now have her attention. Believing that benevolence was now in order His tone became more placid as He continued. "And they are: man-against-man, man-against-elements and the most difficult of all man-against-himself."

Benevolence, you may be interested in knowing, is not always fruitful; and when it fails stronger measures are sometimes necessary.

"Can't," she persistently cut back in to get an answer to what she consider was a simple straight forward question, "You just tell me whether there is, or is not, a heaven and hell?"

"I can! But Can't YOU just wait until I can forcefully pound something into that thick little head of yours about life; it all ties together if you will just listen?

"To get to heaven Miss Hard Head, you have to first live. To live you will have to face at least One of the Three conflicts; maybe All three. You with me?" His voice stern to make the point.

"That's," His tone then calmed down in explaining, "just the nature of life."

"You mean," she was surprised at the way His lower voice seemed to give her an opening to continue her questions, "that all of the troubles of the world can be lumped into just three categories; these three conflicts?"

"That's about it," the temperament of His response indicating that the point had been made and that it was now bordering on being meaningless.

"I..."

"...Don't understand," He again finished her question. Then in a tone indicating He would make one more try, He continued.

"Shelly when I say conflict, in a sense I mean fight or suffer at the hands of adversity.

"Now having said that, yes Shelly there is a heaven. But we deal only in souls; and even there we have conflict. It's just a little different, but for now I'll withhold that explanation"

"Is it," she quickly interjected, "like I have always heard. That it's beautiful and there are no problems forever and ever?"

The off-point of her question caused Him to shake His head and turn His eyes to the heavens. *Dear God,* He thought, *is there no limit to this woman. God help the man she marries.*

"Yes, I suppose," He conceded, "that from your limited perspective that would be an accurate assessment."

"What do people or rather souls do all day. I mean what all can you do in heaven; can you do whatever you want? I mean for example can you dance all night under the stars and fall in love as many times as you like?"

"You mean pleasures of the flesh? Yes, Shelly you can do all of those things for all eternity without end if that is what you desire. But there is something, if you have no objection, which I have been patiently trying to point out.

"In heaven you lose the element of wanting something; meaning anticipating. Whatever you desire, no matter what, it is instantly there; presto! Wish for it and there it is. This means you have no concept of having to earn, plan, save for and work toward achieving a goal.

"And there is no concept of disappointment. Since you don't have to set goals there is no chance of failure.

"Let me put it a different way. You never have to want for anything. You can have everything you want as much as you want, including sex, especially sex. That is what you wanted to hear wasn't it? And of course love affairs, romances, it all becomes meaningless. To what end does it all take you."

"God, I'm..., now I am confused. Heaven is what we all pray for. If we can just get there then we've got it made.

"I mean why is there even the slightest question of whether or not... Are you telling me that maybe when we get there it may not be what we think."

"It is everything you think Shelly, but what I am saying is there is no sorrow, no pain, no hurt, no heartache. In heaven self-indulgence is available like air is on earth.

"You can breathe all the air you want but you can only breathe so much air; right? Think about this. Breathing alone is not enough to make you happy.

"In heaven, *serving and doing for others* is the big sought after prize; not self indulgence.

"In heaven the more one gives of him or herself the happier one becomes. That's what makes it heaven. You can spend all of your efforts doing for others without having to be concerned about taking care of your own needs. The only problem IS finding someone to help. How's that for maybe casting a little different picture on the concept of heaven.

"Let me give you something you can relate too. Earth is the real heaven Shelly. I'll repeat that," He said in a slow concise tone, "earth is the real heaven. The fact of having to earn something makes it have value."

"God is there a hell?"

"Hell is basically being separated from those you love," He responded to the question without any emphasis because He did not want to lose the progress He was making.

"And, yes there are times when souls are separated. But it isn't the searing, molting place of fire which is commonly pictured."

"God," she asked as soon as His response was finished, "is there such a thing as reincarnation?"

"Reincarnation?" He repeated her question while He was thinking. It wasn't something that He particularly wanted to discuss but, the thought came to Him, that it might be a means of getting inside of her mind.

"Yes, Shelly," He spoke in a teacher to student tone, "there are certain ones who ask to come back. Mostly it's the strong-minded, restless souls who can't stand the boredom of lounging around and doing nothing; generally the ones who were naturally forceful when they were alive and possessed an unrelenting drive to succeed. To them it is more satisfying to come back and face the brutalities of living."

"How do they do? I mean the one's who decide to come back? I mean is there anyone that we all know...?

"You mean names Shelly?"

"I'd really like to know...?" her response was in a tone reflecting that she didn't know if it was proper to ask. "If it's all right...?"

At the apparent insecurity of her question God almost broke out into a laugh. His annoyance collapsed, His understanding composure returned and He smiled at the young inquisitive mind.

"Oh I don't mind Shelly," He paused and it seemed to her that He took a deep breath. "Especially if it will satisfy the curiosity of a young mind. I can think of a couple of names; say one name in each type of conflict. How's that?"

"Let's start with man-against-man. Have you ever heard the name General George Smith Patton; United States Army Four Star General. He chose to come back for no other reason than to fight the most formidable army the world had ever known; the mighty power of Hitler's Nazi Germany in the holocaust referred to as World War Two; man-against-man.

"In the man-against-elements category the best example I can give is someone who was a personal friend."

"You, God? You had your own personal friend?" she asked in surprise. "And he left heaven and came back. Why on earth? Who would do something like that?"

God's head was slightly bowed and his mode had gone into an expressionless stare. His emotions stirred over remembering His ol' friend and it was a second or two before He responded.

"You mean his name?" He asked as His thoughts came back to Himself and then continued. "His name, at least the one he used this last time, was Frank Delaney; William Frank Delaney.

"I think it may have been some family name, I'm not sure. But I can tell you this, he was someone who would make you shake your head.

"And," here God paused a longer than long pause as if there was no answer but would go ahead and say something, "in answer as to why he chose to come back I do not know.

"Even I, as his personal friend could not change his mind. To him, challenging the western rangeland was something he had to do.

"With the entire world to choose from he passed up millions of acres of rich fertile farm land; choosing instead to challenge the elements of roughly a hundred thousand acres of the most barren, desolate, brutal land on the face of the earth; and fought it with every ounce of his body to win. I can only assume it was to prove something which is beyond the sane abilities of mortals."

As God was explaining, Shelly unintentionally turned and glanced at the scene of the accident. Everything was exactly the same. There was no moving traffic on the bridge. The black Chevy was still sitting with the grill and opened hood slammed into the concrete wall. And the tumbled bodies of Celia Clair, Lillian and Laura remained motionless against the crumpled seats and dashboard.

God had assured her that time had no meaning but she was still afraid that it would instantly all go away so she rushed to get as many answers as possible.

"God," she addressed Him sheepishly, "is it OK if I talk about myself, I mean can I ask questions about my life?"

"Of course you can ask Shelly. I have no secrets. You may not remember the answers, but for now ask away. There is no hurry."

"God, this may sound silly, but will I get married and will I be happy?"

"Yes, Shelly. You will get married. But before we go any further it's important that we first complete our discussion of conflicts; man-against-himself.

"Your question as to whether you will be happy makes it easy for me to address this category because you are actually what this has all been about. Maybe it would have been better on My part if I had of just came right out and said so in the beginning. But Shelly the reason I am here is I am worried about you and the conflict you are going to have with yourself."

"Me? God, Me? I'm just a young girl. How? I mean what?"

"You are young now Shelly. Before too much longer though you will be leaving the carefree days of youth behind.

"Maturity will come and with it will come the seeds of your destiny; a destiny that by and large will be influenced by your mother's destiny. A destiny that saw fit to take away your natural parents and send replacements, and finally a destiny which has seen fit to give you astonishing headlong determination. How they will all come together is not yet known. Mostly it will become your choice; but brace yourself for this. It will not be an easy road."

Then, to paint the brighter side of the picture He added, "But, the scales are not unbalanced Shelly. You have also had the benefit of wise and loving guidance. Listen to their advise and your fighting spirit will carry you through."

"God," she then asked, "I know that you have matured my mind ahead of my years but even in my maturity I don't understand. Are you telling me this for a reason?"

"Indeed I am Shelly, I am saying that where marriage is concerned it may be someone who is very different. Maybe even odd by most standards; but whatever you do, do not prejudge.

"What I want you to understand is this," God intending these to be His parting words as He started to become less visible.

"The question is not what you want from a man. But what you want from yourself. Heed these words Shelly and in the end you will overcome your own conflict."

"WILL," she shouted to Him as He was fading and the time line of her maturity was returning to her age, "HE BE HANDSOME?"

The missed-point of her question reached Him in the time zone of when He had been a parent. "Shelly," He yelled back as the span was becoming greater, "DO ME A FAVOR." His voice now having a distant sound, "IN THE NEXT TWENTY FIVE MILLION YEARS OF SO, REMIND ME TO NEVER TALK TO ANOTHER TEENAGER."

By then His voice was barely audible but she made out His last words to say, "IT'S NOT THAT I'M AT THE END OF MY PATIENCE SHELLY, BUT I HAVE THIS PREMONITION, IN ABOUT TWO SECONDS YOU ARE GOING TO BE GETTING AWFULLY WET. I HOPE YOU CAN SWIM!"

HE turned for one final look back at the riverboat captain who was pulling her from the murky waters. He then glanced to the bridge and saw the Pittsburgh Ambulance and fire truck and knew that all of His young people would be all right.

Chapter 27

"Ladies and Gentlemen," Frank Buckwilder spoke from behind his large mahogany desk as he slightly leaned back in his high-back leather chair, removed his gold pocket watch from his vest pocket and glanced at the time. "I see that it is eleven o'clock. I believe everyone is here and seated so I suggest we get started." He felt emotionally drained as the reading got underway and hoped that it did not show.

"It is customary," he continued as if there were no personal elements involved, "in these things that a record be made and I have asked my secretary to take notes. Nancy would you please record for the record that on this date of May 14, 1962 at 11:00 A.M. we are gathered in my law office for the formal reading of the Last Will and Testament of Morgan Hays Smithfield who deceased May 11, 1962. Paragraph.

"Present for the reading are: Shelly Patricia Waters, Jenny Sue Craig, Aspen Gerore McGee, Jim Barkus, LeRoy 'Gimmie' Jones and of course myself.

"Not present but named in the Will is his Holiness Archbishop O'Conner, Head of the Pennsylvania Archdiocese. Paragraph.

"Ladies and Gentlemen, we in this room... as well as all of Pittsburgh, have lost a dear and beloved friend. I..." Frank was forced to pause as his voice choked and he turned away.

The room remained silent as the others understood and watched until he regained his composure. He then turned back and in a strained tone, commented.

"Excuse me, I seem to have lost my composure. I hope you will forgive me.

"As I was about to say," He resumed with a slightly shaky but stronger pronunciation. "No one will mourn his loss more than I. All of us could talk at length on Morgan's virtue.

"But I think it would be best if we deal with the matter at hand and save our accolades for the graveside eulogy. Paragraph!"

"Our business today is to distribute his earthly assets in accordance with his wishes. As you may all assume, Morgan and I worked together in preparation of his Will and he asked that I act as executor. It isn't a long Will. In his daily life he preferred things that were simple. The same holds true of his final Testament. Paragraph!"

"As we all know, he had difficulty in expressing his feelings. But in death there are certain things that he wants to be said; things that in life he himself was unable to say. In that context he asked that I convey the words for him. Therefore, in accordance with his request, I now speak in his stead. Paragraph!"

"First...I am speaking now for Morgan," Frank reiterated, "I want to say a few words to my beloved daughter, Shelly. I do not say adopted daughter, because the word causes me pain.

"Shelly, my most wonderful child, I could not have loved you more if you were my own seed. But now I am going to be with your mother whom I love even more.

"The years without Patricia have been long and lonely but now the waiting is over. Mourn not my dying my beloved Baby, but weep a happy tear that the family will at last be together.

"Little Darling my dying thoughts were of you and my hope is for you to have a happy life. We both know that you have a strong compulsion to fight the invincible foe. We have talked many times about the difficulties that lie before you so I will not at this point ask of you, moderation.

"I held you in my arms for the first time when you were only a few weeks old. Moreover, I have watched you grow into womanhood. I know your feelings and emotions as well as I know my own. Underneath your strong exterior there is a loneliness that is almost unbearable.

"As you matured I watched you always searching. I watched as you searched the eyes of passing young men on the street; of working the ticket cage at the Stran and holding the ticket a minute too long as you searched the eyes of the young manhood on the other side of the glass.

I have stood as father and answered the door when young men came to call; but in the end they have all been turned away.

"Darling having said all of that I now want to share my own feeling. I know how much you love your mother. Sometimes I think more than I. In my own mind I have always thought that when your one true love finally arrives, it will be someone who in someway represents your mother. If it will help you to find your way, start looking for that certain something which will satisfy your mother's bond; whatever that may be, only you can know.

"Love him and follow the natural order of life in woman coming to man. Pamper your love and feel it grow until there is a blending and the two of you become just one.

"Do this for me and your mother. When we know that you have found your love, our place in heaven will be complete."

Emotional tears came to Shelly's eyes as Frank was reading and her thoughts flashed back to her final days with Morgan. Thoughts that caused tears to stream down her cheeks. The man who had given the most to bring happiness to her life had lived his own life in chronic pain and died an excruciating death.

Bone cancer had developed in his twisted leg and rapidly spread. Inoperable it grew with impunity and in a matter of two months his life deteriorated until he drifted into semi-comatose. His last days had been confined to a hospital under heavy sedation and she had been by his bedside at the end.

During the entire period of his confinement she had put her personal life on hold. For the care, love and protection he had provided her in her youth she now returned with interest.

Visitors came in numbers each day to pay their respects but it was she who was always there. During the day she left his bedside only to eat or to stretch her legs; her nights were spent half-curled up with a blanket in a stiff Naugahyde visitor's chair.

She slept only in naps, followed by restless thinking. Alone in the dimly lit room she thought about the life of her mother who never had a husband, and the life of this wonderful man who acted as her father but never married to her mother.

Two beautiful loving people whose lives passed incomplete. If only they had been married, how different their time on earth could have been.

Could have been? Where had she heard those words before? 'Could have been' or was it 'might have been'. Might have been. That was it, might have been. When she was in school, a hundred years ago, in a literature class. In some forgotten quote someone had said something like '...the saddest most unkind words of tongue and pen are those that say... what might have been'. How true, she thought. How very true. How different would have been their lives. If only they had been married.

As each day passed and she watched Morgan drift in and out of consciousness she thought more and more about him and her mother standing in a church being married. The picture kept lingering and going around in her mind. As each day passed the fantasy of their marriage expanded and grew; a huge hundred people wedding.

This is my mother and father we are talking about here, she dreamed. *Why the assumption of just a simple little ceremony? Aren't they as good as everyone else?*

Where is it chiseled in stone that it would have been natural for them to have had a simple little no frills wedding? The size of the wedding should equate the measure of love.

From that frame of mind she passed the lonely hours at his bedside by letting her fantasy grow. She started picturing how they both would have looked in a full formal ceremony; complete with wedding gown, tails tux, flowers, organ music playing 'Oh Promise Me', an alter lit by a hundred candles, a saintly looking catholic priest dressed in Ecclesiastical vestments reading the wedding vowels, an exchange of wedding bands...

The fantasy of her two parents finally being together as man and wife made the thought of losing him a little more bearable. Then one night death came to the man she called Daddy Morgan. A little after midnight his eyes had opened to incoherent excruciating pain. He broke out in a soaking sweat and went into jerking convulsions. Almost immediately a nurse had responded, checked the time lapse since his last injection of morphine and concluded that another shot could be given.

She had watched as the nurse pricked a hypodermic needle into the rubber top of a small vile and pulled the contents up into a syringe. Holding the needlepoint up to the light the nurse squeezed until a drop came out and then administered the contents into his arm. Almost immediately he drifted back into a deep sleep, and never woke up; exactly how many hours thereafter she did not know.

After the shot she had sat on his bedside and held his hand for a long time. Eventually she had become body weary and moved back to the Naugahyde chair. As she lay half-curled up she dozed off and it was near dawn before she woke from an uneasy sleep.

Her first notice was that his top cover sheet had slid from the bed and as she was spreading it back she felt his forehead; and instantly knew. His face was cold to her touch and when she felt his wrist there was no pulse.

In a panic she called a nurse and stood silently back as his death was confirmed. As the sheet was pulled up over him she left the room and for a long time wandered aimlessly through the hospital corridors. Then, for the second time in her life, she made a *very important phone call*.

From a pay telephone booth in the lobby her trembling hands dialed the home telephone of Frank Buckwilder. On his end, the demise of Morgan had been expected so the word from Shelly, while bearing hurt, came as no surprise. But the same telephone line that brought notice of his death also brought a preeminence of startling proportions. Shelly related to Frank that there was something she wanted. And the substance of what she wanted brought forth one of life's rarest moments. A moment in which the refinement of Frank's demeanor, the absence of absurdity in his instant thoughts and the grace of his composure all rose to their finest hour. She wanted her mother and Morgan to be married.

There was no expression of surprise or taken back on his part. There was only the calm of a momentary pause in the telephone line while his mind instantly clicked to the legal aspects that would be involved.

The silent line was, no doubt, of little note on his part but as Shelly held the phone to her ear the humming was a transmission of misgivings that she would hear that it could not be done; but then that which she was hoping to hear did come. From the other end of the line came his words of comfort as he said, "I think it can be done"; followed by essential instructions of the first step which had to be taken.

While still at the hospital she gave the order for Morgan's body to immediately be transferred to the County Morgue and put in refrigeration; with instruction to hold until further notice.

Now, three days later the next step was being taken; the reading of Morgan's Will; and the time line of her wish was developing.

As Frank turned to the next page he looked up over his reading glasses at the silent people sitting before him. Jenny and Shelly were openly crying and drying their tears with handkerchiefs; the men were fighting to control their emotions. Frank knew that if Morgan were present he would be embarrassed.

He finished turning the page and continued.

"Next," he spoke as if again explaining, "I will now speak on Morgan's behalf to Jenny Sue Craig.

"Jenny," his tone reflecting Morgan, "now I can tell you. You my most beautiful one, are truly woman magnificent.

"You are more than just a lady; you are a proud lady. You consider your womanhood God's greatest blessing. You unselfishly devote your body, mind and softness to the soothing of the fire that sometimes ravages the souls of good men.

"I can now say this my most lovely woman. I have known you for more than twenty years and never made love to you.

"And yet I have always loved you; and had it not been for my first love, you are the only other woman I could have ever loved.

"So while the torment in me was my own, I have many times imagined that I was the man lying there beside you.

"And in that context my most precious woman I have gone to sleep many many nights with you in my arms. God speed my love."

Frank paused again as he turned to the next page but this time he did not look up. He didn't have too.

He could hear the emotion. He did not want to see, nor did he himself want to be seen.

"Next," he continued, "Morgan asked me to say a few words on his behalf to Aspen McGee.

"Aspen I have always considered you a gentleman and a friend. My life has been richer for having known you. I feel that it was divine providence that sent you to watch over Jenny.

"These things I find comfort in saying. But there is something more; something I could never say before; somehow just because.

"But I have always admired your perception in the business world. You move with the grace of an angel into and out of business dealings and always remain a gentleman.

"Whereas I had to make my living by the sometimes harshness of the street, you always had the insight to glide ever so smoothly into the world of tomorrow.

"A few years ago I had never heard the word computer. Today Shelly has money in her own right because of your foresight into upstart companies such as IBM and Tandy Corp. I can rest easy knowing that no matter what happen she will always be taken care of. My deepest appreciations for all you have done.

"Next," Frank was now proceeding with decorum as he moved forward, "Morgan has asked me to speak on his behalf to his Holiness, Archbishop O'Conner who for the record we have acknowledged is not present but for the record I now speak.

"Your most gracious Holiness I express my appreciation for the help and comfort you have provide me over the years. Many times I have come to you in the middle of the night; times when no one else knew.

"It is unlikely that you will be present at this reading but I am asking that you do me one last favor. As you know a few years back I started and then supported a shelter for the homeless in the Hill District.

"Upon my death I am concerned that it will come to an end. I do not think I could bear for that to happen.

"I realize that it will probably be a great imposition on your part, but I ask that you assume responsibility for its continued operation.

"To aid in the ongoing cost I am leaving an endowment. In addition, there is something else. I have not asked those who are present at this reading, but they know my wishes and I am sure some additional endowments will supplement mine. Remember me in your prayers and may God bless.

"Next," Frank moved on, "I speak now to Jim Barkus, my friend and faithful servant. My life has been easier because of the problems you took off of my shoulders. I always treasured our relationship of joshing each other and of our mutual respect and trust. If I am extremely lucky there will be another Jim Barkus where I am going. It's the first thing that I am going to ask for.

"Fact is," Frank attempted to speak in tones of jest, "if they don't have one I just may not stay. Goodbye my dear friend and may God speed.

Without looking up Frank continued. "And lastly to my wonderful friend LeRoy 'Gimmie' Jones; the man that enabled me to work on the streets. I remember the very first tip you sent to me; an out-of-state truck driver who had a load of produce that he had to unload immediately.

"We bought the whole load for $200.00 and sold it the next day for $1500. Another memory, I can never forget the barge of coal that we picked up for pennies because the operator was being foreclosed.

"That's the kind of Gimmie I understand. Take care my dear friend and may the world be yours at the News Stand."

As the last page came to an end Frank lowered the legal document removed his reading glasses and said. "Ladies and Gentlemen that concludes the reading of the Testament.

"The next order of business is the reading of the Will which is to say the actual distribution of the assets. It is a brief document and there is the probability that it will sound very impersonal. In matters of law, it saddens me to say, that is simply the way things are done.

"I will pause and ask if anyone would like to take a break and visit the wash room? No one? Very well we can proceed with reading the Final Will of Morgan Hays Smithfield to wit;

"To: Jim Barkus, my friend and faithful employee I bequeath the following: (1) One each 1939 black four door Buick presently stored at the Wood Street Garage.

(2) Fifty Thousand Dollars."

"To: LeRoy 'Gimmie' Jones who I have always been proud to call my friend I bequeath the following:

(1) Bought and paid for full title Fee Simple Deed to the 5th Avenue New Stand which he has operated so diligently as a renter for the last twenty five years."

"To: Jenny Craig, the only other woman I could have ever loved I bequeath the following:

(1) One each passenger bus modified with mini berths and painted in the image of a rising Sun over a pale blue sky. Presently stored in the back parking lot of the Trails West Bus Depot. It is my hope that in a ceremony appropriate to the occasion that you will further donated the bus to the Allegheny Historical Society.

(2) My 1/2 (one half) interest in the North Hills Drive-in-Restaurant which we have owned jointly for almost twenty years.

"To: Aspen Gerore McGee who my life has been richer for knowing I have chosen to leave words that I could not say while alive.

"Thank you from the bottom of my heart for watching

over Jenny and Shelly."

"To: My daughter Shelly I bequeath the following:

(1) Liquid assets including cash, stocks, bonds and government securities in the amount of $960,000.00 presently held in the First State Bank of Pittsburgh under the stewardship of Aspen McGee.

(2) Fee Simple title to the apartment located at 427 Wood Street.

(3) Fee simple title to seven theaters of unknown value."

To: Archbishop O'Conner I leave fee simple title to the Guiding Light Shelter for the Homeless in the HILL District and an endowment of $100,000.00 for its continued operation."

Frank Buckwilder then laid the document on his desk and said, "Ladies and Gentlemen that concludes the reading. I must now ask if there are any questions?" he looked at the silent people looking back at him. "No? No questions then this concludes our business and I hereby call..."

"I don't have any questions Frank," cut in Aspen. "But I do have a comment. I know how important the shelter was to Morgan and as a token of my admiration and love for the man I would like to match his generosity by also donating $100,000.00 to the endowment."

Frank was watching as Aspen was speaking and noted that he rose to his feet so that in someway it showed his sincerity.

"Why, Aspen, that's very genero..." Frank was about to say generous when he was interrupted.

"And I would like to make a $100,000.00 contribution," said Jenny as she also rose to her feet. Frank looked at these two proud people who were looking back at him. Standing side by side squeezing each other's hand. Jenny's eyes were red from wiping her tears and Aspen was over compensating in his efforts to control his emotions.

They're looking to me as if I was actually Morgan, he thought. *I'm*

Morgan and they want to know if their contributions please me.

"Jenny, Aspen, I, I don't know what to say..." he searched for words, "except that we know that Morgan is present right here with us.

"And it is an honor for me to tell you that he is standing very proud. He has a smile on his face and he is extremely pleased to have friends such as you. I further speak for him when I say he is touched to the bottom of his heart."

"Daddy Frank," Shelly rose from her chair as she started talking, "am I correct in understanding that I have just inherited almost a million dollars?"

"Yes Shelly, you have. But if you are thinking what I think you are, the answer is no."

"But I want to..." she was about to offer another $100,000.00 when Frank interrupted.

"Shelly, as your legal advisor the answer is no. At least for now. Later on if you still have the feeling, then maybe. But right now, no. We have too many pressing expenses such as probate taxes and so on and so forth.

"Now," he turned more directly to Aspen and Jenny, "what I have just denied Shelly does not hold true for myself. I consider it an honor and a privilege to join you two and add my $100,000.00 to the endowment.

"Very shortly," Frank continued, "we, Shelly and I, are going to be asking Archbishop O'Conner for a very important favor. Very important... More important than you can possibly know. Moreover, we will be asking it as early as tomorrow. In that matter, that is all I can say for now. With respect to all of the other legal detail I will see that the dictates of the will are carried out.

"Now, ladies and gentlemen," he spoke as he was getting up and was surprised at his lack of strength, "that seems to conclude the formalities. If there are no more questions I hereby call the reading to a close."

There was no mention of Frank in the Will, but during the time of the reading a package from Scofield Art Galleries arrived and was left in his outer office.

As everyone was leaving Frank stood by his office door, gave Jenny and Shelly each a warm hug and shook hands with the three men. He was thankful when no one stopped to talk. Now alone in the quietness of his office the reality returned to him that his best friend was gone forever.

With his feet upon his desk he made no attempt to control his emotions. He leaned back in his chair, allowed his head to fall all the way back and rest on the high top back and did nothing to stop the watering of his closed eyes. Finally he wiped the wetness with his thumb and index finger and rubbed it on his shirt. As he sat in his own thoughts he was thankful for the privacy. A moment of privacy that changed when Nancy, his secretary knocked on his office door.

"Excuse me Mr. Buckwilder, I know that you wish to be alone but a package came which is addressed to you."

"What is it Nancy," Frank asked while still letting his head lean back; he made no motion to look in her direction though he did lower his hand from his face. "I really don't want to be distur..."

"Yes sir," she spoke across the room from the half-opened door. "But I think it is something that you would like to see."

"What is it?" he repeated in a tone that clearly indicated how difficult it was to maintain his composure.

"I'm not sure Mr. Buckwilder. It's wrapped but it appears to be a framed painting. It has a note which indicates it is to be opened after the reading of the Will."

Frank sighed and lowered his feet from the desk. "Very well Nancy, bring it in and let's see what we've got."

That attended, what Nancy brought in was Morgan's final gift to Frank; an oil painted mosaic of their combined life and times. A 40"X40" canvas framed in light mahogany, depicting a characterization view of Pittsburgh.

Painted by one of the area's leading artist it portrayed the major events of their two lives. At the top right hand corner, there was an early rising Sun characterized as having two faces. The right-side face was wearing a harsh frown and casting a scornful look down at the wicked complex of Homestead Steel.

In turn, the steel mill buildings in characterization were looking upward wearing the cowardly sweaty face of a pathetic bully who is being chastised for his hideous deeds.

The other of the Sun's two faces is shown with a happy smile which looks out over the skyline of Pittsburgh at the bustling traffic on 5th Av., Wood Street, Liberty Av., Grant St., and the Smithfield Bridge.

Among the things that please the Sun's happy face is the Stran Theater near the lower center. The Stran in turn has the face of a full moon in characterization.

Blended into the Stran marquee is the expression of a big wide smile, dimpled cheeks and down turned eyes that are watching the line of theater patrons buying tickets.

Just above the Stran at near picture center is the Allegheny Courthouse; the place where their court battle was fought and won.

The Courthouse building wears the characterized face of solemn wisdom but with distinctive sparkling eyes clearly revealing that the Administrator of Justice is pleased with the outcome of the trial.

Next to the County Government Complex is Pittsburgh's most celebrated and elegant brothel. Now owned by Jenny Craig can-can girls in painted cheeks and high kicking bloomers dancing on the roofline characterize it.

Just above mid-center and slightly to the right is the characterization of Frank Buckwilder's office.

In suggestion of sanctimonious it is setting above all the other buildings on a white fluffy cloud; carefully reflected on by a golden halo.

Spreading outward from the mosaic center and to the left is the Pepperdine Conservatory; illustrated by beautiful maidens from all the lands including the Orient, the Netherlands and America all dancing in bare feet on a carpet of beautiful flowers.

On past the Pepperdine Conservatory looking to the northeast the terrain breaks to rolling foothill which extends to a purple line of far distant hills; where a towering lady Elm Tree stands sentinel duty with a younger sister Elm Tree at her side.

Looking to the South a winding trail of Longhorn cattle reaches all the way to Texas and Aspen Gerore McGee in oversize is wearing a cowboy hat, bandanna, six gun, boots and spurs and riding a too small Pinto pony.

Crossing the Smithfield Bridge and heading out of town to Jacksburg is a speeding blue bus that is decorated with the golden rays of an early morning sun and carrying an entourage of happy hookers waving from the top of the bus and out the windows.

At the very bottom of the picture the Allegheny and Monongahela Rivers converge to form the headwaters of the Ohio. From there a winding road leads to Lake Erie which is characterized by a north bound 1939 black four door Buick with Morgan and Patricia on top; sitting in the speeding wind and waving back at Pittsburgh.

Two dark rain clouds are also in the picture. One, a smaller one, is pouring rain over the characterization of Dr. Owise's hospital out in Mt. Lebanon; the other a furious dark angry cloud depicting lightning and casting ill will... hangs over the Underground Theater.

Attached to the bottom side of the mahogany frame a brass plate bore the inscription:

> 'Wealth has no measure except in share of friend. And
> mine greater than none other. For that which bares my
> soul has been seen by man another. And in reservations
> not, has still called me friend.'

After he had unwrapped the painting, Frank sat holding it in his lap. At first he just sat and looked. Then he changed to holding it with his left hand and started tracing the features with his right forefinger.

As his manicured soft finger moved over the surface he could feel the uneven edges of the oil paint.

First he touched the face of the Sun and slowly dropped his finger down to the face of Homestead Steel; the place where it all started.

Then his finger moved down and touch the painting of O'Wise's Hospital; the place where Patricia and Shelly had come into the picture.

Next he moved up and lightly put his finger on the Pepperdine Conservatory, closed his eyes and let his mind savor the memory.

But the memories were hollow and frustrating. He wanted more. A feeling from the picture that Morgan was there sharing with him.

He opened his eyes and made a broader attempt. He placed his full flat hand against the center, so that the Stran and his office were both under his palm.

In a voice choked with emotions he asked a question to which there was no answer, "Morgan why did you have to go?"

With the reading of the Will, an event unparallel post mortem in the history of man started its legionary treck. The, then still secret plan, known only to Shelly and Frank, breathed its first breath of new life; without hesitation of second thoughts. On the very afternoon of the Will reading, Shelly shelved her heart-tearing, tear producing emotions and sucked up a resolve that was her inbred strength. In single mind focus, she left Frank Buckwilder's office and from the nearest pay telephone made two telephone calls. The first call was to the Pittsburgh Press where she requested that she might talk to someone who would have been with the paper back in 1944.

"I am trying to locate," she related to the voice on the other end, "the columnist who wrote the lengthy article about Patricia Waters when she died in late December 1944."

"What does this pertain too?" asked the voice.

"It pertains to a favor. Patricia Waters was my mother and I dearly need to talk with the man who wrote the article. I don't know his name but he was a well-known columnist in 1944. It would be greatly appreciated if you could help me."

"Just a minute."

Shelly could hear background talking in what she judged to be discussion among the workers. Then finally the voice came back on.

"Hello, Miss Waters," related the voice, "we can't be sure but some of the older employees think it might have been Seymore Hightower, but he's been retired for several years."

"Do you know where he lives?" Shelly asked.

"Just a minute." There was another pause and again background talking on the other end.

"Hello, Miss Waters," the voice came back, "we think he lives somewhere out in the South Hills area but that's all we can tell you."

When Seymore Hightower answered his telephone Shelly identified who she was and confirmed that he was the Hightower she was trying to locate. She briefly explained the reason for her call and asked if he would consider writing the continuation story on Morgan's death; to which he immediately accepted and expressed appreciation for the honor.

Her second search was at the Post Gazette where she learned the columnist who wrote about her mother's death was Henry Powell; who died some years back. His son however was the Assistant Editor and he would consider it a tribute to his father to write the second half of the story.

Two days later the two reporters were present when Shelly Waters and Frank Buckwilder went into Civil Court in-and-for the County of Allegheny.

Before the Honorable Judge Pittman Wright, wherein Shelly Waters having proved that she 'had legal standing'. Frank Buckwilder, attorney in due course, filed a motion to have the marriage of Patricia O'Riley and Edgar Waters post-mortem annulled. The grounds being desertion.

While extremely irregular, Judge Wright allowed Frank to present his case; agreeing to accept as the best evidence available the testimony of Shelly; the daughter and only child to come from the marriage.

After being duly sworn in, Shelly took the witness stand.

"For the record," Frank began his examination, "identify your- self, give the name of your father and mother, your age, your marital status, where you have lived all of your life and whether you have any brothers or sisters."

"My full name is Shelly Patricia Waters, my father's name is Edgar Waters and my mother's maiden name was Patricia O'Riley. I was born in 1941, I am 21 years old, I am single, I have lived in Pittsburgh all my life and I am an only child."

"Now, Miss Waters, "will you tell the Court what it is that we are asking."

"I am asking that the marriage of my mother to Edgar Waters be annulled post-mortem."

"By post-mortem are you telling this Court that one or both of your parents are dead?"

"Yes, my mother; she died December 24, 1944 from an overdose of sleeping pills."

"What about your father?"

"I don't know."

"Why is it that you don't know whether you father is dead or alive."

"Because I have never laid eyes on the man. He deserted my mother on their wedding night and has never been seen or heard from since."

"You use the word deserted, what does that mean to you?"

"It means that they were duly married by a Catholic Priest, that they spent their honeymoon night in the William Penn Hotel, that Edgar Waters made drunken crude love to my mother and before daylight the next morning while my mother was still sleeping he sneaked out and left."

"And you are the product of that one night."

"Yes, he was never seen again after that."

"How do you know this?

"Because my mother told me…"

"Counselor!" Judge Wright spoke out from the bench. "That borders on hearsay evidence. You and I both know that it is inadmissible."

"I am aware of that your Honor, but if it pleases the Court there is no better evidence available. However I will continue my questioning in proper guidelines.

"Now, Miss Waters, tell this Court the contact if any that you or you mother have had with Edgar Waters and how you have lived"

"I have never seen my father. My mother never saw him after the one night…" "Counselor," cut in Judge Wright.

"Yes your honor. Miss Waters would you rephrase that last statement."

"Yes, in so far as I know, my mother never saw Edgar Waters again."

"Miss Waters why do you want this annulment?"

"Because it is what my mother wanted but never did and the man is not deserving to call such a wonderful woman his wife."

"Your Honor," Frank turned to Judge Wright, "do you have any questions you would like to ask the witness?"

"No, she may step down. But to you counselor Buckwilder I want the record to show I made the following comment. I've known you for many many years and I know you to be as reputable as any man can be. Accordingly, as an Officer of the Court can you, Frank Buckwilder, stand before this court and substantiate her testimony?"

"That I can your Honor. I have known her since she was only a few weeks old and raised her as my own daughter after her mother died. I can swear under oath before this Court that her father has never made any contact what-so-ever with Miss Waters. And while some of her testimony is hearsay I believe it to be true."

"Is," Judge Wright spoke out to a courtroom empty except for two reporter, "there anyone here present who contests the motion before this court?" None answered.

"Will the Clerk please note for the record that there were no objections? Therefore, by the power vested in me by the State of Pennsylvania I hereby grant the motion and the marriage of Patricia O'Riley to Edgar Water, where-abouts unknown, is annulled. This court is adjourned."

The day next the two Pittsburgh daily newspapers carried the story but neither reporter could tell the readers the thinking or motivation behind the annulment. "It seems," wrote Seymore Hightower, "that Miss Waters will shortly be telling all of Pittsburgh something, but as of now we don't know what it will be."

At a pre-dawn hour on a morning thereafter a caravan of four vehicles pulled out of Pittsburgh. Leading the point was a 1939 black four door Buick followed by heavy earth moving equipment and two trucks. The Buick was chauffeured by Jim Barkus and carried Shelly Watters and two newspaper reporters; the whole of the convey being headed east to northeast on a winding two lane road toward a horizon of distant purple hills.

For two hours and a part thereof they traveled the winding miles until they came to a pull-off; a place which was worn wide on the bank of the road caused by years of weekly visit by a man with a silver handled cane.

Shelly and the two reporters were the first to walk the obscure foot trail that bore the evidence of a dragging foot. As the path led across a small creek the water growth sapling trees showed marks of being pushed aside by a cane to avoid racking across a fedora hat. From the creek bed the trail then led upward to the top of a steep hill and the reason for their presence.

Under Shelly's direction, the earth moving equipment and two trucks cut another path up the slope. By noon that day, the lone mature-lady Elm tree and the younger sister Elm had been dug out, loaded on the trucks and were being transported back to Pittsburgh and a new home on cemetery grounds.

In the sprawling rolling acres of the Allegheny Cemetery, Shelly selected a high gently sloping hill with southern exposure overlooking the skyline of Pittsburgh and it was here that the two trees were transplanted.

Thereafter the stately Queen Elm was assigned new duties. In unison with her younger sister and between the two they were to watch over these sacred grounds and make sure that peace and tranquillity forever prevailed.

Of that day, the two reporters reported to their readers of the transplant and... 'of the solemn orders spoken aloud to the two trees by Miss Waters' but still could not offer any reason for her actions. On the other side of the print, readers were starting to share comments, exchanged small talk over morning coffee and speculated. Each day as the reporters continued to report, readers continued to read; anxious to know of any new developments.

In a methodical time line, a new parking area was built at a nearby bend in the cemetery macadam road; the size sufficient to park twenty cars. In no expense spared, it was complete with asphalt paving, guard rails and parking stripes. Nr\ext at the back of the lot a set of steps descended down a slope to a cobble stone foot trail.

At below road level, the winding trail meandered through young saplings trees until it reached a rainbow foot bridge which crossed a small stream; thence the cobble stone path led up the hill on the other side, wound through a rose trestle and ended at the base of the transplanted Elms. This the reporters reported in vivid detail.

At the base of the Elm, the reporters reported the next day, visitors would find a concrete seating bench, a drinking fountain with continuous running water and a birdbath. The reporters told the story; readers read the story and the masses of Pittsburgh started driving out to see.

In rapid moving events, in the middle of the next week Shelly and Frank were able to get back into court; but this time the proceedings were short. Acting as counsel for Shelly, the only living heir, Frank asked for and Shelly was granted legal authority to exhume the remains of Patricia O'Riley to be reburied on the south slope of the Allegheny Cemetery. As the story unfolded the reporters reported, paper sales skyrocketed and the City was becoming spellbound.

The week then following, Shelly was even busier. First she went to Waterman's Funeral Home to make Morgan's funeral arrangements. In looking through their show room she found a decorous, dignified flat top mahogany casket with white satin quilted lining. She ordered two.

She then gave the authority for the Funeral home to assume custody of both Morgan's and Patricia's bodies and to prepare them for closed casket burial. The reporters reported, the public read and the City became a frenzy of speculation.

The next day with both reporters in tow, Shelly created additional curiosity. She went to a bridal shop and spent the morning picking out two ensembles; a bridal gown and a tuxedo.

Two days later the reporters were with her and Frank when they went to visit Archbishop O'Conner and it became public news. She asked Archbishop O'Conner for two services. One that Patricia and Morgan be married postmortem and secondly, that they be buried in a single grave. Services to be held the following Sunday at 1:00 P.M. Public attendance received.

Whereas Patricia's funeral back in 1944 had been a very private affair, her wedding day on this day would be a coronation befitting a queen.

When the proposed wedding was reported in the papers, there had been wide spread speculation among the readers as to whether such a service could or would be performed. In some cases the issue even spilled over into heated religious dispute.

In a divided camp some felt that such a marriage represented the true spirit of Christianity. On the other side were those who considered the act of marrying two dead people heretic and blasphemous. No word was forth coming from the Catholic Church as to whether such a marriage-funeral ceremony could or would be performed. The City hung in suspense.

Nevertheless, when the day came, people in multitude of about five thousand bore witness. That Sunday the spring air was soft and cool. The mocking birds darted from tree to tree, mating season was in bloom, and spring flowers gave off sweet fragrance.

At the base of the two budding Elm trees were two side-by-side caskets; held suspended in funeral arrangement over one large freshly dug grave.

On top of Morgan's casket a black, perfectly pressed tuxedo was laid out; complete with trousers, white studded shirt, black satin cumber band, mid-riff open front jacket, and white gloves.

The top of Patricia's casket was adorned with a white, sleeve-less wedding gown; complete with a half crown silk hat and veil, white pump shoes, a silk handkerchief and adorned with a bouquet of long stem red roses. It took little imagination to picture the bride and groom in formal dress on their wedding day; nervously waiting for the ceremony to begin.

But would or would not the service be held? There still had not been any official word from the Catholic Church. No one knew for sure. Then just a few minutes after 1:00 PM the question was self answered. From the back of the crowd, at the crest of an adjoining hill it was first sighted; a long black limousine slowly coming into view.

There was no mistaking that it was carrying Archbishop O'Conner. As hundreds looked on, the black limo eased through the road lined with parked cars, came to a stop near the graveside podium and the Archbishop stepped out.

Wearing full ecclesiastical vestments, he was ushered from the limo down a carpeted, roped lined passageway where he stepped up to the microphone of the public address system and looked out over a sea of faces.

"Ladies and gentlemen," he started as the crowd became quiet. "We are gathered here today for an unusual ceremony. We are being asked to unite, not the flesh and bones of Morgan Smithfield and Patricia O'Riley but their souls. If..." he paused slightly for emphasis then continued, "we give thought to the notion; it is fitting that we should do this.

"For it isn't the body but the soul which is of importance to our Lord. Our bodies are but the instrument in which we dwell for the short time we are on earth; destined to be discarded at the end of its useful life.

"But it is inconceivable that God would discard a soul. HIS own someday dream is that all of His children will return home.

"Is..., Archbishop O'Conner paused to hold the rhetorical question he was about to ask, "the situation any different among mortals?

"Those among you who have children. Have you not watched your own seed grow; to the end that someday they will leave the nest and ventured out into the world?

"In the natural order of life they will select mates and return home for your approval. And what more proud can a father be than to meet the man to whom his daughter has given her love; or for a mother to meet the girl whom her son has selected for his wife.

"Would we suppose that God would be any less proud over the news that two of His children have found their mates. It is the natural order that the soul, as well as the body, be united in Holy matrimony. That these two will be entering HIS house as a family to dwell everlasting, surely must give Him pleasure.

"It is fitting therefore that we prepare these two souls to enter the house of God as man and wife."

Archbishop O'Conner then looked toward the two caskets and noted that Frank Buckwilder was standing by Morgan's casket and Shelly was standing by her mother's.

"I now ask," he turned directly to Frank as he started the ceremony, "who so stands in proxy to speak for Morgan Smithfield?"

"I, Frank Buckwilder, do so stand in proxy and do speak on his behalf," answered Frank.

"And who so stands in proxy for Patricia O'Riley?" he asked as he turned to Shelly.

"I, Shelly Waters her loving daughter, do so stand in proxy and do speak on her behalf," answered Shelly.

"And you, Morgan Smithfield and you Patricia O'Riley are here of your own free will. So saith you both?"

"So saith we both," answered Frank and Shelly.

"Now having established their intent of total commitment one to the other, let it be said that Morgan Smithfield and Patricia O'Riley are gathered here today to wed in the bands of holy matrimony; to the end that they may dwell in the House of God as man and wife.

"If there is anyone here who saith that this wedding should not take place let thou come forward now or forever hold thy peace.

"Having established that there is no one present who objects to this ceremony, we will now proceed.

"Do you Morgan Smithfield take this woman, Patricia O'Riley to be your lawful wedded wife forsaking all others that the two of you shall dwell as one in the house of God for all eternity?"

"I do," replied Frank.

"And do you Patricia O'Riley take this man, Morgan Smithfield to be your lawful wedded husband forsaking all others that the two of you shall dwell as one in the house of God for all eternity?"

"I do," replied Shelly.

"Then by the power vested in me by the laws of God and the laws of man I hereby pronounce you man and wife."

The ceremony completed, Archbishop O'Conner then added the customary comment.

"Morgan you may hug the bride."

With wetness in his eyes Frank held out his arms and Shelly with tears flowing down her cheeks fell into his chest as they squeezed each other tight.

A silence hung over the crowd. Was it proper to be happy at a funeral? What would happen, each person in the gathered witness crowd felt, if one should start to clap their hands and all the others cast looks of disapproval.

No one knew what was protocol. As Frank and Shelly held each other the crowd silently looked on.

Then as if he himself wasn't sure at first, Archbishop O'Conner remembered his own words. The body is but an insignificant. Two souls had just been married. With that, he announced over the address system.

"My fellow attendees let us rejoice in the happiness of this matrimony."

At that signal the crowd of thousands solidified into one mass exhilaration of cheering approval. Many turned one to the other and shared approval. Men in numbers, came forward to congratulate and shake Frank's hand; women with tears in their eyes gathered around to kiss the bride and groom. To all, Frank and Shelly stood side by side in an acceptance line.

The Sun was starting to drop in the Western sky as the congratulations slowly came to an end. By mid-afternoon the last of the attendees had departed and the cemetery was quiet again. It was time for the burial.

In a mode that was more solemn now, Frank and Shelly held hands as workmen lowered the two caskets into the ground and watched as the earth began to fall.

For Morgan and Patricia, their bodies were no longer needed. Wherever they were, their souls were now united. And, for Shelly, her family circle was finally complete.

Chapter 28

On a mid-April morning in 1968 Shelly Waters was leaving the Royal Theater located on lower Liberty Avenue. She was dressed in her usual uniform of jeans, white blouse with short sleeves, turned up collar, no socks, and brown loafer shoes. She wore no make-up and her honey gold shoulder length hair was pushed back on the sides and held in place by side combs. As she stepped out of the double swinging doors she felt the difference in temperature of the brisk outside air under the alcove. For no reason, she glanced across to the other side of the street and noted the greater number of passing pedestrians. She hoped that their preference to that side was because of the warming sun and not an avoidance of being on the same side of the street as her theater.

In her hand she was carrying a soft leather money pouch that contained the cash receipts from the previous night. Attendance had been reasonably good; not a sellout but over half filled in the late showing.

She paused for a moment and straightened the bills, zipped up the zipper and stuck the pouch half folded over the inside top of her waistband. In a casual inspection of the theater front she glanced up at the floodlights on the underside of the marquee; three were out but in no immediate need of being replaced.

On the outer two sides of the triangle shaped overhanging marquee large red plastic letters displayed the current features:

"Divorce American Style" 'G'

2nd

"Tropical Island Love" 'XXX'

At the young age of twenty-seven she was the sole owner of a seven struggling theaters; struggling because of television. Replacement of the burned out lights as well as the frayed carpet and threadbare seats would have to wait a while longer. Patrons coming to see Grade B movies and X rated porn expected such theater conditions.

Abruptly, her inspection of the theater exterior was interrupted by sounds coming from a distance up the street; jeering voices. Reactively she turned to look; with the full expectations of once again being confronted by protesting, sign-carrying women from some religious or civic group. This time she was not the target. Shading her eyes from the morning sun she could see a gang of teenage boys haggling an adult.

A single adult male who didn't seem to be making any attempt to fight back; presumably preferring the tactics of looking straight ahead, ignoring their harassing and walking swiftly. From where Shelly stood his choice did not appear to be doing much good. The youths were circling in front, jumping ahead at arm's length and mock singing

"Hey, hey, hey sing it loud, sing it clear."

"What's you got in there... Mr. Nipples?"

"Show us what's you got in there... Mr. Nipples."

"Hey, hey, hey, What's that bulge in your pants Mr. Nipples?"

"Mr. Nipples has a nipple, ye, ye, ye."

"Mr. Nipples, Mr. Nipples, when he pees he makes a ripple."

The commotion was moving in her direction and when they reached the front of the Royal, Shelly spontaneously did what she always did; she got involved. She stepped directly into the middle of the disturbance. Reactively her right hand reached out and grabbed the biggest youth by the front of his shirt followed instantly by her left hand grabbing the collar of a second youth. In adrenalin strength she pulled the two together with a sharp cracking of their heads and while still holding them stiff-arm she forced her control.

"OK, OK Billie Boys, that's it! Put a CAN on it! You punks got no respect! WHAT-DO-YOU-THINK-THIS-IS? A free-for-all day?

"Punks! You're all a bunch of Punks! Punks gang up on people. That's what punks do! You know that!"

"We didn't... uh...!"

"Shut up! Punks! You, Harold. How long you known me?"

"A long... uh, a long time Miss Waters. But we..."

"A long time? In that long time have I ever taught you anything about respect? ... WELL?"

"YES Ma'am you have."

"HAVE WHAT?

"HAVE SAID TO ALWAYS RESPECT OTHER PEOPLE."

"And you think running along beside someone like a gang of thugs, you consider that RESPECT? ... WELL. DO YOU?

"What's the matter? You got no answer? Harold, you know better, you too Jimmy, the rest of you."

For all the words she was shouting, they did not reflect her instant concern as she thought to herself. *I really don't need for this to be happening,* she felt uneasy over the number of people who were stopping and gawking. *Not in front of the Royal. Teenage ruffians harassing a mature man, ganging up on the sidewalk.*

At just that moment the man attempted to speak. "Uh, Excus..." but he was over shadowed by Shelly's continued chastising.

"Answer me," she resounded. "What's the matter? You all hard of hearing?" she reprimanded as the three smaller boys were backing off in meekish awe and the two larger teenagers that she was holding were trying to squirm free.

"Yes, Ma'am. Uh, No Ma'am, Miss Waters. No Ma'am we were just teasing, honest.

"We didn't mean any harm. We were just funning; honest."

Sensing that the tension was starting to ease and that there wasn't going to be any hard trouble she relaxed her hold but continued to admonish.

"Why is it you're not all in school? Hookey?" she persisted in making them pay attention.

"No Ma'am, Miss Waters, honest," they all commented in unison as they moved back out of arms length and she sensed exactly what was coming.

In reflex she gestured. "OK SCATTER," she yelled just at the instant when they had all scrambled further back, bolted, and ran. As the crowd of gawking bystanders started to disperse she and the adult male turned and looked at each other; and in reaction both started to speak.

"Well..." initiated Shelly

"Uh, I..." came his voice. "Oh, sorry go ahead," he finished.

"No, uh," she paused looking for words and noticed for the first time that he was about her age. She figured maybe thirty; tall, 6 foot, trim 165 pounds, light complexion with black short wavy hair, black shiny eyebrows that had good spacing, an uplifting brow that brought height and directed attention to his well balanced nose and lips; which had a slight natural opening giving just a hint of his perfect white teeth.

Her first impression being that he was probably a nonviolent man and certainly not feminine or even meekish. So why his reluctance to take a smack at that gang of kids? Lack of self-confidence? An abundance of patients. What?

He was neatly dressed. Brown virgin wool slacks with pleats which complimented his slim waist, argyle socks, brown wing-tip shoes, light tan long sleeve dress shirt with the cuffs turned up, ribbed sleeveless pullover V neck sweater with no tie. The only clue she could detect was a clipboard that he was carrying; under the clip was a writing tablet and she noticed that it had the letterhead, Allegheny Public Schools.

"Street kids," she spoke in the context of the incident now being passed. "They're not really bad. Sometimes they get a little rambunctious but they don't mean any harm.

"I hope they didn't do any damage," she finished with a tone implying an explanation of what was going on. Then as an after thought she asked, "What's your name?"

"Jack, Jack Lamont," he answered her last question first; then turned back to the commotion.

"No, they were... Well, when kids are bored you know how they are. I know them. Not well, but I do know them."

"My name's Shelly, Shelly Waters," she interrupted, passing over his comments and assertively forcing their acquaintance.

"Glad to make your acquaintance," she compelled the introduction by extending her hand.

"Likewise, Miss Waters," he responded in like decorum but was then interrupted.

"Shelly," she insisted; "call me Shelly."

"Shel'ly," he said with a slow pronunciation and a slight nod. "If that's your preference," he concluded as he accepted her hand and slightly bowed in the proprietary manner of a formal introduction.

"*Shelly*," he repeated, the emphasis carrying a tone of chivalry, "if it pleases *ma-lady*, call me Jack.

"My appreciation Madame," he continued the theme of chivalry. "It isn't often that a knight in armor is rescued by a beautiful *deir-dre...* that's old Irish for the *raging one*.

"A rare occasion I would venture," he finished in a final touch of theatrical pun; then shifting to normal vernacular he proceeded with his explanation.

"Like I was saying, I sort of know who they are. Two of them were in one of my classes last year. I haven't seen them in the halls this year so I assume they've dropped out."

As he spoke he could tell from his own words that he was not providing a very clear picture so he moved to the present.

"All of this excitement was really just a chance meeting that they latched on to me. I didn't even know that they..."

"What kind of class?" she interrupted in a tone that she was not really interested in the incident but more in finding out about him.

"What?" he showed his quick uncertainty.

"You said you're a school teacher. What kind of teacher?" she asked in an exacting tone.

"At school, high school; I'm a teacher over at Allegheny High."

"High school teacher?" she repeated. "You, a teacher. Isn't that something? I would never have guess. You a schoolteacher; more like a doctor or lawyer or something like that.

"What subjects you teach?" she finished with a question.

"Psychology and Sociology," he responded. "I'm just a run of the mill, every day, garden variety, friendly neighborhood school teacher thinking I can make a difference."

"My goodness, you are talkative, Mr. Jack 'garden variety' Lamont. So how come you're not in school today?"

"Fieldwork, I'm doing field work," he answered. "We're allowed so many hours per year to do field work."

"Field work?" she asked. Then cut in on her question with another question.

"By the way, why do they call you Nipples? I thought you said your name was Jack."

"It is Jack."

"So why the name Nipples?"

"The so-why," his voice became sternly defensive, "is because they are uncouth, insensitive kids the nature of whom is to verbally assault and ridicule any unsuspecting person within their reach; so that is the so-why."

"So why the name Nipples?" she ignored his tone. "You haven't answered my question?

"I mean, it's not exactly like some of the more common nick names like *the old man* or *head-shed* now is it?"

"That's exactly right," he quickly answered, this time snapping in a stronger defensive tone, "it's not like *the head-shed* or *number one* or *main man*."

"So...?" her tone implying when are you going to answer. She knew that his own words had forced him into a position where he had to respond.

"So, I really don't think it's any of your business."

"Goodness, one of Allegheny High's finest, snapping at the public. What are you trying to hide? You must be trying to hide something to be so touchy?"

"Very well," he assailed, "if you choose to be no less rude, I will tell you. I was born with a birth defect. There, now are you happy?"

Jack's answer caused her an embarrassing silence and for a second she could not respond. Neither did she notice out of the corner of her eye that two men were walking in their direction. It was with a more solemn composure and a slower tone that she responded.

"A birth defect? What kind of birth defect?"

Then in a sincerity that was clearly evident she finished her question. "It's important. I'd really like to know."

"It's called *Penismuliebrity-nipple'glandus*," he blurted out in a manner of confessing-in-order-to-get-it-over-with; and just as he knew would happen he instantly had a feeling of self rage.

God damn it! He thought. *Why in the hell do I always do this! What is this damn compulsion I have to broadcast to the whole damn world what's wrong with me!*

"What in the..." Shelly started to push for a clarification but just at that instant, that, which she had not earlier noticed cut her off.

"HEY HERE GOOD PEOPLE! What seems to be going on?" came an authoritative male voice that startled both she and Jack. In reaction they turned and were met by two men wearing hats and business suits. Shelly recognized one of the men and responded.

"Well, well, well," she acknowledged. "If it isn't one of Pittsburgh's finest. Good morning Detective Casey. You still doing the P.D. proud?"

"I try," came the response. "You know, public servant, golden rule, honor thy mother."

"Especially the honor part, Casey," she chided. "What brings you down to the lower end of Liberty? You slumming this morning?" she chastened in a one-up-man-ship voice.

"Democracy at work 'Salty'," he matched wits by calling her by her street name.

"You know how it is being a good public servant. We have to make sure that we arrest everyone equally. No discrimination of arrest because of race, religion, age or sex gender. That's the great American Arrest Creed."

"Excuse me Monsieur Casey," she rebuked in a tone implying her lack of concern over the threat of being arrested; and by implication the far more important matter of social graces.

"Here I am," she snubbed in a one-up-man-ship, "a graduate of one of Pittsburgh's most elite finishing schools, The Paragon Academy, you may have heard the name," she mocked a southern belle, "Dear me where are my manners?

"Allow me to introduce you to another one of Pittsburgh's finest; only he's on the high school circuit.

"Casey Blackstock of Pittsburgh's P.D." she glanced at him with a condescending look, "meet Mr. Jack Lamont of Allegheny's notorious High."

As she finished she expected the two men to acknowledge each other; but neither one reacted. In a stance of silent animosity she realized that the two were looking sternly at each other.

"We've already met!" snapped Jack in a voice intending a cut at Casey Blackstock rather than acknowledging the introduction.

"Oh?" she reacted in surprise.

"Several times," Jack's voice still icy as he assumed the onus for the conversation.

"Isn't that right Officer Blackstock?" he ended on a resentful note.

"Several... is not necessarily the term I would use Professor," Casey chided in a mocked smile. "You being a school teacher and all. It seems that the term 'few' would be more appropriate; but far-be-it for me to correct a teacher."

"A few? Ha!" Jack answered the clash. "Let me see if I can refresh your memory," came his contradiction as he and Casey continued looking at each other in eye contact animosity.

"Last Monday in front of the Grant Theater, the week before that in front of the Palace and the week before that in front of the South Hills..." he was about to continue when Shelly broke in.

"Hey! Hey, hold on here. Unless I am greatly mistaken those are all my theaters. What's going on?" she demanded; but her words fell on deaf ears as Jack and Casey continued their defiant eye stare.

"Hey!" she made a second attempt, "If, you two don't mind, I would like to hear some words. Spelled w o r d s; either of you comprendy? You know the great American savvy." her voice raised in sarcasm.

"Loitering," commented Casey who was determined to maintain his role of authority by not being the first to blink.

"Our Professor here," he directed his words to Shelly while still holding eye contact, "has been loitering in front of your brothel houses, 'Salty', uh excuse me, Miss Waters; mustn't forget our public servant manners especially in presence of someone who graduated from *ta la da* elite Paragon Academy."

"Loitering?" she questioned.

"Don't listen to him," Jack denied as he broke eye contact with Casey and turned to Shelly. "I've simply been doing field work. Remember I just mentioning it."

"Field work? In front of my theaters? I don't suppose you would care to enlighten me?" she pushed in a demanding tone.

"Go ahead, Professor," cut in Casey. "Answer the lady. Tell her what you have been doing hanging out in front of X rated movie houses for the past few months."

"Not hanging out, you illiterate flat foot," Jack lashed out. "Sociology. For those people such as you who can't read or write the term sociology is an academic course of study pertaining to man and his environment; that means how the environment and man blend together. Psychology; what motivates man to do the things he does. I've been attempting to do sociological and psychological field observation on what impact sexually explicit movies have on the public.

"But you," Jack sharply charged to Casey, "in your pseudo zealousness for catching criminals keep interrupting my studies."

"Perverted," Casey admonished. "Don't you think that's a more appropriate term for standing around and snickering at what kind of people pay good money to go in and see pornography filth?"

"Hey! Hold It Right There! Just a momento Bozzo," challenged Shelly. "Who appointed you judge and jury..."?

"Go ahead," Casey ignored her demand and spoke to Jack. "Tell her Highness here what you told us. What was it you said? 'The evolution of man as it pertains to motion pictures.'

"That was... the explanation you gave us wasn't it? That motion pictures are relatively new to man's environment; fifty years or so. And now it's your job to determine whether sex films help or hurt our social morals?"

"I," Jack was about to speak when Shelly cut in.

"So what did you decide?" she turned to Jack. "Who appointed you judge and jury in deciding what people are entitled to see. Correct me if I am wrong," she yelled, "but I believe it's been firmly established by a United States Supreme Court decision that motion pictures are not a business but a form of Art.

"And as such are protected from undue government infringement by the freedom of speech clause of the First Amendment to the United States Constitution."

"That's an entirely erroneous prospective," Jack rush to clarify.

"Our friend here, Mr. Can-not-read-or-write-Casey is blowing smoke. First of all I don't decide, I observe. Secondly, it is not the position of a sociologist to judge; only to observe.

"But I will say this. The people who do attend your movies seem to do so of their own free will and unless I am mistaken, freedom is the reason we have been fighting wars for the last two hundred years."

"You are right about one thing," Casey responded. "You are mistaken. The laws of Pennsylvania specifically forbid the showing of obscene or pornographic film." At that point Casey Blackstock unbuttoned his jacket and took out a pair of handcuffs.

"And while we are on the subject of breaking the law I find it my duty to tell you Miss Shelly Waters that you are under arrest for violations of Pennsylvania Statute 18, section 4524 of the Penal code to wit, the public showing of obscene material."

"Well, I'll be damn," commented Shelly, "so that's what this whole thing is all about. You're going to bust me again. Casey why'n the hell didn't you say so in the first place?"

"How about the second place," he matched her one-up-man-ship. "In the second place you are hereby under arrest..."

"Wait," she resisted, as he was about to start cuffing procedures. "Just a minute, if you have no objection. First, the matter of money."

"What money," he answered offensively, "if you think I'm going to take a bribe..."

"Perish the thought my dear Casey. I am talking about the sixteen hundred dollars I have here in my money pouch. Now if you will be so kind as to count it here in front of a witness then I might stand a little better chance of getting some of it back. Last time it conveniently got lost; so if you have no objections; count."

"OK Sixteen hundred and twelve dollars; so noted in front of a witness," he answered after counting the contents and assumed responsibility of the pouch.

"Money, money, money, lots of money here," he commented as he sucked in his stomach and pushed the pouch inside his belt.

"The porn business must be more profitable than I thought."

"It makes expenses," chided Shelly.

"And I just bet you have a lot of expenses, like I hear down town some of this porn green is usually spread around in the right places."

"Judging from the fact that I am standing here getting arrested," she answered in defiance, "it appears that my operating expenses have just gone up."

"You know the saying, Salty. Easy come easy go; no pun intended. Now if it pleases her highness let's move it; hands behind your back."

"Who is it this time Casey?" she asked as he was turning her around and putting on the cuffs.

"Now Salty you know they don't tell me those things. When the word comes down I just goes out and does the doings.

"But," Casey paused for affect, "this time you will be happy to know that you are not going alone. We're also going to bring in this here Mr. Professor Lamont."

"What! Him?" her voice rose in surprise as she nodded towards Jack. "You've got to be kidding. On what charge?"

"Oh, we can think up lots of charges. Spiting on the sidewalk, loitering, or what about conspiracy; conspiracy to deal in obscenity. Has a nice catchy little sound don't you think?"

Then abruptly changing his focus he directed his words to Jack. "OK Professor you know the routine. Hands behind your back so my partner here can try out his brand new set of cuffs."

"By the way Casey," Shelly cut in. "Who is this Mr. Silent Clean Cut, rosy cheek, white complexion, slicked back red hair, smiles while he is cutting your heart out, new-hire you have with you; haven't seen him before."

"Ah, par'don my breach of etiquette Madám. By all means, allow me to introduce my new partner. His name is Jeremiah Cole. Jeremiah meet..." but Casey did not get to finish.

"Jeremiah?" she cut in, pronouncing the name with emphasis. "Very biblical. Jer'e'miah, how is it I picture you as being a pseudo Christian, Jer'e'miah?"

"What? Uh, if you are referring to me? I'm sorry ma'am," Cole spoke his first words, "but I'm afraid I don't quite understand."

"OH, you understand all right Jer'e'miah," she again emphasized his name as a dig. "You understand about the radio and TV evangelist programs that are saturating our air ways. Isn't that right? You do understand that don't you Jer?"

Cole did not respond to Shelly but turned to Casey and asked, "Casey, am I correct in assuming that Miss Waters here is under arrest. And if so why are we standing here arguing about..." Being cut off he did not get to finish as Casey interrupted.

"Ah it's not what you think Jer. Salty's OK. It's a game we play. Keeps the job from getting monotonous."

Cole gave Casey a look of disbelief and continued his role of innocence by asking, "What's she talking about? Radio and TV evangelist?"

"What I'm talking about," Shelly barged in to answer the question, "is the articles I see in the *Miami Herald* Newspaper. Miami is down in Florida in case you might be getting confused.

"Let's see," she spoke as if recalling. "What were the headlines? MEYER LANSKY RULES CRIME CARTEL FROM FLORIDA."

"I'm SORRY MA'AM," Cole said as the softness in his young eyes instantly changed to vengeance and shot arrows of poison directly into Shelly, "IF You are IMPLYING SOMETHING, WHY DON'T YOU JUST COME RIGHT OUT AND SAY IT."

"HA!" Shelly said insultingly as she shot back a defiant stare. "I'm talking about your GODFATHER, MEYER LANSKY. YOU DO WORK FOR HIM DON'T YOU? WHAT'S HE WORTH 300 MILLION? At least that's what the paper said."

The reference to the Mafia touched an extremely sensitive nerve in Cole. It was an association term that the mob consistently fought with fervor.

"Ma'am," Cole responded in a tone that he hoped would imply that an association with the Mafia was so ridiculous as to not even merit a resentment.

"I'm an Officer for the Allegheny County Sheriff's Department, and I have no idea..." but he was again interrupted.

"...what I'm talking about," she completed his sentence and then started her own.

"In a pig's rear you don't. What I am talking about is Mafia; spelled M a f i a. You may have heard of them. They're that gob of spit that leaches on society by controlling judges, cops, gambling casinos, the Teamsters Union, dog tracks, Frank Sinatra, George Raft and, lo-and-behold, Radio and Television Evangelist racket right here in our very own little ol' Pittsburgh.

"That last one," she continued before she could be interrupted, "if I was a betting person, why I'd just bet that you wouldn't know one thing about that one would you Jer ol' boy?" And just as she had expected sharp, objections were instantly shouted by Casey.

"ENOUGH!" he ordered. "Back off Salty. You're coming down a little too hard on my main man here. He is, just getting started in the arresting business. So how about we cut him a little slack; you wouldn't want to intimidate him right off would you?

"You want to rob him", Casey continued, "of his self confidence and cause him to develop an inferiority complex? Surely you wouldn't want something like that on your conscious now would you Salty? Just think how guilty that would make you feel. Shame for shame."

"As a matter of fact ma'am," Jeremiah crowded in on his own behalf, "I am a Christian. I simply don't find it necessary to attend some church. And yes, I do support the Word of God that is brought to us by the advent of radio and television. I'm proud..."

"I had a feeling," she cut back in, "that you would promote your affiliations Jer ol' boy.

"Let's talk about those Radio and Television Evangelist shell we? Let's talk about how they daily screaming out over the free air that the world is going to Hell because of the filth, to use their words, in today's movie houses shall we?" she stepped up to his face.

"Let's talk about the man up there doing the preaching while he's dressed in a twelve hundred dollar suit and has more money invested in cuff links, wrist watch and ring finger than most people are worth.

"Thumping that bible and threatening damnation to anyone who dares to short change God..."

"SALTY," came an intruding command.

With her hands cuffed behind her she whirled back to face Casey. The sun was shinning directly into her face so she squinted one eye and tilted her head to where she was half in his shadow and commented.

"Whose side are you on Casey?" she asked in an implying tone. "You know the story as well as I do. You know that I'm not against religion. I believe in God as much as anyone. What I am against is the biggest propaganda scam that's ever been perpetrated on the American people.

"You know and I know that you can't turn on a TV or listen to a radio these days unless you are flooded by 'you-better-send-money-to-God-or-you'll-go-to-hell' Bull Shit.

"We, you and me, we may be on the opposite sides of the fence Casey but you have always been a pretty straight shooter; a puppet for down town but you're OK

"But him," she nodded her head toward Jeremiah. "A 100% genuine hypocrite hiding behind a badge," she paused and gave Jeremiah a quick glance.

"It seems," she insinuated, "very strange that he just happen to be along on this bust. Tell me Jer ol' boy," she turned back in his direction, "I'll bet you even do a little preaching on the side. Is that why they sent you, Jer?

"I've noticed that all you television preaching boys always turn up the threat of Hell and everlasting fire around the first of the month.

"That's when the Social Security checks come in the mail, right Jer?"

"CAN IT SALTY," Casey came down a little more forceful this time. "I can't have you casting dispersions about my new roomie. Jer is just doing his job like I am. As of right now ENOUGH IS ENOUGH.

"Now if you and the Prof will just come along peacefully we have a nice four door unmarked car waiting just around the corner."

"Hey Jer ol' boy," Shelly continued in defiance as Casey started moving her along.

"I run a soup kitchen up in the Hill District; feed about 300 homeless people a day. I can always use some volunteer labor. You know washing dishes, dishing out food, moping the floors.

"I was wondering if you would bring your brand of Christianity over one day a week and help us out. It would really be apprec..."

"SALTY!" Casey commanded in a tone to cease and desist and proceeded with heading toward the car.

"Now, if there are no further objections, let's do it."

At that point Shelly conceded to going along but not before she fired off one last volley.

"Always happy to be escorted by one of Pitts's finest," she returned to her one-up-man-ship, "but Casey I must confess that I am a little embarrassed."

"You mean about being arrested," he answered as they were rounding the corner.

"Why Salty I would have thought by now that..."

"Not for being arrested Casey," she finished her dig; "about being escorted by you in that suit you're wearing. You being such a prominent public figure and all you really should try to keep up with the latest fashions. In case you didn't know it Casey, double breasted suits are out."

In Pittsburgh, the morning newspapers usually hit the street no later than five A.M. On the front page of the next day's addition the *Pittsburgh Press* carried the arrest story. Not headlines, but the next smaller; "Porn Queen and High School Teacher Arrested on Obscene Charges." The *Post-Gazette* went a step further and sensationalized with "High School Teacher-Porn Queen Conspiracy".

Frank Buckwilder, now in his seventies has risen to the very pinnacle of life. His exceptional good looks that sparked so much envy in earlier years have heightened to elegant, genteel admiration. His wavy silver blue hair compliments more than ever the sparkling blue of his eyes and his face and neck have completely escaped the lines of time. In soft creamy texture they remain full, smooth and unblemished.

He has neither a mustache nor a beard. He tried both for a short time but concluded that they bordered on ostentatious and they fell to the touch of a razor. He has never, however, put any such limits on his wardrobe. Always impeccably dressed he had a propensity for light blue, three piece virgin wool suits, white freshly starched dress shirts and deep rose bud red sheen neckties.

His jewelry is limited to two items. On the chain of his pocket watch he wears a gold fob depicting a scale-of-justice that he received over thirty years before as a best friend gift. On his left ring finger he wears an onyx ring that had a vein of pink running through white.

The former he wears in remembrance of the only man he has ever envied. The strand of pink running through the pearl white of the ring stone represents the forging link between the only two loves ever to penetrate his soul; his adopted daughter Shelly and a lady of such aristocratic, bourgeois qualities as to establish Pittsburgh's most elite women's academy.

His current life's pattern is also different than it was twenty-five years earlier. He no longer finds it necessary to go after inequity with a vengeance. Age has brought him eminence and reverence on par with other Pittsburgh renowned men such as William Steinberg, the conductor of the Pittsburgh Symphony; Dr Jonas Edward Salk, developer of a poliomyelitis vaccine and Nicolai Lopatnikoff, noted Russian composer.

He is highly sought after to elevate social affairs, endorse community drives and identify with benevolent causes. As each new social season opens he is highly prized as an escort. At all formal functions of black coat and tie his trademark knows him; a swirling brandy snifter.

Whatever the occasion he will usually be in company of prominent leaders such as the Mellons, Benedums and Heinz; but in mingling small talk he is still the advocate. He never misses an opportunity to nudge and promote the responsibility of the wealthy to provide for the less fortunate; and that power carries with it an obligation to stand guardian for right and justice.

On one such affair he found himself standing in the mingling company of David L. Lawrence, Governor of Pennsylvania Commonwealth. With savoir-faire equal to the brandy he swirled he casually remarked, "Governor Lawrence...that Bill which just arrived on your desk for signature, the 'Save our Children From Obscenity' bill passed by both State Houses of Congress, Governor it seems to me to be a little too harsh.

"Maybe it would be better if we held the power of government in check a little more and not infringe quite so heavy upon the constitutional rights of free speech."

But for all of his social aplomb, the courtroom is still his duty-bound field of front line battle; propelled by the axiom that power unchallenged equates power corrupt. His presence in court, now more than ever, brings an atmosphere of decorum and dignity and it is not uncommon for him to sway a jury in his favor for no other reason than admiration. Even onto a battlefield, grace is respected.

When he arrived at the Court House the next day after Shelly's arrest he was immediately recognized by the Duty Officer and instantly accorded every courtesy.

Without paper work, or waiting in line, he was escorted back to the women's compound by a strikingly beautiful, dimpled cheek, honey smile, pearly teeth, sparkling eyed black female deputy sheriff who chose not to lead but to put her arm through his, walk directly by his side and express her complimentary admiration.

At the compound he knowingly started to take his place behind the yellow floor line but the very polite and accommodating deputy insisted that no such restrictions need apply.

He was very welcome to wait for a moment and the inmate would be brought to him. Thence they were escorted to the Attorney-Prisoner conference room and the female deputy continued her personal attention by bringing a pitcher of ice water and straightening the chairs. When she left, she still had to lock the door behind her but as it closed, it closed with a click and not a slam.

It was the same room in which Shelly and Morgan had shared some eight years earlier; when she was only nineteen.

As she recalled that chapter in her life Shelly felt a small pang of guilt but nothing more. She was older now and her emotions were not so sensitive. Maturity had brought with it an acceptance that life, everyone's life, is usually hard, brutal and more than anything else lonely.

Being in the slammer this time meant nothing more than an inconvenience. In fact it even felt like an integral part of the forging direction her life appeared to be taking; walking in the shadows of Frank's teaching.

It did not go unnoticed when Detective Casey called her Salty. She also knew that she was known as Rebel Rouser and more recently in terms of Agitator and Demonstrator.

She had passed the night in jail by lying on a flat wood bench and tracing a single thread through the time line of her life; one fight after another; all of which she sincerely felt came looking for her and not the other way around. And for whatever reason there was a single common denominator in every one of them; she felt as empty and unfulfilled when each fight was over as she had felt before it started.

Her teens had been wild and she would not trade them for anything. But even back then she got no real pleasure in bringing attention to herself. In many cases she had secretly hoped that one of her other three friends would take the point and stand up against their challenges; but it rarely happened.

By the time her twenties arrived searching had become an inherent part of her existence. Searching for something but as yet she did not know what. While she had never openly discussed the matter with her friends, her needs or at least the essence of her searching, seem to be radically different from the needs of the others. She had often heard the other three using the expression of getting married so they would have a man to take care of them.

Being taken care of in terms of a wife was something she simply could not understand. Why would she need someone to take care of her? Certainly she had no desire to look out for or be dominating over someone else. That part had never been a concern. So what else was there? There was completeness.

For as long as she could remember she simply felt less than complete. Not in the context of being less than whole because of a missing male counter part, but incomplete in the sense of the formula not being finished.

The perpetual forces of her subconscious mind somehow pictured her in terms of connecting or blending a man's body to hers. That was different from what Morgan had said about life's nature order of woman going to a man. For Morgan and her mother such genre seemed exactly right. Morgan was the dominant figure and the picture would have been in perfect balance with Patricia by his side.

But she and her mother were not the same. Her mother's formula would have been complete with the simple addition of a stronger counter part. For herself, however, she somehow knew that completeness for her could only come... from an equal exchange of indispensable needs. Her to her man and her man to her, each providing to the other that certain something, which was so essential, that the absence thereof would totally negate and void the prospects of ever having a fulfilling and satisfying life.

Therefore, she continued to search and as the years passed she watched as her circle of friends, one by one found someone and walked down the isle. With each wedding she felt a little more alone; and for a while during that period of her life her search had been more intense. By her mid twenties she was the last of their foursome to not have dawned a wedding gown; and now in her late twenties Morgan's wish for her was becoming more and more obscure.

A wish that was replaced to a large degree by the influences and philosophies of Frank Buckwilder. She became more involved in demonstrations and more anti-government; central among these being that freedom is the responsibility of every individual; and to challenge without reservation, those who would steal it away.

"Shell," Frank greeted her in the conference room as the two hugged each other, "how they treating you? Make it through the night OK?"

"Good," she answered as they released their hug and lingered holding hands and looking at each other.

"As usual," she filled in small talk. "Hookers and drunks for cell mates. Around eleven o'clock they brought us some blankets, no pillows, everyone sleeps ever how they can; routine."

"How you feel this morning," he talked to relax the situation. "Joints ache, back stiff?"

"Oh, you know. I can't say that it's something I enjoy but in a way I'm used to it."

"So, let's talk some business, what happened this time? Same ol' same ol'?"

"I'm not sure, Daddy Frank. This time there seems to have been a little different twist."

"That twist, does it have anything to do with a school teacher?"

Shelly looked in a quick glance. "How did...?" she started to ask but he raised his hand slightly and cut in.

"The morning papers. Sensationalism. Newspapers have to make money and so they always blow things way out of proportion."

"Oh," she realized. "Sorry but they don't happen to provide us with the latest news in the cell."

Then as if the moment had arrived the two seated, shifted in their chairs until they came to where they were face to face and touching at the knees.

"Daddy Frank, I'm really sorry that I have to keep asking for your help. It's just..."

Frank quickly raised his hand in gesture and slightly shook his head for her to stop.

"Shelly, Honey, you're all I have in this world. Baby you are my only reason for living. All the worldly things that I own, all the supposedly social engagements I have. The kindness with which people treat me. These are all nice; indeed even pleasant and certainly at my age I had rather have them than not have them, but Baby when I pass on, those things too will also pass."

He paused, slightly leaned back, and allowed his hands to come to rest in his lap; a signal for her to relax. Now as always, no matter where or when, their time together was more than just a visit. Just as Socrates, Plato and Aristotle must have held their student in awe, when Frank and Shelly spent time together there was a reverence bonding of the master teaching the young.

On this day, as the two sat together in the Allegheny County Jail his presence induced an ambiance of tranquillity; his way of taking command and establishing the feeling that they had all the time in the world.

Nothing about the situation warranted panic. They were inside a jail cell. Nothing more. Lots of people had been inside that very cell; the construction workers who built it. The cleaning crew. Electricians who replace the lights. Other lawyers and other clients all of whom had passed on through.

"Shelly," he shifted in his chair and took her hands in his, "do you remember the summer of 1954 when you were twelve-thirteen years old and you and I toured Europe? Remember that?"

"Thirteen, Daddy Frank I was thirteen," she responded not overly eager but to show that she was paying attention. "Of course I remember. We flew from Idlewild Airport in New York to Berlin, Germany on a Lockheed propeller driven four engine Constellation."

The manner of Shelly's answer startled Frank. *Amazing,* he thought. *Of all the things that I showed her, she remembers the flight. Simply amazing,* he repeated to himself. *That which is planted in the mind of a child. How long it will live?* Thence he moved on to his point.

"Baby my reason for taking you through Germany and in particularly through Berlin was to make an impression on your young mind.

"I wanted you to see the miles and miles of that war torn, bombed out city. To see the death, destruction, pain and suffering; the end result of Adolph Hitler's ruthless climb to power.

"The final product of a society where the people were too concerned with their individual interest to keep a harness on the Government.

"When," he was starting the words that she had heard so many times before, "in any society, when the people shirk their individual responsibility, power will always gravitate to the corrupt.

"The very nature of a government," he spoke the words she expected would follow, "any government, is the fact that a few in power will control the many."

At that point Frank paused; for whatever triggered the awareness he realized that she already knew all of that so he simply jumped ahead.

"The point is that the power which a society does vest in the few must be kept in check." He paused for effect and then continued, "Shelly, I am saying all of this to make a point.

"When we left Germany we toured the Greek Islands. Remember that? Remember how I talked about Greece being the cradle of democracy.

"And then we contrasted the two. In Greece, the good that the people built has lasted for four thousand years. In Germany, the 'bad' that the 'Government' built lasted less than ten; and will be remembered for four thousand years.

"My thinking at the time was to instill in you a sense of responsibility; an obligation to always challenge that which you think is wrong. And to realize that challenge is not something you do for the approval of others but something you do because it is right."

As he paused he noticed how obediently she was listening but the expression on her face cast a look of confusion. Suddenly he realized how inappropriate all of this was to the present circumstances. In silence he chastised himself. How unfair he was being. His emotions had taken control. He was frustrated that he himself had never been able to achieve all that he was advocating. How unfair, he suddenly realized to place such a burden on the shoulders of his only daughter. He inhaled a deep breath and held while the lungs processed the fresh supply of oxygen and when it was depleted he exhaled.

A sensation came over him that maybe he had always fought life too hard. A fleeting thought that moderation would have been much more rewarding.

He froze at the possibility that he had forged an irreversible destiny in Shelly. The thought caused a chill. Maybe he should just capitulate. His life was closer to the end; hers was just beginning.

"Shelly, Honey after having just said all of that, what I am about to say now may sound very conflicting. But Baby, this running fight that you have with the law over showing X rated movies. Do you really want to continue the present course you are on?"

If Shelly detected Frank's switch it did not show because she answered without hesitation.

"Yes, Daddy Frank, I am certain," She spoke adamantly at first; and then softened her voice in giving her reasons.

"Those theaters," she continued knowing that Frank already knew, "were Daddy Morgan's dream. What he lived for. His life's work. It's what he left behind when..." she did not say the word.

"They are," she emphasized, "his legacy and he left them in my trust."

"Baby I understand all of that," Frank answered reassuringly, "but Honey times have changed and things are never going to be the same. Television has ruined..."

"That's not true," she cut in. "Morgan said it and I say it. TV is just a passing fad. In time it will wash out with the out-going tide."

"Honey," Frank, continued his tone of understanding, "you're not facing reality.

"Baby, TV is here, it's growing by leaps and bounds and there will never be a return to the movie houses the way things were. And Honey, these showing X-rated movies. You are fighting a battle you cannot win."

When he saw that his words were having no impact he rose from his chair and walked a few steps around the room. With his suit jacket pushed back by having both of his hands in his hip pockets he looked to where she was still sitting.

"Sweetheart, he said as he looked down into his daughter's eyes, "I loved Morgan as much as you, maybe more in my own way. But Honey, wanting it and it happening are two different things. Don't you think..."

"No," she cut in. "I know what you are going to say Daddy Frank," a slight watering came as she looked up, "so please, don't say it. I made him a vow, he trusted me and so long as I am able I intend to keep those theaters alive."

Then with a soft tone of determination she continued.

"And if showing sex films is the only way I can keep his legacy intact then I will keep on showing sex films."

Knowing that Frank would not make any further attempt to change her mind she made a final conciliatory statement.

"It's not like they are vile degrading hard core kinky sex. All of my films simply show two people in love making love.

"What's so horrible about that? So the sex organs of the human body are shown. God didn't seem to find them offensive when he put Adam and Eve nude in the Garden of Eden.

"So the breasts of the young women are shown. They are always perfect young breast; and, perfect breast seems to be the criteria the world uses to judge the worth of a woman."

They both knew what she was referring to and neither said anything. Then in unconvincing words she concluded, "Things will get better,

Daddy Frank; it's just a matter of time."

Frank detected the weakening of her courage and his aging heart ached for the lonely young woman seated before him and for the first time he wondered if his well intended teaching had been a mistake. *Dear God, dear God please, have I done more harm than...*

He took a deep breath and wished there was some way he could shoulder her problems but he knew he could not. In tender regret he squeezed her hands and commented.

"There is no need to discuss the matter any further Baby. I know how you ache. Your mother and Morgan are both gone and I know how lonely you must feel." He paused to prepare for the change of subject.

"What's important right now is to get you out of here," he then became a lawyer.

"Shelly, tell me, when the officers placed you and the teacher, what's his name?"

"Lamont, Jack Lamont."

"How are you and Mr. Lamont connected?"

"We're not connected. I never saw him before."

"You mean the officers simply arrested him for being in the presence?"

"Something like that; from what I can gather. He's a Sociology Teacher at Allegheny High School. He was doing some sort of sociology related field work by watching the nature of the people who come into the theaters."

"You didn't know him but you say the arresting officers were familiar with the man, this Mr. Lamont?"

"From the conversation, I would say they were more than familiar. I think he's been watching the theaters for some time and the cops have been watching him for just as long."

"Strange. Shelly...don't ask me why...but I'm getting the feeling that the heat is being turned up again.

"That's something I will have to find out. If I am correct it was no accident that this Mr. Lamont was arrested in connection with you.

"It's my guess that if he had not been there you probably would not have been arrested."

"But why?" she asked. What's he got to do with anything?"

"Publicity my dear; Publicity. The rare opportunity to sensationalize by connecting the sacred name of our public schools to your sex theaters.

"If I am correct the detectives were probably doing nothing more than just watching your premises. Maybe not even that. It's possible that they were simply passing by and saw a golden opportunity to arrest both you and Mr. Lamont so there would be guilt by association.

"And, I might add, it worked. At this very moment I must say that we have an awful lot of bad publicity on our hands.

"As to the why-now, I can't say. The only thing I can guess is that our ol' nemesis, that *un-benevolent* Coalition of Radio and Television Evangelist are expanding their power base. It's a good guess that they have pumped a lot more money into City Hall and have probably bought some additional politicians.

"Baby it goes back to what I said earlier. They are getting stronger and you are getting weaker. Are you sure..."

"Yes, and Yes again, I am sure."

"OK Baby I won't desert you. Now about getting you and Mr. Lamont released.

"Let me ask, when you were arrested? Did either of the arresting officers say anything to you about your rights?"

"Rights, what rights. All we did was jerk each other's chain like we always do."

"Was?" Frank cut in, "there any mention...any mention at all about the fact that 'anything you do or say can and will be used against you'; or any mention that you have the right to have an attorney present?"

"No, nothing like that."

"Are you sure, I mean 100% positive that you were not apprised of any rights."

"I'm telling you Daddy Frank no such words were spoken. Why is it so important?"

"I'm sorry Shel, it's a point of law. A thing called the Miranda Decision. It stems from a 1966 U.S. Supreme Court decision in the case of Miranda v. Arizona.

"In substance is says that you must be informed at the time of the arrest that you have the right to remain silent, that anything you may say or do can and will be used against you and that you have the right to have an attorney present.

"At all preliminary hearing the presiding Judge will usually ask if a defendant has been so informed; if not the case will usually be dismissed.

"The thing," Frank murmured in thought, "is why? I am certain that the officers were fully aware of this. Unless..."

"Unless what," Shelly asked.

"Unless," Frank answered in a disbelieving expression, "they really didn't care one iota about charging you with any violation of law.

"What they really wanted, and what they got was the damaging publicity."

The preliminary hearing for Shelly and Jack was held at 1:30 P.M. before Judge Slater. The Prosecuting Attorney's office was represented by a first year law school graduate and neither Detective Blackstock nor Detective Jeremiah Cole was present.

Frank immediately made a motion for dismissal on the grounds that Shelly and Jack Lamont had not been apprised of their rights.

The motion came as a welcome reason to Judge Slater and over the minor objection of the State's Attorney, the case was thrown out.

By 2:00 P.M. Shelly, Jack and Frank were standing on the outside Courthouse steps. Frank sensing that his work was done shook hand with Jack, gave Shelly a final hug and hailed a taxi.

Chapter 29

After saying goodbye to Frank on the steps of the County Courthouse, Jack and Shelly walked with little comment to a public cafeteria two blocks away and in an open almost empty dining room shared their first cup of coffee. At that hour in the afternoon, the cashiers stood idly by their checkout stations. And it was little noted that this man and this woman were awkward in each other's company; or that the woman followed as the man crossed the room to an out of the way table near a street window.

Neither was it detected that as Shelly followed the man's lead she started noticing his physical features from the back. His shiny black hair was neat and trim and his shoulders were broad and square. In second looking he seemed manlier than her impression the day before. She recalled how he had shown no fear of Detective Casey and wondered again why he had not stood up to the haggling of the teenagers.

Seated at the table, she raised her cup, took a sip of the fresh brew and felt a warming effect. As the caffeine entered her system she realized how tense she was. It was soothing to be free from the arrest, away from the jail, away from the outside street noise and to be sitting in a cool quiet secluded place having coffee. In succession she also realized it was pleasant to be sharing it with the man on the other side of the table.

How come, she had the quick thought; *someone like him has never come into my life?* To her own surprise she did not find it necessary to take charge and be the first to speak. She simply sat with both elbows on the table, held the cup up to her lips with both hands and looked at Jack over the brim. When their conversation did start it fell first to the ordeal of being arrested.

For Jack it was his first time and naturally he was upset. Shelly expressed understanding for his concerns and extended her apologies that he happened to get caught up.

"But tell me," she inquired. "Why were you so hostile with our good friend Casey?"

"Because," he answered in an enunciated tone, "he insulted me by snubbing my profession. Here I am with a Master's Degree in the field of Social Sciences and he has the audacity to view me as a nonentity."

Uh oh, she thought, *touchy subject.* She was about to make some conciliatory remark when he continued.

"The word on the degree," he emphasized, "is Science. I am a scientist. In today's world, though, heaven forbid if you are not a physical scientist. That way you can do things like run out and developing a nice little handy dandy, garden variety type Atomic bomb, fly off to Japan, drop it on Hiroshima, kill a hundred thousand people or so and then you get respect."

"And," she spoke in a rhetorical tone as she took a small sip of coffee and lower the cup, "you think that Casey's snide remarks about my sex films and your profession in the same context is a little undignified?"

"Casey Blackstock is a creep."

"OK," her tone now indicating sincerity, "let's say I add a little of my dignity to off-set Casey's lack of dignity.

"Jack, I ask this in all honesty. Why are you so interested in the manner in which I make a living?

"You think it's easy money, lots of sex involved, what?"

Her remark, the manner in which she spoke, the sincerity in her voice, all caused him to suddenly look at her in a different light. In addition, for the first time he saw her as a person, a woman and not just some obscure owner of sex theaters. In the following seconds before he answered it flashed through his mind that trying to keep a string of run down theaters open by showing X rated movies would be a very brutal way to make a living; and he wondered why she did it. What made her stay in the business against the hammering public opinion; he wondered but he didn't ask.

"In all due respect Shelly," he answered, "I neither condone nor condemn the showing of sexual explicit material. I like to believe that

I have no bias either way. My job is to observe the impact on society; good, bad or indifferent.

"But the fact is, pornography is what everyone is talking about these days. It's saturating the news media; newspapers, radio and television.

"Everyone assumes without doubt that it will be the cause of the world going to hell in a hand basket; and it may well be.

"But how do we know. No one has ever done a 'scientific' study," he stressed the word scientific.

"Wouldn't it be something," his tone implying that enough had been said, "if it turned out that sexually explicit material actually had a positive effect on society."

As he spoke Shelly could feel a warming for this man. A welcomed ally, be it ever so small, had come her way; and she was appreciative for the alliance.

"I'm just curious," she asked. "How did you happen to choose the fields of Sociology and Psychology?"

"Because I wanted to know why everyone else in the world is crazy except me."

"So what did you find out?"

"What I found out is there are no answers, only questions. Everyone's mind is programmed at an early age and it seldom changes."

"What's this programmed you're referring too?"

"Programmed," he took an explanatory breath. "It's a new term which had come into use. It's how they develop computers. How things work. Once a computer is built to, say operate in English it doesn't suddenly change to function in Spanish."

"And you," she asked. "Are you programmed?"

"We are all programmed Shelly. You, me, everybody. Just the circumstances of being born and growing up means that some sort of program has been imprinted in everyone's brain.

"Wherever you were born, whatever your young circumstances, your mind was programmed and it will never change. It's just a fact of life."

"So what language were you programmed in?"

"See what I mean," he replied. "There are no answers. Just questions?"

"OK If there are only questions then how about I ask, are you married, wife, children; the usual things?"

"No, I'm not married or the-usual-things. And for some more of the-usual-things, I don't date. For some of the-unusual things, yes I have dated but I don't date any more."

"And this birth defect," she asked as she continued to hold her coffee up to her lips, "which you said you have. What did you call it? Penna... something or another. Is that part of your usual or your unusual program?"

"Penismuliebrity is the word and whether or not it is part of my programming is none of your business."

UH OH, she thought. She detected the instant hostility and alarming blood rushed to her face. *I don't want to offend him. I don't want to loose him.*

"Uh, sorry, Jack. That didn't come out the way I intended. Bad habit I have of always shooting off my mouth. I really didn't mean to get so personal. Let's change the subject."

Their conversation then drifted to the repercussions Jack could expect in his teaching job because of getting arrested. He felt certain there would be at least two official school hearings on the matter. One would be in the principal's office at Allegheny High School.

The other, the one he feared the most would be the School Board. They had the authority to fire teachers and they had no reservation about using that power. And so the two talked. Teaching was his life's endeavor and he was now facing the possibility of losing his credentials.

Unmindful of the time, almost two hours had passed and it was on that note that they rose to leave. Outside the cafeteria they paused and exchanged telephone numbers. With a parting handshake they both promised to call and said goodbye.

Jack was the first to walk away and Shelly watched as he disappeared into the passing crowd; and continued looking for a long time after he was out of sight.

Her thoughts now back to herself she had three things to do. First she went to the First State Bank and made a deposit of $1,600.00 to the personal account of Aspen Gerore McGee, Vice President in Charge of Investments and left a note to be delivered to his office: Put $800.00 in IBM and $800.00 in Apple.

Secondly, she called Jenny Craig. "Hello," Jenny answered.

"Hello, Mother Jenny this is Shelly."

"Shelly, this is a surprise. Where are you?"

"I'm outside the Bank. I just made a little deposit."

"I see by the papers, my little one, that your fame and glory continues to grow. Hon we just want you to know that you still have the full support of your family."

"Thanks Jenny, that's part of the reason I'm calling. I need a favor."

"If I can Sweetie."

"Uh, it's kind of unusual Jenny, it's not so much for me. It's actually for Jack. He's the high school teacher who got caught up in this mess with me. If there was ever a case of being at the wrong place at the wrong time, poor guy. A real case of innocent bystander. As usual there's a chance that he will end up being a scapegoat. You with me?"

"Hon, I never left you. How can I help?"

"Well, right now his future as a school teacher might be on the line. He's pretty sure he's going to be in for a couple of hearings. His Principal was fully aware of his fieldwork and so that one may not be too bad.

"His big concern is the School Board. Jenny do you think..." but a reluctance from within caused Shelly to not finish her statement.

"Hello, Hello, Shell? You still there?"

"Jenny," her voice still reflecting her hesitation, "Jenny I was wondering. Do you know any of the men on the School Board?"

For the first time in a long while she heard Jenny let out a laugh; a happy laugh that she remembered as a child.

"Shell," Jenny finally said, "Honey you and Jack sleep peaceful tonight; hopefully together but if not at least sleep peaceful.

"In answer to your question, Yes Doll, I do know someone on the School Board; and I know where you are coming from. Leave it to me Baby."

It was late afternoon when Shelly hung up the telephone and she felt a slight hunger pain. From a tired old street vendor she purchased a hot dog and washed it down with a coke. When she was finished she tossed the napkin and waxed paper cup in a mesh wire litter basket and headed for the Carnegie Public Library.

There was a word that she wanted to look up in the six-inch thick, unabridged, medical dictionary. She hoped she could figure out how it was spelled.

It was still twilight when she walked up the flight of steps and entered through the thick glass doors. Inside she went directly to an area on the 2nd floor with which she was already familiar; the section for Medical Reference. This time however she did not reach for the Encyclopedia of Rare and Unusual Genetic Birth Defects. Instead she took down Dorland's Illustrated Medical Dictionary and carried it to a reading counter.

In getting started her opening page was in the A's and her eyes came to rest on:

> **amelia** (ah-méle-ah) [a neg.+ Gr. melos
> limb + -ia]. A development anomaly
> characterized by the absence of limbs.

She looked at the sketch of a newborn child without any limbs and instantly felt the trepidation. *How horrible. There, but for the grace of God, could be me,* she gave her respects.

She then proceeded to turn the pages until she came to the P's where she started running her finger down the alphabet: P-a, P-b, P-e, P-e-a,....

> **penicillinase** An enzyme substance...
> **penicilliosis** Infected with Penicillium usually...
> **penicillus** A brush appearing structure...

penile Pertaining to the penis...

penilloaldehyde An aldehyde
derived from penicillin...

penis The male organ...

penis clubbed A condition...

penis epispadias A..

penis palma'tus A..

Penismuliebrity-nipple'glandus <u>Penis</u> (pe'nis)
[L.] The male organ of copulation. <u>Muliebrity</u>
(mu"le-eb'ri^-te) [L. muliebritas]. 1. Womanly
qualities; the sum of the peculiarities of the female
sex. 2. The assumption of female qualities by the
male. <u>Nipple</u> (nip'l) The conic organ which gives
outlet to milk from the breast (papilla mammae [N
A]), or a similarly shaped structure. <u>Glans</u> (or head)
is covered with mucous membrane and ensheathed
by the prepuce, or foreskin. Penismuliebrity-
nipple'glandus: A rare genetic defect wherein the head
of the male penis develops in the configuration of
nipple; in most cases, but not all, the nipple will be
from 1/4 to 1/2 inch in length and bear semblance
to the female breast nipple excepting the urethra
opening. The body (shaft) of the penis containing
the *corpora cavernosa* and the *corpus spongiosum,*
through which the urethra passes is usually normal.
Penis is usually fully functional including hard
firm erections with the nipple becoming equally
engorged. Corrective surgery is possible to remove the
nipple configuration; however the known attempts
at corrective surgery have not been acceptable. The
likely prognosis will be loss of nerve ending and lack
of expandable tissue to form an acceptable head.

On the outer edge of the page was an illustrative sketch. She stood in silence as she looked at the drawing of a hanging flaccid male penis with a nipple on the end.

She again read the definition, this time more slowly, took one more look at the sketch, hesitated for a lingering moment and closed the book.

And..., that was the instant it happened. As the book snapped shut and she lifted it from the counter, an apocalyptic spark touched a latent power keg in her mind. In a splitting flash as she was putting the book back on the Reference Shelf she experienced an *epiphany*. Something so quick and so powerful as to push the concerns of sex movies and theaters completely into oblivion. Her consciousness was instantly turned backward and after more than twenty years her mother reentered. That which the book's sketch illustrated was the beginning part of her next life.

The apartment on Wood Street was dark, illuminated only by outside streetlights showing in through the windows as she entered, closed the door and turned the dead bolt. Without turning on the inside lights she went to the refrigerator and took out a coke. In the living room she dropped into the recliner, pushed into a reclining position and let her head fall back on the headrest.

Mother, Mother, she thought. *I'd almost forgotten. The only time in my life I was ever happy. How, oh how could I have ever let you slip from my mind. Mother I suddenly realize how much I miss you.* Without thinking she raised the coke to her mouth, took a swallow and the feeling of liquid ignited an old sensation.

Spontaneously the muscles in her mouth thrashed and she let the feeling rise up. In the dark she did it. She put the coke bottle to her mouth and sucked. A small, awkward escaping air sucking sound at first. Then her lips formed a tighter firmer fit and her vacuum grew; again and again she sat in the dark and experienced the sensation of sucking. As she sat in the dark she remembered her mother's breast; and their seat up in the balcony.

The Stran was her one remaining theater that still showed general movies. On this night the last showing would be ending at 11:42 and she knew that the staff would leave shortly thereafter. At some time after midnight she left the darkened apartment and walked the empty street to the unlit alcove of the Stran.

Putting her brass key in the Yale dead bolt, she entered and let the door lock behind. She went up the stairs to the projection booth and from the film closet she took down "The Thief of Bagdad."

With the film threaded and the projector running she left the booth and took a seat; top back row balcony. Alone in the dark, she could hear the projector whirling and watched the initial lights flashing across the screen down below.

As the scene opened she slouched down in her chair and draped one foot over the next row. She recalled how she and Patricia used to sit in that exact same seat and the longing to feel her mother's breast grew stronger.

In the security of being completely hidden she let herself become fully mesmerized as she puckered her lips and made sucking motions with her mouth as the movie whirled away. Fidgety she unbuttoned her jeans, stuck one hand inside and started massaging her tiny button but it was cold and non-responsive.

As the film continued to turn and the desert scenes passed across the screen she concentrated harder. She forced stronger thoughts through her mind about how her little panties had tingled when she held her mother's breast in her mouth.

Then gradually there came a sensitive feeling. As the scenes continued to pass she hugged herself tight with her one free arm, made sucking movement with her mouth, concentrated a harder mind splitting concentration and massaged vigorously; a sensation was coming.

As it started to heighten her concentration became even more mind splitting. It was coming. It was coming. Finally, finally, finally. It looked like she would be able to do it.

She began rocking in rhythm, hugging herself harder, sucking deeper and rubbing faster and faster inside her panties. The milk, she had to taste the milk. It wouldn't happen until she tasted the milk. She gritted her teeth inside her puckered lips and concentrated on the taste of milk. It was almost there.

Please Mother, feed me, feed me, feed me. Please let me do it. She could feel her clitoris becoming raw from the dry rubbing. She wished she had some spit on her fingers but she was afraid of breaking the rhythm.

She could get almost there but then it would fall back and she would start all over. Not to let it escape she would allow her tenseness to relax for only a moment and then work herself up again. She could get it right to the edge but no further. Tingling. Intense tingling. She could hardly stand it but she refused to stop.

As the movie was nearing the end she closed her eyes and concentrated that it was she who was in the arms of Douglas Fairbanks as the magic carpet soared to the heavens. Still, she could not cross over.

Fanatically she rammed the thumb of her free hand into her mouth, sucked it in deep and bit down hard. The sensation of her clinching teeth sent the evasive surge almost over the top. The pain and taste of her own blood but oh God, oh God not quite. She was almost there. Rapidly rocking in the seat she bit and sucked again and again.

Do it. Do it, she ordered herself. *Tie it all together. Concentrate. The soft skin in my mouth. The warm milk. The tingle in my panties when I bit down. One more bite and I can do it. Rub it harder. Use the oozing blood for lubricant, tear some more. It feels good, don't stop, don't stop...* But it didn't happen. *Damn, damn, oh damn,* her mind ached, *why did it have to slip away.*

The movie came to an end and the intrusive bright lights from the ending scene lit up all the way up into the balcony. The trance was broken and her desperate voyage ended without success.

Energy drained she felt weak as she rose to leave. In an unfulfilled state she left the theater without rewinding the film still in the projector.

Back in the apartment she stood in the lighted bathroom and looked at the ragged edges of torn skin on her thumb. From underneath the vanity she reached for a bottle of rubbing alcohol and saturated the oozing teeth marks. She then removed all of her clothes and let them drop to the floor. Standing naked she spread her legs and reached down and lightly explored the damaged to her tender clitoris. From the medicine cabinet she took a tube of ointment and applied a thick coat and rubbed it in.

It was here that she noticed her nude body in the mirror and without knowing why started looking at herself. First turning her head from side to side then looking intently at her breast. Next she turned to a side profile and looked at her solid firm rounded buns; then as quickly as it had started she lost interest and stopped.

Leaving her clothes on the floor she turned off the light and walked in the dark to the bedroom; and done something she had never before done in her lifetime.

Her body nude she knelt down on her knees beside the bed and began to pray.

"Dear God," she started as she rested her elbows on the edge. "This is Shelly. You may not remember me but I still remember You.

"We talked one night a long time ago. The night I was in a car accident. Remember?

"I have seen an awful lot of things take place since then God; and yet nothing has happened. I've grown older and I think a little wiser but I'm still as lonely now as I was then. And for the first time in my life God, it has occurred to me just how lonely You must be.

I didn't realize it back then when we talked but I realize it now. How awesome must be Your worries. And You have no one to turn too; no one to keep You from being lonely. God if it were in my power I would be Your love becau...

"Because I'm so lonely. As I kneel here on my knees I just feel like talking. No wait. That's not completely true. I mean I do feel good about talking to You but I also have a selfish reason.

"That night when You and I talked face to face God, I remember You telling me that I would get married. It's been so many years since then and I was really beginning to wonder why I couldn't find anyone. Well, yesterday I met Jack and he has not found anyone either. And I'm pretty sure that I know why.

"God, I know that on this earth You try to make sure that there is someone for everyone. I don't know if the meeting between Jack and me was by accident or if it was Your doing. Either way God, I am eternally grateful.

She then paused to let him know how important would be her next words.

"God, if Jack is my someone I'll gladly take him. If that is Your intent You won't have any problem on my part. Just please do what You can to make sure I'm acceptable to him.

"Looking at us two through Your eyes I want You to look down from the heavens, see us together and be pleased that us two have found each other. Thank You God and I promise we will do You proud. Goodnight God and I love You."

As she crawled into bed her thumb was beginning to throb. Thinking that it would help if she kept it elevated, she rested her arm up on the headboard, closed her eyes and eventually drifted off to sleep.

Sleep that rose up from the bowels of purgatory and brought her night sweats and soaked sheets. Dreams of catastrophic proportions escalated up from hell and came in the form of pitch black darkness with flashing streaks of lightning in a field of strewn barbed wire, pit holes filled with putrid water, snarled ghostly looking trees and a treacherous rock strewn road.

All around there was thunderous roaring and flashes of lightning. Black raging wild horses with fiery nostrils and steel pounding hoofs came from nowhere and stampeded across her nude huddled body. Somehow she managed to run to a dark farmhouse. A big old two story deserted house with a huge gabled roof and weather beaten siding. Upstairs there was a bedroom with a splintery wood floor a huge four-poster bed, musty smelling velvet drapes and a swag cornice over the one window.

She was alone in the bed. But then Patricia appeared standing at the foot. Nude from the waist up she was holding her elongated breast cupped in her hands as she spoke.

"Come Baby, come to your mother. Mother will feed her baby. You do not have to be afraid."

"No Mother no, I'm too old," she pleaded. "Mother I'm a grown woman now. We can't do that anymore."

But Patricia kept standing there, crystal clear, crystal clear...the nighttime crystal clear view of the bride and the crumpled car. She felt the car smash into the concrete wall, the feeling of flying, now she was falling into the river she could see the water coming up. She was getting closer. Soon she would be in murky icy water.

But there's God. There He is, sitting there in thin air over the river. She stopped falling.

"Yes," God answered her question again and again. "Shelly you will get married. You will get married. You will get married. Make him a good wife. Follow him.

"Who God, who? Who is going to be my husband? I can't see him."

Morgan was standing holding the apartment door half open. How did she get from the old house to the apartment? She was all dressed up and going out on a date.

More dressed up than she had ever been. She was embarrassed at her extravagant clothes. But who with? The date was waiting outside in the dark. Morgan holding the door half open telling her before she goes out,

"Remember what I told you. Your date must represent your mother. Don't forget your mother."

When she went out the door she was suddenly in the library. How did she get into the library at night? What happened to her date? The library was empty. All the lights were on but there were no people. Jack, Jack Lamont was standing there. In one hand he was holding Dorland's Illustrated Medical Dictionary opened up to Penismuliebrity. In the other hand he was holding the Encyclopedia of Rare and Unusual Genetic Birth Defects opened up to Mammopendulopathy.

Patricia, how did she get here? She's in another isle holding her nude breast. Jack is in his isle. Patricia in hers. Both are motioning to her. Should she go to her mother or to Jack?

Where is the librarian? She will be angry for us being in here without permission. What if she calls the cops?

Run, run. Go back to the apartment. But I have to cross the river. Must get up on the bridge wall to cross over. Careful do not stand up on the wall. Careful of your balance. Careful no, no I shouldn't have gotten up here. Too late, falling, falling. It's so dark and cold falling toward the water. God's not doing anything; just watching.

"I am God," said the crystal clear voice. "You must get married."

Landing on a sidewalk without getting hurt. "Thank you God thank you." Run, run to the Stran. Wood Street is filled with flowing mud. Mud she tried to walk through in high heels. The dress she has on for the date is getting muddy at the bottom. She can hardly run in high heels. Why is she wearing high heels? Where are her brown loafers? Get to the Stran. It's safe there.

The alcove by the ticket cage is dark. The theater door is unlocked. Who left the door unlocked? Inside every light is on. Patricia is in the lobby, half nude. She is sitting in one of the big maroon leather chairs. The chair has a tear in the arm.

"Come to Mommie, Honey; you do not have to be afraid. Mommie will hold you and take care of you. Sit in my lap baby."

"Mother I can't I am grown. What will people think?" Think? Who said think?

"Jenny? What are you doing here? Shouldn't you be at the Citadel?"

"Where did Mother go?"

"Remember Shelly, you only have one life, never mind what people think," came Jenny's words.

"Why is everyone crowding so? Morgan here? In the theater lobby with his silver handle cane. How did he get here from holding the door open in the apartment? He keeps saying, "You must represent your mother.""

"Never mind what people think," says Jenny.

"You must get married and build," said God up in the ceiling. Jack is now in the lobby with the library book open. He will get in trouble for taking it out without permission.

"'Ring, ring.' Where is that ringing coming from? Why doesn't it stop? If I can just get to that ringing I will be OK I must get there, but where did everyone go?

Telephone. She woke up startled and sat straight up in bed. Soaking wet with sweat, the telephone was ringing. She grabbed it without thinking.

"Hello," she answered while using a corner of the sheet to wipe the sweat on her neck.

"Shelly? This is Jack. Good Morning. Did I wake you?"

"Jack," she managed a calm answer as her anxiety began to subside. "Uh no, no it's fine. I just woke up. Actually I was having a nightmare and you rescued me."

"A nightmare?" he asked. "You mean like someone was trying to get you and you were helpless; your limbs refusing to move and you couldn't protect yourself?"

"Nonsensical," she answered. "One of those which bounces off all the walls. Anyway how' re you doing this morning; what time is it?"

"Seven o'clock," he answered. "I know it's early but I couldn't wait to talk to you. I was wondering, could I see you tonight? And tomorrow night and the next?"

"Goodness," she responded in surprise. "Did I make that kind of an impression on you?"

"More than that actually but I can't let you know the full extent. Tell me my beautiful *deir-dre raging one* did you think of me last night?"

"More than you will ever know," she responded as she recalled her dreams. "More than you will ever know."

"So?"

"Yes, Jack I find you very attractive. Now let me ask you a question. Am I being offered dinner for the evening?"

"Only if dessert consists of going up on Grand View Drive and doing a little hand holding while we look out over the city lights."

"I have long been a believer in hand holding," her voice now becoming alluring. "How can I refuse?"

"Shelly," his voice abruptly changed to a more serious note.

"Yes," she responded as his sudden switch of tone caused her caution.

"What I just said about hand holding and stuff, Shelly I've been rehearsing that, but when I hear myself saying it, it sounds phoney and I don't like the feeling it's causing."

A non-responsive silence hung in the air and it was an embarrassed Jack who spoke first.

"Shelly? Are you still there? Shelly that didn't come out right either. I...,"

"What is it you want Jack?"

"Wueeee," he let out a long sigh followed by a brief silence. "I think what I want at this point is to tell you the truth. After that if you want to hang up I'll understand. So here goes.

"Shelly the power and strength in you, it overwhelms me. The way you can intimidate people at the blink of an eye. I mean words..."

"You're really romantic Jack, you know that?"

"No, Shelly please. I mean that as a compliment. Shit, another bungle. Now how in the hell am I gonna get out of this. OK let me try to get right to the point."

"Meaning?"

"Meaning that I can't stop thinking about the way you cut Casey Blackstock a new bo-hind in front of the theater yesterday."

"And that's the impression I made on you?"

"No, no of course not. You're the impression, Shelly. God are you a hunk of woman. Your strength and power are just the toping on the cake."

"Jack, I must be missing something here. You seemed to be able to hold your own pretty good."

"HA! It's not the same Shelly. Mine is arguing. Yours is grinding-it-up and spiting-it-out."

"There's a difference?"

"Different as night and day. You get respect I get argument. Nobody pays much attention to me. There's an underlying reason, which I won't to go into right now. But in the game of one-up-man-ship they all look down their noses at me. You with me so far?"

"Jack, it's seven o'clock in the morning. What is it you are trying to say?" She could feel the embarrassment on both ends of the line and bit her tongue for her answer.

"Nothing. It's not important. Let's forget the..."

"No! No!" she cried over the phone. "None of this forgetting business. Damn now I'm the one who's screwing up. It's important, please Jack. Don't hang up. Please."

"Shelly," his tone reflecting his sincerity. "I wanted to use you. I wanted you to cut some people a new rear end for me. That Casey Blackstock performance? You think you could do that again? It's worth a dinner."

"These people whom you seem to think need a new rear end. Could I ask who they might be?"

A paused followed her question and she could feel him hesitating.

"People," he said slowly. "People I work with. But maybe this is all just a fantasy I had. Maybe we..."

"You drive a hard bargain," she whipped in and cut him off. "Is this what you do with all of the women you ask out?"

"Do you think," his tone reflecting that she was accepting his offer for dinner, "I could pick you up at your place, say around seven thirty tonight?"

"Seven thirty will be fine."

Strange, she thought after they hung up. *He said he didn't date and yet it was he who called me.*

Chapter 30

The atmosphere of the French restaurant CAFÉ MARAUX with its casual but motif decor depicting a chateau and vineyard in rural France almost always brings an instant flutter of romance to new lovers; almost but not always. On occasions like the present it is possible for there to be a mutual attraction between a man and a woman, but the elements of romance not being the same as love.

For Shelly and Jack the preliminaries of their first dinner went well enough; not much conversation but an enjoyable twilight, fresh air drive getting there. When it came to their seating they were fortunate enough to get a choice table. A circumstance most probably, but not entirely conclusive, brought on by Shelly. It was her quick palm gratuity to the maitre d' in an instant when Jack happened to be glancing in another direction.

After the water boy, a server arrived in the manner of a stiff, slightly snobbish waiter; who personified the French image by being tall, young, having a full head of black oiled down hair and small trimmed mustache.

The order for drink and appetizer taken, he gave a slight bow, mused a compliment on the selection and briskly disappeared through the swinging half doors leading to the kitchen. In less time than expected he returned holding a serving tray overhead and proceeded to set the table with hors d'oeuvres of Snails Bourgoignonne and a bottle of Roth Chateau young Beaujolais. Jack, approved, ceremoniously sampled the wine and two glasses were poured to half.

Everything was all proper, all elegant and all classy. But in fact of the matter it was out of character for the present mode of these two would be lovers.

They were having difficulty in developing a meaningful conversation and the stiffness of the restaurant wasn't helping matters. Their initial sip of wine was sufficient for a small toast but the taste of the snails brought a mutual whimsical yuck. Thence the situation retreated back to mostly silence.

In awkward attempts at conversation one of them would say "nice place" and the other would agree as "very nice". Apt one to say "the food is supposed to be good". And agreeable the second to say of "hearing the same thing" until the eventual arrival of their house salads of chilled crisp mixed greens garnished with garden tomatoes, Spanish onions, cucumbers and grapes with house made vinaigrette; and their entrée order taken.

It was in the lull after the salad, but not yet to the main course, as they were nursing sips of wine that a few significant lines of conversation did materialize. But the context therein was such that it must have caused any hovering overhead observing angels-of-romance to grit their teeth and slap their forehead in frustration.

Jack abruptly asked, "Shelly, you're awfully quiet. What's wrong? I mean right now, how do you feel sitting here?"

Blunt words, falling harshly upon her feminine ears that were hoping to hear words of compliment on her loveliness.

"I...I don't know Jack," the unexpectedness caused her to stammered. "I mean, I guess I feel like I have just sat down to write a letter and can't think of anything to say. Kind of like trying to get past the first line. How about you?"

"About like a schoolboy instead of a grown man; nervous," he answered.

Ah progress. Angels of romance wipeth thy brow. The two were at least saying words but neither of them had any idea as to where things might be going.

"Jack," the question came out of her mouth, "is there something about me? This nervousness on your part; you've said it before. Like I'm some dynamic force or something that you have to ease up to. Don't I appeal to you; just as a woman?"

He did not answer her question but asked one of his own as they looked generally toward each other across the table but not so much at each other.

"Let me ask the same question," he responded. "How do you see me?"

"How do I see you?" she repeated his question. "How about how I see us? I see you as a man and I see me as a woman sitting at a table for two in a nice restaurant.

"If I were looking at us from someone else's eyes I would say that we appear reasonable normal. What are my feelings? My feelings are we're new, we are just getting acquainted. I feel I'm the woman and you're the man.

"I liked it when you chose the place, I liked it when you recommended the selections for dinner, I liked it when you ordered the choice of wine. I guess what I'm saying is I like it when you take the lead."

Jack did not immediately respond to what she had just said; the part about how she liked it when he took the lead.

In his mind, nobody would ever lead her any place she didn't want to go; not him or anyone else. The mere thought of her being led did not coincide with the dynamics of her personality; and yet he was strongly attracted to her. He did not know what to say so he kept the focus in limbo.

"Shelly, all of these little things you've just mentioned, they're nothing. Well, OK something of course. But in essence they are just the little matters that fall to a man. The thing is," he paused just enough to make his point, "now that I have served them up so to speak, what else can I do. I mean in a sense, now I'm at a loss."

Her response, without her even thinking, catapulted her firmly into the authoritative role.

"Jack, I don't happen to have a Beginner's Guide to First Date Protocol in my purse, but I can think of a few things which would appeal to me.

"You could try telling me I look beautiful, how about touching my hand, tell me whether the candle light reflects in my eyes.

"Handsome man," she purred slightly, "maybe you could try just telling me romantic things. It would make the dinner more pleasant if I could hear them." It was at that instant, possibly sparked by the sound of her own voice that she realized how she had inadvertently stepped into the lead; but as an escape maneuver she gave herself an out.

"Unless," she added, "that's not the way you see me. Maybe I'm not attractive."

"Oh heavens Shelly," his response came in tone that his feelings were just the opposite of her words as he reached over and laid his hand on hers; not squeezing but just touching.

"Not only do I find you attractive but you are so beautiful that it frightens me. There is so much power in you I..."

His comments, whatever they were going to be, were lost as their waiter abruptly arrived with a serving tray balanced on one hand.

"And," the stiff waiter ask, "who has the Tournedoes Au Poivre, twin filet mignon pan seared with peppercorn sauce?"

"Here." answered Jack.

"Very good sir, and Madame must get the Roast Porkloin A L'ancienne slowly roasted and served with apricot rum sauce," he spoke with a snobbish tone as he quickly set the table, refilled their wineglasses, bowed slightly and departed.

There was a minuscule silence as they both looked at the engaging food in front of them. For Shelly her thoughts were quick that she could use the moment to keep the mood going.

"Jack it's all very elegant," she gestured to the sumptuous bill of fare on the table. "You're no stranger to refinement.

"So," her tone implying a question, "why am I hearing you putting yourself down? You must be fishing for a compliment or something. How could you possibly feel even slightly uncomfortable?"

This time it was her hand which reached over took his and lightly squeezed as she passed the onus back to him. Instantly evasive he was not taking. Meaning he would not let the conversation be directed to himself.

"Did," he changed the course, "I hear you mention to our friend Casey Blackstock something about you attending Paragon Academy?"

At the sound of his words a caution flag went off in Shelly's thoughts. *Uh oh, careful. Touchy subject. Don't let this go wrong. Don't better him. Remember, woman goes to man. Don't upstage him.* Wanting to avoid even a hint of pretentiousness she answered in a tone of no importance. "Just a put down, Jack. No big deal."

"No, really," he insisted. "I'm interested. What's the main difference between a finishing school and say a public school."

Easy does it, she thought. *Don't let this get started.* "I suppose," she answered in a tone of indifference as she attempted to avoid the obvious, "the emphasis is a little different, that's all."

"How? You mean they don't emphasize the red blooded American three R's of reading, riting, and rithmetic?"

"Oh they teach those all right," she acknowledged his point but her tone reflected a tactical maneuver of putting the Paragon down.

"But the underlying intent of the Academy is snobbery; how to belittle those below you and kiss the rear-end of those above you".

"You mean the staunch, uppie uppie big wigs rear ends?"

"I mean uppie uppie snobs."

"So what's the magic formula?"

"The magic formula?" she paused and then continued in a tone that she hoped would identify her with him. "The magic formula is pure unadulterated BS. It's all predicated on the premise of elevating one's own standing by cutting someone else down."

"Those," he responded as the conversation seemed to him to be taking a good direction, "are the circumstances in which I usually find myself; on the lower end.

"Now, what I'm after is the secret of getting on the upper end. I mean," he continued as they were eating, "my day-to-day bickering never seems to yield me any degree of success. I'm just wondering what I'm doing wrong?"

Wrong? Where had she heard that before? As he was relating his thinking her mind flashed back to their telephone conversation earlier that morning about his wanting to get even with somebody.

"Jack," she shifted in her chair slightly as she swallowed a bite of food and lightly touched her napkin to her mouth.

"I'm really much more interested in your professional field," she attempted to change the subject. "Tell me what attracted you to Sociology?"

"No, please," he persisted. "Don't change the subject just yet. Is, or is there not, a secret to this game that everyone seems to play?"

The point was delayed for the moment as their waiter arrived at their table and attended to their wine. They both watched in silence as he poured two partial glasses, smiled, slightly nodded and left.

In toast, but not saying anything they raised their glasses to each other, exchange a slight smile and took a small sip. Then without making any comment about the taste of the wine he continued with the subject.

"People who have money seem to always be very proficient at snubbing people. So what's their secret?"

"Is," she asked, "this really the sort of thing which interest you?"

"Not the sort of thing. But I watched you do it. It seems to me you're as good as they come. Maybe you could give me a couple of pointers."

Pointers, she thought. *Pointers about what?* Her eyes came to focus on the man across the table from her and they made direct contact. It was a fleeting contact, from which she got no reading. As a way of delaying her response she took another sip of wine and pretended to hold it on her tongue for the bouquet. She then made two decisions.

First she would respond to his request. After that, the evening had better start taking on some meaningful dialogue or she was apt to get a splitting headache.

"You want pointers?" her tone implying a repeat of his question. "Jack, I can give you pointers. I doubt if you will find the results very satisfying. The essence of the game is to win.

"Not, repeat, not to be reasonable, congenial, or hospitable. It has to be played within the bounds of proper language, socially accepted tone and above all else in front of another player; meaning someone to spread the outcome. Beyond that there are no rules."

"Did," he asked, "they teach you this sort of thing in finishing school?"

She paused, took a deep breath and slightly rolled her eyes. *Where was the end to all of this*?

"I can't speak for other so called finishing school, but yes it's taught at the Academy. They legitimize it by calling it debating. By whatever the name the intent is the same.

"Jack, it's no big deal. It's an acquired skill. Yes, they start teaching it in the fourth or fifth grade. Yes, it does exist. Yes, some people thrive on it. No, I'm not one of them. Yes, it's like anything else. To be good at it, if I can use that adjective, it has to be honed and practiced everyday.

"The secret? The secret is simple. Instantly put your social opponent on the defensive. Ask him or her rapid-fire questions about things of which you have knowledge and hope that they do not. Never allow yourself to be pulled into the position of answering any of their questions but maintain an insistence that they answer yours.

"If it appears they can respond to one subject, jump to another; and finally cut it off with a sharp cut. The termination or ending is critical and for it to be effective it is essential that it be properly executed.

"You must be the one in control, hold one or two seconds of silence, cast a stern contemptuous look without making eye contact, then turn and walk away before they can respond. They'll know, to use one of your phrases, they have been cut a new rear end.

"NOW, if you have no objection, DO YOU think we could talk about something else?"

The chemistry between them became taut after that and she felt a flush over her curt response. In a regrouping mode she searched for a way of easing things. There was something on his mind that was extremely important but she could not seem to pull it out. As the meal progressed they did a lot of glancing back and forth at each other but nothing much happened beyond their exchange of smiles and commenting on the food. Dinner would be over before she would get any inkling.

"Listen Shelly," he made the first mention as they were leaving the restaurant and walking to his car, "instead of driving up to Grandview how would it be if we drove in a slightly different direction."

"Whatever," she agreed. "You're the driver. Any particular place you have in mind?"

"Not a place so much," he responded. "Say more of a trial run of things I hope will come."

In an attempt to guide the conversation toward some romantic aspects she answered with a touch of wit.

"Are you going to abduct me and carry me away to some sex dungeon; I hope."

"Can't ever tell," he replied as they reached his car and opened her door. "Life is full of surprises."

At least that's a little start, she thought. *Try and keep it going.*

"Starting right off," she spoofed. "I like your car."

"This car? A four door Chevrolet? That impresses you?"

"Uh Huh," she hinted as she got in. "It has bench seats instead of bucket seats. It makes it easier to get extra close to the man that's driving; maybe add a little spice to the ride by doing a little leg rubbing."

"This isn't intended so much a ride Shelly," his tone showed no pick up on her gesture. "I had in mind to take a little tour. Some places I want to drive by for you to see."

"Even better," she continued to plug her interest by singing a couple of verses from a then popular song. "...a whirl-round-the-town. Take me dinning, take me dancing... moonlight romancing..."

"Different tour," he said as he looked backward out his window for on coming traffic and pulled away from the curb. "It's a look-see ride while we're getting better acquainted."

"OK, if it's getting better acquainted that you want," she continued her seductive mode as she slid over to his side of the seat, "how about we start by getting a little closer.

"By the way, if I should happen to get the urge will it be OK if I do a little get-acquainted ear nibbling? I don't know if you are aware of this but there's nothing quite like getting acquainted using the

Braille system," she spoke as she was putting her left arm up around his shoulders and her right hand on his leg.

"MMMMM, nice and solid," she squeezed his thigh. "Is everything else about you this firm?"

"Just my determination. Its rock solid firm. I want you to meet some of the other people in my life."

"What?" she pulled back slightly in surprise. "Is that where we're going? We're just getting acquainted ourselves and already we're going to meet other people?" her expression implied an explanation.

"No, of course not"; his tone indicating something different. "Let's just say that this is one of my thinking rides. But as long as we are just driving you might as well be getting acquainted with certain aspects of my life which I hope you will eventually become a part of."

"Aspects, life, part of?" she moved back a little to her side of the seat. "Jack your thoughts and my thoughts seem to be quite different. I'm thinking you-me. You know a little loving, a little turtle-doveing, create a little chemistry, test our hormone level. I don't see where more people is what we need right n..."

"I know, I know Shelly. But if you will just bare with me," he spoke as they enter the North Hill area. "Up here just around the corner; over on the right. See that white house with the big porch?" he slowed the car to a crawl.

"That's where Nat Grover lives," he idled past and then resumed their speed. "Nat is the head of Social Science Department out at good ol' Allegheny High.

"Over here where we are going now, I want you to see Jim Farrel's house. Jim is the High School coach.

"Here we are now. That's his house, the brick with the single car garage."

Shelly was now sitting on her side of the seat and casting nothing more than a cursory look as they drove past the two homes.

Not that that was the end. From the North Hills area they drove in an awkward silence out to the residences of three other teachers; one in McKees Rocks, one in Ingram, and one in Crafton.

As Jack headed the car back into the city he casually remarked, "There now, that wasn't so bad was it?"

"It wasn't so bad Jack, but I don't understand. Is there a reason for all of this?"

"You bet, Shelly-love-of-my-life, these are some of the people I work with. My contemporaries if you will. And before too long I am going to be showing you off to each one of them. This was just a little preparatory work on my part."

"Excuse me if I sound confused," she answered. "But here I am all dressed up in a nice dinner dress, jewelry I seldom wear, light perfume, hair fixed, just a touch of class but not overly done, and you take me for a ride in the suburbs to look at old houses?"

"I know how it must seem Shelly, but you did say something about trusting me."

They didn't make love that night. Shelly let herself out of the car at the apartment and watched as he drove away. Alone in the apartment she went about the business of preparing for bed without displaying any of her frustration. Indifferently she stood in front of the closet and took off her high heels, garter belt and nylons. Her plain but expensive dinner dress she pulled off over her head, brushed out the wrinkles, worked it on to a hanger and hung it to the back of the closet. In the bathroom she removed her complimentary but not ostentatious jewelry and cleaned her face of the earlier applied light shaded make-up.

She went to bed with continued indifference and lay in the dark for a long time and then it all swelled over.

"No, no, no, I'll be damned if I let it end like this," she spoke out loud to herself. "He's my man. I know he is. It's him or nobody. I made you a promise God and by these words I will keep my promise. Just don't take him away. Please."

It was the middle of the following week when her telephone rang. "Hello, Shelly. This is Jack."

"Yes Jack, I was wondering if you were going to call I'm sorry abou..."

"Shelly," he said at the same time. "I'm sorry about the way things went the other night."

"No, no it's OK," she reassured. "I'd forgotten what some parts of Pittsburgh look like at night. I really enj..."

"Shelly," he cut in. "You're more woman than I could ever hoped for," his words rushed out without stopping, "and if you don't feel the same way about me I understand. But Shelly I need you, I want you, I want to fall in love with you and I want us to be together. There. If I had not said it right this minute I don't think... Shelly do you understand what I just said?"

A silence followed his words. On her end Shelly could feel perspiration forming under her arms. She took a deep breath seeking a surge of energy and tried not to exhale too loudly into the phone.

"Jack, what you just said. I've only waited a lifetime to hear. You ask if I understand. Yes, I understand. You need to ask a question like that?

"What I mean is, uh let me do this. Jack I will tell you what I feel. Please just hear me out. I want to tell you. Then, if you are of like mind we can work out our differences. It's just that I have waited so long. I guess I either want to know or not know. Are we talking marriage? I don't think I could stand the pain of another disappointment.

"Jack, are you there?"

"Yes Shelly, I'm here and I think I'm as scared as you. In answer to your question yes, my thoughts pertain to marriage but my scare is that you may not want me. I have some problems. I mean when you get to know me better you may not..."

"Jack please, just tell me."

"Shelly I love you."

"Jack Lamont this is Shelly. Your Shelly and I love you."

"Ouch," he reacted. "Shelly, the way you say that. Coming over a telephone line it doesn't sound exactly the way I had it pictured. Wait, let me rephrase that.

"I mean, I do love you and I mean it. Especially me telling you; but when I hear the same words coming to me it sure sounds awkward. Kind of frightening really."

"Don't Say That!" she raised her voice. "No wait, Jack I didn't mean it doesn't sound good. I just never expected to hear it. That's all I'm saying."

"Shelly there's so many problems we have to work out I just never..."

"Jack, all I ask is for the chance."

"Shelly, maybe you shouldn't make that statement so quick. Make sure you know all there is to know about me first; then make up your mind."

As she heard his words she was sure she knew what he was referring too. Her eagerness was to immediately be reassuring that no matter what, it wouldn't matter to her.

"Jack I already know all I need to know. Just give me a chance to prove it. If you want me to do something just say it."

"Are you sure Shelly? You mean it?"

"Of course. I get the feeling there is something?"

"As a matter of fact, yes. Its a school function this coming Saturday night at the Schenley Hotel; Teacher's Awards night.

"It's a tux and formal gown affair which is put on for the Allegheny County school teachers; a once a year social. I'd like for you to go with me. Part of that showing you off I spoke about."

"That's it? Why Jack..."

"Uh, that's not exactly it Shelly. I'm taking a chance in asking this. But could you come loaded for bear?"

"Meaning?"

"You know what I mean, Shelly. You know."

"Know what?" she pushed him to say it.

A silence followed as she waited for a response.

"Shelly," his voice came back on the wire. "Shelly this is my one big splash. I never in my life expected to have a woman like you.

"And you know how these things are. Everyone stands around looking at everybody else. I," he paused and she could hear his breathing.

"OK," he came back on the wire with sharpness, "I'll say it. I want to rub some shit on their noses. Please Shel.

"Hello? Hello? Shelly?"

"Yes, Jack. I mean I think I'm embarrassed. The way I was dressed when we went out the other night? That wasn't good enough?"

"Heavens Shelly of course it was good enough. Look, I'm out of line. Just forget I asked. It was just something..."

"No, no Jack wait. Just tell me what you want exactly."

"Shelly what I want, what would really please me is if you would dress top on the heap."

"You mean like a Carnegie, or a Heinz or Mellon?"

"Shel..."

"No, wait, I mean, I can do it. I just want to make sure it's what you want."

"Would you?"

"Yes, Jack. Any particular theme you want?"

"Theme?"

"You know, European Royalty, American Fashion, mid-Victorian, high-neck choker, plunging bust line, what?"

"Shel, you know what to do. But as long as I am being offered a choice, something sexy would fit in just fine with what I have in mind."

"OK Top of the heap, sexy theme," she summarized.

"In my mind," she followed up, "it will be an overkill. If that is your desire, one overkill coming up. But tell me, will I ever learn why?"

"I promise. When the time is right, I promise."

As soon as they hung up Shelly made two phone calls. "Hello, Daddy Aspen, how's things down at the bank?" was the first call. "Daddy Aspen how about if I drop by and see you later this afternoon. While I'm there I need to pick up some trinkets from our safe deposit box.

"Maria the Seamstress," was the answer to the second phone call.

"Hello, Maria? Hi, this is someone you haven't talked to in a long time; Shelly Waters. You remember me? Yeah, I know. It has been a long time.

"Maria I have an important favor to ask. I know it's short notice but I'll make it worth your time.

"By this coming Saturday I'll be needing a dress. A special type of dress. Formal affair but walking sex. I have in mind a sleeveless, deep V plunging neck line, wrap around hip hugger skirt cut with a suggestive indentation centered at the crouch; floor length with a waist to floor slit along the side. I'd like it in subdued hued sheen red and I want plenty of cleavage in the boobs so I'll need all of the up-lift you can give me."

In the realm of getting dressed for a formal occasion men seem to have a distinct advantage. No matter what the allowances, women always require just a little bit more time. Jack was on schedule but Shelly still had a ways to go when he arrived to pick her up the following Saturday evening.

"Jack," she asked as she turned to where he was setting on her bed, held up the back of her hair and had him fasten her four strand diamond choker necklace, "are you sure want me to wear this much glitz. I mean, trust me we're going to be out of place."

"Shelly," he was glad her back was to him as he answered, "it's just something I have to do, please?"

"Well, that about takes care of the finishing touches," she continued in front of the mirror and slightly adjusted her dangling diamond earrings.

"A final spray of perfume. "What's you think?" she held the spray bottle for Jack to sniff. "Direct from Paris. On loan to me from Mother Jenny. To quote her 'it's the best damn stuff in her whore house.'

"OK tiger," she was still facing the mirror and looked at him in his reflection. "You go out in the living room and stand by. I've got a couple of more boob adjustment to make and I'll be right behind you; high heels sheen hosiery and diamond garter belt.

"What's you think?" she came out and gave him a fashion model's whirl.

"A banquet!" were his first words reflecting his awe. "A creation of God's most beautiful food. Where do I start eating?" were his second words.

At the party Jack took a forceful lead in mingling. With Shelly's arm firmly inside of his he first accidentally bumped into Nat Grover and his wife Lois.

"Nat," Jack initiated introduction, "Nat I have someone here I would like for you to meet. Nat this is my fiancée Shelly Waters. Shelly this is Nat Grover and his lovely wife Lois."

"Well I'll be," Nat responded as he extended his hand to Shelly. "Jack, you ol' horse thief. Why didn't you make something like this known around the drinking fountain? Miss Waters," he accepted Shelly's hand and held it firmly.

"Jack never let on that he had anyone as uh, intoxicating looking as you," he kept holding her hand and attempting to force an eye contact.

"How nice to meet you, Mr. Grover. Jack has told me so muc..."

"Call me Nat, just plain Nat and may I call you Shelly."

"Of course, please do," she was responding when Jack cut in.

"Shelly is one of our leading citizens, Nat. You may not recognize her in person but I'm sure you have read about her in the newspapers. She's the owner of some of Pittsburgh's best-known theaters. You know, the Royal, Palace, South Hills; all of the good stuff."

"IS that right?" responded Nat while giving her hand a firmer squeeze. "Now, I AM truly pleased to make your acquaintance.

"If you have some spare time sometime and Jack has no objections, maybe we could get to...."

"NAT!" cut in Mrs. Grover. "I'm sure that Miss Waters will be very busy entertaining Mr. Lamont."

The next person that Jack accidentally bumped into was Jim Farrel. "Miss Waters," Jim extended his hand. "I've known Jack a long time. He never mentioned. I mean this is certainly a surprise. You two been together a long time? You say you own the Royal. Uh, could I ask, and I mean this with all sincerity, uh how, I mean those film that you show. Do you take part? I don't mean the actual doing. What I mean is do you get to watch? Maybe supervise would be a better word?"

"Mr. Farrel, may I call you Jim," she pulled him forward by his handshake to where he was rubbing right against her and was forced to look down her dress line. "I like to think that my life style is, shall we say, spicy," she rubbed him with her breast and then lightly pushed him back.

"But if you really want more details. Why you'll just have to ask Mr. Superman himself here."

"Superman? Jack?" he asked in mock surprise. "You mean our very own Allegheny's High Jack Lamont?"

"None other," she purred as she rubbed her spread legs up against Jack and run her fingers through his hair. "Believe me," she purred through her nose and accentuated a May West accent, "I've seem em' all and Mr. Superman here puts them all to shame."

There were other introductions that night. Several more in fact and each one more leading than the one before.

"Why Mr. Gardner," she murmured a southern belle, "you being a physicist and all you certainly must understand about chemistry. Why how could Jack and I possibly get the kind of action we are looking for in a film... unless we give our real life performers some real life illustrations."

It was Cynthia Ann Broader, however, that left the party with a new back side. Jack had mentioned that Cynthia was one of the women teachers who seem to get great pleasure from smearing his nose. Any time the opportunity presented itself, such as passing in the hall, her face would come to a broad smile and with a tone of charmingly patronizing she would ring out her greeting, "Hi there Nipples. How you doing?"

The opportunity to level the playing field came as Shelly was returning from the wash room and could see from a distance that Miss Broader was holding Jack captive and getting her slice of condescends to the circle of on lookers.

"Hi handsome man of mine," Shelly, spoke in a musical voice as she walked up and put her arm through Jack's. "I swear Darling, I can't leave you alone a minute. Who are all of these beautiful people around you. Are they all faculty?"

"Just some of the ones that I work with," he answered unaware of what was coming.

"Who is this one?" she cast a discerning look at a surprised Cynthia

Broader.

"Shelly," he started introductions, "I'd like for you to meet Miss Cynthia Ann Broader. Cynthia this is..."

"Jack's fiancée," she took charge of the conversation. "Tell me Miss Broader, I do hope you don't mind me calling you by your working name. I have such respect, you know."

"Why no I..."

"How long have you been with the school system, Miss Broader? Is this something you do for fulfillment? I mean surly you must have a social position in the community. Do you play the piano?"

"Uh, no teaching is..."

"When I think of teaching I always think of classical music, don't you agree? It seems to be the golden criteria by which other fields of education are measured.

"Of course you know that the history of music is generally divided into six periods: Medieval, Renaissance, Baroque, Classic, Romantic and Contemporary. Tell me Miss Broader, which is your favorite?"

"Uh, well I do enjoy listening to Beethoven whenever I get the opportunity to..."

"Why of course. I am sure that it just slipped your mind that this is generally known as the Romantic Era. Correct me if I'm wrong but I believe that era generally runs from the late 1700's to the early-mid 1800's.

"Uh, I'm not exactly up on the dates, but yes it was along in there.."

"Miss Broader, surely you're too modest. Of the four great composers of the era, Haydn, Mozart, Schubert and Beethoven, which do you feel made the greatest contribution?

"You do know I'm sure," her voice patronizing and cutting, "that Beethoven went deaf in his latter years and yet went on to compose some of his greatest work.

"An inspiration to us all, don't you agree? Music is so enriching.

I don't believe I have ever seen you at any of the performances of Pittsburgh's Symphony Orchestra. The name Boarder. I can't seem to remember seeing it on the Social Register.

"But of course that's of no importance. I'm sure it's just a matter of us always missing each other; or it may be that we simply go on different nights.

"Jack and I always prefer opening nights don't you know. Everybody who is anybody, that sort of thing you understand.

"Really though don't you feel that we're so lucky in Pittsburgh to have one of the world's most renowned conductors."

"Uh, yes I have heard his name..."

"...Is William Steinberg, founder of the Israeli Symphony. We've had him since 1952."

By now Cynthia's mouth was dry and she could feel beads of perspiration on her forehead. Glancing out the corner of her eyes she was seeking an exit when Shelly moved in for the kill.

"Miss Broader, may I ask why do you keep looking past me. Is there something behind me that I should be aware of?"

"Oh, no I uh..."

"Well I hope you will permit me, but I find your lack of social graces offensive.

"Apparently you and Jack have very little in common. I don't understand why he bothers. Now if you will excuse us there are certain interesting people here tonight that we would like to visit with."

She cast a final condescending look, pulled her arm closer to Jack's and softly murmured, "Darling, whenever you're ready."

When the party ended that night Jack and Shelly drove home in silence. When they reached the apartment she opened her own door and had one foot out when he spoke.

"Shelly, I really do appreciate what you did. I..." But before he could say anymore she turned back half around in the seat and put her finger to his lips.

"Shhhhhh," she whispered. "Baby there's no need for you to explain. You're my man and you said it was something you needed. That's all that matters. If you ever decide you want to tell me, I've always got time to listen. For now handsome man I need to go in. Trust me when I tell you that this dress does not feel as sexy as it looks. Goodnight Lover."

Nevertheless, there was a need for him to explain. Many thoughts went through her mind and in hindsight she wondered if she had taken the wisest approach. She fought to keep out the unthinkable thoughts of him being a pantywaist.

She didn't want to be the man of the house. Why was he so reluctant to bid his own way? Why was he so quick to let everyone know that she was the owner of sex theaters? What is his need to be associated with social snobbery?

For all of her wondering, her thoughts never came close to the real reason. That would come a couple of weeks later when she accepted his dinner date. In her mind it was going to be a make-it or break-it date. And for the first part of the evening it looked as if the forces of break-it were going to win.

Starting out under less than amenable feelings, there were no seeds from which anything could grow. The restaurant was not the most elite but respectful; and they were even lucky enough to get a secluded table. A bottle of wine came to the table but the clicking of their glasses lack the element of sincerity. Now and then they would make eye contact but the exchange of slight smiles had no meaning. Mostly they sat in silence through salad, bread dish and entrée; Jack had coffee while waiting for the check.

All through the meal it seemed to Shelly that he did want to talk. Something was just on the verge but not happening. She had the feeling that if he would just bring it out it would be the positive magnetic spark they needed to ignite a common bond.

In her own reading, she felt that he wished she would be the one to start and maintain an on going conversation. On that point she refused. In her mind it wasn't going to happen that way; not this time. So they sat and ate in silence; no comments about the weather, about the entrée about the wine. Dinner came; the food was eaten and indifferently came to an end.

I guess that's it, she was thinking to herself as they rose and were leaving. And then, totally unexpected it started to change. As they left the restaurant the night air felt cool and clean. There was also an immediate feeling of privacy from being alone out on a nighttime empty street.

"Shelly," he spoke and then paused slightly as they were walking to his car, "I have something I really need to say and I thought maybe it could best be said up on Grandview Drive. Is that OK with you?"

"Of course," she answered as they were getting in the car. "But why wait? At the risk of sounding persnickety, I hope you don't have anymore surprises."

His response came after he had pulled away from the curb and was in the flow of traffic.

"Shelly, for what it's worth I feel terrible about what I did the night of the social. But maybe if you know why, God this is embarrassing," he spoke to himself. "Shelly," he was thankful for the darkness inside the car, "would you believe that I am 30 years old and I have never had sex."

A dead silence and a dead atmosphere hung in the car between them. Her face felt an instant blush. The split instant seemed like all eternity. She felt an onus to speak but she was speechless.

"No, wait," he reluctantly continued. "That statement's not exactly true. I tried it a couple of times when I was in my early twenties but it didn't work out. Maybe someday soon you will know why. Just for right now, I want you to know about the ordeal I put you through the other night. You still interested in knowing why?"

"Uh, Yes. I mean I think I do. I, Jack I'm not sure. What I mean it's not necessary. If I'm as truthful as you I should say that my thoughts were a little apprehensive but yes. It would make me feel better."

"Respect," came his one word. "I was trying to get people to respect me. Does that sound strange to you? That a man who has never had sex in his life is looking to acquire a little respect by being out with supposedly the queen of sex movies?

"Interesting isn't it. That I wanted everyone to think I, Jack Lamont, was getting it on with the hottest bit of sex flesh in Pittsburgh?

"Would you like to know why I want and need that respect? Everyone in school knows what's wrong with me. It's common knowledge. Everyone, from student to faculty just assumes I'm sexless. Kids jeer me. The other teachers, men and women, looked upon me as some sort of damaged goods.

"Oh, they treat me nice enough but in the realm of man, woman and sex it's just assumed that I can't get it on with a woman. And that's where you came in. It was selfish on my part but I was desperate for people to start giving me a little more respect.

"The way I figured it was like this. I attend this big to-do with a smoldering, red-hot sex bomb hanging on my arm.

"A walking talking dripping money, dripping sex encounter, light years away from what any of the other men can ever hope to get and at the same time intimidate the shit out of the other women.

"The idea was to give all of 'em the shock treatment. Change their way of thinking. I figured if I could make them believe that I'm man enough to handle something like you then I'd start getting a little more respect; you get my drift.

"So now you know," he concluded as he brought the car to a stop at the top of Grandview.

"So did it work?"

"Oh, it worked all right. It worked damn well. All of a sudden every man on the faculty wants to be my good buddy. I've been invited to become a part of the Wednesday night porker click.

"Women have started looking at my crouch and smiling at me when we pass in the hall. Yeah it worked good.

"It just hasn't been near as satisfying as I thought it would be," the slow enunciation and tone of his voice reinforcing his words.

"The trouble is," he looked out through the windshield into the darkness and said. "It's me. I still know about me.

"Any questions?" he asked as the silence was broken and they got out and were walking to the overlook.

"Did I hear you correctly," she asked, "when you say you've never had an orgasm?"

"No," he embarrassingly answered. "I said I had never had sex. At least not completely. I've tried it a few times with a couple of different girls but nothing came out. For some reason either it, or me don't function right."

"You mean the orgasm or the sex?" she openly asked. "What's the difference?"

"The difference is," he responded, "I do have orgasm, just not with a wom... Oh shit. Never mind. It's getting too deep," he attempted to end the subject.

"So when you do have an orgasm, could I ask how you happen to bring it about? I mean..."

"Shel, please... leave me something will you. How do you suppose?"

Chapter 31

Thunder and darkness that rumbles of terror by day belies the beauty of the heavens at night. Shelly had written one night when she was searching for answers to life. *Is,* the lines continued, *there anyone among us who has not been out on nights when the sky was clear and the blue of the heavens allowed us to look across the universe and behold millions of distant lights. Surely, we think to ourselves, that in all that vastness, there must be answers.*

Feeling small and insignificant we look upward and gaze in silence. Preferring our own solitude to the company of others, we stand in awe as we search the endless horizons.

Those who are looking for love, those who are searching for something unknown and those who are alone and lonely are prone to gravitate to hilltops or mountain bluffs; seeking to be a little closer to the heavens.

Grand View Drive, high above the skyline of Pittsburgh, and its endless blanket of flickering lights has always been such a pinnacle. As Shelly and Jack were holding hands and silently standing on one of the overlooks, other thoughts were also passing through her mind. Thoughts of how she and her mother had frequently come up there and sat.

Once on such a night when they were alone on one of the viewing benches she had crawled up into her mother's lap. Nestled into her favorite position she was about to reach inside her blouse when Patricia suddenly pulled her in close, turned her tiny face up, hugged her tight in her arms and kissed her hard on the mouth. It had been a firm wet lipstick kiss and she could still feel the soft moistness of her mother's open lips; it had felt good and she had felt a tingle. That was then.

Now, in this same instant as Jack put his arm around her, turned to where they were facing each other, lightly raised her face up to his, it happened. The wet moisture of his open mouth served as a conduit and Shelly felt an invisible arc discharge a cataclysmic surge of power through her body.

The surge of Patricia's kiss was the polarizing flash on her mind when some extra terrestrial force from some unknown source of energy arced across some incomprehensible time warp and connected to her current reality.

As Jack's face met hers she ferociously grabbed him around the neck with both hands and their bodies came crushing together as her surge of strength locked them in embrace. In wild frantic passion her lips were on his as their open mouths smashed together in an explosive lip biting, pain piercing, forceful kiss. The continued arcing of the invisible voltage sent her into a frenzy of grabbing, licking, biting his eyebrows and leaving a trail of saliva across his mouth as spurts of pee saturated her panties.

Then just as quickly as it had ignited, it ceased and a feeling of exhaustion came over her as she relaxed her hold.

But a split second later she was struck by a second surge and for a second time she locked him against the guard rail, forced her open lips hard against his mouth until she found his tongue, sucked it out and bit.

And again, she released her bite just as suddenly; but this time it was followed by an explosive request.

"Jack," she asked without embarrassment, "can I see your birth defect?"

"What?" he asked in astonishment; his tongue feeling its own oozing flesh. "What are you talking about?"

"Your birth defect," she repeated with clarity. "I want to see your penis. I looked it up in the library. I know what it is but they don't have any pictures. Can I see it?"

"What on earth!" his words slightly slurred as he was about to express his surprise when she cut in.

"Jack, I can't control this compulsion. I have to see it. Does it really have a nipple on the end; like a woman's nipple?

"It's important. I don't understand it myself. I literally can't control myself; I'm peeing in my panties.

"Inside of me. There are a thousand voices inside of me yelling, telling me that you are going to be my husband; I have to know. I can't wait."

"Shelly!" he managed to take what he thought was control of the situation by squirming free of her hold, "I, Shelly I can't. We can't do that. We don't even know each other.

"I mean," he continued, "do you know what you are asking? Here, right now? Shelly I can't do it. No. The answer is No," he said as he held a grip on her hands.

"It's important Jack. I wouldn't ask if it wasn't important. I have to see if you are going to be my husband," she repeated as she again became the aggressor, crowded him with her body weight against the guardrail.

In reflex he stiffened and momentarily attempted to squirm free. But the amount of hysteria she was unleashing and the frantic of her actions he judged to sbbmit. Would fighting achieve anything? Instead he allowed being pressed back against the lookout guardrail. With her one free hand, Shelly reached down and unzipped his trousers.

As he felt his fly open, any impulsive resistance he may have had simply went limp and he made no more protest. As his body went lax it was a signal to Shelly that he had consented for her to have her way. Now in a more docile mode she proceeded a little more methodical. As he stood passively still she searchingly reached inside his trousers and found the top of his jockey shorts. Blood rushed to his cheeks in embarrassment as she slid her hand inside and found his flaccid penis and squeezed.

Electricity shot through her at her first touch. She hadn't felt the supreme part yet but she knew it was there, the nipple. She searchingly moved her fingers, found the tip and instantly felt the difference in the skin texture.

"Shelly! PLEASE!" he attempted to squirm.

"Shhhhhh Baby. Please, it will only take a minute. Baby please," she begged as she continued feeling the flaccid skin on the end.

At first it just felt like soft skin but as she lightly rubbed it started taking on body; becoming rigid. Her rubbing finger was causing an arousal sensation and despite his wishes to the contrary, he could feel an erection forming.

She was ecstatic as it became harder. She could now make out the full nipple shape; excitingly definable, maybe a half inch. Her lips yearned. There was a sensation in her panties and this time it was more than squirts of pee.

As her excitement grew, she unconsciously bent over to where her head was lower than his and impulsively blurted out, "Jack, when you feel me pinch the nipple, if there's a sharp pain from my fingernails, would you please pop me one on the head."

"What? Pop, are you crazy?"

"No, no, please it's OK. Just pop me one on the head with your hand, if my fingernails cut too sharp. Pleeease," she insisted. "It won't hurt, honest. Please do it right now. With your hand, pop me. I need it."

Yielding to her request Jack gave her a little tap on the side of the head.

"A little harder, harder," she begged as she held his nipple between her fingers and pinched. To her request he then popped her one harder and reactively felt her body stiffen, remain rigid for a split second and they go lax.

As her explosive chemistry subsided she slowly straightened up and in the most natural sequence she brought her hand out of his trousers, her arm went around his neck and they went into a deep embrace. In the seconds thereafter they relaxed and she calmly reached down and zipped up his fly.

In a more feminine mode she delicately put her arms around his neck, pulled herself purringly up to where her aroused breast were against his chest, tilted her head up to his downward glance and whispered, "I love you my Man. Now that I know for sure, I can wait. Ever how long it takes I can wait until we are married."

But her noble intentions about waiting were no match for her warring hormones and a short time later when they arrived at the Wood Street apartment, she would again lose control. His car parked at the curb, he had walked her up the steps to the door and they were exchanging a goodnight embrace. That's when it happened. Her urge reignited, her strength surged, and she grabbed Jack by the arm and jerked him inside. Forcefully pulling him they crossed the dark living room and into the bedroom where their combined bodies fell crumpled across the bed.

He landed under her weight with his feet on floor and she, in her top position, fanatically loosened his belt, unzipped his fly and worked his trousers down around his knees.

Without resistance he remained still as she then worked his shorts down until his penis and scrotum were fully exposed.

Dropping to her knees she massaged it with both hands and could feel it getting firm and erect. She placed her lips down on the nipple until it became fully engorged. Then she took his semi-firm erection half way into her mouth and started stroking.

As the first drops of pre-cum nectar started to flow she said without taking her mouth off, "Pop me. Pop me now."

"NO!" he rebelled. "Why are we doing this this way? If we are going to have sex let's do it the normal way. You have had sex before haven't you?"

"Please Jack, I'm begging." She took her mouth away and looked up. "Please do this for me. Please. Just this once; for me."

"This is crazy," he said, as he became more argumentative and started squirming. She was still on her knees as his twisting got him to the side and he was able to rise up.

"Shelly," he commanded, "get up off of your knees and get in bed. Baby if we are going to do this let's do it the normal way."

Reluctantly she rose and removed her clothing. By the time she crawled in under the sheet beside him he was also nude. They pulled themselves together in a kissing embrace and she could feel it becoming hard and firm. As he worked his way into position between her legs she again reached down and felt the full length of the shaft and the rigid hard nipple on the end. She slid it into her moist vagina and they made love; but nothing happened, for either of them.

At sometime during the night they simply became exhausted from trying. The room became silent and she assumed he had dropped off to sleep. When the first rays of morning light started streaking in through the windows she was still awake and when she could make out his face she saw that his eyes were also open.

"Well good morning handsome man," she snuggled in closer.

"Good morning Doll. You couldn't sleep either?" his hands adjusting her head to a place on his shoulder.

"I thought a lot," she said as her head rested on his chest.

"Same here," he answered.

"What about?"

"Lots of things."

"Such as?"

"Such as," he picked up on her question. "If I asked you to marry me, would you?"

"Why don't you ask and find out?"

"If we got married would you settle down and be a good wife?"

"What does being a good wife mean?"

"Among other things, would you quite running around carrying signs and demonstrating against the Vietnam War?"

"No"

"Would you quite showing X-rated movies in your theaters?"

"No"

"Would you stop fighting City Hall and constantly getting arrested?"

"Probably not."

"It seems to me," he spoke with a tone of questioning his own wisdom, "that being married to a woman like you would be an invite to hell."

"Or heaven," she purringly snuggled. "Don't overlook my special talent."

"Why do you think you couldn't do it last night?" she followed her own words. "I mean was it something I did or didn't do?"

"You? Heavens no Shelly. I have never felt anything so wonderful in my life as you. You are light-years more wonderful than anything I ever had reason to hope for.

"Wonderful woman the problem is me and has nothing to do with you. The problem is it just won't come out. It's a physical thing. The semen just won't come out inside of a vagina. No matter how hard I concentrate it..."

"I can make it happen Jack. Give me a chance. I know it's not normally the way that but..."

"Shelly, no. The answer is no. I just can't do it that way. You're right what you just said about it not being normal. Doing it your way...it's it's, uh, to me it just seems perverted. What would people say if they knew."

"What! Is that what's really bothering you? What people might say?"

"No, if I'm truthful. It's just. Shelly I love you so much. Isn't it enough that we just be near each other; love, kiss, embrace? Is it so almighty important that we have this earth shattering orgasm together? What's wrong with us just, you know... each of us keep doing it our own way?"

"Ha! Talk about something being perverted. Yes Jack, yes it is that almighty important that we have orgasm sex together, ever how we do it. It is the deepest expression we can ever share; and even more. But having to sell you on the reasons is not what I have in mind. What I am more interested in knowing is what is your reluctance? Why are you so unwilling to at least try. I mean it's not like nobody ever did it that way before."

"OK, suppose we, as you say do it that way. What do you get out of it? I mean, I understand for me but what about you?"

"Oh Baby. You will never know. Baby on that note trust me. Just don't worry. The reasons are mine beyond anything you would ever imagine and it would take me a thousand years to explain."

"OK," he said in discussion. "Let's say we do it and it turns out OK

I'm happy and you're happy.

"So in that aspect we're happy. There's still the little matter of all our other differences..."

"JACK!" she cut him off without thinking. But then his tone and the nature of his comment struck her and an alarm went off. How did the conversation get headed in this direction? A moment earlier they were lying in each other's arms speaking of love.

Now all of a sudden he was being defensive. Why? What was going on in his mind? Why was he holding back? These were dangerous waters into which she was not going to be pulled; at least not for the moment.

"Gracious," she responded as she evasively started getting out of bed. "Why didn't you tell me you were such a grouch in the morning before you've had your caffeine.

"One pot of fresh black coffee coming up," she rose and went to the kitchen.

"Shelly," she could hear him putting on his clothes. "Baby I really have to go. I'm late already. I have a very important business appointment."

"You sure I can't give you a cup to go?" she offered as he was tucking in his shirt.

"Next time Baby," they gave each other a token kiss and hugged. At the door she watched as he drove off and then picked up the morning paper.

Back at the kitchen table she poured her own coffee and was about to take her first sip when by happenstance she glanced at the morning headlines, VIETNAM AIR STRIKES TO CONTINUE.

Her thoughts about Jack were instantly obliterated as anger surged through her veins. She read the first few lines about President Johnson's decision to resume massive air strikes and her natural instincts to fight back swelled out of control. In frustration she stood up too quickly and her kitchen chair fell over backward.

In defiance she snatched the paper up and threw it strewn pages across the room. *The dirty damn bastards,* she thought. *Killing more innocent people. Poor wretched starving, dirt-poor people. Killing and slaughtering. Flying nice and safe 30,000 feet up in big Goddamn bombers. Just fly over and drop tons and tons of bombs. Not caring who they kill. Not caring. By the damn I'll not stand by and... I'll get the biggest demonstration this town has ever seen. I'll, something has got to be done. Something...*

But forever action in life, there is an equal and opposing reaction, and this time her determination was not that strong. Perhaps because of the early morning hour, perhaps because she had had a sleepless night or perhaps because of the lonely years of living without love, on this morning her own needs in life took precedent; she couldn't muster the strength. Feeling helpless she reached over and picked up the strewn paper and slumped back down in the living room chair. The odds were so overwhelming. Fighting the industrialists who were making millions and billions of dollars from war profits. Fighting with her own city government over a National disgrace.

Would one more demonstration, one more arrest, one more court hearing, would it really do any good. At that very moment there was something for herself that she desperately needed. She felt herself calming down as she justified to herself; but even that was short lived.

As she was straightening up the pages of the strewn paper the society page caught her eye and a second fire ignited in her stomach.

Unlike the first, though, this one she could damn well do something about. There, in smiling glory was a chapter from out of her past. A picture of a very distinguished looking Dr. Daniel Owise, MD

According to the article he was being nominated to fill the post of Secretary Premier of the United Care Givers of Pennsylvania. In a glowing press release he was acclaimed as a long time Pittsburgh prominent physician who has unselfishly given of his time and money to help the poor and unfortunate. Further, the article continued he would bring the highest of standards to this very responsible but prestigious position. Considerable social engagements would be expected for the purpose of fund raising via social affairs, concert performances and invitation only dinners. So important was the position that only impeccable, credentials were acceptable.

"Well, well, well," she spoke out loud. "Owise, you sorry louse. I may not be able to stop the war in Vietnam but I can sure as to hell do something about this hypocritical bullshit.

"What goes around comes around." Her emotions kept improving as she went to her closet and took down an old photo album. As she turned the pages, she resisted looking at any of the old memories. She had in mind some pictures that had been taken some twenty-five years ago and simply left stuck in an envelope. As she took the aged photos out of the envelope she was pleased to see the color content was still perfect and the negatives were still in tact. She experienced a feeling of elation over what she was about to do.

There in close-up color was dear ol' Dr. Owise in the nude having intimate sex with youthful Detrick Simmons and under-aged Donna Masterson. The Pittsburgh Mirror was always extremely pleased when any such photographs fell into their hands.

Later that morning, when she dropped them into a street corner mailbox, she felt sure that both Morgan and Patricia were smiling down from heaven, knowing that that part of the deal would finally be squared.

In the days thereafter the togetherness of Shelly and Jack grew but their chemistry seem to flounder. The ebb and flow of their relationship was to butt heads by day and attempt to make love by night. In both cases they were locked in stalemate.

On lovemaking they would try until they were overcome by exhaustion. But no matter what the effort or how hard the concentration nothing happened; for either of them.

Still, in its own way their attachment continued to grow. The present passed, spring turned to summer and the fresh air of outdoors became their preferred time together. With school in recess Jack had time on his hands, Shelly was her own boss and so they drifted to a pattern of taking long walks and scenic drives and always talking.

They walked in Point State Park where the Allegheny River and the Monongahela River come together to form the headwater of the mighty Ohio. They walked the winding trails of Schenley Park, interlocked fingers as they strolled the manicured grounds of Pepperdine Conservatory and watched other people as they sat on park benches in Market Square.

It seemed to Shelly that Jack was so well educated but knew so little. It seemed to Jack that Shelly had no idea of what a normal man is looking for in a wife. Instead, it seemed to him, that she went out of her way to look for trouble.

"Shelly," he had asked one day while the two were standing on the Overlook in Schenley Oval, "how much money do you have?"

"Why do you ask?"

"Are you worth a million dollars?"

"Yes"

"Are you worth two million dollars?"

"Yes"

"Are you worth five million dollars?"

"Probably"

"Shelly with all of that money is this all you can find to do in life?"

"By *this*. What do you mean?"

"You know what I mean. I mean running around waving protest signs. Getting in fight, etc. etc. etc."

"And you consider fighting to keep someone from taking away your rights to free speech, to try and hold a ruthless corrupt government in check etc. etc. etc. is just *this*?"

"Shelly, we all have to live in our society. You can't go around tearing it down."

"Wrong. It's our responsibility, nay, our obligation to take an active part in building an ever changing society."

"Wheeee," he let a sound, "Shelly, whatever I say you have an argument for don't you?"

"No, Jack. What I have is a need for you to love me and me to love you. But I can't be something I'm not. Let's put the shoe on the other foot. Why won't you make love to me in a way I know we could be happy? Just tell me WHY!"

"BECAUSE!" he snapped back.

It wasn't long thereafter that their odds started getting even hotter. It started in Market Square as they were sitting on a park bench, each having a hot dog being washed down with a coke. In a lull they threw small pieces of buns to pigeons and uninterestingly watched passing shoppers. But a tension was building and they could both feel it.

"What is it you want out of life Jack?" she had abruptly asked. "I mean do you really know?"

"Of course I know," he answered with a slight snap. "Why do you think I went to college for so damn many years? I want to teach."

"Why? Tell me why you think teaching is so important?"

"It's a good job. You get tenure. Three months off in the summer. Good retirement. Good security."

"I didn't hear you mention anything about developing young minds. Of passing on knowledge. Also that your concerns for the young species come ahead of our own individual well being."

"And you," he responded defensively, "all of this demonstrating you do against the war in Vietnam, going to jail over showing X rated movies, fighting City Hall. That's all for the good of the species? What does it get you? At least what I do is normal."

"What all this tells me," she answered, "is that neither of us know where the other is coming from. So what is it you want Jack?"

"Where I'm coming from Shelly is the same place millions of other normal men are coming from. Good job, wife, house to come home to."

"But you're not exactly as normal as those other millions of men are you?"

"And you are?" he responded offensively.

"Absolutely not. And that is precisely where I'm coming from. It's you, spelled Y O U that I need. I need you specifically because neither of us, as the saying goes, is normal.

"And I'm not fighting with you Jack. I'm fighting that which keeps us apart. And for that I need, no wait, make that we, we need to join together.

"What I mean is why can't we just try pulling together. Do either of us really need to build ourselves up at the expense of tearing the other down? Who knows? If we go ahead and start out having sex my way it might eventually get to where it would work for us the regular way. We might even have a kid."

"Uh huh. I hear you."

"Well, it could happen. In that respect there's no reason why not. Think about it. What if we did have a kid; say a boy. What would you teach it? What would you name it?"

"Ha. Us, a kid? Name it? How about storyteller? He sure as to hell would have a lot of stories to tell. In fact, it sounds so damn plausible; let's plan on it. One kid coming up; birth certificate Name: *Storyteller*. Shelly my mind can't even fathom such a thing. But if we did I have no doubt that your influence over him would be infinitely stronger than anything I could hope to say or do."

"Jack, why do you say that?"

"I have no idea. I mean I'm at a loss for words."

"Yeah, now it's me that's hearing you. Words are not the only thing you are at loss of. You might try looking for the owner of that bull that's seems to be permanently influencing the inside of your head."

"Why do I have the feeling that we have just come full circle? I wonder why that is. Next round coming up. Shelly I get no pleasure in fighting with you. If I wasn't hopelessly in love with you, do you think I'd be putting up with all of this aggravation? Why can't you see that all I want is for you to be a good wife?

"That may be just our point of differences Jack," she pounced. "Where I'm coming from I just want you to be my man; to make me complete. Shit, how can I say this?

"I need you, for you. Because you are you, a very very special one of a kind you. Everything else in my life I can fight on my own damn terms and you know what? I can beat the shit out of anything or anybody, hands down...and win; every damn time.

"Remember our good friend ol' Casey Blackstock? One of

Pittsburgh's finest?

"Ha, ol' Casey would rather have his butt kicked than to have to come down and arrest me.

"But you," she talked without stopping, "you on the other hand, you want me to be a Miss Wife, a housekeeper, a tag along no talk back and Oh! Let's not forget a no-sex deal."

"I hear you," he responded without hesitating, "but I don't think I heard you saying in all of that anything about how you fight with me."

"Granted. OK Maybe I do. Yes I know that it's not something a good wife would do. And I can understand you asking how come?" her tone dropped off as if it ran out of steam. "I guess," she continued in a voice that had little strength, "It's because I'm scared. I'm lonely. I'm afraid of losing you."

"And that's all you need me for?" his stronger voice taking advantage of her weakened position. "The fact that I happen to have some rare oddity of nature which is capable of satisfying your unique sexual requirement. Other than that you can go along on your merry own?"

"You're really something Jack. You know that," her strength surged back to fighting level. "Of all the other words I've said, that's all you've heard. At the risk of calling you a shit head, I could kill you!"

But persistence has its own rewards. Just as flowing water can smooth away stone, if a dream is followed it will eventually come true. For Shelly what she thought was the first small flicker of her dream actually coming true came while they were sunning on a blanket on the shores of Lake Erie. It may have been brought on by the warm autumn sun and the tranquillity of the calm waves lapping at the shore but it seemed to her that his rebuttals were getting a little less opposing.

"You ask where I am coming from," she paused and took a full breath, "I've said this before, but I'll say it again. To me there are two separate parts to life; both being essential.

"One is completeness of the self and the other is purpose and fulfillment.

"Completeness to me means having a mate so absolute that two bodies become one. Fulfillment means putting the interest of the species ahead of one's self."

"What you call finding yourself," he referred back to one of her earlier statements, "I call fighting the world."

"No," she rebutted. "That answer is nothing more than a justification for refusing to look within.

"What is your opposition to wanting to discover what's inside of yourself?"

"Words, Shelly. Those are just words to torment the mind. There is no such thing as finding one's self.

"Who we are, all of us are living organisms. We eat, sleep, attend to body function and strive for a higher rank in our social order; which translates to a higher degree of respect. Anything beyond that, like I say, is fighting life."

The tone of his voice kindled panic. Just when she had thought progress was being made another flare up. She may have misread the signs. What if his change of demeanor was really a prelude to calling it quits. What if he was really just looking for a chance to charge it all up to nagging, tune her out and simply walk away?

But neither could she retreat. Fear gripped her about what to do. The onus was on her and she started perspiring from the pressure of either pushing her point or backing off.

In an all or nothing gamble she drew upon the resources of her entire life and elected to continue but with a different approach. From the teachings of Frank Buckwilder she borrowed support from Greek Philosophy and the meaning of fulfillment.

"Jack," she spoke as she raised up on one elbow and turned to where she was talking directly to him, "Baby don't be angry with me.

"Honey," she justified her words, "it's just the way I was raised. To me the way I think, for me it seems to work. It's been tried and tested.

"Do you know that some four thousand years ago the Greeks figured out that pleasure seeking is a myth? It doesn't exist. According to Socrates and Plato and a few other philosophers, if you want to feel good about yourself do something constructive. They figured out way back then that the greatest pleasure, no wait make that fulfillment, the greatest fulfillment there is in life is to be all that you can be."

"And," she paused for emphasis. "I say this with every thing I believe..., in so much... as you hold back one ounce less from being all you can be..., you will feel cheated by an equal measure."

Her words ended on a note that implied there would be a follow up statement. But she had none. She had expected that he would have an immediate response. But he had none. He simply remained silent with his arm resting across his forehead protecting his eyes from the sun.

She then raised herself up to a sitting position on the blanket, draped her arms over her pulled up knees, looked out over the vast blue-green water and joined the silence.

The morning was getting warmer and she could feel the perspiration on her scalp and sweat dripping under her arms pits.

Fearing that she had sounded too much like she had been lecturing she changed her tone to a small talk approach. Looking nonchalant out to where the distant horizon met the lake she continued.

"Baby, I can't predict what kind of life we will have. No one can predict the future.

"But this much I do know. Whatever life we do have. Wherever we go, whatever we do, I want it to be strictly for us and not the predetermined approval of others.

"Someone once told me that the greatest single thing which has ruined more lives than all other things combined is worrying about what other people might think."

Feeling that the last remark was slanted at him, Jack rose upon his elbows, also directed his gaze out over the calm sun-reflecting waters and responded.

"Meaning that I should live my life as you see it and not be concerned about what all the other members of the faculty think."

"Meaning," she slashed back out of control, "that I think what we should do is fight, fight, fight. I think what we ought to do is continue doing what we seem to do best, and that's fucking fight, fight, fight with each other," she rose from the blanket and started walking down the beach.

"Hey wait Shel...." he rose and ran to catch her. "Baby that didn't come out right. I didn't mean to hurt. It's just that I happen to think what I do in life is important. To me it's a good balance. It lets me do a little good and lets me enjoy a little.

"All this talk about being great. In my way of thinking I'll just leave all of that being great to someone else."

"Jack!" she turned in astonishment. "Honey I'm not trying to change you? IS that how you've been thinking? That it is you? Jack it's me. All this time I've been trying to tell you about me. Don't you understand? For you to accept me as I am," she turned and buried her head in his chest and fought to hold back her hurt.

"Honey you misunderstand me. I'm not finding fault with you being a teacher. To the contrary. I have nothing but the highest respect for the teaching profession and you as a teacher.

"I know I haven't done a good job of telling you where I'm coming from so I'll try once more. Maybe this time I can make it a little clearer.

"The values," she paused slightly in search, " maybe that's a good word, value. To me I put value on that certain something that I pull from deep inside of me. In whatever the course of my life, it's that sincere something which I do because I believe it is right, good, helpful, concern, honest, or whatever other term you care to use," she brought her hand up and wiped away the wetness in her eyes.

"But sometimes I get lonely in that world Jack. It's not that I want to stop doing it. I just want some company. It doesn't have to be a lot of company. Just one, just one someone who is there.

"That way I won't feel like I'm alone in a crowd. Even as I speak Jack, I have no doubt that in your mind I must be crazy. I know that but I don't know what else to do?"

"Shelly," they stood together at the water's edge and he held her head to his chest as he spoke in a consoling tone. "All of this talk about being all that you can be; about being great. I can tell you without hesitation that when the spot light in life is turned off and the crowds have all gone home you will be alone."

"I understand that Jack. That's why I need you. I don't want the end to come like that.

"I can't answer for other I can only speak for myself. But when the final curtain comes down I will know that I measured up. I didn't take more than I gave. Those people who do not know how to give, Jack they endure a hell while they live. I know what's on the other side. I once had an occasion to cross over..."

"Shelly, in your mind what does it take? What were your words, 'for me to be all that you want me to be'."

"Just two things," she meekish replied.

"One, let me be who I am. And two, make love to me; the way I need it. Please Jack," her tone emphasizing her point, "the way you look at love making is not the only way in the world. I say we do it anyway that works. And there's no doubt in my mind that eventually the regular way will work out."

"OK OK OK SHELLY! Please. OK," he abruptly held up his hands and caved in. "Honey I just can't fight you anymore. I love you too much. You are right and I'm wrong."

"Jack, Baby, it's not a matter of who's right or wrong," her tone quickly showing unanimity. "There's no right or wrong involved. It's..."

"No, I'm wrong," he cut in. "I'm wrong but not in the way you're thinking. The way I'm wrong, you're not going to like but I've got to get it out in the open," he responded as they slightly separated.

Standing back so there was an arm's length between them, he deliberately cast a distant look. He took a deep breath, brought his hands up and felt his own face.

"All the things you have been saying," he started as he was bringing his hands down, "Shelly, you think I don't know all of that. I *have* gone to school a few years, you know.

"Somewhere along the way I'd like to think I learned a little something. I don't necessarily agree with everything but that's not to say I don't know something about what you've been saying.

"And, even though I've quarreled about it I've always felt you were right. Not necessarily for me but certainly it was right for you. None of that was ever really the problem."

"WHAT?" she tensed for an explanation. "What did you just say? Did I just hear what I think I just heard?"

"Shel, I uh..."

"All these weeks and months we've been fighting? You mean there's really been something else. I've talked my rear-end off and all the while it's been something else?

"I DON'T SUPPOSE," she raised her voice and her natural assertiveness surged out, "THAT maybe you would be so kind as to enlighten me?"

"Shelly," he started to respond but his voice reflected his uncertainty, "I don't even know if I can find the words. I mean..."

"Meaning what Jack?" she detected his misgivings and her voice quickly became sensitive. "Baby what's so difficult for you to explain."

There was a swallowing in his throat that he did not like. Without answering he took in a deep breath and felt his lungs expand. He closed his eyes and rubbed his eyebrows, searching how to proceed.

In some natural movement he slightly twisted to where they were standing looking at each other. He took her face in his hands tilted it to where they made eye contact for a moment and then started.

"Shelly do you know, really know, how beautiful you are. When I look at the sparkle in your little girl eyes, your perfect unblemished skin, the innocence in your complexion, Baby you are truly a vision of loveliness.

"I've said it before and I suppose I will continue saying it the rest of my life. You are beyond anything I ever expected.

"And if I'm pushed to say it, your lips. God they have the softness of celestial baby skin. No velvet... was ever so smooth and no human instinct more possessive than to call them mine.

"And, forgive me Shelly, but therein lies my reluctance."

"Jack?" her face showed her surprise. "I don't understa..."

"Understand?" he finished her sentence. "If I can I'll try to say it. You are the bed-pillow I have hugged to myself almost every night of my adult life.

"Your lips have brought life to those years of dreams, Shelly. More than loneliness I longed just to be able to feel the touch of lips such as yours. Just to feel the sensation.

"I doubt if there's anyway, anyway at all that you can really understand what I'm trying to say. But after all of those years... never expecting it to happen.

"Even now, at this very moment, you looking up at me. I just want to grab you and weld your mouth to mine. God..."

His words stopped as he looked at her in a cold fear of silence; fear that his next words would be like casting the darkest black soot on the whitest brightest snow.

"Shelly you're asking to have oral sex with me. That means with those lips. I picture it happening and that's when my stomach ties in a knot. I picture your mouth and lips just as I climax, and there it is. And I ask myself, how could I ever bring myself to kiss those very same lips after they have been drenched with my semen?" The last of his words rang to a dead silence. By some unexplainable global catastrophic upheaval all means of communication between the two had just been obliterated........

.... She stood dumfounded.... All of their differences.... All the worry and searching. And there it was..............

That's what all of the months of fighting had actually been all about? Unbelievable.

.... Weak. She felt weak in the knees. What could she say? Embarrassing blood rushed to her cheeks and she could see an emotional hurt cutting across his face.............. Somehow she mustered the courage to make a comment.

"Your own semen. You find that repulsive?"

"I said I was wrong. I..."

"No wait," she put her fingers to his lips. "Ssssss. Just, you wait." At this point she was not going to be denied control.

"You don't say anything...." she said very slowly, "...and I won't say anything for at least a whole minute. This is much too important to say anything without thinking. Ssssss. Let's just relax for a moment and think."

He didn't fight her soft fingers as they remained against his lips. What he did do was to slowly reach down, take her hand and convey a signal for them to return to their blanket.

Still without speaking he dropped down and stretched out. She waited until he was settled and then stretched out by his side. Now looking directly up into the sky each shielded their eyes from the sun by resting an arm over their forehead. The only sounds were the cawing of sea gulls, the gentle splashing of on-shore waves and the heart beat of these two searching people. It was Shelly who after a long while spoke the first words.

"Jack," she softly called his name.

"Yes"

"I'm going to start saying something but if the words start coming out wrong, promise me you'll stop me?"

"Look, Shelly I..."

"No, Jack please. If I talk will you listen. I mean stop me if I start going in the wrong direction?"

"Go ahead, I just..."

"No, please. It's important. If I say just the right words, I'm hoping that I can convince you that it's OK"

"Shelly, I've already said I would do it. You don't have to convince me."

"Yes I do. Yes I do have to convince you. Until you see. Until you know. And until I know for certain that you know, the blotch would always be there. So if I talk will you listen? Promise?"

"I promise," he replied in a reassuring tone as he turned and looked at her.

"As I have been lying here," she returned his look, "I've been thinking of what we might be able to do."

"And?"

"Would you do something for me?"

"Of course?"

"Would you take your hands and feel your face. I know. I know. But please, just do it. Feel the skin and tell me what you think.

"I feel the texture of my skin, my eyebrows, the shape of my nose, my stubble beard."

"Do you have any reluctance? Do you hesitate?"

"No, of course not."

"What if I ask you to feel on the inside of your skin? I mean massage the inside layer. Where the blood vessels, the raw meat, the layers of fat, all of that. Would you feel as easy?"

"Uh, I don't know. You mean actually reach inside and grasp all the blood and; why would I want to do that?"

"I'm not saying you would want to. I'm asking how you think it would feel. Squeamish, scary, interesting, exciting? What?

"Would you feel as comfortable and easy about touching your insides as the outside of your face?"

"Wheeee, I'll say one thing for you Shelly..."

"What if," she cut him off, "we had a great big zipper running right down our front so that we could just unzip it anytime we wanted to?

"What would you think about unzipping your front right now and reaching in and feeling around in, say your intestines? Or maybe feel the ol' heart, give the stomach a little squeeze while you're in there. How do you think you would feel; just feeling all of that nice moist, even slimy tissue?"

"Shelly, you're sick."

"Am I? Why? It's all part of you isn't it. I'm sick but you're not?

"You feel at ease touching certain parts of yourself but not others," she continued uninterrupted. Why is that? Let's take it a step further," she continued without realizing that her natural instincts to defend and hold her course against all turbulence was taking over.

"Let assume that all of a sudden, right here on the beach, this very moment, the zipper just popped open and all of your insides started sliding out.

"First comes a nice big tub of moist intestines, here they come sliding out on your legs.

"What would you do? Lie there afraid of touching them; something which is perfectly sterile. Does it scare you at the thought of picking them up and putting them back in the container?

"Don't like the idea? Yet you'll touch your dirty toes and feet without thinking.

"But heaven forbid that you'll accept as normal the idea of touching anything from your own insides.

"If you get a sensation from touching the outside of your skin, think how your priorities in life would change if you could hold your own beating heart. To watch it pulsate blood through your very existence..."

"CAN..." he pronounced the first word with emphasis and then spoke with a slow, drawn out tone, "I assume that you are telling me all of this to make a point."

"Well?" she felt the easing of tension and asked with a great big dimpled smile, "how am I doing?"

"I can hardly wait?"

"Well, wait no more Sweetie Pie because here it comes. Your semen that you have such a reluctance to see on my lips, here's something for you to think about.

"Think about this. Semen is the essential source of all life. It is the purest of all matter. It is inconceivable that something as miraculous as living sperm would be swimming around in fluids that were not celestial pure.

"To touch it is to feel the blessing of life. To not touch it is to be deprived. Why would you be so squeamish about something that is so absolutely pure?

"Something that is a thousand times more celestial than, as you rave about, my lips.

"Ha," she let out a small mockery laugh at the absurdity. "Semen on my lips Jack; be thankful. If you really want to conger up a picture that will turn you off then do this.

"Picture me running my tongue over my lips, leaving lots of nice wet dripping saliva and then turning to you for one of those nice deep tongue in mouth, spit swapping kisses.

"Ah yes, the absolute act of pure love. Let's do it; and then you can thank me? I have just given you about one hundred billion germs and living strains of bacteria.

"Try it lover boy; you'll like it. Providing, of course you live!"

At that remark all reservation in Jack simply collapsed. He let out a surrendering laugh, grinning shook his head at her innocent analysis and knew that he would love this woman for the rest of his life.

"Baby," the words came out of his half laughing mouth, "I don't think I have ever had anything explained to me exactly like that before.

"You win Honey, God knows you win. What do you want me to do?"

"JACK," she squealed. "Is that a yes? You mean it? Don't say it if you don't mean..."

"Yes, Shel, I really mean it. But I won't be hypocritical. I'll go for the loving but on the other aspects of our differences it'll take some convincing. I may not be as far along in life as you are in knowing who I am. But I can never be you."

"But you will do it?" she rushed for reassurance.

Still half laughing and slightly shaking his head in disbelief he shrugged his shoulders in complete surrender and simply said, "Whatever it is you want, you slightly deranged woman. Just say it. What do you want me to do?"

"Oh Jack," she grabbed him with a squeeze. "Nothing. You don't have to do anything but be the answer to my prayers. It's now up to me. You've just granted me all that I have ever asked for.

"From here on in," she emphasized, "my happiness depends on me and it is an onus that I gladly welcome.

"Oh God I am finally going to get to some relief from my torment. Those ever present lingering frustration that never leaves my crouch finally; finally.

"And," she inhaled filling her lungs to capacity, tilted her head back, looked to the heavens and exhaled with a whoosh.

"I can breath. God, man I love you more already. I'm peeing my panties. And as of right now I have things I have to start doing. Don't ask any questions and don't look to see much of me for a few weeks. I have some dream building to do and some calls to make."

Back at the apartment the next morning she impatiently sipped at a cup of black coffee as she thumbed through the telephone book. She had heard of an engineering firm that specialized in building theatrical stage and set designs.

Her first call was to Bethel Engineering Company where she was lucky enough to get exactly what she wanted; two young engineers capable of making a dream come true.

What she had in mind was renovating an old military blimp hanger-building on Neville Island. This, as it turned out was exactly the type of engineering specialty work they did.

The three met at the defunct blimp hanger the next day and made a walk through inspection.

"Gentlemen," she spoke as they finished their get acquainted tour. "This building is 400 feet long, 300 feet wide and 200 feet high; all open area. The roof is comprised of a bowstring truss and there are no interior support columns. I am holding an option to lease it for ten years.

"When we leave here we will be going to the Stran Theater. I want the two of you to see a movie; an old Arabian Nights movie. Then I will tell you what it is I want.

Inside the Stran the three of them sat up in the balcony and watched as The Arabian Nights flashed across the screen.

"When we get to the flying carpet scene," she told them, "I want you to pay close attention."

As the movie ended she turned to the two and said, "Well, there you have it. Now you know. What I want from you is to duplicate the flying carpet scene in the blimp hanger."

"Flying carpet scene!" questioned engineer One.

"The flying carpet scene," affirmed Shelly.

"You mean you want us to build a platform affair that will simulate flying around in a big high enclosed building?"

"Don't even think of it as an enclosure," she corrected, "the Sahara Desert. More specific the Sahara Desert at night with a million stars, a full moon, blue heavens, rippling sand dunes and an Arabian village to look down on."

"But Ma'am, most of what we see in the movie is trick photography," said engineer Two.

"What you are asking is an actual physical apparatus of some sort, dressed up like a carpet that will travel in and around the building."

"Exactly," she emphasized, "and don't forget the wind blowing effect.

"Ma'am, I don't see how we could..." engineer Two was about to say when he was cut off.

"With roller coaster tracks," interrupted engineer One, as he was sketching on his work pad.

"Coaster tracks?" questioned engineer Two. "Naw, Naw, tracks would never work. There would always be vibration that would detract from the smoothness of riding on air. What we would have to do is use cables and suspend the apparatus from the ceiling."

"Never," countered engineer One, "Cables will sway like a swing. No, it will have to be coaster tracks. Now, we can overcome the vibration with pneumatic wheels," he was sketching as he talked.

"Pneumatic? Well OK," agreed engineer Two as he started his on sketch pad, "that would give us the soft ride we need; good point.

"Also we may be able to design the carpet pad with sponge rubber or coil springs for additional softness."

"Good thinking," said engineer One. "And for the sky we can install a false ceiling with rounded concave canvas. And for the starry night effect we can use small Christmas tree lights barley pushed through from the back side."

"Fine, but not good enough," said engineer Two. "We need millions of lights remember?"

"OK then what we can do is install full lighting directly up against the truss ceiling before we put the false canvas ceiling up, and then just punch in a million pin holes in a pattern to show the Milky Way."

"Just checking you," said engineer Two. "That was going to be my next suggestion. The underside of the canvas can be painted with iridescent paint, midnight blue; and also the walls. On the floor we could paint the Arabian village. No wait we have the entire floor to work with we can build an actual scale model of a village."

"Yeah, and on the village outskirts we can start the desert sand. Now for the ripple effect we can..."

"And for the blowing wind effect we can install circulating fans that..."

Shelly watched as the two young minds became absorbed in their work. It pleased her to see one make a suggestion and the other improve it. She sat silently as page after page in their work tablets were marked up and then turned to the next. Her thoughts drifted to how it would look. She pictured her and Jack sitting with their legs crossed, with the wind blowing in their face.

Somehow the picture did not seem fair. After all it was she and Patricia who first fantasized this dream. Why couldn't all three of them be there to share? That gave her a better feeling of fairness.

Mother, she thought to herself, *I promise that you will always be there with us.* And then it dawned on Shelly where she was sitting. It was the same seat that she and her mother had sat and fantasized in so many years earlier.

"Proof," she said out loud, "that if you do not give up on your dreams they really will come true."

Wheels were now turning. She was instantly restless. Now, she wanted it all to be right now. One morning before dawn she could not stay in bed any longer. She looked at Jack and was thankful that he was still asleep. She needed to get out. Quietly she slipped out of bed, got dressed and eased out the front door.

Outside it was still dark. Morning dew hung in the night air and the streetlights were reflecting across the moist street.

The only sound was a Metro bus pulling away from a corner stop where no one got on. She walked along Wood Street until she came to Market Square. A park that is always full during the day was silently empty at that hour.

A flower vender had just arrived and was putting out his wares. She paused and looked at the buckets of long stem roses and wondered how many young maidens would be receiving a bouquet on this day. As she left the square she turned east and noticed the first streaks of crimson red starting to appear on the horizon. She wondered how many young women had been out all night in the arms of their lover and in wrinkled dress and smeared make-up would just be getting home.

She continued walking east until she was in the Hill District and went passed the Guiding Light Shelter for the homeless. There she saw several derelict men sleeping in the doorway and along the sidewalk; dirty, unshaven and wearing rags. She wondered if their plight was because of a love gone wrong or a love never found.

From the Shelter she walked down Crawford Street to Center Avenue and turned back west. She went past the County Jail and remembered the terrible nights she had spent there for fighting. The irony of it was that she never really wanted any trouble; all she ever really wanted was to love someone and be loved in return.

Neville Island was a major shipbuilding and military base during World War Two. After the war it was declared surplus and all of the property was sold to private owners. The chain link fences having long since been removed, the only evidence of a once secured compound being the remanence of an old guard house.

It was now some nine weeks later, at seven o'clock in the evening, the parking lots were all empty and there was a ghostly stillness about driving past the many empty buildings. When Shelly and Jack pulled up to the blimp building they parked next to a side entrance door.

"Shel," he asked, "what are we doing out here?"

When she did not respond he felt a hurt for asking. He inhaled a deep breath while searching his mind and then continued.

"Baby it's just that you've been very secretive these last couple of months and I haven't tried to intrude. I, I've also notice that during these last few weeks we've given up completely on our attempts at making love.

"Honey," he finished his question, "I just don't know what it is want from me?"

She didn't know what to say so she said nothing. And he said nothing more. Finally in the darkness of the car she spoke.

"It's actually me Jack," she said. "Ever since I was a little girl I have fantasized about making love on a flying carpet. You know the story."

"Yes," he said, "from when you and your mother used to watch the movie in the Stran. You've told me many times."

"Well," she continued, her voice in the mode of a confession. "It may be out of control. I don't know. It may be that I have dreamed about it for so long that it has become a sickness. But in my mind that fantasy is the only place where I will ever be able to have a climax so intense that it will reach the depths of my soul." She paused and Jack said nothing.

"I haven't told you this," she said when she did continue, "but I have spent a lot of money duplicating that flying carpet scene."

"What?" he asked rhetorically. "Are you telling me that you have rigged up some sort of fantasy land inside this old blimp building?"

"It's more than a rigged up scene Jack, it's a work of art."

"But Baby, couldn't we have just fantasized about it in our bedroom. Isn't this going a bit too far?"

"No," she answered emphatically. "No we couldn't have just fantasized about it in the bed room. That's just it. For it to work it has to be real; or at least as real as possible.

"The idea is to be so caught up in the beauty that all of our inhibitions are stripped away. "Hopefully we will become so uninhibited that we become two free souls drifting in the heavenly bodies. Surrounded by beauty so breath taking that it can only be sanctified by an act of total lovemaking."

His impulse was to refute her argument. To relate that fantasies are a figment of the mind; better left in place than pursued. But he did not have the heart. So he held himself in check, took a deep breath and simply capitulated.

"OK woman of mine. Fantasy land it is. We only live once so lets go to the end of the rainbow. It sounds like it would be the most magnificent journey in the world; and I would like nothing better than to be there by your side.

"So why don't we stop wasting time and take our trip to never, never land?"

"Oh, Jack," she cried, "as she threw her arms around him. Oh thank you, thank you Honey. You won't be sorry I promise."

"What is the first thing we have to do," he asked as they walked from the car and she was unlocking the door to the building.

"Well, the first thing we have to do is dress the part; and it just so happens that I have some harem cloths right here in the office," she answered as she closed the outside door and switched on the office light.

"Where is the dream machine," he asked as he nodded his head to the door leading out into the hanger area.

"Patience, Baby. Don't spoil it for me. Here, put these on." She handed him a pair of silk lounging pants, a small open vest and a turbine with a red ruby in the forehead. While he was dressing she was putting on a thin sheen harem suit.

As they finished dressing they paused and looked at each other and their eyes made direct contact. Emotions swelled up as a watering came to both. Two people hopelessly in love and trying desperately to find that one missing link that will bond them into an eternal flame.

"Please dear God," she made one last comment. "Jack don't do this unless you mean it," she shakingly whispered as she hugged herself into his arms. He could feel her trembling as he returned her hug. "I mean it Baby," he said.

"Darling," she talked hesitatingly, "I'm scared. It's my one big shot and I know it.

"It's a dream I have dreamed night and day all my life. And now it's here. Honey what if it don't happen?"

"Sweetheart, it's going to happen," he answered reassuringly.

"But what if it doesn't? If it don't I will never be able to cross over. Maybe," she suddenly offered, "we should wait until we are more prepared; please we can do it another time."

"My most precious woman," Jack assumed the leadership, "listen to me. Right now I could not be more in love with you than if you were a real live angel. What may or may not happen inside no longer matters. The secret ingredient we have been looking for has already happened. It happened right here; just now.

"As of this minute my soul has already left me and has come to dwell with you. So my very wonderful woman, take my hand, let's walk through the door together and take that journey into fantasy land that will last a lifetime."

With a trembling hand she opened the door and took the lead as they went inside. Only one small nightlight was on as she ushered him over to the golden chariot and seated him on a tassel-trimmed carpet.

She then went to an electrical panel box next to the door, threw a series of switches and hurriedly ran to join him.

In seconds, electrical engines started to whine, a small movement in the carpet was felt, and tiny ceiling lights started appearing.

Gradually the carpet started to move. The simulated sky became illuminated in beautiful night-blue color and a big full moon appeared in the eastern horizon. By then the ceiling was ablaze with a trillion twinkling Milky Way of stars.

Then it happened. The carpet that had started slow moving, gradually increased and then suddenly zoomed up into the heaven and leveled off.

In gentle slow movement it then embarked on its long winding journey through the stars. On their cloud, half the size of a living room, with the feeling of soft breezes blowing across their bodies, they lay in awe at the boundless beauty.

Rolling over on their backs with her head resting on his arm they looked up at a sky ablaze with millions of tiny lights. A dark thin cloud was crossing the face of the moon and leaving a feeling of mysterious romance in its wake.

Rolling over and facing down they looked over the side at a sleeping, iridescent walled Arabian village with its cobbled stone streets, stacked houses and arched passage ways all setting in the middle of the desert. In the distance, date palm trees surrounded an oasis well; and beyond that, as far as the eye could see, desert sands were shimmering in the moonlight.

Their ride moved as a breath of wind in the heavens and they cared not where it went. For theirs was a world of beauty before them. Drifting across the desert sky, they were the only souls in the universe.

As they shared these stupendous moments they ecstatically fell into an embrace and frolicked on the huge cloud of soft secure padding. Looking first at the surroundings and then at each other, two faces found the light in the other's eyes.

Shelly sensed a chemistry she had never before experienced and a blushing came to her cheeks. She quivered at the transmission between them. Who should speak? She started to speak but her throat choked and so she said nothing. What should she do? And what she did was nothing; except to feel the increase in her heartbeat. She was totally unexpected of her own reaction.

Run, her thoughts cried. *Run, run! Don't do this. Something's wrong.* But the feel of this man eradicated all reservations. So instantaneous was the return voltage from Jack's eyes that turning back was no longer an option.

In a split instant two souls crossed the universe and were wedded into one. The zenith of their union transcended any uncertainty and all restraint drained away.

Words that she started to say ended in an utter. They had been lying generally side-by-side in embrace as the two bodies blended into one and their movements unify in perfect rhythm.

She instinctively rolled over on top and gently slid down between his open legs to where her head came to the triangle of his manhood. Pulling down the waistband of his lounging pants she reached inside. With a singular motion she pulled out his engorged love muscle and touched the full nipple to her tongue. Softly at first like her mother's breast.

But then, she was hit by a surging impulse and the entire gland went deep into her throat as she impaled her face to his crouch. Her hands grasped the back of his buttocks and her fingernails sunk deep into his skin. Fully ingested in her throat and her nostrils buried in his pubic hair she managed a full sucking in of fresh air, closed her eyes, held and made no motion until the oxygen expired.

She then slowly exhaled and raised her head in a slow upward motion keeping her moist lips firmly tight around the full shaft and then dropped down again. As she repeated the action of up and down sucking strokes a rhythmic pattern set in. Her rhythm becoming more pronounced with each stroke; and each stroke becoming faster. If a stroke was lost it was a loss in rhythm to be regained as quickly as possible. As the crescendo rose she could feel the increased engorging of his rod. Fanatically she worked for that pursued sensation... and then it happened. A gigantic gob of white lava shot out with pulsating force; following by subsequent stroke producing smaller squirts; and all liquefying into a nectar that her mother's breast had once provided. And in that very same instant the burning uncontrollable fire that had been ignited in her panties at childhood was finally released. In wrenching jerking convulsions her feet locked around each other, her legs squeezed one against the other and a torrent of feminine juices gushed forth from her quivering vagina, streamed unabated down her inside thighs and followed by several jerking quivering contractions. A relaxing of muscles and then came the setting in of total tranquillity...

Too exhausted to move she collapsed between his straddled legs with the side of her head coming to rest on his pelvic. As her heavy breathing calmed the only sound came form the barely audible movement of the flying carpet as it continued its unending winding tract through the stars. In the realm of twilight they lay without moving and quietly drifted across the universe.

As some junction in their time travel she came to an intersection of consciousness. She noticed a faint light from the artificial sky casting a glisten on his soft pubic hair and she could see the faint outline of his flaccid penis draped across his scrotum.

Without raising her head she reached out, brought it to her lips and lightly kissed the soft nipple. The tip on her tongue tasting the last traces of nectar. Still not moving her head from his soft mat of hair she then attempted to make it into a coil. A partial loop that brought the nipple to her lips and she gave it a final little kiss before squeezing it in a manner of putting it back into a brassiere.

In a complexity unknown to the minds of others, she then transcended into a world lost to her at the age of three. As her nostrils smelled the still present semen, she drifted back into a dozing trance.

She had finally come to terms with all of the conflicts in her mind. Basking in serenity that only she could know, she softly whispered, "I love you Mother."

The End

.

Afterword
by Dyrel Delaney

The author was born May 8, 1935, Maria Mary Greka on the island of Zakynthos, Ionion Pelagos Greece; in a land that has stood still for a thousand years. Isolated island terrain of sharp escarpments and poor rocky barren soil struggles to produce scattered olive trees and marginal vineyards. Donkey carts led by tired and weather-beaten women trudging down dusty dirt roads in scuffed shoes and time worn clothing are still a way of life.

To this already harsh land there came in 1941 the occupation of Hitler's Nazi forces and the ravages of WWII. During the author's years of ages five to eight her country and home bore witness to massive destruction, fear, hunger, maim, death of her father and a helpless mother who could offer no more than holding her child tight against her own weakened body. Mother and daughter strived to stay alive by hunkering down in the ruins of their home amidst unending shelling; without food, shelter or medical treatment. Death came to the mother in a sleep where the author sat and waited.

In time, WWII came to an end and the post-war reconstruction era begin. Aid from the United States brought the author's first memorable meals, clothes and shelter. In a sequence of one step following another as the reconstruction era came to an end, other United States benevolent programs were materializing.

Significant among these emerging changes was the Fulbright Scholarship program. A foreign policy tool sponsored by Senator J. William Fulbright; who at the time was educator/chairman of the Senate Foreign Relations Committee. In substance the United States Government would bear the expense of foreign students coming to the United States receive a four year college education and then returning to their homeland for the purpose "... that nations will learn to live in peace..." To the thousands of students who applied, the selection was based on one simple criteria; the brightest of the bright.

The author herein was one of the selected. In 1958, from Greece the very cradle of democracy, she came to the United States to learn democracy's rebirth. It was on the campus at the University of California that I came into her life.

In time's course she received her Bachelor's degree and returned to her homeland. In years that passed I eventually follow and we were married in Athens in 1964 and returned to the United States.

My own life's work was our Nation's lands; and to that end my career was to acquire land for inclusion into our nation's national parks. Maria followed my zigzag pattern across the United States until I was eventually elevated to the job of Chief Appraiser of the United States National Park Service in Washington, D.C.

During the course of these years, she successfully completed upper graduate work and was awarded a Master's Degree in Medieval French from the University of California. In the same zigzagging years she also qualified for and received teaching credentials to teach at the secondary level in the States of California, Florida, Tennessee, Pennsylvania, and the District of Columbia. She was certified to read, write, speak, teach and translate English, French, Spanish and Greek and had twenty-eight units in Latin. From Cambridge she held a Certificate of Doctoral Proficiency

Maria lived by the belief that growth can only come from work and sacrifice. In Greek Philosophy, she shared with me, *'pleasure seeking'* is a myth. It does not exist. The greatest feeling that one can experience is to be all that one can be.

Further, in all living things, whatever the life form, the species comes first. In that context, the single evolutionary interest of all species is to promulgate a next stronger generation; in substance, the only reason for living.

In life, vanity is the first thing to arrive and the last thing to leave. And if left unchecked it will stand as a false god to the next generation. Those that hold vanity in check will grow, advance and be held in praise. Those that seek vanity as the light of life, the species will use as filler material. It is an axiom that for something to live something must die. The minute a species ceases to grow stronger, some other species will take over. It is the law and it is welded in strength, not vanity.

There is something else Maria would have me relate. It is called emotions, either a gift, a curse, or a blend of both. The need to love, to be loved, to mate, to share uninhibited inner self is a precious gift. Further to know all there is to know about oneself is the most beautiful voyage that can be experienced and no earthly treasure is greater than owning one's own soul.

In the nature of Plastic Surgery, no surgeon can give you something you do not already own. From your perspective, tell him or her you will keep the $25,000.00 and put it to better use. On his or her part, tell the surgeons to do something constructive for society, like doctoring the less fortunate. Lawsuits bring four years of detestable, vile, obnoxious sewage hell. Sewage to the degree that the loss of life is measured by W-2 Forms and nothing else. To that end money and power can always outspend the victim. In four years of law and courts, no settlement, no offer, no apologies, no remorse, no condolences.

May God Bless,

Dyrel Delaney

Acknowledgments

This acknowledgment is for Laura Connaughton, owner of Laura Connaughton Fine Art and Design. For openers I must first make mention that this all takes place at a time in my life when I am extremely distraught. Certain aspects of this book resulted in the death of the book's author and my wife of thirty-seven years, Maria Greka Delaney. This aspect is further elaborated to some degree on subsequent pages. It is mentioned here not for my edification but to strengthen the acknowledgement to Laura and the tireless work and dedication she put forth to bring this book to market.

How this all started. My wife, Maria Greka Delaney, wrote a manuscript, could not get an agent or a publisher, was advised by a snooty agent to get a face lift and against her better judgment agreed. The surgeon cut her trachea and she died. I, her husband, made the vow that her life's work would not go unfinished and turned to self-publishing. That's sufficient for the present point.

For starters I needed someone that could provide layman's guidance. From the telephone book I started cold calling until the name Laura Connaughton Fine Art and Design drifted down. I didn't have much to go on. Mostly that Laura had previously owned, Queenfish Productions, a multimillion dollar convention design and production company with such big name clients as Barnes and Nobles College Book Stores, General Motors, United Van Lines, WDW and Solomon Brothers. Her assignments took her to such places as Puerto Rico, Cancun, Mexico, the Bahamas Islands, Las Vegas, Orlando, Atlanta, Chicago and New York, etc. Somewhere I picked up a bit of gossip that she had been bought out by some mega bucks conglomerate. When I eventually located Laura, she came with two unanticipated measures of good luck. One, she is the best there is and two, she lives in Naples, Florida.

In our initial meeting, Laura's and mine, my starting point consisted of two elements. One, I was possessed of a distraught, revengeful state of mind. Two, the manuscript which I was determined to get published was in raw form and typed in Microsoft Word. Laura's starting point was to take a quick overview and then inhale a deep breath.

Taking a writer's license I have in mind to share the experience. If, as the saying goes, that there is at least one book in all of us, then there are many readers out there who already have a manuscript written; and brutally have received countless rejection slips. The step from writing to publishing is staggering and brutal. And often in the end, if you want to get published you will have to self publish. Ask not where can an understanding agent or book publisher be found? The answer is nowhere. They don't exist. What does exist are book publishing companies and literary agents who are arrogant, despicable, snooty and generally miserable. Any author's dream, of sending a great story in raw manuscript form, off to the waiting arms of some book publisher, faded from glory with the passing of Hemingway. Yet many keep trying, because they don't know what else to do. In hope after desperate hope, authors grovel and suck and suck.

If and when you get fed up and come to accept that enough is enough, then do what I am attempting to do. I am self publishing. And when I get the product in hand I intend to go out and sell...on the street where I live, door to door, out of my car, at church, at Wal-Mart, a copy always in my back pocket. Note to Self: get some pants with very large pockets. Wish me luck!

With a vow that the commercial publishing industry could kiss my backside at high noon on the courthouse steps I initiated my first move forward. I was able to persuade Laura to take the job. I didn't like the price but I more than got my money's worth. In a general accomplishing time-line here is what she did. First she reviewed the manuscript and explored, then counseled against Vanity Press. (The term actually covers a multitude of back ally publishing hackers that solicit manuscripts from first-time or one-time authors and for a fee send their manuscript to Mexico to get printed on cheap paper and then sell them back to the author. The words Vanity Press are all encompassing; reflecting people's vanity of wanting to publish a book about their grand daughter's summer by the sea.)

One of Laura's first acts was to establish an Internet domain of MGD Publishing (Maria Greka Delaney). In no particular order she then establish and registered with the State of Florida, a Limited Liability Corporation (LLC). Next we jointly proceeded to search for a *printing* company where we could outsource production of the book. To this end Laura spent time contacting and interviewing countless possible printers and binderies. The range for printing quotes ran from $8.00 to $300.00 per book.

In the final analysis Rose Printing Company in Tallahassee, Florida seemed to be the most promising choice. An established, multi-generation family owned business, they seemed to be a good fit. We then took a trip and drove from Naples to Tallahassee and inspected Rose Printing facilities. We were able to meet with the marketing manager, the prepress manager and the owner of the company; and be given a guided tour of the plant. Of noted interest, we learned that their accounts included printings of "Harry Potter" and were delighted with the apparent interest they placed on our project. In addition we ascertained which software programs the Rose Printing were currently using. To insure compatibility, we then purchased Adobe Creative Suite 2.

Thence, the long and tedious grunt work started. Page by page Laura converted the raw Microsoft Word documents to page layouts in Adobe In Design CS2. Also during that time she applied for and received an ISBN (International Standard Book Number) series and a user's manual for International Standards Book Numbering Agency. In other things, she negotiated a contract with Rose Printing, with all the specifications set forth.

While all of the foregoing paints an accurate picture of Laura's effort, there is an additional inclusion that carries even more weight...the factor which merits the most acknowledgment. And that factor is her original artwork that she created for the dust jacket. Here's what happened. A significant portion of *A Mother's Imprint* centered on a historical landmark movie theater in down town Pittsburgh named the Stran. For authenticity Laura researched the historical aspects of numerous famous old movie house of a bygone era. She then hand sketched a design as to how she envisioned the Stran should look. From the hand sketched version she move to actually putting the sketch on canvas. The artist in her painted a 24"x 36" rendition in oils. She then moved to step three, where she digitally photographed the painting using a Konica Minolta DiMage A2 camera with a 7X optical zoom lens. Having done all of the foregoing she then had one final objective. Through the magic of computer design, she put the Stran on the dust jacket, together with carefully selected photographs of my wife, Maria.

That should just about print an accurate acknowledgment. If whosoever elects to undertake self-publishing, Laura Connaughton Fine Art and Design is highly recommended. She isn't cheap but if you can get her she's worth the money. Try email: itsqueenii@aol.com